THE
HIDDEN
CITY

THE
HIDDEN
CITY

A *House War* Novel

MICHELLE WEST

DAW BOOKS, INC.

DONALD A. WOLLHEIM, FOUNDER
375 Hudson Street, New York, NY 10014
ELIZABETH R. WOLLHEIM
SHEILA E. GILBERT
PUBLISHERS
www.dawbooks.com

First Printing, March 2008

1   2   3   4   5   6   7   8   9

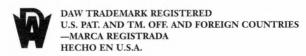

DAW TRADEMARK REGISTERED
U.S. PAT. AND TM. OFF. AND FOREIGN COUNTRIES
—MARCA REGISTRADA
HECHO EN U.S.A.

PRINTED IN THE U.S.A.

This is for Kelly, who waited so long, and who tries, always, to understand the things that come from the heart.

Acknowledgments

This was a particularly difficult book to write, and as usual, was longer than I anticipated. I often disappear inside my own head while writing, but with this book, I approached invisibility.

And so I'd like to thank Thomas, who waited, with near-perfect patience; my sons, Daniel and Ross, who understand that they will *always* be my babies, even if they're in no way babies anymore; John and Kristen Chew, and my parents, who also waited.

Terry Pearson remains my alpha reader of necessity and choice, and held that fort when I was in the (sadly usual) state of complete despair that any book causes any writer, and Sheila Gilbert also waited, with characteristic patience while I struggled with the words.

Jody Lee, as usual, gave me a painting that secretly makes me wonder if anything I'm writing is worth her work.

And the West list, with its constant encouragement and quiet love for the previous books also helped enormously, even if I was absent for long stretches.

Chapter One

405 AA
Averalaan, Thirty-second holding

R ATH CONSIDERED HIMSELF a businessman.
      Besides being something of an expert in the finer arts of item relocation, he also considered himself a linguist, a writer of some renown in the lower parts of town, and, in the same fashion, a scholar.

He did not consider himself a swordsman, although he had been considered promising in a youth that he was well quit of now. Swords were cumbersome, expensive, and an instant magnet for the eye of wary guards, and for that reason, he seldom carried his. The fact that he had not seen fit to *sell* it said something about him; what, he was not inclined to examine more closely.

His hair was still a dark brown although with the passage of time it grayed; he took care not to notice just how much. He himself allowed no stoop of age to threaten his posture, and if the line of his nose, once patrician perfection, was now broken, he fancied that it added some character to his face.

So did the scars, and they were a less fortunate character, especially when he chose to make excursions to the more expensive parts of the Common. But it was in the more expensive arena of the Common that merchants fought their weaponless, almost clandestine duels, and it was in those brick-and-stone buildings, with their expensive windows and deplorably inexpensive guards, that he did most of his trade these days.

He had, therefore, learned a bit of the subtle art of makeup, a fashion he had once despised in his youth. His rooms—he had two at the moment, although that would no doubt change, as he moved frequently to avoid the lingering resentment of some of his clientele—were littered with clothing from all walks of life. Even the highest, although that clothing was also the oldest, and the one he chose most seldom to don.

It held some part of his memory, evidence of the truth of a past he had long since forgotten. Or, if he were honest, tried to forget. Drinking helped, and he drank seasonally for that reason. That, and to dull the Winter pain of old wounds and the breakage of old bones. Empty bottles stood in a neat row in the bedroom's easternmost corner.

Here, too, he had wigs, and face paint that would make a carnival proud; he had fine rings, silver at base, but plated with gold and the occasional real gem; he had heavy necklaces, the wearing of which made him appear to be one of the pretentious people who dreamed of wealth without ever comprehending the social subtleties that truly denoted it.

And he had names, although these were not so disorderly, existing as they did in an inventory contained by memory. One of them was real, if that word had meaning here, in the life he had chosen. He had letters, complete with wax seals, that designated him a courier of choice for any number of well-known merchant Houses; he had letters that designated him the negotiator of choice in the same way. They were written variously in spidery hand, in bold hand, in feminine perfection, and in words that were barely Weston; his inventory in this regard was large.

What he did not have—what he frequently promised himself he would never have—was a companion. He disliked anything that was beyond his control, and always had. He liked privacy, isolation, and the ability to let go of all his many faces the moment he closed the door behind him. Home, as it was always meant to be.

No, he thought, unusually honest on this bright and warm day, *not always.* There had been a time when home had meant something different. A time, later, when it had come to stand for everything he despised.

Now? Contempt took energy.

He marshaled that precious energy, choosing clothing with care. Or with as much care as he usually did, in seclusion; he swept through the piles that were more or less orderly, if wrinkled and somewhat less than perfectly clean, and then deposited a handful of cloth across his bed.

His door came with three locks; his windows were barred. He could afford both, and they were usually the first alteration he made in any place he called home now. All of the things that could be locked, were.

He chose, of all things, worn velvet; he chose a leather satchel that hung across his shoulder, an open display of wealth in the poorer holdings in which he chose to live much of the time, and he chose an obvious long knife. It wasn't a sword; that was hidden in the bowels of his collection of paraphernalia. But inasmuch as his presence could evoke threat, this would have to do. He also whitened the lines of his scars with an appropriate mixture of grease and powder, and darkened the circles under his eyes. His hair, he plaited. It wasn't long, but long enough to suggest a warrior gone soft.

After another few minutes, in which he glanced through his forged credentials, he shrugged and set them all aside. Here, charm—or what passed for charm with Radell, would have to do.

After he had finished, he glanced at the silvered mirror—it was a vanity he could afford, and in fact, one of the few he could not afford to be without—and then he made his way to the door, unlocking each bolt carefully and precisely. He made sure he had keys; he could pick the locks with relative ease, but it was a chore, and likely to be noticed by his inquisitive neighbors. The neighbors were getting to be a bit of a bother; it was almost time to move again.

Exiting, he closed the door, made sure it was solidly locked, and drew breath. Smoke lingered in the air, seeping from beneath the large cracks of poorly-fitted doors. Some of it was cooking; most of it was pipe. None of it was his.

He made his way along the narrow hall, and down steps that made the hall feel wide; navigated yet another long hall and a set of open doors and found himself, at last, upon the streets.

At this time of day, they were crowded. The thirty-second holding was one of the poorest of the hundred, and magisterial guards were encountered seldom; because they were absent, assorted would-be thugs lurked near the buildings or the alleys that occurred between them.

But they seldom preyed on children, and children gathered in the streets, avoiding wagon wheels by a miracle of dexterity and attention that never failed to amaze. They had sticks, hoops, leather balls, and a great deal of noisy energy.

Rath smiled, fake indulgence in the expression, as he met the eyes of some of those urchins, in their poor-fitting, overly worn clothing. They were wary of him almost instantly—friendliness from a stranger often had that effect. But they made way for him, which had been his intent, and he passed them by without another thought.

No, his thoughts were on Radell, on the next possible mission, and the next bag of coins that would make a move smoother.

Perhaps because he was so preoccupied, he didn't notice that this was the day in which his self-imposed exile would come to an end.

He didn't notice that one of the older children had broken away from a group by the far building; she skirted the alleys, giving them wide berth, and made her way toward the Common, her hands in her pockets.

But when she passed by him, he did notice the dull glint of an equally dull knife. His was out of his sheath before he spoke or moved; she was on his right, and the knife, in his left hand. He had always used either hand with equal grace.

Had he been in the Common proper, he might not have spared her another glance; children of her kind were numerous there. But in the streets of the thirty-second? Rare enough. The consequences were higher, here.

She went, with clumsy and obvious movements, for the straps of the satchel that hung by his side. He brought his knife in, to cut the top side of her hand—a warning, and one that didn't require long explanations.

But she brought her dull knife up at the last moment, and his blade skittered off its negligible edge; she kicked him, hard, in the knee, and yanked the satchel off his shoulder as he doubled over.

This was an inconvenience; it was not yet a crisis.

But it became one—a subtle one—when he met her eyes. Brown eyes, dark skin, unruly hair—things that he expected to see on these streets. But her expression was one of shame, of regret, of things that hinted at conscience, even though it was absolutely clear from the prominence of her cheekbones and her pointed jaw that she needed the money to eat.

The expression slowed him, somewhat. Age, perhaps, slowed him more. But neither of these slowed him enough to aid the young thief.

She ran, and he had already covered half her shadow when she suddenly banked right. As if, he thought, she knew exactly what he would do next, and hoped to evade him.

He could outrun her; her legs were short, and she was spindly, exhausted. But he kept pace with her, to see where she would go. The curiosity was out of place, and he hadn't time for it—but he surprised himself. He made the time.

She didn't—quite—surprise him. She didn't head for a building; she didn't head into the holdings. No home, then.

Instead, she turned on her heel and spinning, she ran toward the busiest street in the thirty-second—the one he himself had intended to take.

This, he thought, *is interesting.* And he followed. It was one of his skills. Hunting.

He picked up his empty satchel about fifty yards away from where he'd lost it. He didn't bother to open it and check its contents; he could tell by its weight and silence that whatever it had contained—and it hadn't been much—was gone. The girl was gone with it; the few coins were probably clutched in her hands, and if she weren't careful, she'd lose them to thieves just like her.

Which would serve her right. But wouldn't, in fact, do him any good at all. He stopped for a moment under the paltry shade of the ancient trees that girded the Common, smiled at a market guard, tipped his hat just a touch, and then thought.

With a distinct rolling of eyes, he made his way to the poorest section of the Common: the farmers' market. It was late enough in the day that the food there would be thoroughly picked over; what was left could be had for a fraction of its original asking price, if the child was both hungry and smart.

Having seen her, he didn't doubt the hungry.

And having lost her, his pride wouldn't let him doubt the smart. He made his way through the crowd in silence, regretting the obvious emphasis he'd placed on the scars that adorned his face. It did mean people made room for him—but that room was a hint and a warning if the girl was being at all cautious.

He prowled through the vendors that remained, and they watched him carefully. Some tried to garner his attention by shouting out praises of what was obviously not deserving of praise; the others let him be. They'd seen him, in one guise or another, and perhaps they even recognized this particular choice. It didn't matter; he wasn't thinking about them.

He was thinking, instead, about the girl.

She was nine, he thought. Ten. No older. He wondered if she had a family. Many of the street thieves did—if you considered a prostitute and an absent father family. But most of those children would have made their way home with their earnings; this one hadn't.

Ah.

He could see her back. Could see her talking with a farmer. To his great surprise, the farmer seemed friendly. Not cloying, and not argumentative, the way farmers in the Common market usually were—but genuinely happy to see her. He held carrots in one hand, and something that had probably seen better days—two of them, if Rath was any judge—in the other, but it was the carrots he was offering.

So. She had friends, of a sort, in the Common.

He hesitated, and then stepped back. There were no real shadows here, no convenient way of disappearing. But anonymity had its advantage, and there were enough people in the Common that anonymity was all but guaranteed. He watched the girl pay for the food, and then she surprised him again; she offered the farmer more of the precious coin that she held.

He couldn't see her face; he could see the farmer's. The large man's brows rose slightly in surprise, and then lowered in mimicry of annoyance. It was poor mimicry; it might convince a child of ten, but it would fall flat with any other audience.

Rath waited until the farmer refused whatever she had offered for a third time; waited a little bit longer, to see the girl slowly make her way from the wagon stall, her head bent, her arms cradling the bundle she carried as if it were life itself, which, given her weight and the obvious shape of her bones, was fair enough. She dwindled, dwarfed easily by the adults that were still set on conducting business, until she was out of sight.

Only then did he approach the farmer, and raise his hat.

The farmer's face stiffened in instant suspicion.

"That girl," Rath said quietly. He was a good judge of character, and had intended to open up discussion with some sort of friendly, idle chatter—but the farmer's face made it clear how effective that would be, and Rath hated to waste time.

"What girl?"

"The one you just sold the carrots."

"I've sold a lot of carrots today," the farmer answered. "And I'm about done." He started to close the wagon's back flap.

Rath caught the man's wrist so quickly the man didn't have time to draw back. "Don't," he said softly, "play games with me. The child that just left."

"What of her?"

"You know her."

The farmer shrugged. "I see her from time to time."

"How often?"

"Why do you want to know?"

He almost told the farmer the truth. Almost. Couldn't be certain later why he hadn't. "I was a friend of her mother's," he said at last. It seemed safe.

But it produced another frown. "Her family won't be happy if you don't leave her alone."

"Judging from the state of her clothing," Rath replied, choosing his words with care, "I'd guess her family won't care one way or the other."

The farmer hesitated again, and started to raise his free hand.

"Don't," Rath told the man, lowering his voice. "Don't even think it. I've no interest in the girl in that particular fashion. But I'm curious. She seems . . . different."

"Different how?"

"She hasn't been on the streets for long enough."

At that, the farmer seemed to deflate. "Aye," he said, half-bitter. "Not for long enough. She won't go to the Mother's temple—any of 'em. She's still got some pride in her, and she's honest."

As she'd just stolen his satchel, or at least its contents, Rath was justifiably dubious. He kept this to himself.

"Where does she live?"

The farmer shrugged. "I don't know," he said. "She says she's living with a friend of her father's."

"And?"

He shrugged. "I told you, she's still got some fierce pride. If I had to guess, I'd say she's living under a bridge across the river."

"Why?"

"She's not dirty enough," the farmer said with a shrug. "Look, it's none of my business. But she's alone here, and she looks like one of my daughters. She's polite enough, and she never takes more than she needs. Doesn't take enough," he added, "even when I offer." He shook his head. "She tried to pay me for the last time. When I gave her more than she'd paid for; she didn't check until after I'd gone."

"Thank you." Rath paused, and then added, "Do you know her name?"

"Name's Jay, as far as I know. Jay Markess."

Markess was not a common name. The fact that she had a family name at all was unusual. Radell forgotten, Rath stood in the open sun of the Common, thinking.

Lies are a tricky thing.

And when you tell them to yourself? You can almost believe them. Rath didn't pride himself on honesty. Honesty was for the rich or the lucky. He therefore had no difficulty telling himself that he was now crawling along the banks of the river that wound its way through the hundred holdings beneath rickety bridges and old stone causeways that had been built in better days and still bore the weight of wagons with dignity, in a simple search for the money she'd stolen.

There were men and women on the banks, some cleaning clothing, some cleaning themselves, the latter with vastly less success. There were children here as well, many of them *in* the water. They made a lot of noise, half of it glee and joy, the other half recrimination and tears. None of these children were the one he sought, although he paused to gaze at them all before he continued on his way.

The sun rose, and he considered the water with a little more envy until it started to sink again. At this time of year, it was never cold. Even the nights were humid, and the salt of the sea, miles off, could be tasted on lip and tongue.

But his curiosity had always been his downfall; he was curious now, and he didn't intend to stop searching until he found the girl.

When the sky was crimson, he did.

She was half clothed, and, judging from the way she clung to the shadows of the bridge, not comfortable being so. But she was trying to wash her face, her arms, her hands; she scrubbed at them, dousing them in the running current of the summer river; it was at its lowest. Spring would bring the rains that would cause it to swell, making the lowest of the bridges nigh impassable.

He waited for her to finish, as the minutes passed and the darkness gathered. Color, sunlight dying, could be seen between buildings; the sky above was already revealing the brightest of stars as faint light. The moon was at half, he thought, but there were no clouds. The magelights that kept the streets lit well beyond sundown were high enough above ground that they had yet to be dislodged by thieves.

Then again, the magelights were tended, and often *by* mages, so they were seldom an object considered worthy of theft; too risky.

When she had clothed herself again—in a dry shirt, to his surprise—he made his way down the banks and folded his arms across his chest, waiting to be noticed.

She didn't even look up.

"I'm sorry," she mumbled, her back turned toward him, her shoulders hunched. Her legs were straight and still; she had no intention of running again.

It wasn't quite what he had expected to hear, although he'd heard the whining and sniveling of more thieves in his life than he cared to remember. There was a quality to the girl's apology that those pleadings lacked.

"For what?" He approached her with care, his dagger sheathed.

"For stealing your money," she replied. She turned to face him. "I didn't spend it all."

"You couldn't."

Her curls half covered her eyes, and she lifted a palm to shove them to one side. Because they were still wet, they went. He could see her eyes so clearly, it might have been full daylight.

"You're Jay," he told her quietly, as if she were a wild animal. "Jay Markess."

She nodded. She didn't seem surprised that he knew her name.

"And I'm—I'm called Old Rath in these parts."

"Rath. Like in anger."

"No. It's a diminutive. My sister used to use it, when we lived together." Without thought, he added, "My name is actually Ararath, but I'd prefer to be called Rath."

"Mine's Jewel," she said, scrunching the lines of her face in disdain. "But everyone calls me Jay."

"This is where you live."

She started to say something, and stopped herself, watching him warily. "Yeah," she said, with a shrug. "This is where I live." And then, in a rush, "But only until I can find work."

"At your age?"

She said something rude. He almost laughed. But there was a gravity about her that defied laughter, especially ugly laughter.

"You took something that belonged to me," he told her quietly. "How do you intend to repay me?"

Her shadowed eyes, her sudden, *complete* stillness, told him more than he wanted to know. He wondered what he was doing here, on these banks. Wondered why he had asked her name, why he had spent a long day searching for her.

Head bowed, she approached him.

He reached out, caught her by the chin, and dragged her face up. Beneath the dirt, it was paler than he had thought it. "Your parents—they were from the South?"

"My Oma—my grandmother was." She shrugged. North or South, it didn't matter much.

"Mine are old stock," he replied. "From the North. They don't much like thieves."

"They don't like 'em much in the South either, according to my Oma. At least here, they don't cut your hands off."

"No," he said quietly. "They don't." He looked at her; she couldn't move her face. "Jewel. Jay Markess." He shrugged. "Keep the money. Consider it a loan." He let her go, and her eyes widened.

"I'll see you around," he added softly, retreating from the banks.

Five days later, he found her again. He knew how much money she had taken, and knew how quickly it would dwindle. He had, in the meantime, managed to acquire more of it, but kept it better hidden.

He had gone searching through the old tunnels in the evening as he often did, but when he returned, he chose to eschew the noisy taverns that seemed to blossom only at the fading of the light. He was restless, and not yet ready to return to the confining space of two cramped rooms, so he continued to walk aimlessly, the whole of the night sky laid out before him. He had no particular destination in mind—and he chose to believe this until he found himself skirting the edge of the river.

He had donned clothing that better suited the holdings, and his scars were not so unnaturally prominent. He hadn't bothered to plait his hair; he'd drawn it back over his face, and tied it in a loose knot. He thought about having it cut every couple of weeks during any season that wasn't Summer; in the Summer, he thought about it constantly. But it was a necessary part of his work, and he let it be.

Jewel Markess was on the banks, just beneath the flat wooden slats of her bridge; there was no fire to light her, and only the moon to give her shadow, but he saw her instantly. He approached with care, and waited to be noticed.

She took her time, and because she did, he knew that she'd seen him coming. But she'd clearly been waiting for him to break the silence, as if the breaking were some kind of contest. When it was clear that he wouldn't, she turned to face him. Light on her face was scant; if it weren't for her height, she might have been older.

Her expression was grave. "Rath," she said quietly. She lifted a hand in greeting. The hand shook.

"Jay," he replied, bowing. It was a natural bow, and as a consequence, far too formal.

"I don't have your money yet," she told him. The hand fell, and she drew it across her chest, as if it were armor. "Are you—"

"No," he said quickly. "I was out today. I'm something of a historian, and I found a couple of stone tablets I'm hoping to sell." He wasn't quite sure why he'd said it; it was true, but truth was something he seldom offered anyone. Certainly not a thief in the hundred holdings.

Her dark eyes widened, and he recognized the particular cause of that width. She was curious, but she didn't ask, and wouldn't.

Before he could stop himself, before he could break the fragility of the mood, he pulled his backpack from his shoulders.

"You're not afraid I'll steal them, too?" she asked bitterly. Age, in the words, in the question. Age and self-knowledge.

"Not much," he replied, both smiling and shrugging. "They're heavy, and you don't know where to sell them. Take them to the wrong place, and they'll be thrown out in the garbage heap, and if the proprietor is annoyed enough, you'll follow them." He pulled the lighter of the tablet fragments from the pack and handed it to her, watching how she handled it.

She handled it with care, as if she could tell, just by touch, how old it must be. Her fingers traced the runes that were engraved in the stone's surface, and her eyes followed her hand's movements, absorbed by them. "I can't read these," she said at last.

His brow rose a fraction. "I should hope not."

"Why? I can read," she added. Defensive, showing her true age at last.

"If you can read these," he told her, "you're wasted here."

She ran her fingers across the stone's surface again, as if sensation could be stored and remembered, and then she handed the piece back to him. He touched her hand, meaning the gesture to seem accidental. Her fingers were cold. Death-cold.

The night was warm.

"Maybe," he said, with a shrug, repenting his earlier honesty, "it's the light. There's not a lot of it here." It wasn't the light. He knew it.

She shrugged. "It's night," she told him softly. "There's never much light at night. We could—we could go to the magelight."

"There's hardly enough light to read by there."

"More than here."

He nodded. "True enough. Very well, Jay. Let's go to the magelight." He rose, his knees feeling the damp, and took a few steps up the incline. Then he turned to see if she was following.

It was the wrong thing to do: he met her eyes, her round, dark eyes, and no magelight was necessary to see the hunger in them. It was a hunger he understood; it had nothing to do with food.

"I'd take you to Taverson's," he said quietly, "but these are not items I wish to show everyone."

"They have tables," she offered.

"Everyone in the tavern has ears like an elephant's, and eyes only for another man's business. I have one dagger and no guards. No, Jay, I think Taverson's is out of the question."

Her shoulders listed. She looked so pale, in the early night, he thought her ghostly. And afraid. But she shrugged mutely, and started to turn, to head back down the incline, and away from him.

He didn't want her to leave.

Gods, he was foolish. "Come with me," he said, more abruptly than was wise.

She froze, became even more pale. At another time, he would have been annoyed. But he understood that scars—real scars—were hidden, and for a reason; he felt no anger at all. He did not reach for her; did not offer her a hand.

And because he didn't, she approached him slowly. "Where?"

"My home," he told her gravely.

She hesitated again, torn, and he held out the pack.

She didn't touch it; it weighed about as much as he thought she did. But she nodded.

He led her back to his rooms, pausing between lights to see that she followed, as if she were a stray dog that had been kicked one too many times. Her hair was a mass of curls that caught and trapped the magical light from above; he could see that her cheek was bruised. Wondered, with the sudden heat of unexpected anger, if those were the only bruises she had.

He would have said, *I won't hurt you,* but those were the wrong words. He promised her nothing. She expected nothing. And nothing was safest for both of them.

He was utterly silent as he unlocked his door, aware that she watched not only his actions, but his setting; the length of now dark hall, the step-curved floor of wooden slats that had seen far too much use and far too little repair, the flat and impersonal surfaces of closed doors that extended into shadow.

He had a small magelight which he took out of his shirt's inner pocket, more for her comfort than from any practical need; she watched this as well, assessing him.

If she was afraid, she contained her fear. It was there; he knew the signs well enough, and although the streets had added a patina of opacity to her age, she had not been there long enough to become hardened. But he found he had no desire to inflame the fear or to use it to his advantage, and this was unusual. He had on occasion brought people to his dwelling, and each and every one was worthy of intimidation. When he was doing the intimidating.

But as he opened the door, he almost cringed. He did not, as a rule, have guests; his rooms were therefore not entirely presentable, and the detritus of his many identities lay strewn from wall to wall. It almost made him feel self-conscious, which was both exceedingly rare and unwelcome. "Watch your step," he told her, his voice cooler than he had intended.

Her curt nod was instant and perfect, but then again, she couldn't yet see into his private life. Couldn't yet step across and over it, examining it with her wide, dark eyes. If there was a moment to turn back, this was it, and it was the only moment he would be afforded.

A better man than Old Rath wouldn't even have considered it; he did. She was—by presence alone—a complication, and he abhorred complications; they were always costly, and in ways that mere money did not assuage. But he entered into the room, holding the door wide, and she hesitated in its frame, for entirely different reasons. The first thing her eyes skirted was the dim shape of the obvious bed, seen through the arch that separated the two rooms that contained his life.

He offered no safety but silence; was aware that there was no safety in silence. He let her choose, waiting, the backpack he'd slung across one shoulder dragging his arm down. He wasn't young; it was heavy. Heavy with the intangible gravity that drew her eyes, her attention.

It wasn't because he pitied her that he'd invited her here.

She entered his home, unaware of the singular honor he offered, and waited while he closed the door behind her. She didn't turn to watch him bolt the locks, but he saw her back as he did; he didn't need to look at what he was doing, and it was less interesting, less foreign, than she herself, standing there and flinching with each quiet click.

He opened his hand, exposing the magelight to air and darkness; the darkness made its light grow, and her eyes widened.

"That's expensive," she whispered.

"I didn't buy it," he replied, voice heavy with irony he thought she might miss. He walked over to the table and set it down upon the small pedestal designed for its use. Passed his hand above it twice, each time increasing its offered brilliance.

"Are you hungry?"

She shook her head.

"Jewel, the first thing that I must ask of you is this: while you are in my home—and you may never be in it again—you will not lie to me. Do I make myself clear?"

She met his gaze, held it, and surprised him. "If you already know the answer, why are you asking?"

He laughed; it was quiet, but audible. "Point," he said, raising a hand. "I wanted to see if you would lie."

"I was raised to be *polite*," she replied, the inflection implying clearly that he wasn't.

"And where have your fine manners brought you? To a home of ill-repute." The words trailed into silence as he studied her expression. No, he didn't want to frighten her—but he found that he couldn't help himself; it was interesting to watch her deal with discomfort.

His sister would have slapped him, hard, had she been here. But had she, he wouldn't. He placed the backpack before the magelight holder, and made his way to what passed for a kitchen. The tabletop was littered with an array of dyes, powders, unguents, and the odd piece of clothing;

the counters were likewise adorned, although the shadows leached every-thing of color. He opened a cupboard, pulled out cured, dry beef, and with it a jug of sweet water. The bread beside these was two days old, and it would probably break an older person's teeth. As he wasn't sure if Jewel had all of hers—her adult teeth—he brought that as well.

"Forgive the lack of cutlery, the lack of fine plates," he said with mock gravity, as he placed the food on the table. "I'd offer you wine, but I have a suspicion you don't drink."

"Depends on how thirsty I am," she replied.

"If you're thirsty, wine is exactly the wrong thing to drink."

She shrugged. Her shoulders inched up and down; they were tight and drawn in toward her body, as if, at any moment, she might have to ward off blows. Or other physical violence. It angered him. The anger surprised him. He would have bet money—his own—that he had long lost the ca-pacity for that kind of anger.

He split the beef evenly, and the loaf less evenly; it left a trail of crumbs for the mice. The water he sloshed into ceramic mugs. "Here," he said, handing one to her. "Eat. Drink."

She eyed the food, hunger warring with wariness.

It said much about her that wariness won. "Why are you doing this?" she asked him softly.

"I'm hungry."

"I mean, why are you—"

"I know what you meant; I'm not an idiot. But I'm hungry, and I dis-like philosophical discussions on an empty stomach. If you're determined not to eat, starve. You've probably become adept at it."

That brought a flush to her cheeks, and the color added something. Not beauty, not exactly, but warmth and life. She shoved her hair out of her eyes, pushed something off a chair, and pulled the chair up to the table, sitting down as heavily as her sixty pounds of weight allowed. Reaching over the ungainly lump that was the unopened pack, she grabbed the strips of dried meat and began to eat.

"To answer your question, Jay, I don't know. I have no idea what I'm doing." He swallowed warm water, brushed bread crumbs from the cor-ner of his mouth, and looked at her face in the glow of magelight. At her disheveled hair. At her eyes. "It isn't every day that someone steals my satchel in the streets of the thirty-second. I should have cut you; you were faster than I thought."

She shrugged, chewing slowly.

"I thought leaving you with the money would be enough. I had no intention of seeing you again; I went out for a walk tonight, found these, and started back. But . . . I walked past your bridge on the river." It would always be that to him, even years later: Jay's bridge. "And I saw you there."

"You could have kept walking. Everyone else does."

He nodded companionably. "I could have. But you could have taken what the farmer offered. You didn't. And you offered to pay him for what he did manage to slip you the last time you visited. I don't need to tell you how unusual that is."

As she frowned, he realized that he might be wrong on that last point. "You don't work," he said softly.

"I do. When there's work. When someone needs me. When it's festival season, I can be a runner—"

He lifted a hand, and she let the words trail off. She still had hope. He couldn't decide whether that was a gift or a curse; when one had hope, one always stood on the brink of despair.

"The magisterians would consider your line of work suspect," he told her, smiling to take the edge off the words.

It didn't work. Her face crumpled around the edges, her eyes narrowing in shame. He almost reached out to touch her then, but that would have been a mistake, and Rath had survived to be called Old Rath for good reason.

"When I'm older," she told him, averting her gaze, "I'll work."

"Doing what?"

"What everyone else does," she said. There was no hope in that phrase at all, and Rath decided that hope, in Jewel's case, was a gift. To him, at least.

"What," he said carefully, "does everyone else do?"

She hated the answer, and didn't give it, but she shot an accusing glance at him, and held his gaze.

"No lies," he said softly.

"I wasn't going to lie," she told him. "I just wasn't going to answer. You said you weren't an idiot. You figure it out."

His shadow flickered as he moved; the magelight, unlike inferior candle flame, was steady and constant. "Sell your body?"

She nodded.

"It's not a good life," he told her. "And it's usually a short one."

"Shorter than this?"

"Less respected."

She snorted. Not quite what he'd expected, but he was willing to let it play out. "It shouldn't be," she said, after the pause had grown long. "I own my body. It's mine to sell. It's honest. Stealing isn't."

"Jay—"

"It's true," she continued, her earnestness at odds with the subject. "At least that way, I'd be giving something back. I try," her voice dropped, "to steal from people who look like they won't starve if they lose a few coins. I try not to take more than I need. But I—"

Silence.

"There are men who won't pay you," he told her quietly. "And men who will beat you if they think someone else has."

She said nothing.

"Jewel."

Looked up.

"How long have you been living by the bridge?"

She shrugged. He knew, by the quality of that forced nonchalance, that she could tell him to the day how long it had been. But he didn't press her. Instead he rose and untied the leather thongs that bound the backpack shut. Her eyes shifted, watching his fingers work the knot. She didn't offer to help him.

But her hands jumped up against the tabletop as he pulled the two tablet fragments from their resting place and laid them out beneath the light, runes taking shadow and making shape of it.

"Were you born here?" he asked, as he carefully arranged them so that they were oriented for her view. They were cold to the touch. Almost as cold as her hand had been, come new from the river.

She nodded, still staring, her fingers now fluttering as if they were trapped by some unseen force of air. "At least I think I was. This is the only place I remember."

"And your parents?"

"Not my Oma. My grandmother," she added, as if Rath couldn't be expected to know the old Torra word. He did; he didn't enlighten her. Enough that she talked at all.

She hadn't looked away from the engravings, but her expression was slowly shifting into something that looked like disappointment. If disappointment could be said to be shattering and crippling. "I can't read them," she whispered. "It's not—it wasn't the light."

He said, "If you cry, I'll throw you out. I cannot abide tears in a child."

"I'm *not* a child."

But you are, he thought, as he carefully moved the stones so that the runes faced him. *And, gods help me, I have no idea what I'm supposed to do with a child.*

"This," he told her, lifting the stiletto he had chosen as the most convenient pointing device available, "is an R."

Her forehead wrinkled; the lines would fall away the instant her expression shifted, and it did so a dozen times in a minute. As she shoved her hair out of her eyes again, he asked, "Does your hair always do that?"

"All the time."

"And you haven't cut it?"

She stared at him, and the shadow of poverty crossed her face.

"Never mind. That was a stupid question. And in compensation for the stupidity, I will allow you to ask any three questions that come to mind." He turned back to the tablet. "It is not in the form of the R you would normally write; this is not Weston. It is Old Weston, and it has not been spoken in the Empire since well before its founding. It is, however, the root of the Weston you do speak. Can you write it?"

She nodded. It was hesitant, but he caught no lie there. "Who taught you?"

"My father, mostly."

"Good man."

"He was," she whispered. For a moment, the tablets lost her interest, and her gaze fell inward. Rath couldn't divine, from her answer, any specific truth; he had seen monstrous men who were, in the end, loved by their children, and that twisted love was a bitter, bitter legacy in the open street.

"In Old Weston, the letter forms used for engraving were very precise. The men and women employed in the carving of this particular tablet were probably Priests."

"Whose?"

"I can't answer that question."

"Can't?" she said, her eyes suddenly sharp and bright, "or won't?"

His smile was reward enough. "Smart girl."

"Does that count as one of my questions?"

"No. It wasn't stupid enough. But back to my point: the engravers were artists, of a kind. They worked with chisels, and judging from the absolute uniformity of these curves, I would say those chisels were magical in nature. The R looks much like any other letter form; the letters carved here were intended to be almost of a kind to the uneducated eye."

"Did people read a lot then?"

"That," he said, "counts as one question. It's not quite stupid, but I'm not that generous a man, as you will quickly discover. No, it is our belief that when these were engraved, writing and reading were done by very few."

"You can read these, though."

"Not a question. You're a clever girl, so I'll let that one by. Yes, I can read these."

"How?"

"I studied Old Weston. I hated it, at the time. My friends—such as they were—were out in the sword yards, or out on horseback, or out in the country hunting all manner of vice. My grandfather was a strict old bastard, and had no patience for such time wasting; I learned from him." He winced, remembering how often blows had been part of that experience.

"Does anyone write Old Weston now?"

"Not that I know of," he replied. "And I'll count that as half a question. There is a possibility that the Priests still write it, when it suits them; it is certainly spoken in some of their more odious, long-winded ceremonies."

Her mouth rounded in an O of shock, and he was almost ashamed at how pleased he was by the reaction. He really *had* spent too much time in self-imposed exile.

"That's an M?"

His brow rose and fell. "Yes, in fact, that is an M. And in the middle of a word. You have a good eye."

"These aren't from the same place, are they?"

"An extraordinarily good eye. No, they aren't. The larger piece will fetch a higher price."

"Where did you find these?"

He smiled. In truth, he had expected that to be her first question. "It's a trade secret. And I," he added, "am a trade of one."

"Tell me what they say."

"The first," he said, "is a snippet of praise. I believe it's from the base of an old statue; the statue itself exists only from the knees down, and there is no name here to indicate who was being honored by its erection. The second, longer and flatter, is from the base of a cenotaph."

She frowned, turning the word over and over. After a moment, she gave up. "A what?"

"A large, stone coffin that rests above ground. Usually in a crypt."

"You—you robbed the *dead?*"

"That was your second and a half question. And it was suitably stupid." He shrugged. "The dead don't care, Jay. No matter what your Oma told you, no matter what your parents might have said—the dead simply do not care. But the living *do*. And every fragment we find, every piece of ancient Weston, gives us information about the society that once laid claim to the city and the Isle."

"You're going to take these and sell them?"

He nodded quietly. "I have friends in the Order of Knowledge upon the Isle."

She drew back from the table, staring at him, her expression shifting between awe, fear, and a very stark envy. "I've never been to the Isle," she said at last.

And Rath knew that he was a complete idiot, an utter fool, because of what he said next.

"Would you like to?"

She stared at him. Turned away. Surprised him. "They'd never let me across the bridge."

"Not dressed like that, no."

"I don't have any other way to dress." There was no bitterness in her voice; none of the anger he might have expected. There was simple acceptance. Of life. Of fact. She stood, pushing the chair back so gently it made no noise. "Thank you," she told him gravely, "for dinner."

She made her way to the door and reached for the locks. He wasn't afraid of losing her; she couldn't reach the topmost one. But he rose, leaving the most valuable objects in the room by the light.

"Jewel Markess."

She turned at the sound of her name, listless, but no longer afraid. He had earned at least that much this eve—her lack of fear.

"If you could have any one thing—anything at all, accepting the fact that the dead cannot return—what would it be?"

"A home," she whispered. "A place of my own."

He nodded. "You have one more question."

"Half a question."

"Ask."

She shook her head. "I'll save it," she told him. "Can you—can you let me out?"

"I could. But it's not safe in this holding at this time of night."

"I have a knife."

"Do you know how to use it?"

"You saw."

"Good point." He was a damn fool. He should have known better than to lay food out for a stray. Should have known better than to coax her here, to his stronghold, his place of impermanence. Well, he would be gone soon enough. "I have a favor to ask of you."

Her eyes once again darted through the arch. To the bedroom, which was at least as messy. Anger, unwelcome, almost made its way to the surface of his words.

"If you live to be sixty," he told her curtly, "that will never be something I ask of you. Do you understand? I realize you mean no insult, but I *am* insulted, and I am not a man you wish to offend."

She said, "I don't understand you."

"No, child, you don't." She didn't even bridle at his use of the word. "And I doubt that you ever will. I can hardly be said to understand myself these days. If I thought they would find you a decent home for a few days, I would turn you over to the magisterial guards."

She knew, by that, he wouldn't.

"I work alone. I have worked alone for most of my life, and I admit there was a time when I resented it. I was younger then. But never as young as you."

She still waited, her palm on the flat surface of his door, a few inches beneath the final bolt.

"You cannot live with me," he continued, "for reasons that might, if you are very unlucky, become clear to you. But tonight, I would like you to stay."

"Why?"

"Because I don't want to go out again, and I don't wish to find your body in the streets. I don't want to go to the bridge and find it abandoned. In the morning, you can leave."

All of her hesitations were almost linguistic. He could read them, but slowly, as precisely as if they were words being formed with care.

She nodded, and let her hand fall from the door. Her eyes were ringed with dark circles; she looked pale. Too pale. He rose and went over to her; he touched her arms and her hands, but not her face.

They had gone from the cold of the river to something just slightly too warm. He cursed under his breath. Lifting her, he carried her to his bed, and shoved aside the pile of clothing that occupied the center. "Sleep here," he told her.

"But it's your—"

"That wasn't a request. I am not yet finished my study; it will be a few hours yet before I require sleep. I have a bedroll; I am not always situated in such luxury." The irony was lost on the girl.

She closed her eyes.

It was dark enough in the room that he could pretend she wasn't crying. "There's no door," he told her. "If you need me, call. I'll hear you."

"I won't—"

"In the morning, if you are still ill, we will go to the Mother's temple."

Her eyes widened, then. She caught his hand in hers, crushing—or attempting to crush—his palm. There was more than a little strength in the grip, but not nearly enough.

He disentangled himself and rose. Paused beneath the arch. "I smoke," he said, "when I work. Do you mind?"

She didn't open her eyes. Didn't nod. But he knew she was not yet asleep.

Chapter Two

H E DID NOT TAKE HER to the temple, although she burned with fever. She would know, from that, how much of a liar he was. Being a liar had never bothered him. It bothered him now only because it might set up expectations which he could not possibly fulfill.

And as that was, in general, the *purpose* of a lie, Rath took no comfort in the momentary flicker of decency. Although he seldom maintained a residence for longer than a year at a stretch, although he could wear four different faces in the course of a single day's work, although he could speak three languages fluently, and seldom frequented any establishment enough to be considered a regular, Rath disliked change. As there was so little about himself that he considered fundamental, he was facing a sea change now.

Ignoring that fact took a bit of effort. But being with the child at all took effort, and he buried the one in the other.

Rath took care, while she slept, not to touch her face; her hands were hot enough that he had no need. Her breath was shallow, but clear; her skin was free of rash. She needed water, he thought. He found water, poured it into a wineskin, and dribbled it between her lips. She woke, her eyes wide and almost wild; they saw someone else. They did not see him.

He knew this because she smiled, and the smile was so desperately *open*, so entirely unfettered by the caution that had marked all of their interchanges, it was almost painful to watch. She reached up and clutched the wrists of the hands that held the skin, babbling in Torra, and at that, in children's Torra, the broken beginnings of adult language in the making.

He let her. He did not intrude upon the delirium by trying to answer any of her questions; he continued to drip water into her mouth.

As it fell, drops catching light across the corners of her mouth, her face, Rath wondered, idly, if this would be the year he finally died. This softness was not in him, had not been in him; he would have sworn it before the judgment-born, those golden-eyed spawn of the god who could not be lied to. Some lies were buried so deep, they looked like truth, tasted like it, lived like it. Until the moment they turned on you, biting, as her bright eyes bit, in hidden places. He could not move until she closed them. But she did, at last, giving in to exhaustion and fever. Only then did he pry his wrists free of her slender fingers to leave her side.

The sun rose; he closed the shutters. He had curtains, but they were leftovers from a time when the state of his living quarters had been some part of his pride; he had not used them since he had abandoned a house in the middle part of town, where poverty such as Jewel's was myth or debacle. That had been five moves past.

"You can't live here," he told her, because she couldn't hear him.

He left her when the sun was high, and went to the market. He did not take his tablets; he took only a handful of coin, and with it, bought food. He took some small pleasure in the bickering that passed for negotiation between a poor farmer and an apparently hungry man, but did not linger; he was afraid that she would wake.

Not that she could leave easily; she couldn't reach the top bolt on the door without aid, and in her current condition, pushing a chair to the door would probably exhaust her. But if she tried to climb the chair, she'd probably fall, and he'd find her in an injured heap across his precious clothing.

He'd have to clean it up, he thought, as he sidled his way through the market throng, satchel heavy by his side. He glared two thieves into invisibility, insulted a merchant selling what could be passed off as jewelry only to people who'd never actually owned any, and paused to buy wine.

Then he was gone, leaving the Common to wend his way back to the thirty-second holding, his keys warming in his hands as he clutched them. Why this girl? Why *this* one? He shuffled through the static images that he called memory, trying to see some subconscious similarity between those people and this child. He failed utterly. His life, in youth, had had little to do with the lower part of the hundred holdings, and the girl's dark, curled tangle of hair, her dark eyes, the dusky skin that spoke of Southern heritage, had been well beyond his ken. Not even the servants in the house of his once proud family had been born to Southerners; his mother had detested the way they looked. She found them dirty, and thought they were all probably thieves.

He had detested his mother, in like fashion. In ignorance, he thought, with a shade of bitterness. Life had taught him much about his early self, and not all of it was valuable. He went in through the front doors of the building and made his way up the stairs, enduring the suspicious glance of the most elderly of his neighbors in the process.

"No, Mrs. Stephson," he said, for perhaps the hundredth time since he'd moved in, "I haven't seen your cat." The cat, legend in the tenement, had been missing for well over a decade, and she was certain that it was in someone's room. It was a gray cat who answered to the name *Belle,* she told him, in that hushed confidential voice that was just one side of insanity—and at that, the wrong side. He'd once been tempted to tell her that he'd eaten it, just to shut her up. Luckily, the temptation hadn't been as strong then as it was now. Magisterial guards hated to be called out for no reason, and Rath had no doubt whatsoever that she'd march straight to the nearest station to demand that they deal with him. And while he could probably assure them, after they'd spent more than five seconds in her company, that he had not, in fact, eaten her cat, there were things in his rooms that would demand more complicated explanations.

He left her as quickly as he could, curbing his tongue, and unlocked his door, stepping into the relative safety of home. He locked the door behind him. The old woman was foolish and addled, and given half a chance, she'd follow him, her litany of woes growing with each step.

She was, in every possible way, unlike the child he *had* let in.

Jewel was where he had left her, but she was no longer sleeping. Nor was she fever-witted; her brown eyes were large and clear, her expression, made gaunt by lack of food, lucid. She had bunched the sparse coverlet in her hands, and she sat against the headboard, staring out at his strange world as if it were the only world she could see.

She did not start or otherwise move as he entered the bedroom, but she looked at him. "My last half question," she said, surprising him.

"What of it?"

"If you can't answer it, does it count?"

He almost laughed. "You have a life as a merchant ahead of you," he told her. "Or a lawyer."

She said, "Can you find work for me?"

He almost said no. But he looked at her carefully. "How strong are you?"

She held out one bony arm. "Not very," she admitted. "I think I used to be stronger." Her eyes did all the pleading she would allow herself.

"You can't live here," he told her again.

"I know. You're moving at the end of the month."

His brows rose. Pale brows, but that was the curse of his birth, and he hadn't bothered to dye them this week. "I am, am I?"

She nodded listlessly. "You won't give notice. You'll leave money in an envelope. For the landlord. No note."

"I will?"

When she failed to answer, he left her, going to the kitchen to empty the satchel of its contents. He'd bought too much meat, too much fruit, too many things. The bread was fresh; he inhaled the pleasant aroma, held it in his lungs. There was nothing of death or sickness in it, and it was a long moment before he exhaled. From the safety of the kitchen, he continued to speak. "How do you know that?"

"I just know."

"It's not what people normally do."

"No. If they leave without notice, they don't usually pay. Why do you?"

He thought about lying, because it was what he was accustomed to.

"No lying in your home," she said, as if she could hear the thought.

"No lying from *you*," he replied, almost pertly. He put the food in a basket. He hadn't lied about the lack of plates or cutlery, and perhaps he should have; honesty was a habit, like any other addiction. "What I choose to say in the comfort of my own home is entirely my own affair. It's a privilege I pay for." He walked back into the bedroom and sat on the edge of the bed; it creaked under his weight. Although he wasn't large by Imperial standards, he was not a small man; he could make himself look smaller than he was in subtle ways, and in Jewel's presence, he usually did. He dispensed with that pretense for the moment; he wanted to appear vaguely threatening. There was safety in that. "Here. If you can, eat."

"Why?"

"Is that your question?"

She shrugged. Her hands shook. The food she had eaten the night before had blunted the edge of her hunger, but she was growing. To his eye, not enough. "How old are you, Jay?"

"Ten."

He nodded.

"What did you do before you decided to live under a bridge?"

The question made her brow furrow. "What did I do?"

"That's what I asked."

"You mean—like work?"

"If you worked, yes."

She curled in on herself. Her attempt to make herself smaller was entirely unconscious, and he let it pass, although the posture was enough of an answer. "I helped my mother," she said at last. "I helped her at home. I went to the Common with her. I helped sew our clothing," she added, "but not the important stuff."

"Important?"

"My father's clothes," she said, her voice softer, low enough that he had to lean over to catch the words. "My father worked," she added. "My mother sewed when she could find the work. My Oma took care of me before she got sick."

"And after?"

Jewel bunched more fabric beneath her birdlike fingers; the sun-faded blue seemed rich and dark against the color of her. "After, I helped my mother." Wooden words. "She died less than a year later."

"And you were left with your father."

She nodded.

"What did your father do?"

"He worked. When he could. Sometimes he worked at the port. Sometimes he worked in the warehouses near the port." Her lids were veined, fine, pale jade against the surprising white of skin. She didn't close her eyes often in sunlight, he thought. "He died in an accident. At the port. His friend brought me the last of his pay.

"While he was alive, I took care of him," she added softly. "I went to the market. I kept our home clean. I tried to fix his clothing, when it needed mending." She glanced toward the shuttered windows, as if seeking sight of escape. As if there were anywhere to escape *to*. "He taught me, in the evenings. Before he started, when my Oma was alive, we used to listen to her stories. When it was cold, we'd build a fire. When it was very cold," she added. "I like your pipe."

She was such an odd child.

"After she died, the stories died with her. My mother tried, but she'd never liked them much. My father didn't know them. So he—he taught me to read. Instead. He told me that I could find stories that way. By reading."

"If you have the money," Rath replied, without thinking. "Books are expensive."

She nodded bitterly. "I found that out."

"What else did he teach you?"

"To write. To handle numbers, at least a bit." She let go of the blanket and spread her hands flat, palm down. "To use a knife. To kick a man. To run."

"In your apartment?"

"In our home."

"He didn't expect you to run very far, then."

She didn't answer his momentary smile with a smile of her own; she was guarded again. Against hope, he thought.

"Yes, I'm leaving."

She nodded; she didn't flinch, didn't ask him why.

"But I'm curious. How did you know?"

Her eyes were flat as slate, dark and lifeless. "I know," she said, shrugging. "I saw it."

Were he a different man, he would have assumed that she had gone through his things in his absence—but he knew what he owned, and knew as well that there was no sign among the piles of cloth, the bottles and unguents, the dyes and even the quills that he kept for his own letters, few though they were, that would give her the information she possessed.

"You won't take me with you," she added.

He was an accomplished liar. Truth, he used seldom, because it almost always caused pain. "No," he said quietly. "I can't. Eat."

She ate. "I can't pay you for this," she told him, around a mouthful of meat. She ate the meat first.

"No."

"You don't care."

"Not much." He watched her. The light would persist for some time, even with the windows shuttered; the shutters were broken, and he hadn't cared enough to have them replaced; there were bars across the panes.

"You're not eating."

"I'm not hungry," he told her.

"Yes, you are."

His genial smile was becoming a bit of a chore; he let it slide free of his face, discarding it. What was left, he couldn't say. He watched her. She ate. There was a lot of silence, and in it, he saw that she was, at last, afraid.

But it was fear that had an odd texture to it; she was not afraid for herself; not afraid of him. He was not accustomed to children, and the lack of familiarity had never galled him before; it did now, because he found that he could not read her expression clearly.

And that he wanted to be able to.

"You can stay for another night," he said at last, giving up.

"Can I leave?"

"If you—" He cursed. "No."

And she surprised him by smiling. It was a glimmer, like light, that changed her face. "Was that stupid enough to be my last question?"

He stood suddenly, and turned away from her. It was easier to speak when he didn't have to watch her face change with each word, each sentence.

"I won't be leaving for another two weeks. And you won't be well for another three days, if I'm any judge. Stay."

"Why?"

"You had your question," he said sharply. "And unfortunately, I've wasted most of the day in the Common, and not to my own ends. I have a matter of some urgency to which I must attend."

"I didn't ask you to—"

"No. If you had, you wouldn't be here."

"I don't understand you."

His laugh was curt. "That makes two of us." He walked over to the table, lifting his leather backpack. Thinking, as he slid it over his shoulders, that she *would* weigh less. That she did.

"My Oma told me something," she said, while his back was turned to her.

"Only once?"

She laughed, and then coughed; she must have been halfway through a mouthful of something. "You have no idea," she said, when she could talk. "More than once. A hundred times. Maybe a thousand."

"What was it?"

"That we don't leave our debts unpaid. And if we can't pay 'em, we don't accept them either."

"That sounds like something an old woman would say." He turned toward her, fixing his cuffs. He should change, and knew it, but also knew that it would make her skittish.

"So . . . I can't pay for this."

He was a *very* accomplished liar. "I'm almost an old man," he began.

She snorted. "Don't tell me you're lonely," she snapped. "Or that you want company. Because you *hate* company."

"Do I?"

She was mutinous in her silent response. Fire there. Spirit.

He shrugged. "I hate complications," he said, correcting her. "Company, I can take or leave. If it's decent company. And Jewel?"

"What?"

"It's not nice to accuse a man of lying."

"It's true."

"Truth is not an excuse for bad behavior. I have to go. I'll be back, but late. Don't wait up."

She folded arms across her ribs, sinking back against the headboard, her face slowly graying. Fever, he thought.

"Drink the water." His voice was rougher than he had intended. "Drink all of it. Do *not* try to walk. Do *not* try to unlock the door."

"And if someone comes?"

"Ignore it. Unless they break the door down, in which case, you have my permission to extemporize."

"To what?"

"Improvise." He frowned. "Ignore everything else I've just told you and make it up as you go along."

"Do I need your permission to do that?"

"You need my permission to breathe while you're in that bed. Or in my home. Is that understood?"

She nodded. "Yes. Yes, Rath. I understand."

Then maybe, he thought, as he reached for the highest of the bolts, *you can explain it to me.*

As if she could hear him, she spoke. "The man you're going to see," she whispered.

He could hear her. But not well. With a resentment that was vastly more natural than charity he turned and walked back to the bed.

She had shrunk. The bed dwarfed her. The threadbare counterpane seemed miles wide as it stretched to either side of her spindly legs. "He'll have you followed," she told him. "If you come here, he'll know where you live."

His brow rose a fraction. "Who is he?"

"I don't know. I don't know his name. He's big. And bald." She was wrong on two counts. He did not correct her. "He wears dark clothing. Two knives, but I don't think they're both obvious. I don't know who he is. But he'll have you followed."

"Interesting. Do you know why?"

She shook her head, as if she was already caught out in a lie. "I think it's the tablets," she added, voice dropping into inaudibility.

"Who?"

"I told you, I don't know—"

"Who will follow me?"

And her eyes widened a fraction, her voice losing some of its quiver. "I don't know," she told him. He cursed roundly, and reaching out without care or subtlety, he placed his palm flat against her forehead. She was burning. He had seen this before; fever came and went at its own pleasure. Sometimes, in the end, it came to stay. He could not be certain, with Jewel, that that wouldn't be the case.

Maybe the delirium of fever made her talk.

But he was a man who had survived by trusting his instincts; fever or no, he had to ask more. "How do you know that he'll have me followed?"

"Because he orders someone to do it," she answered, sliding away from him, although she did not try to avoid his touch.

"And does he give any other orders?"

"I don't know." After a moment, she repeated the words, but they were louder, and they bristled with pain and anger. *"I don't know."*

"Enough. Enough, Jay. Promise that you'll stay here."

"Unless someone breaks the door down."

"Unless someone else enters my home."

She swallowed. "My Oma used to say—"

"That you shouldn't make a promise you couldn't keep." When her eyes grew wide, he almost laughed, but it would have come out in anger. "She was right. Promise that you'll wait."

She swallowed. Her lips were cracked. He wondered if she'd keep the food down. "I promise," she said.

And her voice was a little girl's voice. A lost voice. It cut him, and he had exposed enough of himself—carelessly, ignorantly—that she *could* cut him, just by speaking.

He left as quickly as he could and tried not to look back.

The streets of the thirty-second holding were shutting down almost imperceptibly. The sun was still high enough that some children scattered their sticks and stones throughout the street, their voices raised in laughter, a mix of joy and mockery so common he might have been anywhere.

But their parents were at the windows and doors that girded the street itself, and one by one, those children were being called inside. For dinner. Or safety. Women were beginning to leave different doors, in gaudy dresses and ugly, garish paint. They would not linger here; this was home, and very few of their customers could be found in the thirty-second.

He was not, and had never been, among them. Because of this, he could smile, or nod, and they would return this pleasantry. He did not treat them with diffidence, but he didn't treat anyone with diffidence, and they knew it.

"You look a right mess," one of the women said.

"And you, Carla, like a vision." His grin was brief, answered by hers, although she took care not to show her teeth; she was missing a few too many.

He checked his satchel; it was a nervous habit. The streets were long and narrow when he departed the main road, and they were framed by alleys and tall buildings, neither of which held any friends. Rath had killed men on streets such as this, without hesitation or noise.

But in truth, he didn't relish the opportunity. It was a messy business, the killing of men, and he had seen, time and again, acquaintances who had slid from the precipice of necessity into something darker. He had taken care not to become them. Not through any particular moral conviction; he'd long since given up on those. No; the magisterial guards were clever, they saw well, they found the bodies, and it was hard—if one continued to add to the dead—to avoid their detection.

The Common was closing down by the time he reached its outer perimeter; he made his way past boarded stalls, saw flags coming down their poles as their weary owners closed up for the day. Morning started before sunrise, and they had some distance to travel before they ate; they paid only enough attention to assess any threat he might offer.

He, of course, offered none.

He walked past the lengthening shadows cast by the Merchant Authority, and banked right, a sharp right that would lead almost instantly to the
row of buildings, glass windows like an unholy temptation, that housed
the city merchants properly. They were adorned by the usual guards, and
where guards were not present, the magisterial patrols were frequent.
Here, the source of the taxes that ran much of the city was at its most
dense; only across the bridge on the Isle itself was more money gathered.

He seldom crossed the bridge.

Had he not already made the decision to move, he might have traversed
it this eve, and made his way by carriage to the Order of Knowledge upon
the Isle—but any negotiations that involved the truculent scholars and
mages upon that Isle took weeks. Oh, the money was better—and no
doubt, the man to whom the tablets were eventually consigned would go
there himself—but if money was time, it was not, in this case, time he
could afford.

He tipped his hat to guards; they were not familiar to him, but they
were familiar enough with his contact that they nodded in turn. Bored
nods, all, which was as it should be. Had they looked at all tense, Rath
would have backtracked quietly and returned on a different day; merchant guards were like personal weather vanes, and Rath was allergic to
trouble.

He paused at last in front of a set of old doors; they were wooden, with
large glass panes. A ridiculous name in gold leaf traced a half circle at eye
level. *Avram's Society of Averalaan Historians.* Avram was an Old Weston
name. Like the man who purported to own it, it was pompous; unlike that
man, it was succinct. The sign itself was lettered in mock-ancient style,
which made it hard to read. Rath had never understood the point of having a sign that was difficult to read.

Signage, however, was not considered one of his areas of expertise, and
as he wanted money from the man who had commissioned it, he kept his
opinion to himself. He knocked twice and waited.

A beard brushed the other side of the glass, and a familiar glower could
be seen just below Rath's eye level before the lock was turned and the door
swung open.

"You're late," the man hissed. "Two days late."

Rath nodded. "My apologies," he said. "I was detained."

"I don't want to hear about it."

He never did. Which was why Rath liked Radell. Radell, who now went by the name Avram, was about ten years Rath's junior; he had grown a beard because he could dye it, and it added—or so he thought—years to his face. His face, wide and flecked by early exposure to sun, was pinched and pale.

"Is this a bad time?"

"Yes," Radell hissed. He looked back, into the shop. Rath couldn't easily discern what he was looking at; the contents of the store got in the way. Shelves stretched from the front of the store into shadow, each as tall as the ceiling. They housed antiquities—most fake—and books; they also kept dust, spiders, and silverfish in great abundance. Radell lived with those. He had paid the mage-born to make certain that the larger insects that came with the warm ocean clime never crossed his threshold, but he was at heart a cheap bastard. Besides which, he thought the cobwebs made the store look more distinguished. Which was true, if by distinguished one meant that it looked as if almost everything sat there, untouched, unmoved, and definitively unsold, year after year.

"I'll go," Rath said, backing away from the door.

But Radell's shoulders had already done their forward slump, and in Radell, that was a sign of graceless resignation.

"Avram?" A deep voice drifted out of the store's back room. As back rooms went, they were easily the most modern and cheery part of the establishment; they were certainly the cleanest. They were also only opened to persons of import. Rath, on occasion, managed to gain entry by dint of his ability to find "unusual" items.

Such as the ones that now weighed him down.

Rath's smile tightened. He now bore an expression similar to Radell's, but for distinctly different reasons. He knew at once that this customer was of import; that he was a *private* patron, which usually meant monied; that he was either extremely rich or frequent. He also knew that Radell lived in dread of the day that Rath cut out middlemen. Thus, Radell's reluctance.

Rath's was different. He valued middlemen because he valued privacy; he valued Radell because Radell could lie like the proverbial rug—and it was Radell who was required to come up with the ludicrous back story of ancient wonder which was the foundation upon which Rath's items would then be placed on display. Rath, more prosaic, disdained the cheap jaunts into imaginary tales that wouldn't have impressed a smart child. He also valued the privacy that came with being anonymous.

Ah, well. He had already decided that it was time to move.

"Avram, is there some difficulty?"

Radell's face did the jump from resignation to obsequiousness. It was, in all, a brilliant display—something that even Rath had to marvel at. "No, Patris AMatie, no difficulty at all. Please allow me to introduce one of my associates." He bowed, his beard clearing dust from the floorboards. With that much middle, Rath wondered how he could maintain the bow without overbalancing. But Radell had stores of athleticism reserved for just such occasions.

The Patris—if indeed he *was* a Patris, and Rath privately doubted it—came at last into view.

He was a good six inches taller than Rath, and his round dome of a head gleamed in the light of the lamp he had carried from the back room. His clothing, austere, was perfectly cut, and fell from broad shoulders to floor in an almost august drape of black. He wore a beard, but it was cropped close to his face, and veered down his chin in a sharp point—as unlike Radell's facial mess as a beard could be. He radiated both confidence and power.

Perhaps, Rath thought, he did Radell a disservice; if this man was not a Patris, if he was not one of the patriciate that ruled the Isle—at least in monetary affairs, for he was clearly not one of The Ten—Radell could be forgiven for making the assumption.

"Patris," Radell continued, when the man had taken as close a look at Rath as Rath was comfortable with, "this is Wade."

"Wade? I see." The man extended a hand.

Rath, carrying the pack in his hands, made an exaggerated display of its weight, excusing himself from the social nicety of actually taking the offered hand. Rath was a good actor; there was no awkwardness in the refusal.

But . . . the man noted it.

"Wade does odd jobs for me," Radell continued, stepping in front of Rath, and bowing again. The bow lent dignity to the word "scraping." "And if he is not always timely, he is *very* reliable."

"He is the man upon whom we have been waiting, then."

Radell colored slightly. "Yes, Patris. My apologies. There was some difficulty—"

"Yes, yes," the Patris said, lifting a large hand. "If you will proceed," he added, looking at Rath. "My time grows short. I am a busy man."

Radell ushered them into the back room. Light, magelight, adorned the walls in four places, and the furniture gleamed with new oil; the chairs, curved arms beneath velvet pads, had been placed around a flat, wide table. The table was almost made gaudy by the intricate carvings that circled its perimeter; the legs curved and ended in wooden paws, in mimicry of some great Southern beast. The wood was dense, ironwood or perhaps cherry; it was stained so dark it was almost black, although paler streaks of grain could be seen in the light.

Nothing in this room was sparse or subtle.

Rath, silent, placed the pack upon the table. He failed to take a chair, but the Patris did not. Seated, the man was more impressive. He could almost meet Radell's eyes on a level, and Radell was standing and unconsciously—or self-consciously—wringing his hands; he, too, remained standing, as if at attention.

"Patris," he said, "wine?"

The man shook his head. "Not tonight, Avram, but I thank you for your offer of hospitality. I am eager to see what your associate bears with him."

Rath wanted to be gone, and quickly. But he was meticulous and careful as he removed each of the stone pieces from his backpack, orienting their carved runic surfaces toward Avram's distinguished customer as if he did nothing else with his life but serve.

He watched the man's face.

The man watched him. It was . . . unnerving. Very little in Rath's life was unnerving in this particular fashion.

"These?" the Patris said at last. He spoke to Rath. The single word carried enough authority that Radell did not seek to answer; he waited nervously, his silence loud.

Rath nodded. He didn't trust himself to speak, and this, too, was rare. Too much unsettling had happened in his life these past few days. It would be good to be quit of them.

The Patris picked up the larger fragment. His eyes passed once across the carved surface, and he frowned. "Where," he asked, "did this come from?"

"I'm afraid, sir, that I can't say," Rath replied. He kept his tone modulated, his words almost as obsequious as Radell's had been.

"Can't, or won't?"

"Can't. My job was simply to retrieve these items from another of Avram's associates. If you are interested, I can ask."

"I am interested." He put the piece down. Picked up the second. His gaze seemed cursory; he barely touched the stone. "They are genuine," he told Avram. "I will take them both. I will also," he added, before Radell could begin to speak about his favorite thing, that being money, "take any other such items as can be found."

Radell looked suitably hesitant. It was only half act. "Patris, I have many customers, and if I—"

"The first," the man said quietly, "is worth three thousand gold crowns to me. The second is a lesser piece; I will pay you fifteen hundred."

Radell almost choked on his tongue. It would have been funny, in other circumstances.

But Rath found little amusement here. Patris AMatie bore no medallion; he was therefore not one of the historical scholars that were scattered like market litter throughout the Order of Knowledge. Nor was he one of their mages, or if he was, he chose to hide the fact. It made no difference; in either case, he had named a sum that was three times the best value Rath could have extracted from a member of the Order.

"I will write a bank note," the man continued. "If you will draw up the paperwork, Avram?"

Radell was still standing there, fish-mouthed.

Rath stepped on his foot.

"Of course, you will want to hold these pieces until the funds have been transferred."

"No, no, I wouldn't hear of it," Radell said. He'd managed to reel his tongue in, and it was flapping as usual. His hands were a colorful accompaniment; they were waving. "You've always been the *best* of customers; I trust you *completely*."

"But not so completely that you're willing to disclose your sources," the man replied, with a mock smile. And it *was* a mock smile; it never touched his eyes.

Radell failed to notice. Had the failure been deliberate, it would have said something about Radell's wisdom; that it wasn't also said something about said wisdom.

Radell ushered Rath out of the room. "I'll get ink," he told the Patris, "and my best paper." As if he had second-best paper. Which, given it was Radell, was probably the case. When the door was behind them—but not quite closed—Radell caught Rath's sleeve. "I'll give you half," he said. Funny, how little of the instant pandering remained.

Rath nodded.

"If it weren't for me, you wouldn't even have a customer for this stuff," Radell continued. "And, of course, I have my establishment to think of. It's not cheap, having a real store in the Common."

Rath nodded again.

Radell's lungs ballooned anyway. The sum of money had obviously closed down the part of his brain that controlled his mouth.

"Avram," Rath said coolly, "I said *yes.*"

"And I—I—you said yes. Right. Half."

"And if you start rubbing your hands together, I'll break them."

Radell looked hurt. But he shoved his hands into his belt loops; he knew when Rath was serious. "You don't like him?"

"I don't care one way or the other. Like the Patris, I, too, am a busy man."

"Of course. Of course you are. Not timely, but busy."

"Give my regards to your customer," Rath continued, as he made his way to the door. "I'll be back sometime next week to collect my money."

"Will you have anything else for me when you come?"

"Don't push."

"Right. Right. Well, you know your business, and I know mine. It's good to see you," he said, practically shoving Rath in the direction Rath was heading anyway. "Good of you to drop by. See you later."

It took Rath six hours to get home.

Six hours, five of which were spent attempting to elude pursuit. A pursuit that he wouldn't have noticed had it not been for the words of an orphan girl with clear, dark eyes and hair that looked like an accident.

The tails were *good.* Far too good. He saw the obvious man first, although obvious was perhaps an uncharitable word. Had he not been looking for him, Rath wouldn't have seen him at all. The man was dressed as if he lived in the holdings, and teetered as if he'd been drinking in their famed taverns; he even reeked of alcohol, and at the distance that Rath kept, this said much. But his expression was a little too strained, and his gaze a tad too alert.

He lost the man quickly enough. An hour.

And when he lost him, he should have relaxed. Should have. Instinct made him far more careful than he would otherwise have been. Instinct, and fact.

Rath had arrived without notice at Radell's door. There was no way that the Patris could have known he was coming; Rath had told no one. Certainly not Radell. But on no notice—on none at all that Rath could conceive of—he had set up a tail. Had he had guards—any guards—in Radell's shop, Rath would have been less surprised; easy enough for one of the men to leave by the back door. Rath had done it himself on numerous occasions.

But there were no guards. The man who had followed him had appeared out of the proverbial nowhere. And because he had, the hour spent walking in wide and awkward circles, in a neighborhood that Rath knew better than well, didn't feel quite right. Losing the man, far from easing suspicion, honed it. He kept on walking for another half an hour; found himself by the riverbank. The bridges were still. If people were living under them, as Jewel had done, they slept, or they had no way of lighting a fire. At this time of year, it wasn't necessary.

He threw stones into the moving current, pulled his pipe from his pocket, and smoked a little, thinking. Worrying.

This was Jay's bridge. He shook his head, started to walk. The distance from riverbank to building wasn't great; the holdings here were packed with buildings, and the street was as wide as a wagon, if that. The mage-lights shone building-side, and the occasional person walked beneath them, favoring that light.

Rath walked toward the occupied part of the street, and then he smiled; it was a cold smile, Winter in a face. He emptied his pipe, tucked it into his satchel, and began another aimless tour of the city.

The second tail was so much part of the shadows that Rath had failed to notice him until he was in the middle of the thirtieth holding. He did not teeter, did not attempt to make himself part of the living landscape that defined the poorer holdings; he simply failed to be seen.

Or tried.

Rath shrugged, uneasy. This would not be the first time that he had been followed—not the first time that the men who followed were trained professionals. But it was the first time that he spent a useless hour in an attempt to lose a pursuer.

Whoever he was, he might have been one of the almost legendary scent hounds of the Western Kingdoms.

Two hours later, and he was still being followed. His fingers brushed dagger hilt as he considered—and discarded—that option. Something about the grace of the man, moving almost unseen between buildings, beneath lights, spoke of competence—and no one that competent would be an easy kill. No one that competent could fail to note, at this stage, that he had been sighted.

It became a game, but Rath had never been fond of cat and mouse; he hadn't the temperament to be a cat, and being a mouse had less than no appeal. Rath varied his pace, running in quick bursts and stopping just as quickly; turning into alleys that led nowhere, and leaping tall board fences that led into scant yards and more alley.

No good.

He even dodged into Taverson's and stayed for an hour, taking a bar stool and watching the entrance. It was late enough that men and women came and went, but none of them were his pursuer. He eventually paid for the drink he upended in a potted plant, and negotiated his way out the back; the man was there. Shadow, not light, and waiting. But he, too, kept his distance; he hadn't come for a fight.

In the end, Rath chose utter lack of dignity as his escape route; he waited for the familiar sounds of a magisterial patrol, pitched his voice as high as it would go, and screamed his lungs out. He had heard men scream in terror, had heard them scream in pain. He had a good memory for sound, and he used it to his advantage; he blended knowledge with experience, and then ran as if his life depended on it.

The heavy steps of men in a sudden panic grew at his back. They grew, he thought, with a grim satisfaction, in exactly the same line that his pursuer would take. He had minutes before his pursuer would manage to hide himself from the patrol, and he made use of them.

It was enough. But it was barely enough.

It had been a long, long time since Rath had twitted a patrol in that fashion. He'd had the excuse of youthful exuberance, a lost bet, and rather too much alcohol behind him, but that hadn't counted for much when the very annoyed magisterial guards had deposited him on the grand steps of his family manor.

It had also been earlier in the evening, and if youth wasn't an excuse, it was a guarantee of a fast recovery; he was not so young now, and the last sprint made itself felt in the building quiver of fatigued muscles. It had been a *long* day. Too long. It was good to be home.

He made his way up the stairs, stopped at the door, and fished his keys out of his inner pocket. They were the only thing of worth he now carried, and he was grimly happy to be rid of the tablets; he couldn't have escaped the guard while carrying them, and it would have pained him greatly to leave them behind.

He was practical enough that he would have done it, however. He had proved, time and again, that he was good at leaving things behind.

Rath made his way to the bed in the darkness, and then stopped; had he been given to dramatics, he would have slapped his forehead. He had forgotten, in the lull of relief, that his bed was occupied, and not by a person who would be happy of his company.

He fumbled for a moment, retrieving his magelight; he palmed it carefully, folding his fingers over its heart. They glowed red in the room's night. As his eyes adjusted, he looked down at the longed-for bed.

Jewel lay dead center, her legs straight, her arms on the outside of the counterpane. Her hair covered her eyes and splayed in flattened curls against the mattress; he had no pillow. He listened for her breath, trying to judge by its regularity whether or not she slept.

"You can stop pretending," he finally said. "I'm the only person who has keys."

Her eyes opened. It was hot enough in the room that her forehead glistened evenly. Sweat, in the fevered, was not a bad sign.

"Did you sleep at all?"

She nodded.

"I told you," he said grimly, "that you are not to lie to me here." He approached her slowly, and as he did, he opened his fingers one by one until the light was bright.

"I'm not. I slept."

"When did you wake?"

She was mute. After a moment, she shrugged. In a small voice, she said, "I wasn't sure you'd come."

"I was followed." He sat on the bed. She didn't move away, although the mattress sagged with his weight. "By one competent man and one expert."

"*Two?*"

"Two."

"Do you know who sent them?"

"I know now." He paused, and then rose and set the light in its pedestal a room away. It was a good light; it grew bright at his back. When he returned, he said, "I have a name. I have no idea if it's a real name.

"I'll get you water. Wait." He picked up the wineskin on the bed table, and gave it a squeeze. It was empty. Good girl.

"I don't need—"

"Wait *quietly*."

He padded into the kitchen, removed his boots, and dropped them. He loosened his shirt as well, and briefly considered pouring some of the water over his head to cool it. But there wasn't a lot of water, and he wasn't of a mind to go to the nearest public well to get more; he filled the wineskin and returned.

Jewel took it from his hands; her own were shaking. Her eyes were a little too bright, and he touched her forehead as she sat up and almost overbalanced. She was hot, but the fever was not—yet—high. He watched her drink; watched her cough and splutter.

"Jewel," he said speaking in as measured a tone as he could, "I am not angry. And I will not touch you."

She said, "I know."

"Then stop being nervous. I find it annoying."

She nodded.

He stopped himself from rolling his eyes. "I've had a change of plans," he said quietly.

"You're leaving tonight." She looked at his hands, and the wineskin still fairly full of water, at the counterpane, at the spot behind his left shoulder—at anything but his face. As if, by doing these things, she could hide her expression.

And gods, her expression; it was so muted, so subtle, and so utterly obvious, he found his voice gentling, as if it belonged to a different man. "There is no tonight left. But yes, I'm moving sooner than I had intended."

She pushed the counterpane off her legs and tried to slide off the bed; her thighs hit his hands, and she stopped. "I'll go," she whispered.

"No," he said, resignation stronger than surprise. "You won't. Not yet."

"I'm sorry—I—"

"You repaid the debt—any debt—that you might have incurred; if your Oma's advice troubles you, remember that. You owe me nothing as of tonight. I doubt very much that I would be moving at all had I been followed here. Or, rather, I doubt that I would be moving to a destination of my own choosing."

Her hands were shaking. He reached out and caught them in his own, noticing, as if for the first time, how small they were. He had asked her if she was strong, and he knew that she was; her strength was not defined by something as simple as muscle.

"I lied," he told her quietly.

She said nothing, but her eyes—they must be close to tearing. She didn't blink.

"I'll be packing." He rose, and as he did, he bent to pick up a cloak that lay half under the bed. It was speckled with bread crumbs, and he shook it absently, folding it with care.

"Rath?"

"What?"

"What lie?"

"I don't like children much," he replied. Which would only confuse her. Then again, he could probably say anything at this point, and it would only confuse her. *How have you survived this long?* But he wasn't certain if he meant the question for Jewel or himself, so he didn't ask it aloud.

Instead, continuing the rhythm of retrieving and folding his various pieces of clothing, he said, "I've never liked children much. They talk. They blubber. They get in the way."

She did none of those things. She waited.

"And they ask too many questions."

He heard the rustle of cloth. Turned to see that she'd pulled the counterpane up, until it rested in folds beneath her sharp chin.

"I won't leave you here."

"I can't stay, if you're gone." She was shivering now. Chills, he thought. The fever was climbing. It would help if she coughed, if she said her ears hurt, if she broke out in boils or a rash. These, he was familiar with.

She couldn't see his grim smile. "You probably won't survive. You're ill. That's another thing I hate about children; they get sick too much."

He discarded something. There was always too much to take with him, and anything that he couldn't carry didn't concern him.

"Now *go to sleep.*"

"But I—"

"I can't carry you," he continued, ignoring her attempt at words. "And you need your strength; you'll have to walk."

Her brows rose, or what he could see of them did; she didn't even push her hair out of her eyes. No defiance left in her. He missed it, a little. Gods, he was a fool. He folded more clothing, piled it beside the magelight. Turned his back on her, as he would often do, because it was easier to talk that way.

"I consider my life to be worth vastly more than a meager handful of copper coins."

"They were silver," she told him.

"Are you ever dishonest?"

"I stole them."

"Good point. Now shut up. Sleep."

"I can't. You're talking to me."

"Most people find that my 'talking to them,' as you so quaintly put it, is an aid to sleep, not a hindrance."

She snorted. Weakly.

"Very well. I consider my life to be worth more than a handful of silver coins. Or gold coins, if it comes to that. In fact, it may come as a surprise to you, but I consider my life to be of more value than pretty much anything under the sun."

"My Oma used to say that. Not about her life, but the bit about under the sun. I think it's Southern."

"Thank you for the lesson," he said dryly. "Now pay attention, because I also consider *my* lessons to be of vastly more import than yours." But he said it gently, and he cursed quietly when he realized that he had turned to look at her, his hands falling still.

"I am therefore in your debt. And, mindful of the words of your Oma, I am not happy to *be* in your debt."

He knew what she would say next, and unfortunately, she didn't surprise him. "I didn't save your life. He didn't tell them to kill you; he only told them to follow you."

"In my profession, Jewel, they are often the same thing."

"But you can't be sure."

"You haggle like a merchant—a merchant intent on giving away everything of value, rather than selling it to make a living. Now *shut up*."

She laughed. Wrapped the blanket more tightly around her. He grimaced, picked up the cloak he had folded so carefully, and threw it on top of the counterpane. She felt cold enough now that she didn't protest. He touched her forehead; the cold was very, very hot.

"I now owe you my life. Nursing you back to what passes for health on the streets is not going to unburden me—but it will have to do. When I leave, you will come with me."

She started to speak, and he glared.

"If you thank me, I'll hit you. I am *not* saying that you can live with me. I'm saying that I'll keep you until you can at least walk out the door without collapsing." There were so many questions that had to be asked. He wanted to ask them now.

But he thought he knew some of the answers he would get, and he was dead tired; he didn't want the bother of dealing with them.

Her wide eyes still followed his every movement. And he found that he couldn't work while they did; he felt haunted. So he sat on the bed again, caught one of her hands in his, picked up the wineskin in the other. Cursed her genially in three different languages. The tone of voice obviously mattered more than the content, because she smiled vacantly, and her eyes began to film.

Gods save him from tears.

He had nursed wounded men before. He had sat by their sides while they died. It was both easier and harder than this.

Chapter Three

WHEN RATH LEFT in the morning—after what felt like an hour's rest—Jewel was sleeping. She had turned away from him, and her back was exposed; her arms crossed her chest, her hands covered her shoulders, and her knees were tucked beneath her chin. She covered such a small area of the bed, it seemed a pity to waste the space.

He rose and changed while she slept, taking the time to drag his lank hair into plaits; he took nothing out of the boxes that he did not need. He also chose to forgo his hat; a hat was almost its own character, and he needed as little character as possible. He took his satchel, made sure it was heavier than usual, and then paused to look at Jewel.

She hadn't moved. When he touched her forehead, she stirred, but not enough to waken; she was becoming accustomed to his intrusions, slight as they were. She was not burning, but often fever was at its ebb in the hours of dawn. It hadn't broken; it hovered, like a cloud in the sky of her body.

He told himself he should take her and dump her on the steps of the Mother's closest temple. Told himself forcefully, decorating the declarative sentences with as much foul language as he knew. And then, having failed to convince himself, he made his way to the door, unbolted it, and let himself out. He was very careful to bolt it at his back, and he stood outside in the hall for long enough that other movement in neighboring apartments could be heard. He realized he was afraid to leave her.

This annoyed him enough that he did.

The farmers were making their way through the streets from the East gate. The Common itself was only slowly coming to life, and the streets were as barren as they would be while the sunlight lasted. During the stormy months, the market day was of necessity shorter; Rath was glad that this particular move had not been undertaken during the Winter.

But he watched the flags rise in the Common, and then turned away from them, heading deeper into the hundred holdings. Rath knew how to get around the old city. The streets were of passing convenience, but they were not his only form of egress; they were just the safest, and as he did not wish to draw attention to himself, he followed their course, whistling tunelessly as he walked.

He needed a neighborhood that was harder to traverse without some knowledge of the holdings; he also needed a place in which the landlord was more eager for money—timely money—than answers. Although it was commonly thought that all forms of debauchery took place in the oldest and poorest of the hundred holdings, Rath had found that common wisdom was generally not wise; there were monstrous men everywhere, from the highest of walks to the lowest, and if one knew the city well enough, any holding was safe.

Or that had been his early experience.

In the last couple of years, the whispers had grown steadily, and the fear that spread with them had grown as well. It was not his fear, but he felt it. Wondered how much he would be aware of it had he not promised to nurse one sick child back to health.

And to what end? She would be healthy, yes, but the streets would be her home; she had some skill at reading and writing, but no way to offer those skills to an employer who would find them useful. The absurd desire to aid her was exactly that: absurd, a fool's hope. She would go to the streets, they would devour her, and if he chanced upon her again, years from now, she would be a hollow shell of the girl who had offered a farmer money for food he had thought to give her in charity.

And that, he told himself angrily, was *not* his problem. He owed her; he would pay that debt and be quit of it.

But she had given him a warning that had quite probably saved his life. He hadn't asked her enough yet. Not enough to be certain. If he could be certain . . . he shook his head. If he could be, what then? He was in no position to exploit anyone. The girl herself clearly didn't understand the value of the warning she had offered; she had offered it with so much hesitation, he guessed that she was accustomed to a much colder response. He wondered if she would have spoken at all, had it not been for the forceful warning of a dead, old woman, and the girl's natural fear of obligation.

At best, he might introduce her to someone who would prize that gift, and force the child to use it.

And that left an unfortunate taste in his mouth.

The thirty-second holding melted into the thirty-third; guards were seldom seen, but when he heard them, he avoided them on general principle.

He visited several tenements, made mental lists of them all, and found them wanting. This was a part of the process of finding the right place for any given stage of his life, and normally, he didn't resent it.

But time was of the essence, as the saying went, and he found his mood souring with each dead end. By the time the sun was at its peak, he was in the thirty-fifth holding, and he had just walked into the seventh building, holding a dialogue with his stomach that would have embarrassed a man with more impeccable manners. Once, that might have been Rath.

The reminder did nothing to shore up his mood, and the smile he gave the landlord was forced enough that the landlord hesitated. Rath, knowing that he was better than this, forced that smile into something that resembled a natural grin, and the landlord shook his head, muttering something under his breath that Rath didn't care to hear.

This time, instead of taking stairs up, he was led down a hall to a set of stairs that descended. Sunlight vanished slowly until they reached the end of that narrow flight, which opened into a single hall, if hall was a word that could accurately be used. Rath didn't have to duck; neither did the landlord. Someone of Patris AMatie's stature would have had to, and this was oddly comforting.

There were window wells at the height of the hall; they let in a brief glimpse of both street and the back alley—an alley that had once, by the look of it, been a garden. The building itself was not as tall as many that Rath had lived in; it was, however, a good deal broader. There were decayed fringes of stonework at the foundation, and along the outer walls; someone with money had once lived here. He was either long dead, or long gone, his life relocated to the more fashionable districts within the holdings. The home that remained was skeletal, and instead of housing a single family with a retinue of servants, now housed several.

The architect had never intended that, but architects were responsible for something done in a moment of time; what became of their work was a matter of economics and the ebb and flow of history.

"This is the only set of rooms I have available," the wiry man said over his shoulder. He carried a lamp, rather than a magelight, and the flicker of fire contained in glass made all shadows dance and quiver. Even Rath's.

"These halls," Rath said quietly, "are they wood?"

"They are now."

"And before?"

"Dirt. Stone. I don't know. I bought the building from someone who had a few gambling debts he couldn't pay down fast enough."

Rath didn't ask. The man offered no more about the former owner, but he did continue to speak in his grating rasp of a voice. "There are only these rooms, in the basement. There are windows," the man added, as he stopped in front of a solid door and pulled out an ostentatious ring of keys. "But they're not good for much. I've had them barred," he added.

Rath doubted that the bars would be any good. He'd have to examine them from the outside. "No neighbors?"

"The ones above you."

Better. "How much do you want for the place?"

"I get paid by the week," the man said. "Five silver crowns."

"Four."

The man shrugged. "Four and a half."

Rath said nothing; the door slid open. It didn't creak; it was in good enough repair. "These rooms—they don't have an exit of their own?"

"They do. We don't use it much," the man added, his eyes shifting to the side. "The frame's warped, and the door needs to be leveled. It takes an ox to pull it open. Or two."

Rath nodded. He walked through the open door and into a small hall. The hall—in repair that was only slightly better than the one that led from the stairs—contained four doors, two to the left, one to the right, and one at the end. "Four rooms?"

The man shrugged. "The fourth's not much. It's storage."

"You use it?"

Again the man's eyes shifted sideways. "No."

Rath liked men whose expressions gave almost everything away; it made them easy to read, and easy to predict.

The air in this place was cool. And Summer was hot enough that this appealed to Rath. "What's in the storage room now?"

"Old furniture," the man said, just a shade too quickly. His voice had gone slick and oily in the scant syllables. "Look, use the three rooms, and I'll give them to you for four crowns. The storage room's unfinished."

"You could have—"

"There are floors there, flooring, but it's old and rotted. My nephew broke his leg falling through them. I wouldn't suggest you try."

"What's beneath the floor?"

"Dirt." Again, the man spoke too quickly.

Rath kept his smile to himself. He tried to make a mental map of the building, tried to gauge the depth of the basement. "Four crowns," he said quietly. "When do the rooms become available?"

"They're available now."

"Good." He pulled his satchel off his shoulder and made a show of fumbling with its buckle. The man drew closer, the ring of keys rippling in the lamplight. He seemed eager, which was generally a bad sign.

"Two weeks up front," Rath said.

"Fair enough."

"Do you have a curfew?"

"What, do I look like your mother? Don't make a lot of noise, don't bring your business here, and don't cause problems with the magisterians. That's all I ask."

Rath put eight coins in the man's key hand. "Don't bother," he said, as the man looked for some place to set the lamp down. "Leave the door unlocked; I'll want to change the locks myself."

"You leave me copies of the keys."

Rath stared the landlord down. "I'll pay a month up front," he countered. "And I'll pay per month ahead of time."

All men were merchants if you dug deep enough; some required only the barest of surface scratching. The landlord bickered and whined, but his heart wasn't in it; he went through the motions because to do otherwise was to imply that the rooms were empty for a reason.

Which, clearly, they were. Rath didn't ask, largely because he didn't expect an answer that would be either truthful or useful.

When the landlord collected his money, he gave Rath what would pass for a friendly nod in a bar brawl, and retreated. "Don't change the lock to the building's front door," he said, "or I'll call the magisterians."

Rath nodded absently; he doubted that the locks of the front door were even in passable working condition.

*   *   *

He'd left Jewel alone for most of the day; had to. He stopped at the Common farmers' market, and then forced himself to go to the well and wait in line, avoiding bored boys with buckets. He filled two waterskins, spoke pleasant, empty words to one of the two grandmothers who minded children far younger than Jewel, and then departed.

Jewel was waiting for him when he opened the door.

Her eyes were sleep-crusted and heavy; she rubbed them as he slid bolts back into place and looked at the neat and empty rooms. "I've called for a carriage," he told her quietly.

"You called a carriage *here?*"

It was a reasonable question. He approached and touched her forehead; she grimaced. It was not a wince; it was a child's complaint. "You're still running a fever."

"Why do they say that?"

"What?"

"Running. A fever."

He shrugged. "I don't know. Possibly because people get hotter when they run for too long. You're still hot. Is that better? Here." He handed her a waterskin. "I've brought food as well, and I expect you to eat it. I'll be moving things into the carriage while you eat."

"No one calls a carriage to the thirty-second holding," she mumbled.

It was true.

"Is it because of me?"

She would always surprise him. This was the first time he realized it, or perhaps accepted it. But because she wouldn't believe him if he lied, and because the only reason *to* lie was to put her at ease, he nodded.

She looked pained. Was, he realized, in pain. Fever pain; her skin was probably prickling at every touch, every contact. Her stare was slightly glassy. Rath looked out at the sun, and down at the shadows it cast. Evening was coming. He'd waited too long.

"Forget the food," he told her roughly. "But drink the water. Drink both of these," he added, handing her the second skin. "Now."

She lifted her arms; they were shaking. He could not bear to watch her fumble with the stopper, and opened the skin himself. Water dribbled down the corners of her mouth, and from there, down the front of her rumpled shirt. He almost shouted at her, then. To be careful. To drink carefully.

But the cloth of her shirt darkened, and he saw the way it clung to her ribs. He hated poverty.

"Jewel," he said, his jaw stiff, "I won't be in your debt."

"What?"

"You'd better survive this."

She said, "If I don't, do you think my father will be waiting for me?"

"He's dead."

"I *know* that. I mean, in Mandaros' Hall. In the long hall." Her dark eyes were a little too wide.

"I don't know, never having been dead," he said curtly. He did not speak of gods, and of his general contempt for people who relied on them; if she took comfort in their undeniable existence, he was unwilling to part her from it. "And I don't intend for you to find out. You can die on someone else." He started to say something, thought better of it, and lifted the heaviest of his chests. This one was the oldest, and it was also the finest, although the humidity of the years had caused it to bow slightly with age. Grunting, he made his way to the door.

"You locked it," she said.

He cursed.

"You locked it for me," she added, her voice dropping.

It was true; he had. He'd been thinking of her. "If you apologize," he said, through gritted teeth, as he unlocked the bolts, "I swear I'll hit you."

"You swear a lot."

"Not until I met you."

She snorted. Choked. But she was drinking, and that was enough.

She was the last thing he carried down to the waiting carriage. That the carriage *had* waited spoke more of the expense of its hire than it did of the driver; the man was clearly nervous this deep into the holdings.

His nerves didn't get any better when he saw what Rath carried; Rath had bundled Jewel up in the counterpane, but her bare feet dangled free of its edges; it had been done in haste.

"I didn't pay you to gawk," Rath snapped. "And I certainly didn't pay you to ask questions."

The driver did neither, or attempted to do neither; he managed not to ask questions.

Rath carried Jewel into the coach and slammed the door, juggling her negligible weight in his lap. She was barely conscious, but she frowned as the carriage started its creaking, bumpy motion through the streets.

"I always wanted to ride in one of these," she said. "But it's not very comfortable."

"You will find, with time, that very little that you want is comfortable. At least, not when you've achieved it. Now hush."

"Why?"

"Because I can barely hear you over the wheels."

She nodded and settled against his chest. It was almost dark; the mage-lights above were beginning to shed brilliant light in a hazy glow. The streets were misted; they tasted of the sea.

"We're going to live in the dark," Jewel told him.

He didn't ask her how she knew this. He brushed the hair from her eyes instead, so that she could see him nod.

Some items of furniture could not be conveyed by carriage; he had left bed and mattress in the now empty rooms that had, a day ago, been home. But he had brought bedrolls and sleeping bags, one of which had seen some use in the North. He ceded that one to Jewel, and laid her out against the floor of the smallest, and emptiest, room. The landlord hadn't lied; there were window wells just below the height of the ceiling, and they fronted the building's east side. The bars—he had had the gall to call them bars—were a simple, rusted net, something meant to keep garbage out. Where garbage was not a determined thief.

Rath would fix that over the next few days.

The waterskin was almost empty. "Drink this," he told the child. When she didn't answer, he opened the skin and dripped water into her mouth, watching as she swallowed. At night, her fever was at its height, burning its way through flesh.

He thought she was asleep. She caught his hand, dispelling that comfortable illusion. "Rath," she whispered, the word dry and almost silent. "Will you go out tonight?"

"Not tonight."

She nodded, and did not speak again.

He did, but the words were soft and foreign, and interlaced with their cadence was the beginning and end of an old song his nanny had favored.

✻   ✻   ✻

The next three days were—in the usual rhythm of Rath's hectic life—quite boring. Ordinary. Things that he had, in a foolish, distant youth, disdained.

He left Jewel sleeping on the first day—when she would sleep—and saw to the fitting of new locks and new bars. The man responsible for the work was an old friend.

"Don't like the look of the neighborhood," he said, as he worked.

Rath shrugged. "It suits me."

"It suits you, yes." The bars were thick, but they were harder to place than normal, given where they were situated.

Rath rolled his eyes. "What is it, Taybor?"

"Last I heard, you had sworn off women."

"Sworn at them, as I recall. So?"

"And I've never heard it said that you had much interest in children."

Ah. "You think so little of me?" he said softly.

"I'm here, aren't I?" Taybor grunted as he worked a bolt into the outer brick. Rath would not live in a building that had no brick; the bars were too easy to dislodge, otherwise.

"Yes. As always. Not that you're doing the work for free."

"The wife wouldn't like it."

"She wouldn't like being used as an excuse much either, unless you've got a new wife I haven't met."

Taybor's laugh was a short burst of sound, just shy of a snort. But there was genuine affection in it. "Same old wife," he said, with the hint of a smile. "Same old shop.

"But I'll tell you, Rath, if she were here helping out, she'd tan your hide."

"I am *not* involved with a *child*."

"No. But she's here, isn't she?" And he nodded to the window beneath the bars he was erecting.

"She's here."

"Why?"

"Do I ask you about your business?"

"Frequently."

"That would be considered making polite small talk in other parts of town," Rath replied. "It's not as if I actually care."

Taybor laughed again. He was a short man, almost as wide around the chest as he was tall, with a shock of hair that would be called red in anyone's estimate. None of the girth could be called fat, although his wife, Marjorie, often did. She was, on the other hand, the only person who could without suffering for it.

"Marjorie would probably approve," Rath added.

"Oh?"

"The girl's ill. No, I don't know with what. It's not the usual Summer diseases—at least not the ones I've seen."

"You've not caught anything?"

"Not yet." He would have coughed, but he didn't trust Taybor's humor to extend that far. In the Summer, the crippling disease was not a joking matter, and many healthy men were suspicious of anything that could lead to it.

"So . . . you're being a nursemaid, now?"

"Business is slow," Rath said, with a shrug. "Good work," he added, as he made show of examining Taybor's bars.

Taybor snorted. The sound was not unlike Jewel's snort, except for the nose that emitted it. The older nose had been broken at least once that Rath personally knew of. "That slow?"

Rath shrugged. "I found her by the river. She was living under a bridge." He paused. "She'd stolen some money."

"Yours?"

"Would I care if it were anyone else's?"

"Not usually, no. Then again, you wouldn't usually bring a thief home and put her to bed either."

"I should have blackened both her eyes."

"Marjorie wouldn't have complained much, if you explained why."

"Hah. You've forgotten your wife's temper."

"She does have a bit of a soft spot for starving children. Comes from all that work in the Mother's temple, I imagine. You want me to take the kid?"

Yes. Yes, Rath wanted that. But the word that came out was No.

"You're going soft, Rath," Taybor said, as he stretched his shoulders and stepped back to examine his work. He stood on the bars; they took his weight. "Door, too?"

"Same as usual."

It was too much to hope that the conversation had ended, although Rath did try to steer it in a dozen other directions. Taybor was a good locksmith, and a passably good blacksmith as well—but he was ferociously focused; once he'd glommed onto something, he let go when he was good and ready. Rath had seen bulldogs with less of a grip.

"If you're going soft," Taybor said, as he examined the single lock on the door, "you should be about ready for another line of work."

"That is getting dangerously close to the thin line," Rath replied.

The lock being examined was beneath Taybor's contempt. He spared it a cursory, damning glance, and then set about disassembling it; Rath held the magelight. There wasn't enough to work by otherwise.

"Thin or no, Rath, I mean it. If you've taken this girl in, you're changing. If you're about to tell me you're not, I'll believe you—but in that case, it's no life for a girl."

"And life under a bridge, starving slowly, is?"

Taybor's friendly face folded a moment in what passed for a thoughtful expression. "No," he said at last. "I assume she's got no kin?"

"None that are living."

"She told you?"

"More or less."

"No siblings?"

"None that she mentioned." He paused and then added, "She *is* feverish, Taybor."

"Meaning you haven't asked."

"As a rule, I don't ask more than I need to. Information is—"

"I know, I know. The Mother's temple—"

Rath shook his head.

"Look, I know you don't hold much with the gods. I'm fine with that. But the people there do good work. Marjorie—"

"Let it go." Rath leaned up against a wall. "It's not as if I intend to keep her."

"You don't?"

"Do I look like an orphanage?"

"Not much." The lock disassembled—along with the doorknob— Taybor looked up. "What do you intend to do?" Friendliness had ebbed from the tone; what remained was steel. Taybor was good at working with that.

"I intend to see her healthy," Rath replied, choosing his words with care. "I want her out—but I'm not going to turn her into the streets of the thirty-fifth when she can't even walk."

Taybor's gaze was unflinching and unwavering. He stared at Rath until the silence was long past uncomfortable, and then shrugged his broad shoulders. "Be careful, Rath. Children grow on you."

"So does fungus."

Taybor chuckled and began to reassemble the door with a different locking mechanism. The bolts would follow. "Never thought I'd see the day," he said.

Rath didn't deign to reply. If the only bad to come of Jewel was laughter at his expense, he could live with it.

But he heard her cry out, and tried to look casual as he leaped past Taybor and into the hall beyond his bent back.

"Jewel," he said, throwing the door wide.

She was sitting, her eyes wild.

He caught her as she struggled out of the sleeping bag and stumbled blindly toward the door, as if he were invisible. She didn't struggle; as her feet left the floor, she stilled instead. She was hot.

"What is it, what's happened? Are you in pain? Do you need to throw up?"

"They told me you were dead," she whispered, as her arms crept up around his neck.

He knew that she was delirious. But he didn't tell her that she was wrong. Instead, he cradled her, his eyes closed, his hearing attuned to her ragged breath. When she slept again, he put her down, loosening her grip.

Taybor was standing in the door's frame. He shook his head. "I tell you, Rath—"

"Shut up, Taybor. Just—shut up."

The locks finished, Rath sat by Jewel. He had taken the time to visit the well—actually, he'd taken more than enough time, because he'd had to *find* it first—and had come back with water of dubious quality. He fed it to her, sitting on cramped knees by her side. He needed to find a bed, but that could wait.

She woke seldom, and when she did, she was listless. The defiance and the caution that had defined her had been swallowed; she had become entirely fever. He knew that the fever would either break or consume her, and he was unwilling to leave until one or the other had happened.

Taybor came by later in the day. He had two large baskets, one in either hand, when Rath opened the door for him, and he handed them both to Rath without comment.

"I don't think she'll eat," Rath said.

"Idiot. They're for you."

Rath was momentarily nonplussed, but it didn't last. He paid Taybor for the food. Taybor took the money; long years of friendship had made clear the danger of offering Rath anything that resembled charity.

In this, Rath and Jewel had much in common.

But before he left, Taybor offered to take Jewel to the Mother's temple again.

Rath said, "You win. She is not going to the Mother's temple, now, tomorrow, or the day after. If you hear that I died in the next week, you can come and fetch her."

Taybor's smile was slight. "It's not a contest," he said, but he was grinning.

"You're keeping score."

"Happens I am. Don't tell Marjorie."

"You don't tell her I'm living in the basement of a hovel in the thirty-fifth holding with a sick ten year old, and I won't tell her anything."

"Done. Rath?"

"What now?"

"If you weren't such a damn ornery cuss, I'd tell you I was proud of you."

"But I am. Don't."

"You fix to move again, give me a bit more warning next time."

Rath's smile was genuine. Taybor was one of the few men living that he trusted.

Two days later, the fever broke. Jewel had lost pounds—how many, Rath didn't care to guess—and her skin was pale and tight over bones that were far too prominent. Her eyes were ringed black, her cheeks hollow. But she would live.

Rath left the magelight with her. Given his own lack of familiarity with the new rooms, it made navigating more hazardous; he kept his boots on to protect his toes. His wooden chest was still closed, and the creep of mess and debris that characterized home had had no chance to start; the rooms were as neat and tidy as they would ever be.

The kitchen—if it could be graced with such an elevated description—

did have a vent to the outside; it was covered with new netting, and it was narrow enough that not even Jewel could fit an arm down the pipe. He didn't like it, but he didn't much like the idea of Winter without a woodstove. He busied himself, but did not cook anything; he mashed fruit, doused bread in milk, brought out soft cheese.

He carried these back to Jewel's room—and stopped himself from thinking of it *as* Jewel's room.

She was lying on the floor; she levered herself up on her elbows as he entered, and made to rise. He frowned, and she subsided; his frown was ferocious. Lack of sleep, and the uncommon occurrence of a gnawing worry, had conspired to rob him of any ability to project charm or friendliness.

"I feel funny," she told him, as he knelt by her side.

"You're weak," he replied.

"I know. But I—"

"I mean, you're weak from the fever. You haven't eaten much. You've barely been drinking water."

"Rath, I can't—"

"Do *not* start that again." He put the basket on her stomach, and helped her to sit. "Can you eat?"

She nodded. Her eyes were wide, seen as they were through unruly fringes of hair. Humidity hadn't done much to straighten the curls.

"Then eat."

"What about you?"

"I'll eat when you're finished."

She stared at him for a long time. "Can I at least say thank you?"

"No."

"Oh."

"Look, if your Oma is watching from Mandaros' Halls, she can damn well wait with the lectures."

Dark brows rose.

"I'm tired," he added. "And I'm not about to apologize for that in my own home."

"Have you left at all?"

"None of your business."

She ate a bit of the fruit, and her eyes widened again. He said nothing, watching her. Something too close to relief threatened to overwhelm him. Losing battle.

She ate for a while in silence, as if eating was new and fascinating. But silence, with children, rarely lasted. "What do you do?" she asked.

"You don't have any more questions."

Because she was ten, she nodded.

"But I happen to have a lot of them, and I want you to be healthy enough to answer."

Healthy enough was another two days in coming. Rath went out to market at the end of the second day; it was a longer walk, and he had to admit that the squalor of the thirty-fifth was worse than he'd remembered. Then again, he'd never actually lived in the thirty-fifth holding before; he wondered how long he would stay, now that he was there.

He stopped at Radell's shop.

Radell was alone; in the middle of the day, he often was. It was hard to imagine that he had enough custom to keep the storefront going, but the two pieces that Rath had brought would keep the shop open for some time.

Radell brightened when Rath walked through the door, and then sagged when he realized that Rath wasn't carrying anything of interest. "I suppose you're here for the money?" He managed to make the question sound vaguely accusatory.

Rath nodded.

"You'll be back with something soon?"

"Not for another week or so. I'm following a lead," Rath added.

"Good, good. No," Radell told him, as he ducked beneath the desk and fished a key out of a strongbox that wasn't actually locked, "I don't want to know anything about it."

"Has the Patris returned?"

Radell shook his head, almost mournfully. "He's a peculiar man," he said, because there was no one to hear him, "and a bit particular about things. But as you can see, his money's good."

"Impressively good."

Radell's eyes narrowed. "You think it's too good?"

"Everything is," Rath replied, with a bored shrug. "When did he start visiting your establishment?"

"He's been a customer for about three years. Maybe longer, but he didn't buy much until three years ago. He's particularly interested in Old Weston artifacts and books."

"And he knows enough not to be tempted by most of your antiques."

The emphasis on the word was not lost on Radell, but the younger man took no insult.

"Do you know where he lives?"

That, on the other hand, was coming close to a danger zone. "Why?"

"I'm curious. I have no desire to deal with him directly," Rath added. "As you should well know, by now."

"You deal with the Order of Knowledge."

"From time to time, yes. When I think that what I've found won't be of interest to your regular clientele."

"You should let me be the judge of that."

Given his taste in signage, beard, and clothing, Rath had formed distinct opinions about Radell's judgment. He was politic as ever, and kept these to himself. He considered telling Radell about the fact that the Patris had had him followed; the idea that Radell had arranged it never crossed Rath's mind.

Because Radell truly did not want to know anything about Rath's business. It was better for all concerned that way; if an item went missing, and the magisterial guards chose to pay a visit—as they often could—Radell wanted to be able to truthfully trumpet his ignorance.

It was sound practice.

The magisterial guards were part of the Magisterium, and they served the Kings. If the situation warranted it—if the man or woman who had lost a treasured heirloom had enough political pull—the guards might show up with one of the judgment-born. Or one of the bard-born.

The judgment-born, golden-eyed all, were sons of their father, Mandaros, the god of judgment; they could not be lied to, and they could discern, if they were trained, elements of criminal activity. They could be trusted, however, to be exactly what they appeared to be; they could not be bribed to lie, one way or the other.

He numbered none of them among his friends, but he did not disdain or despise them; they did what they were born to do, no more and certainly no less.

The bard-born—any of the talent-born—were different. They could not be detected by the simple expedient of looking at and noting the color of their irises, and they owed their power to an accident of birth, rather than a remote deity. They therefore felt free to make those alliances that seemed to suit them, and they did so without the natural compulsion of an immortal parent's blood to guide or bind them.

The bard-born were, however, almost always associated with one of the bardic colleges. In Averalaan, Senniel was that college, although many Morniel bards also ventured to the capital, to sing in its many courts, and tread in the shadow of lives of privilege.

The talent-born had more—and less—power than the god-born. One could not lie to the judgment-born, any more than one could live without drawing breath; one *could* lie to the bard-born, with enough training or experience. The bard-born were sensitive to a man's voice. Rath, sensitive as well, but in a different fashion.

On the other hand, Rath could not, at whim, use his voice as a tool of command; he could not use voice alone to give orders that must be obeyed. He could not sing in a way that could captivate a crowd of thousands; he could barely sing in a way that didn't instantly sour wine-mellowed men.

Radell, a nervous little weasel of a man, albeit a fairly wealthy one, hadn't the control to hide behind words. Luckily, he hadn't the ego to deny the weakness; he avoided it, instead.

"Patris AMatie is not one of the mage-born, Radell?"

Radell shrugged. It was an uneasy shuffle of motion. "How would I know? He doesn't wear the medallion," he added.

"I noticed the lack."

"Well, then. It's none of my business."

"Unless he chooses to use magery to burn down your fine establishment."

Radell looked shocked. Was, probably. He was good enough at acting that it was difficult to tell. How a man could be that good at acting, and that bad at lying, Rath was never certain.

"I think not," Radell said at last, fidgeting with his mess of a beard. "Where else would he go to find his antiquities?"

Rath didn't answer. Mostly because Radell would have plugged his ears and shouted a lot in response. But of the talent-born men and women that Rath had met, it was the mages he distrusted instinctively.

The healer-born, he had visited once or twice. They were bound by their odd power, and they were protected by a heavy squad of guards at almost all times. Life and death was literally in their hands. But the causing of death? He had never heard of it. Although they, like the mage-born and the bard-born, were in theory free of the taint of the gods, they were bound by their talent, and their fealty to it ran deep. The healer-born often worked at the side of the Priests and Priestesses in the Mother's temple; no more needed to be known of their habits.

Radell dumped a large sack on the table; it made a delightful noise. "It's gold," he said, almost apologetically. "I asked for smaller coin—I know you prefer it—but you know bankers."

Rath shrugged. "Smaller coin in that amount would be more obvious than even I would like. Thank you," he added, meaning it. "I'll be back."

He made certain that he was not being followed. At the height of day, it was, oddly enough, far easier to do.

He even considered taking a well-earned drink at one of the more expensive taverns in the market proper, but decided against it; Jewel was still recovering, and he didn't want her to be without food or water for longer than absolutely necessary.

Burdened by both, he finally made his way home.

Thinking about the talent-born.

Jewel was not only not sleeping when he opened the door, she was not in her room. She was in the kitchen, tidying invisible mess. At least that's what he assumed she was doing; she had a bucket, a rag, and all of the cupboards, some of dubious quality, were open for her inspection. Her hair was tied back, pulled up and over her eyes, although much of it had worked itself free of the binding.

She looked exhausted.

"What," he said, standing, his arms full, "do you think you're *doing?*"

She almost fell off the chair. Managed to right herself by grabbing its high back. "I'm cleaning," she said, in as pert a voice as he'd yet heard her use.

"I can see that."

"Then why did you ask?"

Rath considered pulling the chair out from under her. Instead, he walked over to the negligible counter space, and dumped the contents of his basket. "I'm going to guess," he said, in a voice that was definitively unfriendly, "that that water didn't get into the bucket on its own."

"I went to the well," she told him. She picked up the wet rag—which was blackened with dust—and dropped it into the water.

"You . . . went to the well."

She nodded. "It was a bit tricky to find."

"Did I not forbid you to leave?"

She shook her head; more hair fell free. "That was at the last place," she added, as she picked up the rag, wrung it dry—or as dry as she could with her slender hands and lack of muscle—and clambered up on the chair again.

"Get down from there this instant."

She looked across at him; she could meet his eyes with ease, given the added height of the chair's legs beneath her. "I'm not finished yet."

"You *are* finished."

"The cupboards—"

"I don't *have* anything to put *in* the damn cupboards."

"You can store some of the food there," she told him. Her voice quavered slightly, but her chin came up. She was working hard for her defiance.

"Jewel—"

"Jay."

"Jay, then."

"Yes?"

"What exactly do you think you're doing?"

"I'm cleaning."

"Yes, I can see that. Why?"

"Because it's dirty."

The absurd desire to strangle her came and went. "Jay, you are *not* in my debt."

The rag stilled, and she looked deflated. "I thought I could, you know, clean up a bit. Before I left."

He gave up. "It is dirty," he admitted. "But so are you, now."

"I'll wash up later."

"In the river, you mean."

She said nothing.

"Jewel—Jay—you are barely well. You spent over five days burning with fever; you ate very little. I do not intend for you to return to your river home until you are fully recovered. This," he added, taking the bucket from its place beneath the chair, "is *not* going to help.

"I brought food," he added. "If you feel you *must* do something useful, do something with the food. Make dinner. And," he added, "eat."

"I don't want your pity."

He looked at her, then. "I know. But sometimes, in this life, we just don't get what we want. Or, to reverse that, we get an awful lot of what we *don't* want. And we learn to live with it. So learn."

She was bristling with resentment.

"Here." He handed her a long, slender dagger. "I don't have another that I'm willing to let you use. You cut yourself, you can bleed."

"Yes, Rath," she said, sullenly.

He started to walk out of the kitchen, and paused in the door. Without looking at her, he said, "I don't pity you."

"Then why am I here?"

"You're out of questions, remember?"

He walked out, and heard something hit the counter heavily. Probably her fist.

It had to be tonight, he thought, as he inhaled. The slender stem of pipe was crooked in the corner of his mouth; pipe weed burned in orange embers, and he watched the smoke leave his lips. He sat on the floor of the largest of the three rooms, missing his furniture. He would have to get a desk. Another chair. The small table, he had taken with him.

Tonight, or never. She wasn't going to stay for much longer; even if she collapsed two blocks from the apartment, she was going to try to leave.

He had thought she might try, instead, to stay. To make a life here. She was such an odd child. Or perhaps, he thought, with a tinge of bitterness, she was too damn new to the streets.

Or she didn't trust him.

That, he could understand. There were whole weeks when he didn't trust himself, and she would not be the first person that he had disappointed bitterly in his long life. Nor, probably, the last, if it came to that.

She knocked at the closed door, and he rose to open it. Her hands were balanced beneath a large basket; she had cut bread, made sandwiches, sliced fruit. The waterskin hung over her left shoulder like a huge sack; everything about his life seemed designed, in that moment, to make her look smaller and weaker.

He gestured to the table, where the magestone lay exposed, and she marched past him, and put the basket down, mindful of its contents. Then she stood there, uncertain.

"Sit down," he told her, motioning with the pipe.

She looked at it, and a smile, brief and slightly pained, changed the shape of her mouth; her angry defiance ebbed. She picked up the basket and brought it with her, placing it carefully between them.

"I have my Oma's temper," she told him. It was obviously something she had heard often, in her childhood.

"Then it's a good thing I have no dishes. I imagine you would have thrown a couple."

"At the wall."

He nodded, as if this were normal.

She said, as she had said once before, "I like your pipe."

The words were not wrapped in fever, but memory gilded them.

"Your father smoked?"

She shook her head. "My mother never liked pipes much. My Oma smoked, though."

"Your Oma sounds like a remarkable character."

She looked suspicious, and he could see her repeating the words to herself, sifting them for mockery. She came up with none, and nodded. Guileless, this child.

He took a sandwich out of the basket, and after he did, she followed suit. She ate slowly, watching him, her eyes dark in the room. "We never bought much fruit," she told him, eyeing the contents of the basket with open suspicion.

He offered no response, and after a moment, she shrugged. "I try not to steal from people who need the money." Clearly, the presence of fruit made him one of those people. He didn't bother to mention the gold. He was fairly certain she wouldn't touch it. But she was a child; he wasn't at all certain she wouldn't mention it. And he now lived in the thirty-fifth.

"I know. You told me. I've heard it before," he added, "but in your case, I find myself believing it." He stopped eating for a moment to put the pipe out.

She watched him.

The fever had earned him some leeway; she wasn't so wary as she had been. That would, no doubt, change.

"Jay," he said quietly, "I have a few questions. I want you to answer them."

She nodded.

"You gave me a warning, a few days ago."

Nodded again.

"Why?"

She shrugged awkwardly and put the sandwich on the floor before her feet. He would have to buy plates. Or napkins. Or something.

"I didn't want to be in your debt," she said at last. "And it was the only thing I could think of. To pay you off."

He nodded. "How did you know that I would be followed?"

She winced and looked away. "I'm not—"

"I don't care what the answer *is*. I'm not a magisterian; I'm not your father. I will trust you not to lie to me. But whatever it is that you say, say it without fear; I only want the answer as you see it."

"I'm not supposed to talk about it," she told him, voice low. Her hands found her feet and she bent over them in a remarkable display of flexibility. It would have made him feel old, but he doubted that in his youth he would have been able to do the same.

"Your Oma told you this?"

She shook her head. "My mother."

"And your father?"

"I don't think he—" She looked at Rath, and then away. He guessed, correctly, that she would do a lot of that before he'd finished. "He never talked about it."

"Why?"

"It didn't matter." There was a curious flatness to the words. Like the flatness of a door that had been slammed shut, and locked for good measure. Rath had doors like that; he let it be. "It didn't matter, to him."

"What did your Oma say?"

"She called it—she said it was—" Jewel shrugged, and shoved her hair out of her eyes. It was a nervous habit, he realized, because there was very little hair in her eyes. "Thunder and lightning."

He frowned a moment, assessing the words. "You mean because lightning comes before thunder?"

She nodded. "I think so." She wasn't going to eat.

Not while he talked. He cursed curiosity and necessity, because he had no intention of stopping. "Did you often . . . see things? True things?"

She met his gaze, held it, examining him. Looking, he realized, for signs of mockery. He was deliberate and careful; he offered none.

"I saw a dog die, once. With my mother."

"Before it died?"

She nodded. "My mother couldn't even see the dog. And after, when we found him dead, she was upset. She told me—she told me that I was never to speak about it."

"Why?"

"She thought I—she thought people would blame me."

"Your mother—did she grow up in Averalaan? Was she born here?"

Jewel frowned. "I . . . I don't think she was born here," she said at last. "Why?"

"Because there are no witch hunts in Averalaan," he replied. "People might think you strange, but they wouldn't—" He stopped himself. The god-born, people knew and trusted. The fortune-tellers that cropped up like boils during any festival season of note in the city, people considered charlatans. At least publicly. Privately, they sought them out, exposing hands for their inspection, dumping damp tea leaves, shaking canisters of old bones—probably chicken bones, he thought bitterly. One or two of the fortune-tellers were expensive; they had crystal balls, and possibly some minor mage-talent that they had managed to develop without the tutelage of the Order of Knowledge. But they spoke in the pleasant riddles most likely to part people from considerable sums of money, and they told them more or less what they already knew, adding, at the end, what they *wanted* to hear.

Rath had visited them on a lark when he had been a younger man. A much younger man.

Experience had taught him many things about people, and one of them, time and again: no one liked to listen to something they didn't *want* to hear. Not about the future, if it involved them.

"Let me rephrase that," he said at length. "People couldn't blame you for whatever it is that you see."

"My mother—"

"Your mother was a superstitious woman."

She bristled.

"I'm sorry. I did not know your mother. It may be that she was worried about you; that she wanted to make sure you were safe."

This comforted Jewel enough that her eyes lost that spark that spoke of incipient rage.

"But . . . what you told me was true. Is it always that way?"

"What way?"

"True?"

She shrugged and looked away. Ill at ease. "I don't know," she said at last.

Something occurred to him. "The first day we met—"

She shrank in, her shoulders curling down.

"You knew that I would try to cut your hand."

She swallowed.

"Can you always do that?"

And shook her head. "No." Her voice was a little girl voice.

"What you told me—did you decide to look?"

She shook her head again, looking even more miserable.

"So you can't do it on command."

"On command?"

"Whenever you want."

"I *never* want," she said, the words low and intense. "You don't know what it's like—"

He held up a hand, to forestall the words.

But she shook her head. "You can't know what it's like. To tell people things. To have them not *listen*. To watch them go away and die forever."

He didn't have the heart to correct her usage of "die" and "forever." He waited a beat, and then said, as casually as he knew how, "So you can see when people die?"

"No."

"But you just said—"

"I can't see it," she continued, as if the words were burning the inside of her throat, her mouth. "I can't always see it." She ran her hands through her hair and shoved it to one side. "Only sometimes. Sometimes I can see it."

"When?"

"I don't know," she said bitterly. "It just happens. Sometimes I just see it. I can look at you, and I can see you dead. It doesn't last," she added. "And I can't just call it back. And sometimes I *don't want to look.*"

He could well imagine.

"I know if it's going to happen to *me*," she added, and there was more bitterness in the phrase than in any other he had ever heard her utter.

She waited. Was waiting, he realized, for his reaction. As if she knew what it would be.

He picked up the emptied pipe and went through the motions of filling it, not because he wanted to smoke—although in truth, he didn't mind—but because he sensed that this would set her at ease. Inasmuch as she could be.

"But I don't see it, not always, when it happens to other people. Not even the people I care about. I *know* when they're dead," she added bitterly. "I know, then. But sometimes, not even then."

"So."

"It's worse when I'm dreaming," she added, and at this, she shuddered. "I see things, and I *know* they're true, but I *don't understand them*." She swallowed. "Sometimes my Oma would try to help me. Sometimes she would tell me it was just a nightmare. I knew it wasn't," she added. "But it didn't matter.

"Sometimes," she added softly, "I know when something bad is going to happen to me—and it doesn't matter then either. I can't get away." Her eyes closed, pale lids. He wanted to touch her then, but he thought if he did, he would never let her go.

And neither of them would be free.

"Eat," he told her, instead, and far more gruffly than he had intended.

Chapter Four

THE TALENT-BORN.

Rath waited until Jewel had finished eating. This, combined with the earlier foolishness of cleaning the kitchen—which still inexplicably enraged him—had exhausted her, and she was nodding off, her legs crossed, her hands barely able to keep her head and shoulders off the ground. He told her to go to her room, and she nodded listlessly, failing to notice—as Rath had—that he had called it hers.

But although she agreed in principle, she had had some difficulty in practice, and in the end, he had scooped her up off the ground and carried her there. In the dark, punctuated by his pipe's scant light, he had tucked her in.

"Promise," he told her softly, "that you'll stay in bed."

"Rath—"

"Promise that you won't leave without saying good-bye. In person. I don't want a letter—you'll make a mess if you try to find ink, added to which, I don't have enough paper, and I hate to lose it when words will do."

"My Oma said—"

"I *know* what your Oma said, Jay. You told me, remember?"

But she clearly didn't. The fever had taken much, hidden much. "I can't," she said forlornly.

"You can, or I won't leave."

"Ever?"

"Ever."

She considered this for a moment, a sleepy drawn-out moment, and then she whispered the promise. It was the last thing she said before sleep overtook her.

Bard-born. Mage-born. Healer-born. Maker-born. These were the common talents; one could not live in a city as cosmopolitan as Averalaan and fail to at least have brushes with men and women who were born with these gifts. Any of the four, if discovered, could lead to prosperity and safety.

If, he amended grimly, discovered in time, and by the right people. There were stories of mage-born boys and girls who had destroyed whole villages before their unchecked talent had consumed them; these were told by Priests and Priestesses of any temple across the Empire, cautionary tales meant to frighten the parents of young children.

There were darker stories yet, of healer-born children who had been discovered and taken for personal use. These were spoken of less often—far less often—as if in the speaking, the speakers might be tempting the unscrupulous to attempt to do the same.

The bard-born were possibly the most common; theirs was the most subtle of the powers, and existed to a greater and lesser extent; the men and women who used the voice, as it was often called, used it to entertain, to move, to plead.

And the maker-born? They were the merchant class of the talent-born. The Guild of the Makers had no monetary rivals in the Empire. The talent-born could work in their compulsive and obsessive silence within the grand halls upon the Isle; they could work in the lesser halls in the large cities that were scattered across the Empire. Their work commanded the highest of prices, and it could not be mistaken for the work of lesser craftsmen; there was, in each detail, a sense that life had been captured or perfected. Maker-born artists were legend, but the maker-born turned their skills to many things: jewelry, furniture, mirrors—anything at all that caught their attention.

Had Rath been able to choose a gift, it would have been that one—but Rath, like the vast majority of citizens of Averalaan, had been born without the grace of even this faint touch of magic.

But there were other talents, older and rarer.

Seer-born.

Rath sat in his room, listening for any sound that Jewel might make, acutely aware now of the possible significance of her nightmares. The word itself—seer-born—felt like something out of the dark side of dreaming to him.

Not only had Rath never encountered a man or woman who claimed to be seer-born—not even the fatuous fakes in the festival stalls were bold enough to claim that—he had never heard of one that wasn't part of some historical lay. And those seers were of a stature that Jewel, at ten, could not possess. They were also more reliably, more wildly, powerful. At their whim, and by their word, whole armies marched, and baronies rose and fell.

If she were seer-born, and she fell into the hands of the right person, she would never have to worry about hunger again.

But she was ten, poor, and barely schooled. What were the chances, he thought bitterly, that she would fall into those hands? If she was willing to parlay what she could barely be brought to speak about into something that she could barter and sell, what were the chances that she would actually be believed?

The pipe went out six times as he thought in the darkness, giving up on the idea of sleep. If he had been a different man, he could answer those questions. If he had chosen a different life, avenues that would aid the girl would now be open to him.

But had he, he would likely never have met her; he would never have chosen to live in the hundred holdings, where her poverty would draw her to him.

As it was, he didn't need to be able to see the future to see hers. It was here, in the holdings, starvation giving way to desperation, and desperation to a short, miserable life.

Unless he could think of a way to use the girl himself. If he could somehow do that, he could justify her presence here. For both their sakes.

Health had curbed part of her tongue; it had given excessive rein to the other half; she was, as her family had told her, possessed of a temper.

"Jay," he told her, opening her door, "it's morning. You can get up now."

She practically leaped out of the sleeping bag; he wondered how long her promise had actually kept her tethered. She was a bit paler than she had been when she'd first taken his satchel, and she was a lot thinner, to his eye.

"I want to ask a few more questions."

She shriveled.

"I believe you," he told her, speaking quietly. He was amazed at how easily his tone conformed to her, and he wasn't certain he liked it. "And I want to know more."

She shrugged. "I told you everything."

"You told me everything you could think of telling me," he countered. "Just this, then. Do you always know when you're in danger?"

She frowned. "Not always," she said at last.

"And when you do?"

She shrugged. "Sometimes things just feel *wrong*. Bad wrong. I avoid those, if I can."

"Like what?"

"Some parts of the holdings."

"Always?"

"No, not always. Just sometimes."

"People?"

She hesitated. "Sometimes."

"Me?"

"I knew you didn't need the money," she said at last.

"I didn't look like a—"

"No, you didn't. But—I just *knew*. You didn't. You wouldn't starve."

"If I asked you to stay, would you stay?"

She became utterly still. He couldn't tell what was going on behind her face; her lips were thin, and her eyes were fastened on loose stitching. "Why?"

"Because I think you might be useful."

"How?" The single word was muted, almost dead.

"The warning—"

"I *can't* do it all the time," she said, and a hint of something that might have been anger showed through. "If you asked me now—if you told me where you were going—it wouldn't make a difference. I don't *know* when these feelings are coming, Rath. They're not—I can't count on them." She took a deep breath. "And if you think you can, and that's why you want me to stay . . . I can't stay."

"But that night—"

"I heard him," she said. "I heard him first. Like in a dream. I thought I was dreaming," she added.

Fever. He nodded. Rose. "How much do you know about this city, Jay?"

She shrugged. "The Isle's that way," she said, pointing. She was, however, pointing in the wrong direction. "And the Common. Some of the other holdings."

He rose. "I'm going to the market," he told her, and held the door open. "I don't think you're strong enough, but getting out of the darkness will probably do you some good. Do you want to come with me?"

She hesitated.

"I don't want you to run off," he added softly. "I'll find you, if I have to." Wasn't certain why he'd said it. He'd been counting the days until he was rid of her. Would have sworn he'd be glad to be rid of her.

She would have, too. So much for sight.

He shrugged. "It's up to you."

And she nodded.

"I'll have to teach you a few things," he said, as he walked. His long stride had to be shortened considerably in order to make certain that Jewel didn't lag behind. She shadowed him, casting furtive glances toward all the intersections, all the streets.

As if she was mapping routes of escape.

Rath didn't begrudge it; he begrudged the fact that she was so damn obvious about it, no more. It was, after all, what he did. While she looked, he readjusted his backpack. She'd noticed it, of course. She hadn't asked.

"What things?" she asked, to show she'd been listening.

"Things that I do," he replied. It was evasive. She noticed. "Jewel, one day, you *will* be on your own. You can learn a trade—even one as lowly as mine—or you can ignore the opportunity. It's not easy work; it's barely safe. And I can't guarantee that it will keep you in money. But if you pay attention, and if you have *any* dexterity, it *will* keep you from starving. It may even keep you in wood during the Winter months."

She nodded slowly. "It's not reading or writing," she said.

"You can do that, or so you said. And no, it's not."

She clearly wanted to ask him why, but he'd tired of that game. Or perhaps he tired of making excuses that he only half-believed himself.

"You can make yourself useful," he added. "You can keep my place tidy, if that pleases you. I'd ask you *not* to darn my socks or mend my clothing; much of it is delicate."

"But Rath, I don't know what you *do*."

"Does it matter?"

She looked away. Enough of an answer. He lowered his voice, touched her shoulder. She let him.

"I survive," he told her quietly. "I try not to steal from anyone who'd miss the money."

If she noticed the gentle mockery, there was no sign of it on her face.

"And at the moment, I'm not required to steal much that belongs to anyone who'd miss it."

"But you—"

He held up a finger to his lips, and she fell silent.

"Come," he said quietly. "I have something to show you."

Rath liked his secrets; he had to, he had so many of them. He had told Jewel his name; he wasn't certain if she'd forgotten it, and didn't care to ask. He was not, by nature, impulsive, and on the rare occasions he had been, he'd paid for it. Certainly a high enough price that he avoided it like the plague.

He was therefore slightly angry at himself, because having learned this lesson time *and* again, he had given in to impulse. He caught Jewel by the hand, and he led her into a building. It was much like the building he called home; long, squat, a few stories in height, and made, at least at base, of stone blocks. Ancient quarries had been emptied in the construction of this part of the holdings; he wondered what had transpired, in the movement of history, that had in the end deprived it of wealth.

She knew that he was exposing something; she was quiet. Not still; she couldn't be, and follow him. But she said nothing. Her brows, covered frequently by hair, could not be easily seen, but her eyes widened often, and she wore her curiosity openly across her face. One day, he thought, she would lose the ability to be surprised.

He wondered if he would be there to see it go; to see its slow decay. He didn't, he reminded himself, like children. Jewel was a child. Therefore . . .

"Be careful now," he told her, sharply. "Here." He handed her the magestone he'd taken out of his pocket. "If you need the light, open your hand fully. But open it carefully; I don't need to tell you just how much that cost." On the other hand, he doubted that her previous home had been lit with magelight, so perhaps this was optimism on his part. He was seldom guilty of optimism.

He led her round the back. There, boarded over—badly—was a chute that led toward the basement. All of the old buildings had them.

He lifted the board with care, and her eyes rounded; she looked over her shoulder repeatedly, as if at any minute she expected to see a magisterial guard patrol coming round the corner.

"It's the thirty-fifth," he told her. This didn't seem to have the same meaning to Jewel as it did to Rath, and he let it go. Instead, as he pushed the board aside just enough that there was room to squeeze through, he said, "Part of this building is rotten. The joists were worm food decades ago. No one lives in the west half, unless they're very, very desperate."

"There are a lot of desperate people in the holdings," she said quietly.

"Desperate people don't usually have the wherewithal to get medical help when the floor disintegrates and they break a leg—or worse. Trust me. There are mice, rats, a dozen cockroach clans—but no people." He paused and then added, "Don't even think it. The river is a lot safer, and it's a lot more pleasant."

"It's more exposed," she told him.

"Depends. The roof has collapsed over there." He pointed. "You get rain and sunlight. They've rewalled the east half of the building; it'd cost more than it's worth to try to recover the west." He began to gingerly slide himself between the board and the ground; Jewel looked at him, her fingers a fist around the smooth magestone.

"It's safe enough below," he told her. "More or less."

"You—you want me to follow you?"

A dozen sarcastic replies tried to jam themselves between his gritted teeth. "Yes."

She nodded. She'd gone that particular shade of pale that meant she was afraid, and given what he'd just said, this showed that she was sensible. He seldom resented sensible people so much.

Funny, how even the untrustworthy wanted to be trusted. "Don't climb down until I call you."

She nodded again. "Shouldn't you take this?" She held out the magelight; it looked like a flat stone in the light of day, a thing of no value to anyone who wasn't five. Or ten.

"Not here. I know the way."

Easy to say. He took a deep breath and caught the edges of the chute in both hands, and then lowered himself the rest of the way down; he dangled for a moment, his fingers closing reflexively before he forced them to open.

She heard the dull thud; he saw her face in the light of the space between slat and chute. Reorienting himself, he said, "Now. Put the stone in your pocket. Or your mouth, if you don't have one; I don't want to lose it." To her credit, she didn't hesitate; she struggled through the opening—and made it look difficult, which, given she was half his width, would have been risible in other circumstances—and then froze, her hands holding her weight high above the ground.

"I'll catch you," he told her. "Let go."

She hesitated for another beat, and then, for just a moment, she was falling. His arms were wide, but it had been many years since he had caught anyone; he was clumsy, and a little too rough, as if she were an object, and not something that needed to, say, breathe.

As if she were a rare object, something of value.

He thought he knew, as her head hit his chin, who she reminded him of, and for just a moment, he froze, thinking of sunlight, of trees, of a vast estate. Of himself, in younger years, when he had had a noble name, and the course of his life had seemed so straightforward.

"Rath," she gasped. "I need to breathe."

Almost word for word, as if she could see memory. But he realized that he was holding her tightly enough that breathing might actually be a problem, and he let her drop gently to the ground. He couldn't see her face; his eyes were still acclimatized to sunlight and open street.

He was thankful for it, because it meant she couldn't see his.

It took him a minute to find his voice, to find words, to remember that that life and this one were separated by many, many things. But it took her more than a minute to fish the magestone out of her shirt, and by the time she had, he was ready.

"This way," he told her, holding out a hand.

She took his, without any hesitation. As if she had stepped, new, into a different life. Smart girl.

He led her down the rough incline. "There's a break in the floor here," he told her, when he stopped short and she thudded gently against his back. "And we have to go down again. It's a bit more tricky, and there's less light. Can you hold the stone up?"

"Yes."

"Good."

"How do you do this when there's no one to hold the light?"

"In the dark," he replied, with a shrug. "I know the way," he added. It was half bravado, and half truth; he seldom entered the underground from this building. It was too exposed.

But Rath had always had a memory for geography. For the feel of the ground beneath his feet; the feel of stone, or the smooth, polished slats of hardwood; the feel of broken cobblestones; the feel of grass, and where grass had gone wild, undergrowth; the nubbled width of great tree roots that lay exposed to sun and air. He could navigate the grounds around his home with his eyes shut by the time he'd turned four, and he sometimes did, to show off. He wondered if he were giving in to the same desire now.

Either way, it didn't matter. If he was showing off, it was for the benefit of a girl whose home had long since vanished beneath the weight of poverty and loss; what harm could there be in it?

Oh, the lies. The lies he could tell himself and believe.

He lowered himself down, through this second hole. It was larger than the first, but more jagged; the wood was old, and splinters lodged themselves in his clothing, scraping the skin of his chest, his shoulders. He should have brought rope.

But then again, had he thought to bring it, he would have *been* thinking, and it was unlikely that he would now be here, with a stranger. This, after all, was *his*.

When he landed, he landed on stone. The stone was cracked, but the crack was clean, and the stone itself hadn't crumbled. He reached out, felt nothing but air beneath the flat of his extended palm. The halls here were wide.

Wide enough, easily, for two. It wasn't always the case. He looked up; he could see Jewel clearly; the magestone was in her hands, and its light traveled up the underside of exposed skin; her chin was tilted toward her neck.

"Can you see me?"

"I . . . think so."

"Good. Throw me the stone. Don't worry; if you're not good at throwing, it'll bounce—but down here, there's no way to lose it."

She swallowed and nodded. She was, as it happened, not terribly good at throwing, but not so bad that the stone bounced off Rath before it struck ground; he considered himself lucky. He bent, retrieved the stone, and dropped it between his feet; they were planted apart.

"Now," he said calmly, "throw yourself down as well."

"But I—"

"Don't try to hold on to the edge of the floor—you'll get a dozen splinters in your hands, and the floor will fold anyway."

She nodded.

"You can close your eyes if you want."

The nod froze. Clearly, at ten, she disliked obvious coddling. "I want to see," she whispered.

"Then look. But you can't sit up there all day; I can't get back up that way."

Her eyes rounded, and he almost laughed. He must have smiled, because she frowned in return, looking like the little princess of defiance. Her lips thinned, she took a breath, held it, and jumped.

He was ready for her the second time, although the distance was greater. Maybe because it was greater. Or because there was no sunlight, no hint of blue sky, to invoke unwelcome memory. Here, he was Rath, and she was—Jewel.

"If you can't get back up," she said, from the perch of his arm, "How are we going to get out of here?"

He did laugh, then. "Wait," he told her. "Wait and see." And it occurred to him that although he'd long ago left childhood and its lie of a promise behind, some part of him retained the desire to share secrets. It was absurd; a secret, once shared, was utterly broken.

But they were both broken in some fashion, this child and he. He let her go, and bent, retrieving the stone for a second time. He handed it to her, wordless, and she palmed it in the same fashion.

He didn't tell her that this was something that shouldn't be spoken of; he didn't forbid her to speak of it. He knew, looking at her face, that he would never have to. She was good at hiding truths, and the bigger they were, the better the chance that they remained hidden.

"Come," he said, as he might once have said to another girl, decades past, "I want to show you something."

And oh, her face.

He had let her hold the magestone for her own comfort—or so he'd told himself—and he even believed it for a few yards. But . . . her face.

It was pale in the unnatural light—the only light—and her dark eyes, rounding so perfectly they might never have a different shape again, made him see the world as if it were new; as if he had never walked these stone halls before, never touched their scored surfaces, never paused to examine the runed Old Weston along some of its unbroken edges.

Wonder woke in her face, her bedraggled angel face, as if she, too, were awakening; as if descent were all of her reality. He waited for the questions; they were slow in coming. Words had deserted her, and they were caged only in the lines of her expression. It was an odd gift.

He led her down the hall; it was a long hall, but not an endless one. He thought, from the feel of the stone that had gone into its construction, that it had once been open to sky, perhaps an enclosed cloister; it would never see day again.

But he acknowledged the fact that he might be wrong; there was, in his estimation, magic in these stones; magic to withstand the travails of weather, of storm, the pettiness of simple erosion. The great cracks that girded walls and floor were clean, and in evidence almost everywhere; they could be crossed with ease, and Rath was fairly certain they had occurred centuries past.

He had often wondered what great cataclysm had broken these halls; had driven them down, into the depths of earth, and away from the sight of a city that numbered in the tens of thousands. When he could, he had tried to glean information about Averalaan before the ascension; before Veralaan the Founder, whose name the city still bore, had returned from the land where gods and mortals might meet, two sons by her side, to reclaim—to remake—the Empire.

But in truth, if the information existed, it existed in fragments of Old Weston, kept under lock and key by the most pompous of scholars the Order of Knowledge had the misery to train, and no amount of persuasion or money could grant him the easy access he desired.

Information would, but that would lead to this, and this was not something he wished to surrender. The only time in his life that he had regretted his decision not to pursue the scholarly arts had been when he had first discovered these tunnels, and even that regret was not enough to grant him the endurance necessary to pass the exams and examinations required to become a member of the Order of Knowledge.

He knew roughly where he was; he had explored tunnels like this one for the better part of five years, gathering and hoarding knowledge. He had never drawn a map, because that might be discovered; he was well aware that anything he owned could be confiscated, either by magisterial guards or thieves, and he would be damned if he made their lives richer or easier. Let them find what he had found the hard way, if at all.

And yet . . . he glanced at Jewel again. She was lost, and willing to be lost, and the look she gave him said all of this clearly.

"It's not a dream," he said, more gently than was his wont. "It doesn't vanish."

She reached out and placed her hand against a wall, following it with her fingers. Traced the crack that broke what seemed, to the eye, to be otherwise seamless stone.

"Yes, it's real." He walked slowly now. "The ground here is solid," he told her. "But up ahead, you have to be careful; the cracks in the floor are wider than your thighs, and if you don't pay attention, it's easy to break a leg."

"You haven't."

"My thighs are lamentably wider than yours."

"Oh." Magic had robbed many a grown man of a sense of humor; she was a child. He smiled, but she didn't notice, and therefore didn't bristle.

"Where does this go, Rath?"

She had found her voice.

"Everywhere," he replied softly. "It's not all hall. In some places, the surfaces are rougher; in some places, the walls give way to cavern. I think," he added, reaching for her hand both to steady her and warn her about the upcoming gap in the floor, "that the caverns used to be open space. The halls—like these—were either parts of buildings or causeways."

She was quiet, absorbing the words. Trying to make sense of them. He almost told her not to bother.

But she crooked her head to one side and said, "Who lives here?"

It wasn't quite the question he'd been expecting; it certainly wasn't the first one he'd thought to ask. "No one."

She frowned.

"Jay?"

"I think . . . I think someone must," she said at last, hesitancy punctuating the sentence in a way that grammarians would have loathed.

He stilled. "Why do you say that?"

She shrugged. There was something less than casual about the movement.

"Jay."

"I don't know," she whispered. He knew, then, that if he asked again, the words would be the same, but louder. He didn't ask.

But it had been so empty here, so devoid of life and life's complications, that it had truly never occurred to him that anyone could actually live in these spaces. And the thought wasn't a welcome one.

He led her, at last, to the end of the hall they'd followed in such careful silence. The wonder that had briefly transformed her face still lingered, but curiosity's sharper edge had grown as well. "Can you read this?" she asked him, kneeling briefly. In the corner that ground and wall made, she had found a long stretch of runic engravings.

Before he could answer, she said, "This is the same. As the writing on the stones."

"It is not the same."

"The same language." She corrected herself without hesitation. "The same forms. Look."

Bright girl. He nodded, and when he realized that she hadn't looked up, added, "Yes. It's the same."

"This is Old Weston?"

He nodded again.

"What does it say?"

"I'm not certain. It's too fragmented. I am not a scholar," he added quietly. "There are those who are; they could tell you what the words might be. But even the scholars could only give you their best guess."

"Because there's not enough of it?"

He nodded again. "They work by context. The greater the number of words, the greater the likelihood that they'll be able to tell you what the passage means. The language is ours, or was, at some point. Come," he added softly. "There is more to see."

She nodded, and rose again.

He led her into the cavern. It was, in his estimation, the easternmost point of this underground city, this vast mausoleum in which all history lay fallow. The cavern's rise was rough and uneven; great points of stone jutted from it, visible only as the magelight brightened, and leached of color by shadow. Bats lived there; he'd seen them take flight once or twice in his early treks through the streets. They were silent now. Sleeping. As if, even without the sight of sun's light, they lived by rhythm of day and night.

"You . . . found those tablets here."

"Not here, but close."

She looked up, and up again; he thought he'd have to catch her when she overbalanced. Nor was he wrong. He'd fallen himself that way, once or twice, losing his bearings, his sense of the earth beneath his feet, to the glory, grim and dark, of the heights that passed for sky.

"If necessary," he told her quietly, "you can escape into these tunnels and find refuge here. You can cross the thirty-fifth holding, and most of the rest, without being seen. The hardest part is finding a way in; you can't, in the newer parts of the city. It's only in the holdings proper that the entrances can be found."

In the distance, he could hear the movement of water; it sounded cold. "Come," he added.

She nodded again as she stepped out of the passage and into the open street. And it was a street; this much could be seen because the exterior walls of other buildings now faced them. They were broken, like the wall was: cleanly, the cracks slender, their edges still sharp. Some of these buildings had once had doors, but the doors—wood all—were gone; their frames remained, arches of carved stone, some bearing words, some only a mark at the height of the keystone, and some the likenesses of odd faces. Pale faces, things that had no rendered expression.

Jewel stopped before one of these, and reached up; she was about three feet too short to actually touch anything. But the face itself was framed with hair that seemed—to Rath's admittedly jaded eye—to move or grow; it flowed around high cheekbones, and then fell to either side, following the downward march of the door frame.

"It used to have eyes," she said.

He frowned. "It has eyes."

"That's just stone. But it—it used to have eyes."

"Interesting. What color?"

"Blue," she told him, her voice barely a whisper. "Blue and orange."

"Can you see who lived here?"

The wonder collapsed and she looked at him as if he were an idiot. He failed to make it worse, and after a moment, she passed beneath the arch, leading, where a moment before she had been content to follow.

He had explored many of the buildings in the labyrinth, but by no means all of them; he did not remember this one, and moved more cautiously because of it. "Be wary of the floor," he told her softly.

She nodded, this time without any resentment for his gently offered warning. She held the magestone aloft, walking slowly; she was so light, he thought she might pass over the softer ground without falling. It was something that he could not be certain of doing himself.

The building was not small. Jewel walked from room to room, looking; the rooms themselves were empty. In one, and only one, a stone table lay, as if it had been disgorged from the floor; in another, empty, a basin that might once have been either a fountain or a large bath. No water remained. Rath gestured to Jewel, and she obliged his wordless request; she knelt, and light spread in an even blanket to either side of her legs.

The floor was marbled stone, and where dust was swept aside, it still gleamed as if new. Bath, he thought, and rose. Jewel rose with him, bright shadow, and only when they were both standing did she continue her odd search. It wasn't methodical, as Rath's searches were; she had come unprepared to the tunnels, and although she was aware that he had taken some items from it, she did not seek those items for her own use.

Instead, she hoarded knowledge, as he had done the first time, the first ten times, he had made his way down to this city under the City. Rooms passed, some smaller, some larger, and by dint of curiosity, she made her way at last to what looked like a small vestibule. There were stairs.

"Don't," he told her shortly.

"The stairs aren't good?"

"The stairs, in the undercity, are the most structurally delicate parts of any building."

She nodded, but he saw her eyes upon those steps, and after a moment, cursing impulse, he examined the flat steps; they were stone. Marble, he thought. Like the marble in the bathing room. "Yes." It was a curt word.

She was on it—and the stairs—like a carrion creature. But he didn't have to tell her to move slowly, and he didn't have to tell her to pause at the height of the flat the steps reached for, for he saw what had drawn her. Wondered if she had seen it herself, in shadow. Or in vision.

A statue stood, arms out to either side, palms exposed. It was carved in loose-fitting robes, the drape of which fell from shoulder to ground with austerity. No belt bisected or impeded its fall; no rope, nothing. The gentle swell of breasts implied that the figure was a woman's, but the woman after whom this statue had been carved had been slender—too slender for

Rath's taste—and young. Adult, but not yet hardened by experience or the necessity that made, of life, a constant battle.

The robe's hood was drawn back, and the woman's hair fell from her forehead, parting in a peak. It was of a color with the rest of the statue, gray with dust. Jewel's height, he thought she must have been, maybe a few inches taller. She watched them approach with sightless eyes, her gaze unchanging.

Rath had never tried to take statues from the buildings. They were too large, for one—and perhaps that was chief among the reasons. But he saw the other in Jewel's expression: she was staring up at this pillar's face, and her own lips were slightly open, as if she were searching for words.

"The maker-born made this, didn't they?" she asked him quietly at last.

It was not, as it often would not be, the question he expected. But he nodded, as if he could be certain of the truth of agreement.

"Did she live here, do you think?"

"I . . . don't know. It is almost certain that she died here," he added.

"Why?"

"Because most of the people who lived here did."

"How do you know that, Rath?"

"There are bodies," he said at last, and reluctantly. "Skeletal bodies. There are one or two that appear to have mummified." When her brow creased, he shrugged. "They're dried out," he offered. "Like raisins are dried-out grapes."

"Here?"

"I don't think I've been in this building. But in others, and in the caverns, yes."

"Were they wearing anything?"

Astute question. "Armor," he said quietly.

"You took it."

"Yes."

"And sold it?"

"Yes." He shrugged. "They're dead, Jewel. They want for nothing."

"Not even peace?"

"Ask Mandaros," was his curt reply. "There are other dead, but properly buried. No," he added, "I didn't dig them out of their cenotaphs."

When her brows furrowed again, he gave up. "Coffins," he reminded her. "Big stone coffins."

She nodded, and then continued to walk.

When she was within an inch of the statue, and before Rath could think to react, she reached out and touched one of its exposed hands, placing her own pale palm against its stone one.

He couldn't see her expression, but he didn't have to; he was just behind her when she shuddered, her hand jerking away. She collapsed slowly, and he caught her, four steps down. Her eyes, open, were white.

He shook her; she lolled. For a moment he thought she was dead—but the moment passed; she was breathing, and if the breath was labored, it was there.

The statue was there as well. And all thoughts, all regret at the idea it could not be moved, were gone when he looked at it closely; it was no longer a pale alabaster, covered in dust and the webs of time; it was a pale, flesh color, and its open eyes were blue.

"Do not disturb the Sleepers." Its lips seemed to move, its hands seemed to fold, fingers curling into fists. *"Do not disturb the city. What sleeps, sleeps, until the End of Days."*

Maker-born? He whistled, shaking slightly. No simple maker had crafted this statue, this slender image. An Artisan had labored here.

"Let her go," he told the statue grimly.

As if it could respond. But blue eyes met his, and he acknowledged the fact that he had almost never seen the work of an Artisan in his life; among the maker-born, they were rare, and guarded; their power was legend, and rightly feared, for their works were imbued with a magic that not even the mage-born could understand, let alone duplicate. If rumor was true, the Kings held such artifacts as part of their office; Rath put little faith in rumor.

But here . . .

"Long we worked, and hard. Long we toiled in secret. Long we lived, and in pain, we died, in the coliseum, for the amusement of our enemies. But the time has come, has been coming: the gift of Myrddion has been called forth, and it has come from the earth, in time.

"She is not yours," the statue continued, in its flat, but undeniably feminine voice. *"And her time is not yet come. She will wake. You will teach her many things, Ararath Handernesse. You will teach her things that neither you nor she will understand for many years. She will find what she seeks, and you would reject it could you, but you are a fool; you cannot protect her. You know this, and she knows it as well, although she will not wake to its truth until your time is long past.*

I will give you the gift that it is in me to give. Two women will define your life long after your life is forgotten. And in your turn, Ararath, you will define, unknowing, the fate of the greatest of The Ten Houses upon the Isle in your new Empire.

Take Jewel Markess from this place, but tell her: Do not wake the Sleepers."

"Will she understand this?"

"No more than you do. The time for understanding has not yet come. I tell you this for the sake of peace, both yours—and mine. I have been waiting. Tell her," the statue said, and its voice fell silent, color ebbing until it stood, at last, as it had stood when Jewel had approached it.

She stirred against his chest, for he held her, cradled in his arms. Her eyes slowly rolled down, brown replacing thin-veined white. "Rath?" she whispered.

He nodded grimly. He wanted to lecture her, but held his tongue; she had touched a statue. He had done worse, in his time, but never with this effect.

He set her on her feet, and she stood, swaying, the statue now above her. Her hand shook as she lifted it. "The girl—"

"There was no girl," he said gently.

"There was. She—"

But he shook his head more firmly. He did not speak of what the statue had said. He had spent the whole of a life learning to ignore an order, or several if it came to that, and he was not about to obey someone who was, by any sane measure, long dead.

"Come, Jay." He forced himself to use her chosen name; his came naturally to her lips. "It will be dark, soon, and we must be out of the maze by nightfall."

"Why?"

"Because getting out requires a bit of light and some luck. Neither of which we'll have if it's moon-shy."

She nodded then, but her eyes were anchored to the statue's face, and he had to lead her down the stairs, watching as she took them slowly, walking backward.

They came out of the maze just beneath an old building in the thirty-second holding. The sun was settling past the horizon; the night sky was deepening its blue, unfettered by clouds or mist. They stood on the boundary between two worlds, and it was the one they had left behind that still anchored them.

She turned to him quietly. "Rath?"

He nodded.

"Our place." The word had slipped from her without conscious thought; he didn't correct it.

"What of it?"

"Is it—does it lead here?"

He smiled. "You're wasted here," he told her, taking her hand. "I don't have an answer yet. But it's in the right place, and my suspicion is that it does."

"Good. I want—I want to spend more time below ground."

"You might have to," he replied. "Money isn't a problem at the moment, but it usually is. And I have furniture to buy. You might even want a bed."

"Can you teach me?"

"To do what?"

"To read Old Weston?"

"I can teach you to read what I can read," he answered. He pushed her into an alley as the familiar sound of a guard patrol approached. They waited in breathless silence as the steps grew louder, waited a little longer as they retreated.

"But I want you to promise me one thing before I do."

"What?"

"Nothing that comes from the maze—from what I call the maze—goes to anyone but me. I will sell it. I will find a buyer."

"But I—"

"That's not a request. It's not a point of negotiation. You will agree, or I will never take you down to the maze again, and if you find your way there, you'll likely starve."

She was keen-eyed, this Jewel, this urchin. "It's because of the man who followed you, isn't it?"

"Yes," he replied curtly. "Because of that man, or men like him. I know how to lose men like that in the streets. You don't. Your word, Jay."

"I promise," she told him.

He wondered how long it would be until she regretted it. Could not imagine, staring at her wide eyes, her intense expression, the *earnestness* of her, that it was he who would, in time.

Buying furniture proved an exercise in frustration for Rath; to Jewel, it was a curiosity. She could ask a hundred questions without opening her mouth, and she bobbed from foot to foot, as if compelled to expend her enthusiasm by motion.

She had not lied, however; she knew how to read and write Weston. She could also speak a respectable amount of Torra, the language of the Southern refugees, and as Rath's Torra was far less smooth, this was welcome.

It came as no surprise to him that she went, when she had the money, to the same farmer in the Common that she had visited when she had next to none; no surprise that she would insist on doing so, time and again. The farmer, thick, garrulous and older, was always happy to see her, and if he spoke gruffly in Rath's presence, he seldom spoke to Jewel without affection.

As the weeks passed—and they passed, a bed eventually appeared in the underground rooms they called home, chairs joining them, and at last, a large desk—Rath gave her an allowance. He didn't choose to tell her how to spend it; instead, he told her how much of the rent she had to pay, and how much of the food costs. He watched to see if she would be in the unenviable position of being forced to borrow money—from Rath, of course—in order to cover her shortfall in the first month.

She wasn't. Her mother—or her father—had taught her numbers in perhaps the only way that counted, in the hundred holdings: she knew how to budget. Knew that plenty was followed by privation. Her iron box, one of the few items that she had retained from her old home, was seldom empty.

But he felt a twinge in the Common, a month after she'd become part of his life, when she made her way to the farmer, coins in hand, and stood silent while he finished transacting his business. It was late in the day; too late to buy produce, besides which, she had already come this way in the early hours of morning.

"Jay?" the farmer said, looking as surprised as Rath chose not to.

She handed him the coins. Silver lay nestled among the copper; it was not a small amount. The farmer's brows rose and fell in one sweeping motion, adjusting the tenor of his expression. Before he could speak, however, she lifted a slender hand.

"It's not for me," she told him quietly.

Whatever he had thought to say was lost as her words penetrated his thick skull. He was certainly capable of suspicion—Rath had experienced this firsthand on the day that he'd met Jewel—but he seldom offered that suspicion to Jewel. It hovered on the edge of his face, seeking purchase and finding none.

When he did not speak, Jewel pushed her hair out of her eyes. "It's for the others," she said quietly.

"What others?"

"The other children like me."

His smile was genuine, and if it held a trace of bitterness, the bitterness did not work its way into his voice. "There are no other children like you," he told her fondly.

She had the grace to redden. But not to retreat. In Rath's growing experience, retreat was not a word that Jewel understood. Not in any emotional sense.

"You help," she told him quietly. "It's not just me."

The farmer was silent.

"I want to help, too. I have a job now. I have money."

"You should save it," the farmer began.

She cut him off. "I want you to keep this. Use it, when you see children like I was."

He hesitated, and Rath could see instantly that she knew she'd won. She put the coins in his hand—a hand that dwarfed hers in every possible way.

"Aye," the farmer told her. He didn't count the coin.

"One day," Jewel told him firmly, "I'm going to live on the Isle. One day."

The older man smiled. "I hope I live to see it, lass."

"You will," she said firmly. Child's voice, teetering on the edge of a determination that wasn't passive; that didn't wait.

But as they walked back from the market, as they passed beneath the flags of the Common, and crossed the long shadow cast by the Merchant Authority itself, Rath watched the girl who dogged his steps. He had invited her into his life. He had made that decision.

He regretted it briefly. What he could say of Jewel—that she did nothing by halves—had been said of Rath himself, many, many times.

Looking up, she saw his expression, and her step faltered. "What have I done this time?" she asked. The words were more defiant than the tone they were couched in. She was slender shadow, cast by sun, against the perfect stones.

"Jewel—"

"Jay."

"Jay," he corrected himself. "Why did you do that?"

Her turn to look confused, but she wore confusion openly, as if it were a promise. "Do what?"

"Why did you give that farmer your money?"

"It was mine to give," she said.

"I'm not accusing you of a crime," he replied, aware that he was half lying. Aware that she knew it. She was too perceptive by half, this girl, this sometime stranger.

They were silent for another three blocks, weaving in and out of foot traffic and the occasional empty wagon with the occasional tired horse to give it right of way.

"The money's yours," Rath finally said. "And you don't have a lot of it."

"Some people have less."

He was tense now. "A lot of people have less. What of it?"

"What's the point?" she asked him, stopping, her hands finding their perch on what existed of her hips.

"The point?"

"Of *having* the money."

"Not starving," he replied. "Not freezing, if the Winter's bad. Not running around half naked because you can't afford clothing that fits you."

"And I'm not. Doing any of those things."

"You were," he said darkly. "And you may well be, again."

"But I'm not *now*."

"Now is nothing," he snapped.

"Now," she countered, "is all we have. All we can be certain we have."

"Jay—"

"It's *my* money. And if I can't help people in any other way, I can at least do this."

Faded echoes of other arguments. He looked at her, down at her, seeing in her youth the fire that had once burned him. Had once hurt the whole of his family, in ways that an impoverished girl from the holdings could *never* understand.

"And what of the people who care about you?" he asked bitterly. "What of the people who need you?" And then he stopped.

Because she was staring at him, her eyes slightly rounded, as if she could see through him. She said, "I don't understand."

And Rath, cursing himself, started to walk faster. It often worked; she had to work to keep up, and much of her words were lost to the effort of breathing. But not, alas, today.

"Rath—what did you mean?"

"Nothing."

"The people who cared about me—the people I loved—they're all dead." She hesitated. Reached out for his sleeve, the elbow pressed tightly against his upper body. His hands were fists; she wouldn't touch those. Not now. "Except for you."

"And I care about you?" he said, turning on her, his words so sharp she stopped following.

He had to listen to catch her reply.

"Yes!"

Not worth the effort. He crossed the invisible boundary between the thirty-second and the thirty-fifth holdings before he relented, not trusting the streets. Or their occupants. "Yes," he said, although it sounded like No. "I should have known," he added softly.

"Should have known?"

"You remind me of someone. I didn't see it, because you look nothing at all like her. If I had, I would have left you by the river."

"But—but why?"

It was a fair question. Rath was not of a mind to be fair. "Because you *are* like her, Jewel."

"Did you love her?"

He laughed. "We all did."

She hesitated, and he almost appreciated the tact. Coming from Jewel, it was rare.

"Did she die?"

His laugh was bitter, ugly, something that he had thought himself long past uttering. "No."

He let her attach herself to his shirt. "I don't like her."

"Don't you?"

"No."

"Why?"

"Because she hurt you," Jewel replied, with the ignorance and ferocity of a child's loyalty.

There was no point denying it, although he longed to. He did nothing instead; it seemed safer. But safety was a different country now.

Safety was, for Rath, a thing that existed solely in isolation. He had forgotten that.

Had chosen to forget it.

Jewel was here now, and for the moment, she was his.

But the act of determined generosity was the beginning of a long tale, and one he knew well.

"Who was she?" Jewel asked quietly.

"Her name? Her name was Amarais," he replied. "She was the best thing that our House had ever produced; the child upon whom our grandfather showered all pride, all affection, and all hope. We loved her," he added, because he thought it necessary. "And in her, my grandfather saw the rise of his House, and our fortunes; he saw the hope of political ascendance that had long since been eroded by lesser men." His gaze skirted the streets; the coming shadows contained buildings that he had not seen in many, many years.

"What happened?"

"She left us," he replied. Remembering, now, the long months that led up to that departure, and the long months that followed. Remembering the woman who was *not* this child.

"Why?"

"Why?" Bitter word. "Because she thought her duty lay elsewhere. Because she thought she could do great things, better things, for those in need."

"Oh." There was a very Jewel-like pause. "Did she?"

"It depends," he replied, "on whose needs." And then he lengthened his stride again, taking care not to dislodge the girl who shadowed his life. His expression made clear that he would answer no more questions; that he had already answered too many.

Chapter Five

R ATH RARELY TOLD Jewel where he was going. He would disappear, usually when sundown began, and he would lock the door
when he left. For the first ten days, he gave strict instructions about those
locks, and they were pretty simple: Don't bloody well open them.

When she started to look mutinous—not at the instructions, which
were sensible enough, but at the *tone* in which they were delivered—he
stopped telling her. But he didn't say where he was going, and aside from
that one journey into the undercity, he didn't ask her to accompany him.
If that's where he was going at all.

Her first vision, fevered, had shown her nothing of the underground; it
had given her the sound of a dark voice, and a glimpse of Rath being hunted,
no more. She didn't know for certain what he did when he was gone.

Jewel accepted this. Partly because she didn't want to know, and partly
because, for the first month, she was desperately trying to be *good*. And
useful. Either of these would have kept her quiet at home. But home
wouldn't have been this empty place, these blank walls. Only pipe smoke
lingered in Rath's absence; although there was dust in plenty to be found
among Rath's personal things—and Jay knew, as she cleaned them all,
much to his dismay—they hadn't been in the dank basement rooms for
long enough to let much gather otherwise.

She had three buckets, one for cleaning and two for water; she had
a wide slat, with ropes, across which she balanced those buckets when
Rath at last decided she knew her way around the holding and let her go,
unsupervised, to the well. She had a broom, several rags—most of these

old clothing that Rath had discarded when they had become too damaged to be useful in other ways. The holes and rips were always of interest to Jewel, but their stories lay fallow; he gave her that *don't ask* look, and she was compliant. She didn't.

But she didn't have her Oma. Her father. Her mother was dim enough in memory that absence didn't linger in daily tasks; the reminder came in the dark, when she lay aground in the sleeping clothes that Rath had given her. Then, it was harder.

But during the day—when he was awake—Rath began to teach Jewel things that he thought she should know.

There had been scant argument offered, and all of it from Jewel.

"You won't always live here," he told her quietly. It wasn't meant as a threat. It was hard not to take it that way. "You'll move. You'll have to." He paused, his smile grim. "One day, I might not come home. Have you thought about what you'll do then?"

Every night.

Every night when he *didn't* come home. When the locks were quiet, the hall silent, the night too ominous in its stillness.

She could go back to the river.

But it would be better if she could go back later. And because she knew it, because she had always tried to be practical, she began to learn what he offered so brusquely to teach her.

How to pick a lock.

How to pocket small items without being noticed.

How to read—more, and write—more. These last, he was particularly aggressive about.

"I *know* how to read," she told him.

Kindness was no part of Rath's vocabulary. He'd handed her a book. She'd taken a look at the stylized letters, the odd brush strokes, the way they glittered in the right and wrong light, and she'd haltingly tried to tell him what she saw.

Hated the smug silence that followed, but swallowed it anyway, and began to work harder.

Numbers, in the third week, followed letters and locks. She had only a very basic understanding of numbers, and he was distinctly unkind about her abilities.

But he left her with her studies, left lamp oil, lamp and candle. He knew, without asking, that she would lay awake until the door opened.

When it didn't, she would watch the sun rise through the window wells. The light was slow to reach the floor, dribbling across flat, worn slats with a kind of wary brightness that never alleviated all of the shadows of her daily life.

On one such day, she rose. There was some bread that was hardening nicely—if you wanted a rock that was easy to lift—in the kitchen, but not much else. The water was cool, but safe to drink, and she did that, waiting, her hands dripping over the bucket.

She swept the floors. She played with the inkwell. She fingered the covers of Rath's many books. Without Rath standing over her shoulder, they didn't hold much of interest; they weren't stories, after all. Just faceless words with the occasional brilliant picture and letters that were almost pictures in and of themselves.

The waiting was hard.

No, the waiting was impossible. And because she'd done with it, and her body was stiff with uncertainty, she dressed, pulled boots—Rath's gift—over her feet, and found her father's money box. That there was money *in* it was also Rath's gift.

"We won't always have money," he told her softly. "But if we have none for the next six months, we'll still see the Winter in and out without worrying for the cold."

She took a handful of silver coins out of the box, and counted them carefully. She had always liked to play with coins; to line them up, to stand them on edge, to make them spin, while their sides caught light. She had also often liked to bite them or put them in her mouth, and this was a habit that was strictly frowned on by her Oma. *You don't know where that coin's been*, the old woman would say, rapping Jewel's forehead sharply with the flat of a bony palm.

In my mouth.

You don't know where else *it's been.*

She was no longer that child, and she didn't put coins in her mouth. Instead, she put most of them back. But not all. She needed some of them for the market.

She disobeyed Rath for the first time. Not the last; that would come much later. Climbing up on a chair to reach the highest of the bolts, she opened it, and then opened all but the last.

Hesitating for a moment, she returned to his newly swept room, his precious paper, his ink. She picked up the quill that was hers—

identifiably so, because the end was chewed so badly—and scrawled a quick note.

And then she let herself out.

The bolts were beyond her current skill, but the lock itself was fairly simple; she pinned it shut. She didn't have keys, but didn't worry; Rath did.

"Lefty."

The boy who belonged to the name looked up. He had to, if he wanted to see the face of the man who'd called him. The man—a big, bald farmer who was almost famous for not calling the market guards too often—knew Lefty well enough by now not to try to say much to him.

Lefty almost liked him; he didn't know the farmer's name, but then again, barely remembered his own. He nodded, and the farmer smiled. It wasn't a mean smile, but it seemed, to the young, gaunt boy, a sad one.

He didn't understand why. The farmer was obviously well off. Had to be, to have that big wagon and all that *food*. He had sons and a daughter who often helped him sell when the market was busy. Lefty knew this because for months they'd only dared to sneak by the wagon when it *was* busy. And the daughter was pretty, besides. She wasn't always nice, but that suited Lefty. It was often the nice ones that were the most dangerous.

"Where's Arann?"

Lefty shrugged, nervous now.

The farmer's smile changed. "It's all right," he said, speaking in his loud buy-my-stuff voice. "I can see him now." The farmer had also noticed that Lefty didn't like quiet voices.

Arann came out from between the stalls. Lefty smiled and ran to meet him, fitting himself into the larger boy's shadow. He lifted his hand and pointed to the farmer, and Arann nodded.

"There you are," the farmer said. He now looked relieved, which made sense to Lefty; it was how he felt when he saw Arann. Arann was the only person in the holdings that Lefty trusted.

"Farmer Hanson," Arann said, nodding.

The farmer smiled in reply. It was a different smile. Sad, yes, but stronger. "You've grown," he told Arann. Most people—the ones who talked to them at all—said that every time they saw him.

Arann shrugged. "It's the clothing," he told the farmer. "It's shrinking." He paused and then added, "You have work for me?"

"Tomorrow, if you'll come by. I'll tell the market guards."

Arann smiled. "We'll be here."

"Wait," the farmer said, as they turned to leave. Arann turned instantly, and just a little too quickly. The farmer handed Arann a basket. "Eat. Bring it back in the morning."

Arann nodded. He never questioned the farmer's gifts. Because he didn't, Lefty knew they were safe.

"Come on, Lefty. Let's go home." Clutching the basket tight now, large hands cradling it against his chest.

Jewel made her way to the market. Out of habit, and because it was almost on the way, she stopped by the old well when she saw a familiar bent back. The woman to whom it belonged looked up, her facial lines beginning to harden into what seemed a perpetual frown.

But the frown froze, and the lines shifted as the woman squinted. "Is that Jay?"

Jewel nodded. "Can I help?"

"Where's that young man of yours?"

As Rath was old enough—easily—to be Jewel's father, she snickered quietly. Elsie was a tad hard of hearing, so this was safe. "He's out working," Jewel said, in a much louder voice.

"It's good that he's found work. I worry about you, you know." But the old woman handed Jewel the heavy bucket and preceded her down the street, as if she owned it. She walked on hard canes, and those canes could be used to startling effect if someone was actually stupid enough to come too close.

Jewel had seen it half a dozen times. Had almost been victim to it once.

"You're certain you're all right, dear?" Elsie said, when they reached the narrow building she called home.

"I'm just going to the Common," Jewel replied. In truth, the bucket was damn heavy, and she was struggling with it; her arms were shaking when she set it down. "To buy food. Should I buy anything for you?"

"No, my useless son will do that." Elsie sniffed. "And he'll come home with yesterday's vegetables, mark my word."

"They're cheaper."

"Not when he buys 'em, they aren't. If I were younger, I'd go to the Common myself and give those thieving farmers a piece of my mind."

As Elsie often gave away pieces of her mind, it was a small wonder she had much of one left. Jewel, wise in the ways of this particular type of woman, kept that opinion to herself, because not only did Elsie have a mind of her own, she had a temper to go with it. She said her good-byes and turned toward the great trees that marked the Common so visibly, even at this distance.

Her hands were in her pockets when she left, and silver cooled her palms. She knew that some of the farmers weren't above a little game of merchant trickery, but she also knew who they were and how to avoid them.

And when it came right down to it, there was really only one farmer that she ever wanted to see.

He smiled broadly as she approached his wagon, and his sons dispersed when he barked at them. Jewel had become accustomed enough to his voice that she could—barely—make out which rapid barks meant what.

"I swear," Farmer Hanson told her, as she stopped in front of the wagon, pushing herself between the small gap two larger people left, "you've gotten taller."

"It's just you," Jewel said with a grimace. "I'd've noticed."

"Aye, and maybe it's just that at *my* age, you only get wider and shorter." He laughed. "What'll you be having today?"

Jewel was eyeing his vegetables as the question floated past her. He didn't tell her not to touch; he'd long since given up on that. When her Oma had come to the Common, she had inspected *everything*, and her sight—as she'd explained in a rather annoyed tone—wasn't all it used to be. Everything was touched, lifted, looked at, sniffed.

This is how dead people lived on. Jewel's motions were almost exactly the motions of the older woman, absent only pipe and narrowed eyes. She took her time, partly because she enjoyed her brief conversations with the farmer, and partly because the inspection itself demanded lengthy consideration.

Farmer Hanson waited. Not quietly, but he did wait.

When Jewel had chosen her vegetables, and the luxury of fresh apples, she held out her coins.

The farmer took them, counting them with care. His coins replaced some of hers, but she'd brought far more than was necessary. She always did, when she had the money. Until Rath, that had been never.

"Your change?"

She smiled. "Keep it."

"You've paid me now for anything you might have taken," he told her.

"It's not for me."

"Who is it for, then?"

She met his eyes and held them, her own very serious. They always were. Farmer Hanson seemed to enjoy this particular conversation—he must, they'd had it so often.

"For others like me. But not as lucky." She held his gaze, a smile escaping her earnest expression. "If it weren't for you—"

He shook his head. "There's enough money here to feed a lot of children like you. Especially given how much you used to eat."

"Feed the ones you can," she told him quietly. She shifted her basket. "While the money lasts."

She started to walk away, but he called her by name, and she turned; he hadn't finished speaking. Today the conversation took a slightly different turn.

"There are a couple of boys," he told her, lowering his booming voice. The market noise forced Jewel to draw closer, and Farmer Hanson opened the small gate that separated his clients from the men he affectionately called his useless sons, making clear by that gesture that he wanted her to join him. As she obeyed the wordless invitation, Jewel wondered if there *were* any other kind of son, given how often she heard the phrase. But there was no malice in it.

"Boys?"

"Aye."

"Who?"

The farmer hesitated for just a minute—old habits—and then said, "They call themselves Arann and Lefty."

"Well, the first one sounds like a name."

"The second one is a name as well, or the only name the lad'll answer to. He's missing two fingers on the right hand, and it's crippled. The right hand," he added, just in case she hadn't heard him.

She had. "They come here?"

"When they can," the farmer replied. "Just like you did. You might have seen them."

She took in the whole of the Common at a glance, and the farmer winced. "Aye, well, you might not."

"What about these boys? You like them?"

"I like them as well as I did you," was the unusually quiet reply. "They're street kids," he added. "And they don't have family they care to live with, if they have family at all."

"They're part of a den?"

He shook his head and frowned.

Fair enough. It was a stupid question. "You're feeding them?"

He nodded again. "The older boy, Arann, is big. He's strong, too. When I have work, I pay him." He held out the hand that still contained the remainder of Jewel's coin. "But this is enough to actually clothe them. It's getting cold," he added, still quiet. "And Arann outgrew what he wears about a year ago. Maybe two. He's a big lad."

"Is he simple?"

"Not in the head, no. He's canny enough."

"Then why is he—" Jewel stopped speaking for a minute. "If he's big enough, he could find a place with a den, easy."

Den was not a word that Farmer Hanson liked or approved of, and Jewel cringed as his brows grew into one long line across his face. Luckily, it didn't last long.

"He could, yes. But Lefty couldn't. Lefty is smaller than you are. I don't think he's any younger, but he might be."

Jewel met the farmer's gaze. "You want to use the money to buy clothing for them?"

"Mark my words, there'll be snow this Winter. The rains are already falling cold for this time of year," the Farmer replied. "And if you see clear, yes. I would. You should meet them, Jay. I think you'd like them. I think," he added softly, "that Arann would like you."

Jewel shrugged uneasily. "I couldn't do anything for them," she said at last. "But you can keep the money. Use it any way you'd like. You see 'em. I don't. You'll know what they need."

She started to walk away, and then turned. "You like this Arann because of Lefty, don't you?"

"They're not kin," the farmer replied quietly. "But they might as well be. I think Arann would die before he abandoned Lefty. And they live in the poor holdings, Jay. If he were a different boy, I wouldn't have noticed him at all."

Jewel nodded.

"They'll be here come morning. You should come, if you can."

"Why?"

Farmer Hanson shrugged. But he slipped the money into his generous pockets, a generous man, richer in every way than Jewel Markess, but poor enough that he couldn't help everyone he thought needed aid. He did what he could.

Which was why Jewel liked him.

"Maybe," she said.

Home, this month, was the boarded remains of one of the old buildings in the thirty-second holding.

They'd found it at night, and Arann had pried just enough of the boards loose that they could squeeze in. Of course, given how big Arann was, that was most of 'em. They tried to put them back. It was always better if no one could tell where you lived.

They'd been caught before.

Lefty's secret guilt: They'd been caught, but Arann would have been okay if he'd been willing to leave Lefty behind. A lot of den leaders would have taken Arann on in a second—he was big. Strong.

Lefty? He was neither. And his right hand, the hand he always tried to keep hidden, had once been his good hand. He might have been useful for begging, if he were just a bit younger or prettier. But he'd never be a thief. Never be muscle.

He was no good to anyone.

Everyone had always told him that, and if Lefty dreamed otherwise, he always woke up. He knew it was true.

Arann was older than Lefty, and even knew his real birthday. He was smarter than Lefty, too.

But how smart could he be? Any time he'd had the chance, he'd never left Lefty behind—and no one was willing to take them both. Some offered, but Arann didn't trust them. Lefty didn't either, but that was almost beside the point. The fact that den leaders had been willing to lie meant Arann was valuable. And in the holdings? Accidents happened. All the time.

Any time Arann wanted, he could find a place, a safe place with a large den.

Instead, he found places like this one.

There were two rooms that could be lived in, sort of. The floors, though, tilted toward the door that divided them, as if they'd been built for mice, and nothing heavier. Lefty felt safe enough crossing the floor—but he worried about Arann.

Arann didn't like it when Lefty worried, and he could always tell, even when Lefty didn't speak.

Like now. Arann held out the farmer's basket, and Lefty took it. He was hungry. They both were. Aside from river water, they hadn't had food for almost two days.

"Eat," Arann told him, watching. "But remember what happens when you eat too fast."

Lefty nodded absently, thinking.

The rains had started to fall cold. In the Summer, it didn't matter, but Arann said that Winter this year was going to be bad. Really bad. Lefty didn't ask him how he knew—he'd probably asked someone. Maybe the farmer.

Cold could kill.

The rooms had a fire grate, but even if they'd had the money for wood to burn, Arann didn't trust it; he said it was too old, too dirty. There were gaps in the roof, and the west wall leaned out. The night they'd found the place, Arann had tried to lean against the outer wall, but it hadn't done any good. In the end, he'd given up and shrugged. It was better than nothing, now that the rains were starting.

Lefty began to empty the basket, folding the small cloth that had been laid over its contents as well as he could before he set it aside; it belonged to the farmer and it had to go back. They didn't want the farmer angry at them.

Not when he offered them things like this. Bread, old apples, some dried-out cheese. No meat, but there almost never was. "Arann?"

"Not hungry," Arann said.

Lefty looked at the food, trying to ignore his stomach and the way his mouth had started to water. "Liar."

Arann didn't answer. For a minute or two, it was real quiet. When he spoke, it wasn't much better. He ran his hands—whole hands, strong hands—through dirty, dark hair, and expelled all his breath.

"You're never going to get bigger if you don't eat more. You always want to be that size?"

"I ain't never going to be big," Lefty replied. "Not like you."

"You're at least two years younger. You're just slow to grow, is all."

Neither of them believed it. Lefty folded arms half the size of Arann's across his chest, which was even smaller. "I won't eat if you won't."

Arann glared. Lefty glared back.

But it didn't last long. Lefty never lied to Arann, and Arann knew when he was serious. He sat on the floor, and it made a frog's noise in protest. "What are you going to do if something happens to me, Lefty?"

Lefty handed Arann some cheese. He didn't feel like talking.

Rath didn't come home.

Jewel did, picking the one lock she'd shut behind her. Holding her breath, as the door swung open; listening for something other than the almost inaudible creak of oiled hinges. Standing, a moment too long, one foot on either side of the threshold. This was home.

And this was too good to be home for long. Jewel wasn't too old to daydream; she was just this side of too old to believe in them. She'd set the basket down in order to play with the lock, and she shoved her hair out of her eyes before picking it up again. She didn't think Rath was dead. Couldn't be certain, and *hated* that. Gift, as Rath called it, or curse, as she did, was like a damn cat—it came and went as it pleased, and she could no more order it about than she could cajole it.

She dragged the basket into the narrow hall, and then pushed the door shut. Her stool—a low-backed chair—joined her at the door as she slid the bolts home; no point in pissing Rath off without reason. She alighted and ran into the room that was in theory his private place to search for some sign that he'd been and gone—but she found nothing disturbed.

She ate alone. The light grew and shrank, and with it the shadows from the window wells. She offered Kalliaris a prayer, asked her to smile, and then played at dagger work for a stretch of time. Rath was still conspicuous by his absence, and the whole of the apartment was silent. Jewel hated the silence.

Silence was the thing that made clear that no one was home. And in her life, that meant that there was no home. She made noise. Spoke to herself. Tried to sing. Found no comfort in any of these activities.

Night came, and with it, more silence; the streets emptied, and in the thirty-fifth holding, the sound of foot patrols was sporadic and undependable. She ate again, sparingly. Thought about Farmer Hanson, his sons, his daughter, the wagon in the Common. Thought about her Oma, her father, the shadows their absence also cast.

Thought about the friends she didn't have, and what that would mean to her if Rath *never came back.*

When sleep came, it came by surprise.

The rains fell cold.

The night passed, the quiet broken by the sound of water against the crumbling roof. There was no thunder, no bright flash of crackling light; it wasn't that kind of rain. Not a storm, just an endless, insistent drumming. Lefty was asleep before it started, and awake before it ended, if it ever would. Some rain was like that.

The floor by the wall was wet, and damp everywhere else. They couldn't stay here much longer. Even the mice were huddled in distant corners, like balls of standing fur.

Arann was snoring. Lefty didn't kick him—not yet. The sky was still dark, and if they didn't see the sun rise, it would come anyway.

The streets—smaller stones giving way to slabs as the Common grew closer—would be wet, weeds slippery and heavy to ground. There were no real windows to look out of; Lefty lifted a board. Got his head wet when he stuck it outside for just a minute. He didn't much mind; it would get a lot wetter on the way to the Common, and the rain didn't show any sign of letting up.

"Arann?" he said, nudging the older boy gingerly with his toe. Had he much else to throw, he might have chosen to wake him by standing against the farthest wall and tossing whatever he could find—but Lefty's aim was damn poor with his left hand, and he didn't much like to use the right one. Besides which, Arann didn't *always* wake badly.

Lefty never tried to wake him from nightmare, though. He knew enough to know how very unsafe that was.

Arann was not a heavy sleeper. He rolled away from Lefty's toe, and was half on his feet before his eyes were open. His hands were fists. But this wasn't a bad sign; Lefty just stood very, very still until those fists began to unbunch, and Arann's expression went from glassy to *here.*

Sometimes it took minutes; today, it took seconds. Lefty was lucky. "I left you some bread," he said. "It's a bit hard."

Arann shrugged. "That's what teeth are for. While we have 'em." He looked at Lefty's wet hair, and grimaced. "Raining?"

Lefty nodded.

"We're not late?" The last said with as much anxiety as Arann ever showed.

"Not yet."

"You should have let me sleep, then. I was having a good dream."

"Good dream, bad dream—they're all just dreams."

Arann started to eat, and then stopped. "You didn't eat anything." It was as much of an accusation as Arann ever made.

Lefty shrugged, uneasy. "You're doing the heavy lifting, not me."

"What did I tell you?"

"I forget."

Arann snorted. But after a moment, he ate. Because it was true: This morning he would do the heavy work, and that always made him hungry. Without the work, there would be no food. For either of them.

The rain kept falling, and Arann's chewing was the only other sound in the sodden, abandoned building. It lasted minutes—which was as long as the food lasted—before Arann rose. "We'd better get going." He paused, and brushed off bread crumbs; by the time they got home, the mice would have the floor cleaned.

Lefty nodded, pulling his clothing tight. It wasn't that hard; in spite of everything either of them said, he *had* grown some, and the clothing was old. Not so old that it was threadbare like Arann's, but old enough.

They slid out past the loose boards, and stood up as the rain fell, faces turned a moment toward the thin gray cloud that was all of the sky.

Nothing closed the Common.

It was a truth that the City thrived on. Summer, Winter, rainy season or rare snow—the merchants and farmers who had things to sell came, their wagons laden, their tempers indicative of the seasonal inconvenience, whatever that happened to be. In the Summer it was the heat and humidity; in the rainy season, it was the cold and the damp. People were good at complaining; there was always something that they could find to complain about.

When she wasn't the source of that complaint, Jewel found it amusing. You could tell a lot about people by the complaints they made. Her Oma's complaints had always been a continuous stream of words, interrupted by pipe smoke and the occasional affectionate nod. But there was, in her sharp observation, very little malice; she complained because it was one of her few indulgences. Or so she often said; she didn't much like it when Jewel joined in. The phrase, "I'll give you something to complain about" still lingered in memory, and it made Jewel both wince and smile.

Farmer Hanson's complaints were not her Oma's, but they were kin to them; he complained about his sons, about the lugs that tried to obliquely court his working daughter, about the customers who bruised his produce, the customers who tried to pay him less than it was worth, and the customers who were stupid enough to think anyone else had better food.

He complained about his back, his arms, his shoulders; in the rainy season, some joint or other was always aching, and he mentioned his left leg frequently. Apparently, at one time or other, it had been broken. He was in fine form as Jewel approached his closed wagon; he was setting up the tarps that would cover the stall, and, of course, complaining about the speed at which his sons moved—which would, according to the good farmer, beggar them all. His sons seemed to take this in stride. They were big enough, well-fed enough, not to worry about being beggared.

Jewel had decided to observe. Rath still wasn't home, and she'd risen before dawn, waiting in the silence until she couldn't stand silence for another minute. She fled it; the Common was never silent. Rath had been teaching her about moving in the streets; with and against the flow of the crowds; about disappearing, reappearing, remaining hidden while standing in plain sight.

He, unlike the farmer, seldom complained; his face would tighten, his lips would thin, and she would feel the weight of his frustration and disappointment—in silence. She missed the words most.

Rath talked when he had something to say. And clearly, he didn't have much to say to a ten-year-old orphan.

If she hadn't learned enough to merit Rath's approval, she'd learned just enough to remain unnoticed by Farmer Hanson. She stood by the roadside to the Northeast, watching as the Common filled. Waiting for some glimpse of the two boys he had mentioned.

She didn't have long to wait. As the sky grew paler, and the rain continued to fall, she saw them break through the crowd in a bit of a rush: A tall, broad-shouldered giant whose age she couldn't guess, and a small, spindly boy who looked younger than she did. The tall boy wore clothing that probably hadn't fit him for a year—which made him look big and awkward, to Jewel. Most of it was a dark brown, but rain did that. He also carried a basket that was incongruously neat.

Jewel pulled her own vest a little closer, shoving hair out of her eyes. The only good thing that could be said for rain was this: When she pushed her unruly curls to one side, they stayed where she'd shoved them. Out of her eyes, so she could *see*.

It was hard to tell what color their hair would be when it wasn't plastered to their faces, but their faces were flushed; she was certain they'd run at least part of the way.

Their breath came out in thin clouds as they at last reached the farmer's side. The large boy handed the farmer the basket, and the farmer set it aside.

She couldn't hear what they said; she could hear the farmer shout at his sons. He had no unkind words for the boys, and this told her—more clearly than anything else—that he pitied them.

Just as he had pitied her.

Her Oma would have been furious; pity was somewhere below charity in her rank of acceptable behavior. But her Oma was dead, and Jewel didn't mind pity. Maybe, when she was old and smoked a pipe, she would.

Or maybe never. She couldn't understand what there was, in pity, that her Oma despised—her Oma had pitied many people. To Jewel, pity meant understanding.

The large boy began to help the sons erect the standing cloth canopy. He was strong; she could see that clearly because his thin shirt clung to his back, wrapped around the contours of muscles. She thought him a bit like Rath; he didn't speak much.

The thin boy, who wasn't put to work at all, did, but only to the large boy; he avoided looking at anyone else. She could see his breath come out, again and again, in a thin cloud. He was shivering, and he had his right arm shoved under his left armpit. Jewel hadn't Wintered in the streets, but she recognized cold when she saw it because her family had often been too poor to buy wood for burning.

Still, cold or no, his left hand was waving back and forth as he talked. He didn't seem to be able to stand still. But the giant wasn't annoyed by this; he seemed to both expect and accept it. Every now and then, he would answer, his breath a short grunt.

Boxes came next; the rainy season had a different rhythm than the humid, hot one, but people still had to eat. Now was the time when those who had money would begin to stock up on the things that would carry them the month or two of cold before things started to grow again.

Jewel had heard tales of the Northern lands, the farthest edge of the Empire; she had heard about the constant snow. She wondered what they ate, and how, those people who were trapped there.

Was very thankful not to be one of them. Averalaan saw little snow, but when it did, people died.

And as she stood watching, her arms wrapped unconsciously around her upper body, she suddenly *knew* that this year, there would be snow in Winter; that it would be cold, and bodies would lie frozen in the streets.

She didn't try to talk herself out of believing it; she had long since given up that particular lie. It would be cold. She would have Rath.

And the boys?

She understood why Farmer Hanson had asked her about the money, about clothing. *Mark my words,* he'd said, although he usually said that. She wondered how he had known. Maybe his plants grew differently, if they grew at all when it was cold; theirs had.

A visceral desire to *be* rich warmed her for a moment with its sudden ferocity. Because if she were rich, she could give Farmer Hanson enough money to clothe every child he managed to stumble over and care about.

The work was done before she had finished with the dream of such riches, such largesse. She almost missed it, she was so involved in her momentary anger at the gods, the city, the world in all its injustice.

But the large boy stood still now, his arms by his side, waiting for the farmer. Customers had started to arrive, and his daughter was slowly being swamped; the sons were ordered—loudly—to make themselves useful. Which wasn't exactly fair; although they were wet, Jewel was pretty sure that half of that water was sweat.

The farmer handed the boys the basket they had arrived with; if it was noticeably heavier, it was hard to tell. The large boy carried it with unconscious ease. The farmer said something else, and the two boys stopped to listen. The large boy nodded.

They began to walk down the rainy street, heads bowed against the sudden sea wind that made the rain colder and harsher. The street itself wasn't crowded by Common standards, although it was by any holding standard. Jewel watched them dwindle.

And felt her stomach knot, her voice catch—although there wasn't anyone to speak to—as the large boy stopped to wait, patiently, for the smaller one to catch up.

Arann. She did not speak the name out loud. Was surprised that it had come to her at all. In the cold, her skin was pale, her eyes wide and round, but not unseeing.

She should have hesitated. She *should* have stayed her ground, said nothing, done nothing. Could not have said, later, why she hadn't; Rath's warning was ringing in her ears, louder and more doom-laden with every stride she took. She forgot about being invisible; it took too much time.

The causeway opened up.

She could see its mouth; could see the market guards that stood, drenched in their obvious armor, by the gate. And she could *feel* the rattle of wagon wheels, the movement of a skittish horse, the sound of thunder. Lightning. It broke through the tall trees without hitting them, illuminating gray-green sky.

Someone was coming, late, to market. And in a hurry. People could get out of the way, or they could be run down.

Would be.

Jewel had the sense, as she ran, that she would do this again; that she had done this before. The former, she couldn't argue with; the latter was impossible. But Farmer Hanson had been *right* about these two boys, and in a way that Jewel, at ten, did not understand. Or couldn't put into words.

She put what she could there instead: She shouted two names. Arann. Lefty.

Had she been a man, things might have been different. Had she had that low, loud growl of a voice, had she armor or weapon, had she looked in any way like a city official or a magisterial guard, they would have bolted.

She looked like Jewel—drenched, curls flat as they would ever be along the top and sides of her face.

The large boy looked up, his face creasing in a frown, his eyes narrowing into a squint and a question. The younger boy, Lefty, tried to find a shadow to stand in. There wasn't one, but he didn't seem to notice the lack.

Just by the gates, they stood, watching, their backs toward the street. She pushed her way past people; knocked at least one over. Late apologies would have to do—if they were needed; she could hear very colorful Torra following in her wake, as if she were a ship parting water.

She *had* to reach them.

She had to reach them in time.

Arann's frown shifted as he saw, at last, where his name was coming from. He didn't recognize her—how could he?—but the difference in age and size made her no threat.

She was breathing heavily by the time she reached his side, and she couldn't speak above the grating rasp of cold breath, wreaths of mist hanging between them. Instead of words, she reached out, grabbed his arm, and *pulled.*

She might as well have tried to move Farmer Hanson's wagon. Arann's frown deepened, and with it, she saw worry.

She turned instead to Lefty. Found breath, although it was thin. Found her words. "You've got to move," she told the younger boy. "You can't stand here, you can't walk the way you were going to walk."

Lefty looked up at Arann.

And then he looked at her.

She couldn't hear what he said to the large boy; she could hear, instead, the sound of a wagon; could almost taste blood, hear the brief crunch of snapping bone as the wagon at last careened around a corner, and the boy, horse, and nailed wood and heavy cargo, met in an act of fate. Arann would turn. Arann would drop the basket he held, grab Lefty, and *throw* him. Jewel *knew* this.

Lefty? He'd be bruised. Scraped.

And alone.

She lifted a shaking arm, and pointed. "A wagon's coming," she told them. "It's heavy. The street is slippery. The driver is stupid. The horse can't see well; it's rainy.

"Arann will be hit by the wagon."

Lefty looked. At the girl. Listened to her words. Even met her eyes. She was taller than he was, but she wasn't hunched over to avoid the rain and hoard warmth. She wore clothing that fit her, but she was thin, and her eyes were dark with lack of sleep.

But her words were sharp and terrifying.

Lefty reached out with his good hand, caught Arann's arm.

Arann was staring at the stranger as if she were mad. Lefty? Yes, he thought she was crazy. But not dangerous crazy. If she carried a weapon at all, he couldn't see it. She had come here alone; if she was part of a den, they weren't with her. And she'd run.

As if someone's life depended on it.

Lefty wasn't smart, not like Arann. He believed in stupid things. Old stories. A better life.

Mostly, though, he believed in Arann.

He did what the girl couldn't; he pulled, and Arann followed. "It doesn't matter if she's crazy," Lefty said, his voice more urgent than the girl's because he wasn't winded. "Does it? What can it hurt?"

Arann still hesitated, and the girl was turning a pale shade of white. He started to ask her a question, and Lefty's grip became more insistent.

"Move." He waited half a beat, and then added, "Please."

Arann allowed himself to be dragged to the side of the road, beneath the shelter of awnings and the suspicious gaze of merchants who were not quite busy enough to ignore them.

And the wagon came crashing round the corner, its wheels almost off the ground, horse's muzzle flecked with foam, eyes wide. There was a *lot* of shouting, a lot of swearing, a lot of anger, in the street they had just left.

But not Arann.

Lefty's mouth was hanging open; he closed it and looked at the girl who had followed them as if she were afraid Arann would change his mind.

Arann removed his sleeve from Lefty's grip and Lefty let it go; his fingers were suddenly slack, and his hand was shaking. Cold, he told himself.

Liar.

The girl was now looking at the ground, and her hair had slid down her face and into her eyes. She wasn't pretty. She wasn't scarred. She was frightened, but Lefty could sympathize with that. People bumped into her and she tried to move out of their way, mostly succeeding.

Arann looked at the wagon as it passed by. Watched it moving; watched the market guards running after it, their voices more threatening than the voices of the people who had come to spend money here.

"What's your name?" Arann asked her, when it was quieter.

The girl looked up, and up again. Most kids did, when they met Arann. But she straightened her shoulders, thin shoulders like Lefty's, and said, "Jay."

She seemed afraid that Arann would ask her something else, but she didn't know Arann. Arann shook his head, drew the basket closer, and said, "Thanks."

*   *   *

Jewel stared at him.

Had to. What he'd just said made no sense, and it took her a minute to actually hear the word he did say, rather than the ones she was dreading.

After a moment, after more waiting, she realized that Arann wasn't going to say anything else. He looked down at Lefty, and thanked him as well.

"I guess," Lefty said, shuffling from foot to foot, "you aren't as crazy as you look."

His first words to Jewel. His eyes were still hesitant, and they still turned to the side when she looked at him. As if she would hurt him. As if she could.

"Where are you going?" she asked them both.

"You don't know?" Lefty replied.

She stared at Lefty. This, this was more along the lines of the expected. "No," she told him, voice flat. "I have no idea."

"But you knew—"

"Lefty," Arann said, in that *shut up now* tone of voice.

It wasn't a threat. Lefty shut up anyway. Shuffling. Cold. Colder than he had been when he'd been struggling to catch up to Arann.

"You have a place?" Jewel said, when they were quiet again. Rain fell in a sheet, as if the gods were emptying buckets. Thunder spoke for them all. Lightning changed the Common for a brief second.

Arann nodded. "You?" he asked her, after a minute.

She nodded as well. "It's in the thirty-fifth, so it's a bit of a walk. If you—" Rath was going to kill her. If he ever came home. "If you want, you can come to my place. It's dry," she added.

Rath wasn't home. For the first time ever, Jewel felt relief rather than worry at his absence. She motioned Arann and Lefty into the apartment, and closed the door behind them. Hesitated for a minute before shoving the bolts home. Arann stared at them as they slid shut. He even reached up to touch the highest one—the one Jewel needed a stool for.

They dripped on the floor in the hall for a while, Arann touching the bolts, Lefty touching nothing. There was a long, awkward silence, and Jewel realized that if it was going to be filled, it was going to be by her.

She was good at that; too good for Rath's liking.

"This is where I live." Or maybe not too good.

"It's *all* yours?" Lefty asked her, his voice pitched to whisper, his eyes wide.

"Not all. I share it with a friend." She hesitated, and then added, "I've only lived here for a couple of weeks. Before that, I was by the river."

They both looked at her then.

She shrugged, meeting Arann's gaze, and trying to catch Lefty's.

"This friend of yours," Arann began.

"He's older," she said. "He hates questions, and he doesn't talk much."

"How'd you meet him?"

Jewel shrugged. "In the street," she replied. "You hungry?"

Arann nodded and lifted his basket; Jewel motioned it away. "I wasn't well. He brought me home. Well, to the other place. This is sort of new."

"You work for him?"

"Not yet." She met Arann's gaze, daring him to put into words everything that lay behind the question. He didn't. When she was certain he wouldn't, she turned and went into the kitchen. Stuck her head back out into the hall when she realized they weren't following. "Food's in here," she told them both.

"She has a whole room for food?"

Arann looked down at Lefty. "It's a kitchen," he told the smaller boy.

Lefty nodded, and Jewel knew the word probably didn't mean much to him. But he didn't want to look stupid. Fair enough; she hated that herself. She pulled a chair over to the table. There were only two. The other one was in the hall, by the door, and as she left the kitchen to retrieve it, she told Lefty to sit down.

When she came back, dragging the chair across the wet floor, he was seated uncertainly, his legs hanging over the side, his feet tapping ground. Well, his toes anyway.

The kitchen was cramped, narrow, cut by cupboards and one measly counter. But she had the idea that these two were used to small spaces, besides which, her room had daggers and other mess that she didn't want strangers to see.

She pushed the second chair toward the table, and told Arann to sit. Arann hesitated for a fraction of a minute, and then he joined Lefty. But he was still and watchful, where Lefty seemed almost frenetic.

She began to cut apples, cheese, and bread. There were plates, but again, only two; Rath didn't believe in owning more than was necessary. And Rath never brought friends home. If he had any.

Her mother's upbringing took hold. They were *guests*. Jewel didn't need to eat, not yet, and they were obviously hungry. Hungry and wet. She was wet, too, and dry clothing was in easy reach—but she wasn't an idiot; even if Farmer Hanson *did* like these two, she wasn't about to leave them alone in Rath's place.

But she had a sense, watching them, listening to their silence between slicing, that had she *had* her own place, she could have. There was something about Arann that she instantly trusted. Instinct, not feeling, but her instincts were usually pretty good. Good enough to trust.

So she dripped, as they did, standing while they sat. When she was finished, she brought two plates to the table and put them down, one in front of either boy. "We have water," she added.

"Seen enough water today," Arann replied, with just the hint of a smile.

Lefty looked at her, and Jewel waited. When she realized he wasn't going to ask, she went and fetched him a cup of water and put that on the table as well.

"What's that?" Lefty asked Arann, as if Jewel weren't really there. He pointed to the wood stove.

"For burning things," Arann replied. "It's warm in the rainy season."

Jewel nodded. They'd always had a stove, but they hadn't always had firewood for it. Rath wouldn't have that problem.

Arann looked at Jewel when he was halfway done. He chewed, swallowed, and straightened up slightly. His expression was friendly. "You went to market for something?" he asked her.

Had she actually *bought* anything, she would have lied. But there didn't seem to be much point; she'd already exposed the only thing she could do worth lying about. "Yeah," she said. "Farmer Hanson asked me to stop by."

"You know the farmer?"

"Same as you," she replied. "He didn't catch me stealing food. But he did let me know he knew."

"You work for him, too?"

She shook her head. "I'm not big enough. Like Lefty."

"What did he want you to stop by for?"

"To see you two."

Arann was quiet. After a moment, he said, "Why?"

She shrugged and went back to the counter; it was easier to answer this question when he wasn't looking at her face. "I have some money now. Don't know how long it will last. I buy everything from him," she added, "and I still have some money left over. I told him to keep it. He wouldn't until I told him it was for other kids. Like me."

"He wanted you to help us?"

She shrugged again. "Maybe." And turned. "Look, you're wearing clothing that didn't fit you a year ago. And it's the rainy season. And it's going to snow this year. It's going to be a damn cold Winter. I gave him enough money the other day that he thought about buying clothing for you."

"Jay," Arann said quietly, "how long have you been in the streets?"

"My father died this year. In the shipyard."

Arann nodded, as if that explained anything. Maybe it did. She looked at them, started to ask them the same question, and stopped, seeing the way Lefty tried—always—to hide his right hand. Seeing the start of a pale, slender scar on Arann's forearm, where the sleeve was just too damn short to cover it all. Seeing the hunger in them, the lankiness, the darkness of skin that spoke of too many different kinds of exposure.

There were stories in all of it, and none of them stories she could ask for. They lay across skin and beneath it, hidden and private.

"I know you've had it harder than I have," she said quietly. "I know that *so many* of us have it harder than I did." She hadn't, truly, until this moment. It was something she knew, the way one knew a boat existed, but not the way a sailor knew the truth of its wood and its sloping motion across the water.

"It doesn't matter to me, what you've done. In the streets," she added, "we all do what we have to. I've done things I'm not proud of. And I'm certain I'll do more of them, if there's no way out." She wiped her hands on her tunic, and looked at them both.

"You can't live here," she said quietly. "But if you need help, come here, and I'll do what I can to help you."

Arann met her gaze and held it. There was something in the set of his tight mouth that reminded her, inexplicably, of her Oma. But he didn't say what her Oma would have said. He swallowed it.

Jewel wondered if the streets could have forced that bitter swallow out of her Oma; she doubted it.

Lefty rose and looked at Arann, and only at Arann. But when he spoke, he offered an almost inaudible thank you.

Funny, how manners did matter. Even here, in the thirty-fifth holding, between children whose parents no longer existed to care about them.

She saw them out, letting Arann unbolt the high lock because it meant she wouldn't have to drag the chair from the kitchen to do it herself; there wasn't much room for a chair, herself and Arann; Lefty was so slight he hardly made a difference.

When they left, she leaned against the door, listening for their footsteps. She listened there a long time, and silence returned again to the home she shared with Rath.

Those two boys were strangers. And they didn't talk much. But by presence alone they alleviated the silence she hated, and although she knew them only as boys that Farmer Hanson trusted, she found herself missing them.

Chapter Six

RATH PAUSED AT the door. It was late; dawn had not yet wedged itself across the horizon, but it would, and light—what there was of it, in these cursed and interminable rains—would make itself felt. Had, in fact, already begun to make itself felt. He was exhausted, bruised, and hungry.

But he was also instantly wary.

Although he had left strict instructions with Jewel, his absence had been long enough that he expected her ability to obey them to flag. Bending, he touched a slender wire; the door had certainly been opened.

It was not, however, open now. He unlocked the bolts and felt them resist the key in his hand; humidity had thickened the door slightly. The lock, however, turned smoothly and he let himself in. He carried only a magestone for light, and the light it cast was low. A single word brightened it, revealing the long stretch of empty hall, and the closed doors on either side.

He was aware of movement to his left before he turned to lock the door behind him; Jewel was awake. He wondered if she'd slept at all, and waited, as the sounds of rustling cloth drifted into the creak of floorboards. Not even a mouse could wander here without evidence of its weight.

Jewel's door opened. Her hair was more of a mess than usual; clearly, she'd tried to sleep while it was wet, and had achieved a flattened wedge composed of dark curls that still trailed the edge of her eyes.

"Rath?"

Tired, he nodded.

She trudged past him before he could speak—not that he intended to—and went into the kitchen. Paused, came back, and pulled the mage-stone from his palm. When she had first come to live with him, she had chattered constantly. It had taken a week or more before she finally realized that the chatter set his teeth on edge. He had survived this long by living alone, and knew it in a way that he could not easily dislodge.

She said nothing. He walked past the kitchen to his room; the satchel he carried was heavy, and he wished to deposit it someplace that wasn't his shoulders or his back. By the time he finished, she had also finished; he heard the knock at his door and he grunted.

She pushed it open with one hand, carrying a plate with another. "I went to the market," she said quietly. "You must be hungry."

As he was, he nodded almost curtly. He spoke a word and the light dimmed; she would see the bruises in the morning, and even if she was too wise to ask what had caused them, the worry would shadow her eyes. Her concern was more than he wanted to deal with now.

But she stood in the door, having put the plate on the flat of his desk, and she watched him for a long time.

Long enough that he realized she was waiting for attention. "What?"

She started to speak, stopped, and shook her head, retreating. He wanted her to retreat, and did nothing to stop her.

Morning came quickly, and Rath was inclined to ignore it. Jewel, on the other hand, did not; he could hear her steps, the clattering of things in the kitchen, the movement of the bucket as it hit the lower left leg of the table. He had to remind himself that she was ten; she was so determined, it was easy to forget. Or perhaps, if he were being truthful, he wanted to forget it. Living with a child had been no part of his life's plan, and it caused him a distinct unease every time he saw her when she was quiet, or sleeping, or pensive—because at those times, she looked her age.

At those times, she reminded him of a past that he loathed, and he could feel that old anger spill over. A bit of a bind, that; he hated the chatter and the noise of animation, but the lack of it had other costs.

He watched her disappear with her buckets, the brace slack against her slender shoulders. He'd taken the time to follow her three days running, and had seen for himself how she interfered in the lives of strangers, making them, by the odd kindness of her actions, less strange. Less threatening. She helped the elderly, she chided the young, she paused to play at sticks and hoops with some of them while she waited her turn in line. She talked. A lot.

Her flyaway hair in her eyes, her skin pale, her lips turned up in a smile, he regretted almost everything about her life, although he knew little enough about it. What she had said, and what she had not said, made little difference; watching her, it was clear to Rath that she'd been wanted, she'd been loved, and she'd been protected. The protection had not been gentle, clearly, but it had planted the seed of a similar instinct, and he watched its slow flowering with a kind of dread fascination.

Seeing, again, another girl.

Another life.

After the third day, he didn't bother to trail after her. "Jewel."

"Yes?" Her voice drifted in from the hall. He heard the scrape of the chair as she dragged it to the door, and wondered if she would live long enough in his shadow that she would one day be able to leave without standing on it.

"Wear the oiled shirt. It's raining."

He knew she wouldn't. She hated the smell and the feel of it, and it was far too large for her. Anything that made her look younger was instantly despised. The door opened, and the door closed. Rath waited until she was gone, and then began to eat. The rain fell against the window as wind caught it; the patter of its fall shifted as the same wind did.

He felt certain that she was going to do something stupid one day.

But he had, and he knew better. He'd invited her into his home.

When Jewel returned, an hour and a half had passed. The well was almost flooded, but it was also almost deserted. Only people who had no money or space for rain barrels stood in the diminished line, hair hanging about their faces, buckets slipping in wet palms. She'd carried water for a spindly older woman before she'd filled her own bucket—had, in fact, paused to empty her buckets in order to ease their weight while she carried the bucket of a stranger. The old woman was familiar, but not enough that she chose to tell Jewel her name; Jewel was polite enough not to ask for what wasn't offered. Street polite.

Jewel was determined that the old woman would one day offer her at least a name, and she was persistent. Today, although there was little cause for it, the woman had actually smiled, her slack lips rising on the left, and only the left, side of her face. She spoke about her daughter, a woman that

Jewel had never seen. Given how old the woman was, the daughter was either ancient or dead.

Which was why Jewel never asked. Street polite: never ask. Just accept.

After she returned with the day's water, she left for the Common with a handful of coin and an empty basket. Rath was in his room, and the door was closed. She stood in front of it, dripping, her hand an inch from its hard surface. But in the end, she chose not to knock. Rath was busy.

Rath was always busy.

Jewel's suspicion that Farmer Hanson had no clue where Arann lived was borne out by a short question. The farmer, huddled under the lee of his awning, spread his thick hands in the tail end of a long shrug that started with his shoulders and stretched down the rest of his body. "I don't know where you live either, if it comes to that," he told her, when she looked at him in silent disappointment.

"He didn't come today?"

The farmer shook his head. "He's got food enough to last another day or two, if they're careful. He's not," he added, "a greedy boy. And he's not, more's the pity, a thick one. He knows that I'll make work for him when I have it—but he's smart enough to know how often that isn't."

"And Lefty?"

"He never comes without Arann."

She knew that as well, but had felt compelled to ask. She couldn't say why. "I'll see to their clothing," she told him, as she picked over fruit that had already, by the looks of it, been handled by a hundred people.

Seeing her expression, the farmer snorted, and mist left his lips like the thin stream from an invisible pipe. But he didn't defend what was left of his food, and she didn't insult it. Worse than this—far worse—had kept her from starving while she'd lived on the banks of the river. She filled her basket, lingering by the stall in hopes of actually seeing either boy.

Hope was scant, and it stung.

"If you see them," she said at last, "tell them I'm looking for them, okay?"

"They know how to reach you?"

"They know where I live," she replied, with an almost guilty smile.

The farmer's smile was unfettered; broad and wide. "It's getting colder," he said, looking up, his gaze focused on the sky the awning hid.

She nodded. "It'll get colder," she added softly. "But Arann's not much for charity."

"He'll take it," the man replied sternly.

"I know. But he won't like it much."

"We all have to do things we don't like."

She made her way home, thinking of Lefty. Not certain why, and not much liking it. Her breath was a wreath that followed her, and she found herself clutching the basket as if its bent, threaded thatch was a blanket. Cold, yes. Too cold for Arann.

She took the straightest route home, pausing only to rescue a cat from a bored child—or to rescue the bored child, because with cats it was hard to tell—and made her way in through the door. It wasn't raining hard; it was raining; the key was slippery and cold in her hand, and she dropped it once, adding colorful language to the bend of knees as she retrieved it. The sky was gray, which was not her favorite color, but it cast less shadow.

Rath's door was still closed; she could see that clearly as she entered the front hall and made a small puddle as she stood, shedding what water her clothing could no longer contain. She went to the kitchen.

Stopped in the arch.

Rath was seated at the table.

And beside him, hunched and white, was Lefty.

Of all the people she had thought to find here—

"Jewel," Rath said coldly. He raised a pale brow as she met his gaze. "Is there something you forgot to mention?"

The whole of her answer was to hand Rath the market-heavy basket. He took it without comment, waiting for words she didn't have. She passed him—it was about two steps, as the kitchen wasn't large—and came to stand beside Lefty.

To stand, in fact, between Lefty and Rath.

Lefty was staring at the table. And Lefty, she saw, was *bleeding*. He didn't look up. Was afraid to look up. His eyes were fastened to wood grain as if the table were his only anchor.

"Lefty," she said, pitching her voice low, but forgetting to strip it of urgency, "what happened?"

Lefty began to rock. His feet didn't touch the floor. His left hand was in his lap, and his right, shoved under his left armpit. His shirt was torn in two places, and his forearm—left arm—was adorned by an ugly gash.

Uglier, she thought, by look than in fact; it wasn't deep. She couldn't see bone. "Why didn't you tend it?" she asked Rath. This time, she worked to keep accusation out of the words.

"He was not of a mind to be, as you put it, *tended*. Had I not caught him, he would not have been of a mind to enter the apartment at all."

"He's frightened, Rath."

"He should be. Why is he here, Jewel?" Jewel, not Jay. Rath was annoyed. But his voice, even and calm to the ear, gave none of that anger away. She suspected it was why Lefty was still seated.

"I don't know," she snapped back. Shoving wet hair out of her eyes, she knelt by the chair; it was uncomfortable in the cramped space. "Lefty," she said, not touching him, not trying to catch his eye, "where is Arann?"

"Jewel, who *is* this boy?"

"I met him at the market," she replied, wishing Rath was someplace else. Preferably someplace far away.

"And you told him where we live?"

"I brought him home."

Rath rose, shoving the chair back. "And the other boy you mentioned?"

"Same."

He started to head out of the kitchen, and Jewel turned suddenly and caught the leg of his pants. She would have caught his arm instead, but she didn't want to rise too quickly; she didn't want to panic Lefty. "Don't leave," she whispered. "Not yet."

"Jay," Rath replied, relenting, some of the unnatural stiffness leaving both voice and face, "how often have I told you not to get involved with strangers?"

"I haven't kept count," she replied, "And I'm bad at numbers anyway."

"Not," he said severely, "*that* bad." He shook his leg free and found his place in the frame of the kitchen door, bracing himself against it. Waiting, as she had asked.

"Lefty," Jewel said quietly. "We don't have much time." And as she said it, she *knew* it was true. "Where is Arann?"

Lefty shook his head. "We were home," he told her, although he would not look at her face. "We were just home. It was night. It was raining. The mice ran away."

Rath was utterly still. Frustrated, but watchful.

Jewel was almost dancing in agitation, which was impressive, given the crouch. She took a guess.

"Whose den?" she asked. "And which holding?"

"It's the thirty-second," he answered. The words came out quickly, the syllables running together in too little breath. He suddenly pitched himself forward, feet hitting ground, chest hitting table edge.

"Whose den?" she asked again.

"Cliff's."

The name, of course, meant nothing to Jewel. She looked at Rath quickly, almost afraid to take her eyes off Lefty, although if Lefty bolted, he'd have to get through Rath. Rath nodded slowly.

"Where?"

"They tore the boards down," Lefty said, to no one. "They came in."

"How *many*, Lefty?"

Lefty held up his hand. Left hand. Five fingers. Jewel would have to teach him to count. Different day, she thought. On a different day. "What did they want?"

"Money. Arann."

"You don't *have* any money."

"Food."

"You ran?"

"Arann threw me out. I scraped my arm on the board. I—" His eyes widened, and Jewel could see the water that filmed them, the reddened whites around a pale brown. "I ran." He looked at her then, for the first time. "He *told* me to run."

"And you came here."

From his expression, it was clear that he would never be able to tell her why. And it didn't matter.

Rath stared at Jewel. Watched her face pale, her eyes widen, watched her expression slide into the peculiar absence that sometimes took it for seconds at a time. Often when it did, she didn't choose to speak, and he didn't choose to interrupt her. He had come, in such a short passage of time, to *trust* the girl.

And she had dragged two strangers into the hidden heart of his life. He should have been furious. And on some level, he was.

Cliff. Cliff's den. Cliff's gang. He knew the name, and knew the boy, although to Jewel, Cliff would not be a "boy." Rath thought him eighteen, possibly nineteen. He had seen Cliff's group in action twice, and had observed them with disgust but little concern; they would be magisterial prison fodder within the six-month, if that long.

Child gangs were often tolerated if they did little damage. In the holdings, death was not uncommon, and children were allowed some leeway in their awkward attempts to survive their orphan years.

But unhindered, those children grew into something less tolerable, and less tolerated. Cliff was long past heading that way; he had almost arrived. Had there been a decent war, in either the North or the South, he would have been pressed into service—if he could be found. As it was, he was slowly creating his own war.

Rath said, "Jewel, watch the boy." He left the kitchen. Heard her low, familiar tone, and the boy's less familiar silence. This, he thought bitterly, was Amarais. Amarais all over again. His sister.

The one Rath had once admired.

The bitterness was hard. The anger was worse.

Rath knew what he should do. Knew it, as he approached the closed door that led to his personal room. Recited it, in growing fury, as he entered, kicking aside the clothing that allowed him to play at belonging to any walk of life his work demanded.

He didn't change, but he didn't need to; he had expected to work uninterrupted for most of the three days that research required. He should have left the girl by the river. Or in the emptiness of his former apartment, a squatter who could be easily and quickly removed by whoever rented the rooms after he no longer required their use.

He made his way to the bed, which was new, and then found the ground with his knees, the flat of his palms pressed against newly sanded boards. They still creaked with his weight.

He found his sword. The sword that had been his grandfather's gift when he had reached the milestone age of fourteen. It was a reminder of everything he had chosen not to be—and had he been a more sentimental man, he would have rejected the sword along with the rest of his life.

But it *was* a damn fine sword; it had cost a small fortune when the commission for its creation had been passed to the Guild of Makers. It kept its edge almost indefinitely, it was lighter—by far—than any sword its length and width had any right to be, and it was long, immune to damage caused by water. Or blood.

He grabbed its scabbard from its unceremonious resting place beneath the bed, and drew it out.

The best advice he had yet given Jewel Markess: *Don't get involved*. But that was the nature of advice; given, but not always followed.

He looped the belt around his hips, adjusted the fall of the sword, and retreated from the room, closing the door firmly—and a little too loudly—as he did. Then he walked back to the kitchen, and stopped just shy of the doorframe, listening.

He thought the boy might be crying; it was hard to tell. Rath had seen many damaged children in his chosen life—they became damaged adults, and often dead ones, and in truth, he had seldom mourned their passage.

But this boy—Lefty, as Jewel had called him—was different. He had developed no scar tissue behind which to hide; he was an open walking wound, shying away from all contact. It really was a miracle that he had come here at all, given that he wouldn't even look at Jewel.

And Jewel was too young, too new, too unscarred, to free herself from that obvious pathos.

"Jay," Rath said, stepping into view. "Bring the boy. Watch him carefully. Here," he added, and tossed her a dagger. She caught it, her hand moving almost without thought, her eyes widening slightly at the unexpected weight of the sheath in her palm. "You remember what I told you about how to use it?"

She nodded.

"Good. Forget it all. Do not draw it unless you lose sight of me, or I fall. *If* I fall, run first."

She said nothing.

"If you do not give me your word that you will obey me in this, I will not leave this apartment. Neither will you."

She darkened. The red really was a lovely highlight to the faint auburn streaks Summer had added to her hair. He could see the decision play out in the tightening of her lips, the narrowing of her plain, dark eyes. She nodded.

It was enough.

"You, boy," he said to Lefty. "I would leave you here, but I don't know where your friend *is*. I have some suspicion, but it would be best if you took us to your home first."

Lefty said nothing at all.

But he looked at Jewel, this time.

And Jewel, damn her, said, "You can trust Rath. You have to, for Arann's sake."

The boy was white, white, white. Only the bleeding gash on his forearm had any color at all.

"Lefty. Trust him. I do."

To escape her words, the unwelcome weight of them, the certain truth in the speaking, Rath leaped toward the door, slamming back the bolts. His step was light and graceful as he crossed the threshold; their steps were loud and ungainly as they followed.

He turned back to Jewel, and only Jewel. "Jay."

She nodded.

"Remember what I told you about swords?"

She nodded again, and gave him a warning glance.

He ignored it, ignored the boy. "I don't play with them. If the sword is drawn, there will be death."

They ran. Lefty's gait was awkward, and Jewel could tell, from the way he favored his leg, that it wasn't only his arm that the ragged boards had caught. Still, it wasn't broken, and if he looked strange in his bobble, he still *moved*. He was crying. Not weeping; that would make noise. All of his breath was visible, he was so thin.

She was angry.

It wasn't the last time she would be angry like this, but it was almost the first. She didn't know how old he was, and she had no time—or breath—to ask; she only knew that he *felt* young to her. A child. Someone her Oma would have curbed her tongue around, and protected simply because he needed protection.

He's not a bad boy, she could almost hear her Oma say. Smell of familiar pipe smoke, like an echo of time, was a physical memory; the rain didn't wash it away.

Instead, it washed dirt away, made exposed stone slippery. Rath was surefooted as a cat; Jewel stumbled once or twice. She righted herself with difficulty because she was holding onto Lefty's hand. His good hand. His fingers were white as they clutched her palm; had he had any strength at all, he would have crushed it. And she would have let him.

Rath was pale and wet; he was also frustrated. Jewel knew it because she'd grown to know all of his silent moods. She wondered if Lefty would notice, and decided she didn't care, which took effort. Her hand was cold. When Lefty slipped, she tightened that hand, half-dragging him to his feet.

"I won't let you fall," she told him, her lips almost pressed to his ear. Felt the words more than heard them. As if, she thought, they were distant thunder.

He looked at her.

"He'll be okay," she told him. Meaning it.

"You can see that?" he asked.

She wanted to lie. Really, really wanted to lie. But she'd never been good at it, and even for comfort's sake, she couldn't do a decent job; this time, it was Jewel who looked away. Pulled him along, moving as fast as he could, but not faster.

"Jay," Rath said.

She stopped instantly. His voice was quiet. As cold as the coming winter. If snow were a man, it would be Rath at this moment.

"Lefty," Rath added, his back toward them both, his shoulders a perfect line, his right elbow bent so that his hand could lie casually atop his sword's hilt, "this is the street?"

Lefty nodded.

"He says yes," Jewel told Rath's back. She didn't ask why he'd asked. Instead, she gathered Lefty, as if he were something precious she could carry. The whole of his slender body was pressed against hers, back to chest, rain wet and shaking. He was shorter than she was.

His right hand was juggled loose from its mooring; she could see that it was missing fingers. Blunt stubs had been scarred—seared, she thought, to stop bleeding. She didn't cringe. She didn't ask. But she bit her lip, and the skin between her teeth broke.

Lefty wasn't talking.

Rath wasn't talking.

But in the distance, someone was. At least one person. Maybe two. Ugly voice, either way, heavy as if with drink or anger. There was a certain humor that was almost indistinguishable from fury, and it was an ugly, primal sound. Jewel's body tensed as the noise reached her ears, and Lefty's tensed as well. He backed up, as if to flee, but there wasn't any place to flee *to*; she had him, and intended to hold on.

Rain, more rain. Jewel hated the rain.

Her teeth chattered with it. Her vision blurred. Her hair grew weighty and dragged its curls into her eyes. One day, she was going to shear her head. Baldness had a certain appeal.

As did nervous thought, any thought, that had nothing to do with Rath.

He had a room in which he had two sticks, a carpet, and a whole lot of nothing else. He made her practice with those sticks until her arms were shaking with their weight. It was one of the few times his mouth never stopped moving, and all of the words he uttered were sharp, curt, and disapproving.

But although he had called it sword practice, those sticks and this sword were so utterly different she had never truly appreciated the connection. Didn't appreciate it now as the right hand tightened around the black hilt of the long, double-edged blade that hung from the leather strap encircling his hips.

All noise was the noise of steel against steel; the mouth of the scabbard scraping the edge of the blade as the two parted. Rath's stance changed; she could still see his back, but beyond it, now, the distant figures of large men. Younger than Rath. One of them wider. None of them taller.

And none of them armed with a sword.

They hadn't noticed Rath. In fact, they seemed not to notice much; they were standing in a loose circle, and they looked to be doing an ugly, visceral dance composed almost entirely of jerky leg motions.

Kicking. Stomping.

They were ruddy in color, at least from this distance; they wore old clothing, but it seemed to fit them. The clothes were dirty, and some torn. Gray, brown, a hint of green flashing—these, the poor light was still capable of revealing. Morning light, edging toward noon. No sun. Little shadow.

She couldn't see their faces; she could see the backs of their heads. Hear their voices, unrestrained now. The street was almost empty, but not quite; men and women were pulling children, or themselves, to either side of the street, toward buildings, doorways, and away from violence.

Once, she would have been one of them.

She was ashamed of it.

Because she could see, as Rath strode forward and she followed at a safe distance—at a distance that Rath would never have considered to *be* safe were it not for his presence—that Arann was stretched across the ground. His back was turned skyward, his arms pulled around his face in an attempt to protect his head. She could see mud across his exposed skin, where the torn edges of a too small tunic ended.

His hands were red and bloody, and red was a startling color, here, where there was no color.

What little light there was was not enough to make Rath's steel glint. His steps were quiet, and he did not speak a word. They didn't seem to notice him.

Not until Lefty did the unexpected: He screamed.

Jewel froze; the scream went through her; she could feel it almost as clearly as she could hear it, and her arms tightened. Good thing, too; Lefty suddenly erupted in a frenzy of motion, kicking and flailing, the right hand's deformity forgotten. Had he been a little larger, he would have broken free.

As it was, she could hold him. She *did*. She spoke soothing words, nonsense words; had she been able to free a hand, she would have slapped him just to get his attention. She'd seen that done before; seen it work.

But here? She just held on. He scratched her face, her cheek, his palm smacked her left eye, hard. She almost bit him.

Didn't. Because as she looked up, she could see that his screaming had silenced all other sound. Had stilled all motion except Rath's.

The street to either side of the road went on forever in Jewel's vision; the buildings, squat and low on the east, taller and in slightly better repair on the west, were like a broken frame. Weeds flattened by rain and heavy feet provided color, and the pocked stone of what had once been a solid road formed the base of the tableau; above it, the heights were gray.

In the center, five men turned slowly to see who had made the noise. Lefty stopped struggling now that he had the attention he didn't actually want.

That attention was scant; if they noticed Lefty, it was cursory. Rath's sword was out; he held it across his chest. She could see that much. Could almost—but not quite—tell what stance he had adopted.

Five against one.

Rath's lessons, his harsh words, overlay the silence as Jewel watched, Lefty in her arms. They were his audience; the five men who also watched were different: they were his enemies. Two against one were bad odds, but in the right circumstance, they weren't impossible.

Three against one was a guarantee of death, unless the one was an expert and the three were incompetent. Anything else? A quick, fast run.

But Rath wasn't running.

Some part of Jewel wanted to scream at him to do just that; some part of Jewel was tensed to sprint. Had she not been holding Lefty, she would have. But had Lefty not come to her at all, Rath would be in his study, with whatever it was he'd managed to cut out of the heart of his beloved maze. And she would be in her rooms, or in the kitchen, struggling in a different way with the language and the lessons that Rath insisted she work through. There would be no rain. There would be no death. The walls would be pale, and dry, and clean. Not a cage, but a fortress.

One of the men spoke. He didn't step forward. But he did draw a long dagger. It was not the equal of Rath's sword. Jewel, no weaponsmith and no expert, could see the truth of that comparison anyway.

"We've no business with you," he said, nodding to the others. They pulled away, forming up in an awkward line, their shoulders almost touching as they also drew the weapons they carried. Weapons that they hadn't used against Arann, or he'd be dead.

"Good," Rath replied, stepping forward, the motion graceful, deliberate. His sword didn't waver. His voice didn't either. It was low, the single word; low enough it shouldn't have carried. But Jewel could hear it so clearly she knew that it had. "I've come for the boy," he added.

"He's not for the taking," the man replied. Ugly man. Face scarred, chin thick, lips rising over a prominently chipped set of teeth. From here, she could see them.

"No," Rath replied quietly. "He's not. Step aside."

The man snorted. He said something Jewel didn't care to catch, and Rath stepped forward quickly. It wasn't a run; it was a leap.

Jewel stayed her ground. She couldn't draw dagger—and knew that Rath would only be distracted if she did, because he'd *know*. The best she could do—the only thing she could do—was to stay far enough away that she wasn't something to worry about.

Or something for Rath to worry about.

That, and hold on to Lefty.

"He's alive," she said, in Lefty's ear.

There was motion then. Five men. One man. Everything happened quickly. Jewel had never seen Rath fight before. Everything he had taught her so far had been about *not* fighting.

And she was sure, watching him, that this *was* a fight. He seemed to know exactly where to be, exactly where not to be, exactly where to thrust sword; he never stopped moving once he'd started, but every step seemed so deliberate it was like a dance.

He offered them no warning. Made no threats. He didn't posture.

Instead, he killed. And this, Jewel had never seen either. She watched not his blade, not his feet, not his hands, but his face when it was turned toward her; pale and composed, it was shorn of any emotion at all. His eyes were wide and clear, almost gray in the clouded day, as if they were mirrors and reflections, nothing more.

When you draw a sword in the streets, it's not a game. It's not part of a tournament. It's not an act of status or prestige. You draw a sword, you use it. You use it quickly.

Yes, she thought numbly. *Yes, Rath.* Nodding, his words made real only by this act: the falling of bodies, the gout of arterial blood, the sudden screams of voices that were horrible in the silence that followed their end.

Three men ran. The leader was not among them.

The green flash of cloth that had been tied round his forehead was still green; it was forest green, she thought, because of the rain. The water. Hunter green.

The second man had fallen across Arann.

Only when Rath wiped his sword across his sash and sheathed it did Jewel let Lefty go. They both stumbled as her arms loosened, as if they had held each other up.

But Lefty kept stumbling, the awkward motion propelling him toward the body that was slumped over Arann. Over the only person in the world that Lefty trusted.

Rath said nothing as Lefty approached. He didn't try to meet the boy's eyes; he didn't try to touch him. Instead, he grimaced, bent, and lifted the body he'd made, rolling it to one side with an audible grunt.

Jewel approached as Lefty knelt in the mud, his knees absorbing the dirt. And the blood. He was touching Arann's arms, Arann's back.

"It's time to leave," Rath told Jewel, without looking at her.

She almost shrugged. "It's the thirty-second holding," she said, as she watched Lefty, and only Lefty. "If anyone bothers to call the magisterians, they won't be here for a while."

"Count on Kalliaris to frown," Rath replied grimly. "She's smiled on your boy—on both of them—and that's the most we can expect from her in one day. Tell Lefty to get out of the way."

Jewel looked almost dubious. "Arann's big," she began.

"Move him, Jay."

Jewel nodded, and crouched beside Lefty. "We need to leave," she told him, as gently as she could. "We don't want the magisterial guards to ask us how these two died."

Lefty didn't answer. In fact, from his expression, Jewel would have bet that he hadn't heard her at all. She cringed and then reached out to grab the smaller boy's shoulder. *"Lefty."*

He looked at her then, and she was sorry she'd touched him. His eyes were round, red, almost wild; he looked like a caged, injured dog. She'd had enough experience with injured animals to know danger when she saw it.

She pitched her voice low, kept it soothing, and carefully lifted her hand. "He's not dead," she told him, putting as much force as she could into the words without changing their cadence or tone. "But if we don't move him, he will be. It's cold, it's wet, and he's injured."

"I can't carry him—"

"You don't have to, Lefty. We're here. Rath is here."

Wide-eyed. Too wild.

Jewel took a deeper breath and held it until she was uncomfortable. Rain wet her lips, her face, made her hair even more cumbersome. At least this time she could shove it out of her eyes. She turned her attention from Lefty to Arann.

Touched his forearm, saw that it was bent. And not at a joint. "Arann," she said, daring urgency and volume.

To her great surprise, Arann moved. His moan was most of his answer. Answer enough. "Rath, I think his arm's broken."

"If it's just his arm, he's damn lucky."

Thank you, she thought, but she was smart enough to keep that to herself. Rath didn't like sarcasm when he wasn't the one using it.

"Arann, we have to move. Lefty needs you to move."

The giant boy's face rose from the cushion of dirt and stone. It was a mess; bleeding, nose broken, skin abraded.

"Jay?" he said, incredulous. Shaky.

She nodded. "Jay," she said softly. "Can you . . . can you get up?"

But Lefty was weeping openly. "I'm sorry," he said, gulping air, swallowing it as if it were liquid. "I'm sorry, Arann, I'm sorry, I'm sorry."

"Lefty."

Lefty froze and then turned to stare. At Jewel. At her eyes.

"Arann needs you to stop the damn crying. Do you understand? He needs you to be stronger."

"Arann," Lefty said, although he was staring at Jewel now. "Arann, what do I do?"

"Listen. To her." Broken words. Wheezing breath.

Rath was her shadow, although she hadn't seen him move. Jewel broke eye contact with Lefty as she became aware of him.

"Ribs," Rath said quietly. "That was quite a beating." His frown made him look older than she'd ever seen him look, although she couldn't say why. Not then. "It's going to be hard to move him. Hard to carry him. I don't know if his ribs have pierced his lungs or not."

She didn't ask what would happen if they had.

"Boy," he said to Arann. He held out a hand, inches from the arm that didn't seem—at least to Jewel's eye—to be broken. "You have to stand, if you can. I have to know how much of your own weight you can bear."

Arann reached out and caught Rath's hand; the older man stiffened as he caught Arann's forearm and elbow and began to lever him up off the ground.

Arann's legs held. But blood trickled out of the corners of his mouth. Hard to tell if teeth would follow. Lefty did a little dance of anxiety. Jewel caught his shoulders and held them in a death grip.

And he allowed it.

"Legs aren't broken," Rath told her. "It's not that far from home," he added. Arann swayed. Rath slid an arm under the boy's arm, taking care not to put weight against his side, against the ribs.

Together, slowly, they began to walk away, leaving the dead behind.

It took hours to get back home. But if it had taken days, Jewel would have spent them gladly. Some words were curled on the wrong side of her throat; her throat was thick with them, and she couldn't speak. She wanted to tell Rath something, but one look at his face made it clear that whatever it was—and she honestly didn't know—it would have to wait. Maybe a day. Maybe forever.

Lefty was hers to watch, for the moment. Arann had told him to listen to Jewel, and he had always done what Arann told him to do. She *knew* it, and was oddly comforted by the knowledge.

Money was not a problem. Not yet. Not for months yet.

A doctor, on the other hand, *was*. The thirty-fifth holding was not exactly a popular place for doctors, because no one who was living in it had money, and doctors didn't work for free.

The Priests and Priestesses of the Mother did, but the nearest temple was over two holdings away, and the Priests didn't like to leave. They were happy enough to see you if you came to them—but getting to them when you could barely walk and could breathe even less easily, was a bit of a challenge. Jewel knew it all.

But she didn't care. Arann managed the stairs down to the apartment. He managed to lean against the wall while Rath opened up the bolts and the locks that separated home from the rest of the world. He managed to stumble in, Rath balancing his growing weight. He even managed to smile at Lefty, and had there not been so much red in that smile, Lefty might have taken comfort from it.

Jewel took command instead. She opened the door to her room, threw everything that was on the floor to one side or the other in unceremonious haste, and flattened her bedroll. It was a Rath castoff; he'd obliquely offered to buy her a bed when she'd managed not to get herself thrown out of his life in three months. Where "when" was a lot like "if."

"Careful here," Rath told her, as Arann's knees collapsed. Arann's weight was suspended for a moment between them, and Rath's brow rose slightly when Jewel managed to both stagger and hold up.

Arann's clothing—the clothing that was two years too small—had been torn; it was threadbare enough that sneezing would have done that. Jewel hesitated for just a moment, and then she began to unbutton the shirt front as Rath very carefully lowered Arann to the ground. She couldn't quite remove it, and suspected that it would have to be cut away.

"Keep an eye on them," Rath told her quietly.

She nodded.

He made his way to the door, passing Lefty, who failed to either acknowledge him or be acknowledged by him, and turned once he'd reached the frame. "Don't answer the door if anyone knocks. Unless," he added, voice heavy with sarcasm, "there are *other* friends you've failed to mention who might be in need of rescue."

"Just these two," she said, staring at Arann's closed eyes. The left one was almost swollen shut, bruise purpling to black; she couldn't remember what color his skin had been. Now, it was red, purple, black. "Lefty," she said, as she knelt on the creaking boards. "Get the bucket in the kitchen. There's a towel hanging on the far wall beside the cupboards—grab that, too."

Lefty did as she ordered because it *was* an order. "Don't touch anything else," she called out after him. "We can worry about food after we've cleaned Arann up."

From the look of Lefty, it would be a day or two before the thought of food occurred to him.

"Rath's gone for a doctor," she added. "He's got enough money. He'll find one stupid enough to come here."

And, she knew, he'd *hate* that. She wondered if it would mean they had to move again. Rath wanted no one to know where he lived, or how. Arann couldn't be moved without some kind of stretcher, and a couple of strong men to carry it. Either way, he'd opened himself up to discovery.

Because of Jewel.

And Jewel would care more later. Now, as Lefty returned, lugging the bucket, the rag of a towel thrown over his dirty shoulder, she knelt against the ground. Towel hit water; she wrung it out carefully, and just as carefully began to sponge Arann's face clear of dirt. Everything about her was gentle. She knew how to do this. Even four years ago, when she'd truly been a child, she could do this much. For her mother, when she was ill. Or her father. For her Oma, although her Oma complained constantly, words like a stream of thin smoke.

She took care not to press against his side—either left or right—or his chest; she took care not to apply pressure to his broken arm, although she did slowly remove the dirt there as well.

"What are you doing?" Lefty asked, sitting in her shadow. Staring at Arann.

"What?"

"You're humming."

"Was I?"

He nodded.

"I don't know," she said. "My Oma used to sing, sometimes. And sometimes she'd just hum."

"Who was she?"

"She—oh. You're not a Southerner. She was my grandmother. *Oma.* That's the Torra word for it."

"You knew your grandmother?"

She nodded. Didn't ask him if he'd known his; the question made it obvious.

"Arann knew his mother," Lefty said quietly. "I mean, really knew her. He liked her, I think."

"I liked mine, too."

Lefty said nothing else. He didn't offer to help her, either; instead, he stared at his hands. At his right hand, exposed, as it hovered above Arann's face.

"He'll be all right," she told him. And as she said the words, she smiled. Soft smile. Certain smile.

He wasn't stupid. Awkward, yes. Frightened, yes. But stupid? He could see her expression clearly, and she saw the line of his shoulders relax; saw his hand begin to tremble.

After a moment, he said, "Can we stay here?"

A question she wondered herself. "Until Arann's well," she told him. "At least until then." She straightened her shoulders and dropped the cloth back into the bucket. "There's another towel on the floor. By the far wall. I think. You can dry off."

"What about you?"

"I'll wait. I'm not as cold as you are. And I'm not as wet."

He was smart enough not to call her a liar.

Chapter Seven

THE DOCTOR CAME and went. He was watched at all times by Rath, but not with the suspicion that Jewel would have expected. If the doctor—whose name she never heard—was not a friend like the locksmith was, he obviously knew Rath from somewhere. He had thin lips, pale white hair, and a pinched face; his skin was highborn white, and his eyes a crisp, cool blue. He was not a young man. Not even compared to Rath.

He was certainly less friendly.

But Rath trusted him to know what he was doing. Arann's arm was splinted—which caused a lot of screaming, while Rath restrained him—and his sides were bound.

"Make sure he stays in bed." As the doctor said this, his brows drew in; the floor wasn't much of a bed, in his opinion. He didn't bother to say it in so many words.

"For how long?"

"At least two weeks. He's cracked three ribs, but he's lucky; they didn't pierce his lungs. His legs are bruised. They'll heal. His arm will heal properly only if he doesn't try to use it."

"He can use it in two weeks?" Jewel asked.

The doctor replied—to Rath. "The arm will probably take four to heal. He's young. If he were your age, Ararath, it would be at least six. At *least*." The man carried a large black case. He had opened it for bandages, and the bracing pieces of wood he called a splint; he closed it now with a distinct snap. "I do not consider this wise," he added, as he stood. It was clear that he was not accustomed to kneeling. His pants were too fine, and far too unwrinkled. They were also—or had been, when he'd arrived—very clean.

"Thank you. That will be all."

But the older man had not yet finished. "I answered your call," he continued, "because of our history. Your family will, of course, learn of my visit."

Rath said nothing.

"And they will ask questions. I consider them inconvenient," the man answered, "because none of the answers will be to their liking. Ararath, Handernesse is still open to you. Will you not reconsider your choices?"

Rath said nothing again, but it was a louder, colder nothing. At this point, Jewel would have backed out of the room quickly and closed the door for good measure.

The doctor, however, seemed either ignorant of Rath's growing anger, or immune to it. Maybe it would be something she could learn, with age.

"Very well. Understand that I had to ask."

Rath nodded curtly. "I will, of course, send money."

"Of course."

"You will not bill Handernesse."

"No. It was not to Handernesse that I was summoned. But it was," the doctor added, the lines of his face shifting suddenly into weariness, "because of Handernesse that I chose to respond. I do not understand."

"No. You don't."

"But if you can find it in yourself to show charity to these, you might find it—"

"Enough." Rath bowed. It was a perfect bow. As perfect as his sword stance, and not, Jewel realized, much different in meaning. It was a warning.

The doctor accepted it. "Keep him warm, if you have the wherewithal to do so. Keep him dry."

Rath nodded, and showed the doctor out. Jewel heard the bolts of the door being drawn; heard them being slammed home. Then she heard his stillness, the silence of breathing.

Lefty had hidden in the kitchen the entire time.

"Jewel," Rath said, when he at last left the door and returned to her room, "these two are your responsibility. You found them. You led them here. I expect you to watch them. I expect you to stop them from doing anything stupid."

"Rath—"

"No, I did not walk the streets of the holding with my grandfather's sword in order to leave the boy dying in the street. Two weeks, the doctor said. I give you two weeks."

She nodded. It was more than she should have hoped for. But less than she had. Still, two weeks was a toehold in an open door. She could work with that.

"I have business to attend to. I will be in my study, and I *do not expect to be interrupted again*. Do I make myself clear?"

"Yes, Rath."

"Get Lefty out of the kitchen. They will stay with you," he added. "If your room is crowded, you have no one to blame but yourself."

She nodded, striving for meek. Almost achieving it.

But when he left, she rose and retrieved Lefty. "Did you hear what he said?"

Lefty nodded.

"We'll have to find bedding," she told him. "And in this rain, it's not going to be comfortable. But I've got some money left."

He nodded again. Looking at her room as he did. It wasn't a small room. In her old apartment, three people wouldn't have made much dent in it. She'd lived with four in a smaller room. A colder one.

"He said you could stay."

"For two weeks."

She caught his face in her hands, and his eyes rounded in sudden panic. But she held him there anyway, waiting until his breath was less short and sharp. "You've lived in places for less than that," she told him, forcing his gaze to meet hers. "And a lot of things can change in two weeks. We have to be good," she added. "And we have to be quiet while Rath works. But maybe if we are, two weeks will be a long time."

Lefty tried to nod, but it was hard with her hands on his cheeks. She let him go slowly.

Thinking that she should have been worried.

That it was stupid not to be worried. Rath was angry, cold angry, and that was always bad. He probably wouldn't speak more than two words to her all day. And all of the next day.

But worried wasn't what she felt. And cold wasn't there either. "You can help," she told Lefty. "We'll take care of Arann for now."

He was looking at her, waiting.

"I know you trust Arann," she said, picking up the cloth from its wet resting place. "You've known him a long time. I want you to trust *me*."

Lefty said nothing.

The words hung in the room, a simple adornment to plain, painted wood, flat slats, and the accumulation of only a few weeks of life with Rath. Blankets. Clothing. Daggers. The odd piece of paper, two slates, chalk. An empty basket, a full bucket. A lone metal box.

"Family's a funny thing," she said, as she released Lefty, knelt, and once again began to stroke Arann's face with the towel. "I never had brothers, you know? I always wanted one. Well, an older one.

"Now I have two."

"But we aren't your brothers."

"Not yet," she said, and she felt the hum in her throat, her grandmother's pensive, wordless song. "But if we stay together for long enough, you will be."

As if he could hear the words, Arann's eyes opened. Or at least the right eye did; with the left, it was kind of hard to tell. "Lefty?" he asked. But he asked it of Jewel.

She nodded, smiling. "He's here. He's safe."

"Why . . . here?"

"He came," she told Arann, understanding at last the odd source of her happiness, "to get me."

Arann's lips were also swollen; they were damp enough not to crack as he moved them. But she pressed the cloth against them, stilling his words. "And I," she said, as she did, "came to get you.

"I always will."

Spoken words. Intense words. A smile framing and containing them. As she said them, she knew they were true. Not in the way that she had known the wagon was coming; not in the way that she had known how little time Arann had if they were to rescue him. This was a different sort of gift.

Choice. Promise.

Her first, but not, although she did not see it clearly, her last.

The first week passed slowly. Rath would have appreciated it had it passed *quietly*. Had he been able to blame the boys for the arrival of noise, he would have thrown them out in a minute, promise to Jewel notwithstanding. They were hers. He acknowledged this because it was safe, and because it was true. She didn't see it, of course. Her ignorance was bitter, appalling, and entirely in keeping with her age.

No, the noise was hers. The chatter. The speech. The endless drone that accompanied her jaunts to the kitchen, shadowed by Lefty; the endless humming as she tended Arann. The stories that her Oma told, broken by pauses and poor memory, which she offered the boys when the night had fallen and the streets were entirely off limits. She did not have the storyteller's gift, and narrative came in fragments.

To Rath, it was almost agony.

To the boys, it was different. Perhaps they had come to the streets so young the memories of such stories and songs were precious and distant enough that these broken imitations were not insulting. Or perhaps they had never been offered them at all.

A closed door should have impeded all words.

Which meant, of course, that Rath—as if he were Arann or Lefty—was listening for them, straining to catch them even as they annoyed. It had been many years since he had killed a man. He had killed two a week past, and for what?

A crowded, noisy home.

He set his pen down; work was almost impossible. Instead of pen, he lifted pipe, packing the bowl with damp leaves. Everything in the air was damp. The farmer thought the rain would stop in a day or two, and Rath was inclined to believe him. How much of that inclination was wishful thinking, he let be. Other thoughts disturbed him.

If he had left his sword beneath his bed, if he had chosen not to become involved, Jewel would have gone with Lefty. She would not have returned.

Perhaps he could have found her; finding things of value was his specialty. But what he would have found, he couldn't say. Had she been injured, he might have brought her here, and it might be she who lay abed. She might learn, the harshest possible way, what life on the streets entailed for far too many.

But the glimmer of understanding, the stiffness of posture, that she had showed on their first meeting implied some understanding. He had never asked. Did not intend to ask now.

Restless, he got to his feet. Upon his desk, carefully wrapped in cloth padding, were two plain, gray bowls. Their basins covered both his palms when spread side by side; they felt delicate, but like so much that appeared fragile in this city—above ground or beneath it—they had had to be more; they were almost whole. One was seamed with a crack, the other was perfect. Both held a single carved rune in their center, and both were adorned with a longer series of similar runes around the edge, a circlet of words. He thought they were offering bowls, and he was not certain of their manufacture; they were so smooth, they might have been glass—but the fracture was not the type of crack that glass took.

It was a pity that they were of a single color. Still, they would certainly be of value; how much value depended on his ability to retrieve meaning from the fragmentary writing; time had worn key letters, changing their shape and meaning.

He set his jaw, sat, and began his work again.

He had traced the letters with care, choosing to use eye and hand rather than to take a rubbing. Five times he did this, substituting single characters where they were not distinct enough. In the magelight, their ridges cast short shadows; he worked by these.

As he did, he heard the whisper of a name: *Kalliaris*. His pen stopped; his chin lifted, as if he had been momentarily touched. Perhaps he had; the door surrendered syllables, mute but distinct.

Jewel was reciting the list of gods. She always started with Kalliaris; Kalliaris was the goddess of Luck, both good and bad, and it was upon her smile or frown that Jewel's life depended. He could hear neither of the boys. He could pretend that they did not exist, and perhaps that was for the best.

Rath was a rather good liar.

He woke in the morning to a sharp knock. A very sharp knock. He was out of his bed, pale blue sheets on the floor, before he realized where he was. Nightmare had come and gone; it was a graceless visitor.

"What?" The curt word was not an invitation.

Jewel knew it. Through the door, she said, "I'm going to the Common." She paused and then added, "I've been to the well. It's not raining hard. Can we get a barrel?" and then, before he could reply, "Can you watch Arann while we're out?"

He was tired enough to say, "No." He was awake enough to say it quietly. "I'll check in on him."

She didn't answer. He heard, instead, the slight shuffle of her feet as they receded. Only hers; Lefty apparently hadn't accompanied her down the hall.

Rath was surprised that the boy was willing to accompany her to the Common. But as he was awake, he picked up the blankets, dumped them on the bed, and groped his way toward his chair. It was in the same position as he'd left it when he'd finally dozed off for the third time; the light in the room, never bright, streamed gray from the window well above.

He was hungry.

This was the first morning that Jewel had actually allowed him to *be* hungry.

Lefty's gaze was glued to the door. Jay pushed the chair to its usual position, and opened it; she pushed it aside, and waited. Lefty still stared, but his gaze now traveled down the empty hall that Rath didn't own.

"Lefty?"

And turned to the door behind which Arann slept. He slept like a dead man. It made Lefty uncomfortable. But not so uncomfortable that he hadn't thought to warn Jay about the dangers of being too close if she was going to try to wake him.

"I'm not throwing things at an injured boy," she said sharply. But she didn't try to wake him. "He needs to sleep. The doctor said so."

"Where are we going?" Without Arann.

"To the Common."

"Why?"

"We need food."

"Oh." He looked at his feet. He was more than passingly familiar with them, and with the boots whose soles flopped open with a squelch in the wet weather. He had no socks. He hadn't had 'em for a year.

But his toes looked funny.

"And you need clothing," she added. "And boots."

"Boots are hard to steal."

She nodded, expression serious. "They are. If you want them to fit."

"You can usually only grab one."

She nodded again. As if she'd had to. Or had to think about it. Her boots, on the other hand, were in one piece. "We don't need to steal them. Not yet."

"And clothing?"

"Not that either. But we need to get to market before everything good is gone. It's late." She handed him the basket that he hadn't really noticed. Given how big it was, that said something. "I'll carry it when it's full. If you're going to stay here, you have to be useful."

He shrank a few inches.

"Lefty," she said, drawing closer, her height greater because she wasn't slumped, "you *can* be useful. You can't be Arann. Don't try."

"But he's big," Lefty said, swinging the basket as he followed her. His leg hurt, but it was only bruised. His knee was swollen. He didn't tell her. "And he's smart. Smarter than me."

"You told him to listen. To me. The first time. And you came *here*," she added. "You saved his life twice. How is that stupid?"

The hall got shorter; the front door got closer. Jay pulled keys out of her pockets; they were shiny. New. Lefty stared at them as if they were coin. He stared, as well, at the door itself; it was thicker than any door he'd lived behind, and it seemed new. The walls here were straight. And dry. He couldn't see holes between them and the floor.

"Not stupid," she said, as he caught up with her. The rains weren't so bad, this morning. But the air felt colder. He was shivering by the time they'd gotten most of the way down the block and had hit the intersection marked by limp trees and flattened weeds.

"No," she said softly, her breath a cloud. "Why'd you come?"

He shrugged. "Don't know."

She shrugged back, motion part of the conversation.

Lefty twisted the basket's handle between his hands—his good hand, and the hand that he was ashamed of. Ghost fingers ached. There were still days when it felt like the fingers were *there*, even if no one else could see them. "I thought you could save him," he said at last. He didn't look at her face. But he wanted to. He wanted to see her eyes.

It frightened him, the wanting.

"And we did," she replied, careful now. The streets weren't as crowded as they were when it was warmer or drier, but the wagons still passed by, and there were always larger groups of men that had to be avoided. "You were right. And you did what Arann couldn't. Remember that."

"I did it for *me*," he told her. "Not for him. I did it because I can't live without Arann. He's big. And he's smart. And he protects me."

She nodded. "You protected him."

"But I *didn't*—"

"You didn't use your fists. You didn't use a dagger. You didn't wield a sword. You ran, yes. But you ran *to* something, not *away* from it. You're not Arann. He's not you. If you were both the same, you wouldn't be friends." She paused, waiting for a wagon to amble past. Not looking at his face, not looking at his hands.

"I'm not big," she told him softly. "And I'm not as smart as Rath. Maybe I never will be. But I don't believe that big is everything. I think—I think that you can be stronger. Just different strong, is all."

His toes were wet. "What if I don't?"

"Believe it, or want to be?"

"Either."

She shrugged. "Doesn't matter what we want, does it?" This time, there was a familiar bitterness in the words. "Only matters what we *do*."

They walked. Jay was quiet for a long time. Lefty noticed the buildings on either side; noticed faces in the open windows, where shutters had been pushed back for air. There weren't many.

The trees that ringed the Common were dark, the leaves hanging like wet cloth. Some of them. The rest? They covered the ground, making the dirt less muddy. When had they dropped? Why did he notice?

"We're going to meet Helen," she told him. "That's her name. I know you don't like to talk to strangers. She doesn't either. But she talks to them. She's a bit harsh, and she can't hear all that well, but don't tell her that; it makes her grouchy."

"Who's Helen?"

"Seamstress. Or something. She makes clothes."

"Jay?"

She nodded.

"Why are you doing this?"

"It's going to get cold, and you need new clothing. Not as bad as Arann does, but he can't walk, and you can."

"I mean why are you helping us?"

"Do I need a reason? Why did Rath help me?"

Lefty frowned. "Because you can see things."

"See?" Her voice was soft, still visible. "You *are* smart." Sad.

Lefty didn't want to upset her. Wasn't certain why, although he should have been. She was going to feed him. And Arann. She was going to buy clothing. Upsetting her might take that all away.

"I want to help," she told him. "And you need help. Shouldn't that be enough?"

He shook his head.

In the streets, there were no gifts. There was what you could steal, if you were clever or fast enough. There was what you couldn't. There was barter, and some things—some things you had to pay for in ways you couldn't imagine, if you were lucky.

Lefty had never been lucky.

But he *wanted* to trust her. It frightened him, the wanting. He needed Arann. He needed to ask Arann why.

And he couldn't. Silent and obedient, he followed Jay like a shadow.

Helen was smoking a pipe.

Jewel almost closed her eyes as the scent drifted in the still air, wreathing her face. Lefty coughed. The cough caught the old woman's attention. Her eyes narrowed in her perpetual squint. "That you?" she asked Jewel.

"It's Jay," Jewel replied.

"You said you'd be bringing a large boy."

Lefty lost a few inches.

"I will. But he had an accident, and he can't walk much right now. Or the doctor will kill the rest of us."

"Doctor, eh? Rath called a doctor?"

Jewel nodded.

"I guess I was wrong. He *is* good for something. You, boy, come here."

Lefty, having no one else to look to, looked to Jewel.

Jewel nodded.

"He's not simple, is he?" Helen snapped.

"He's really, really shy," Jewel managed to reply. Some hint of anger colored the words anyway, and Helen straightened slightly, unfolding. She wasn't actually that small a woman, but years spent hunched over needlework made her seem smaller and older than she was.

She waited, imperious, while Lefty approached; at the last minute, he caught Jewel's sleeve in his left hand, and dragged her with him into the stall. Out of the rain. There wasn't a lot of room, and Helen's son frowned at them both—but as his mother was smoking, and as her lips were pursed in that "don't argue with me or else" frown, he said nothing. Loudly.

"Shy," the seamstress said. She reached under her chair, and brought up an old wooden box with a cracked leather strap as its only lock. She undid the knot that held it—and the faded lid—in place, and opened the box. Needles shone in the sparse light, stuck to the sides of spools and spools of colored thread. These weren't what she wanted, and her hands were callused enough that the pricking of careless fingers didn't even register.

Instead, she pulled out a long, flat piece of cloth. Or leather; it was thin and supple, worn along the edges; it was obviously meant for something other than making tunics or shifts.

"What in the name of the Mother are you wearing, boy?"

Lefty pulled Jewel's shirt. Jewel answered. "The only clothes he has. They're a bit small," she added. She wasn't at all surprised when Helen snorted; pipe smoke streamed from her nostrils, as if she were a dragon gutted of flame.

"Aye, they're small," Helen said at last. "And cheap." She snorted again. Lefty did not, clearly, find this comforting. But he didn't find it so threatening that he fled, and Jewel considered this a good sign.

"We can't afford expensive."

"Aye, you can't. But you can afford better than temple castoffs. Unless Rath's been gambling again."

"Rath doesn't gamble."

A gray brow rose. "I suppose he doesn't drink either?"

Jewel shrugged. She couldn't remember Rath drinking much of anything but water, and even that, he seemed to prefer to do without.

"Does he still smoke?"

Jewel nodded.

"Good." She lifted the thin strip, and motioned to Jewel, who stepped forward, dragging Lefty along. She wondered if he was ever going to let go.

"He's a small one."

"Name's Lefty."

"Is it, now?"

Jewel nodded. "That's what he calls himself, at any rate."

"Lefty, come here."

Lefty dragged himself forward. He stepped on Jewel's foot as he passed her, and Jewel's arm went with him.

"This," the woman said, "is a measure. It was given me by my uncle.

I'm going to slide it round your chest, and along the back of your shoulders. And here, from your neck down to your butt. Oh, and your arms, too—so you're going to have to let go of Jay sometime."

He looked at Jewel, and Jewel nodded, encouraging. When he didn't budge, she added, "It's going to get cold."

"You're sure?"

"I'm sure."

"But Arann—"

"When he can come, we'll bring him, too. His clothing is worse than yours, but he's still too small for Rath's."

Helen was businesslike and curt, but not so curt as she was with Rath. Her voice was almost gentle as she turned Lefty round; she moved quickly, but all of the movements themselves were deliberate and obvious.

"You have to stand straight," Jewel whispered.

And watched as he tried.

Helen wrote things down on the slate she also pulled up from under the chair. The chair was her cave. And her throne. Jewel had only really seen her stand up once or twice, to measure Rath.

She finished quickly, and when she was done, Lefty pressed himself into Jewel's back, waiting.

"I can do it for four silver pieces," Helen said. She lifted a hand and glared at her son. "Rath's business is good, and we charge him a lot more. We can do this for his friend."

The son's lips disappeared in a thin line. He muttered something about joining the beggars, and his mother muttered something about cutting his leg off so he'd look right at home.

"How long will it take?"

"Three days, unless it's urgent. You said these were the only clothes he had?" When Jewel nodded, the woman sighed. "Two days, then. I can't do better. And I can't promise you a decent color; I'll use the ends for things, so it's going to look a bit of patchwork."

"If it's warmer than this, and it fits, who cares?"

Helen laughed. "You'd be surprised," she told Jay. She emptied the bowl of her pipe and looked at it, eyes still narrowed. Not looking away from its fine wood grain, she added, "You're not like Rath, girl.

"But you'll be good for him, in the end. He shouldn't be alone."

"He likes it that way."

"What we like and what we need aren't always the same. Like the clothing," she added softly. "Go on, now. Basket's empty, and Farmer Hanson will be waiting."

Jewel nodded and reached into the satchel she carried on the inside of her tunic, just above her belt. Then she paused. "You know Farmer Hanson?"

"Aye, it happens I do. I make clothing for his useless sons." She chuckled. "And his daughter, if it comes to that. You want to bargain with those sons, if you're short money, though. Daughter's a dragon."

"How did you know I—"

She waved a curled hand, brushing the words away.

"Pay me when I'm done. You're good for it. And if you're not," she added, with a grim smile, "Rath is, and I'll charge him more."

She was humming as they retreated; humming and smiling, the pipe upside down in its bowl. Jewel smiled as well.

"Jay?"

She nodded at Lefty.

"You like her?"

"Yeah, I like her."

"Good."

She paused a moment, breaking stride, her feet getting a little wetter, his reminding her that she had at least one more stop before the farmer. "Why?"

"She's scary," he whispered. "And she smokes. I don't like burning things."

Jewel touched his shoulder, slowly and gently, as if he were an injured dog that she had almost earned trust from. She didn't speak, but she understood, then, why Arann had kept him safe all these years. Because she certainly wanted to.

Farmer Hanson was happy to see her. Happy to see Lefty. "Where's Arann?" he asked, before Jewel could interpose herself between them.

Lefty, however, looked down at his feet. No answer there.

"He's at my place," Jewel told him.

"Yours?"

She nodded. "He had a bit of a problem with—what was his name? Cliff?" At Lefty's nod, she continued. "But we found him in time. He's seen a doctor," she added, voice low. "A *real* doctor. From the upper holdings, even. Rath brought him."

The farmer wasn't as impressed with this as Jewel had been. "How bad was it?" he asked, the stall momentarily forgotten. And rain, too, as he stepped out from beneath the awning.

Jewel frowned. "It was bad enough. He's in bed. He has to sleep. The doctor said he can't move for two weeks, but after that, he should be fine."

"And you'll keep him that long?" Meaning, of course, Rath.

"I'll keep him longer," she said, meeting Farmer Hanson's worried gaze with an intensity that was, although she did not know it, much older than her face.

He held that gaze for a moment, and then he smiled. It was a wan smile. "I was worried," he said quietly.

"Me, too. But Lefty came to get us. And Lefty's staying with me, as well."

"Good. You keep an eye on them. I'll have work for Arann when he's fit."

Her smile was brief. "We're late," she said, taking the basket from Lefty's good hand. "Is there *anything* good left?"

Which, of course, changed the expression on the farmer's face instantly. She was sorry to see it go, because she wanted the approval of this generous, avuncular man, but Lefty wasn't, and Lefty needed the comfort of the familiar far more than she did.

The dreams were bad.

In her own room, in isolation, they were bad enough—but in a room with two boys, one who was under strict orders *not* to move, they were worse. She woke screaming, as she often did; Rath had learned to wait when he heard those screams.

But she bit her lip, tasting blood, as she became aware that two sets of eyes were now watching her. Lefty's, in the dark, were wide and round; he was out of his bed and in the corner, his hands across his face, almost before she had stopped.

Arann was also out of his bed, or rather, out of the bedroll. He struggled toward her, turning from side to side as if seeking the threat.

"Jay—"

"*Lie down,*" she whispered. Had there been an "s" in either of the words, she would have hissed.

Arann didn't immediately obey, which added guilt to the horror of nightmare. This one wouldn't leave her. It clung to waking, and she could see, imposed upon the safety of her four walls, her closed door, the open streets of the holding at night; the soft glow of magelights, the sound of running feet.

The sound of high breath, sharp breath, young voice.

Her own?

No.

"Arann," she said, struggling now to make her voice as normal as possible, "I had a nightmare. That's all. Just a nightmare. You've *got* to lie down. Rath will kill me if he has to call the doctor again."

Arann nodded slowly, and she realized that he wasn't—quite—awake. He was ready to fight, and in his condition that would be suicide, but he wasn't awake. Wasn't quite himself. She made a note to herself: No screaming.

Which, given the unpredictability of her nightmares, was going to be damn hard.

"Lefty—" she stopped. Lefty, cowering in the corner, was holding a dagger. He'd picked it up where she'd thrown it—near the wall. Near the corner of the room. But Lefty, unlike Arann, was awake.

This type of awake, on the other hand, had no safety in it.

"Lefty, put the knife down," she said, her voice low and measured.

He wasn't interested in listening. This close to sleep, there was only one voice he could hear.

Arann groaned in pain. The sudden movement, the standing wariness, had been costly. But he grimaced and turned to Lefty. "It's safe here," he told the wild-eyed boy. "We're safe. Put it down, Lefty."

Really, really no screaming, Jewel thought. But she waited, and after a long, long moment, Lefty let the dagger drop.

"You have nightmares often?" Arann asked, keeping his words casual, and keeping the pain from their surface. He eased himself back to the floor.

"Sorry."

"Don't be. Lefty has 'em as well. He's more quiet, though."

"I'll try harder."

"Is it about your—is it about why you—" Arann coughed.

"No," she answered, understanding both the question and why he had asked it. Lefty had not moved. She knew he'd sit in that corner until morning light finally made its way through the window well. The covered well.

154 ◆ Michelle West

"What was it?"

"A girl," she answered quietly. "A girl Lefty's age. Even smaller than Lefty."

"What was her name?"

"I don't know." Reflexively, she added, "Is."

"Is?"

"What *is* her name."

Arann shrugged, and winced. "What is her name, then?"

She started to say, *I don't know*, but when she spoke, the word she used was, "Finch."

"Isn't that a bird?"

Jewel shrugged. "My parents named me Jewel," she said bitterly. "People are stupid about names."

"Where do you know her from?"

"I don't," Jewel said, lying back on the floor, as sleepy as Arann. Which is to say, heart pounding, eyes filled with night.

"You don't know?"

She shook her head, and pushed hair out of her eyes, although there wasn't much point. Rath had the magelight, and the light in her room wasn't. "I don't know."

"But you know her name."

She nodded.

"Is this like—"

"It was a nightmare," she said firmly. Because she wanted to believe it. Rath was a good liar. But it was one of the things that he would fail to teach Jewel, time and again, although he thought it the most useful of his skills.

"What happened?"

She closed her eyes. "It was a nightmare," she said, but the tone of her voice was entirely different. "There were boys, I think. Older boys. They were chasing her. In the streets."

"Which streets?"

"I don't know. Old holding streets. I think—" she paused, and *did* think. "She ran past Taverson's place. The hole. She ran past Fennel's."

"They're not in the thirty-second."

"No." She was thinking. "The moon was wrong."

"Wrong?"

"I could *see* it."

Which she couldn't, tonight. Or last night. Probably not tomorrow night either. "I could see moonlight. Some stars. Not many stars, though." She paused again, and then added, "I could hear water."

"River?"

She nodded. "Not rain. It wasn't. Raining."

Lefty's head rose, chin trembling. He still hadn't moved. "It's going to stop raining in three nights."

"How do you know?"

"Farmer Hanson."

"He's wrong more than he's right."

Lefty had the grace to look indignant. She loved him for it.

"How many?" Arann asked softly.

"I don't know. I couldn't see them; I could hear them. They were shouting to each other." She tried to pick the voices apart. "Maybe three."

Arann said, "I can't get up by then."

And Jewel nodded grimly. But she said, "It was only a nightmare."

The room, silent, was answer enough. They'd seen the cart. They knew what only might mean to someone like Jewel. And, to her surprise, they cared. Lefty, terrified. Arann, injured.

She wanted to ask them how long they'd been living alone. Alone without adults. Alone without Oma. Alone without Rath. Because she *knew* that they shouldn't care. Not about a girl they'd never heard of; not about a simple nightmare.

She wanted to keep them. She wanted them here.

And she knew Rath would be fit to kill if she brought anyone *else* to his home.

"It was nothing," she told them both, forcing her voice to sound sleepy. "It was just a dream. Forget about it."

In the morning—and it was later than normal when Jewel finally crept out of the room—she went straight to the kitchen. Lefty was dozing in the corner, the knife at his feet. Arann was snoring loudly, and the sound of his breath was a rattle that made her wince every time she heard it. Not a snore—her Oma had been the queen of all snorers—but something worse.

She cut bread and cheese, and pulled out strips of dried meat; she cut apples, and added those to the mix. Gathering them all on the bare tablecloth, its red hatch lines faded to pink, its white a uniform gray, she bunched them together and carried them back to the room, leaving them by Arann's side.

She took the two plates, and made breakfast for herself and Rath. These, she carried silently down the hall, pausing at his door. As her hands were full, she kicked it.

He answered it instantly, which was unusual. There were dark circles under his eyes, and he looked as if he might bite her head off and toss the plates down the hall—but that was the morning face she was most accustomed to, and she waited.

He pulled the door open and let her in. His room was a mess, but it always was when he worked, and he had expressly forbidden her entry to clean it. Her tidying, he said, made everything impossible to find; the mess was its own geography, and he hated any change in terrain.

But he watched her as she set his food on the table.

"You had a nightmare," he said, as she put her plate down beside his. It wasn't a question.

She nodded, pulled the only other chair in the room to the table, and leaned against the soft back. This chair had arm rests; it was Rath's smoking chair. When he bothered to sit in one. Tobacco smoke lingered in the cloth; pipe smoke. A comfort.

She could see the bottle of ink, the quills, the paper that contained the runic writing of Old Weston—Ancient Weston—that he was attempting to decipher. She almost asked him about it, but his expression forbid intrusion.

"I had a nightmare," she said at last. She was hungry. She began to eat.

Rath waited. When it became clear that she would eat rather than talk, in itself something she seldom did, he sighed and joined her. Fifteen minutes passed, the sound of chewing the only sound in the room.

"What was it about?"

Her hesitation was marked. Everything she did was, by Rath; there was nothing he didn't notice. "A girl," she said at last.

"A . . . girl."

She nodded.

"Someone you know?"

"No. But . . ."

"But?"

"I know her name."

He closed his eyes. "How old is this girl?"

"Lefty's age, I'd guess. Maybe younger. It's hard to tell. She's not very big."

"Pretty?"

Jewel considered the question for a while, dried meat softening between her teeth. "Maybe. I don't know."

"What was her name?"

"Her name *is* Finch."

"She didn't die?"

"Not in my dream."

He said nothing. A lot of it.

"It was a dream," she said, faint hope guiding the words.

"I heard you scream," he replied, with stronger accusation.

She nodded. "I don't know why," she told him, although he hadn't asked. "She was being chased by men. Or boys. Older than us," she added, aware that it wasn't a useful distinction to Rath.

"Why this girl?"

"Rath, I don't know."

"And the boys chasing her?"

"I didn't see them clearly."

"You often see them clearly."

This was, she realized, what had been bothering her. He was right. She did. "I know. I heard their voices—"

And stopped, and met his eyes.

They were open, and staring. "What did they sound like?" he asked casually. Always a bad sign.

She was ahead of him, now. "Yes," she whispered.

"Like the man who ordered the tail."

"Like that. But louder."

"Jewel, need I remind you that I require privacy to work at all?"

"No."

"Good."

They finished eating in silence, both aware that they had resolved nothing.

Chapter Eight

RATH WAS FINISHED for the day.

Had, in fact, been finished before breakfast. Although he hadn't looked it to Jewel's inexpert eye, he'd also been awake. Her screams usually had that effect. Had the boys not been with her, he would have joined her, because he knew her well enough to know she'd be awake.

He had chosen not to, because he didn't wish to panic her guests. And, yes, he was aware that "guest" was fast becoming an inaccurate word, but he clung to faint hope.

The only neat pile of papers in the room was on his desk; beside them, once again carefully wrapped in cloth, were the two bowls he'd taken from the maze. He was aware that he should wait at least a week or two before he attempted to unload them. He almost considered bypassing Radell—*Avram's Society of Averalaan Historians* had caused him some small trouble, and he expected that both it and he would be watched should he enter it again.

But he had a fondness for the stout, mendacious man with the fake beard, and a certain fondness for the money. The fact that the last two items had been sold for so good a price gave him the luxury of time, and he briefly considered crossing the bridge to the High City to seek out the Order of Knowledge.

The money would not be as good; the information, however, would be better. He had not yet ascertained the use of the bowls themselves, but he was almost certain they were magical in nature. And handing something magical to Radell's new clientele made Rath decidedly uneasy.

So, too, had Jewel's dream.

Since she had recovered from her fevered state, she had had only dreams and the instinct that guided her daily life; she had offered Rath no waking vision, no clear guidance. Until this morning, he'd allowed himself to believe that she'd forgotten everything she'd said while the fever burned high.

But while Rath was an accomplished liar, he liked to lie only when it suited a purpose. The man who had tailed him had been so competent, serving ignorance did not serve Rath's sense of self-preservation.

Finch, he thought. He wondered how literal the dream vision was. Wondered if there were, in fact, a girl smaller than Lefty who bore that name. On another day, it wouldn't have mattered.

But it did now.

Because in her dream, the men who were chasing this child were also akin to the man who had tailed Rath. He had no illusions. If Jewel was unwilling to speak of the death of a child, he allowed her that comfort; he allowed himself none, because none was needed.

If she were indeed being followed—and at speed—by three such men, she had no hope of eluding them.

In and of itself, this was not his concern.

But Jewel now knew it, too. And he had been gods-cursed foolish; he had not only gone to the rescue of one endangered boy, but had then summoned a doctor, at some personal cost that had nothing to do with coin, and had even allowed the boy—and his shadow—to stay.

She was not going to leave the nightmare alone. He had asked a single question, and she had instantly understood the whole of its import.

Grinding his teeth, he rose from his squat on the floor, and reached for his leather satchel. He carefully placed the bowls within it, cushioning them further with the thick weight of a shirt, and then topped them with his frustrating writings. Only when this was done did he change.

Velvet, he thought, with a mild sneer. A hat. New pants, new boots. He paused by the mirror, winced, and made ready to shave with cold water; the morning was passing him by. He was a perfect, elegant fop in shades of deep blue when he at last finished.

Good enough for the High City, if he chose that route; certainly good enough for Radell if he chose otherwise. He kept his options open because, in the end, the disposition of his artifacts were not his chief concern.

The Patris was.

What were the odds that men such as the one who had followed him—missing success by the expedient of an unpredictable patrol—served anyone else in the hundred holdings? And why, if they served that Patris, were they hunting an urchin in the poorer streets of the city?

Questions, and Rath hated questions. Mostly because he'd discovered with time that they had answers, and the answers were almost always worse.

Farmer Hanson had not heard of Finch, at least not by name. That much wasn't a surprise to Jewel. But he also couldn't identify her by description. Granted, a terrified, tiny girl wasn't the easiest to comfortably describe, but the farmer had always had keen eyes.

Like, say, now, as he helped her with her basket. "Arann's fine?" he asked her.

She shrugged. She'd left Lefty at home with Arann, which was strictly against Rath's orders, and had come down to the Common, ostensibly to shop.

"You said she's smaller than Lefty?"

Jewel nodded.

"You're certain she's on her own, that she has no family?"

And nodded again. Because she *knew*. "Her hair's longer than mine, and I think it's lighter. It's hard to tell. I only saw her at night. Her skin's pale, though, and she's all bone."

Farmer Hanson raised a brow. "This would be the pot calling the kettle black, hmmm?"

Jewel shrugged. "She's shorter. Than me."

"What was she wearing?"

Good question, given what the street orphans usually owned: what they wore, and nothing else. Jewel started to answer, and then frowned. "You know," she said quietly, "that's a damn good question."

"Language, Jay."

"Good question, I mean," she corrected herself. "I think she was . . . I think she was wearing a *dress*."

"Here?"

She nodded again. "It was gray, I think. I mean, it wasn't fancy. Maybe it was a—what do you call it?"

"A shift."

"Or a nightshirt."

"If she has that, she's not alone."

But she *was* alone. Jewel looked up at the sky; she got a slow face full of drizzling rain for her trouble. The clouds were heavy, but pale; no thunder waited in their folds.

"Jay," the farmer said, reaching out to touch her wrist. He was one of few men who could, without causing her to flinch or pale.

"What?"

"You can only do so much."

Which made almost no sense.

"You took Arann and Lefty in, and if I had to guess, Rath's not thrilled."

"Not much, no."

"You mean to keep them."

Her eyes widened, and then she had the grace to redden. "Is it that obvious?"

Farmer Hanson shrugged. He punctuated the movement with a sharp word to one of his useless sons, as he so often called them. He spoke more fondly to his daughter. "It's obvious enough to me, but you've always been a strange one. This girl—where did you see her?"

"I'm not sure. Maybe the twenty-fifth holding. Maybe the twenty-sixth. Near Taverson's."

"At *night?*" He looked scandalized. It made her smile. Although he didn't trust Rath—because, she thought, he didn't know Rath—he had come to think of the odd man as her guardian. And guardians did not let girls out near Taverson's in the evening. Not if they weren't looking for a different type of customer.

She shrugged. And tried to lie. "I saw her before. Before Rath."

His brows rumpled in the middle. Really, Rath would be embarrassed.

"You stay away from there."

"Yes, sir."

"Good. Where was I?"

As she didn't want a lecture, she tried to retrieve her hand without reminding him. He held on.

"You've done well," he told her, voice gentling. "And I think you'll *do* well. But you can't save everyone."

"I know," she said bitterly. Thinking of her father. Thinking of her gift. Hating them both, for just a minute. Because it was always like this. "But I *have* to try. You understand that, don't you?"

He met her gaze and held it. "Trying," he said at last, "is good. It always is. But failing? Everyone fails, one time or another. It's how you deal with failure that counts, in the end. It's the successes that you're known for—but it's the failures make you what you *are*."

She looked up at Farmer Hanson for a long time. "Farmer Hanson?" she asked, in her politest voice.

"Yes?"

"Could I just be adult now?"

He laughed, but the laughter trailed off, and she knew—watching it die—that he was thinking about his children, their childhood, and hers. "It doesn't get easier," he told her quietly.

"It *has to*. It has to be easier than *this*. My mother used to tell me I had my whole life ahead of me. I don't *want* my whole life ahead of me. I want it behind me. I want to be whatever it is I'm *supposed* to be. I want to be listened to. I want to be able to make a difference. I want to—"

"To save people?"

She looked at him. "You do."

"You have, Jay. But you can only do it one person at a time. And you can't save everyone. You couldn't even *meet* everyone in your whole life, if you did nothing else.

"But it's a dream," he added, bending slightly to bring his eyes level with hers. "It's a *good* dream. Some people dream their life away. Some make goals of their dreams. If you don't fail, it only means you didn't try."

"And do people always fail?"

"Not always, but not never." He shouted at his sons again, and turned away. It was busy enough that she let him go.

When Rath returned, Jewel was in his room. The paper he prized so highly was laid out against his desk, and the inkwell was to one precarious side. She had quill in hand, and ink on her lips and fingers; she had never been a neat child.

He said nothing; she had ears, and she had obviously chosen to ignore his approach; to keep her place on his chair, two volumes of ancient history beneath her in order to give her the height she needed to make proper use of the desk. Red leather, worn and faded, was not the cushion he would have chosen, and he was annoyed.

But not so annoyed that he failed to notice her work, and when he saw what it was that she attempted, the annoyance evaded his slight grip. Straight lines, with names marking them; small squares with words in their centers. Radial lines going out from the Common at the heart of the holdings, and slinking into the different districts that comprised the old city.

A map, he thought. A poor map. But not a poor first attempt. Taverson's was marked, and by it, the old warehouse that was known as Fennel's place. It was occupied by squatters; it wasn't safe—or warm enough—for anything else.

The map was not to scale. He wondered if she knew it, if she knew what scale was, and if she cared. Her hair was pulled up and out of her eyes, but curls darkened them anyway. Flyaway curls, dark eyes. This child, he could almost come to care for.

He came to stand by the desk, and as his shadow interrupted the light—the magestone light, whispered to brightness—she looked up. Rubbed her eyes, and left a trail of black along their lower lashes. "You're back early," she told him, no guilt, no guilty start, in the words.

He nodded, and removed his blue velvet jacket with care. "My client's abode seemed . . . under observation."

She nodded, but it was clear from her expression that the words had passed in one ear and out the other without catching on anything in between.

She said, "The moon was out. And it was almost full. I think I know when the dream happens."

He said nothing, draping the jacket with care over the armchair. He found his pipe, but he did not choose to sit; instead, he stood by her side, placing dry leaves in its flat bowl.

"It's supposed to stop raining in three—in two—nights. But that's wrong, for the moon, isn't it?"

"The full moon is at least a week off. You said it wasn't full?"

She nodded.

"In which direction?"

"I don't know. A day before. A day after. Maybe two."

He could have been proud; he'd taught her that, and she'd actually listened. He would have bet money she hadn't heard half of the words.

"I don't know where it starts," she added softly. "And I don't know where it ends. But I know that she runs past Taverson's. And Fennel's place."

He nodded, and lit the pipe. Smoke was slow to fill the room.

"I'm going to wait by Taverson's," she added, standing. "I know she runs near the river. I think I know which direction she'd have to be coming from."

"You are *not* going to wait by Taverson's."

"I can wait inside."

"No, you can't."

"It's lit, it's crowded, it's—" She couldn't quite manage to say the word safe. "It's better than waiting by Fennel's."

"Jay, you have no idea what you're up against."

"No. And maybe she does. I don't know. I only know she's running. And she should stop right here." And she pointed to Taverson's on the crude map, her nail burnished with magical light, darkened with a line of ink. She looked at him then.

"I have to try," she told him calmly.

He could have spoken the words before she had; he had heard them all before. "Arann won't be able to help you."

She nodded.

"Lefty—"

"Not Lefty." And waited.

"This is not the fight that Arann's was," he said carefully. Pipe smoke left his lips.

She nodded. "I know. I don't think we'll win if we fight. I wasn't going to fight," she added, as if it weren't obvious. "I was just going to help her run."

"I spent an entire evening attempting to outrun one of these men, if your nightmare is accurate. And I have training. You have next to none; she has less than none."

"I know." She stood, tucked the quill absently behind her left ear, and after a moment, carefully moved the map. Rath considered it a minor miracle that she didn't upend the inkwell.

"And if I forbid it?"

She said, "You will."

She was such a frustrating child. "Jewel," he finally said, "If I agree to attempt to intervene on behalf of this child, will you stay here?"

Her smile was a quirk of lips, something that touched only her mouth. "I can't," she told him, although her voice was quiet, rather than defiant. "I'm her age. I'm *like* her. She's—she'll be—terrified. She won't stop running if she sees you. You'll just look like one of the—"

He lifted a hand. "Thank you for belaboring the obvious." When it looked like she was about to continue, he turned a thin frown on her. Which stopped her mouth. In the brief respite, he inhaled pipe smoke and exhaled it in rings. She was right, of course. "You can't bring her here."

She said nothing to that, but that was about all he expected. "Understand that this is *not* something I would normally do."

She nodded.

"But . . . three such men—even one such man—in the holdings is cause for some concern." His smile, still sliver-thin, was cold. "I am not a man who desires competition, especially not competition that can afford to hire competence in such numbers."

"Competition?"

He sighed. "Sometimes, Jay, you're old enough for your age I forget how young you are."

Which caused her to bridle. Ten, it seemed, was somehow a magically transfiguring age; it had two digits, not one, if you knew how to write or count. And she did.

Sullen, but not so sullen that she could ignore curiosity, she said, "How are they competing with you? Aren't they willing to buy everything you find?"

"Yes. Everything. Without question."

"This is bad."

"It is if, as I suspect, their desire to acquire stems not from greed or obsession with ancient history, but from a desire to make certain no one else sees any of it."

She frowned. "But that would mean—"

And his smile was less sharp, and far more indulgent. "Yes," he said, setting the pipe in his bowl. "It means they either know about, or suspect, the existence of the maze beneath the city. And they want it to remain secret."

"You want it to remain a secret."

"Because I'm *greedy*," he replied, "and it's my source of income."

"And they don't need the money."

"Not apparently, no."

"Which means—"

"Enough. Yes, that's exactly what it means. I will help you find the girl," he added quietly. "But you will do *exactly* what I tell you to do."

She nodded, and the taut line of her shoulders, the pinched narrowness of her lips, relaxed. "Rath, I'm—"

"I know."

"It's just that she's—"

"Jay, I know. You are what you are. I knew it before I took you in. I should have left you by the riverbank. I didn't," he added, "and this is my penance." He closed his eyes, tilting his head toward the door. "I think Lefty is restless," he said at last. "Which means Arann is awake. Tend to them. I have . . . other things to tend to." He lifted his jacket from the back of his chair, and paused by the window. Rain. More rain.

He disliked the oiled cloth as much as Jewel did, but he could not afford to look like a bedraggled thug; not where he was going. He found it, folded in a corner, and began to unfold it, keeping distaste from his expression.

"I may not be back tonight," he told her. "And I may not be back during the day. I understand that if I tell you not to leave, you'll leave anyway, and as you are so terribly pathetic at the art of prevarication— lying, Jay—I will not waste our time. Be careful. Buy food as you need it; bring water. But, Jewel, if someone comes to the door, do not let them in."

The Proud Peacock was, by anyone's standard, a stupid name for an inn. Rath privately thought the owner had named the place after himself; he was that type of man. Officious, self-important, and condescending. Which were his good points.

He was balding, and his head gleamed in the open flood of light that girded all visible walls; magelights, of course, and set in a way that their glow could not be mistaken for anything as common as lamplight or fire. He wore fine velvet, silk velvet, a deep burgundy offset by a cream shirt with ostentatious ruffles; his hands were girded by rings that could in no way be mistaken for tasteful, and his smile was like oil.

His expression was a great deal less friendly when Rath appeared than it had been for the couple that preceded him, but he was a cautious man; he examined Rath's clothing as if he were calculating its worth—and Rath was certain he was, and had its value down to the coppers the lace cost—as he clapped his hands and servants appeared to take Rath's outer coat. Rath wore a sword openly, and the innkeeper hesitated as he stared at its pommel. In the end, the man decided to ignore the weapon; Rath was certainly not the only armed man in the room. That most of the men were guards was not at issue; Rath was not dressed as a guard.

"You'll want a table for one?"

"No. I've accepted an invitation; I believe you will find I'm expected."

"Your name?"

Rath did not so much as tense. He gave the innkeeper a name from a list of names, each one slightly pretentious in its obvious Old Weston roots, and each, fake.

The man went away, which was a relief; Rath disliked him. His return, however, was vastly more supercilious than his departure had been, and the bow he offered Rath made Rath want to kick him. Rath, however, wanted to kick most of the men—and women—he met, and had mastered the art of self-control. When he had been a much younger child, it had eluded him entirely, and only by the grace and will of his sister had he managed to behave in a way that did not disgrace his House.

A bad sign, to think of his sister here.

He followed the man, ignoring the babble that accompanied him; it was long, it was pointless, and it would have been—had he chosen to mind it—irritating.

But as he approached the table at which a lone man sat, and at that, an older one, he assumed the carriage and bearing that he had chosen to reject, and became Ararath of Handernesse.

He bowed to the seated man. "Patris Hectore," he said quietly.

The Patris, Hectore of Araven, a merchant house that was both old and well-regarded—inasmuch as any merchant house could be—nodded. The nod was meant both as acknowledgment of the name Rath had chosen not to use and as a dismissal of the hovering innkeeper. The innkeeper was not a fool; he hovered for only a moment longer, and then left.

The table was a fine table; it was covered by pale linen, and the vase in its center was a gleaming silver that housed a single, pale blossom. The plates were china, edged with silver; the utensils silver as well, warm with a patina of age. Everything hinted at delicacy and expense; the crude, thick utensils of the poor commoners was not to be found in the Peacock.

The chair Rath occupied was dark, unscratched, well-oiled; it was high-backed, but padded and comfortable, as ostentatious as the mage-lights that adorned the dining room.

But the Patris seated across from Rath was dressed in a much less pretentious fashion; he had reached the age and station in life where pretense was for those who lacked substance. He wore linen, not velvet or silk; his fingers were free of all jewelry, save a single signet ring. His name was well enough known that the rest was unnecessary, but even had it not been, he would have disdained high court fashion. It was for this reason, among many, that Rath trusted him.

"Ararath," the Patris said, after Ararath had taken his seat.

Rath nodded. "I appreciate the honor you do me," he replied. The phrase was formal. But it was also genuine.

A gray brow rose. Hectore's gray was the gray of steel, not age; he was neither young nor old, and to Rath, he looked like the human epitome of the Northern wolf. There was always an edge of danger when one dined with Hectore, which was why Rath chose to dine with him at all.

"You look well," Hectore said quietly.

"And you. I hear that you resolved the difficulty with the Northern trade route."

The man nodded. "You heard that, did you?"

"Half the city heard it. On the other hand, half the city has heard that the Princess Royale has been engaged at least fifteen times in the last five years."

Hectore laughed. It was a rough laugh, deep and offered without hesitation. "Not the same half, surely?"

"Almost exactly the same half. There is always a grain of truth in the most outrageous of rumors."

"Oh, indeed. The Princess Royale would make a fine wife for an ambitious man. And there have been many ambitious men in the last decade."

"She is, from all accounts, uninterested in ambition."

"That, I believe, is heard by far fewer people than the half city you claim."

"And is therefore more likely to be true."

"Indeed. You haven't changed much since we last met, Ararath."

"I've had little cause to change."

"Little cause, but not none." He paused, and then added, "Amarais seems to have done well by House Terafin." It was a probing comment. The question in it hung between them for a long moment, and Rath wondered if his answer would be the price of admission. A pity, if it were, as he would not tender it.

"I have little business with The Ten," he replied, cool now.

"And The Ten, little business with you," Hectore conceded. "She is not unlike you; she is not unlike the girl she once was. And she, like the Princess Royale, has never sought marriage as her entry into the world of influence and power."

"She never needed it. Had she, she would have married in a heartbeat."

Hectore frowned. It was, as his laugh had been, genuine. "You underestimate her, Rath. Or you overestimate her. She is not—"

"She is ruthless; she will sacrifice everything in order to achieve her goals."

"Indeed. I will not gainsay you. But her goals themselves define the worth of the sacrifice. Enough, Ararath. I will let it go. One day, perhaps, you will do the same."

Wine was brought by silent men; it was carried in a crystal decanter, a deep, red liquid not unlike the color of the innkeeper's coat. It was poured while the men sat in silence; when the servers had retreated, they resumed their quiet speech.

"Why did you contact me?" Hectore asked, as he lifted a crystal stem between his large fingers.

"I wish information," Rath replied, lifting his glass in turn. "Narayan," he added, as he tasted the wine.

"Indeed. I believe it was favored by you in your youth."

"Much was."

"What information would you have of me?"

"Merchant information, if you have it. Gossip, if you don't."

Hectore raised a brow. "I am not overfond of gossip," he said quietly. "But I keep an eye on the Merchant Authority."

Rath smiled. "This would involve a very small portion of the authority; perhaps it would bypass the Authority entirely."

"Not a trade route, then."

"No."

"Very well. You've piqued my interest, and I'm inclined to help you, if only to hear the question."

"There is a Patris in Averalaan, a man whose name was previously unknown to me. He is not unpleasant in countenance, but he is not friendly."

"That describes a great many of the patriciate."

"Indeed. This one, however, has an interest in the antiquities."

"And money to spend?"

"A great deal, or so it appears."

"His name?"

"Patris AMatie."

Hectore frowned. The frown was like a vintage of its own, with hints of various lingering experiences in its creases.

"You've heard of the man."

"I've met him," Hectore said at last. He set his glass down. The frown had settled across forehead, darkening eyes. "He does a great deal of trade in the Authority, although he is—as you surmise—new to the stage; he has been but ten years in Averalaan."

"Where does he hail from?"

"The North, or so it is said."

"You have some reason to doubt him?"

"I have reason," Hectore said, offering the wolf's grin, "to doubt *all* men, Ararath. Even you." He sat back. "The bread here is fine, and the butter sweet. Break bread while we speak."

"What does he deal in?"

"Minerals," Hectore replied. "And ocean jewelry; pearls of some quality. It is an odd combination. I have not heard that he is a scholar or a sage of any note; nor have I heard that he has any particular interest in the antiquities, as you call them. Be more specific, Ararath."

"I will be as specific as I can," Rath replied, with care. To lie to Hectore was difficult; better to skirt truth, and let the gaps be. "He has an interest in artifacts that pertain to ancient Weston culture."

Hectore ate as he listened. "And he is willing to spend coin on these?"

Rath nodded.

"Is he a fool, or has he some method of determining what is genuine?"

"He has some method," Rath replied, "but he did not have—to my knowledge—a mage-born member of the Order of Knowledge in his employ."

"I would say that he would be an ideal customer, then," Hectore replied, keen-eyed now.

Rath nodded. "I would have said the same."

"But?"

"His interest is strong enough that he had me followed on the one occasion we met."

Hectore nodded, neutral.

"He did not know—could not know—that I would arrive when I did; he did not have, to my knowledge, guards waiting. But clearly, he had the establishment with which I deal watched, and when I left, two men attempted to follow. The first was good. The second was unnaturally good."

"Not so good that he was not detected."

Rath failed to mention Jewel. "He was good enough that he should not have been detected. It took me almost eight hours to lose him, and I had to resort to a use of the magisterial guards that was beneath my dignity."

At this, Hectore laughed. "You care a great deal for your dignity, given how little of it you possess."

"Things scarce are a valuable commodity, where they are wanted. I believe—"

"Yes, yes. You may use my words against me; I'm particularly fond of those ones."

"The second man was in the Common. Fair enough. While most of the expensive trading is done in the High City, items of dubious origin seldom make their way across the bridge."

"Dubious origin is such an unfortunate phrase."

"I was rather proud of it."

"You must have coined it when you were younger."

Rath shrugged.

"And so he had one good man in his employ. This is cause for concern?"

"For me? It is some cause, but you see clearly, as always. I have reason to believe he has employed others as competent."

"And they?"

"They are in the old holdings. The thirty-second, possibly the twenty-sixth."

Hectore frowned. "Why? There is little of value in either."

Rath nodded.

"Very well, Ararath. I will spend time and resources to see what I can discover about this Patris."

"Discreetly."

"Oh, indeed. If he made an impression on you, discretion is necessary."

"I would not have you shoulder the cost of the investigation if it is costly."

"Of course not. I'll bill you. It's not my usual line of work," the merchant added, "and I am therefore free to set my price. Can you be reached in a reasonable way?"

"No."

Hectore rolled his eyes. "Then reach me. Give me two weeks."

"I have perhaps three days." Rath grimaced. He reached into the inner pocket of his jacket, and handed the Patris a rolled parchment. "Burn it," he said softly, "when you have word. I will come."

Hectore's brows rose, and Rath felt a moment of genuine pleasure; it was so rare that he was able to surprise his father's old friend. "This must have been costly."

"It was . . . barter. But yes, it was costly." He watched as Hectore slid the paper into a similar inner pocket. "I am not involved in anything illegal," he added, before the merchant could speak. "Were I, I would not have come to you."

"Believe it or not, Ararath, I wasn't going to ask. Whatever decision drove you to this place, drove you; it drives you still. But I cannot think that it has so changed you."

It had. Hectore knew it. But if there was honor among thieves, Rath reserved it for men such as he. They ate in companionable silence, and Hectore spoke for some time about the shifting alliances among the merchant Houses. He failed to mention Terafin, but Rath could hear the unspoken House name in the gaps.

Only when the meal was almost at an end, did Hectore let his discretion lapse. "You thought the House War would devour her," he said quietly. "You thought she would die."

"I didn't much care," Rath replied.

"That is not the word that was carried to me by my informants." He lifted a hand. "She survived. She did better than survive. House Terafin is first among The Ten, and Amarais is without peer."

"She walked away from Handernesse," Ararath said sharply. Unwilling to be drawn into the source of old wounds; unable to let them bleed.

"Do you know who would have taken the throne had she failed?"

"No."

"Become a better liar, Ararath. Or a better actor. You know. The House would have been a much darker place had she not played her game of war; it would have had the power to inflict a great deal of damage on those with no ability to defend themselves. Amarais understood this."

"Handernesse fell."

"It fell," Hectore said softly, "because you left it."

"I was *not* what she was. Not to my father. Not to my grandfather. Her desertion killed him."

"Aye, perhaps there's truth in that. But he understood her, in the end. And had he been younger, had he lived up to the potential of his youth, he might have *been* your sister for a different generation. You judge harshly."

"She wanted power. She took what she wanted."

"Men want power for different reasons; it is what they do with the power that must be judged, and sometimes, it is history that is the best judge; not those who live under its rule.

"And what did you want, Ararath? What is it you want *now?*"

"To be left alone," was the swift reply.

"And yet you are here, and I am here, and your request has some of Handernesse in it, whether you admit it or not. It is for that reason alone that I will aid you as I can." The old man's eyes dimmed. "But I have misgivings, Ararath. I will not lie. You were never a fool, and if you choose to be blind where your sister is concerned, it is your only blindness.

"If you would take my advice, I would offer it freely."

"You've always offered advice freely."

"To my godson, yes. To others? They pay. I have a reputation of my own to maintain."

Rath waited, understanding that he owed Hectore of Araven this much. Costly, yes.

"Make your peace with Amarais. Make your peace with her decision. Leave this place; I fear it will devour you."

"It has not devoured me yet."

"No. But the wise do not depend on Kalliaris' smile. Only the desperate and those without choice do that. You are not the latter; do not become the former."

"And is the sundering of all ties of blood to be so easily forgiven, so easily forgotten?"

"Blood, in the Empire, has never been the sole deciding factor of worth. The Ten are The Ten not by birth, but by competence and ambition."

Ambition was, in Rath's vocabulary, the most bitter of words. Before he could speak, Hectore continued.

"The oaths we make as children, we mean. It is what defines us. But the inability to live up to those oaths is the coming of adulthood. Sometimes, in order to make something, you must break something. Believe that it was costly for her."

"It does not seem costly from here," Rath said bitterly.

"No," was the quiet reply. Hectore had finished. He was wise enough to know when a wall was unbreachable.

Clouds reflected light, making the night a paler shade of gray than even moon's light could. Rath had walked the perimeter of the block in the Common; he had skirted yards and outbuildings, seeking, in shadows, some sign of a vigilant watcher.

Finding none, he chose to approach Radell's. Light still shone in the window above the ridiculous sign. *Avram's Society of Averalaan Historians* was a foolish, grand boast, but it had kept Rath in clothing, food, and information—each of them precious.

He knocked at the door and waited a few moments before knocking again. There was a bell, its pull stained by water and tarnish. He touched the strands of linked metal that formed its chain, and after more time had passed, he pulled it, listening, as the bell—its ridiculous brass bowl on the other side of the door—tolled his presence. He did not look back; if someone saw him now, they saw him. To run, to hesitate, to attempt to find shadow where none existed, would make him more of a curiosity, not less.

A bleary-eyed Radell opened the door without apparent surprise. He stepped aside, and Rath slid in.

"Where have you been?" Radell asked, when the door was closed, and the light in the store called up by his hiss of a keyword.

"Lower the lights," Rath said, by way of reply. The curtains, such as they were, were half drawn; the streets were lost to reflection.

Radell, accustomed to Rath's odd moods, bid the lights dim, until Rath could see the silent streets, the cloudy, listless night. It was cold, humid, but still; the sea winds had not yet begun their Winter howl.

Radell rubbed his eyes. His ridiculous beard was in need of dying; the dark layer showed half an inch from his jaw. "Where have you been?" he asked again. He would probably ask the same question again regardless of whether or not it was answered; it took Radell some time to fully wake. Normally, he never asked a question this intrusive, but Rath was accustomed to ignoring such questions when they did arise.

"I've been acquiring a few items that might be of interest to your new client," he replied, with just a trace of sarcasm.

Radell's hands fell away from his eyes as if they were scales. In many ways, Radell was like a child: greedy, easily distracted, and prone to fits of almost unholy glee. The wakefulness that had eluded him on his stumbling walk from the rooms he occupied above the store to the door now hit him fully; he was entirely himself in the clap of two overly padded hands.

"When can I see them?"

Rath did not bother to hide his disdain.

"Rath—"

"Showing them to you will mean nothing," Rath replied. "But showing them to your client, much. I am unwilling to leave them with you, as I believe them to be of value; they are delicate, and easily broken."

"What are they? Can't you at least tell me that?"

Rath almost snorted. "What," he said sharply, "were the last items that sold for such a high price?"

Radell frowned. "Pieces of stone," he said at last, wilting slightly.

"Pieces of stone," Rath sighed, looking at the back side of the letters the curtains didn't obscure. "Yes, they were that." He touched the curtains. "Have you seen the Patris lately?"

"Two days ago. But I can contact him at any time."

"Good. Tell him that I have, in my possession, items that may be of interest; tell him that you are uncertain—"

Radell puffed up, like a little bird in winter. "I *know* how to speak with my clients!" His outrage was only partly for show.

"Indeed. I forget myself. I will return in three days, but in the early evening, after the market has closed. If he is unable to meet me at that time, I will attempt to arrange another meeting; I am busy, however, and it may be some days."

"You won't go to the Isle?"

"No, Radell. Not to sell these. Not unless they prove of little interest."

Radell nodded, asked a number of pointless questions, and then yawned. It was a terrible yawn, a thing of yellow teeth and indescribably poor acting. "You woke me," he said, as he lowered the arms he had raised in an overly obvious stretch above his head. "And I need my sleep."

"Of course. Forgive me." Rath bowed. It was a half bow, and it was inflected with every nuance of sarcasm that Rath could produce, all of which was wasted on the over-focused dealer.

He knew that Radell would instantly go to his desk and compose his letter; he half expected that Radell would wake some poor, desperate fool and send the message before morning.

Which suited Rath; he himself now had work to do.

Arann was able to sit up, which was good. He was in pain, which was—according to Jewel's Oma—also good, because in his case, it meant he was still alive. Jewel had taken a few years to get comfortable with her Oma's definition of the word good. His left eye was less swollen, but more discolored. He had all his teeth. He could breathe, but his chest was very tender.

And Jewel had to admit that he was a far better patient than she had ever been. He was quiet, for one, and he ate and drank whatever he was given; he never complained, and his only worry seemed to be Lefty, who still shadowed him for most of his waking hours.

Jewel envied them, some, when she had time.

But her worry about the unknown Finch took most of that time, and left envy in second place. She tried not to let the worry show, and Arann was in poor enough health that he didn't notice it.

But when she had been working in Rath's office for an hour, the door slightly ajar, she was surprised to hear a creak; the door itself being pushed slowly inward.

The map she had retrieved lay before her and she'd added what she could to it. Had even gone out of her way, on her daily excursions to the Common, for just that purpose. Taverson's by day wasn't very crowded. She'd added the river, a few footbridges, and the people who lived beneath them. She'd added street names, and cross streets, the better to plot an escape route.

If she'd had the courage, she would have attempted to figure out just how it was that magisterial guards traveled the holding; they seemed to only be present when they *weren't* wanted. But the magisterial offices in the holding were intimidating enough that she had lingered across the street for a few minutes before losing all nerve. What was she going to say? *Hello, I have nightmares that sometimes come true, and I'd like you to patrol in front of Taverson's on one of these four nights because I think a girl will be in danger?*

They'd treat her like Mrs. Stephson and her endless tales about her cat. Or worse.

As she was adding another street, the door opened fully and she turned. She didn't expect Rath; the step was wrong for him. But she was surprised to see Lefty, even if he was the only other person who could be walking in on her.

He came to stand by the desk, avoiding her gaze. She'd grown so used to this, she hardly noticed. She still noted that he had a habit of stuffing his right hand into his left armpit, but she understood why.

He waited for a full five minutes in silence, and when it was clear that he wasn't going to talk, she went back to her work.

"You can write," he said softly. As if it were a miracle.

"Some," she replied. "Not as well as Rath."

"Can you read?"

She bit back the first reply that came to mind, and forced her voice to be soothing. "It's hard to write if you can't read at all."

"Oh." He drew closer to the table, drifting as if his feet weren't actually touching the floor. "You can't draw."

"No," she replied, again biting back bitter commentary. "I'm not very good at that. I don't think Rath is either, though."

"Can you do numbers?"

"Numbers?"

"Counting. Adding things."

She nodded hesitantly. "Some," she said at last. "I'm not good enough at it, yet, but Rath is teaching me."

"Could he—" Lefty stopped, his teeth shutting so quickly she could hear them click.

She tucked the quill between her hair and her ear, and turned in her chair. Well, Rath's chair. "I'll teach you," she told him quietly. "And I'll teach Arann, too, when he's better."

"We can't pay."

"No. I can't either," she added, "but it didn't stop Rath. And it didn't stop my Oma or my father."

He stared at her.

"They taught you things?"

She nodded. "They tried. I wasn't always good at paying attention. I wish I had, more."

"Why? I mean, why did they teach you?"

The question was so strange to her that it took her a moment to even understand it. When she did, she wanted to hug Lefty; the urge was so strong she was almost off the chair before she remembered who she was dealing with. She kept her hands to herself.

"I ruined my mother's life," he told her, his voice matter-of-fact. As if it were weather, and not his life, that he was talking about.

She *really* wanted to hug him. Wished she was with Arann, because Arann would know what to do.

"You didn't choose to be born," she told him.

"Neither did you."

She nodded. "My father taught me because he hoped I would make it out of the holding. That I would find a job someplace with a rich, fat merchant. A better life."

"Why?"

"He was family. I was family."

Lefty said nothing. He started to drift away and stopped, his back toward her. His voice was like nothing she'd heard him use before when he spoke next. "If you teach us," he asked her, his good hand on the door, "does that make us your family?"

But he didn't wait for an answer. He left the question in the air, hanging there as Jewel stared.

You don't get to choose your family, her Oma had often said, usually when she was annoyed at a member of said unchosen family. Jewel couldn't remember the first time she'd heard it; she couldn't remember the last time, either.

Your family are the only people you can count on. That, too, had been her Oma's saying. *Blood is thicker than water.*

Only when it dries, Oma.

You can't trust strangers.

No. She knew it. She'd learned it early. But as a child, the definition of *stranger* had been loose, imprecise. It simply meant people you didn't know. Or didn't recognize. Sitting alone in Rath's room, her makeshift map drying, black ink a sign that she still hadn't mastered the use of the damn quill, she acknowledged again that she had *no family.* But she wasn't alone.

And if a stranger was a person you didn't know, what did they become when you *did* know them? How much had she known her mother, long dead; how well had she understood her father, or her Oma? She had accepted their love as something that was almost unconditional; she had given back whatever it was a child gave back, not questioning its value.

The map was flat.

She looked at it, and after a moment, she pushed her chair back, reached for the widest of the drawers in Rath's desk, and opened it. Inside, there were two slates; they were heavy and large, and Rath had threatened her with several kinds of death if she dropped them. This made her as careful as she ever was.

She picked up pieces of chalk, their odd shapes leaving marks on her hands, and she trudged toward the open door, sparing only one glance for the map in the making, the strange girl some part of its network of ragged lines and poorly written names.

She had done what she could. For today, she had finished. Hating it, fearing it, she did what she had been taught to do by her Oma: she found the other work that needed doing, and she minded it ferociously.

"Lefty," she said, as she walked down the hall toward her room, its door also ajar. "Arann." She entered, holding the slates—the one Rath used, the one he had bought for her—and sat, trying to look Rath-like.

Lefty, seated by Arann, looked up.

Arann looked at her as well. "Jay?"

"I was thinking that while you're lying here doing nothing, you could be useful," she replied. It was what her Oma might have said, and she said it while looking at Arann. "Lefty, take the slate. *Don't* drop it. Today we're going to learn letters."

Chapter Nine

A T RATH'S AGE, the past was a bitter terrain, and the elements that loomed large cast sharp shadows along the thin edge between history and story. He could not be certain which of the two drove him; the facts—for he prided himself on rationality—or the emotions those facts evoked; the certain sense that he had made his choice, and must abide by it, or make a lie of the whole of his adult life, or the gnawing uncertainty that the choice itself was suspect, that pride, with its bright and bitter edge, held him now, cutting him and strengthening him, always with cost.

On bitter days, the struggle was so clear it could paralyze.

Danger often dispersed paralysis. It was why he sought it so frequently. But in choosing this particular danger, he was walking the line, rather than escaping it.

He resented Jewel Markess more than he could find words to express. He resented her quiet determination, her stupidity, her naïveté; he resented her willingness to literally follow a dream that would devour her. He resented her presence in his life, her attempts to be helpful, and the quiet way in which she had insinuated two strangers, two boys, into his home.

But more, he resented what she represented. The streets had not yet had time to tarnish her; they had time to frighten her; they had time to scar her—but the scars that she had taken had somehow perversely opened her up to a compassion that Rath himself had turned away from in his early years.

She was a living accusation. And, of course, she was ignorant of this fact, as she was ignorant of so much. He had thought—he admitted it now, as he walked across the holdings to another meeting—to remake her. To teach her what he himself had had to learn in order to survive, even thrive, in the subtle open market of the poorer holdings. Had started to do just that.

And she? She had begun to learn. To pick his locks. To read his books. To write. To add, subtract, handle numbers at some base level. She had learned when to sit in silence, when to wait for his word, when to speak first; she had learned when it was safe to interrupt him, and when it was *not*. She'd even learned to accept the threat of his absence, the possibility that he might not return.

He had thought only of that.

But, of course, he was foolish. Should have known it before he started. No lesson ever went one way; lessons were not like rivers, flowing toward the ocean. They were, like his sword, a thing of two edges. He was learning, once again, to live in the world.

To live, to his surprise and growing anger, in hers.

And in Jewel's world, in a world that bordered on starvation and isolation, a stranger named Finch had incalculable value. A boy named Lefty who would not meet Rath's gaze, no matter what Rath said or did, no matter how Rath chose to approach him, and a boy named Arann, who was their conduit to Lefty. She had rescued them not once, but twice, although she knew it would anger Rath.

She had nothing of her own; everything was Rath's. Had he seen to that? Had he done that on purpose?

Or had he simply hoped?

And what, he thought, kicking a jutting piece of road from its wet moorings, had he hoped *for*? He almost turned back.

But she had the simple power that he had, unknowing, granted her: the pain of her disappointment. He was not certain, if he sent Lefty and Arann on their way, that she would not feel compelled to join them. That would be best. He would be free.

As free as he had been the day his sister had announced that she was leaving Handernesse. The words of the statue in the maze returned to him, unbidden. He kept walking.

The rain fell.

Arann and Lefty spent the day learning—or trying to learn—the

Weston alphabet. Jewel's hand was not Rath's; her letters were not as clear, as bold, or as consistent. Her temper was not Rath's; it wasn't quiet. When she was frustrated, it showed; she pulled her hair out of her eyes, she cursed the slate, she dropped the chalk on Arann's outstretched legs.

But she persevered. They did as well. It was awkward, this half-blind leading the blind. She forgot things, and had to backtrack, which added confusion. But it was clear that she had no intention of giving up, and Arann's quiet nod to Lefty made it clear that neither would they. It was a start.

Arann couldn't physically lift his arm to write, but that was fine. Lefty couldn't either, and that was less fine. In the end, she settled for memorization, which made her letters look *even worse*.

She broke for lunch, and made it, standing in the kitchen. Lefty snuck in and stood beside her for a long time, watching her, listening to the sharp thunk of knife against board as she cut apples and hard cheese.

"Can I help?" he finally asked.

She started to say no, because his right hand was in his armpit, and his left hand was not, in fact, the hand that he had favored. But the no caught between her teeth, and she found something for him to do. Because he had to, and she saw that clearly.

A gift, a different gift, from her life: Her Oma's words. Always, her Oma. Her father and her mother had been busy enough with the work they could find, and her mother's death had come early; it was her Oma she had shadowed, her Oma who had taught her much of what she understood about life. If her father didn't agree—and he often didn't—the apartment was a lively storm of argument, pipe smoke, and sound; banging on tables, scraping of chairs against the floor, banging on walls (although that was usually the neighbors).

Her Oma often spoke Weston when she dealt with strangers; she spoke Torra at home. Jewel spoke both, and her Oma had insisted that if she was going to learn to read Weston she could damn well learn to read a real language.

She wondered if either Arann or Lefty spoke Torra; half of the people who lived in the holdings did, at one level or other. Half didn't. She didn't ask. Weston was going to be work enough, for now.

As was lunch. Lefty had been given the job of arranging food on two plates, and it looked like a mess. But it would probably look worse after it was eaten, as her Oma used to say, and Jewel nodded her approval, giving him one plate to carry.

As they left the kitchen, she felt an odd twinge, and wondered where Rath was.

Rath was at home in the smoke-wreathed den. It was called a tavern by people who only viewed it from the outside—something considered intelligent by many of those who had viewed it at least once from the inside.

It was not unlike a story or a bardic lay in feel; it was dark, and shadowed, not through any mystic atmosphere, but rather by the fact that it was half a story down, and the windows were sparse. Den was a better word for the place. In fact, it was the only name he remembered it having. The Den.

Not of thieves, sadly, although this was more accurate than he would otherwise have cared for. No; here there were mercenaries, old soldiers, and the young who had made their way back from the borders of various skirmishes to the North or South. Many of the men who would frequent The Den had once been sailors, and Rath had never cared enough to ask where they docked when they had cargo; had cared less about what that cargo was. Better not to, in this place.

It was why he felt comfortable here; not caring was perhaps the only rule by which the men—and the occasional woman—who negotiated at its ancient, warped tables played.

The scent of pipe smoke blended with the smell of ale and slightly sour wine. Fat boiled in pots in what passed for a kitchen, and that, too, was a strong odor; more pleasant than the sweat and dirt of the road, although that was severely lessened in the colder season.

The chairs were hard, and often as warped as the tables; the spindles that held the backs together were rickety as holding fences. Nothing about The Den was new or shiny; there were no peacocks here.

Nor were there men of Patris Hectore's stature, although stature here was measured in an entirely different way. Instead of rings or gold chains, one bore scars, and openly. Weapons were almost a necessity, and by presence alone, they were sheathed. A bar brawl here ended in death. Usually several, although they happened seldom.

There were no obvious bouncers; there didn't have to be. The men who jointly owned The Den were some of the old sailors—where old was a relative word—that Rath, or any of the patrons, practiced their scant diplomacy on. The owners didn't like fights. It cost money and time. Therefore, they didn't let them last long.

The Den was housed in the thirty-first holding, not far from the invisible border that rammed up against the thirty-second. Gossip—or information, as it was more politic to call it—could be had here; its worth was often determined by how much money one laid down, either at the tables, or into palms. But not always. If something big was happening, it was a whisper and an undercurrent that informed even the postures of the people who were carried by it.

It was for information that he had come, but not solely for information. He took a seat at a corner table, not because he wished privacy, although it was his usual preference, but because it was one of the few tables that were not occupied. The rains drove people indoors; that and the turn of the season. Ships moored in port for much of said season, and men who might otherwise find gainful employment were left to fend for themselves; to spend or hoard the money they had managed to make during the hotter clime.

Day or night, it made no difference.

Still, from this vantage, one could see the whole of The Den and its occupants. Some, he recognized instantly, and by the lowering of chin or the raising of mug, he was acknowledged. Others were new to him, and he spent some small time evaluating them by the clothing they wore, the posture they adopted, the scars they revealed. He found the watching of interest, as he often did; although he was never certain why he was aware of it, some people had a substance to them that was not precisely gravitas, but nevertheless went below the surface and spread there, like old tree roots. They could dress like every other man present, they could speak the same words, they could utter the same threats—but there was something akin to authority in them that others did not possess.

It was very like danger, in this place. In others, it was less obvious.

One or two of the newcomers had that substance, and he studied them more carefully. He did not speak with them; did not attempt to make contact. They would notice him or not, and over the passage of months, they would evaluate him by their own standards, becoming familiar with his presence.

A man joined him at his table, and Rath smiled. It was a genuine smile, and if there was no affection in it, there was respect—as much as anyone could expect in The Den.

"Harald," he said.

"You're not drinking," the tall, fair-haired man replied. He wore a leather eye patch that was not decorative; Rath knew this because he had been in the fight that had cost him the eye. Not on the wrong side, as it happened—which in this case simply meant not on the side Harald was fighting *against*.

Losing or winning counted for little. Survival counted for more.

"I'll drink when one of the sailors notices he hasn't any of my coin in his pocket," Rath replied, with a wry smile toward the busy bar.

"Aye, it's a busy day." Harald draped himself across the back of a chair, after first reorienting it. He sat with his back to the wall; as it was a corner table, there happened to be two walls, and Rath's back was firmly toward the other one. Old habits, but not bad ones. "Haven't seen you here in a while."

Rath shrugged. "I've been busy."

"I haven't. I'm bored."

Harald bored was about as useful as Harald drunk. Drunk *and* bored, on the other hand, was a little more excitement than Rath currently craved. This hadn't always been the case. "How many of those have you had?"

Harald laughed. He knew why Rath had asked. "I'm just a grunt," he replied, tilting the mug between his lips. "I'm not much for the numbers."

"I'll grant you that. I've seen you at the tables."

Ale came out of Harald's nostrils and dribbled down his beard as the large man choked on a laugh. Rath guessed that Harald had only just started.

"Bored? That could be useful."

"Depends."

"On?"

"How deep your pockets are today."

Rath shrugged. Harald drank. There was a subtle shift in posture. In both of their postures.

"You've been here a lot lately?"

"Aye. *The Winter Whore* has docked." The name of the ship was *The White Lady*, but Harald was colloquial in all things. Rath found it amusing, inasmuch as he found anything amusing. The rains had not yet deprived Harald of the brown of sun, and the salt sea winds had added their heavy creases to the younger man's face. Hard to tell that Harald *was* the younger man, now. Rath wondered if anyone could.

There was some advantage to be had in age, but only up to a point. A man in his prime, in The Den, was a man who was canny enough to survive all misfortune. A man beyond that? Not likely to survive much longer. Rath played the middle, here. He understood the value of danger.

"Rath?"

He nodded, his gaze sweeping the crowd. As Harald's was no doubt also doing.

"You notice anything strange about the magisterians in these parts?"

"The thirty-first?"

Harald shrugged. "Not in particular. But in the old holdings." Which was his way of saying the poor ones.

Rath frowned. "Stranger than the fact that they're here at all?"

"The fact that they aren't."

"I've run into patrols."

"And they're frequent?"

Rath shrugged. "As predictable as they usually are. Why?"

Harald's turn to shrug, as if the gesture was something that could be traded back and forth. "Curious," he said.

As Harald, like the rest of The Den's occupants, considered curiosity a venal sin, Rath turned to look at him, shifting in his chair. A drink, or the forceful offer parading as a request that resulted in one, had failed thus far to materialize.

"Curious because?"

"Jim's gone missing."

"Jim? The red-beard?"

Harald nodded.

"I didn't know you were friends."

"We're not. The sonofabitch owes me money."

"Good enough reason to disappear."

Harald laughed. And shrugged. "Maybe. But he left everything at his place pretty much untouched."

"You know this how?"

"I broke his door down and rifled through his stuff."

"I take it he owes you less, now."

Harald's smile was thin. "He has a girl there. Maybe had. Fiona. You know her?"

Rath shook his head.

"She's got a temper."

"So did Jim." He paused and then shook his head. "I take it she was *in* Jim's place when you kicked the door in?"

"Pretty much."

"You're still walking."

"She slammed the side of my head with a pan."

"You've got a thick head."

"That was one of the kinder things she said. She seemed to think I'd have to pay for the door."

"You corrected that misunderstanding?"

Harald shrugged. "Would have. But Jim's been missing three days. He didn't take a lot of money with him, not that he had much. He also didn't take more than a dagger or two. Wherever he was going—and she thought it was the Common—he didn't go expecting to stay a few days."

"She told you that?"

Harald frowned. "You're sure you haven't been drinking?"

Rath nodded; it *was* a stupid question. "What did she want you to do?"

"Find him, more or less."

"She went to the magisterial halls?"

Harald nodded. "Two days ago."

"They find a body?"

"They took a report."

"A report?"

Harald nodded.

"That's more paperwork than they'd do in a year, in these parts."

"That's what I thought." He emptied his mug and dropped it on the table; it rolled in a clumsy circle, trailing the last of the ale.

"I take it there were no bodies?"

"If there were, they didn't offer to show 'em to her."

"All right. That's unusual." It was. Missing people weren't uncommon in the older holdings. They weren't *entirely* common; the rule of law, if shoddy, was still in force. But if someone came to report a missing person, the magisterians usually took them to look at the bodies that had been retrieved from either the river or the streets.

"You said her name was Fiona?"

Harald nodded.

"Which holding?"

"The thirty-fifth."

"But if Jim was on his way to the Common—" Rath stopped. He didn't have a map of the holdings, but he didn't need one; he knew where Jim lived. Knew, as well, what the route to the Common from Jim's place looked like, unless Jim was trying to lose someone, in which case it was anyone's guess.

"This along the lines of what you came here looking for?"

"No. Who was Jim working for?"

"Judging by his debts? No one." He shrugged.

"Was he planning to?"

"At the Common?" They both knew it was the wrong season for press-gangs. If Jim went, that wasn't the method of his departure.

Rath nodded. With a forced wry grin, he added, "Too early in the morning for thinking."

Harald raised a brow. "What did you come here for?"

"Word," Rath said quietly. "Of anyone new in the holdings." Quiet was relative in The Den.

Harald's voice dropped. "Maybe," he said at last. "You have someone in mind?"

"Not by name. Money, maybe," Rath added, after a pause. "And a number of very competent men."

"Competent how?"

"About how you'd expect."

Harald looked uneasy. Given his size and his general demeanor, this was two things: Nigh impossible and bad.

"I'll take that as a provisional yes."

"Take it as you like. Don't attach my name to it."

"Anyone in The Den working for someone new?"

Harald said nothing, loudly. It was enough. As a drink failed to materialize, Rath looked at the doors; watched people entering.

"You working?"

Harald shrugged.

"I'll take that as a provisional no."

"What do you want me to do?"

Rath told him.

To Jewel's surprise, Rath was home before dinner. He knocked at her door, and both Lefty and Arann tensed; Jewel got up quickly, more for their comfort than Rath's. She left her room, the two slates in use a reminder that she wasn't technically supposed to pillage Rath's quarters. The door, she shut quietly and firmly behind her.

Rath was covered in a fine patina of damp dust; she knew where he'd been for at least part of the day. His backpack hung flat and limp against his shoulders, though; if he'd found whatever he'd been looking for, he hadn't brought it with him.

"Jay," he said softly. He removed the velvet jacket as he spoke, glancing at it with mild dismay. This was as much expression as he ever showed. She took it from him as he turned back to the door and bolted it.

She nodded.

"I need your help."

She nodded again. "I can't wash this—"

"Not with *that*," he snapped. His eyes were almost glittering in the pale gloom of the hall as he held out the magelight he always carried with him. "Hang the jacket up in my room. Over the chair back," he added. "Not the armchair."

"You've eaten?"

His expression made clear how endearing he found being mothered. She backed off. Given his current mood, she also backed away. It was involuntary, and it caught his attention.

He closed his eyes and drew a long breath, straightening his shoulders and schooling the lines of his face. Eyes still closed, he said, "I'm not angry at you, Jay."

"You *are* angry—"

"Not specifically at you. I'm angry, yes. I'm also a sane man; I have no intention of throwing you out or beating you." He opened his eyes, and held out his open palms, one still glowing brightly with magelight. The underside of his chin was lit with pale gold, and his eyes were ringed with shadow.

There was a long pause that Jewel had no intention of breaking.

Rath, to her surprise, did. His voice was softer, and there was something akin to regret in it. "I forget how much of a stranger you are. Or I am, to you. There are reasons I live alone, when I've the choice. This is one of them; I've never been known for an even temper."

She had seen him frustrated before. But anger was different. And he knew it.

Still, his hands were open and empty, and he held himself still, as if *she* were the wild or injured creature. She tried to meet him halfway. "What—what did you want me to help you with?"

"The maze," he said curtly. There was edge in the words.

There was wonder, momentary and not unalloyed, on her face, and her mouth was half open because he stared at her until she remembered and shut it. "You want me to go back to the maze?"

Annoyance, a familiar twist of facial geography, answered the question. "No," he said, just as curtly. "I *don't*. But at the moment, I don't see any good choice."

She said, "I'll tell Lefty we're going out."

"You won't."

"But—"

"We're not going out." He reached into his hidden pouch and pulled out a small key. "We're going *in*." His eyes narrowed. "Have *you* eaten?"

"Everything on my plate," she responded promptly. It would annoy him. But then again, on some days, everything did. He had promised he wouldn't hit her. She chose to believe him, but she wasn't against pushing the line a bit, just to be certain.

"Good." He failed—probably deliberately—to hear any cheek in the words. "Put your boots on."

She slid back into her room.

Lefty and Arann were sitting side by side, just a few inches too close together. She smiled at them, and it was an encouraging smile.

"He's mad about the slates, isn't he?"

She shook her head. Bright smile, all around. "He's just pissed off in general. Probably some deal went bad."

"Should we leave?"

"And go where? No, don't answer that. Arann," she added, "If you leave, I'll break your legs. I swear."

Given the difference in both their size and age, it wasn't much of a threat, and it was taken as the sign of affection it was. He nodded. She bent and hooked the back of her boots on her fingers; they were heavy and solid, reminding her that Arann needed to visit the seamstress and the cobbler in the Common.

"Keep an eye on Lefty."

"I'm not the injured one," Lefty snapped.

Both she and Arann turned to stare at him; his back was stiff, and although his right hand was cradled in his armpit, the left one was bunched in a loose fist.

She almost laughed. Lefty had snapped at *her*. And Rath was about to take her back to the maze. The day had turned out so much better than she'd expected. Firsts all around.

Arann muttered something to Lefty.

"Well, I'm not," Lefty replied, shoving his left hand under his right armpit and staring at his friend.

"This," Arann said heavily, "is what he's *really* like."

Jewel laughed. "I like it better," she told Arann.

"You won't," was his dire warning. But she could see the half smile on his face, and the strain of hope. She could answer neither easily. "Stay in the room," she told them both, "until Rath calms down."

That much, they could obey easily.

Boots retrieved, Jewel joined Rath in the hall. He waited with more or less patience while she shoved her feet into them. In the apartment, she hated to wear them; they were stiff, and they rubbed the back of her ankles raw. After she stood up, she pulled her hair out of her eyes and tied it back over her head with a kerchief. It wouldn't stay there, but it was as much as she could manage.

"Where are we going?" she asked, although she suspected she knew the answer.

"To the storage rooms," he replied.

Her point.

After the incident with the statue, Rath had promised himself that he would not bring Jewel back into the undercity unless it were an emergency and her life depended on it. So many broken promises were the stones that formed the cobbled street his life had followed. This was just one more. But it held more weight than he would have liked, and he felt the breaking of it more keenly than he had any recent oath.

Because it was silent, and offered to himself.

He had two keys to the storeroom. They were the last keys that he had had made; the last lock that he had overseen. Although the mechanism had been left with him, he had not chosen to install it while Jewel was awake, and it had taken three days of surreptitious work to achieve some semblance of secrecy, as she was always underfoot.

So much for his work, his secrecy.

He reminded himself that she was a *child*. This did not have the desired effect. Looking at her—looking down on her—he could see both vulnerability and determination, and it was a combination that was unsettling in its familiarity. Her eyes, the standard brown of Southern descent, were wide and almost unblinking as she watched him turn key in lock; they burned, in their own way.

And he would have let them burn quietly, in the safety of his home, had she not introduced the two orphans. Arann, almost Rath's height and width, and Lefty, smaller than she. The ghost of a girl he had never seen was wrapped up in the mystery of Jewel. Finch, she had called her.

"This," he said grimly, "is for Finch. I hope she's worth the risk."

Jewel's eyes widened. She bit her lip. Pushed her hair out of her eyes—although it wasn't in them. All her nervous habits came and went in the moment between the lock's welcome click and the silent movement of the new door.

"I don't know," she told him, as he stepped into the dark, lifting his hand so that the light reached its greatest height. He had called this room a storeroom, as had the building's owner, but he had chosen to store nothing in it. The floorboards, as the owner had implied, were in poor repair. Where poor repair meant they wouldn't hold the weight of anything heavier than a starving mouse. He tested the floor almost gingerly, regretting the lack of a pole.

"What don't you know?"

"If she's worth the risk."

Rath shook his head. So much potential power in that child, and none of it understood. Not by Jewel herself. He let his breath leave him in a forced, loud exhalation, the only other sound in the room save for quiet breathing.

"She's worth the risk," he told her, without looking back. "Stay to the side of the room; keep to the walls."

"How do you know?"

"The floor is—"

"About Finch?"

"How could I not?" He countered, taking his own advice. "You had the vision," he added. "We'll need rope here. Do you know where the rope is?"

"In your pack?"

"Not the one I was wearing. The older one."

"The big one?"

"Yes. That one."

He heard her leave, and waited, continuing his cautious examination of the floor. She returned quietly. Good girl.

"Rath?"

"Yes?"

"What did you mean? About how I could not know, I mean."

"You're not going to let her go," he replied evenly. It was hard to do it; he wanted to snap. But in the darkness, in the sudden danger of eroded architecture, he hoarded his impatience. "No matter what I tell you, no matter how much danger you'll wind up facing, you're not going to let her go."

Her voice was a child's voice when she answered. "I can't." It was also a whisper.

"I know. If I thought it would help, I *would* throw you out. You've been enough trouble as is." Before she could stammer or freeze, he lifted the hand that didn't contain the light, cutting off her words. "But you've *also* saved my life."

"We're even," she began.

"In more than one way, Jewel. And I imagine, if you survive this, you'll save my life again."

"Don't." The bitterness was heavy. It added years to her voice. "I've never been able to count on—"

"I know. The holdings will kill me eventually." He turned, then, exposing something he hadn't realized was hidden until this moment. "I accept that. I chose this life. But you? You *didn't*. Arann didn't, and Lefty didn't. And I expect you to survive the life you eventually *do* choose. Do you understand, Jay? Jewel?"

She didn't, quite. He could see it in the way the light played up the lines of her face. "No."

"I know. I want you to learn whatever I can teach you because I want you to have the choice that I did."

"And make the same choice?"

He could not answer the question. He would never answer that specific question, not directly. "And make the choice that seems wisest to you at the time," he told her, but the words were thick.

She was a danger in too many ways. He longed, deeply, viscerally, to be rid of her. And he knew, at this moment, that it would almost kill him.

"Help me," he said, trying to bury emotion, trying to deny attachment. "Those boards."

She started toward them and he snapped her name; she froze. "Lie down," he told her. "Lie as flat as possible. I'm going to tie the rope around your waist; if you fall, you won't fall far." He knelt by the wall and placed the magelight on the ground, passing his hand over it and whispering the word that would brighten its glow.

She waited as he wrapped the rope twice around her almost negligible width, and knotted it with care. Then she did as he had bid; she lay flat against the creaking, unfinished planks. She didn't wait to be told to move; she moved, deliberately, toward the center of the floor, sliding on her stomach, the dust and damp the only scent in the room. Rath braced himself, one foot on the floor and one knee for balance; he also looped the rope several times around his right arm, and he spoke to her, not giving orders, but giving instead the slow encouragement of an even, smooth tone of voice.

The floor gave, as he expected, the boards suddenly tilting toward the darkness of the nothing beneath them. They creaked; something snapped. Jewel didn't fall, but she slid forward, her palms against rough grain. She'd have splinters for sure, but he could remove them later; splinters didn't kill. Infection, on the other hand, cost limbs.

The floor here was so damp it took a while for the boards to snap, and they didn't so much snap as disintegrate in sharp pieces. Jewel did fall then, and Rath felt the rope around his arm go taut, instantly cutting off all circulation. He heard the whoof of her breath as it left her in a rush, felt the rope twist as she momentarily struggled with the sensation of suspension.

When she stilled—as much as she could—she was a weighty pendulum with a slow arc. He inched forward, lowering himself to the floor and giving the rope some play. It, too, was rough, and it scraped the skin off his arms, pulling the pale cream of undyed linen against his skin. He reached for the magestone with his free hand.

"I'm throwing the light down," he told her. "If you can catch it, that's good; if you can't, let it drop."

"But what if it—"

"We have the money for another," he told her, "and I'm not without backup." Again, he kept his voice soothing and calm.

She impressed him; there was no panic in her voice when she told him she was ready. He rolled the stone toward the large hole she'd made in the floor, and managed not to wince as it followed the incline of that hole and disappeared, taking most of the room's light with it. The storeroom had no window wells, no external light.

Which, given the undercity, was what he expected; it was also how he worked. He could see the brightness of the light vanish, and listened for its fall.

The rope twisted against his arm; he was thankful that Jewel was still street-thin, a gangly child. "It's—it's hit ground," she managed to tell him.

"How far down?"

"I'm not sure. Maybe ten feet?"

"I'm going to lower you down."

"Good. Because the rope is crushing my stomach."

He chuckled.

"Do we have to go up the same way?"

"We won't be able to. We'll come up—" He stopped himself. "You'll see."

She said nothing, and he began to edge himself along the same floor that had buckled beneath her weight. The floors were actually worse than he'd expected, and he would have to have them replaced in their entirety, which meant strangers—even the ones he called friends—in his private space.

He'd worry about it later.

Now, he just hoped that the floor held him for long enough that Jewel made it down without injury. He listened as he moved, as he let more rope play out. The rope itself was a good ten yards in length, and far too bulky—but he'd discovered that this had its uses, and the more expensive rope made by the maker-born required both a public presence at the Guild and an assumption of some rank.

He wished for neither.

The rope went slack, and he felt his shoulders relax.

"I'm down," she told him. "And I've got the light."

"Good girl. Hold it, now; I'm going to come down after you, and I'm likely to hit the ground rolling."

She understood what he meant, or at least he assumed she did; he crawled on his stomach to the same point that had swallowed Jewel, and the planks beneath him gave about two feet earlier. He was prepared for this, and he managed to make the fall a rolling fall.

Dragging a trail of dust and old cobwebs, he managed to gain his feet; Jewel had pressed herself into the walls to give him a clear path should he need it. Smart girl. Her fingers gripped the magestone too tightly, and he stood, showing her that he could, before they relaxed.

He was standing on packed, oiled dirt; the walls were of rough stone and were covered in fine, green algae. The earth wasn't much of a house-keeper. But this, this was what he expected. He motioned for light, and she brought it, stepping gingerly, the rope now loose around her waist and her almost nonexistent hips.

He smiled; the light touched his face, lending it no warmth. "I was right," he told her. "This is the right place."

He pulled another silver circle out of his inner pocket. "Compass," he told her. "I've never navigated this entrance to the undercity, and not all of the pathways in were preserved. Let's hope this one was."

She nodded, and fingered the knot he'd made. He shook his head. "Leave it," he said firmly. "It's not a guarantee of safety, but we've another level to go before we're in the real maze. If you fall, I'll catch you."

"And if you fall," she said, just sharply enough that he tasted fear, "I'll fall with you."

He shrugged. "Soft landing," he told her, "if you can control yours."

He began to walk, and Jewel, to follow. Neither spoke. The ceiling— such as it was—was adorned by the occasional tree root; they had to duck a couple of times, but this, too, was normal. Rath felt a sense of solitary peace, even with Jewel at his back. This, this was his home in some fash-ion. Dark, yes, and unknown. But not unknowable.

He'd found the maze some five years back. Perhaps he'd been looking for it. Its black caverns, its white buildings, its old facades—they seemed to call to him in their perfect silence, as if they were the tombs to which he would at last be brought. No one lived to be old in the holdings. Not when they lived Rath's life.

Had he not found the maze at all? He wasn't certain what he would have become. What he would have chosen to become, having left Han-dernesse, as his sister had done. But he had. And its secrets were *his* se-crets, waiting at last to be spoken.

The hall, such as it was, was twisted; it was not of a uniform width, and there were at least two sections that had to be navigated with care. He turned sideways, edging between two dirt walls; Jewel, at least, did not have to make this contortion.

But he wanted to see her face; to see the wonder on it. He had witnessed it once, and it was a gift that he wanted again. Time and familiarity would destroy it, as it destroyed all mystery—but it had not yet begun to decay, and he could not resist a backward glimpse as he offered her his hand.

She took the hand; hers was trembling. She followed.

And he found, to his surprise, that this hall ended in steps. They were stone steps, but the stone itself was worn in the center; at one point, many feet had come this way, leaving slow evidence of passage only in the gentle slope of what had once been flat stone.

"This," he told her softly, "is unexpected."

"Is it safe?"

He nodded. "As safe," he added, "as anything in the undercity can be."

"What are we looking for?"

"An exit," he replied. He could almost see her wilt, and he kept his smile to himself, although it was a fond smile. "We can look at buildings if you like; there will be one or two that we must pass through to reach where we're going."

"Where?"

"You'll see."

"Rath?" Jewel looked at his back. Linen caught light, and because it was pale, Rath seemed almost luminescent in the darkness that knew no sun.

"Yes?"

"Can I afford a stone of my own, if I find something worth any money here?"

"Yes. You can probably afford one now."

"I can't," she told him softly. "Not if I want to feed Arann and Lefty. Arann needs—"

"Clothing. Yes. And boots. But, Jay, you have more than enough for that."

"It's not my money," she said flatly.

"It's yours." They'd had this argument before. "Were it not for your interference, there would be no money, because I wouldn't have been there to collect."

She ignored the words. "And maybe Finch, too."

"They will not *all* fit in your room."

"My family fit four people in smaller rooms before."

He shook his head. "As you insist. As long as they're not in *mine*, or spread out in the training room, I will not argue."

She walked in silence for another long moment, taking the steps as if they were magic—and illusion, at that—and could disappear at any second, dropping her sudden weight. But she stopped once or twice to touch them; to feel their cold surface against her palms. To judge for herself the truth of his words.

"How far down does this go?"

"I don't know. You can count the steps if you like; they're not much more than a foot in height, possibly less. This is a gentle incline."

She counted for a while, and gave up. Counting was something done on a slate, with numbers; counting these was like losing the experience, or rather, like flattening it, like making it something it wasn't.

The rope was a slack thing between them. "Rath?"

"Yes?"

"How is it that no one discovered the maze before you?"

"I don't honestly know."

"I mean, there must be other people who've come into basements or chutes before."

"Possibly. But when people fall into something, their usual concern is to *get out*."

It felt wrong, to Jewel. The wrong answer. She was uneasy here, and couldn't say why. But she didn't mention it precisely because she couldn't, and Rath would ask. The feeling was strong, and it made her neck prickle; goose bumps, she thought.

The last step opened up onto a flat causeway that was visibly cracked in many places. It was gray, in the magelight. She thought it would be gray in *any* light. But it felt safe to her, and she relaxed; it was good to have her feet on solid ground. Even if that ground was so far beneath the ground she was used to, bodies didn't make it this deep.

The thought disturbed her in a different way. "Are people buried here?" She asked him. "I mean, in the ground, not in cenotaphs?" She forced herself not to add, *you know, the ones you rob.*

His face in magelight, he turned, lifting a pale brow. "You ask the oddest questions," he said at last. "But I think there must be bodies buried here. You've seen some remains, and this *was* a city. All cities have their dead."

"Do all cities demand them?" she asked. The words left her lips as if they were foreign, and he looked at her oddly. She realized she'd asked the question in Torra.

Was surprised when Rath answered her anyway, although he answered in Weston. So Rath understood Torra, even if he had never chosen to speak it.

"All cities," he said softly. "But I think especially this one. Do you know your bardic lays?"

She shook her head. "We didn't see too many bards."

"Most bards wouldn't know the lays of which I speak," he replied. "And I speak mostly to myself; it's a habit. It's seldom that I have company here that is not my own." Her hand was still in his, and he tightened his grip; it was meant to reassure. Or she thought it was.

They walked across the stone together, and it opened up into a darkness that was utterly unlike Averalaan at night. Here, the magelight was dwarfed, as it had been the one other time she'd followed him. She saw a building ahead of them, and stopped.

Her mouth was a half-open O of surprise.

"Yes," he told her quietly. "This is a part of the undercity that you did not see the first time you visited. Do you know what that is?"

She shook her head.

Before it, steps that were the length of a city block beckoned, and above those, recessed on a flat that held square pedestals, were four statues. Some were headless, or missing limbs; some were hewn, as if by stone sword, at waist, leaving only legs, some portion of torso, nothing to identify them. Funny, how faces mattered. But they seemed sentinels of a bygone age, and they stood between what had once been doors. The frames themselves were arched and came to a point three times Jewel's meager height. Maybe four. She looked up; they seemed tiered, these doorways, and if wood had once graced them, nothing did now; they opened up into blackness, as if they had always been open arches.

"Into this place," he said softly, "I do not travel."

And as she edged toward the stairs, she felt it: a subtle prickle of skin, a sharp unease. "Me either," she whispered, leaning into his back, almost unaware of the motion until she felt him stiffen. She pulled away.

Rath did not say another word, but led her past it, the magestone now cupped slightly in his palm. The city was dead; empty—but he shielded his light as if he himself did not believe those words.

But it was here, and only here, that that was true.

"The city," he told her softly, "was not uniformly buried; there are buildings that might have been palaces, and what remains of those are crypts. There are others that might have been bathhouses—at least judging by the placement of the fountains. Homes of the powerful. Come," he told her, and she followed. Not, given that he held her hand, that she had much choice.

But this was his place. There were streets, although it was odd to see streets with a ceiling, no matter how high, odder yet to see them and feel so strongly the absence of the magelights that were scattered so precisely throughout the city, no matter which holding they occupied.

"Where are we going?"

"I believe," he told her gently, "that it was once the home of either artists or the maker-born."

He turned corners, and she tried to mark them, to hold the direction of the turning in memory. To Rath, memory was important; possibly the most important of the attributes that she lacked. Here, just the two of them again, she wanted his approval.

As much as she had ever wanted her Oma's, perhaps because at least with Oma, she was guaranteed a sharp affection. Rath guaranteed nothing.

It was damp, here; the rains must have a way of seeping through dirt, through the closed sky. "The tunnels," he told her, "are extensive. It's only in a few places, such as these, that they open up into the remnants of the old city."

"What city was it?" she asked softly.

He said nothing for a long moment. At last, he said, "I do not know the name. I will not ask it; the Order of Knowledge might have some answer, or perhaps the bards—but to gain their insight, I would have to give too much away. Remember this."

She nodded, even though he couldn't see it.

He paused at last in front of a building that was so tall its upper floors vanished in darkness. She wondered if they were still there, or if they had been crushed when whatever cataclysm that had swallowed this place had occurred.

Otherwise, it was a structure that almost dwarfed the street; if it had had grounds, the way the fancy manors did, someone had built roads across it. The front of it, the facade as Rath called it, was flat, and seemed to be almost seamless stone; what seams there were were like fault lines, cracks that looked like webbing or roots as they traveled down the length of wall.

There was a large door. Easily the largest door that Jewel had ever seen—except, of course, for the absence of door itself. Stone was molded and formed, and ran from ground upward, ending in an arch that, unlike the peaked architraves of the other building, was also composed of a series of smaller stones. In the center of that arch, one of these stones was larger than the rest, and a symbol was engraved upon it; it glinted in the magelight.

"Is it gold?" she asked him softly.

"Gold," he said with a shrug, as if gold were of no consequence, "or magic. From this vantage, it's impossible to tell, and I've never tried to climb the facade. Not everything that seems solid is." He paused and turned toward her. "From here," he said quietly, "take nothing. I have items that we can sell."

"Is there anything *to* take?"

"Much," he replied, "but not without effort, and the sale of it would be costly in ways you cannot imagine." He hesitated, and then shook his head. "I take," he said quietly, "things which might *possibly* have been passed from father to son for generations; things that the poorest of the people in the holdings might conceivably own, in ignorance of their value. Or things, like the stone, which might be found at the entrance ways to the maze itself.

"The maze has many uses, and if it were to be discovered, one of them, at least, would be gone."

She waited.

"I travel, here. I can pass unseen by those it is better to avoid. I can move from the thirty-second to the heart of the Common and back, should I desire to do so with no witnesses at all."

She didn't ask him when that might happen. It was wisest not to know. But he surprised her. "I will teach you what I can, Jay. And you will find that the ease of passage is not without its use. This is today's lesson, and I have neglected your tutelage almost shamefully of late; I have been much occupied. Are you ready?"

She nodded.

"Then come. Enter the stone garden."

And he led her through the open door—if indeed it was that—and into the darkness beyond.

Chapter Ten

THE STONE GARDEN, he called it, and if Jewel had wondered why—and she had—the wonder shifted, becoming something else entirely. She had heard of rock gardens before, and they made no sense— how did one *grow* rocks? And why would one bother? You couldn't eat rock, after all, and it wasn't particularly pretty.

But *this* rock?

She reached out to touch a trailing vine. Felt the hard, smooth flat of a leaf beneath her fingers as dust came away in her hands. The trellis upon which these vines grew was rock as well, but rock with grain, as if it were a testament to wood, to things that lived and died.

She saw leaves, and bowing stems, things without color, and she almost heard the wind through them; felt a hint of a sunlight that would never again reach this place.

Rath let her hand go, and she wandered almost without thought; here, she found flowers, whole flower beds, each flower different; some budding, some blooming, and some at the end of blossom, petals almost falling from round centers. She found roses, but they were odd roses indeed: trees, trunks thick and knotty, branches, thorns still sharp, just above her head. Touching them, she exhaled; she blew dust in a cloud past her lips, left blood in its wake. None of these things were alive; they were all stone, although not the same kind of stone; some were smooth and some porous, and in the light of a day that would never come, she thought the subtle shades of gray would have hinted at color in a way that not even living flowers could.

"Makers," she whispered.

"I think it must be so," he replied, his voice muted and hushed. She turned to look at him then; found him close to her shoulder, where the light he carried might illuminate this hidden wonder. She had rarely seen Rath in any state of reverence, and perhaps reverence was the wrong word—but it was damn close.

"Even the least of these," he told her quietly, "would be almost beyond price, could you pick them. But they would never grace this garden again; there is no life here, and no renewal. It is, and it is what it was meant to be: eternal. Only the living dies," he added softly.

There was a path, and he led her along it, but they walked slowly; they had to. She paused, often in shadow, and light came as he returned to her side, to see what had caught her eye, and what, her hand. She could not help but touch the plants that had been carved in stone. Could not believe that they *had*, in fact, been carved; she thought they must have been shaped, and grown, by the hand of an Artisan.

"Is it all like this?" she asked him as she rose for the fiftieth time.

"I cannot say. Much of it, yes. Understand, Jay, that this is a work that affects each witness in different ways; what you see and what I see are at once the same and utterly unlike. I have seen gardens that might surpass this one in color and form; that might be considered the more beautiful by those with an eye to appreciate it. I would be surprised if you've seen more than flower boxes."

She couldn't argue with him. It was true. But this stone garden made her long for a sight of the grounds beyond the gates in the richer holdings.

"Who lived here?" she asked.

"I told you—"

"I mean, were they good people?"

He froze, and the look he gave her, softened by magelight, was an odd one. "Good?" he said, as if it were a foreign word.

"Good as in not evil."

He reached out to touch a rose petal. "Does it matter?" he replied at last. "I think the men and women who lived in *this* place and created *this* garden were not concerned with good or evil; they were concerned with beauty, with truth rather than reality; they made something they hoped would last."

She said, "It matters."

"Why?"

And shrugged. "I don't know. I don't think I could do this—this garden, this work—if people were starving outside my doors. Or worse."

"Why? People will always be starving. If not directly outside your doors, then beyond them. People," he added, letting his hand fall away, "will always be dying. And if you stop your life's work because of them, what work will you ever do?"

She shrugged again. Thinking of Arann and Lefty. "I don't know. Could I make that my life's work?"

"To know?"

She shook her head. "To save them." She saw the stiffness in his shoulders, in the sudden straightening of his neck, and wondered what she said that was so wrong.

"It won't last," he told her, voice cold.

"Neither will I. My father didn't. My mother didn't. My Oma didn't. Does it matter if it lasts?"

"Can you ask that, while you stand here, in this garden?"

She was silent.

"Can you understand that you can spend the whole of your life fighting—both literally and figuratively—to achieve something as fragile as peace? That, having given your life to it, you will lose it, either before your death, or for certain, after it? What will your life have meant, then?"

"Rath—"

"No. I will not speak more on this." He was not speaking to her. She *knew* it. And wondered about whoever it was he *was* speaking to. Her Oma had told her that the past was like a whole other country, with different rules, and no way of changing anything. She saw that in him now. It was the first time she had ever seen it so clearly.

"It will mean," she said distinctly, "that I'll have *tried*."

"And failed," he said bitterly.

She bent, now, before a perfect stone blossom. Gray, dusty, webbed; she touched it, and the webs clung to her fingers, becoming part of her. "These were never alive," she told him.

"I'm aware of that," was his cool reply.

"But if the person who made them had never *seen* life, they would never exist all. They don't grow. They don't change. They can't change," she added, "anything."

"Beauty can change much."

"Depends," she said, rising as well. "Depends what you find beautiful." But even saying it, even defiant, she felt a pang as he led her away from the stone garden. Because it *was* beautiful, and in a way that life could never be: It was perfect.

"And maybe," she continued, although he was no longer speaking, "if people saw people *try,* they'd try, too. Maybe then we'd have something like the garden, but alive."

"You're young, Jay."

"I won't always be young."

"No. I was young once. And now? I'm Rath. Come. We've spent much time here, and we've a little ways to travel."

He led her beyond the building; the light's radius was so small, it was gone as if it were dream. Someone else's dream. The width of the streets narrowed, and part of the road was blocked by fallen stone, the collapse of walls. Rath navigated these with deliberate care; he was slow, and heavier than she, and the stone teetered beneath his weight. He went first, always, testing these stones and their give, although it was clear he'd passed over them before.

When it was safe, he signaled and she followed, finding foot and hand-holds where she had to climb. Nothing was so tall or forbidding that he offered to use the rope he carried, and although she scraped skin off her knees and elbows, she didn't complain. The dust was like a second skin by the time they'd cleared the ruin, and nothing in it could tell her what the wall had once hidden from the view of passersby.

Beyond the ruin, there were tunnels. If they had once been narrow streets, they were now a mix of stone and earth; she thought the ground must have sloped toward the city above, although she couldn't be certain.

Rath motioned a halt, and she sat heavily upon the ground. It was difficult to imagine that the hard dirt beneath her legs led to the stone garden, and only in thinking this did she realize that they had not entered the building proper. She wondered if it still stood. Or if it, like the ruins, had folded from within, leaving great passages blocked by chunks of sharp stone that were larger in all ways than she.

Rath held his compass in the glow of the magelight, consulting it briefly. "Here," he told her quietly.

She squinted. Ahead, darkness, and behind, darkness; Rath was her only light, and his feet were pale shadows. She wanted to speak to the magestone, to tell it to brighten. Had she been at home, she might have tried—but this was more Rath's than any room in the apartment they shared, and she acknowledged it by silence. Sometimes silence served best.

He turned a corner of sorts, a rounding of earth and stone that seemed worn by some sort of liquid. It was cold to the touch, and Jewel touched it only once.

"The ground is solid," he told her. "But we'll ascend, soon. Be ready."

By which he meant: be quiet. This hall was narrow and less well formed. "This is nearer the street," she said, almost without thinking.

"Why do you say that?"

"The narrow tunnels are."

He turned; the light caught his brief smile. "Good. Could you find your way back?"

"Back?"

"Home."

She hesitated, right and left a memory, and at that, a jumbled one. "I—might be able to."

Not the right answer, but from his expression, the one he expected. "We have two days," he told her softly. "In two days, the answer must be yes." And he led her down the hall.

It trailed into darkness before Rath stopped. "Here," he told her, and pointed, his hand brushing the low ceiling. "Can you see?"

She couldn't, until he lifted the magelight and held it almost against the earth. Or what she had assumed was earth. There was a small crack in the uneven surface, and it looked as if it were made of wood.

"There's an entrance?" she asked him, surprised.

"It leads to a subbasement. Half height; when it's really raining, it's much less pleasant." With care, and a bit of a grunt, he pressed against the wooden slats; they moved up. There was no hinge here. What had appeared to be a trapdoor was merely a set of boards, and from the look on Rath's face, a heavy one. He grunted once as he lifted it an inch or two and slid them to the side.

Then he knelt, and handed her the stone; the compass, he slid into his inner pouch. "Up you go," he told her. "Don't stand quickly; you'll hit your head."

She braced herself on his shoulder with her left hand, holding fast to the magestone with her right, rising as he rose. He was careful. But she was light, and she did graze ceiling in spite of his warning. It was four feet from the slats, if that. She wondered who had boarded this entrance up in the first place, because there wasn't a similar one anywhere above it that she could see.

Something skittered by her feet. She hoped it was a mouse. Or mice. Or a hundred mice. She *really* hated rats. Spiders, she could live with— mostly because she could step on them. Bugs with shells were a bit more of a problem because they were usually larger and rounder, and her weight wasn't a guarantee that they would go crunch.

She heard Rath whisper her name, and forgot about bugs. "Sorry," she murmured, holding the light above the hole as she moved. The ceiling here was low enough that he needed no help to get up, which was good, because she wasn't in a position to give him any.

Arann, now, that would be different. If he were here.

Rath unfolded as much as he could, crouching on the balls of his heels, knees bent. He grimaced and began to crawl, stomach facing the ground. She motioned to the board, but he shook his head, and she left it; it was hard to navigate around the opening; there was barely enough space for Rath to climb through.

"Where does this come up?" she asked him, hunching as she walked. She could crawl, but she didn't particularly like the look of the ground, and walking wasn't as difficult at her height.

"You'll see," he replied.

Her first impulse, when he pushed against the short, short ceiling, was to frown. Her second, better impulse, was to hold the magelight for him. Her third was to notice that he once again pushed boards up and out of the way. These were, on the other hand, like a trapdoor without a hinge; heavy, but obviously made for the purpose of covering a hole. "Rath—"

He held a finger to his lips, and she shut up.

She could hear noise, the sound of voices, in the distance.

"Give me the light," he whispered, and she handed it to him without thinking; voices, even in the distance, were often a sign of danger.

He crawled out of the square opening, and after a moment, she saw both his face and the light. "Can you get up on your own?"

She nodded, and caught the lip of the entrance with her hands; she didn't weigh much, but her arms weren't strong, and she struggled to swing her leg up, to gain purchase. He watched her for a moment without comment, but he didn't try to help her.

Minutes passed; she managed at last to emerge, and when she did, she was surprised. She was in a storeroom. It wasn't used for anything important, that she could see; a broken chair, a chipped table, some trays that were literally dented. Make that four broken chairs. But the room itself was a normal room, and she could see a door between two of the chairs.

Rath pointed to that door. "This is the tricky part," he told her, smiling. He paused to brush the dust and dirt from his clothing, which had the effect of smearing it. The tunnels were damp. She looked at her own clothing with some dismay, but she'd been dirtier than this before. Not, on the other hand, since she'd come to live with Rath.

"Beyond that door," he said, voice still low, "is another storeroom. Which *is* in use. Supplies are there, and the owner of this place doesn't much care for thieves."

"Is there another way out?"

He shook his head.

"Will anyone notice us?"

"Probably."

"Is the door locked?"

"That's the funny thing. The owner is a damn cheap bastard, and the answer should be yes. Not that getting out would be a problem," he added, "If you've been paying attention to anything I've taught you."

She nodded.

"Getting *in* would be. And getting in is crucial. Do you understand?" All in a low, even tone, as if he were talking to a frightened animal. Or a small child. She tried not to bridle. Succeeded because she was, in fact, frightened.

"No one will comment on our presence here if we don't appear to be furtive. The tavern is busy enough, if we've paid attention to time."

And if we haven't? Jewel paid attention to time by sunlight, damn it. Of which there wasn't any.

Rath pushed the door open, and Jewel saw instantly that he was correct. Saw, as well, that *this* door swung in, which was a good thing; it was half blocked by canvas bags. Lumpy bags. Potatoes or apples, by her best guess. There were bags of heavier, finer cloth, and she thought those must be flour. The second storeroom smelled, to Jewel, like wealth; like life. She saw barrels by the far wall, and realized they were on one side of a door.

"It's late enough in the day," Rath told her, maneuvering his way around the sacks that were laid out across the floor, "that they've gone to the Common and come back. Never try this in the morning," he added softly.

It was Jewel's intent never to try this *at all*.

He pushed the door open, and the distant noises became almost over-powering. The subtle scent of food gave way in an instant to the smell of smoke, ale, cooking oil, burning wood. And sweat. Rath stepped into the back rooms of Taverson's, and smiled as Jewel joined him. Taking her hand, he led her into the main room, bypassing a set of swinging doors behind which a man was cursing loudly. And colorfully.

The bar took up the west wall, and tables and chairs—chairs similar to the broken ones they had first encountered—took up the rest of the place. Most of those were occupied by men and women who were eating, drinking, and arguing. Someone was playing a lute, and only half badly; no one was telling him to shut up, at any rate.

No one seemed to notice they were there.

She gaped.

"Taverson's," he told her, smiling slightly. "Food to be had, of a sort, for a price. They won't serve you ale at your age," he added, "but it's swill, so count yourself lucky. When you look older, you may have to actually buy some if you don't want to be tossed out."

Rath entered the dining room, found a table, and took a seat. "We look a mess," he said with a grimace, "but that usually means faster service."

But not, at least to start, friendlier service. The man behind the bar came out with something that could be called a scowl—except ten times worse.

Rath, however, laid his purse upon the tabletop, and as it was not obviously empty—and more to the point, in much better state than his clothing—the man's snarl diminished into something approaching politeness. He took Rath's order; Jewel was too intimidated by his height, width, and general bulk, to say a word.

Only when a woman came by with a tray that had two mugs, one small and one large, did Jewel relax. Because the woman took one look at Rath, plopped the tray on the table, and tried to hug him.

Rath endured this, to Jewel's surprise.

"I didn't recognize you without your beard!" she said. "You've been avoiding us. Carl, you lout, you didn't say it was Old Rath!"

The lout was behind the bar, and he looked up at his name, but his glare didn't change in any significant way.

"And who is this?" the woman asked.

"A friend," Rath replied, in a voice which discouraged further questions. Or should have. She asked anyway, and when Rath didn't answer, she turned that friendly ebullience on Jewel. Jewel didn't know what to say, and stared at the tabletop.

Thus defeated, the woman retreated, and returned about fifteen minutes later with food. It was warm, and it smelled good. Which was enough for Jewel.

Rath watched her eat. "Remember," he told her, as she ate, "to go past the kitchen quickly. It's likely that you'll be noticed, but you'll also be followed, and Taverson's not as bad as he looks; he'll try to stop your pursuers, or at least question them. It won't buy you much time," he added. "But the time it does buy will have to be enough."

She looked at him, forgetting to chew. The food was hot, but not hot enough to burn her tongue. It lost flavor, however, as the import of his words sunk in. She suddenly understood why he had brought her here. Taverson's.

She knew that the unknown girl would run by Taverson's. At night. Moon near full. And she had told Rath that she intended to wait for her someplace, thinking that he wasn't really listening.

A lesson, for Jewel. Rath always listened.

"If the girl is lucky," he told her quietly, "she won't be pursued by three men. If she is unlucky enough to be pursued by three, leave her be."

But as he said it, she watched his expression; his eyes were only slightly narrowed, and they were unblinking; his lips were neither compressed nor turned down in a slight frown; they were utterly neutral. It wasn't a request. But it wasn't an order either. He knew that if she were here, she would act.

Had brought her here because he knew it.

"Eat," he told her, with a genial smile that never touched that appraising gaze. "And eat well. I need to drop coin here, and I'm not particularly hungry."

"Why do you need to spend money?"

"Because, in case you hadn't noticed, greed overcomes suspicion in almost all walks of life. If I am here, and I spend money and tip well, nothing more will be said of my presence."

"And a lot about your absence?"

That caught him unawares, and evoked a smile. She was surprised at how much it changed his face, and because she hadn't his ability to hide behind her own, he saw this at once, and the smile was gone. "Could we take some of this home?"

He started to say no, and his eyes narrowed. "What you don't finish," he said at last. A concession to Lefty and Arann. "I don't want her thinking I run an orphanage, and I *certainly* don't want to give her the impression that I'm starting a less charitable form of business. Even greed has its limits."

Over the next two days, Jewel woke early in the morning; she went to the well, came back; went to the Common, came back. Made certain that Lefty and Arann were fed.

And then she and Rath went into the storeroom and vanished from sight for hours.

Rath wasn't kind. He was just short of openly derisive, which made the work harder. But it was work that needed to be done. The first run, from the apartment storeroom to Taverson's, was first; they would eat there, speak a bit with the owner's wife, and then, instead of leaving by the front doors, would leave by the storeroom there. This made Jewel less nervous than it would have otherwise, because Rath was *there*. He could make excuses, lie if necessary, and do both so perfectly that his presence in off-limits places seemed natural.

But he never had to.

She learned quickly. She watched the gray of endless rainy sky, and for the first time in recent memory, blessed rain; it meant she had time.

On the morning of the third day, Rath took her on both runs, and then, when they had made their way out of the storeroom, he returned to his room in silence, motioning Jewel to follow.

"Here," he told her quietly. "This is yours. Lose it, and you replace it; it was costly." He handed her a small, white stone, fire its heart. She was speechless as the cool surface touched her palm. "I trust you know how to use it?"

She nodded. A magestone. Her own. "I'll pay you—"

"Not now, Jay. Maybe later, when I'm in a merchant mood." At first, enthralled with this gift, she failed to notice that he was in the process of laying out clothing. He did this every morning, and the clothing varied greatly in quality.

But when he began to lay out his weapons, the magelight lost some of its shine; glinting steel did that. There was enough of it. And she didn't recognize some of the dagger sheaths, they seemed so like clothing.

"Rath—"

He shook his head. Opened the curtain that hid the window well, and its scant light, from view. She saw a dim hint of blue, and after a moment, realized what this meant. "What if it's the wrong day?" she asked him.

"Is it?"

"I—I don't know."

"Then we'll have to make educated guesses," he replied, turning back to the bed on which so much was laid out. "The sky is clear. The moon is not yet full."

She nodded. Drew breath. "Where are you going?"

"What did I tell you, Jay?"

"That I'm not allowed to ask that question."

"Good. Why are you asking?"

Her gaze lit on the daggers, and didn't move.

He donned them, wrapping them around his thighs, as if they were pants, or part of his pants. She wanted to touch them, and wanted to avoid looking at them. She managed the latter, and that took effort.

"Throwing daggers," he said, without looking at her face. "There is a moderate chance that I will not come home this eve."

She swallowed, and he turned to face her. "If I don't come home tomorrow, however, you're free to leave. Take your money, and take mine; if I'm not back, I probably won't have use for it."

She wanted to tell him not to go. The words almost left her lips. She *knew* he would be in danger. That the dagger sheaths would be at least partially empty; that he might be injured or killed.

She could say none of this.

But he saw it in her face, as he often did. He shook his head. "Never play cards," he told her.

"Not for money."

"Not for anything." He picked up his jacket and his satchel. The latter, he glanced at with some regret, as if he were certain he would lose it.

Finch.

A stranger. What was her Oma's rule? Family came *first*. And Rath? Was he family? She struggled a bit with the question. Not, certainly, by her Oma's blood definition.

"You don't have to leave yet," she said at last.

"I do," he replied. "I want to be in the Common for a few hours before I make my appointment; I want nothing at all to be traced here."

"You'll be followed when you try to leave the Common," she told him, her voice low. And certain.

"Will I?" His smile was odd. It was utterly unlike the unguarded amusement that had changed the whole cast of his features in the tavern; it was, however, genuine. In spite of this, she took a step back. This was a Rath that she seldom saw, and in truth, she didn't like it.

"Jay," he told her quietly, as he walked toward his door, "Have I forgotten to mention that I am not, at heart, a *nice* man?"

She shook her head. "Not forgotten," she managed to say.

"Good. I'm not. It is because—entirely because—of this fact that I may be home on the morrow."

And she realized, then, the significance of their first conversation in Taverson's. "You're going to draw them away."

"I? I am merely going to present something to the man I believe employs them. If they are, as you so quaintly put it, drawn away from a young orphan—if she is that—it will have little to do with my orders.

"If you don't remember by now how to follow the tunnels between Taverson's and here, you won't be back either."

She swallowed, nodded, and opened his door for him. Tried not to look at his back as he left, because she knew it was all of Rath she would see. Rath wasn't one for good-byes.

But after he left, she looked for a long time at the maps she had drawn with such determination. They were crude, and Rath had criticized them sixteen different ways, but they felt important enough that she simply curled them into a roll and stuck them on the edge of his desk.

Everything was sharper in the light of the open sun, this reprieve from the rains of the winter season. Even the smell of the streets was changed, the damp, heavy scent of moldy, wilting leaves giving way to a dry breeze. The streets were crowded with the old and the young, children and those who minded them; games were being played with sticks, stones, crude leather balls. Shouting and laughing punctuated the turn of those games, and Rath allowed himself the luxury of observation, seeing beyond the running, slender bodies of the underfed, the buildings that housed them, the open windows, the clothing that could be safely set out to dry.

Rath set out for the Common, moving slowly and without any obvious concern down the streets of the twenty-fifth. He had, of course, chosen to take the tunnels to arrive there; once there, in a territory that was in no way home, although it was familiar as all the poor holdings were, he lingered, letting himself be seen. He was neither dressed too richly nor too poorly, although he was on the edge of the former, and he did catch attention, stares, and the very youthful pointing that was instantly cut off where there was someone older and more experienced to notice.

The question of Jim's disappearance still disturbed him, and he had briefly considered spending the morning doing research into just that—but after consideration, he decided that it might trigger the type of interest he could not afford on this particular day. Later, he thought.

Later was a different country.

He did not go to the usual merchants that punctuated Jewel's daily routine. He desired no questions, and they would ask them; he desired no evidence of the life he actually lived. He could be almost certain that he was unobserved by anyone in a position to harm him, but almost was a far cry from certainty. And if he was called Old Rath in some quarters, there was reason for it. None of them were in evidence today. Were he in the right frame of mind, he would not be here.

Jewel's existence changed all frames of reference. He had not thought to accept this when he had first found her so unusual. He barely accepted it now. But he had, and he did, because he was here. Radell had been informed; Radell had set up the meeting—and although Rath had made it clear that he waited upon the whim of Radell's important client, he was completely certain that the meeting would take place. He was less certain that Radell's lovely shop would not be overrun by magisterial guards by the meeting's end, however that end played out.

Part of the way it played would be determined in the Common. Rath made his sauntering way to one of the few inns that were of note at the edge of the Common; it was near the Merchant Authority, and as such, was often frequented by men who had money and power. For the most part, their choice was a matter of convenience, and the more ostentatious of the new merchants chose to adopt rooms upon the Isle; the address itself was worth the doubling in cost.

He entered one of the four sitting rooms that the inn—dubbed the speckled egg, for a variety of reasons that had nothing to do with its actual name—possessed. It was the most informal of the four, the most formal being a ladies parlor, with appropriate chairs, tables, and service.

Still, informal was relative; it wasn't Taverson's. He was met at the door, and after he introduced himself by yet another name, was led into the room, with its low seats, its mock homey environment. The tables and chairs were old, but they were designed for comfort and a long stay. He took one, and waited.

He almost rose to leave when he saw the man who entered the room; it was not the man he was expecting. Patris Hectore, his godfather, was noted and noteworthy, but the man who had come in his place—and no other could have sent him—was both more and less so. Less, in that he had no official position, no title, and no obvious wealth; more, in that he was deadly.

Rath had once seen him kill, and it was Rath's opinion that the man would have been at home among the Astari, the almost legendary body of men and women upon whom the Kings depended for their safety. They were the bane and the fear of the Empire's patriciate; they were despised and watched by even The Ten. He was not, however, Astari. Or if he was, he had not claimed the association publicly.

He did not rise. Instead, he forced himself to look as relaxed and comfortable as any man who found himself in the speckled egg.

"Andrei," he said, as the dark-haired man joined him. "You look well."

Andrei was not, in seeming, a man who enjoyed small talk. But he was more than capable of it, and he smiled politely, and with an efficient sort of friendliness that could put hardened merchants at their ease. Rath, hardened by different things, was instantly on his guard.

Then again, around Andrei, he always was.

"The Patris sends his regrets," Andrei said, after asking after Rath in the politest of ways. "He finds himself unexpectedly detained in a meeting of some import to his House, and he begs your understanding and your patience. Matters of the House, of course, are his primary concern.

"But you are his godson, and he did not wish you to be left waiting for any period of time; he asked that I join you for the day."

Too much in those words to assimilate at once. While Rath digested them, Andrei ordered wine. It came quickly; the service was both efficient and unobtrusive. Rath couldn't name the vintage, and didn't care enough to try; the wine tasted like bitter water as he swallowed.

"Did he ask you to convey a message?" Rath asked at last, noting Andrei's clothing. It was workmanlike, but it was not the clothing he usually wore; it bore no obvious hallmarks of wealth, nothing to indicate that it was expensive. Andrei wore no sword, of course; as a servant to the Patris, and not a bodyguard, a sword was not only not required, but could be viewed as an active insult.

It was also not necessary.

"He asked me to convey a message," Andrei said, nodding agreeably. "Understand that, given the time constraints, he could not write it out himself, and he did not choose to dictate it; I am therefore quoting from memory, and memory, as you know, is often . . . unreliable.

"You asked about a Patris AMatie, a man who has been involved with the Merchant Authority in minerals and pearl trading. He is known to the Patris, albeit not well; they do not overlap much in their business interests. Because they do not, information about Patris AMatie was more difficult to obtain than it might otherwise have been." He smiled, and took a small stone out of his pocket.

This, he set upon the table between their glasses. He spoke a soft word, and passing his hand over it, he met Rath's gaze. Nothing about his expression changed, but his eyes grew colder.

Rath was impressed in spite of himself. The stone must have cost a small fortune. Hectore, of course, could spend a small fortune without noticing its loss, but he seldom chose to do it among the Magi. To the eye, it seemed a magelight; it had the right shape, the right color, and the right activation key.

But many things could be activated by word and gesture. This one? Silence, of a sort.

"What are we now speaking about?" Rath asked, with just the hint of a smile.

"Hectore's family," Andrei replied. "His troublesome sister and her unmarriageable daughter, his troublesome nephew and the possible difficulty his brother might be experiencing."

Not just silence, then. Rath shook his head.

"Yes," Andrei said, "it was costly. The more so because he did not have it to hand; it had to be crafted, and in speed. This may return to haunt us," the man added, with a small, sharp frown. "But I am known to serve your godfather, and the discussion would not be out of place among the merchant class. If we are overheard, we are overheard."

"And if someone is looking for magic?"

Andrei's brow rose a fraction. "They will find it," he said with a shrug. "It is stronger than the average magelight, but not by much, and not if the person searching is not looking directly at the stone."

"You think of everything."

Andrei shrugged. "I have to," he said softly. "And, of course, I have a few questions of my own, Ararath."

"As long as they don't involve Handernesse, I'll endeavor to answer them."

"I doubt that. I doubt that highly."

Rath smiled. His expression was not that different from the one Andrei wore. "Why did my godfather send you?"

"Because our investigations were . . . unsuccessful."

"Which means you can tell me nothing about the Patris."

"We can tell you that he appears to be sponsored by Patris Cordufar."

Rath whistled. "That's an old House." Not rival to The Ten in size or power, as some of the merchant houses had grown to be, but lineage, in the Empire, counted for much. "Is Cordufar still associated with The Darias?"

"Yes. House Darias has found that association profitable, and Patris Cordufar is not hurt by the association. He has not sought to better his standing with a more powerful House, but there is always risk in that.

"AMatie was brought in about ten years ago. From where, it is not clear. And I doubt that clarity will ever come of the investigation."

Rath frowned. "What else?"

"Very few men were willing to speak of Patris AMatie at all."

"Not unusual."

"But it is. He does not appear to be married; he does not appear to be otherwise involved. He keeps to himself, although he has a fine house upon the Isle. He has five servants; they are all men of roughly my age. They arrived with him when he arrived in Averalaan."

"You didn't try to speak with any of them."

"No more would anyone try to speak to *me* of the affairs of Patris Hectore. I did not see wisdom in making the attempt, however."

Which said much.

"He does have money. He uses it in odd pursuits. He is known to the Order of Knowledge as a hobbyist scholar."

"Everyone who is not a member of the Order is known that way," Rath said, with just a trace of annoyance.

"Indeed."

"His areas of expertise?"

"Ah, now that is interesting. It appears that he has some interest in knowledge of Ancient Weston."

Which was disappointing. "That much, I knew."

"Then I will add to your knowledge. You knew Member Haberas?"

Rath frowned. It had been months since he'd seen Haberas, but he knew the old man well. Truculent and wheedling by turns, he was the foremost authority in Ancient Weston writing in the Empire. "I know him."

"You knew him."

Rath's frown froze. "When?" he asked softly.

"Two months and seven days ago."

"How?"

"That *is* the question. He was found dead. He is an old man. Had he died of age, there would be no difficulty. Indeed, it was assumed that he *had*."

"But?"

"One of the Magi—Member APhaniel or perhaps Member Mellifas— has an investigation pending on the circumstances of that death. The magisterial guard has not been called," he added.

Rath did not ask how he knew about an internal investigation ordered by First Circle mages of the Order of Knowledge, not because he wasn't interested—he was—but rather because he had known Andrei for far too many years to expect more than a frown for an answer. Instead, he waited.

"Patris AMatie is a man of almost negligible needs. His food is the same, day in and day out, and it is sparse. Only when he entertains— which he does seldom—does it differ."

"Who does he entertain?"

"Merchants of the Guild."

"No other—"

"None whatsoever. If he has a private life—and I concede the possibility—it is conducted entirely off his grounds, and there is no trace of it that could be found on short notice." Andrei leaned back, lifting the wineglass that he would not actually drink from. He frowned, however, as its scent wafted beneath his nose; he was a very picky man, and his expression clearly said, *I have no intention of paying for this.*

Rath had no intention of causing a scene, however, and grimaced.

"Hectore believes that you have encountered AMatie in professional dealings in the Common." The neutrality of the statement bordered on the absurd. Rath, however, did not laugh.

"Given the deadline—"

"It was a *request,* Andrei, no more."

"Given the deadline that you imposed upon the gathering of information, it is not beyond belief that you intend to have similar dealings with him again. It is, of course, why I am here."

"Not to ask questions about the details of those dealings."

"That is beneath you, Ararath. Your godfather is fond of you, and has always been fond of you. I personally think that you hold on to too much, and for far too long, but my opinion is neither wanted nor relevant. He is concerned for you, however, given the death of Member Haberas. Is there cause for concern?"

Rath nodded quietly.

"Good. I hate to waste my time."

"So do I." Rath looked out the windows. He had grown so used to his dwelling that he had almost forgotten how much he liked sunlight. "The meeting is not for some few hours yet."

"And where will it take place?"

"Radell's."

Andrei raised a brow. Rath cleared his throat. "Avram's Society of Avealaan Historians."

Andrei nodded, although half of his attention had already wandered. "Will it not, at that time, be closed for business?"

"Radell is never closed for business when vast sums of money are involved. He is *always* willing to accommodate any customer who has spent thousands of crowns in his establishment."

"And you have something to sell?"

"Of course. Antiquities," he answered, before Andrei could ask. "Two bowls that were, I believe, used for household offerings. No, I'm not certain to which god. But I believe them to be genuine, and I will offer them to the Patris for his inspection this eve."

"Good. If things go well, we will not meet this eve."

"And if they do not?"

Andrei's smile was marked and cool. His gaze grazed Rath's daggers, and he added no words to his meaning. There was no need.

Had Rath been a prouder man, he would have refused Andrei's oblique offer. But pride he had left behind, when he had left Handernesse, and in truth, Andrei was more competent than most of the men Rath had met, or fought beside, in his life.

"I'll see to the bill," he said, rising.

"I wouldn't advise you to pay it," Andrei said, lip curling as he plonked the glass down on the table. "This is almost sour."

"I'm not of a mind to have a loud argument with the establishment's owner on this particular day," Rath replied. "Had I been alone, it would be different."

Andrei's smile was unexpected. "You've grown cautious, Ararath, if not wise. Good." He rose. "I will make my report to your godfather, if I have no cause to meet with you again." Andrei retrieved the stone he had placed on the table. "There are things at work here," he said softly, just before he pocketed the stone, "that I do not fully understand. Be wary."

Rath nodded and watched Andrei depart. With him went what little Rath retained from his life in Handernesse, and for a brief moment, he missed it. But brevity in such longing was always wise, and he shunted it forcefully to one side. He would sit here alone for another hour before he once again made his round of the Common.

He knew Andrei would already be out in the street, watching. Suspected that Andrei could identify all five of the men who served the Patris AMatie; if they were present, Andrei would know.

If they were dangerous? He would know that as well.

Rath almost regretted Jewel's absence. Her sight was so skewed and so unreliable he could not direct it or force it—but when it came upon her, when she had what she called her feeling, he learned much.

Jewel, he thought, *be ready. Be careful.*

"But where *are* you going?" Lefty stood in the frame of her door. Arann was on his feet, but he didn't look exactly comfortable; the doctor had said he would be in pain for some time, and he was to do no heavy lifting or work.

"Out," she said curtly. Which was not entirely true, but *in* had connotations which she was unwilling to share with anyone.

"Jay." Arann's voice. Arann, who had abandoned his bedroll, and who walked, slowly, to stand behind Lefty. Who, in fact, gently shoved Lefty to one side. Lefty threw him a mutinous glance, but held his peace. She had seriously misjudged Lefty, and was coming to understand how much only now. He had slowly accepted her presence, which she expected; he had started to meet her eyes, and there were whole hours that went by in which he now forgot to stick his three-fingered right hand in his left armpit.

But with this slowly growing trust came a sharpness of tongue which she would have bet money was beyond him. Given that it was her own money, she was just as glad she hadn't. Rath, the sonofabitch, would have taken the money anyway.

If she could ignore Lefty—and that was arguable—it was impossible to ignore Arann. When they were out together, Arann did all their talking, but Arann actually spoke very little.

"I can't talk about it," she said. Which was true. "Rath will kill me." Which was less true, although she had her suspicions.

"Your nightmare," Arann said. He, too, could surprise her. He was big, yes, and because he was often silent, because he was honest whenever he *could* be, it was easy to think of him as stupid. Well, okay, not *stupid*, but not perceptive.

She shrugged. "I'm sorry. It was just a nightmare. I have them all the time."

His brow rose. Gods, she was *such* a bad liar.

"This 'out' that you're going to," Arann continued, when she lost even the will to try to maintain a lie, "has something to do with that girl? Finch?"

"What makes you say that?" she asked, stalling. She had some time to kill. Not a lot, but some. She and Rath had gone to Taverson's every day, and had eaten there. Rath had introduced her to everyone, and they had taken note of her. She was to eat there, a late meal, and alone. Alone in Taverson's at night was not the place Jewel wanted to be—but Rath said she'd be safe enough there *because* they now felt as if they knew her.

"Sky's clear," Arann replied.

She frowned.

"You said the sky was wrong, that you could see the moon."

"Did I?" She honestly didn't remember. The nightmares did that to her. Then again, Arann had hardly been *awake*; it was unfair that he remembered more than she did.

"Jay."

"You can't go with me. Not where I'm going."

He met her gaze and held it. "You took your daggers," he said softly.

She changed tactics, a Rath word for fighting. "I want to keep you both here," she said, voice low and as intense as she could make it. "Do you understand? I want you both to live here. With me. With us.

"You try to follow me, and I can't even guarantee that *I'll* be able to stay when Rath finds out. And he will."

"I don't think Rath's as bad as you think he is," Lefty told her, meeting and holding her gaze.

"Doesn't matter what you think. Or what I think. Only what Rath thinks." She paused, and held out a hand, palm out. "I need you both to stay here. I can't say it clearer than that. You decide."

Lefty looked at Arann. Arann looked at Lefty. Neither spoke for a long moment, and when someone finally did, it was Lefty. "It's up to her," he said, shrugging awkwardly. "Rath's not here either, and I'd bet he's out doing something to help Jay."

Mostly, Jewel hated stupid people. But she realized at the moment that they had their advantages. She gazed down the hall at the storage room, and shrugged. The rope was in place. All she had to do was get to Taverson's, eat—and her stomach wasn't up to much in the way of food—and get to Finch before whoever was following her did.

And truth? She would have loved to take Arann with her. For safety, and for comfort. But his size, his strength, and his age hadn't done him much good so far. She told herself this as firmly as possible.

"Don't open the door," she told them, as she walked toward it.

"We know."

Chapter Eleven

THE MOON WAS NEARLY full. The skies retained the clarity of early afternoon, rare at this time of year, and the sea breeze was mild. Rath would have appreciated the evening walk at a different time. But the scenery was like so much stage dressing; he noticed it, but it did not move him. What might, he could not yet see: the men who hid in shadows, in the Common. Shadows, in any light, were always present where so many buildings were planted so tightly together. With the exception of the lands upon the Isle, this was the most expensive land in the City, and possibly the Empire. As it had been long since Rath had entertained the notion of owning much, he could admit that his knowledge might be out of date.

But he had never wandered far from Averalaan. In all her glory, in all her dinginess, she was his home. He had crossed several boundaries to be where he was, and in the crossing, had better come to understand all parts of her nature. Or all of the parts that could be understood.

The magestone that Jewel so envied was cool against his palm, its light guttered by the pocket of his jacket. Did he understand it? He could use it, certainly. He could evoke the brightest of its lights with a word, and dim that light again with a gesture. But utility and understanding were different creatures.

As a boy, he had dreamed of becoming a mage. In that previous life, all elevation, all power, seemed to be a grant of birth. But talent? It was not, like lineage, a thing which could be easily determined or quantified, and those gifted by its mysterious powers could come from any walk of life;

they were special. He could not now think of the boy he had been without wincing, he still remembered him so clearly.

Rath had never shown any sign of that—or any other—talent. Neither had his sister, or his friends. And eventually, the desire to be special had gone the way of all boyhood dreams, all futile romances and unrequited desire, crossing the dangerous threshold of envy and bitter resentment, to something that, at last, resembled calm acceptance.

He wondered how the mage-born saw the world. If they looked at a piece of wood and stopped to wonder how it came to be, examining it with the same momentary curiosity with which he examined their handiwork before turning again to other things. He wondered if magic was, in any sense, truly magical to those who labored with it. Wondered what surprised them, aside from the general—or specific—stupidity of other men.

Wondered what could kill them. Member Haberas was a scholar of the Order, but he was also mage-born and trained. He spoke seldom of that training, mostly because it did not seem to interest him much. Things dead, things gone, things hinted at in brief fragments—these were where his sense of unraveling mystery lay, and in his aged, wrinkled face, with its perpetual frown, they were the only things that could wake the eye's sparkle, speaking of a boyhood that was long past. But, regardless, he lived within the confines of the Order, content—barely—to let men like Rath bring him the things which he so valued and so delighted in; he did not, and had not, sought the adventure of their discovery for his own.

The Order of Knowledge was almost a fortress, although it didn't need to look as ungainly as one. It was hard to get in without a Member by your side; it was hard to leave without the same Member, which, in the case of the absentminded, could provide hours of amusement for the unwary. It was impossible to steal anything without magical aid, and as most of that aid lived in the building, Rath had never tried. Not, of course, that he hadn't been tempted, but even the temptation was simple curiosity rather than acquisitiveness; he wanted to see for himself what happened when he made the attempt.

So, reason followed, Member Haberas, if indeed he had been murdered, would have had to lead his murderer into his private quarters. Or another Member of the Order could have served this function. There were often bizarre rivalries between men of knowledge. Rath didn't begrudge them these tiffs, these angry postures; knowledge was, after all, their coin.

The third possibility, that someone had gained entry and exit without notice, did not bear scrutiny.

But Rath thought about it anyway, as he casually glanced at the streets. They weren't empty—they almost never were—but the people were scattered, and traveled in ones and twos. In the evening light, the colors of their clothing were muted, but they were not poor. The market guards generally cracked down on that sort of obvious trouble an hour before the stalls began to close.

But the Common wasn't walled, and if the market gates were in theory the easiest access to be had, they were not, by any means, the only one. On the other hand, Patris AMatie came openly, and it was likely that he, at least, would arrive by those gates. What would be interesting would be the knowledge of who arrived with him, if he did not travel alone. That would have to wait.

The pack on his back felt alternately too light and too heavy as he walked. He did not look back; he listened, but no more. If he were now being followed, it was of little consequence; both he and any who followed knew where he was going.

Radell's shop had one magestone in the fake but ambient lamp that hung windowside. To either side of his pretentious establishment, similar windows were dark, curtains drawn across them from within. One, however, had a guard posted; it was a jeweler's storefront. The man looked bored; he straightened visibly as Rath passed him by, his armor clinking at the shift in posture. Rath met his gaze and nodded politely, no more.

It began here, a few yards away from a bored man with wide shoulders and a pale scar across his forehead; it began with a knock on a door. Where it would end, Rath couldn't begin to guess—but he had hopes.

Radell had taken the time to dye his beard again. He had taken the time to make sure that his underpadding was properly positioned so it hung in the appropriate location over his belt; he looked almost genuinely old and sage as he swung the door wide and stepped to one side. This level of pretension, when the shop was dead quiet, would normally have been enough to elicit some sarcasm from Rath.

"Wade," Radell said, with just the slight dip of his unruly chin, "the Patris is waiting for you."

And probably listening, if Radell was being this formal. Rath was surprised that Radell actually remembered which of the many made-up names he'd used the last time the Patris had been present; Rath remembered it because it was distasteful. Wade, as far as Rath was concerned, was what one did in shallow water of either persuasion.

"Avram." Rath's bow was all the sarcasm he allowed himself, and it failed to make any impression on the density that was Radell's greed. "Is he alone?" he added quietly.

Radell frowned. Clearly, if this was an act, Rath, as an actor, had severely sidestepped the lines assigned him. He failed to repeat the question, and Radell, grotesquely aping obsequiousness, led him toward the private room at the back of the still dusty store.

It was, by contrast, spotless. Everything was gleaming, and a tray of small crudités lay at the center of the ostentatious table. Patris AMatie sat in one armchair, his hands upon the rests. Seated, he was still an imposing presence—one that almost demanded silence. Or fear. He was, of course, perfectly attired, but he still chose black as his color; there was a flash of something that might have been jewel red at the base of his throat, no more.

He had no guards with him.

"Wade," he said, lifting only his chin. His eyes were dark, and his gaze unfettered by an apparent need to blink.

Rath, however, bowed. It was not a bow of equals, but it was graceful enough; let him think on it.

"It has been some time since Radell has sent word to me, and I admit that I was beginning to feel a certain . . . disappointment. The pieces you brought the first time we met were of great interest to me, and I look forward to seeing what you will offer me this eve."

Rising from his bow, Rath decided against the other empty chair in the room, and after a moment, Radell occupied it. His supposed girth fit it neatly, but his hands didn't press against the rests; they were troubling the edge of his beard.

All this, Rath noticed as he removed his pack and set about unbuckling it. He was deliberate in his movements, and spent neither more nor less time than necessary; nothing about his movements implied that he was in a hurry. But he wanted to be quit of this place as quickly as possible.

He unwrapped the bowls with care. This, he would have done had he been seated before a fractious Member of the Order of Knowledge, although perhaps he would have moved more slowly. He found amusing the anxiety and greed that such Members often showed, and he liked to extend it.

If the Patris was greedy in that traditional sense of the word, none of it showed on his face. In fact, nothing showed on his face at all; it was like a stone mask, dark eyes almost livid with the intensity of his stare.

He handed the Patris the first of the two bowls; the one with a cracked seam. Patris AMatie took it without comment, moving from the armrests for the first time since Rath had entered the room. Rath watched him turn the bowl over in his hands, and watched that frozen face for any sign. Of what?

His hands were dry. He was silent.

Even Radell seemed slightly cowed; he started his usual babble, but the words rarity and valuable were the only words which were notably audible. Given that Radell could outshout a poor farmer hawking his wares at the market's busiest hour, this said much.

"Where," Patris AMatie said at length, "did you find this?" He set the bowl upon the table, leaning slightly forward.

"It's a family heirloom," Rath replied, with the practiced ease of a habitual liar. "A man of my acquaintance has fallen on hard times, as so many of us do. He did not consider it of worth or note; the writing along the rim, in his eyes, was a pattern, no more."

"And you failed to inform him of its value?"

"Value," Rath replied, just as easily, "is in the eye of the beholder."

"Do you know what it was used for?"

"This one? Nothing much. It's cracked," he added, with a slightly apologetic smile. "The other, which is similar, was used for water, but it wasn't considered decorative enough to be used often."

"You have another?"

Rath nodded, and went through the same process of unwrapping and revelation. He handed the second bowl to the Patris, and the Patris made some show of studying it. It was a poor show, even to Radell, who nervously cleared his throat five times.

"I assure you," he began, but the Patris lifted a large hand, and Radell swallowed the rest of his words. Given how many of them there usually were, it was a small wonder he didn't choke on them.

"I will take them both," the Patris told Radell, but his eyes never left Rath's face.

"The price—" Radell began.

"Three thousand crowns for the cracked bowl; five thousand for the whole." The words were delivered without inflection; had they been spoken by any other man, Rath would have bet money that the speaker was bored. And far, far too wealthy for wisdom.

But not this one. "You are aware that the marks upon the rim are Ancient Weston words." It wasn't a question.

Rath shrugged broadly. "They're faded in places," he said. It had frustrated him greatly in his attempts to take good etchings. "And I confess that my understanding of Ancient Weston is poor. I made some assumptions based on these," he added, pointing to a random set of runes. He noted the subtle shift in the Patris' expression, and wondered what he had just pointed at. He noted the section of the rim, no more. "But I have not had time to confirm those suspicions. Do you recognize the runes?"

The shrug was theatrical. "As Ancient Weston, yes." A pause, a deepening of the glitter of black eyes—eyes that should never have been able to reflect light in quite that fashion. "No one else has seen these?"

"No one else," Rath replied smoothly, "is willing to better the price you paid for the last pieces I delivered."

At this, the Patris did smile. Rath preferred the mask; there was something in the smile that was almost feral. It was also brief.

The Patris rose. "I will leave these in your care," he said, looking at Radell for the first time since Rath had entered the room. "And I will send the agreed-upon sum on the morrow."

Rath began to wrap them up again; it was habit. Radell was almost insensate with that peculiar joy that comes from vast sums of money, and he didn't trust the little merchant not to damage the ancient bowls.

"You are an interesting man," Patris AMatie said to Rath, as he walked toward the door, blocking the only exit. He stood there, the frame inches above his head.

Rath tilted his head slightly in acknowledgment. "And you, Patris, are a wealthy one. I admire your ability to collect these items, but I confess that I see little of value in them beyond your interest."

"That is all that is required."

"As you say. I hope to do business with you again."

Patris AMatie smiled. "As do I." His words were a whisper, something soft and dark.

What Radell heard in them, Rath couldn't say—but it was clearly not what Rath heard. The little merchant gathered the bowls in his shaking hands and headed toward the door. AMatie stood for a moment, his hand upon the frame—and Rath thought they would collide, Radell was now so oblivious.

But at the last minute, the Patris moved, allowing Radell to leave. Rath, no fool, trailed after him, keeping as little distance as possible between them. It would have been unseemly in other circumstances, but Rath had no desire to remain in a room with the Patris.

And he suspected that the Patris knew it.

Radell went to his desk. Rath stood in front of the mess for a few minutes, and then said, "I'll be back in a few days." Radell barely looked up, but did manage to nod, and Rath knew that he could have said eight thousand crowns instead, and it would have made more sense to the merchant. He would try to dislike it more later. The Patris was also in the back of the store, and he lingered like shadow cast by unwanted light.

It was difficult to ignore him; Rath had already chosen his mode of behavior, or he might have switched into the fawning and obsequious, to better gauge the man's reaction. He suspected, on the other hand, that it wouldn't have much effect.

"I do hope to meet with you soon," the Patris said quietly. He spoke to Rath, and Rath nodded briskly.

"As do I," he said, "when I have something of interest to offer."

In the silence, the words "of interest" twisted. Rath bowed formally, as the difference in their obvious ranks demanded, and rose. He turned and walked out of the shop, his gaze toward the door and its gaudy window, the magelight still bright on the other side. He saw, as he reached for the door's tarnished brass, the unmoving reflection of Patris AMatie; the man's eyes were clear and unblinking.

Rath wondered, for just a moment, if Radell would survive. He was fond of the merchant for a number of reasons, not the least of which was his money. But he was not so fond that he was willing to die with him, and in Patris AMatie, at that moment, Rath saw and felt only death, and the stillness of the assassin before the blade falls.

He pulled the door in, took a breath, and stepped into the bracing wind of clear night, bright moon, and the whisper of the hunt.

Wondering, as he did, what Jewel might tell him now, if he had been willing to risk her.

*   *   *

Jewel cursed Arann and Lefty in both of the languages she knew. Cursing in Torra had been an early delight—when her Oma wasn't present—and cursing in Weston had come later, in an excited, bartering exchange of foul words with a young boy she'd met in the line to the well near her old home. His pale hair and startle of blue eyes marked him as Northern, at least by birth, as did his reddened skin. The Northerners, it was said, lived in a land of near-perpetual Winter, and no one burned in the Winter sun. Jewel, dark-haired and ruddy, had looked as much his opposite as a bored child of the city streets could. She'd said something in Torra, and when he asked what she'd said, told him what it meant; he brightened visibly and told her what the Weston word would be.

It had been one of the more useful things she'd gotten from a stranger. She thanked him for it again, although she'd never asked his name. Nameless boy, she thought, and one of many.

But mostly she thought about strangling Arann and Lefty. Had they just shut up and left her alone, she could have taken the tunnels, and been in Taverson's by now. She could mark the moon's height, although she hadn't thought to do it until Rath had asked where, and above which building, she had seen it in her brief glimpse of Taverson's. Nightmare vision was clear and strong. She could answer.

And because she could, she could pay attention. While cursing in Torra and Weston. She cursed under her breath—when she bothered with breathing. The thirty-fifth holding at night was no place she wanted to be—and she was not only in it, but walking its streets. Its empty streets, so like a different country she almost failed to recognize the buildings in front of which small children played during sunup.

Why can't I just come up through the storerooms?

It will be busy enough they'll be in use. They see you as harmless, Rath added, unaware of how the word had stung, but if they find you there, they'll see you as a thief, and you'll be out on your backside long before it's time. Take the maze to the thirty-second, Jay. Be as careful as I've taught you to be, and enter as obviously as possible through the front doors.

You'll need to leave by the other doors, and that will be the only time you'll use them.

She had to reach the tavern.

And because it was important, she tried to remember every damn word Rath had ever said about walking without being seen. It didn't help much, though; the echo of her own steps dogged her, making her spin on a heel every time she was near an alley.

In the end, more for comfort than utility, she drew one of the two daggers Rath had given her. He had taught her how to hold it so she didn't slice her own fingers off, and had taught her where, so that sweat didn't make the hilt slippery enough that it ceased to be hers at all. She pointed out that she'd carried a knife the day they'd first met, and his snort of derision made clear what he thought of that knife.

He had also refused to be distracted by an argument about where that knife had gone.

He'd tried to teach her how to throw—but throwing knives was difficult, and in the end, she'd managed to get up to lousy by dint of stubborn effort.

Neither of the daggers was balanced for throwing. She'd do more damage throwing a large rock, and be just as likely to hit anything that needed hitting. A stray glance at the pools of dark street that existed between the magelights didn't immediately surrender sight of such a rock.

Kalliaris, she thought, desperate now, *smile.*

And then, without thinking, added, *Smile on Rath. Smile on Finch.* It was best, with the goddess of luck, to wish luck for someone else, a superstition that Jewel usually forgot to heed.

She held the dagger close to her side as she walked; its flat brushed her thigh. The sea winds were higher than was usual at night, and she briefly wondered if they meant a storm was coming—but the night was still clear, and if there were clouds, the wind would have some trouble blowing them here in time to hide that moon.

Whenever she heard footsteps, she froze. But it was deliberate, this chosen paralysis; she found a building with an open door, and hid a moment as the steps passed by; she found an alley, and crouched on her heels as far from the street as she could, without losing sight of it. She hated walking at night, because it made her feel small and isolated—but she had to admit that night had enough shadows.

She listened for screaming. Or steps that fell quickly, rather than slowly; she listened and watched the moon and cursed, and cursed, and cursed. But even cursing, she began to edge through the streets, and the cross streets; toward the river. The river, she knew. Bridges, banks, places where garbage was momentarily strewn—she wasn't at home there, but she could be almost safe.

Almost would have to do. She'd dressed warmly, which was good. The night was cool, the breeze a bite of sensation across exposed skin. Shivering, she almost cut herself, and decided that maybe the dagger was better in its sheath.

Awkward sheath, Rath-sized, it butted against her ribs no matter how she adjusted it, reminding her of all the ways in which her life and Rath's didn't fit together. But he was out here, in the streets of the holding, and beneath the same moon.

The Patris didn't bother with an obvious tail, this time. Or if he did, obvious was too simple a word. At night, the Common was as brightly lit as most of the Isle, and although the street onto which Radell's ridiculous shop faced wasn't empty, it might as well have been. He saw a slender boy duck out of sight, and smiled; he knew the look. If that was what the Patris had hired this time—

Knew the look.

But the scream? It was high and terribly brief.

Time, Rath thought, to get moving. He didn't look back; didn't pause to see if the boy emerged running. Because he'd heard similar screams from older throats before, and he knew that whatever emerged wouldn't appreciate a witness.

One man's cowardice was another man's wisdom. The most important rule Rath had learned about fighting was that survival was the only thing that counted. He listened as he walked, his stride so wide Jewel would never have been able to follow, and in the darkness, he thought he heard footsteps.

But turning, just once, as he banked sharply around the circle that surrounded the Common in a rudimentary road, he saw nothing that might have made those steps. He saw magelights, on storefronts and above them, and he saw windows, much like Radell's, whole panes of glass unbroken by simple lead bars.

It was the windows that caught the corner of his eye, not the street itself; the street was still. But across the surface of those reflective panes of glass, a shadow moved. One, perhaps two; their forms were indistinct because they were in rapid motion. Nothing appeared to cast those shadows, and Rath felt the night grow cold indeed as he realized exactly how he had managed to miss the last man who had followed him so cunningly.

Magery. Here.

And if Andrei's stone had been expensive, whatever now hooded his followers from sight was something that Rath would have sworn could not be purchased; it was, by Imperial decree, illegal without a writ from the Magisterium. All magic beyond a certain base level was.

And whoever was following him either felt confident enough that a writ might be granted, should it be required, or they didn't intend to see him take complaint to the magisterial authorities. He was betting on the latter.

He began to run.

When she heard the slow steps of a larger group, Jewel once again found an alley to hide in. They were coming down the street, and they were accompanied by voices; she thought they must be either drunk or close enough as made no difference. Loud voices, men's voices.

Unlike Rath, she had no certain sense of where the holdings changed number; had no certain way of knowing when she had left the thirty-fifth for the thirty-whatever. She knew moonlight, and the moon's position seemed to have shifted by slow degree between the buildings' heights. She also knew that she couldn't afford to be seen. In the weeks since she'd been with Rath, she'd lost the hungry look that clearly said she had nothing worth stealing.

She crouched, waiting, as the steps grew louder and closer. There was no anger in the voices; she might have thought them happy, had she heard them in the safety of her Oma's arms, in a different life. But happiness in the holdings meant many things, as she'd discovered, and she had no intention of adding to the wrong kind.

Waiting was hard, this last time. She felt a wrongness as she crouched that made her want to run, and she held on to her knees, grinding her chin into them, and trusting the shadows.

Mistake, that, to trust shadows.

Or bridges. Or rivers. Or even Kalliaris.

The steps went by; she hid her face, her hands, things that might show the wrong glimpse of color if someone was actually paying attention. She stopped breathing, as if breathing was more audible than the song they were singing. Weston song, rude words melting into syllables and laughter.

When she lifted her face again, when she pulled shaking hands from around her shins, she looked up.

Saw the glint of a dagger, when her own hand was empty.

*   *   *

This was not the plan, but so few plans survived. Rath ran, and his steps were the light steps of a fencer or a dancer, things he might once have been, had he chosen to weather life behind the walls of the manor that had once been home. He did not choose grace for show or even for comfort; he chose it because it was the most silent way of moving. What vision would not easily surrender, hearing might.

And he heard steps, now, heavy steps, scraping across the cobbled stones as if made by steel boots. Fast, he thought. He could not guess at the size of the men who made them. Had they not been so close, he might have chosen to enter the tunnels, but the tunnels were their own form of treachery to one in flight, and if he were cornered there, there was no guarantee that he could stand and fight.

If one could stand and fight against something that couldn't be seen.

Still, hearing surrendered what sight had only barely hinted at, in the windows of merchants and light: there were two. Jewel had spoken of three, and this meant that—if all supposition, all guesswork, all folly were accurate, she faced only one.

"They're gone."

Not the words she expected to hear, surrounded by walls in a narrow passage between two buildings. But the voice was also not the voice she expected—and as she allowed the words to actually make sense, she also realized that the person who uttered them was young.

Maybe her age, maybe a bit older or a bit younger; it was hard to tell. He was thin, bone-thin, but taller than Jewel, and half his face was obscured by hair. Then again, half of hers usually was as well, the difference being that when hers was in her eyes, she shoved it out of the way.

In the shadows of the alley, it was hard to see his expression, given that a third of his face was hidden.

"You should do something about your hair," she said, risking first words without exactly choosing them.

He shrugged, almost bored, as if he'd heard it all before and didn't care. But he hadn't been crouching, and she hadn't even heard him enter the alley. Wondered which way he'd come.

He was wearing clothing that didn't fit him, but unlike Arann's, his was on the large side. It was heavy, and the color was hard to determine;

something dark. Either he was part of a den, had a family, or was a much better thief than she had ever tried to be.

His knife hand didn't shake.

"You know them?" he asked, still holding that dagger, and still staring down at her.

She shook her head. "And I didn't want to," she added, slightly defensively.

"No," he said softly, "you don't."

As she had assessed him, he now assessed her. Low whistle, but still a boy's whistle. "What are you doing out here?"

"Hiding."

"Ha ha." The dagger came closer, but it had to; the boy did. His pants, she thought, were also on the large size. They were rolled up over bare feet, exposing large ankles. Which answered one question: He was a better thief. "What are you doing out here at night? Running away from home?"

She shook her head.

"Not a smart thing to do," he added, and for a moment, there was an edge of anger and bitterness in the words. She thought he might threaten her. He looked as if he were deciding.

Rath had taught her how to fight, sort of. Most of the lessons simply centered around how to cause enough pain that she could then run away. She unbent slowly, her palms out, watching the boy's face. Faces gave the most away, when there was anything to give away.

His was shuttered like a window against the Winter rains.

"I'm trying," she said, making a bitter decision of her own, "to save someone's life."

She saw a brow rise into the length of hair across forehead. Just one, though. "By hiding in an alley?"

"I'm not going to save anyone if I need saving myself," she snapped back. Then, "My name's Jay."

"Like the bird?"

"Like the letter."

"Letter? Oh, you're educated." The dagger shifted. "Well-off girl. This is not your part of town."

"I live in the thirty-fifth."

"You work there?" The word work had unmistakable meaning. At one time, she would have hated it. A year ago. Maybe less. Now?

236 ✦ Michelle West

"No." No pride in the word at all, just fact. Fact and moonlight, the knowledge that it was moving. "Look," she said, "you're hungry, right?"

"Do I look hungry?"

"Aren't we all?"

That stopped him for a minute. "Who are you trying to save?" he asked at last. "You have family here?"

She shook her head. "Dead. My father was last to go. In the shipyard."

"You belong with a den?"

She almost snorted. "How? What would I have to offer?"

It was the right answer, sort of. "Then who are you trying to save?"

"Some girl," she said at last. "Named Finch."

"Finch?"

"Like the bird."

"Friend of yours?"

"Hope so."

His single visible eye narrowed, as if he thought she was making fun of him. But because she was a lousy liar, and because everything—as Rath constantly pointed out—showed on her face, the narrowing didn't turn into a glare. "You're trying to save someone you don't know?"

"Something like that."

"So you're stupid."

"That, too." Not that she didn't want to slap him for saying so, but the moon—the damn moon—wasn't staying still. "Look," she added, balling her hands into fists and lowering them to her sides, "if you're going to try something, can you do it now? Because I don't have a lot of time."

He stared at her. "Maybe you're crazy," he said at last. "My name's Carver." To make his point, he twisted his knife in the air. She wondered when he acquired it, but only briefly. "You said something about food?"

"Food? Oh. Right. I'm going to Taverson's. You know it?"

He shrugged, which could have meant anything.

"But I have to get there soon."

"Meeting someone there?"

"Hope so." She paused, glanced out into the street. "Can you use that thing?"

He shrugged again.

"Well, don't use it on me. If you want, you can follow. I can feed you there; I have to eat something anyway." And two people were safer than one. Not that, at this age, two people amounted to much. "Where do you live, anyway?"

"Somewhere around here."

Which was fair enough. She had no intention of telling him where she lived. But she winced when she saw his feet.

"The old ones fell apart," he told her. "It ain't cold yet. I'll find better."

She was just hoping that they let him in.

Rath retraced his wide steps as the city streets darkened. The sound at his back made it clear that his pursuers were never far enough behind that he could take advantage of the terrain and his superior knowledge of the holding. If, indeed, it was superior.

The reflective surface of glass, blended with light, had given him his only glimpse of the men that followed him, and if he strayed farther from the circular road, he would lose that. The holdings were not known for the quality of their windows; not the ones he knew well. And the ones that he'd have to cross featured gates and fences as the roadside attraction. He couldn't climb them quickly enough to make use of them either.

All this, on the run. To stop was death.

Living was incentive.

Taverson's was crowded. That much, they could hear from three buildings away. It made Jewel stop dead in her tracks, but Carver was careful enough that he didn't collide with her back. Instead, he waited. She took a deep breath, and the wind brought the scent of smoke and sweat to where she waited. Apparently, the crowd at night was either larger or a whole lot louder.

She wasn't certain which she wanted, but she approached the swinging door, trying to straighten up. She needed to look taller.

Carver actually snickered.

With a pointed glare at his bare feet, she shoved the door open and stepped in. The light was bright enough that she had to blink, and if it hadn't been, the smoke was thick enough to cause the same reaction. The noise was almost overwhelming; so much for her plan to sit still and listen hard. Not that it was the plan, but she'd had hopes.

She looked for the familiar barmaid, and saw no one. Given her height, it wasn't much of a surprise. But there was a clear path—of a sort—from the door to the back where most of the tables were, and she began to make her way toward them, looking at people's feet.

"Hey, you!" She jumped. The voice was familiar. It was, in fact, Taverson's voice. But louder and a lot less friendly. Not that it was friendly to start with.

"No, not you," he added, and she realized that shouting was his only available method of being heard. "The one behind you. You!"

Carver. She turned; he was standing there, chin tilted up in awkward defiance. She reached out and grabbed his shirtfront, her fingers closing around cold buttons and a handful of heavy cotton. He was surprised enough to lose the growing expression, and off-balance enough that he stumbled. "Put the damn knife away," she shouted in his ear.

He looked at it in surprise, and then flushed. Made him seem younger, which made her more comfortable.

"He's with me," she said, in the same shout, as she turned to face the tavern's owner, keeping Carver behind her back by the simple expedient of the shirt leash. From where Taverson stood, he probably couldn't see Carver's feet. She hoped.

This good news did not diminish the tavernkeeper's annoyance. "With you? Rath know about this?"

She nodded vigorously, hoping that the smoke was as thick as it looked.

He snorted, and she could swear there were eddies in the air that followed the sound, traveling through the room.

"Take a seat at the back," he shouted. "Both of you. Stay out of trouble. You!" He shouted, at Carver again. "I see anything shiny that isn't round and copper, you're picking up your own teeth before I throw you out. Got it?"

She tugged on the shirt, hard.

"Yes."

"What?"

"Yes, sir!"

"Good. Now scram."

Jewel dragged Carver toward a table that looked sort of empty; it was crammed up against a wilting, yellow potted plant. She was surprised it wasn't dead because, if she'd had to live here, she would be. Only one man attempted to get in their way, more out of amused malice than any real threat, and Marla, swinging her way out of the back kitchen, kicked his knee. "This isn't the right time of day, Jay," she said, in a loud, loud voice that didn't quite sound like shouting.

"I'm sorry."

"Can't hear you, love. But don't worry. We'll take care of you." She waded past, and people got out of her way.

"What do you want to eat?" Jewel shouted, in Carver's ear.

"What?"

And gave up. She couldn't see the street from here; she couldn't see the moon. She'd expected the door to be open, and it wasn't. The streets might as well have been in a different holding. And the moon in a different sky.

Getting home wasn't going to be the problem she'd been terrified about. It was getting to Finch in time, and that one was infinitely worse.

She turned to look at the stranger she'd dragged into the tavern, trying to think of some excuse for leaving him here. Trying to think at all.

Carver's feet hurt. It was warmer in the tavern than he'd been in two days. Smokier, but he'd trade smoke for rain, about now. Or heat. He would have massaged his toes, but he didn't want to look weak or pathetic. That had costs.

Jay? Jay. Was staring at him. He tried to meet that odd look with a glare, with what might pass for a glare, if she could see both his eyes. She kept pushing her hair off her face, and it kept springing back; he wondered what it must be like to have hair that stupid. Might have asked, but truth was, he was starving, and he wanted food. Whatever food she'd buy. He could save the rest of the words for later.

His stomach had stopped aching sometime yesterday. He'd had water—water was easy—but although he'd come up with an unexpected bonus in the form of an unconscious drunk man, food was just damn scarce. It was the feet, really. By the time he'd managed to roll the man over and unbutton his tunic, strip off his pants, he was already beginning to groan—and the shoes, way too big, couldn't be had in safety. He cursed himself as he ran; he should have started with the damn shoes first.

Bare feet could be seen by the market guards a mile off. They weren't harsh, but they didn't budge; he was entirely unwanted in the Common. Fair enough, because he had no coin to spend but charm and sleight of hand; it was a game that they both understood, and even if it ended in death, it had its rules.

Finding this weird girl had been an accident.

He couldn't decide if it was Kalliaris smiling or frowning. Gods were perverse, and what they gave with one hand, they could take with another, and backhand you in the process. Carver didn't trust the gods.

Carver didn't trust anyone.

But was he going to feel threatened by a girl? She was, what, nine? Ten? Hard to tell, and hard to ask. She had a dagger; he'd seen that right away. Wasn't completely certain if she knew how to use it, but was completely certain he knew how to use his better. Things would have been different, had his brother survived the den fight.

Bitter memory. Hungry memory. All the "what ifs" in the world. Jay was frightened. He knew she was scared when he saw her crouching in the alley, but that made sense; he wasn't hiding in it himself for no reason. Not that the Harricks were hunting him, at least not tonight, but they took what they could when they had the chance.

There, surrounded by old brick and warped stairs, fear was normal. He wondered if it was normal in a tavern, because he hadn't really spent much time inside one. Hunger didn't deprive him of senses: What he smelled, what he could see—the dying plant, the wide, tall men, the golden glasses and dull tin mugs—and what he could touch, he would remember. Beneath his hand, he could feel runnels in the flat, hard surface of the table. Someone had started to carve something here.

Someone had had something to carve. A dagger would have done the job—but Carver had nothing he wanted to leave behind in something as dead as wood. It didn't bleed, and it didn't scream.

Then again, it didn't cause bleeding or screaming either, and maybe that was the point.

The big woman with the dark hair and the slightly saggy cheeks came round a wall made of men in different textures; bearded, red-haired, gold-haired, bald and dark; tall, short, fat, thin, things in between; wool, leather, cotton shirt darkened at armpits and chest; smoke everywhere, like tendrils of mist. Heavy, smelly mist.

But big and old, this woman seemed to part that mist; it didn't swallow her, and the men wavered, falling a step to one side or the other as she almost pushed her way past them, carrying a full tray. There was leftover food on some of those plates, and Carver, had he been a different boy, would have wept in outrage at the waste.

But not here. Not here, where everyone would notice, and he would draw attention of the unwanted variety. If there was any other kind of attention.

The woman disappeared into the swinging door in the far wall, and when she emerged again, the tray she carried was less unwieldy, less a mass of teetering dishes and waste. She elbowed someone out of the way, and Carver heard the man's bark of annoyance, but not the actual words he used. From her look, they didn't bother her.

Then again, from her look, nothing did.

His stomach woke and growled; he would have been fatally embarrassed had it not been so damn noisy. Jay's lips were moving. He couldn't hear a word she said. It didn't matter; the large woman was making her way toward their table; whatever she carried, it was meant for them.

Two days, and the food he'd had before had been cold and almost moldy. Bread. A shriveled apple that had rolled off the back of a wagon and into the street, bruised and unnoticed by anything but mice. They had taken small bites, but he didn't care.

If he'd been able to catch them, he'd have eaten the mice as well.

She placed big bowls on the table; they were steaming. She put a spoon and fork to either side of the bowls, and offered them large cloth squares. Between the bowls, she dumped a basket of cut bread—and as much bread as he'd had in weeks—and then she was off again, shouting something into the suddenly unimportant distance.

Jay tried to grab her elbow, to touch her—her voice wasn't loud enough to do that on its own. But she missed.

Carver didn't care. He picked up the spoon in a shaking hand, and shoved it into the stew in front of him; his mouth tasted of dry salt, and his throat tightened.

For his trouble—this lifting of spoon to stubborn mouth—he burned himself. Couldn't withhold the yelp of pain, couldn't spit out the chunk of potato. His eyes watered, and he wiped them clear with his sleeve.

When he looked up, he met Jay's dark eyes, half interrupted by hair. Hers and his. He couldn't tell her he'd burned his mouth. He couldn't expose that much stupidity.

But she rolled her eyes, shaking those tight, awkward curls. The fear was still in her; her shoulders were tense, and her back was hunched slightly, as if against an expected blow. That, he knew.

He expected her to eat. He really did. Even fear couldn't stop him, and he was almost too giddy to feel it. But she rose instead, cupping her hands around her mouth, bending across the table, her sleeve trailing the sharp edge of cut bread. "I need to go outside for a minute. Wait here!"

It occurred to him that she intended to leave him here, with no means of paying for what he ate.

She saw it, too. "It's already covered," she shouted again. "Mother's blood, I swear."

The stew was too hot. Carver ate the bread instead, waiting. Watching, as he chewed, the back of the strange girl as she tried to traverse the same narrow gaps in the crowd that the big woman had made larger simply by frowning.

Gods, he was hungry. The stew was hot. If it hadn't been for the bread—which was quickly disappearing, this would have been like stories of the Hells.

The night air enveloped her like the answer to a prayer she hadn't known she was uttering; it was clear and cold, and although she reeked of smoke, it didn't. She'd always liked pipes; she had never imagined that there would be a time when she would need to escape them. But the moon—

She was late, she thought, wild now. Late. After everything that had happened—

Finch.

And as the hair rose on the back of her neck, as her skin suddenly went that particular cold that was part fear and part something she'd been born to, she heard at last the ragged, heaving breath of a high, light voice, and from the vantage of Taverson's door well, she saw a small figure careen around the corner three buildings down the road. In the moonlight, shift torn, shoes slapping the undersides of her feet because the soles had started to come off, came a girl that Jewel had never seen.

And knew, in an instant, as Finch.

Rath slid into a narrow alley used by servicemen; it was girded, on either side, by the finest of the shops in the Common. He turned, silent, on heel, breathing too quickly. He no longer felt the evening cold, except as a trace in his lungs. Across from the shops that served as tactical protection were similar shops, two clothiers, one gallery. Each had pretty, colorful displays, and the magelights here were fine and bright; the gallery had somehow managed to mask that light so it fell in shades of different greens, as if to suggest forest without substance. It was very contemporary, a work that was based on a subtle appreciation of the nuance of mood.

Rath's not-so-subtle appreciation was reserved for the windows. He watched them, drawing his daggers. It was tricky to be silent, here, and the light would catch the sheen of his blades' flats; he chose the throwing daggers. But here, at least, the narrow walkway was one good man wide, no more.

Not perfect for the sword he'd carried. He might draw it later, if it came to that.

He heard pursuit, but only barely. It was almost as if the men who followed, unseen, walked barefoot across the perfect cobblestones of this stretch of the Common. He listened for breathing, for the sound of exertion; the men were good. He heard none.

But in the windows across the street, all bay windows, glass facing him and facing, as well, to the sides, he caught again the vague glimpse of his pursuers. They moved quickly, traversing one angled pane, but he was certain, now, they were two.

Two shadows, and tall; one man slightly wider. He could not see the reflected gleam of a weapon in either of these passing impressions. It should have made him feel safer, but oddly enough, it made him more wary, if that were possible. He shifted the left dagger in his hand, lifting his left arm, slowly, always slowly, as he watched. Trusting his aim to reflections across the passing fancy of current fashion trends: a ball gown that trailed from shoulder to temple train in a deep, deep blue that spoke of money.

He waited, judging distance. Trying to see where they might stand— in mid-street, if they were confident of their illegal magical tools. They crossed the dress again; the front facing portion of the bay was at an angle to where Rath now stood, protected by a lip formed of buildings, an open, silent mouth.

He raised his right arm, as his left held steady, and counting as the shadows wavered and flickered, a mix of light and surface, he took a guess, and threw.

The trajectory of daggers in flight ended in seconds; he heard them hit. There was no response, no grunt, no sound, and the daggers hung suspended in air for just a moment before they wavered, as the reflections did, and disappeared.

He drew two more, but held them as his intended victim finally responded. With laughter.

They were close, now, and they could see him; he did not have the advantage of seeing them in turn. Listening, tense, he retreated two steps. Let them come one at a time.

Jewel bounded up the three stairs that led to the recessed door, taking them at once. The girl's eyes were dark—it was night—and wide, her mouth was open, lips obviously cracked. Too much breathing, too quickly. Her ribs could be seen through the tear in her shift, and a long, thin streak of beaded blood was her only jewelry.

She came running down the street, clinging to the side that held the magelights, as if light were somehow important—a street instinct. She almost passed Jewel, her flight was headlong and unseeing; Jewel reached out to grab her arm.

The girl shrieked and started to lash out with fists that were far too small—and awkward, and wrong, thumbs on the inside of curved knuckles—and Jewel pulled her close, shouting one word over and over into her ear: Her name. Finch. Finch.

"Finch!"

But the name didn't do it, and without another thought, Jewel grapped the girl by the shoulder and slapped her, hard. That, in Jewel's experience, could seldom be ignored. Jewel had never been able to ignore it.

The girl stiffened, and then she said, "You have to let me go—he's after me—"

And looking over Finch's shoulders, which were a good six inches or more shorter than her own, Jewel saw a man jogging around the same corner that had given Finch, whole, into her keeping.

Their eyes met, Jewel's and this stranger's, and Jewel almost froze in place. Something about this man was wrong in a way that was so utterly foreign, so completely dark, Jewel wasn't certain what it was. But she could taste screaming in the silence, as if it were her own.

"My thanks," he said, in a soft purr of a voice.

All of her hair stood on end. Goose bumps that had nothing to do with the cold, nubbled her skin. He seemed to her, in that instant, to be a leisurely and unerring bolt of lightning, but darker, and more dangerous.

He had slowed to a walk, and his lips were turned up in a thin smile that didn't expose his teeth. She couldn't have said what he was wearing, because for the first time since she'd made the streets her home, it didn't matter. Rich, poor, or something in the middle—it would tell her nothing she needed to know.

Finch was utterly silent. Wide-eyed. Hair clinging to her forehead, flat and mousy. Thin as Lefty. Completely alone.

Or she would have been, in the moonlight, on these streets. But she had Jewel, and Jewel had just enough strength to tear her gaze away from the stranger's—tear was about the right word, it was so damn hard—and drag Finch down the stairwell. It was clumsy, but it was fast, and the stranger hadn't been expecting it.

He was fast.

Had the door been hinged in a different way, had it been locked, had it required more than a shoulder to shove it on its inward trajectory, it would have been over then.

Finch didn't speak at all; she was white, her cheeks flushed in a way that made them look garish. She stumbled forward, and Jewel let her shoulder go and grabbed her by the hand instead. She began to drag her through the crowd, and any direction that was away was the right direction to pull her.

But the crowd was thick, and Jewel had none of the authority of Marla, Taverson's intimidating wife. The men swore at her, or shoved back, or worse, failed to notice her at all. She moved so damn slowly, all the waiting and planning, all the nightmare in the world, wasn't going to mean a damn thing to anyone outside of the Halls of Mandaros.

Because if the stranger caught them, they were both dead. And not a quick death either. Jewel knew it, and as strongly as she had known almost anything in her life.

"Taverson!" she screamed, her hand crushing Finch's delicate fingers so tight they ceased to tremble. "Trouble!"

She couldn't even see the tavernkeeper. She could see the back of the tavern, the kitchen wall, the swinging doors; she could see the crowded tables around which standing men pressed because there wasn't enough room for more chairs. She could see smoke, and dead things in pots, and—she could see the stranger's shadow, even in this light.

As if it lay across her, as if he had already cut his way through the crowd that she couldn't part.

What she couldn't see was Carver. The table, two full bowls untouched—or as close as made no difference—was empty. She reached for her dagger with her left hand, and turning, shoved Finch behind her.

The stranger was close. Men did move when he walked by; she would have run, but they were older and less easily frightened. Or they were stupid. Or they weren't his intended victims.

His eyes were dark, and they caught the light in the tavern and held it, glittering like jewels without the benefit of facets. Surface, there. She could hardly see the whites of his eyes. Couldn't, in fact.

He approached; she backed up. Finch backed as well, as Jewel at last let her go and shifted the dagger to her right hand. She knew it was stupid. Useless. Didn't know how or why, and didn't care, because it was all she had.

He passed the last man, and then there was a small space in which they stood, two girls and a tall man in clothing that Jewel still couldn't see clearly, it meant so little. Long arms. Long fingers. He stretched out, slowly, reached for her face. Her dagger flashed in reply, and he laughed.

But he didn't laugh as much when a bar stool struck him full in the face from below.

Wielded by Carver, and dropped by him as he turned to meet Jewel's eyes. "Don't stand there," he shouted, "Run!" The exit was blocked; the stranger had teetered, but he hadn't fallen.

Carver looked around, and then his gaze caught the kitchen door, and he nodded toward it. He'd looked the place over, of course. Just in case they needed to get out fast, and not by the front door.

It was enough. Jewel turned, caught Finch by the hand again, and made her way past the dining room's last tables, past the inner wall of the kitchen.

They ran together. Carver was longer of leg, and he drew his dagger. She didn't bother to tell him it would do no good—what was the point if it made him feel safer? But she led him away from the swinging door, pressing a finger to his lips before he could shout incredulity into a single word or ten.

He hesitated, but only briefly, and then he, too, followed. They all ran.

And at their back, she heard Taverson's loud exclamation, wordless in the rumble of too many voices, and she knew that he'd noticed that someone had started a fight.

Hoped that she hadn't killed too many people before it ended, and prayed that one of them wasn't Taverson.

Chapter Twelve

JEWEL REACHED FOR the storeroom door. She'd seen Rath do it a dozen times, but her hands still shook. The storeroom was open, which was good. At this time of night, it was *also* likely to be used, which was bad. She pushed Finch through the door, waved Carver in, and stepped in herself, shutting the door as quickly as possible. At this time of night, quiet counted for nothing.

It was dark; she could hear Finch and Carver breathing, but neither spoke. The door muffled the sounds of shouting, but didn't quell them entirely, and she leaned against the rough wood, fumbling in her pocket for the only thing of value she owned: the magelight.

Its weight in her palm, she spoke a single word, and light gradually illuminated the sacks, the walls, and the faces of two strangers.

Carver whistled.

Finch, still pale, only stared. She lifted a slender hand almost without thought—and dropped it to her side again when thought caught up with her.

"I'm Jay," Jewel told her softly. "And we can't stay here."

"There's not much way out," Carver began grimly, but she lifted her left hand, palm out, the universal "shut up."

She led them to the second storeroom's door, moving as quickly as the light allowed. "Here," she told Carver. Can you open that?"

He frowned, approached the door, and knelt. She snorted. "It's not locked," she said. "Just—open it, will you?"

Gaining his feet again, he pushed the door, and it gave.

"Go in. You, too, Finch." She followed them. "Close it," she added, as she stepped through.

Carver snapped a salute.

She might have hit him, but not yet; not when Taverson's was still so close. Death receding, they listened. She wondered how much they would fail to hear once she had them in the tunnels. Worrying about what Rath would say when he saw Carver was so far down the list—

"Jay?"

She had listed to one side, seeing light, window, shadow, a dark blue dress at an odd angle. Shaking her head, she flinched.

"Jay?" Carver said again.

She said something very, very rude in Torra.

And Finch, silent until then, said sharply, "What is it? What's wrong?"

Jay looked at the pale girl then. "You speak Torra?" she asked, almost surprised. And in Torra. The girl nodded quietly. Jewel's use of the language seemed to comfort her—probably because she'd never met Jewel's Oma.

"Follow me now," she told them. Trying not to see windows, and the odd slant of night sky; the tilting of moon, round and full. Seeing some of it anyway, imposed across the orb in her hand, as if moon and magelight were, for a moment, one.

She led them to the heavy boards. "This is sort of a trapdoor," she said, and it sounded lame, even to her ears. "I can go first, but someone has to hold the light." It wasn't what she'd meant to say; she didn't want to be parted from the stone. Not only was it Rath's gift, but it was life: they wouldn't make it through the tunnels without it.

Carver stepped up and held out a hand. Carver, the strange boy with a dagger—a dagger he hadn't even tried to use. Bar stool was better, though, she had to give him that. The stone? She hesitated for just a minute; he ignored the hesitation, waiting.

"Where are you taking us?" he asked, as she pushed the board out of the way. It would have made more sense to give the damn thing to Finch, who was smaller, and less likely to be of help. But she hadn't, and, as was so often the case, made do.

"Does it matter?" she countered, sliding the wood across the floor and listening to the labored sound of her breath. Of metal against metal. Of something that might have been laughter, had it not been so cold.

Rath.

What was it? Why now? Since she'd met Rath, Jewel would swear everything about the cursed gift that marked her had gotten so much *worse*. She shoved her hair out of her eyes, and then shoved the board as far back as she could. There was just enough room.

"No," Carver said at last, and she remembered that she'd asked him a question. Didn't remember what it was.

She looked into the darkness. "Here," she told Carver, pointing at exactly where she wanted him to stand. "Hold it here."

He nodded, and kneeling beside the hole in the floor, he held out his palm, just as she had done. "There's floor there," he said at last, but he sounded doubtful.

"We either go there," she told him grimly, "or there." And pointed to the door. To what lay beyond it.

He didn't even try to tell her that their pursuer was just one man. Nodding, he sidled over, keeping his hand steady. She caught the edge of the floor in her hands, and swung herself down.

"Okay," she said. "Drop the stone."

He did. Just like that. Just as she had, when Rath had first taken her into the maze of tunnels that lay beneath the city streets. She moved to one side. "Finch next," she told him.

Finch didn't hesitate. Possibly because she was worried that Carver would push her if she did. Hard to say—what did Jewel know of the girl, after all? That she would die if no one tried to help her. Not a lot to risk a life on, really.

But she had. Finch landed awkwardly, but she weighed so little, it probably didn't matter. She fell, stepped on the hem of her shift, and stumbled again. Even with the light, it was awkward here. Carver landed perfectly on his feet. His bare feet.

"There's rope there," she told him. "Beyond the hole. It's in the pack—can you carry it?"

He nodded. "You planned this?"

"Well, it didn't get here by itself." She wouldn't need it. She knew the way. But she couldn't quite bring herself to leave it behind. "Can you drag the boards across the hole?"

He was taller than she was, but not as tall as either Rath or Arann; he had to struggle, and it took a long time. But he managed. And the tunnels? They were quiet. The tavern suddenly seemed like it was in a different holding.

She held the stone she'd retrieved with care. "Follow me," she told them quietly. "It's safe here."

"Where is here?"

"Tunnels. More dirt than stone, but still there. I think—I think there's stone there as well."

Carver touched the rough earth that formed the wall here. "How far do they go?"

"You'd be surprised."

"Good surprise or bad?"

"Good. I hope."

And Finch turned to Carver. "I'm Finch," she told him gravely.

"I'm Carver," he replied, raising a brow. Maybe both; Jewel could only see one. "Jay came here tonight to save your life."

"You didn't come with her?"

"I came with her," he said, and his stomach growled. He failed to notice, and Finch failed to notice; Jewel didn't ask him why he hadn't eaten. "But I—"

"We met each other in an alley," she told Finch, "Just outside of the thirty-second holding."

"When?"

"About an hour ago."

The *is she sane* look crossed the younger girl's face, but it didn't linger. It would probably be followed in quick succession by *how did she know* and *was she involved in this*. Not that Jewel cared. She started to walk and they followed.

She knew the way home. She had done this run a half dozen times. But she had never done it so quickly; she was so far ahead of Finch and Carver that she heard one of them hit the ground with a thud, and realized that the light went where *she* did. When she turned back, she saw Carver rubbing a knee; he looked at her and said nothing. Not even loudly.

"Jay," he said, as she waited for them with dwindling patience, "where are we going?"

And she meant to tell them *home*. But what came out instead, and that in a rush of syllables—was, "The Common." The minute those words left her lips, she *knew*. And knew, in a different way, that she had never made the run—if there was one—to the Common from any part of the tunnels.

There had been wonder, for her, when she had first ventured after Rath into these mysterious byways. There had been more, and quieter, on her second journey. She had thought—when she could think of anything other than the possibility of failure—that she would have the time and the opportunity to offer some glimpse of that same wonder to Finch. Well, and Carver, too, now that he was here.

But a darker understanding was working its way through her now, as she stood, the stone granting light in her shaking hand. What the tunnels meant to her, what they might mean, was lost to urgency. There was no magic here, no otherness, no sense of wonder—there was fear, and it overshadowed everything less primal.

"This way," she told them both. *"Hurry."*

She led them over broken stones, fallen walls; she led them between four pillars that had been sheared off at the height, and rested in darkness above. She led them down open roads, across which lay the crumbling ruin of what might have been a walkway, the light in her hand shifting too softly to give her any hint of what type of stone it might be. Gray was everywhere, and if it was broken by the occasional glint of something brighter and more colorful, it didn't matter. She heard Finch's brief Torra, more prayer than curse, and there was wonder in it.

She banked left, and then right, into a narrower section of what she thought of as street, given the ground that she walked on. Stopped once, along a crack that was three feet in width. Enough to jump easily, at Carver's height, or so she hoped.

He stopped and looked at her. She didn't tell him to jump.

"Rope," she told him softly. "There's a thing sticking out from that wall. What is it?"

Carver, standing close to the "thing" in question, turned to examine it briefly. He proved himself to be no Rath; he shrugged. "It looks like a bowl. You know. In the wall."

"Does it come off?"

He pulled.

"Just—sit in it."

Carver did as she ordered. He sat. "If it comes off," he told her, his butt conforming to the cold stone hollow, "it's not coming off with my weight." He didn't add that he was the heaviest person present because it was pretty damn obvious.

"Good. Rope," Jewel said again.

He *was* bright. He shrugged the pack off his slender shoulders, pulled its straps free of an extra yard of cloth that threatened to twist there, and set it on the ground. She came back so that he could see the knot he had to undo, but it was a waste of her time. "You can jump that?" she asked him.

"If the rest of the road is as solid as where we're standing, yes."

She nodded. "Finch," she told the younger—and smaller—girl. Her tone changed as she met wide eyes. "You've got to be able to jump this. Can you?"

"I—I don't know."

"Take the other end of the rope. Carver, tie one end to either yourself or the bowl—I don't give a damn which. If she falls, you have to hold her weight."

Carver nodded again. He hesitated, and then tied the rope around his waist in a knot that Jewel wasn't certain would hold. Neither, it appeared, was he; he caught the slack in both of his hands, and waited while Jewel looped the rope around Finch. Hers was a better knot, but she'd had Rath standing over her shoulder and frowning in that despicable silence of disapproval as she'd struggled to learn how to tie the damn thing.

She'd hated him for it until this moment.

"Finch," she said, when she gave the knots a tug, "we *need* to get to the Common. We need to get there quickly."

Finch said nothing; her nod was a pale movement of white skin and mousy hair. Delicate chin, delicate cheekbones—she was a bird, Jewel thought. But she couldn't fly. Jewel led her to the edge of the gulf. And then led her back, as far as the rope's play would allow. It was a long rope. "Taking a running jump at it," she told the girl, touching her by the shoulder.

Feeling the tremor that Finch hadn't—wouldn't—put into words. The words she said, so quietly that Carver couldn't hear them from where he stood, were unexpected. "Are you going to save someone else, like you saved me?"

"Gods, I hope so," Jewel whispered back, liking the girl. Unable not to like her.

Finch nodded, then, and showed that her diminutive spine must be made—as they often said—of steel; she bent slightly, shoulders hunching, head down, and then she built up as much speed as the short distance would allow. Her knees were off in her first attempt, and she only barely made the other edge; she foundered there for a moment, her arms cartwheeling as she found—and fought—the fear of falling, the truth of gravity.

Jewel did not touch the rope; she was afraid to grip it too tightly, to unbalance the edge upon which Finch teetered. But she saw that Carver's hands were steady, and that he had eyes for Finch. If she fell, he'd be ready.

Jewel was counting on him.

And that surprised her. She'd known him for a few hours, and the first thing he'd done was to pull a dagger on her. But he hadn't used it. Not yet. That was as much as she could hope for.

That, and that if Finch fell, his weight would somehow manage to balance hers. But Finch managed to throw herself forward, and she fell there, heavily, the thin lip of rock tinkling in small pieces into the abyss below. Jewel held the magestone. She hated to part with it.

But in the struggle between hate and necessity, there wasn't much doubt about outcome; she waited until Finch was across the divide and on her hands and knees. "Can you untie it?" she asked.

Finch nodded.

It was sort of true; it took agonizing minutes, and a few Torra phrases that were on the outer edge of ear-whackingly rude, and then the rope unwound itself. But Finch was still crouched on the ground.

"I'm next," she told Carver, as he pulled the rope in and she tried not to notice the way it slid first out of sight, into the darkness. "Finch?"

"I'm okay."

"Good. Catch the magelight. If it rolls, it won't be hard to find." And she threw it. Throwing the stone was easy. Finch, as aware of its value as any poor orphan could be, scrambled after it, still on hands and knees; only when it was in her hands did she rise. Holding it carefully, but not cupping it, she approached the opposite edge of the fissure.

Jewel took the rope and repeated the process of wrapping it around a waist. But it was hers, and her hands shook. She'd not yet mentioned to Rath how much heights terrified her, because she was always wary of his incredulity, and the derision it implied. He was afraid of nothing. She wanted to be like him.

Especially now.

It's not height if you can't see the bottom, she told herself. She backed up to the same distance Finch had, and then said to Carver, looking across the divide, "I'm heavier. And clumsier."

And then she ran. Her knees bent at the right moment, and she leaped, trailing rope, her eyes closed at the last possible instant. Finch caught her hand as she, too, teetered. Finch pulled her down.

Jewel nodded at Carver. She caught the rope around her waist, just as he had done, moving back a foot from the edge. Two feet. Three. Finch joined her, placing the stone safely on the ground, where its light could still be seen, but couldn't so easily be lost. Her hands were slight, small, and utterly still as she grabbed the rope.

"Now," Jewel told Carver. Carver nodded, and picked up the empty pack, which Jewel had entirely forgotten.

He leaped with ease across the distance. Envy might have made her snap something at any other time—but not this one.

He untied the knot at the same time she managed the same feat at its other end, and they shoved the rope back into the pack.

"Let's go."

Jewel almost missed the intersection. In fact, she did, and had walked ten yards before she felt the wrongness of the direction. She didn't put it into words; no point. Instead, she retraced the steps in a hurry, and found a small opening in a wall. It was just that, no more; no archway announced its presence, no stone frame formed its mouth. But this was where they had to go.

"I don't know what the ground is like," she told him softly. "But we're close to the City, now."

"And the Common?"

She nodded. There was a lot of prayer in the single motion, but none given voice. "These are like the first tunnels we took."

Carver nodded again.

They began to walk. Where there was room, Finch walked by her side, wanting—drawn to—the comfort of light. But there wasn't always that much room; they walked single file, and even ducked or crouched, as the tunnel began its slow incline.

"Where is this going to come out? Storeroom?"

"I don't know."

"Will there be people there?"

"I don't know."

He stopped asking questions.

"You're going to have to wear something besides that dress," Jewel told Finch, when Finch tripped on its hem for the fourth time.

Finch nodded. But her expression made clear that that something wasn't something she owned. The tunnel ended suddenly in something that looked like a door. It made Jewel nervous.

But Carver approached it, examined it, and shook his head. "Not used," he told her.

"How can you tell?"

"The lock's rusted."

"Great. Can you get it open?"

"Depends on how rusted."

She waited. Finch waited with her. After he struggled for a moment, Jewel gave up and pushed him out of the way. Took pins from her hair that weren't actually of any other use, and began to work her way through; it wasn't a difficult lock. Well, the parts that *were* lock.

She thought she heard a click. It could have been a snap. Shaking her head, she put a shoulder to the door, and Carver tapped her. "Hinges," he said, pointing.

"What about them?"

"Wrong side."

Reversing direction, she tried to tug. Was surprised when it opened; surprised enough to fall over.

Finch came to the open door, light in her hand, and they went through into more tunnel. But this time, the ceiling seemed slightly different. Jewel began to look for the telltale sign of board or hole. She found it. "There," she told Carver.

Carver nodded. "Me first, or you?"

"You go. You're taller."

He gripped the edge; some of it crumbled, but he just adjusted his handhold. Then he swung his legs up, and disappeared. His head reappeared. "A basement, I think. You coming?" And he offered them a hand.

She sent Finch up next, but not before throwing Carver the light. She followed.

The basement—and it was that—was dark and somewhat musty; there wasn't much in it. Wood. She looked to the side and saw it then: a chute. It was a relief.

"We go up that way," she told him.

He nodded.

There was a wooden hatch over the chute. It was rotten, and it was nailed down; clearly, this wasn't used. But she had some leverage, now, and with Carver at her side, she managed to push it up, sticking her dagger between two nails and using it like a pry bar. Rath would have been grinding his teeth, if he were here.

But as it popped open, she froze.

She could hear voices.

One of them was Rath's. That one didn't bother her. But the other two? Like the man at Taverson's, *everything* was wrong with their voices. Everything. And there were two. And Rath was tiring.

He fought his way down the small alley, bleeding from a dozen insignificant cuts. Tallied, they were not as insignificant as he would have liked, but they bothered him less than the certainty that they were meant to tire, not to kill; killing him should have been simple. His blade had connected with something any number of times; he couldn't see the damage he caused—if any—but he could hear a brief snarl, some hint of annoyance.

Had the alley been wider, he would have drawn sword, but it wasn't, and he had been taught to let the terrain dictate the fight. Not that his teacher had ever chosen to cover this particular example; he had, like Rath, assumed that his attackers would be visible.

Rath took a step back, listening. Straining to hear motion, something across the ground, something scraping the walls to either side—any hint, any clue, of where his attacker was, and from where he might choose to strike.

What he heard instead was a shout:

"Left, now!"

And he recognized the voice instantly, obeyed it instinctively, flattening himself against the left wall.

She came up behind him, making far more noise than either of his attackers, her shoes slapping the stone and wood to either side. He would have shouted at her, would have given some warning, would have told her to run—but she spoke again. "Dagger, Rath, low right!"

She could *see* them.

She could see them, and had figured out—somehow—that he couldn't.

She held a dagger in either hand as she moved just at the periphery of his vision, her arms too thin and too lacking in strength to do real damage.

But too thin or not, here she was, her head barely brushing his shoulder as she moved forward into an alley that could not safely contain two people standing abreast.

They were two men, tall men, dark-haired and dressed in torn clothing that might once have been finer; it was hard to tell. They weren't wearing armor, so they weren't guards; they weren't wearing anything that made them part of any organization Jewel knew. Then again, she wasn't Rath, she knew damn few.

Her hands gripped dagger hilts as if they were rope and she were in danger of plummeting. No, as if they were rope, and someone at the other end was depending on her ability to *hold on*. Her hair was in her eyes, but she barely noticed; she couldn't take her eyes from the men for an instant.

Because she *knew* they didn't want to kill Rath. And that they were perfectly willing to kill *her*.

They didn't seem to be bleeding as Rath was, but he'd hit them, no doubt. They were only as wide as Rath, but they had chosen to enter the alley in single file. She could see the second at a distance, a body's fall, no more. He was watching her intently. He was smiling.

They were *both* shimmering, as if she could see them through a curtain of orange and gray. She hoped that Carver and Finch had stayed put, because she didn't give much for their odds. Or hers, if it came to that.

She twisted to the right, bending slightly, as the man who had been attacking Rath drove his blade toward her vitals. He moved so fast, she hadn't seen him strike, but her body was already contorting, and her dagger struck him in the bend of elbow before he could pivot to take advantage of her odd position.

Had she been stronger, she'd have cut off his arm.

As it was, he snarled some and withdrew, but not much. And she saw that whatever she'd managed to do, it wasn't quite enough to make him bleed. Wondered if, in fact, he bled at all. It wasn't a comforting thought.

It was all the thought she had time for.

She lost sight of Rath, and of the man attacking her; she had a glimpse of the alley, of the things that lay beyond it, of her hair in her eyes, the folds of her tunic, things that she *could* see when she was moving, and moving again, in something that was too awkward to be a dance, and far less graceful.

But each time, she avoided being skewered; avoided losing fingers or hand, avoided losing an eye. Everything Rath had taught her had vanished; she was Jewel Markess, and she relied entirely on instinct, on the things that came so quickly, she had no words for them.

She wanted to tell Rath to run.

Rath moved instead, his blade coming in where hers did, and striking in a different place. All of her blows were awkward, and she couldn't see what Rath was doing clearly enough to judge his—but his had a force behind them that years of training would never give her.

And even that—it wasn't enough. Whatever it was the men hid behind, it seemed to protect them.

She could do this for a while. Longer than she could have before she'd met Rath; she'd had food, and shelter, and warmth to strengthen her, to give her endurance. But not long enough. The men didn't even look tired. But why would they? They had the advantage of—of—she paused. It almost killed her.

Light saved her life.

Strange light, a different color, something that fell from the heights like grains of shining sand, like solid rain. She heard words follow in its wake, and she looked up as Rath shoved her roughly to the side; she could see, at the height of three stories, someone looking down.

The words he had spoken were haunting because she could hear them clearly, and would never be able to repeat them; they lingered in the air as the light trickled out—from his hands. His hands, palm down, shining palely.

The rest of him was dark as night—darker, really; the light that he had cast out did nothing to illuminate him. But granular, those specks of light began to eat away at the gray-and-orange nimbus that surrounded the two would-be killers, until neither color remained.

Jewel could see the men as clearly as she had before—but now that the orange-gray curtain was gone, Rath could see them as well. She started to speak; the men themselves paused as they realized that they were suddenly no longer protected. They both carried long knives, heavy belts, wrist guards; they both wore boots that seemed too light for the season. They hadn't bothered with dark clothing, although in this light the exact colors they'd chosen were muted; Jewel tried to place the style of dress, and failed.

One looked up, and Jewel looked with him; the man upon the building to the right leaped down into the alley, his hand grazing the building's side for the whole of his descent, as if he weighed nothing, less than nothing, and air was a chute he could follow. He landed in perfect silence, and in his hands, she could see weapons. They were daggers, but they were oddly shaped, things that she might have expected to find below ground, where all ancient things lay.

"Well met, Ararath," the man said softly.

Rath nodded grimly. "Stay back," he told Jewel.

Nodding, she retreated as far as Carver, and stopped. Carver, whose dagger was out, and who stood sentinel above the old chute, watching and waiting as if he had no other purpose.

I told you to stay down, she thought. The words wouldn't come. Instead, she said, "Where's Finch?"

"She's down below. It didn't sound safe."

"It's not." But she could *breathe* now. She could shake.

"He another friend you don't know?"

She shook her head. "He's Rath," she told him. "I've known him for weeks now."

Carver snorted. "You're crazy, right?"

"Probably."

She watched Rath's friend—old friend, by the use of the name—walk toward the men in the alley. She watched Rath do the same. "Come on," she told Carver, pointing at the chute. "Let's go down."

"Why?"

"It's safer?"

He started to argue, but someone screamed, and screaming usually had one of two effects on homeless children. This time, he retreated.

Finch was waiting for them, her hands over her ears. When she saw them both, she relaxed, but only slightly; the night air carried the sounds of real fighting, real pain. *There would be death,* Jewel thought.

"Should we go somewhere else?" Carver asked her, nodding toward the tunnels.

She shook her head. "I'd just get lost," she told him ruefully. "I don't know how to get back."

*   *   *

It was a short fight.

Andrei's presence was not the mixed blessing it so often was, and nothing he did this eve would tarnish his reputation, should Rath be foolish enough to actually speak of it to another living man. The daggers Hectore's most famous servant carried, oddly ornamented even in the dim light, were more deadly than any that Rath had wielded; they drew blood.

And fire.

The fire was disturbing; a brief flare of orange light that flickered with blue heart, the shape and size of a man. Twice. The screams were loud, but they lingered only in memory; ash had no throat, no lip, no way to utter cries.

Rath watched as they died, these men who had been sent to take him. He sheathed his daggers slowly, his face utterly impassive, his expression calm.

"You were lucky," Andrei said, sheathing his own blades without comment.

"You were late," Rath replied.

Andrei nodded quietly. "Forgive me," he said, kneeling in the alley as if in penitence. What he was actually doing, however, was disturbing a fine sheen of ash with his knees, his gloved hands. "This is not the best news," he said at last, looking up at Rath's face.

"They weren't mage-born."

"No."

"And those—"

"These?" Andrei said, touching the dagger hilts. "They were a gift."

"From?"

Andrei shook his head. "Poorly done, Ararath."

"My apologies, Andrei. I am . . . not at my best, as you find me."

"Indeed." The man rose. "It was not clear to me that these men were here at all. Had they not run across the boy—"

"Boy?" Ah. The single scream.

"He is dead," Andrei added quietly. "But his death was enough. I was prepared for some difficulty, but not of this particular nature. I was forced to retreat for a moment. I did not think they wanted you dead," he added.

Rath, looking down at a jacket that could not be repaired, shrugged.

"But a question, Ararath."

"Yes?"

"The girl."

Rath turned to look back at the empty stretch of alley. "Girl?"

Andrei's smile was tight. "As it pleases you. But Ararath, be cautious. These . . . men . . . are not the men you have played your dangerous games with in times past."

"Who were they?"

"I am not entirely certain myself. I have some contact with the Order of Knowledge, but it is a fractious order, and the contacts that I do have are reticent."

"Your daggers?"

Andrei nodded. "They were delivered to my hand when I made inquiries about the death of Member Haberas. I will have to return them," he added, without regret. "And in return for their use, I will be compelled, by rules of hospitality, to surrender what information I've gained.

"Rath, if that's what you prefer to be called, quit this game. It is beyond you. Do you understand? It is beyond *me*." He ran a hand through his hair; it was an uncharacteristic gesture. It almost made him seem human.

Rath merely bowed. "I am in your debt. I am, again, in the debt of Hectore."

"Your godfather counts you as blood-kin; he requires no such accounting."

"Of course not. But that changes nothing. The Patris AMatie?"

"Do not play games with him. What dealings you have had, Ararath, must come to a close here. He will know, of course, if he does not already know." Andrei offered Rath a brief bow. "I must return to Hectore, and you to your home. If I have information for you," he added, "I will find you."

No other man could say that with such confidence, and Rath had no doubt that it was well-placed. He turned, then, as Andrei did.

"If the girl is mage-born," Andrei's voice drifted back, "have her tested. She is young, to come into her power—and there is a risk."

"She is not mage-born."

"Good."

"How so?"

"If she were, and she were already evincing some power, it could destroy her if it were not discovered and trained; I have heard it is not a pleasant death, and in all likelihood, she deserves more. In my opinion, she saved your life."

*   *   *

Rath slid down the chute, and almost collided with Jewel. Not a good start. He righted himself, and Jewel managed—barely—to get out of his way. So that he could clearly see not one but two children, standing just above the tunnels that he so prized.

He looked a mess, even to Jewel, but he didn't appear to notice, and if he didn't, she couldn't. That was one of the unspoken rules that governed their life together.

"This is Rath," she said quickly. "Rath, this is Finch. And this is Carver."

"Carver?"

She shrugged. "I didn't name him."

"You brought him."

"I'll explain it later."

"Good. I look forward to it. How did you *get* here, Jewel?"

"Jewel?" Carver repeated. She hit his shoulder.

Rath ignored him.

"I followed the maze," she told him. "I—"

"Later, then. Do you know how to get back?"

She shook her head.

"Let me lead, then. I think we'll stay clear of the streets for the moment." He paused. "Don't use this tunnel during the day."

"I don't think I could find it again," she offered, as he drew a magestone out of his pocket.

"Good."

She was going to be in *so much* trouble.

They made their way home, sticking to the tunnels. Rath was not in a mood to offer wonder. He was not in a mood to share words either. He led, and Jewel took the rear, bracketing the two orphans with light. If it was dim, the darkness of the undercity was so complete it didn't matter.

They crossed the crevice with ease; there was less urgency, and Rath was easily heavy enough to bear their weight. He asked Jewel how she'd crossed it the first time, and she pointed to the pack that hung awkwardly, across Carver's shoulders. But it seemed that in this, at least, she'd done well; he nodded grimly and said nothing more.

Only when he led them, at last, to the apartments he called home did he pause. He leaned against the storeroom wall, and looked at the door; it was locked, but it was a lock that he could open in his sleep.

He didn't. "Two more," he said, voice heavy with something that was suspiciously devoid of anger.

"I didn't mean—"

"You never do. The boy?"

"I met him in an alley."

"And you trusted him enough to expose us all?"

"Yes." And then, stronger, *"Yes."*

Rath nodded curtly, as if he had expected no less. "Carver," he said quietly.

The boy nodded. He was wary of this adult in a way that he had not been wary of either Jewel or Finch. Which made street sense; Jewel and Finch couldn't hurt him, even armed. Rath could.

"And Finch."

The younger girl nodded as well, wrapping arms around herself, as if against cold. Or inspection.

Rath turned and opened the door. He made a show of retrieving his keys in the scant magelight, but no one was fooled. He didn't need them.

"Jewel will show you to the room she occupies. There are two other children here, and they—as you—are her responsibility." He opened the door and held it, waiting. They had to almost scrape past him to reach the hall. Jewel went with them to the room; Arann and Lefty were in it, waiting in a tense silence that dissolved slowly when they saw who stood in the door.

Arann rose slowly. And towered. "Jay?"

She nodded. "This is Finch," she told him, although she looked at Lefty as well as she spoke. "And this is Carver."

"Carver?"

"I, uh, met him in an alley."

"Is everyone going to do this?" Carver asked, lounging in the frame, like a very young version of Rath. He'd drawn his dagger to make a point; Arann was a lot larger than he was, in height and in width.

Jewel smacked him hard in the chest, to make a different point. "Put it away," she snapped.

He raised a brow, his hair flat against his forehead and a third of his face. Dark hair. Dark eyes. Prominent bones forming the jut of jaw, the height of cheek. But after a moment, he sheathed the dagger.

"I'll feed you," she told him.

"Something that won't take the skin off the roof of my mouth this time?"

"Something like that. You don't draw that here. Unless there are intruders. You never draw it if you don't mean to use it."

"I do," he told her grimly, softly, "because I *don't* want to use it."

She started to argue, but Arann lifted a hand. "He's right," he said quietly.

"Not here, he's not. He can play games outside. This is my place."

"Rath's place?" Lefty asked.

"Mine. This room and everyone in it."

Carver whistled. Jewel still couldn't. And she couldn't snap her fingers either. "There's room on the floor. Not much bedding yet," she told them both. "I—there's some for Finch, but I didn't expect to find you."

He shrugged. "I can sleep on the floor. At least it isn't wet."

"And it's warm," Arann told Carver.

Jewel stared at Arann. Arann, sensing it, met her gaze and shrugged. "You brought him," he told her, starting something that neither of them knew would continue. She felt it, though; the force of his words, the weight of his unexpected faith.

Faith was an odd word. It existed in both Weston and Torra, but it was colored differently in either language. Arann used Weston. It was the brighter coloring, the cleaner shade.

"This is your den?" Carver asked her as she turned toward the kitchen.

"No."

"Then what is it?"

She shrugged. "Arann," she replied, nodding to the giant. "And Lefty. He's kind of shy."

"And me?" Carver asked, following her as she left the room, his bare feet slapping the wooden floor.

"Your feet are bleeding."

He shrugged. "They'll stop."

She made her way to the small kitchen in silence and began to assemble food in a basket. No sense in plates; there weren't enough of them.

"Why?" he asked quietly.

"Why what?"

"Why did you try to save someone you don't even know?"

She shrugged. "Why didn't you stay in Taverson's? Why didn't you eat?"

"Burned my mouth."

"Why did you hit that man with the stool?"

Carver shrugged. Looked at the floor. "Stabbing him would have got me thrown out."

She laughed. It was an unexpected rush of sound, nerves driving it. "The stool would have got you thrown out if Taverson figured out you'd done it." She looked up, met his gaze, and held it. "You have anywhere better to go?"

"Not tonight."

"I owe you a meal. I'll feed you." She looked at his feet. "And I'll buy you boots, or something. Your feet—"

"The old ones fell apart. They were too big, anyway."

"When did you lose 'em?"

"Couple of days ago. I don't know." The gaze that had tried to hold hers became evasive.

She held up a hand. "You helped me," she told him quietly. "I didn't ask. I couldn't. I didn't know—" She threw the words away, chose different ones. "You helped me. I owe you."

"I'd say Finch owes me, if anyone does."

"She didn't ask either."

"She's smarter than she looks." His tone took a turn for the bitter. "What's the point in asking?"

Jewel couldn't really argue with that. But she was what she was; she did. "What's the point in *not* asking? What different does it make, one way or the other? Sometimes you get what you ask for."

"Sometimes," he said, stone-cold words, "you don't know what you're asking for."

She nodded then. Thinking of Rath, thinking of all the things she hadn't asked for. Not in words. Maybe never in words. Thinking of his ruined jacket, his blood in thin welts across chest, ribs, cheek; thinking— knowing in a way that was less certain and more natural than gift—that he had almost died because he'd known that she would try to save a stranger.

Wondering what the cost would be, if she stayed here. Not to her—but to Rath.

She finished cutting bread, apples, hard cheese. "Take these," she told him.

He took the basket.

"Stay in the room, with the others."

"Where are you going?"

"To talk to Rath."

He waited another moment. "My name," he began.

"I don't care."

"I want to—"

"I *don't care*, Carver. Whatever you've done to survive, you've done. Telling me isn't going to change a damn thing." She swallowed, turned to look at him, at this accidental boy who had hit death in the face with the seat of a bar stool. "What you do *when you're here*, I care about. That's the only thing that matters. That, and tonight."

His gaze was odd. She watched it waver, wanting to be elsewhere. "I'm not part of a den," he said at last.

"Good."

"I'd be part of yours."

"I told you—I don't have one."

He nodded, then, just before his stomach spoke. Embarrassed, he retreated.

Jewel waited until she heard the click of the door; her room, occupied by four strangers, and shut against the world.

Then she walked to Rath's room, and knocked.

The door slid open; he hadn't really shut it. He was sitting, jacket still shreds across his back, in the chair in front of his desk; the magelight was in its stand and a quill was moving steadily in his right hand. Paper's edge curled to either side of the words that seemed to anchor him. He often wrote at night.

And she often let him.

This night was different. She entered his room and shut the door quietly—and carefully—behind her. His pen continued its quiet scratching. She walked past him, to the cupboards above the chest he kept locked. She pulled out two small jars and a long, white roll of something that reminded her of cheesecloth.

He looked up as she approached him in silence, the jars and the bandages in her hands. There was no accusation in his face; there was nothing in it at all; it was closed. Intimidating.

But she'd come for a reason. She touched the shoulders of his jacket, avoiding what she assumed would be his glare. To her surprise, he let her remove it, and began to unbutton the shirt—also ruined—that lay beneath it. Blood was a red conversation on that shirt. The rest, the welts and cuts, were shallow enough that they didn't expose bone and sinew. She'd seen worse.

But these were personal in a way that even Arann's broken ribs, bruised eye, swollen lips, hadn't been. She removed the lid from one of the jars, and with shaking hands, she dressed each wound. His pen stopped at some point, but she didn't mark it; there was something compelling and soothing about the dressing of these wounds.

"The bandages won't stay," he told her quietly, as she began to play out the long strip. He caught her hand, sticky with unguent, before she could touch his cheek. His eyes were lined and dark, his face gaunt.

Old Rath, he'd called himself, the first day she'd met him. And he'd seemed old to her—but not the way he was now. It frightened her. She could see the bones beneath his skin.

"Do you know what you're doing?" he asked her softly, holding that hand. He would not let her touch his face.

"Disinfecting the cuts," she replied. But it was the wrong answer. Or perhaps the right answer to the wrong question.

She wanted to touch him to make certain he was real. And alive. She couldn't tell him that. She couldn't have said that in her old home either, when her mother and father had been alive, and her Oma had been at the center of the universe.

"How many, Jewel?" he asked.

She knew what he meant. "I don't know," she answered, just as softly. "I only meant to save Finch. That's all."

"I know." The words were uninflected. "I've seen it before. In someone else. But not like this," he added, lifting his cut arm. His smile was almost bitter. "Then, it was all theory."

"It's worse," she told him.

"The seeing?"

She nodded. "Since I met you, Rath."

His gaze fell to the words he'd been writing. His cursive script was both strong and almost illegible. "Four," he told her quietly. "Will you keep them all?"

"Will you let me?"

"For now, Jewel." He shook his head, and his smile was strange; she didn't understand it. It was shorn of both sarcasm and edge, but it was also shorn of mirth, or joy. It cut him, she thought. Knew it was true, and didn't know why.

"You'll find others," he told her.

"You're seeing things, too?"

"Just you, Jay. Jewel Markess. Just you." He paused, and then let her hand go. "And perhaps myself, clearly. You're like a mirror," he added, "and it is not a kindness."

She wanted to ask him what he meant. But she knew the rules, even if he seldom bothered to put them into words. What he didn't offer, she couldn't ask for. Not here and now.

"Go back to your den-kin."

"They're not my den."

But his smile was still there, shifting in the light, gathering different shadows that showed the many lines that edged the corners of his lips.

She went.

Chapter Thirteen

JEWEL HAD NEVER lived in a *quiet* room with this many people before. If she were honest, she had no memories of the time in which she'd lived with this many people at all, although her Oma had often spoken about them with some pride. She was always proud of the things she'd done, and the words had survived, some echo of that dim voice, when the memories themselves had been devoured by age and time.

It was crowded, but it was less crowded; the arguments that time had worn into patterns—between her father and her Oma, between her father and her mother, between Jewel and either of her parents, or sometimes both—had been a part of the house in a way that the quiet here had never been.

Her first task, in the foreign quiet of this new morning, was a visit to the Common. She took Finch and Carver, and after a moment's hesitation, asked Arann and Lefty if they wanted to come, too. Arann had been told not to move much, but it was getting damn cold, and the cold couldn't be good for him. Just to the market, for clothing. Just that.

Arann nodded instantly, a sure sign that the "rest" was finally driving him insane. Lefty looked at Arann. He had momentarily lost his voice in the presence of Carver; Finch didn't seem to scare him.

Then again, Jewel couldn't imagine Finch scaring *anyone*.

Rath was either sleeping or out. His door was closed, and she didn't knock on it because she didn't want to know. Disturbing Rath was never a good idea anyway.

The skies had lost their clarity; the open face of the sun once again obscured itself with clouds. But the air was distinctly chillier than it had been, and it hadn't been all that warm to start.

Finch, in thin shift, was almost shuddering when they reached the outer door and threw it open. Jewel had offered her clothing, and Finch had—much to her surprise—mutely refused to take it. She was here, and she obviously trusted Jewel at least enough to stay—but the rest might take time, and Jewel wasn't certain how much of it they had.

"Finch," she said, her voice inflected with an echo of her Oma, "I'm already minding one sick person. I *do not* need another. Is that clear? Put this on. It doesn't fit, and yes, it's ugly, but it's not exactly warm outside, and. Well." She held out one of Rath's many jackets, aware of how small it would make Finch look. How much smaller. Rath's training was good for something; she could hold her arm out in that position for a long damn time.

She had to prove it, and the silence as she did was damn awkward.

Finch eventually gave way, without once breaking it.

"Why was that man after you?" Jewel was breaking the one cardinal rule about the past, and she knew it. The past, as she had told Carver, wasn't her concern. And it shouldn't have been. But in the clear light of sun, it *was*.

Finch shook her head.

"You were alone?"

And nodded. The nod was wrong. Everything about it.

Carver said nothing. His visible eye was narrowed, and he turned to glance at Arann, who said more nothing. Lefty shoved his hand further into his armpit. If they'd been walking slowly enough, he would have shuffled, his shoulders stooped and his head down.

Jewel inexplicably wanted to hit them all. Not hard, and not to cause damage—more to get their attention. Well, maybe not Finch. Her Oma had had that habit for all of Jewel's waking memory. But, she reminded herself, she wasn't her Oma. And hitting them wouldn't do much good.

"Why are you wearing a dress?"

More silence. But this time, Jewel wanted to hit herself. She did not ask Finch where her parents were. Or who. In fact, given that Finch now looked like a prettier, skinnier version of Lefty, she thought it might be best if she never asked another question again. In her life.

Carver gave her a *look*.

Arann deliberately didn't.

But Finch said nothing at all, and that was worse; it was in her eyes, and her face, her unbruised face.

Given how she felt, Jewel surprised herself, and not in a good way. "Where were you, when you met that man?"

Silence.

"Could you get back there?"

Carver's eye widened and he shook his head; his hair slid across his face, and beneath it, his skin was both pale and unblemished. He really was almost handsome; his face was like the face of a storybook patriarch's son. But his feet were bare.

Finch had stopped walking entirely, which caused them all to stop, stillness radiating outward slowly, like the opposite of ripples in still water when a stone falls.

It was Arann who said, and very gently, "She doesn't mean to take you back there."

Finch looked at him—looked up at him—her neck stiff, her eyes slightly rounded.

"She went to get you," he added, in his reasonable Arann voice. More of his voice, Jewel thought, than either Finch or Carver had yet heard. "It sounds like she risked her life, even. You think she did all that to take you back?"

In a low voice, Finch replied, "They'll pay."

"Oh, they'll pay," Jewel said, her voice bright as new steel.

"She meant money," Carver told her curtly.

Jewel shrugged.

"Why do you want to know?" Carver's hand had fallen away from his dagger. Jewel wasn't certain when it had started to reach, and Rath would have been really annoyed at the lack of awareness.

"I think—I think it's important," she said at last, and lamely.

"Why?"

"They—he," she corrected herself, "came from that place, somehow. It's a connection."

"I saw him. *You* saw him. You want to *ever* see him again?" Carver's gaze was intent, intense.

"Not that way, no."

"Then leave it alone."

But she couldn't. Not yet. The Common trees were drawing closer as they resumed their walk. "Were there others, where you were?" Pressing, pushing the point, when she knew better.

Finch closed her eyes, which was answer enough.

"See?" Jewel said to Carver, or to Arann, or to no one in particular.

Carver looked at Arann. "Is she crazy?"

Arann shrugged. "Good crazy, maybe."

"Look," Carver began. "How exactly did you *know* where she'd be?"

And Lefty spoke his first words to the strangers; he said, "She had a nightmare."

Jewel closed her eyes.

In the market, they were good children. Which meant silent children, hands out where everyone could see them. The guards at the gate stared at Carver's feet long before he'd actually reached their disapproving glares, and Jewel was tense for a moment because she was preparing an argument.

It wasn't necessary. At this time of day, the guards were harried enough that they were willing to let the merchants fend for themselves, and although they issued a curt warning to the group, they let them go, crushed in a press of moving people who didn't have the time or inclination to stop for the simple suspicion of a couple of armed and armored men.

"We're going to the cobbler's?" Lefty surprised them all by asking.

Jewel nodded. "That, and Helen. She'll want to see Arann. She said so. And it can't hurt to bring Finch and Carver, too." But the words came out on their own, and without much thought; Jewel was occupied with other concerns.

The cold. The food.

The place Finch had managed to escape from. Oh, Hells, almost entirely that place. She couldn't *see* it, and she didn't fancy more nightmares. But she also didn't want to ask Finch any more questions; the ones she had asked were intrusive enough that the girl was pale.

The cobbler looked up when they entered; his door was actually narrower than Jewel had first thought it, although she noticed this only because Arann and Carver collided in the frame, and stopped there.

While they did their quiet juggle for position, she approached the merchant. "I need shoes," she told him. "Winter shoes."

"You don't," he said, with a grimace. "I'm surprised you got that one past the market guards." He nodded at Carver, who had managed to turn sideways and slide in past Arann, without dislodging the older boy. "And the girl?"

"Her, too. Unless you think you can repair what's already on her feet."

Merchants were famous for their mendacity, but this one was one of Rath's. He looked at Finch for a moment, and shook his head. Seeing more than her feet. Maybe too much more. "I can repair those," he said at last, "but I don't think they'll last the Winter if she grows much."

"Then we'll need new ones for her as well. Oh, and Arann."

The biggest of her charges stepped up at the mention of his name. He was quiet, as he always was, and utterly still; his gaze, unlike Carver's, didn't flit from edge to edge, taking in everything in the room that might not be nailed down. Jewel knew the look well, but struggled to ignore it. No point in alerting the already alert cobbler.

He dealt first with Arann, and worked in silence. Finch was next, but he handled her differently; he didn't touch her feet, not even her ankles; didn't do more than tell her where to stand, and on what. He was careful not to meet her eyes too often, and when he did, Jewel saw why: he couldn't keep the pity off his face.

She liked him.

She told herself that she liked him. She had to.

"How long will this take?" she asked, more gruffly than she'd intended.

"About five days for the three of them."

She nodded, but it was a curt nod. "You can't do 'em sooner?"

"Not at a decent rate, no."

"It's going to get cold. Carver, at least—" she pointed.

"I know. But I've got only one apprentice worth anything, and I've other customers as well."

"Then I'll pay the indecent rate."

He gave her an odd look, and she met it, her own gaze defiant. After a few minutes, he shook his head and said, "All right, girl."

Clothing was next. Finch and Arann were examined and measured by Helen, and if the cobbler had taken care not to touch Finch, Helen felt no compunction whatsoever. She was firm; the unlit pipe clinging to the corner of her mouth made her words difficult to understand, but she made do with pointed gestures and a lot of muffled cursing.

Where the cobbler had demanded five days, Helen demanded the opposite; she refused to let Finch leave her ragged stall without clothing—warm clothing—on her back. As she put it.

Finch was embarrassed and grateful by turns, but said nothing. Arann, however, was less of an emergency in the eyes of the old woman. Although she had clothing she considered suitable for someone his size, she wanted a day to adjust things, and Jewel nodded.

"Jay?"

"Hmmm?"

"Pay attention."

"Yes, Helen." But it was hard to pay that attention. Something about Finch, something about the way she hadn't answered the question, the last one, made Jewel uneasy in a prickly way.

She couldn't figure out what it was.

But she knew who would.

Rath was waiting for them when they made their way home, carrying a basket heavy with food from Farmer Hanson's stall. The farmer was by far the friendliest of the three merchants; he asked the names of the newcomers as if Jewel was one of his children, and she answered in a like fashion. "The boy's too skinny," he told her, leaning over his produce as if he were the epitome of largesse. "And the girl as well."

"So's Lefty."

"Lefty has Arann."

"They have me."

The farmer's smile was a warm one. "Things must be getting crowded at your place," he told her.

"Not that crowded. I've lived in smaller rooms."

"Good." He handed her apples, and potatoes, and the bread that should have been gone by this time in the day. She took them all, paying for them. He failed to take the extra money she habitually offered. "You'll need it," he told her, glancing at Carver's feet.

Carver's feet were of interest to everyone.

She shook her head, her snort coming out in a brief, pale cloud. "Let's go," she said, to everyone at large. And like a small, unruly mass, they followed where she led, and she led them to the apartment; Rath entered the hall at the same time they did, but from the opposite end.

He looked only at Jewel.

"Room," she told everyone else. Arann had the basket, and she paused. "Lefty? Can you help feed everyone?"

"What about you?"

"I'll take care of me."

He nodded. Without even looking at Arann.

Jewel closed the door and leaned against it, staring at Rath. He had retreated into his room, had taken the seat he favored, and sat looking up at her as if he expected her to say something Really Stupid.

This was oddly comforting, because it was a very familiar expression. She almost hated to disappoint him, and since she was half certain she wouldn't, she took a deep breath and met his eyes.

"If," he said quietly, "you are about to tell me that another child is in need of rescue, let me tell you to keep your nightmares to yourself."

She shook her head. "No nightmares," she told him gravely.

His expression indicated that he was not comforted.

"But I talked to Finch. On the way to the Common."

"And?"

"She had to come *from* somewhere, Rath."

"So did you."

She shook her head fiercely. "Not the same. She *was* someplace. She escaped. They—he—chased her."

"Jay. Jewel. I think your involvement in Finch's life is now maximal. Does it matter where she came from?"

It wasn't the answer she was expecting. She wasn't certain what she had been expecting, but this was wrong.

"It matters," she told him, keeping her voice even, "because whoever her pursuer was, he must have known where she'd be. He went to wherever it was—he probably didn't expect her to run. Not the way she was dressed. He was going to kill her, Rath." She paused. "They," she added in a much quieter voice.

"They failed. She's here. I think it unlikely that they will find her again. I have work," he added politely. But his eyes never left her face.

"It's just—"

"Just what?"

"Whoever they were, they must know. They must be *there*."

"Where?"

"Where she was. The place she escaped from."

The eyes closed. "Jay—"

"I'm right. I want to find out where she was. I don't want her to go back—but I think, if she tells you what she can of the place, you'll know where it is."

"I doubt—highly—that she will volunteer that information."

Better than Jewel had expected. But not by much. "She'll tell you."

"What makes you so sure?"

"Because she wasn't the only prisoner." Prisoner. The word left her tongue so easily, she knew that was exactly what Finch had been.

"She told you this?"

"Not—not exactly."

"Jay—"

"Look. It can't be legal. Whatever it was. It *can't* be. We can get the magisterians—we can send word. They don't have to know it comes from us—"

He lifted a hand. She stopped.

"Must you interfere in everything?" he asked quietly.

"Not everything, Rath. But they were going to kill her. And if they couldn't kill her, they might settle for someone else who's trapped wherever she escaped from. You know that."

"Yes. I do."

"Why? What could she possibly—"

"I *don't know*, Jewel. I don't know, and at this point, I am not entirely certain it's safe *to* know." He rose. "Do you know how you get to be old in these holdings, doing what I do?"

She shook her head.

"By knowing what to avoid, and when. This is something to avoid."

"But they're after you as well," she told him.

"Yes." The word was bleak. "And it's not just me. I'm of little consequence, but not none. They cannot find me; if they could, they would never have attempted to take me in the Common. Here, there's safety."

"Only for us."

"Only for me," he replied, the threat in the words absolutely clear. "Leave it be, Jay."

But he knew she wouldn't.

Or couldn't. He could not say with certainty what drove her, although he'd done nothing but observe her for weeks. He'd taught her some simple dagger throws, and some very simple unarmed combat, but she was not the most apt of pupils in that regard; she was small, and if she was flexible, she had little strength.

No, her strength lay in what she called instinct. She should have died, in the alley.

He had no special sight, no talent, no gift of birth—but he knew, far better than she, that she should be dead. And Rath? He would be left with the body, and a few odd memories; he would be left with her flotsam and jetsam, the children she was making a responsibility of the type he had assiduously avoided for all of his adult life.

That she hadn't died was a miracle. And it was entirely hers. The others? If they had such gifts, they had yet to evince them—and Rath very much doubted they ever would. Yet she had dragged two of them, a girl probably a year, maybe even two, younger than she, and a boy her own age by look—he was lanky in the way that the young are—across the tunnels in a blind and desperate run.

To reach his side.

To save his life.

He pulled the chair out from under its place at his desk, and unlocked the writing flat, lowering it gently while it creaked. Dark green leather bore faint marks, faint impressions, the occasional dark stain of ink gone wrong. He covered it with paper.

She was half right. That there were men with either talent or very illegal magical equipment in the lower holdings was a threat that could severely curtail his activities. He had not survived, as he had intimated, by ignorance. If he had no intention of tangling with them again, if he had every intention of following Andrei's oblique advice, he could not do so blindly.

But the weight of her years—her lack of years—was almost more than he could carry. He had seen the two only when Andrei had intervened. Had seen, for himself, that Jewel was not hampered by their invisibility, their lack of visual substance.

And had seen, last, what reminded him most of his sister, his treacherous sister, in the curve of her spine, the straightening lines of her shoulders, the trembling of her slender arms, as she had drawn her own daggers and entered the alley, bypassing him with ease because she was so slight.

Odd.

To see his adult sister in the much smaller spine, the much slimmer stretch of shoulders; to see her patrician face in the ruddy complexion of a child who was half Torra by birth, and all Torra by personality. She had drawn the daggers she could barely wield, had dragged the children into a danger only she could sense, because of *Rath*.

That was the heart of his ill-ease.

That, and the fact that, without Andrei's intervention, he could do *nothing* to save her. He had saved her life, he reasoned—if such feeble and pathetic attempts at justification could be graced with such a word—when he had brought her home, to this one and the one they had abandoned. He had fed her. He had, against all better judgment, gone through the streets of the holding wielding his sword, to save the small giant and his maimed shadow.

And he was coming to realize just how much that would mean if she died.

How far did her talent extend? He had never mentioned his suspicion, his growing certainty that she was seer-born to anyone, and if Andrei guessed, he would keep it to himself. But in failing to mention it, he was depriving himself of information; the information he had gleaned had been from story and near-myth. Who *had* a seer? Who could answer the questions that threatened to propel him into a fight he had no hope of winning?

And if he found a man—or woman—who was capable of answering his questions, would he still manage to keep Jewel hidden from them, from their use?

He wrote a letter slowly, thinking of these things.

And thinking, too, that Jewel would not be content to remain here while she sensed a different threat.

Perhaps, he thought grimly, he should have waited until the cold had truly set in; until the loneliness and fear had resolved itself, at last, into the desperation that truly made orphans in the streets. She might have been broken then.

But seeing her, that night, with no hope of victory, he thought instead of futility. She was, in the end, what she was.

And he had lost one such woman to House Terafin.

He had no desire—he admitted it, the quill digging deep furrows in the soft paper—to lose another.

He finished his letter, and folding it, rose.

It was time to talk to Finch.

* * *

Rath fit in the room.

Jewel reminded herself of this fact a dozen nervous times. She'd been in more crowded rooms. Her father's friends had sometimes come home with him from the docks and the shipping yards, pulling up the crates and boxes that served as chairs when company was present, and jamming themselves around the table, as much as they could.

But Rath was different. He took up more space than any four of those men, just by standing in the doorframe.

"Jay," he said, although he used the tone of voice reserved for the more formal—and therefore more despised—Jewel. "This is Finch?" His gaze traveled in a small arc, and landed more or less on the right person.

It was a *polite* question, since he damn well knew the answer. And polite, from Rath, meant something. Not usually something good.

Finch nodded.

"Jay tells me that you managed to escape from . . . someplace."

Her second nod was a good deal more hesitant than the first.

"Do you know which holding it was in?"

She frowned. Which Jewel took as a no. Rath, no idiot, interpreted it correctly as well.

"Where were you living, before you ended up there?"

"Twenty-eighth," she said promptly.

"With your family?"

The silence that followed the question was terrible.

Rath lifted a hand. "Finch," he asked softly, "how did you get to where you were . . . held?"

"Walked." To Jewel, and in Torra, she added, "Make him stop."

"He understands Torra," Jewel replied quietly. She hesitated. Carver had stiffened unexpectedly, and this probably meant he understood it as well. First time he'd given a sign. "Finch—you left someone behind. There's a chance we can help them."

The younger girl's shoulders had folded in on themselves, the new weight of clothing suddenly far too large for her frame; it was as if the heavy cloth was swallowing her without a fight. "I didn't know her before I—before that place," she said softly. "I still don't know her name. She was—I think she was your age. Maybe older. Dark-haired. She had a scar—" she stopped for a moment, lifting a hand to her mouth. Jewel hoped dinner wasn't about to be wasted.

"She told me—the boys and the girls—some of them are just disappearing. I'd only been there two days—I—"

Jewel slid an arm around her shoulder, standing now between the girl and Rath. "She helped you." No question there.

"Yes. I don't know why," she added. "She told me when to run. I think—I think she knew the man. Or recognized him." She paused. "There's always a guard. Sometimes two. It depends on who . . . " She looked up, her face so pale Jewel thought she might faint. But she didn't. "On who's visiting."

"How did you get past the guards?" Rath asked, his voice softening.

"Her."

"You don't think she's still alive."

Finch, again, offered silence.

"Rath—"

"I need to know where," he said grimly.

"Is it a—"

"Yes. Sometimes they're called brothels. They're highly, highly illegal."

As if that mattered, here. No, Jewel thought, *here*, in this room, it *did* matter.

"It's new?" he asked Finch, bending his knees and reducing his height, as if by changing his posture he could diminish the threat.

"I don't know."

"In a house?"

"A big house."

What big meant to Finch was not clear. It meant something to Rath, and Jewel hoped it meant the same thing. Language was tricky, that way.

"Not one of the tenements? Or the courtyard buildings?"

She shook her head. "A house."

"It has to be new," he said to himself, rising. "Finch, I'm sorry—but I need you to help me now."

"I'll go," Jewel added.

Carver said, "We can all go." He failed to notice Lefty. But Lefty failed to say a word.

"Out of the question," Rath told them firmly. "One of you, maybe. Arann. Jewel. But not all of you. You'll be noticed by anyone with an eye, never mind two. And at the moment, we're *not* going anywhere.

"I need to know as much as possible about the lay of the land."

They all stared at him, except for Jewel.

He smiled a tight, frustrated smile. "I need to know what things look like," he said, speaking slowly, as if to children or idiots. "I understand that it's difficult to speak about," he added, "but this girl probably saved your life. Do her the kindness of attempting to return the favor."

And Finch straightened her shoulders, took a deep breath, held it for a moment, and then began to speak.

It came as a shock to Jewel to hear the growing strength of the younger girl's voice.

The Den was busy. Late afternoon would shade into evening, and then it would be *really* busy. Rath was indifferent to either state. He waited at a table by the back; the corner he preferred was already occupied, and as he didn't wish attention, he left it that way.

The strangers that he had noticed a few days past were not present; if they were lucky, they had work. If they were unlucky, it was the wrong work, and if Rath was unlucky, it was both wrong and in his way. It wouldn't be the first time.

Still, he waited. He had paid Harald, and if the pay was not precisely a patrician sum, it was good enough to guarantee that Harald paid attention. As much as Harald ever did.

Half an hour passed. The sky was no longer clear, but the clouds were thin and promised drizzle, not rain. Rath had forgone the oiled overcoat that made all men look like canvas sacks with legs; in this, his vanity was allowed some rein.

Harald, however, had no such vanity to be pricked, and Rath recognized him by movement, more than sight; he had a particular way of walking into a room as if he owned it. And because he almost did, other men had a way of making room to let him pass unhampered. Then again, Harald was known here; getting in his way on the wrong day was like offering a gift to the gods of bad temper, such as they were. In this case, they were probably named Harald or Haraldess.

He pulled the hood off his face as he approached Rath. "You drinking?" he said heavily, and pulled a chair round, shoving its back against the rounded lip of the table.

"Demonstrably," Rath replied, lifting a mug.

"It's not empty," Harald said, with a shrug.

"I've only been here—"

"Stow it."

Rath inclined his head. "What do you have for me?"

Harald raised a fist.

One of the sailors—the youngest, although with the three it was hard to tell—made his way through the crowd with a tray. He dropped the whole thing, three mugs, in front of Harald. Either Harald had been here more frequently than Rath, or the sailors preferred him to be more mellow than he clearly was.

Harald paid. And counted the change. His heart, however, was not in it, and he counted poorly. Rath, from his vantage, could see this clearly, and chose not to comment on it. He noted that the sailor, a few coins richer, didn't either.

"Yes," Harald said, after he'd drained half a mug. "I have what I think you want."

"Names?"

Harald shook his head. "But there are a few startups. Last three months. Maybe six."

"That would be during the shipping season."

"Yeah. When the rest of us were out."

Rath was silent for a moment. "The magisterians?"

"I've got a friend of a friend," Harald replied, leaning slightly over the table. He was careful not to upend any of the ale he'd paid for.

Friend of a friend. Rath almost shook his head. "Magisterian?"

Harald nodded. "He was transferred out of the thirty-fifth about four months ago."

"Better job?"

"The same job."

"Then why?"

"That's the funny thing. No reason given. Just—out."

"Anything unusual going on in the thirty-fifth?"

"Funny you should ask."

This was Harald; Rath waited. He even feigned patience. Which, for Harald, would simply mean he didn't try to hit him or draw weapon on him.

"There was some kind of shake-up. Not in the Court or the Magisterium, but down near the ground. Shifts were changed or rescheduled. Timing was marked."

"The patrols are supposed to be random."

Harald shrugged. "Funny coincidence."

"Frequency?"

"That seems to have gone down as well. Apparently, some of the merchants—"

"In the *thirty-fifth?*"

Harald coughed ale. "That's what I said."

Rath shook his head. A child could do better, if a lie had to be fabricated; these weren't the rich holdings. "Merchants, then. Go on."

"Some of the merchants—who pay the taxes—weren't happy with the quality of patrols they were seeing. So patrols have been diverted."

"Someone's being bribed. Did you find out who?"

Harald shook his head. "Thought I'd leave that to your fancy connections. But it's the thirty-fifth," he added. "I'm not sure any of that money is going into a *bank*."

"Tell me about the rest."

Harald hesitated. He emptied the first mug and almost tossed it aside. But he wasn't in the mood to deal with the person it would have hit, and he forced himself to drop it on the table instead; Rath caught it before it rolled off and hit floor.

"There are rumors," he said carefully. "Just rumors."

"I'm a gossip. What are they?"

"No one's got anything. No proof. No street address."

Rath nodded again.

"But some of the uptowners have been making their way into the thirty-fifth." He paused. "And possibly the thirty-second as well."

Rath's face was carefully neutral, which looked very much like boredom to those who didn't know him. Harald knew him well enough.

"What are the uptowners buying?"

"Time," Harald replied. "Someone went through the thirty-first and the thirty-second, talking to some of the street families, some of the poorer ones. And after that? Some of the kids went missing."

Finch.

To his great surprise, Rath was angry. He was also cautious enough to contain it, for now.

"You haven't lived here long enough," Harald said, lifting the second mug. It was so easy to forget that cunning and intelligence were cousins. But he was sober, and his eyes were a shade too dark. "You've got work for me?"

"Not yet."

"Too bad." His fingers were white. Rath almost laughed, but it would have been the wrong laugh for this crowd.

"You look like you're about ready for a fight."

Harald nodded.

"Where?"

And shrugged, a bear's shrug, the stiff oilskin creasing as it followed the motion. "I'm not sure I'm considered reliable enough," he said at last. "And I wasn't exactly gentle when I was getting the damn information."

"Be careful. How many?"

The question caused the mug to stop halfway to Harald's mouth. It came back, table-side, and rested there. "You know I hate kids, right?"

Rath nodded.

"They're whiny. Stupid. Weak."

And nodded again.

"I don't want a handful of screaming kids following me around."

"Trust me, they won't be following you."

"How much money are you offering?"

"Standard rates."

"Standard for what?"

"Small job. High risk."

"Well, The White Whore won't miss us. Much. Maybe six. Eight. Depends."

"On what?"

"You're not the only man hiring."

The second half of the information. "Who is?"

"You'll see him, if you stick around."

"Name?"

"No name. At least none I've heard."

"You don't like the look of him."

"Not much. But I've been around. I hate being dockside. I hate the ground; it doesn't move. And the hires? They're never going to see ship-side again."

"Why do you say that?"

"Hunch."

Good enough. "If you can get me eight, get me eight."

"Up-front money?"

Rath frowned. But it wasn't a deep frown. He pulled a small purse from the inside of his jacket and tossed it at Harald. Harald didn't bother to count what was in it. Then again, watching Harald count was its own special hell; Rath was grateful.

"Where?"

"I'm not exactly certain."

"You've got an idea."

Rath nodded. "Meet me tomorrow; we'll go before the Common opens."

"Where?"

"Looseboard and Trail."

Harald laughed. "The thirty-fifth."

"It's not like you'll have to worry about magisterial guards."

When Rath returned, he was in a mood that would have been foul had he spoken a single word. He saw Jewel and Finch in the kitchen; saw Lefty hovering in the corner. He didn't even look at them. Instead, he passed them by, his eyes narrow, his lips thinned.

"Jay?" Finch whispered, when his door slammed shut.

Jewel's knife was in the middle of a large carrot; it had stopped there. "He's not happy," she said quietly.

Lefty snorted. Jay was beginning to think that the quiet boy who wouldn't meet her eyes was preferable to this one.

"What is it? Is it us? Have we done something wrong?" Finch was shaking. Quiet. "Are you going to be in trouble?"

Jewel forced herself to laugh. It was awkward. "I'm *always* in trouble," she told the younger girl. "You take this. Get Arann to help you and tell him if he cuts the board again, I'll hit him." She let the knife go, and it clunked against the counter as the carrot rolled.

She made it to the open frame, and stopped there. "Finch?" she said, without looking back.

"I don't want to go back," the girl whispered. And then, to Jewel's relief, added, "But I will, if you're there."

"I'll be there." She left them then, and went to Rath.

He wasn't sitting. He was standing in the center of the room. His shoulders were tense, and his back was toward the door, but he clearly expected Jewel, because he didn't jump or turn when she entered.

"You found something," she said.

He nodded. "Finch—"

"She'll go, Rath."

He turned, then. "She was sold," he told her quietly.

"I'd guessed." The words were just as quiet. Bitter. Hers. "Maybe she had a lot of family. Maybe they were starving." Her words as well, and she couldn't believe she was saying them.

Clearly, neither could Rath.

"They're poor," she told him, as if that were a defense. A defense against her own anger, her own helpless rage. "And it doesn't matter, because *I* want her. I'll never sell her. I'll never give her up."

"Given what we risked, you'd better mean that." He lifted a hand to his forehead. "Given what we *will* risk, you'd better remember that."

"I'll go with her."

Rath nodded, almost absent. It was damn cold in the room. "At dawn," he told her quietly. "Have her ready."

"The others—"

He met her gaze. Held it. And after a long, long moment, he looked away.

He was giving in. Jewel was almost shocked. But chasing shock, other emotions followed. "You don't think we're only going to find one other person," she said, softly.

He stared at her for a minute, and some of the stiffness left him. She wasn't certain it was an improvement. "I would never have taken you in if you were stupid," he told her, almost fondly. Almost angrily. "But there are days when I wish you were. No, I don't think it's just one person. And no, I don't know what we'll find.

"But you were right; Finch would have run from me. And if I'm right, we're going to need people that children won't run away from."

People. More than one.

Rath had three sets of boots.

He surrendered one to Carver. They didn't fit. But not fitting, they were still far better than the bare feet the cobbler couldn't cover for another two days. The boots were old, and soft; worn at the heels and in other places. They were covered with dried mud. Jewel knew where he wore them.

But if Carver were quick, he'd know, too. She had almost suggested he stay here; his expression had stopped her. It wasn't like Rath's; it didn't have his arrogance or his particular certainty. It held, instead, a different kind of certainty, and beneath it, a desperation she didn't understand. Might never understand, if the gods were kind.

His fingers trembled as he struggled with the eyes and the laces, crossing them in the wrong way as Rath watched. Rath seemed to have that effect on everyone.

Everyone but Arann, who, dressed, was grim and silent. There had been a bit of an argument between Arann and Lefty, and Jewel could guess what it had been about. But Lefty, hand shoved into a pocket instead of his armpit, was quiet in his jittery defiance.

Where Arann went, he would follow. He clearly didn't think Arann was ready for this. And Arann, just as clearly, didn't care.

"You can use that?" Rath asked Carver.

Carver looked blank for a minute, and then he hesitated. "If I have to."

"Good. It's the only time you should ever even be considering it." His gaze was cool as it lingered on Carver's hair. Jewel almost *felt* him stifle the coming lecture. "Jay told me about the bar stool. That was clever."

Carver didn't beam. Didn't even smile. But he did straighten out a little, and that was something.

"We're going to meet a number of men. They'll all be armed. Some will be in armor, depending on how their gambling went; some won't. None of them are your friends." He gazed around the room at the handful of boys, at the two girls. "But *if* you run into trouble, let it chase you to where they're waiting. Got it? They won't talk to you. They *will* fight for you." He paused. "I'd prefer you wait outside, if we find the place we're looking for.

"But if you don't, I'll accept that as well. You've all seen the streets. You've an idea of what they mean. I don't know how much death you've seen. I don't know how much real fighting. You follow us in, and you will. Do *not* attempt to join the fighting. You'll find that in the chaos, you probably won't be able to tell who's on our side and who's not.

"Understood?"

They nodded in unison.

"Your job," he continued, "is to try to guide or help the children who might run *out* of the building while the fighting is going on. They won't go near my people; they won't go near their guards. Or any of the other adults on the premises. If they don't run, we can do something for them, maybe. If they do . . ." He shrugged.

And Finch said, in a quiet voice, a steel voice, "Some can't run."

Rath nodded, as if he expected no less. He took one more look at them, and then he made his way to the door.

"Don't talk," he told Jewel. "Tell the others: don't speak. What they're doing isn't legal. What we're doing isn't either."

"But we're doing the—"

"Right thing?" He grimaced. But he said nothing else until they had filed out of the apartment, past him; until he'd locked the door at their backs. "Maybe," he told her softly. Just that.

Day felt like night, as they walked.

People did not quite crowd the streets; it was a little too early for that. But buckets borne across bent shoulder and straight back alike were beginning to make themselves seen, and the sun's light, faded, pearl and gray, colored clouds moved by wind. This was dawn, in the rainy season. The clarity of the day had passed, and the morning was cold.

Cold against cheek and exposed hand, exposed throat. Cold in other ways. Jewel looked at Rath's back as he led them; he walked more slowly than was his wont, but did so with a grace that belied impatience.

She trusted him, and in ways that she had never thought to trust her father, when she had lived with him in the quiet and illusionary safety of their home. She could never have asked him for *this*. When her Oma had lived, she might have asked for a story that contained it, no more; she might have imagined, in the dark, humid confines of an evening bed, those ancient arms around her, that she could live in those stories, and be of them.

But that was dream, and the waking was harder than she could have imagined. In dream, she was a great leader, an intrepid explorer, a woman revered for her heroism by the faceless, adoring masses. In dream, she could save not only lives, but baronies and kingdoms; she could sit by the right hand of the Kings themselves, or even *between* them; she could rove across the windswept sands of desert that glittered like golden death for as far as the eye could see.

That was her Oma's gift to her: the ability to dream. And yet . . . without it, she would not be here. She would not think of being here.

Here was a place of death, or the fear of death. Here, Rath ahead of her in dark clothing, the finery of jacket set aside in favor of the absolute length of blade, she could imagine losing him, in ways that she had not—until the end—imagined losing her father.

She had asked for this.

Not in so many words. Never that. If she were entirely honest, she could say that he had decided it, and she merely followed.

But if she hadn't learned how to lie to Rath's satisfaction, it was because she was simply no good at lying: she knew he would not be in this street, on this chill morning, without her. Carver walked by her side, to the left; to the right walked Finch. She wore clothing very much like Jewel's—it would have to be, coming from Helen, as almost all clothing did—but she didn't look at Rath's back as she walked; she looked at her feet. At the weeds that passed beneath them. At the shift in the road as Rath turned a corner. There were no real shadows cast, not in this light—but had there been, Jewel was certain she would have looked at those as well.

Rath paused. "Jay?"

She whispered Finch's name. Finch hesitated a moment, and then nodded. "I think this is the right way."

Rath's nod was both the same dip of chin and entirely different. There was a curt certainty to the motion that spoke of purpose, not fear.

Jewel wanted to *be* Rath, for a moment. To be older, to be that certain. She was his shadow, instead, and it galled her. But not so much that she was made stupid by envy or inadequacy. She couldn't afford to be. He'd made that clear.

So much else was unclear.

Her father would have *died* before he'd parted with her. Her Oma would have killed him, had he tried to sell her; to bargain for her as if she were a thing, and not his blood, his kin. They would have starved, all three, and almost had, time and again—but they had done it *together*.

Finch . . .

She seemed so quiet, so fragile. Jewel had seen old women who seemed the same—but the fact that they *were* old, in these streets, said something; spoke to some part of her that understood how strength was measured. Was Finch that strong?

She certainly didn't seem it, to Jewel. Her steps were shaky and small; she moved so slowly, Jewel wanted to tell Arann to pick her up and carry her. Maybe another time. Maybe never. Because Finch *was* walking, and maybe that's all that Jewel could ask of her.

Carver's hand was on his knife. He was taller than Jewel, and he looked older—but his eyes were dark and a little too round. He knew—probably better than Jewel herself—what they might face. And he had no reason to want to face it. He was an accident. Something that her curious vision hadn't granted her.

But she *knew* he wouldn't run. Not here, not yet. Maybe not ever. She wanted to ask him why. Or why not. But she didn't.

Nor did she ask Arann, but it didn't occur to her to ask Arann; he was almost as tall as Rath, and he was so utterly solid as he walked, Lefty to his left, the open street to his right. He watched Rath, but not the way Jewel herself did; his gaze often slid to the people that were beginning to fill the street, to make their walk less solitary.

She almost tripped over Rath because she was looking at Arann. Rath's pinched expression was all the admonition he allowed himself, but she felt it keenly.

"Be on your guard now," he told her, as she righted herself.

She started to ask him why. Stopped. The answer was there, in the streets, creating as it walked—as they walked—a widening circle of silence and flight.

Armor didn't gleam in this kind of light, and besides, it wasn't that kind of armor; it was pitted and dented and tarnished; hung in rings that could be seen through the gap of overcoats and over the thick, undyed padding beneath it. There were flat plates across the chest of one man, a man who wore an eye patch across a scarred face. His hair was the color of sand on the white beaches at summer's height, and his skin was sea skin.

He was the leader, she thought.

She put out an arm; Carver walked into it, and stopped moving. Finch had stopped a few steps back, and Arann now towered over her, without a word, Lefty also cringing by his side.

"Gentlemen," Rath said, and Jewel privately thought a Weston word had *never* been so misused. "Well met."

The pale-haired man with the odd beard and a single eye spit to one side. "I've seven," he said grimly.

"And the eighth?"

"He'll recover."

Rath shrugged. It wasn't friendly; Jewel guessed he knew who the eighth man was, and didn't much care whether he recovered or not.

"Who are these?" The stranger said, almost snorting. Like a bull. Or a stir-crazy horse.

"They know the holding," was Rath's evasive reply. "And they may prove of some use." He paused, and when the man's face failed to shift into something like acceptance, added, "They're *mine*."

The man's shrug was almost the same as Rath's had been.

These are the people we're supposed to hide behind if we need protection? She almost said it. Had to bite her lip to stop the words from tumbling out, one over the other in a heated rush.

But she put a hand on Finch's shoulder, and Finch stilled. No one spoke.

"Well, they're quiet enough."

Rath said nothing. He might have been one of these towering, ugly strangers. Except for the dirt and the obvious scars.

"Finch," Jewel whispered.

Slowly, Finch began to walk.

Chapter Fourteen

ARMOR MADE NOISE. The wrong kind.

Jewel had to speak loudly in order to be heard, and as she was speaking to Finch, she had the tendency to lower her voice, not raise it. She wanted to tell the men to either go away or stop moving for a minute, but when she turned, Rath's sharp look made her teeth snap shut.

Finch, however pale she was, nodded. To Jewel. And to Rath. Rath listened to her quiet voice, reading her lips and their motion; there was no way the sound could carry to where he stood. But what he gleaned was enough; he turned to speak curtly with the man who wore the eye patch, and the man in turn barked at the others.

If they were supposed to be approaching quietly or without notice, it was an utter failure; the streets were now empty for as far back as Jewel could see—which, given the bodies of armored men, each taller than she was, wasn't perhaps as far as usual—and as they rounded a corner, it cleared in front. Sort of like the movement of a gigantic broom.

She hated to cause that fear in children, because she knew it so well herself. Her gaze grazed Lefty, but Lefty was almost Arann's shadow; she couldn't see his face, and his hands were still shoved in pockets. By no means did all of Helen's tunics have them; Helen must have noticed the way Lefty tried to hide his right hand.

Carver seemed a little less lost than she was, as if he knew the neighborhood. Given the expression on his face—or the utter lack of one—Jewel guessed that whatever he knew wasn't worth sharing. She'd told him his life before Taverson's didn't matter, and inasmuch as she could, she'd told the truth. But she was curious. Rath said it was both her strength and her weakness, and he hoped she lived long enough to be able to tell exactly when it was one or the other.

She had seen Rath draw his sword once. She had seen him fight twice. She was aware, as they walked, that she really didn't want to see a third time. The stories of old—her Oma's grand stories of life in a sea of sand— had somehow failed to mention the brutality and the swiftness of death. The glory of causing it, yes, because that was Right. Funny, how wrong Right felt when she could actually *see* it.

Her dagger hadn't managed to cut skin. She'd tried.

And she wondered how she would feel if somehow she'd succeeded; if it would haunt her. Wondered if today was the day she'd have her answer, and regret her question.

The streets widened out as they followed Finch's directions—directions that were becoming quieter and more hesitant with each step she took. She was reduced, in the end, to pointing, and her mute nod, her mute shake of the head, should have caused pity.

In Jewel, it caused the beginning of something like anger—except that it grew, and grew, and grew. Someone else had brought Finch along these streets. Someone else had given her to the men from whom she'd barely escaped.

Jewel reached out and caught Finch by the hand. Finch's hands were shaking—it was cold and damp—almost as much as Jewel's. But not, Jewel thought, for the same reason.

The buildings they passed grew wider, although they were still tall. Fences began to line the street, but they were a legacy of older times; they were broken in places, and rusted in others, and whole sections leaned in toward the ground. Although the streets were wide, they could barely be called streets in places; there had been stone laid here, once upon a time—but it had cracked, and whole patches of weeds, which had sum-mered and grown, stood waist-high where carriage and wagon wheels had failed to crush them. Rainfall made patches of mud, where stones had been pulled up or removed entirely, and in those patches, deeper puddles had been formed by the fall of heavy feet.

This much she expected, although she skirted the edges, mindful of the fact that she now held onto Finch.

The buildings began to flatten, sometimes literally, but more often figuratively; the fences in one or two areas were, if not new, then at least kept up. Not that the grounds—such as they were—beyond those fences were cared for in the same way; there, with no wagons and no running children to squash them down, they looked like a wild harvest, some city version of farmer's fields gone bad.

Still, there were trees that had grown up on either side of the road, and no one had yet been enterprising enough to cut them down for Winter wood. She wondered at that; they wouldn't have survived for long in the holding where Jewel had spent almost all of her life. They were not so tall or grand as the trees that marked the Common, but then again, no trees were—and no one with half a wit about them tried to take an ax to *those* trees.

She looked at Rath.

Rath looked at Finch, and Finch swallowed.

He lifted a hand, and the movement rippled backward, as the men who followed came to a slow halt, fanning out in the street. Across from the fence that was in passable repair were houses tightly packed together; small houses, with narrow fronts and even narrower stairs.

They seemed almost fine, to Jewel, but not compared to the large house that hid behind gates and weeds, rising above them in the distance.

"Here?" Rath asked.

Finch managed a nod.

Rath looked at the man with the eye patch, who frowned a moment, as if he were thinking. Then he nodded.

"Jay."

Jewel looked up at Rath.

"We're about to take out the gatekeeper, if there is one. You will stay back with your friends until we've entered the building. Is that understood?"

She nodded.

"Carver," he continued.

Carver's nod was a lot stiffer. It was also really minimal.

"We cannot be entirely certain that all of the men we're looking for are *in* that building. They may well reside in the smaller residences across the street."

Carver nodded again. Slow nod, and measured.

"You've said you know how to use that dagger. I trust you meant it. If you need to use it, you'll know. Watch that row," he added. "If more than one man comes out, it is *not* the right time." He turned to Arann, met his gaze, and then offered him a nod.

"Jay."

"We'll wait."

"Good."

The man with the eye patch lifted an arm; it was a signal. Without another word, Rath and his friends drifted down the street, following the line of the fence until it came to a gate. If the gate was locked, it didn't seem to matter; they opened it somehow and then charged out of the street.

There should have been yells, or horns, or something; there was only the sound of armor and heavy feet. Even breath didn't make much sound, although she could see it rise like a thin, thin mist, in their wake.

"Where did you find him?" Carver asked her, after they had gone.

She shrugged. "In the streets. On the way to the Common."

"I wouldn't have gone near him."

"I was hungry."

"Begging?"

She snorted. "What do you think?"

He laughed. But she saw that his eyes were on the thin houses that stood too close to the street; that they flickered over the shuttered single windows that stood beneath their steep, peaked rooftops. "I've never been hungry enough to try to steal anything from someone like him."

She shrugged again; she wasn't proud of what she'd done, but it didn't shame her completely. "I knew he didn't need the money. He wasn't going to starve if he lost it."

"And that mattered?"

"To me. Then. It probably wouldn't have made as much of a difference in the Winter, though."

Lefty said, loudly enough to be heard, "Liar."

She glared at him.

And then, before she could speak, she heard what she'd been waiting for. What she hadn't known she'd been waiting for.

The loud cries of men. They all froze then, their words lost a moment to fear.

To Rath's surprise, there had been no guard at the gate. Perhaps the early hour worked to their advantage, in this; the clientele that were attracted to a building such as this were no doubt men who traveled at night, and by magelight; they were not poor men.

The building was not new, and it was not well maintained, except in the loosest sense of the word. It was, clearly, occupied. At one point, perhaps two centuries ago, it had been a very fine building. Now, it possessed the squalor of all fallen things, grace turned on its edge, its dingy glory a reminder that all things of value must fade.

Not a welcome reminder. Never that.

The doors were not as old as the building itself; nor, Rath thought, were the shutters that graced several windows that had once held glass. The walk from the gates to the steps that led up to the door was also newer, and it had been laid out in haste, or by incompetent craftsmen. The steps, however, were solid stone, and if they sloped in the middle, they were not obviously cracked or broken.

They bore the weight of armored men, and they were wide enough that those men could fan out at different heights. They wanted to be as close to the building as possible; some of the windows weren't barred, and the most obvious defense—the crossbow—was probably lying beside some sleeping thug's bed. None of Harald's men relied on crossbows, probably because they couldn't afford them.

The doors were locked. Rath thought they were probably barred as well, and from the inside. He took the time to pick the lock, and tried the door to confirm his suspicion; it didn't take long.

"Can we break it down?" one of Harald's men asked.

Harald cuffed him across the side of the head. "Only if we use your thick skull as a battering ram." He looked back at Rath. "Left or right?"

Rath considered the two large windows—real windows—that fronted the manor. These, too, seemed newly added. He could see the drape of drawn curtains, and between these, a glimpse of something that resembled a parlor. Not even a poorly appointed one at that.

"Left," Rath said quietly.

Harald shrugged.

The windows themselves were not level with the ground; they were level with the height of the stairs, whose gentle slope was deceptive.

"Sorn!"

A long-haired man—braided hair, no fool—stepped up; he was carrying a club. A large club. Harald knelt, cupping his hands together. "Darren."

Another man, with drawn sword; he sheathed his weapon with a grimace. Rath knelt, facing Harald, his hands also cupped. He grunted at the weight he was forced to bear; he'd gotten used to Jewel and she was probably a quarter the size.

"Get the door unbarred," Harald snapped. "If you can. We'll come up by the window until the door's open."

They hoisted the men at the same time, and glass broke, cracking rather than shattering. Three times, the club hit the window; the third time, and the panes fell, forced inward by the strength of the blow.

Good damn glass, Rath thought. If he'd had any doubts, they were gone with the windows. This was the place.

Sorn and Darren disappeared, and two more of Harald's men stepped up, sheathing their weapons. They were through the remnants of the window when the first cries were sounded.

The doors swung open, and Rath and Harald almost collided in their race to be through them before they swung again. If their purpose here could be considered—in Jewel's quaint usage of the word—good, their intent was more practical; they wanted to take advantage of sleeping, unprepared men, and they wanted to do it *quickly.* Harald's Northern ancestry did not carry with it the complicated rules of Northern engagements in battle. Or perhaps he considered this less a battle, and more an extermination of vermin. It was hard, with Harald, to be certain.

Rath didn't have that problem. There was no honor to be had in fighting; there was no honor to be found in killing. Having made the decision, there was the simple fact of the thing. That and the imperative of survival.

He was in the foyer—and it was the ghost of what had once been impressive; there was no massive chandelier to light it, no pristine carpets to cover it; instead, there was faded paint, faded wood, and a grand, twisting staircase that rose to the flat of the second floor.

It was there that Harald's men headed, and it was there that they were met. Rath, behind them by seconds, saw what he'd feared: a crossbow. He took in the man who wielded it only after. Saw that he was poorly dressed, and unarmored; that his face was shadowed by what might one day be a beard, and his eyes were wide.

But the bow was steady in his hands as he swung it down.

Rath's hand dropped to his leg and he drew a throwing knife; he leaped up the stairs, thankful for the vanity of their width, their open climb, and threw the dagger.

It struck the man's shoulder, and the man cried out; the bow wavered and the string twanged. The bolt flew wide. Reloading was not an option. After a few seconds, neither was breathing. Rath didn't stop to check the fallen man; if he wasn't dead, he was no longer a threat.

"Jay," Arann said quietly, when the cries had died into stillness and Jay had begun to walk the length of the fence.

She turned and looked back at him without speaking.

"Rath told us to wait."

She nodded, but she looked to Finch. "How many?" She asked quietly. The wrong type of quiet.

Finch stared at her for a moment, drawing her tunic more tightly around her. "I don't know."

"You had a chance. To run. Someone *gave* you the chance."

"Duster," she said quietly. *You said you didn't know her name.* But if Finch remembered the lie at all, it didn't show. "She told me her name was Duster."

"She was the only one?"

Finch shook her head. "I didn't see many others," she added, eyes scraping the road.

"How many did you see?"

She shook her head almost violently. "I heard them. I don't know how many."

Jewel looked at Arann again, and then swung round to Carver. "We have to go," she said at last, and pointed to the mansion.

He hesitated. His dagger was a simple, flat blade, and rain fell like mist in the streets, threatening steel with rust. He finally said, "You sure?"

She nodded.

"How sure?"

"Just . . . sure."

"I'm in." He looked at Arann, and then at Lefty and Finch. "Maybe you two should stay—"

Lefty stepped closer to Arann, which shouldn't have been possible.

Finch said nothing. She looked at them slowly. "You can't fight them," she said quietly. "They'll kill you all."

"We're not alone here," Jewel snapped. "Rath's in there. With his friends. Who all have swords. It's not our job to *fight*; it's our job to *find*." She hesitated again and then spit out a curse in bitter Torra. "We don't have *time*, Finch. Arann, you stay with Lefty and Finch. I'll take Carver."

But Lefty caught Arann's sleeve, dragging his arm down; Arann bent to the side and Lefty said something in his ear. It had been a week since he'd been this spooked, this word-shy. Jewel hated to see it.

But she understood that here, Arann was the source of comfort; she waited.

Arann unbent. "We go together," he said quietly. He looked at Finch. Looked down at Finch. "Stay with me," he told her.

She was pale as light on water. But she nodded.

Jewel began to move.

Rath was, by nature, a suspicious man.

There were four bodies in the hall in a handful of minutes, none of them his. None of them Harald's either; the morning was not kind to the men who dwelled here. Nor should it be.

But . . . it felt wrong. Too easy. He walked to the first closed door in a wide hall, and tried to open it; it was locked.

The lock was a pathetic one; Rath could have picked it in his sleep. But putting his weapon down was harder than he would have liked, even surrounded by Harald's men. He bent, retrieved lockpicks, and opened the lock. Then he motioned them away from the door, and, turning the lock, threw it open, hunching down.

The room looked empty.

There was a bed to one side, a small dresser, and, incongruous here, a large, rectangular mirror. The mirror was new; the silvered glass hadn't tarnished or yellowed. It was also clean.

Harald entered the room, looked about it for a minute and then pointed, with his sword, to the bed. Or rather, to the floor beneath it. Not empty, no. One eyebrow rose—oddly enough, the brow above the patch. Harald's way of asking a question.

Rath shook his head. "Leave the doors open," he said quietly. "We don't have the time to gather the occupants; that's not what we're here for."

He stepped back into the hall.

"If they're scared enough," Harald said quietly, "they won't leave."

"We can worry about that later."

Harald gave him an odd look. Rath shook his head in reply. It wasn't quite signing, but close enough; they'd been in fights before. The large, Northern man snapped an order. One of his men had picked up the crossbow.

From down the far end of the hall, men emerged. They were better armored than their dead compatriots, and two carried crossbows; the other four carried swords.

Six men. Harald's man shot down the length of the hall just before they charged.

Jewel's slow walk became a jog, and when she cleared the fence, she began to run. She couldn't say why, but she didn't need to; in her old life, it would only have gotten her in trouble. She didn't precisely forget about the others that followed; Carver kept pace with her, no matter how hers changed. But reaching the manor doors had become, in the brief span of minutes, *urgent*.

They knew it. Carver actually out paced her; his legs were longer, and it became apparent that he'd spent a lot of time on the run. From what or who didn't really matter. Arann was slower; he had Lefty and Finch in tow, and he meant to watch over them.

But when their gaze met briefly, Jewel understood that part of the reason he did it was for *her*. To free her from the worry and the fear. To let her think.

They made their way into the foyer just in time; the doors slammed shut at their backs with enough force to splinter the damn wood. And just for good measure, the bolt dropped.

They all jumped and spun, and saw . . . nothing. Closed doors, that was all. Carver looked at Jewel. "Should we open them?"

She shook her head. "We can't," she told him quietly. Staring at the doors. At the faint orange light that now ringed them, burning nothing but vision.

"Why exactly did we want to be on the *inside* of the manor?"

Jewel looked up the stairs. A body lay perched on the flat above, his arm trailing blood down old carpet. "Up there," she told Carver.

Carver hesitated, and then nodded. But he let her lead the way, and as she took the steps, she slowed. Not because she felt danger, not precisely; she *heard* it. The sounds of swords clashing. The sounds of running men. Orders, barked with so much edge they didn't sound like words anymore.

"Jay?"

"We need to get them out," she told him. She would have whispered had she the choice; she had to speak loudly enough for the words to carry.

Carver was smart; he didn't ask her who they were.

Four men down. One of Harald's; three of their enemy. Three were standing, and they held the hall. But they weren't terrified.

And they weren't *good enough* not to be. They faced seven armed men, and they fought, but they fought as if they were waiting. For reinforcements, Rath thought. The hall was wide enough that swordplay was possible; the ceilings were high enough that even Harald could swing his broadsword overhead. They could fight side by side without endangering each other.

Rath *was* good enough. He brought a fourth man down, and that left two. They backed down the hall, retreating rather than fleeing.

It was wrong. Something about it was wrong.

Jewel saw the first open door, and she ran for it; Carver made it there first. They had to cross the hall, had to step over a body, had to leave the safety of open steps and the promise of flight behind.

They also had to ignore the men in the hall yards away. Lefty froze; Arann caught him by the shoulder and dragged him into the room. He caught Finch as well, but they left the door open, and Arann was the wedge that would *keep* it that way.

Jay looked at herself in the mirror; saw her companions, Arann by the door where the sound of fighting was clearest. He didn't look out into the hall; he kept watch over Lefty and Finch. Carver whistled at the sight of the mirror, at his face in it; she kicked his ankle, and pointed to the bed.

But it was Jewel who got down on her hands and knees, as if she were a much younger child, and Jewel who crossed the wooden slats of bare floor until she reached its edge. It was Jewel who looked under the hanging folds of creased, blue counterpane—a color she would always despise after this day—and Jewel who lifted it high, exposing more floor and the child who had taken shelter beneath the bed.

He was curled up there, watching, and his eyes widened when he saw her face. There was enough shadow beneath the bed that she couldn't see all of him clearly. But he had no weapon. "I don't have time to explain," she told him, keeping her voice level with effort, "but you can't stay here."

His eyes widened further, and then narrowed. "You're new here," he said quietly.

"I'm not here," she answered. "Or not for long. We've come to get you *out,* but we don't have much time."

The boy covered his face with his hands.

She would have slapped him if she could have reached him. "We don't have—"

She heard shouting from the hall. Adult voices, raised in something that wasn't quite panic.

The boy shook his head. "They're here," he whispered, his face going pale. "They're—they're here."

Jewel said, "I know. We have friends," she added. "But we can't stay here long."

The boy shook his head again, and if the men outside weren't panicking, he was.

Before Jewel could shout—and she was close—Finch dropped to the ground. Finch who was smaller, slighter, quieter. She nudged her way past Jewel, almost pushing her to one side. "I was here," she told the boy quietly. "I was here, and I got out."

Jewel saw the boy's face as his expression transformed it. "You were that girl—the one who ran—"

She nodded. "I came back."

He looked at her as if she were crazy. But fear of that kind of crazy was just a little bit less visceral. "How do I know—"

"Duster helped me," Finch said quietly, as if she had expected doubt.

The boy nodded slowly. Slowly, his face undergoing the contortions of confusion, hope, and a lot of fear. "She didn't get out," he whispered.

"I know. I—" The words failed her for a moment. "I couldn't wait for her. She told me to run."

What Jewel hadn't managed to do, Finch did; she talked the boy out from under his meager fortress. He unfolded slowly; Jewel thought he was her age, but his face was bruised, and his arms—where she could see them—were scraped raw. His hair had cobwebs in it; enough to add dust and a gray net to a dark brown mess. He was, she thought, a pretty boy. Not in the way that Carver was, though; there was no danger in it.

She had no room for anger. She had no room for it, but it crept in anyway, darkening her vision. He was wearing a thin tunic, thin pants—poor clothing for the weather. She could see where the cloth had been torn, and through it, could see his ribs, and the bruises that lay there like purple fingers.

"I'm Finch," Finch told the boy softly. "Finch. We won't leave you behind."

The boy swallowed. Jewel noted that he didn't give her—give them—his name. He was still counting the probable cost. It made him shake.

"Do you know where Duster is?"

And look away.

Two men joined the two who were injured and bleeding at the wrong end of the hall. They were good; Rath hadn't heard them move at all; hadn't been aware that they were coming. All of his instincts were honed, and if he wasn't as fast as he had been in his youth, his experience more than made up for it.

And all of that experience told him to run.

Were it not for the contents of the letter he'd sent, he would have. Because he'd seen men like this before, and not enough time had passed to dampen the impact of recognition. They weren't afraid; they were smiling.

Cold smiles. Their eyes, in halls that were flooded with light at their backs, were dark and unblinking; they walked with a silent grace that Rath knew he had never possessed.

They carried swords.

"Harald!"

Harald grimaced. "Trouble," he said.

"Pull your men back."

"For two?"

"Do it."

A crossbow bolt flew between them and landed almost dead center; clearly, if Harald's men were too down on their luck—as they liked to put it when describing the habits that usually deprived them of whatever they'd earned in the shipping season—they'd enough experience with crossbows to know when to fire.

But if the aim was true, it was also instantly demoralizing; the man staggered back at the force of impact, but that was *all* he did. He didn't even bother to remove the bolt; it jutted out of his chest at right angles, an unspoken threat.

* * *

Arann called Jewel, and she nodded grimly. "More doors," she told them. "I can't open them all."

Carver, quiet until that moment, shrugged. "I can open half of them. Or at least as far down the hall as the fighting."

The fighting. Jewel drew a deep breath. Or tried. What she took in was shallow, like a gasp, a series of gasps. Rath was there.

She was here. It was the here she had to concentrate on. She slipped out of the room, Carver her shadow, and on to the next door. It was locked. Carver broke away, kneeling by the door opposite Jewel's. She wanted to watch him work; to judge—from the vantage of meager skill—how good he was. She didn't have time.

Not even to waste on a thought like that one; her hands were shaking so *damn* much, Rath would have been Winter itself had he watched her work. But the lock clicked. She pushed the door wide, hoping to the Hells there weren't any guards in it.

And there weren't. There was another boy, who looked up as she entered. He hadn't the sense to hide under the bed; he hadn't the sense to hide in the closet—because this room seemed to have one, tucked to one side and behind the long mirror.

In fact, he hadn't much sense left at all, to Jewel's eye. His stare was dull, almost disinterested. His clothing was clean, but also unseasonal; his feet were bare. His hands were thick hands, and his arms, thick as well; he was shorter than Arann, wider, his eyes a blue that no sky knows. Because when the sky was blue, it contained light, sun's light; there was none of it here.

He stood up from the bed as she watched him. The sounds of swords were closer, and there was no Arann blocking the door, nothing to keep it open. But even the sounds of shouting didn't seem to register on the boy's face; his jaw didn't tense. He said nothing, waiting.

As if this were his life, truly his life; as if all fighting had already been done, and everything lost in the attempt.

She'd heard the word "broken" before, even heard it used to refer to people, but she'd never seen it so clearly. Not even Lefty, who jumped at the sight of his own shadow, was broken like this; he still had fear to drive him.

And Arann to care for him.

Not even the fact that she didn't have to talk him out from under the bed was a comfort, here. The mirror that she looked into—and away from—was contained in the prominent bones of his cheeks, the squareness of his jaw; a dim little voice said, *this could have been me*.

She didn't even try to argue with it.

"We have to leave," she told him.

He nodded.

"We have to leave now."

He nodded again. When she left the room, he followed, moving slowly and carefully, avoiding eye contact with anything that wasn't the floor.

She looked across the hall, saw Carver emerge, dragging someone by the arm. A boy. Another boy. His hair was the color of dark carrots, and his face, pale, showed freckles, but no bruises. He looked bewildered, but not afraid. New here, she thought. Too new.

But why were they all boys?

Before she could ask, Carver said, "How many more, Jay?" And he looked down the hall. A man was reloading a crossbow. And cursing. In fact, a lot of men were cursing.

Without thinking, she answered the question. "Just one." And then stopped, as thought caught up with her mouth. Her eyes narrowed. But Carver was without guile; he had asked because he expected her to know.

He was pale, and he had his dagger firmly in the hand that wasn't dragging out the room's occupant. But he wasn't ready to run. She thought, then, that her Oma would have liked this strange boy.

Carver took him to Arann; Jewel's silent charge followed without a word. But Carver's? He looked down the hall, his green-brown eyes widening. *He* had flight in him.

"One more where?" Carver asked, and looked down the hall. There were six doors; they could probably reach two of them without risking limbs to the swordplay.

Jewel had reached Arann's side. She now turned to the first boy, the one Finch had rescued. "Which room is Duster in?" she asked him quietly.

"None of these," he replied.

The silent boy, the boy who had guttered eyes, seemed to hear the words at last, and he flinched.

Jewel had no right to judge him. And had she *time,* she would have let him be. He'd suffered enough.

But he had the answer, and she needed it.

"Where?" she asked him, more brusquely than she'd intended.

"Up," he whispered. And as he did, he pointed.

Down the hall. Toward the thick of the fighting. Jewel followed the direction and her eyes came to rest, briefly, on the two men who stood sentinel there, smiling in the face of Rath and Harald and their men.

She forgot how to breathe for a moment, and almost took a step back. But she forced herself to stand her ground, to say *nothing*. Because she was aware that all eyes were on her, and some of those eyes were almost vacant; she couldn't afford to fill them with fear.

Or terror.

She could not go through the men. None of them could. "Finch."

Finch was white. But she nodded. And pulled the boy's arm down, so that it rested, again, at his side. He didn't flinch when she touched him; he made no attempt to free his hand. And Finch, the smallest person here, held that hand as tightly as if it were all the money—or food—she possessed in a very unfriendly world. She had been so terrified of returning, she could barely take steps, but here, at last, she had found something that was worth holding onto. Someone who needed her.

It surprised Jay, and even above the din and her own growing agitation, it was a good surprise. A welcome surprise.

"There's another floor?"

"I think so."

"Okay. This is a big place. That can't possibly be the only way up." She turned to Arann. "I want you to wait downstairs," she told him. "With the others."

"And you?"

"Carver and I are going to find a different way up." She turned and headed down the stairs.

"Aren't you going the wrong way?"

"No."

"But—"

"There won't be more stairs from here," Jewel replied. "And we won't reach those ones alive. But I've got a couple of ideas."

The redhead turned to her. "Good ideas?" he asked dubiously.

"Compared to going through the fighting? Yes."

"Jay—the door—"

She shook her head. "It's closed," she told Arann firmly. "And I don't want you touching it until I tell you to."

"But—"

"What?" She tried not to grind her teeth. And tried to breathe. *What in the Hells am I doing here?* But she had an answer to that. And it was a good answer, shorn of defiance but not determination. "It's magicked," she snapped. "There's a mage here. At least one. I don't know what will happen if you try—but it doesn't look safe."

"How can you tell? Hey!" Arann had stepped firmly on Lefty's foot before grabbing him by the arm. He all but dragged poor Lefty down the stairs.

They huddled in the foyer. Jewel tapped Carver on the shoulder, and Carver nodded. "The rest of you stay here. Unless the wrong people come down the stairs."

"What are we supposed to do if—"

"Go through the windows in that room; they've already been broken."

Arann nodded. The cluster surrounding him moved toward the open door of the room she'd pointed out. But one of them broke away, and came toward Jewel and Carver.

Finch.

She was shaking, but her hands were balled fists. "I'll go," she whispered. "I'll go with you."

"There's no point," Jewel told her. "You don't know this building well enough to be useful. And it's safer—"

"I know Duster."

Jewel wanted to argue, but the words wouldn't come. Truth often had that effect on her tongue. And Finch had talked one boy out from under a bed when Jewel herself couldn't manage. She nodded.

Together, they went toward the doors at the far end of the foyer. They were a dark-stained wood, and looked very fine—far finer than the carpets on which they walked, or the faded patina of the walls. There was a mirror here—it seemed to be a theme—but this one hung across the hall like a painting.

This, Jewel thought bitterly, was where customers came. This was supposed to pass for wealth.

And it did, and Jewel despised utterly all men with power and money. She wished, for just that second, that she had come at night—at night, when there were customers who could see them, be terrified with them, and join the dead who lay like afterthought in the long hall above.

She wanted them to be afraid.

She wanted them to be trapped here, like they were.

She wanted them to burn—

She almost stopped walking as Carver pushed the doors wide. He ran into her back, nearly knocking her off her feet.

"Fire," she whispered. She turned to look at them, at Carver and the very surprising Finch.

Finch couldn't get any paler. Carver could, and did.

"Where?" he asked.

"Here," she replied, her eyes wide, "Everywhere. They're going to burn the house down."

"It would take a lot of fire to burn *this* place down."

"Not that much," she told him. "Not to start." And then she pulled herself together, took a deep breath, and ran. The hall behind the closed grand doors was narrower than the hallway above. It was also a good deal shorter, and it ended in a T, bracketed at either end by doors.

"This is why we have to hurry?" Carver asked her.

She nodded.

And he waited, again, as if she knew what she was doing. She hated it; it was a burden she didn't want. But without it, she doubted that he would follow at all.

"Right," she said softly.

Carver nodded, and began to run down the hall. Finch followed Jewel. The door at the end wasn't locked, but it was a pathetic excuse for a door.

It opened into the kitchen.

As kitchens went, this was probably cockroach heaven. The water that lay in the buckets to one side of the counter that covered the wall to their left seemed brackish or slimy. Not that she wanted to drink it. There were plates on that counter, piled in a precarious heap; there were—of course—cockroaches crawling across their dirty surface. The counter itself was a thick, warped wood.

Insects scurried when Jewel and Carver raced by. Jewel didn't stop to think; there were three doors into the kitchen, but one of them they'd already passed through, and the other went in the wrong direction; probably to some fancy room meant just for eating.

She led them to the other door, the far door, and paused there.

"Safe?" Carver whispered, crouching slightly, his dagger in his hand.

She nodded, and pushed the door open. It made a lot of noise, and it wasn't easy—but she could see why; a mop and a bucket were pressed against that door. As if they had ever been used. She kicked the bucket aside. Beyond the kitchen were stairs; they went both down and up. They couldn't compare to the foyer's grand spiral; they were narrow and dingy, and what light there was came through the cracks of shutters more warped than the counter.

No glass here, she thought. No carpet. Just stairs with a railing that looked suspiciously rotten. She stuck to the walls and began to mount them, hoping they didn't come out anywhere near the second floor.

At least they were visible. Had they been otherwise prepared, Rath would have lost Harald in the first few seconds; as it was, Harald chose to be cautious. Where cautious was abandoning, for the moment, the overhead swing for which he was so famed. It always had momentum and strength behind it, but it left him open, both at beginning and end.

Harald liked to play the part of a berserker; had he actually *been* one, Rath would have assiduously avoided him. Then again, had he, it was likely he would have been dead ten years ago. Anger, in combat, was almost never your friend.

It wasn't Rath's.

Because Harald chose to be cautious, because he chose a conservative stance and a thrust that would give him room to maneuver should he require it, he survived the shock of having his sword almost bounce. He managed to bring it up in time to parry, and the parry sent him back two steps; although the blow itself looked like an exploratory thrust, it was anything but.

Whoever these two were—*whatever* they were—they were good. At least as good, Rath thought, as Rath himself. But Rath had had the money and prestige of an old House behind him when he had begun his long years of lessons; he wasn't so certain that these men had that advantage. They didn't need it.

Rath, having fought them once, didn't waste his throwing knives; he didn't waste his swordplay either. He moved carefully, fighting defensively because defense was the only way he would survive. Survival was almost everything.

But in this case, it wasn't everything. He hadn't come here to die; he hadn't come to flee. Flight, given his previous experience, was a very poor option. He let fear show; he let it guide the muscles around his mouth, his eyes, the creases in his forehead; he let it be, for a moment, exactly what it was.

He made a play of swordsmanship, in the wide halls, sun streaming just out of reach through the long, long windows that had been rebuilt. These men seemed to cast no shadow, or rather, it seemed part of them, inseparable from them—something that would have existed in the absence of light.

It was a few minutes' work, to seem good enough, and frightened enough, to draw them out, to make them step forward and retake ground that their dead companions had surrendered.

He ignored the voices of the men at his back; ignored Harald. Concentrated instead on two things: the man he was fighting, and his own dagger, unsheathed, on his belt. One of two, it had been a gift from Andrei, and on short notice, it had probably been a very costly gift.

With Andrei, the cost was written afterward.

Rath fought as if there might never be one.

But when the moment came—and it did—and the man to his front deflected a blow in such a way that it pushed Rath's sword wide, exposing his chest before Rath could step back, Rath pulled a dagger in his off hand, and drove it into his adversary's chest. It helped that his enemy didn't even bother to make the attempt to get out of its way.

But this blade—this one, small, ornate, incredibly ugly to Rath's more cultured sense of aesthetics—bit. Rath let it go, and swung his sword in, and this time, it, too, cut.

They weren't invulnerable, these men, these unwelcome strangers.

But when the fire started, Rath noted where: at the opening of the wound the dagger had made.

The steps didn't open up as they reached the top of the second set; they continued higher, but a door was closed and contained by wall. Jewel looked at it. "Second floor," she muttered, and Carver, who was seconds behind her, nodded. They looked at the door for a minute, and then left it, racing up the last of the stairs. Or the last two flights; the ceilings here were high.

They stopped only once: When a roar shook the building. It was short, but loud, a thing of fury and pain. Finch had plastered herself against the wall, and she raised shaking hands to her ears. Had it gone on forever, she might have remained where she was standing.

But Jewel hopped back down the stairs, grabbed her arm, and drew her up them; the soles of Finch's shoes, half unattached to their uppers, flapped and made uncomfortable noise as she struggled just to keep up. She didn't let go until they reached the last door; it was at the top of the thin flight, and it was closed.

It was also, to Jewel's eye, old. The handle was almost black with the tarnish of age and neglect—if it had ever been anything but neglected. She had a feeling that the powerful didn't often take these stairs, either up or down.

"Locked?" Carver asked, as she stood there, catching her breath. It was silent again. She twisted the knob, and shook her head.

"We're waiting for an invitation?"

Jewel gave him a look, and he laughed. There was fear in the sound, but most of it was pure defiance.

"That looks like an old lady glare," he told her, as the sound faded. She was surprised at how much better it made her feel, because she had never quite heard a laugh like it. Certainly not from her Oma, whose laughter, when it had come, had come most often with barbs and bitterness.

Your Oma came from a harsher place than this, Jewel's mother used to say, in the days when that laughter had bothered Jewel. *And kindness was frowned upon by her gods.*

Jewel wondered about that as she pulled the door open. How much harsher could a place be, and still have gods at all?

Rath had time to draw the second dagger, but only barely; he certainly didn't have time to wield it. The fire that was now consuming the man he had fought continued to burn—but the fire that suddenly shot toward him in a swirling orange-and-yellow beam had nothing to do with the weapon.

If he had wondered—briefly—whether or not he faced mages, he stopped then. He almost stopped breathing, and had it not been for the sudden impact of one of Harald's men, he would have been a pyre.

Instead, the fire stove in a wall. About nine feet of it, as if it were a fist.

Rath had time to see the wreckage that might have been him; he had time to turn his gaze in the direction from which the flame had sprouted. He did not have time to attack the creature, and the dagger he carried was so ridiculously designed that he didn't risk a throw; it wouldn't have gone far, and he wasn't about to be parted from the only weapon he had that he was certain would work.

The man whose palms were still cloaked in flame had eyes that were black; if there had ever been whites there, they were lost. The fire devoured his clothing, deformed his armor, washing away all signs and symbols of things that were merely mortal.

What was left in the fire's wake, what walked at its heart, was something entirely different.

Rath could speak the Northern tongue to a lesser degree; he understood approximately half of what Harald shouted.

The important half. He was sounding the retreat in his deep and resonant tones.

The creature—there was no other word for it—looked at Rath, and only Rath, as he and Harald began to back their way down the wide hall, watching the fire burn. Almost casually, it peeled away some section of that flame and threw it.

Rath lifted his dagger almost automatically—damn fool thing to do—and the fire parted as it sheared the edge; the edge was glowing, faintly, like sunlight.

But what that fire struck, it burned, and flame, not wood or plaster or paper, was the shape of the building that contained them all.

"Harald!" Rath shouted, still wielding the dagger, "get the kids—get them out!" And he continued to back away. His weaponsmasters had always said that the difference between a retreat and a rout was the difference between living and dying. The creature watched him, and began to walk slowly toward them all, keeping the distance between the moving Northerners and himself static.

Chapter Fifteen

THE DOOR OPENED into a dark hall. If there was sunlight in the rainy season, none of it reached this place; not even through the gaps between doors and floor. The hall was a narrow thing, with floors that would have creaked at the weight of a mouse; they groaned as Jewel stepped on the boards. She reached into her pouch and pulled out the magestone that was her prized possession. Passed a shaking hand over it, speaking words of illumination. It brightened.

And the sounds from below drifted up through the floor, muted but unmistakable.

She stopped; Carver stopped as well, although he did it by once again running into her back. "Jay?" Quiet voice now, shorn of humor.

"It's started," she said. "We don't have much time."

They looked down a hall packed with small doors; each one could have opened into a closet. She counted twelve; the hall wasn't long. At the other end, however, was a door.

She ran toward it, ignoring all the others, and heard the floor's evidence that her companions were following. The door wasn't locked, which was good; it was stuck, which was bad. In this weather, old doors and warped frames seldom went together well.

She tugged on it for a while, and then Carver shouldered her aside. Which would have been more comforting had he Arann's brawn behind him. As it was, he strained at the door for a moment, and then Jewel tried to add her weight to his.

When it did open, they all fell over—because Finch was literally right behind them.

It was helpful, because while they were disentangling themselves and finding their feet, the other side of the door didn't seem as threatening. But when they stood, they hovered in the frame for a moment, because in its fashion, it was.

It opened, not into another hall, but into a vast room; the room had rails in the center, and odd diagrams on the wall. They might have looked like paintings, but they had no frames; they were drawn on heavy parchment, something that might have once been attached to a very large cow. They covered the wall opposite the door, and in front of those drawings was a single long table with no chairs to gird it. To her left—east, west, north, and south had been swallowed—were other doors.

There was carpet here, but it was the same faded carpet that adorned the hall from the foyer. A few more footprints weren't going to make much difference.

"Jay," Carver said sharply, as she walked toward the far wall with its lines and its unframed drawings, squinting, waiting to see what they resolved themselves into. She gave him a quick glance. "Time?" He said, the single word urgent.

She nodded, but she walked in the wrong direction: instead of the doors that led elsewhere, which were much wider and much finer than the one they'd entered, she continued to approach the drawings. And frowned. "They're . . . maps," she said at last.

"What?"

"Maps. They're supposed to be pictures that tell you where things are."

"What things?"

"Streets. Stuff like that."

He frowned. "You can read that?"

She started to nod, and then stopped. Because, she realized, she *couldn't*. She could see that there were street lines, and could even see where names had been written in dark ink beneath them; she could see the squares and ovals that must have been buildings, and they, too, contained words. What she couldn't do was read them.

But she could recognize, in their shape and form, some of the letters that she had seen on the few items Rath had chosen to show her. "Carver, give me that knife," she told him.

"You've got one—"

"Sorry. I forgot." She drew the knife Rath had given her, the knife she wasn't accustomed to wielding, and took a closer look at just how these drawings were fixed to the wall. Nails. Several in each.

"We need these," she told him firmly.

"What, all of them?"

She nodded. "There are only three."

"They're not small."

"Just shut up and cut them down, okay? *Don't* cut the lines, whatever you do; just cut around the nails."

He looked as if he would argue, which would have been bad. But he didn't. Instead, while Jewel worked, he chose the map farthest from her and began his own work as well. He was better with the knife, even if hers was sharper; either that or his map hadn't required so many nails to hold it in place.

They met across the third one, moving toward each other in a frenzy. It was hard to get the knife under and around the topmost nails; their flat metal heads were high above the ground.

Carver had dropped the first map, just as Jewel had done, in a heap on the floor. When the last one came down, Jewel caught it, and noticed that Finch was on her knees, rolling the other two carefully into what looked like thin carpets.

"Heavy?" Jewel asked carefully.

Finch shook her head. "Not too heavy. I can carry them." When Jewel opened her mouth, she added, "And I can't wield a knife."

Carver said, "She's got a point. Do we really need those?"

Jewel looked at them, hanging over Finch's slender arms as she cradled them. "I think so," she said at last, hesitantly. "I don't always have the answers, Carver. I don't always know."

"But you—"

"I don't always get them *in time*." He wasn't stupid. But he held her gaze for just a little longer, and something dangerously close to pity seemed to flicker in his eyes. "But—I hate to see them burn."

"Better them than us," he muttered, his expression becoming one she was more familiar with. She felt a pang of something like gratitude.

She had to agree with that. And being agreeable took a bit of work, most days. "Doors," she said abruptly, and looked toward them. Two doors, side-by-side, wood gleaming like something new. Brass handles, as well—and they were either new or well-tended; she suspected the former. No one seemed to take much care with this place.

Carver approached the doors first; they were rectangular, and a little tall. Then again, the frames that held them were tall; those, she suspected, were as old as the house. Wood trim trailed out from either side of the doors in a thin, dark line.

She pushed them open, and they opened outward, into a larger hall.

Carver frowned as he joined her. "You smell it?" He asked.

She nodded. Smoke. The not-distant-enough scent of wood burning. "Finch, stay with us. Don't get lost. And don't let those doors close."

They entered the hall quickly. This far from the fire—and Jewel *knew*, for a moment, where it burned—the smoke hadn't yet managed to reach them. The hall looked clear; were it not for the smell, she could have pretended they were imagining things.

But pretense took time, and she'd wasted enough of it. There were two doors in the hall, and each was tall and wide. Jewel approached the nearest door, and twisted the handle; it stuck. She knelt instantly beside it, and pulled out the finer tools of Rath's less savory trade: lockpicks.

Carver watched her as she worked. She wished—for just a minute— that it were Rath, instead, because she made no mistakes; she worked quickly, but everything fell into place as she did, and that almost never happened.

She'd have to be grateful for the lessons; Rath wouldn't see the results. She heard the mechanisms inside the door click, and she stood. "Ready?" she whispered, almost to herself.

She pushed the door open.

The room was a much larger room, and perhaps, in a different life, it had been a very fine one; what remained was in no way fine. There was a large bed, yes, and a large standing cupboard—what had Rath called them?—on one wall; there was a window with real glass, and with equally real bars, through which gray light poured. There were curtains, but they were tasseled, held back.

And there was a girl.

She wasn't on the bed, or even under it; she sat against the far wall. Her hair was long and dark; it was also matted; some of it clung to her face, and some to her shirt. Her eyes were the bruised of beating, not lack of sleep, and her lip was split. Her wrists were also cut, but not deeply.

She looked up as they entered, and her eyes were the same color as

Jewel's—the brown of Southern descent. They were not flat and lifeless; she hadn't withdrawn. She was dressed, but the clothing was tattered.

She frowned, seeing Jewel, seeing Carver. The frown thinned as she saw Finch, and her eyelids closed over that dark black-brown as her head sagged forward into her arms.

But Finch said, "We've come to get you out." She spoke in Torra.

The eyes flickered open.

"And we don't have much time," Jewel added, speaking in Torra as well. She looked over her shoulder. "They've set fire to the damn building, and it's going to burn quickly."

The girl's grin was a lopsided, bitter thing—if it weren't for the curve of her lips, Jewel wouldn't have identified it as a smile. "You brought an ax or a pry bar?"

"Neither. Why?"

And the stranger stood. As she unfolded, as her arms fell away from the knees that were curled into her chest, Jewel saw that she wore a manacle, which was attached to an intimidating thickness of chain. And wall. "I'm not going anywhere," she added softly.

"Duster," Finch began.

"You shouldn't have come. You were the *only* thing I did right in this place. You shouldn't have come back."

"And you shouldn't have—" Finch couldn't even say the words. "I would have ended up here," she finally managed. "Instead of you."

Duster's eyes were a narrow hint of something dark and cutting. "Not here," she said at last, her glance flickering over the walls. "Not for you."

"Yeah, well, she's here." Jewel snapped. "We're all here."

"Must be something about Finch," Duster said bleakly. "Everyone wants to help her."

"Except for the people who want to kill her, you mean?"

Duster shrugged, the corners of her lips twitching between a smile and a frown—neither of which was pleasant.

"Well, surprise! We didn't come here for Finch; we already had her."

The eyes widened slightly; they now looked normal, rather than hunted. If, by normal, one meant almost predatory. It was hard for Jewel to decide; something about Duster's face, something about her physical posture, spoke of danger.

"This wasn't Finch's idea."

Jewel considered lying, but only briefly. "No."

"Yours?"

"Mine."

"Why?"

"Because you did help Finch," Jewel replied.

"Friend of hers?"

"Just another stranger."

Duster shook her head. "What've you got in mind?"

"Getting you out of here before we all burn to death."

"So . . . you brought an ax?"

"No. I'm a thief. I brought lockpicks. Don't kick me in the face." Jewel made her way to Duster and knelt by her ankle.

"Jay—"

"I know." She could smell the fire burning. Couldn't see it yet. Her hands were shaking as she pulled the lockpicks out; the lock itself was both simple and heavy. A padlock. She hadn't had much experience with those; Rath didn't favor them.

Then again, he couldn't—most padlocks were usually on the wrong side of the door. "Finch, Carver—pick up those maps. We're not leaving them behind."

She didn't look to see whether or not they'd heard her; she worked at the damn lock. Duster kept still; her foot might have been nailed to the floor. Even her breathing was so silent it couldn't be heard.

Jewel had never been that good about silence. Then again, she hadn't had to be; she wondered about Duster as she worked. About who she was, how she'd become whatever that was, and how in the Hells she'd wound up here. Duster wasn't like any of the other children they'd rescued.

"Jay—"

"Not yet, Carver."

"The fire—"

"I *know,* damn it." She shifted picks, choosing the finest, the narrowest—and the easiest to bend. The other, she shoved back into her hair; her hair was good at keeping whatever got stuck there.

The lock clicked; she felt it more clearly than she heard it. She said something in Torra, half prayer and half curse, and then pulled the manacle open. The hinges were sticky and stiff; they opened slowly.

Duster was on her feet before Jewel had finished prying them wide. She offered Jewel her hand, and Jewel took it, rising quickly. "Can you run?" she asked.

Duster grimaced. Looked down at her bare feet. "Sometimes faster than others."

"This would a good time for fast." She turned to Carver; he carried two of the maps; Finch cradled one beneath her delicate jaw. "Back the way we came," she snapped.

Carver nodded.

To Duster, Jewel added, "Unless you know this place well enough, follow. If you need help, ask for it. We don't have time for—"

Duster shoved Jewel forward. "I'll follow when you're moving. So move."

Carver, closest to the door, leaped through it, and Finch followed; Jewel was right behind her. But she'd chosen the rear for a reason. She kept an eye on Duster.

Duster didn't like it much, but she didn't complain; they both knew this was no place for an argument.

The hall was full of smoke; it was a thin smoke, an acrid mist that eddied slowly beneath the tall ceilings.

Jewel drew her sleeve to her mouth and nose, breathing through it. Aware that Carver and Finch, hands full, didn't have that option. She almost told them to drop the maps—but she couldn't quite make herself say the words.

The maps—like Duster—were things she couldn't leave behind.

But the fire was below them. They could feel its heat in the floor, especially Duster. They ran into the wide empty room that still had bits of parchment nailed to the walls; they ran around the long table and toward the open door. There was no pursuit here, but none was needed; the fire was enough. It would take the floors from them; it would devour the walls and the fine wood, the faded carpets, the doors, both old and new.

They reached the servants' hall—Jewel had figured out that much in the short time she'd been here—and ran past the closed doors toward the narrow flight of rickety wooden steps.

These, they took quickly, with small leaps and jumps, using the walls as large, flat rails. Jewel stopped Carver from leaping down the half flight that ended in the door to the second floor, and he didn't argue, but when he gained the small flat, he reached out with his palm and drew back much more quickly.

The door was hot, and smoke plumed out from beneath it. "It's worst here," she told him, half meaning it. "Let's move."

"The others?"

"They're well out, by now." She silently added, *They'd better damn well be*. She glanced at Duster; the girl didn't seem even slightly concerned at what remained of her thin clothing. She followed Jewel.

It was the first time they would run this way, Jewel in the lead and Duster her shadow. Jewel caught the image as it flew by, as real for a moment as the walls, the curved steps, the threat of fire. She wanted to turn and touch Duster then, to fix her firmly in the here and now, but she didn't dare. If Duster was nonchalant in appearance, she was—she had to be—approached with care.

And care took time.

They made their way down the steps, sent the metal bucket clattering in a spin, and grabbed the mop. Or rather, Jewel did. Duster's brows rose into the tangle of her hair, but she said nothing.

They left the kitchen; Jewel led them, not back into the hall that ran to the grand—well, almost grand—foyer, but rather, into the dining room. It was empty, and it wasn't exactly dirty; there were no dishes here, and the chairs looked new. But the ceiling was patchy with water damage and poor paint; the makeover, such as it was, was simple and dirty.

There were doors from the dining room that led to the foyer, and doors that led to the sitting room. Carver started toward the foyer, and Jewel shouted his name. When he looked back, she shook her head. "Touch the damn door," she said, her voice low.

He touched the handle instead, and cursed loudly. "Good call." He would have said more, but the mansion spoke for him; it *cracked*.

"That'll be the stairs," Jewel said grimly. "Come on. Sitting room."

Duster bridled and stopped just short of the closed doors. Jewel knew why. "It's day," she told Duster. "Morning. If the bastards who visited are anywhere, they're up in their expensive homes in the high holdings; they won't be waiting for you there." She saw, instantly, that this was exactly the wrong thing to say.

Wrong, but necessary. She pushed the doors open, and hoped that Duster would follow her. Not trust her, not precisely; saving her life hadn't earned that. If anything would.

Because in a life like this, salvation could be just another trick. Had they not all been about the same age, had Finch not been with them, Jewel wasn't certain how it would have played out.

But the crack of timber was its own imperative, and Duster, last through the doors, entered the sitting room.

This room *was* a fine room. The care that hadn't been taken elsewhere had been concentrated here. The carpets were new, and thick, a dark, deep red that reminded Jewel of Rath's wine. There was a low, plain table that gleamed; it was unmarked by anything but a silver vase that was, at the moment, empty. There were cabinets that rested against the far wall, and behind the clear panes of diamond-shaped glass, bottles of different shapes and sizes, and cut crystal glasses that she almost stopped to pocket. They'd break, or she would have.

The chairs were also fine; the wood, dark and oiled, the velvet armrests and the rounded padding on the chairback a match for the carpet they were trampling. And beyond them, beyond the new mantel that girded an old fireplace, beyond the framed paintings that hung above it, curtains that were edged in gold. They were drawn.

Carver shifted the weight of the maps into one arm, and shoved those curtains apart, exposing the full height of windows in a bay that stood some six feet above the flower beds beneath the window. At least the beds weren't fancy; they were mostly—like the rest of the grounds—composed of weeds.

Jewel hefted the mop in her hands, and began to break glass.

"Chair would be better," Duster offered.

"We can't lift them," Jewel replied tersely.

Duster tried. "Good point." She looked around for something else, disappeared, and came back wielding what could only be called brass sticks. "For the fire," Duster said. "But they'll do."

Jewel nodded. They lifted their chosen weapons—brass and wood—and swung them wherever they could reach.

Glass flew in shards, falling outward. The sharp edges that remained in the frame were struck again and again by brass rods.

Jewel looked at Finch and Carver; they both had boots. So did she. Only Duster, barefoot, risked shredding skin against what remained of the windows.

But bleeding was far less painful—and deadly—than fire. "You ready?" Jewel asked her.

She nodded.

"Finch?"

Finch looked at all of them, her eyes wide. Then she moved toward the window, map still in arms, and her eyes widened. "I see Rath!" she shouted.

"Anything else?"

"His friends. Some of them. But, Jay . . ."

"They're not alone."

She shook her head. Her face was white.

And Duster came to stand beside Finch; she was a good four inches taller, and if her face was bruised and her hair was clumpy, she looked, for a moment, more regal somehow. Certainly more dangerous. Her eyes followed Finch's gaze, and her lips thinned.

"They're not going to make it," Duster said softly. "And if we join them, we're not going to make it either. There's a back way—"

"There isn't," Jewel replied grimly. "There's a lot of fire, and the joists on the second floor have fallen." She paused, and added, "The fire started at the back end of the building on the second floor; it's spreading now."

Duster raised a brow. "You saw this when we weren't looking?"

"Something like that." She pushed her way past Finch and looked out of the glassless frame. The weeds were burning, but they didn't burn for long; they were wet. Everything outside was, except for the man who wore fire like a cloak. Mage, she thought, and swallowed.

"He hasn't seen us," Carver said quietly.

"Do you see Arann?"

Finch shook her head. "Duster—your feet—"

"Better than fire," Duster said curtly. "Can you climb out on your own?"

Finch nodded. The two looked at each other for a moment, and then Finch whispered something Jewel couldn't hear. Duster cuffed the younger girl in the side of the head, but not so hard that it was meant to actually hurt.

She looked up, met Jewel's eyes, and offered her a crooked smile. "I've always had a weakness for birds," she offered with a shrug.

And before she could really think, Jewel said, "Why did they keep you alive?" It was entirely the wrong question. And it was the only question that mattered. Jewel knew this with more certainty than almost anything else at the moment.

"Long story," Duster replied. But her expression had stiffened, and her eyes had gone that shade of wary that hinted at upcoming lies.

"Right. Story later." Jewel looked at the men who were battling their way back down the path. The mage didn't press them; he threw fire, and Rath seemed to split it in two with the wave of his hand.

No, she thought, squinting, not his hand. He was carrying a dagger. And from the look of it, not a normal one either. Some of Harald's men had made the fence, and the gate that lay slanting from old hinges. She half expected the gate to slam shut, but it didn't.

Still, she now knew why the doors had closed so suddenly, sealing them in.

"Stay close to the mansion," Jewel told them all, as she grabbed a handful of curtain and laid it against the window frame, protecting her hands. She raised herself up to the window, and then swung her legs over the other side, falling into the beds beneath it. They were mostly flat weed, but that was better than the mud they would otherwise have been.

She turned, looked up, and lifted her hands. "Throw the maps down first," she said, sparing a backward glance over her shoulder. Fire had always mesmerized her.

But a faceful of map was a good antidote; it completely blanketed her head. She heard a muffled snicker as Carver dropped down beside her, and managed to lift the map enough to catch the expression that accompanied it. But he retrieved the map and rolled it back into something that could be carried; it looked like a really tattered rug. He then looked up as Finch threw the next two down. He was more agile than Jewel; she had to admit that.

Finch came next, and almost right behind her, Duster. Suspiciously right behind; Jewel wondered, watching them as they fell, if Duster had pushed her. As if she could hear the question, Duster looked up and met her gaze; she held it briefly, and broke it with a shrug.

Fair enough. Had Jewel been the one left behind, she'd've pushed.

Duster's feet went from white with a few red streaks, to brown in the space of a few steps; the air here was cold, but not enough to freeze ground. And, on the bright side, if they stayed here much longer, they'd be warming their hands over the city's biggest bonfire.

She looked down the side of the building, past the steps that led to doors that would probably never open again. There was no sign of Arann or the rest of her—her friends. Charges. Whatever.

He'd been given instructions; she hoped he'd followed them. If he had, he'd be well quit of the grounds, with Rath and his friends between him and the only thing left that was a danger.

She couldn't understand why the man kept his distance; he followed, but he followed at the exact pace that Rath retreated, no more. She could see Rath's face, could see the narrowed movement of his eyes, the occasional movement of his hands. The dagger, there.

It was *cutting* the flame. Where fire struck its edge, it split, shunted to either side of Rath. And Rath remained where he was as Harald's men retreated farther. One had a crossbow, but nothing to put in it. The others? Swords, but not useful ones. She wondered about that.

And wondered how long Rath would last. He wasn't tired yet. But the mage who followed him? She could see his back, and only his back, but she *knew* he was enjoying this. To him it was a game.

"Carver," she said, and held out her hand.

He placed his dagger hilt into her palm, and she looked at it as if it were rain-worms. "What am I supposed to do with *this*?" she asked.

"Girls," he said, taking it back, "are weird. What did you want?"

"A map."

"Which one?"

"Any one. I don't care which. And I want you to take everyone else over—there." She gestured broadly to the right. "Get to the fence, if you can. Get to the gate. There's no way it's closing any time soon."

"What are you going to do?"

"Help Rath," she said grimly, taking one of the maps they had worked so hard to pull down from the great rooms above.

"You're going to help him with one of those?"

"Probably only one of these," she said. She tried to project confidence; it was one of Rath's constant refrains. "My guess?"

He was staring at her; she could almost see his other eye as the wind kicked his hair back. "Guess?"

"Dagger's not going to do much good if those men are holding their swords."

"It's better than nothing."

"No," she said quietly. "It's exactly nothing."

"This one of your—"

"Shut up, Carver."

He saluted. Sort of. More important? He caught Finch by the arm and began to lead her away. She held the other two maps; he couldn't take her hand. But Duster drifted behind them more slowly; she was watching Jewel.

And Jewel knew better than to give orders to Duster. Maybe one day. If ever.

Well, let her watch.

Rath was not yet tiring. But yet was a precarious word on which to balance survival. Had he been in any other fight, he would have taken a position at the rear—it was one of the tangible benefits of being the one to hire men, rather than the other way around. This confrontation, however, differed in a single important way from any other he had chosen to engage in: He had in his possession the only effective weapon which could be wielded against this flame-robed, black-eyed man. To run was not only to court death, but to wed it. And to stand behind a row of men whose weapons were of little use was to surrender them needlessly.

Rath had never prided himself on his ability to lead; nor indeed had he any desire to rule or command. He had been content, if not to follow, then at least to choose his own path. The Patriarch of Handernesse—his grandfather—had believed in a way that was in parts visceral and in parts paternal, the adage about power and responsibility.

In some measure, Rath found, he must have absorbed the lectures he had cared so little for. Tiring, he retreated, his attention upon two things: the man whose fire he split, and the men whose lives he had endangered. He wondered, briefly, if Andrei would make an appearance; it would be welcome, but it was not to be looked for.

And in the end, it did not come.

What came instead, what he did not realize he dreaded until the precise moment he saw her clearly, was Jewel Markess. And she carried, of all things, a small rug that she set flapping in the wind, held as it was by small hands. Small fists.

He bit back the warning that rose behind clenched teeth, and his skill was such that he, unlike Jewel, could see her without betraying her presence. But it was harder than he would have either expected or predicted; she was not yet eleven. And she was not, he realized, a child. Not truly.

She moved toward the man who burned, unerringly; the damp grass smoldered in his wake, and smoke managed to wend its way above the sodden ground as he passed over it, blanketing it with flame. She couldn't see his eyes, Rath realized. But see them or no, she had to understand the danger; there weren't many men who could walk in raiment of fire, and of those, very few who would have dared the Laws of the Empire to do so.

And yet . . . and yet he saw what she intended, and it evoked a sharp sense of pride; it had to be sharp, to cut through the fear.

No dagger in hand, no weapon that could harm him, she approached him, and at the last moment, her legs almost trembling, she tossed the carpet up, and up again, controlling—but barely—its fall.

It fell over the eyes, the face, the shoulders; it fell and began to darken slowly as the fire consumed it.

And it bought Rath the time he needed.

Gone was caution, gone retreat; he lunged forward the moment the rug billowed down, moving as his enemy sensed its fall, the immediacy of a shadow he did not control.

Rath risked the dubious caress of flame and fire, for fire gouted, wild, released in a circular blast that traveled outward in a thick, dense ring of heat and death.

Jewel was gone before it struck her, but only barely; he could see her retreat as he stepped in, lunging through the fire itself with the dagger's blade, cutting a literal path in a substance that should have given inches of steel no purchase.

The tip of the dagger broke robe and skin, moving slowly through both, as if they were illusory, something fitted awkwardly over stone or steel. He put his shoulder into the single thrust he was given as the creature raised his arms; he saw golden light flare when the dagger at last bit home.

More than that, he left to fate; he released the hilt and leaped back, disarmed. He made the dubious safety of the gate, the hinges listing slightly with Harald's weight.

The Northerner's face was dark with blood, and his nose would bear a scar for the day's work. But it was still attached to his face. He offered Rath a grim smile, a dark smile, as he held the gate open. "Didn't think you were going to make it," he said, nodding genially.

Rath shrugged. It was all he could offer for the moment; his attention was upon the grounds. "Where," he asked, without looking, "are the other children?"

"Well past the fence to the east," Harald replied. "One of mine is with them; they don't like it much, but I don't think they've run." He paused, and then added, "I think your mage has run out of flame."

Rath nodded.

"That's a brave girl you've got there," Harald said with grudging approval. "And not a stupid one either. I thought she'd take the boy's knife."

"I'd have cut off her hand myself if she'd done anything that idiotic."

Harald raised a brow. The patch that rested below it had been slit in the blow that had almost dislodged the man's nose, and the socket that had once contained an eye lay exposed. It didn't make the Northern face look much more threatening than it already appeared. "She's off by the far window," he added.

Rath nodded. "Finch is with her."

"Another girl as well. And a boy."

"Good. I think it's about time to leave."

"Well past, I'd say."

But Rath lingered until Jewel had decided for herself that the danger was past. She spoke words that he didn't catch to her companions, and then walked slowly over to what should have been a corpse. She paused to look at what was left of her sole effective weapon. Frowning for a moment, she touched it with her toe, and then frowned more deeply.

What in the Hells was she doing?

He had his answer a moment later; she picked the damn thing up. Looked under it, as if for a hole in the ground, some escape route that the large, flame-robed man might have taken.

She found, instead, what was left of Rath's dagger, and she touched that with care. In fact, she wrapped her hand in the carpet, and picked it up by the hilt. Only then did she look up to see him, and when she met his eyes, she smiled weakly.

He nodded. He could manage that.

But words failed him for a few minutes longer, and in the space of those few minutes, she had assembled her den, and she had dragged it, motley odd thing that it was, down the broken stone that had, in grander days, once been a narrow road.

Carver carried two carpets, rolled and bent over his arms; Finch and the latest stranger walked hand in hand, and it was hard to tell which of the two—the slender, young Finch or the dark-haired, bruised stranger—was in command. Certainly, the new girl looked as if she should be vacant-eyed or terrified.

But as she approached and Rath could clearly see her expression, he revised that thought and then threw it out. She wasn't terrified.

"Jewel," he said.

"Jay," she replied, her voice a little on the low side.

"Jay, then." He leaned in, so that his words only had to carry a very short distance, "that girl—I think it best that you leave her."

"Her name's Duster," Jewel told him quietly. She looked at Duster as she spoke. "I'm taking her with me."

"She's—" He hesitated. He knew what he might say to another person—to almost any other person. But to Jewel? The words would have no meaning. What experience she'd had of life had been sheltered; if it had been marginal, it had been safe.

Duster? No.

"You can't trust her," he told her instead.

"No," Jewel replied gravely, surprising him. "I can't. Not yet. But I will."

He let it go, then. He had no choice. "The others are waiting for you," he said, standing back. "And I think you'll be more of a comfort than Harald will."

She looked up at Harald's face and forced herself not to recoil—but Jewel's face was as expressive as it always was.

Harald, however, was not offended. He even smiled. It was meant to shock or scare. And because she was Rath's, she knew it, and it annoyed her instead.

"Duster?" Jewel said, touching the strange girl's shoulder with just the tip of a finger.

Duster turned to look at her. "I want to stay," she said quietly.

"We can't."

"I don't care if you stay. I want to watch it burn."

Jewel frowned for a moment, as if trying to make a decision. "It doesn't matter. No one's in it."

"I was."

"Yes. You were. You aren't now. But if we stay and watch it burn, we'll be caught here."

"By who?"

"Magisterians," Jewel replied quietly. "If we're lucky."

Duster stiffened. "And if we're not?"

"You tell me."

They squared off, his Jewel and this orphan girl. And into their uncomfortable and unfriendly silence, Rath spoke. "Jay's right," he said quietly.

"The men you want aren't there. And if you stay here, and they find you, the loss of this building won't matter.

"You want to watch it burn? Watch it, then. But you'll probably never have a chance to make them pay."

She was young. Had she been another ten years in the streets, she wouldn't have blinked. Wouldn't have been tempted by what he seemed to be offering.

This was vulnerability, of a type. But not a welcome one. She nodded slowly.

Rath turned and walked down the street, skirting the gates, his own gaze drawn to the fire that now raged in the open, broken windows. Mage fire, yes, and strong at that.

He frowned. "Jay," he said, aware that the others listened. "What are those?"

She looked at him for a moment. "Maps," she said at last.

Of the answers she could have given, this was not one he'd expected. "Maps?"

She nodded. And held out the one she carried. "I picked up your knife," she added. "It's not very . . . practical."

"Practical," he replied, as he took it from her hand, noting its blackened metal, "is only in the doing. Remember that; just because someone looks rich, bored, and lazy doesn't mean they aren't dangerous."

She frowned. "Rich is usually—"

"Never mind. Come. We've been too long as is." But his gaze fell upon what she held, and in turn, he held his questions.

He almost made a detour to the Mother's temple in the twenty-fifth holding, but one look at Jewel's compressed lips told him how successful that would be. He would have this argument with her, when they reached the safety of his apartments; for the moment, he chose to retreat into the pragmatic. He counted.

Lefty. Arann. Carver. Finch. Duster. Three other boys whose names he had yet to discover. And, in their midst, Jewel Markess. Nine children. He doubted they would all fit in Jewel's room, but had no doubt at all that he was going to make her try; let her bear the brunt of her impulsiveness. Rath would.

They were silent when they left the thirty-second holding, but their silence unfolded, peeling back in layers as if it were an onion, one thin word at a time. Lefty's hand was in his armpit, its customary sheath, but his eyes were darting back and forth as if they were moving of their own accord; he practically crossed them. Arann hovered over the rest of the children by at least six inches, although Carver, in Rath's estimation, would one day equal his height.

He wasn't certain what the other boys would do or be. The redhead was chatting almost amicably with Finch, who was doing her best to keep up—mostly by nodding. The other two kept as much to themselves as it was possible to do, but to Rath's surprise, Lefty spoke to them.

Not loudly enough to be heard, and not loudly enough—at first—to get much of a response. But where Arann was intimidating, and Harald and Rath were terrifying, Lefty, his hand hidden, his shoulders hunched as if to avoid a constant rain of blows, was the opposite: he was like them. Too slight to be either dangerous or independent; too damaged to be of use.

And if Lefty felt safe enough, here, to speak, then there *must* be some safety. Rath could see the understanding, although he wasn't certain the boys themselves would have put it as succinctly. They were underdressed for the weather, and the rains—and curse the skies, it was raining—caused their thin, pale shifts to cling to their skin, exposing too much.

But Duster? She kept to herself. The boys seemed to know her, and they weren't precisely afraid of her, but they weren't entirely comfortable either. She enjoyed that; he could see the slight malice of her smile. And shook his head again, as he saw Jewel's wet curls grow tighter.

This was not the end to the morning that he had envisioned. But he was accustomed to the idea that all action had consequences, and he accepted these as his natural due; no good deed went unpunished, after all.

Harald and his friends drifted off well before they made the thirty-fifth holding. If Rath had encouraged them to leave—and he must have—Jewel couldn't quite tell how; they stopped a moment, and spoke in low tones among themselves. She couldn't understand a word they said; it was Northern, all of it, and that wasn't a language she knew.

Her Oma had always found the Northerners annoying. Or terrifying. Living in a desert, it seemed, was a good deal less difficult when the desert wasn't made of snow. To Jewel, they had seemed the same: death, either way. But her Oma had had her own ideas, and she always shared.

They made an odd procession as they walked through the streets. If there hadn't been so many of them—and if four of them hadn't been so strangely dressed—it would have been easier for Rath. As it was, Jewel could tell how uncomfortable the visibility made him; he was curt, cool, and at a slight distance for the entire walk home.

He didn't stop at the Common. He didn't stop by the well. The latter made sense—they had no buckets—but it still struck Jewel as odd. They made their way home, and only when Rath had ushered them into the hall of the apartment—and they were crushed between its narrow walls—did he seem to relax at all.

"We may have been followed," he told her.

She winced. But she kept her peace.

"You can use the drill room," he added, "if you need the space. It might be best for now."

The last two words kind of hung in the air.

She did her best to ignore them. It didn't last long.

"Arann," she said quietly as Rath made his way to his room and shut the door behind his back.

Arann nodded.

"We don't have nearly enough food for everyone. We don't have enough water. We don't have enough anything."

He nodded again.

"We can manage food and water, for now. I need you to come with me," she added, in case this wasn't obvious. "And I need everyone else to sit in that room—*that* one—until we're back. Leave Rath alone. Carver?"

Carver nodded quietly.

"You stay. Finch—feed the others whatever you can find in the kitchen that isn't moving."

Duster stepped in her way. "You give the orders here?" she asked, in a voice that was quiet.

"Rath does," Jewel replied carefully. "It's mostly his place."

Duster shrugged. "If you say so."

"I say so."

"There are more of us at the moment."

Quiet kind of grew in a ripple. "I'd like it to stay that way."

"You work for him?"

Quiet could be so very loud. Jewel knew she'd have to have this conversation with Duster; she didn't want to have it *now*. "As much as he'll let me," she said. "You want to talk or eat?"

Duster's eyes were dark. She would have said more; her mouth opened. But Finch stepped between them—and as there wasn't much between to step into, it was awkward.

"She saved me," Finch said to Duster. And to Jewel.

"For what?"

Finch hesitated. "I don't know," she replied. It was safest because it was true.

"You trust her?"

"I trust you."

If Duster could have snarled, she would have; her whole expression twisted suddenly into something feral and dangerous. Jewel would remember it later. Wondered, now, if she would ever forget it. Trust was obviously not a word that Duster liked—either to use or to hear.

Rath was right about Duster.

Jewel knew it. "You saved her," she said evenly. "You figure out why. Don't take it out on me."

"You saved her," Duster snapped back. "You know why?"

"Yes. She needed me."

"I *don't.*"

"Probably not." She looked at Arann, and nodded toward the door. He could reach the bolts. "Does it matter?"

"Do you know why they kept me?"

"No. I don't care either." It wasn't true. But Jewel made it true, for now. "I didn't make the rules. I didn't follow them."

"They'd've sent you away. Broken you, and sent you away."

Jewel nodded. "But they didn't. And we're here. You want to be them? You want to do what they didn't?"

Duster's eyes rounded. Jewel was afraid—for just a minute—that Duster would hit her. Or try. But her eyes subsided into narrowness, and her hands uncurled. "No," she said curtly. "Not me." She looked at the door that Carver stood beside.

Jewel waited until Carver pushed the door open. There was another awkward pause, while the three boys whose names she didn't even know let their gazes bounce off the walls, the door—anything but her face or Duster's.

Carver kicked one of them, and he jumped, reddened, and left the hall; the others joined him quietly, which left Finch hovering by the kitchen.

"Go," she told Carver.

"Lefty?"

"He'll come with us."

"Right. Anything I should—"

"Don't scare them."

Carver shrugged. "One of them—"

"Carver."

He nodded, gave her an odd look.

Duster caught it as well. "I don't aim to start a fight I can't win. You can take your hand off the knife."

Jewel frowned and saw that Carver's hand *was*, in fact, curved casually around the hilt of his dagger. His expression was serious; he meant to wait.

She couldn't bring herself to tell him Duster meant no harm. She even tried, but the words wouldn't work their way out.

"She's not bad," Finch said, to no one in particular. "She helped—"

"Don't remind her," Jewel replied.

But the words broke Duster's mood, some. The way ice broke over water that was cold enough to kill you anyway if you were walking on it.

Duster walked past Carver slowly, measuring him. He didn't take his hand off the knife, but he made no move toward her; he simply held the door until she passed through its frame.

"Jay," he said quietly. Just her name. But it was all he needed to say.

She looked at the ground by Carver's feet. Saw what lay there, in a heap. "Leave them," she told him quietly. "We're going to get food."

He hesitated, and she added, "There won't be any trouble you can't handle."

Chapter Sixteen

FOUR HOURS LATER, two candles down, Rath heard the click of
the door at his back. Although he had gathered his papers in a more
or less orderly pile to his left, and the inkstand, with quill to grace it,
stood to his right, the only thing that occupied the focus of his attention
were two dull blades. Flat ornate daggers, golden-handled, with runes
that were so stylized it was almost impossible to recognize the language;
they seemed to be so ceremonial no one had thought to sharpen them.

He knew; he'd tried cutting paper and cloth, and while the paper
eventually gave, the cloth hadn't budged. He had studied those words,
attempting to glean what information he could from their letter forms;
he knew them as Old Weston, but they were a style of Old Weston that
his scholarship had seldom encountered.

But there were other engravings, on hilt and handle, that gave clues.
Old, old blades, these; they bore the marks of something that resembled
either fire or sun, and given the shape and curve, worn in places, he chose
to see them as sun's light. As, in fact, light.

"Where did you get them?" Jewel asked.

She had opened the door, of course, and she had padded in near silence
across floors that shouldn't have allowed it. He felt a momentary pride
in this accomplishment, and if he knew that the attempt at silence had
been made because she feared his censure for this long, long day's work,
it didn't lessen the pride. He wondered, briefly, if anything would, and
turned in his chair to look at her.

Her arms were full.

The work that she had done, to walk into the room so quietly, was made more impressive by the fact that she was overburdened. She carried these rolled objects as if they were an offering, and he allowed it.

But when she approached the table upon which he was working, he let that go. "Jewel," he told her quietly, his voice skirting the edge of frustration, "the decision to go was, in its entirety, mine. Two men died."

"More than two."

"Two of any worth."

She nodded quietly. If there was a day to argue about the value and sanctity of life—and Jewel Markess, odd urchin that she was, might be the only child present in his home who would even think the attempt worth making—it was not this one.

"These," Jewel told him, surprising him as she so often did, "are mine." Her arms tightened. "I found them. I brought them back."

He raised a brow. She seldom played games of any note, and although the daggers lay there, demanding both questions and answers, he found himself interested in this one. "Granted," he said quietly, waiting.

"But this," she added, rolling her head to take in the whole of his room, and by implication, the ones beyond the door as well, "is yours. You paid for it. You found it."

Ah. He now understood the opening gambit of a clumsy negotiation. He gazed at the light that came in from the window well above, broken by bars, and landing like spokes across the surface of the desk; it was the reason he had chosen to work instead at this table. The odd breaks in light, the bars of shadow, discomfited him.

"I can't send them away," she continued, and this—this came as no surprise at all. "You've seen them, Rath."

"I'm not sure you'll be able to keep at least one of them. And no, Jewel, I don't mean Duster."

She closed her eyes; her dark lashes, in the magelight's glow, made her face seem pale in comparison. Too much shadow, here. Too much odd light. She seemed to have carried it with her, and he wondered how it was that he hadn't seen it the first time they'd met.

"You want information," she told him. "And you pay for it. I want *them,* and I'm willing to trade what I have. Let them stay with us."

"Jewel—"

"I know we can't stay here forever," she added. She seemed oddly deflated; her words had a peculiar flatness to them that he associated with—with vision. "You'll make us leave," she added. "I don't know why. I don't know what we'll have done wrong. But you'll make us go."

Although it was a future he had contemplated, and in earnest, he himself could not see the manner of its arrival. He said nothing. Instead he rose, and moved both paper and ink, setting them on the desk. They were there, after all, more as companions than as useful tools. He had not touched them at all, save to place them where they might be touched should he need them.

He took the daggers last, and set them on the bed.

"What information do you think you have that's worth another four people?"

She put the bundles down, and lifted only one; its edges were darkened. "These," she told him, and she laid the one she held flat against the table, where it draped on all sides like a thick cloth meant for no other purpose. He would have spoken, but she continued.

"I think this is magicked, somehow."

"You can see that?"

Her frown added lines to her face. "No. Not—not like the doors."

"The doors, Jewel?"

"The ones that were barred. You didn't get out through the doors," she added.

"Arann seemed to think it unwise."

She smiled briefly at that, some echo of his own sense of pride, given the quiet giant was nowhere in sight. But brief was the correct word; the smile vanished. "They were . . . orange. They glowed orange."

Not to his vision. Not, certainly, to Arann's. He said nothing, however.

"It's a map," she added.

He looked at the parchment, the hide upon which so much had been drawn. He did not touch it, however; he was aware that he had not yet finished the negotiations she had begun, and he was willing to let her continue, although the presence of the lines and the words beneath them, the large ovals, the squares, and the odd, small circles, made it difficult.

"I thought it would burn. When I threw it over the mage, I thought it would burn."

He nodded.

"But it didn't. I think these were important," she added, "to the mage. Or the mages. I think they were willing to burn the house down because they knew these wouldn't burn with it."

"And you took them."

She nodded quietly. "I wouldn't have, if it weren't for—" She shook her head. "They looked like maps to me. But I've seen the maps of the city, and this isn't them."

He knew; they were his maps. "You didn't seem so eager to study my maps," he said, with a hint of wry humor. "I wouldn't have guessed you would choose to take maps from the manor; there were other things of value there."

"I took everything of value there," she replied quietly. "And these, as well."

It wasn't subtle, but then again, Jewel never was.

"It would cost much to magic something of this size," he said, his eyes on the lines that denoted streets. She was, of course, correct; this was not Averalaan. "Minor magics, some scrambling, perhaps keying the maps to individual eyes—those would be less expensive. But to protect such things against destruction?"

"You said people do it. For paintings. And other stuff."

He nodded. He had. But these were not the same. He stared at the map that lay there, following a line that plummeted off the table's edge. "What do you think these are, Jewel?"

Her hesitation was awkward; silence was as close as she came to a lie. But she wouldn't lie to him in his own house; he had set that ground rule early, and she abided by it. "The undercity," she said at last. "I think these are maps of the undercity."

"What makes you say that?"

She wanted to shrug; he saw it, and knew why: she wanted to appear to be in control of this exchange. And she so seldom wanted that control. But in her mind, lives depended on it, and he let it pass without comment, curious to see how it would play out.

But her answer was not the answer he wanted. She bent at the knees and retrieved another of the three maps; this she laid over the first. He could see where they'd cut it down, and wondered what type of magic had been placed upon them; certainly, the ability to be impervious to edged weapons had been demonstrated clearly by the man who had almost killed them all with his flame.

And by the others.

But that enchantment was absent, had to be absent; he could see where daggers had done their sloppy, quick work.

When she had flattened the map, and centered it, she touched its surface.

The lines beneath her finger began to glow. Jewel frowned; it was clear that she was uncertain as to whether or not Rath could see the effect. But it didn't matter; the line took pale blue light and spread it in a thin wedge. Her fingers ran along it, and stopped at a large rectangle that receded for some distance, bound on the other side by another line that sloped in a gentle curve. The map continued its odd glow, and Rath realized that the lines touch invoked did not conform entirely to the lines drawn on the parchment itself. Magic indeed.

"I think," she told him quietly, "that this is the stone garden."

He nodded; he could almost see it. A rough series of calculations might tell him the scale the cartographers had used. He bent over the map, and she stopped him; she rolled them both up, lifted them, and waited. Solemn child.

"They're ours," she told him quietly.

"Ours, now?"

"I didn't take them down on my own; I couldn't have carried them out on my own. Carver helped. Finch helped."

"You could sell these," he began.

But she shook her head, her expression wary. "You wouldn't let me sell them," she told him. "And because you won't, it means they have value, but only to you."

He nodded, and then he graced her with a rare smile. "You've done well," he told her quietly. "And yes, Jewel Markess. In exchange for these, I will allow you the use of two rooms."

"Rath?"

"Yes?"

"Will you let me look at them, sometimes?"

He started to say something clever, but her expression stopped the words. "Yes," he told her quietly. "While it is safe, I will let you look at them."

Her shoulders seemed to collapse a fraction, and he realized, with surprise, that the act had been no act; she did value the maps in and of themselves. Under other circumstances, she would have kept them.

And she would have accepted his refusal to allow her access in return for the rooms that would house far too many of her wayward children. Her den.

He smiled.

"What's funny?" she said sharply.

"Your den," he replied.

"My what?"

"They're yours, Jewel. To heal or to lose."

She shook her head.

But this, he would not allow. "Whether you accept it or not, you've already become their leader. Arann would follow you anywhere now. And I think young Carver as well, although I'm less certain why. Finch wouldn't follow you into a fight—but that's not her gift.

"And the others? They'll come to you, sooner or later. They'll learn to trust you. And you, little Jewel, will understand how much of a burden that trust can be."

"Trust is a gift," she began.

"Only until you fail it," he replied. "And at your age, I think failure is certain. Remember that. Remember, the first time it happens, that it is only one failure. And remember this as well: How you deal with that failure will define not only your life, but theirs."

He would have said more; he meant to. But he had come close to skirting the sharp edge of his own past, and the words that he had offered were not his words; they were his grandfather's words, come back to haunt him in the only way they could: from his lips.

And they were true—but Rath's truth was not, yet, Jewel's. It was bitter, and darker.

"Go," he told her, more harshly than he had intended. "I have business to attend to."

"Here?"

"I'll go out in an hour or two."

She nodded.

Duster wore a russet shade of brown, and it didn't suit her. The sleeves of the winter tunic were rolled up at least twice by the look of them, and the hood that hung from the shoulders seemed to have a spine, it stood so stiffly behind her messy hair. She wore pants that didn't match, but these were both tighter and shorter. Her feet were still bare. If Helen could be cajoled into parting with clothing that had yet to find a wearer, if she could be talked out of the need to use her measuring tapes and sticks, her wealth of straight pins, the cobbler wasn't so generous.

The other three were dressed in a similar fashion; the clothing was obviously meant for small adults, and little thought had gone into color or size; they were either green or brown. But it was better than what they almost weren't wearing, and they all knew it. They knew, as well, that clothing that actually fit would be waiting, soon.

They looked up as she entered the room.

"I'm Jay," she told them quietly. "Did everyone else introduce themselves?"

Lefty nodded, and then frowned. "This," he said, nodding to the red-head, "is Jester."

She raised a brow. "Jester?"

"What, it's worse than *Carver*?"

Jewel shrugged. He had a point. "I don't care if you call yourselves Mouse and Rat," she replied. "I don't care if you want me to call you Mouse or Rat. I don't care how you wound up at that place; it's gone, you're not going back. But if you've got someplace else to go back *to*, that's fine as well. It's awfully crowded here." She waited.

No one volunteered the location of a home. She hadn't expected they would, but had to make the offer anyway.

"Jay *is* my name," she added quietly. "It's short for Jewel." She lifted a balled fist in warning. "It's a Southern name, sort of. And it could have been worse. I wouldn't bother to tell you about this, but Rath uses it when he's annoyed. Which is often."

"Finch is my name," Finch said quietly. She looked lost in this crowd. Or almost lost. But her quiet had no fear in it, at least not for herself.

"Arann's mine. Lefty's not—"

Lefty kicked him. Arann didn't appear to notice.

Jewel turned to look at the other two boys. One, silent in a way that implied the remnant of defiance, finally said, "Fisher." His face was almost all jaw, and his eyes were small and bright; blue, which was a bit startling given the darkness of his hair. He wasn't tall, but he didn't give the impression of being small or underfed either.

Jester. Fisher. Duster. She turned to the quiet boy and almost turned away. There was food in his lap. The fact that it was there at all meant he hadn't touched it. Jewel looked at Finch, and Finch looked at the floor. As if his lack of appetite was her failing, somehow.

Jewel made a note to herself: Don't put Finch on kitchen duty. But Finch was good in the damn kitchen; she was neat and very tidy, and she organized space; she also took up so little of it you could actually stand beside her without having to dance around the jut of her elbows. Jewel made no guesses about what she'd done when she'd had a family. She didn't even wonder how big—or how close to starvation—it must have been.

She just hated them blindly.

And if Finch did, she wasn't about to say it. Not yet. Maybe never. It was hard to tell—Finch had been on best behavior, at least by Jewel's standards—since she'd come to Rath's. Maybe in time, when she was truly at home here, she'd let go.

But maybe this was just the way she was.

The boy who was silent was also dressed in Helen's half-price castoffs. She wondered if he had struggled or argued or ignored what had been offered. Asking was awkward, so she didn't, but she stored that one for later as well.

"He's hurt," Lefty said quietly, nodding to the silent, motionless boy. "He just sits there, staring at the wall. He doesn't like loud noises," he added, as if that were helpful. As if it weren't obvious.

But loud noise had defined Jewel's life with her Oma, so maybe it wasn't.

"How hurt?" she asked softly.

Lefty glanced up at Arann. Arann's silent expression was enough of an answer. "We could take him to the Mother's temple," he said at last.

She started to say no and stopped. The Mother's temple, according to her Oma, was a place that you went when you had no other choices; when you were so down on your luck, all you had left was pride or death.

But she'd never seen anyone like this boy before either. She started to ask another question, and then stopped. Duster had crossed the floor; Duster now knelt by the boy. Jewel wanted to grab her by the shoulder and drag her away, and curbed the impulse with difficulty.

She didn't trust Duster.

But Duster had made clear how much of a burden she thought trust was. How much of an insult.

"He was there for longer than I was," Duster told them all, her eyes on the boy's profile. His hair was a pale gold, and his eyes were a more natural blue; his cheek was bruised, his lips were slightly thick, and purple to one side.

"What was he like, when you first saw him?"

Duster looked up. The warning in her expression was sharp as a knife. Then again, everything about her was.

Jewel accepted the criticism; she'd broken one of her own rules, without thinking. What he had been didn't matter; what he was, did. She nodded quietly at Duster, and Duster's response to the silent apology was an odd frown; it was a tightening, a whitening, of lips. An expression of pain. She hovered there, as if it were the only place she was at home. "He tried to help me," she said, after a long, long pause. "I owe him."

"What did he call himself?"

"Lander."

"Why?"

"I think it was short for Alexander, or something like that. I don't know. I never asked." Before Jewel could ask anything awkward, Duster added, "it was best not to know. Anything. Because anything we did know—"

"Could be discovered."

Again, Duster gave her an odd look. "You weren't out on the streets for long, were you?"

Jewel shook her head. She had something to prove here, but it wasn't going to be proved by posturing, and it wasn't going to be proved in minutes, or with a few words. "I was lucky," she said at last. "I tried to steal something from Rath."

"Tried?"

Jewel shrugged.

"And he took you in?"

"I don't understand it either."

Duster shrugged. "How do you pay for it?"

And Jewel, understanding the place that had been their prison, didn't even have the energy to bristle. "Not like this," she said quietly. "Never this."

"And would you?"

"I—I don't know."

Duster's eyes widened slightly. "That's not a no."

"It would have been, five minutes ago."

"I know."

"Oh?"

"Arann looks like he wants to hit me for asking."

Jewel turned to glance briefly at Arann; he looked pretty much the way he always did to her. "I don't know what I'll be forced to do, to survive. But Rath says that the only thing that counts is survival."

Duster nodded. "He's good," she said quietly. And then she smiled. Jewel preferred it when she didn't. "He doesn't want me here. He doesn't trust me."

Jewel shrugged. "He's willing to have you here anyway."

"He must trust you a helluvalot."

"Some." She shrugged.

"I don't run with a crowd," Duster told her. "I did, once."

Jewel waited. Just . . . waited. And it was hard.

Lefty rescued her. "You ran with a den?"

Duster nodded. "You think I couldn't make it?" Edge in the question, but it was blunted; she clearly didn't think much of Lefty, but he wasn't a threat.

"Better than I could," Lefty said, with just a hint of shame.

"Your friend with a den?"

"He's with Jay," Lefty replied firmly.

"This your den, then?" Duster's face had become all angles; the line of her jaw sharp enough to cut. It was a challenge. Again.

Jewel gave in to the inevitable. "Yes," she said quietly. "It's my den. You in or out?"

"Not much of a den," Duster replied. "Maybe those two," she added, nodding at Arann and Carver. "But none of the others."

"Depends."

"I've been in the streets. I know what it takes to survive 'em."

"So have they."

Duster turned to Carver. "What's the deal, then?"

Carver shrugged. He didn't blink. He looked to Jewel instead, making a point.

"What do you *do?*"

"We live here," Jewel replied.

"To eat."

"I've got some money. We find things," she added, putting pauses between the words. "We give them to Rath, and he sells them." It was more or less true. "He cuts us in."

"You steal things, he fences them?"

"No."

Duster shrugged. "Fine. You 'find' them. What holding do you run in?"

"This one."

"And your territory?"

Jewel said quietly, "This place."

"I mean—"

"I know what you meant. Any idiot would. We're not thugs. We don't mug little old ladies by the well."

"You ever gone into the fancy holdings?"

"Not farther than the Common."

"But they let you in?"

"We buy things there."

Duster shook her head. She would have risen, but the boy by her side reached out slowly and caught the hem of her tunic in his shaking hands. He didn't speak, but he didn't have to.

"I'm not an idiot," Duster said, half crouched. "I know that nothing comes for free. You rescued us. I'll give you that."

Sarcasm was not a good bridge. Her father had said that, when he was trying to teach her not to be like her Oma. Jewel bit back words her Oma could have said.

Duster seemed to have been waiting for what Jewel struggled to hold back. When Jewel won—barely—Duster shrugged and asked a single question. "Why?"

"Because you saved Finch," Jewel replied evenly. "Just that."

"And the others?"

"Because they were there."

"But you knew."

"Knew what?"

"Who held us." It was almost a question.

Jewel said, quietly, "Rath had his suspicions. He must have, or we'd all be dead."

"And you came anyway. Are you stupid?"

Jewel nodded. "And not," she added, "your kind of stupid."

"They had friends," Duster said quietly. "In high places."

"People like that usually do."

"You don't want to meet their friends."

"Not really."

"But you will, if you're here. Or your friend will. They were *mages*. They had power. And they weren't working for themselves."

Jewel gave up on the ask no questions approach. "How do you know that?"

"I met one." Duster had stiffened; she held her ground, the small patch of floor over which she crouched by necessity. The boy had not let go.

Jewel nodded, because she heard the truth in the words. Knew that if Duster could lie to her, now was the time. She felt it clearly, as if it were vision. Curse and gift.

"If he was so powerful," she said carefully, "we'd be dead. We're not. They are. Friends in high places aren't all on their side." She paused, and then added, "We want to stop them."

"Stop them?"

"From—from this. From taking—from this."

"You can't even *say* it."

"I don't have to."

Duster shrugged. It wasn't a casual motion. "Your friend has something I want."

"What?"

"Information. If he gives me what I want, I'll stay."

"And if he doesn't?"

"I'll find it out on my own."

Carver stepped forward, and Jewel lifted a hand. She couldn't look away from Duster's face, from the round darkness of her eyes, the absolute determination of her gaze. Even had she wanted to.

"What will you do with the information, if we can get hold of it?"

"None of your business."

But Jewel already knew the answer. "Have you ever killed a man?"

"Once."

"When?"

"In a fight. My life or his."

"This isn't the same."

"It's worse." Duster's words were almost a growl. But there was implacability in them. And Jewel knew that she herself would go to Rath, that she would ask; she could see this clearly, almost as clearly as she could see how it would end.

"I'll ask him," she said quietly.

Duster waited. "You want something."

"Everyone does."

This seemed to suit Duster, who shrugged more comfortably, if you could do that and still bristle. Jewel was reminded of the fact that her Oma had also hated anything perceived as charity. As pity. What Finch

had accepted in silence, what Arann and Lefty had accepted with gratitude, what Carver accepted without thought, Duster would abhor.

"What?"

"I want to go with you, when you go."

Duster's face crinkled a moment, lines of confusion lessening the anger
that was so bleak and powerful. "When I go?"

"To find him," Jewel said. *To kill him.*

The confusion didn't so much ease as deepen, until it looked very much
like anger.

Before Duster could give voice to it, Jewel added, "I won't ask him, if
you don't promise."

"I don't need your help."

"I wasn't offering to help you."

"You wouldn't be able to." The contempt in the words caused Carver to
take a half step. Before Jewel could lift a hand, he stopped himself.

"No. I wouldn't. But . . . I won't stop you," she added quietly. "And in
the end, that's almost the same."

"It's nothing like the same."

"No one helped you," Jewel told her quietly. "And you ended up there.
If one person—or two, or ten, Hells, I don't know—had, you wouldn't
have. The people who watch and turn away—they didn't actually *hurt*
you; they didn't—" She shook her head. "It wasn't their hand that held
the knife. My Oma used to say that," she added. "But if they had lifted
a hand before it had started, it *would never have happened.* I'm going to be
there with you. I won't try to stop you. You'll do what you have to do.
Not doing anything? It *does* matter. It *is* the same."

"If it were," Duster said, her voice as low as Jewel had yet heard it, "I'd
have to kill them all."

"Them?"

"Whoever you're talking about. Those people. The ones who watched
and did nothing."

"I think," Jewel said, choosing her words with as much care as she
could, "most of them are already dead."

Duster's shoulders dropped an inch or two.

"Finch ended up in the same place," Jewel continued quietly. Hard to
speak quietly. "And Fisher. Lander. Jester."

"They're not the only ones. You think you've saved them? You think
you can give them a better life?"

"Better than that? I already have."

"For how long, Jay?"

"For now. Now is what we have," she added bitterly.

"You sound like a damn Priest."

"There are worse things to sound like. You promise?"

"I'll think about it."

"You do that." She paused, and then turned to Arann. "You, Carver, the other three—you sleep in the drill room. We'll sleep here for now."

"Rath's okay with that?"

"We worked something out."

Arann's frown appeared slowly and gradually, like the waning of sunlight. It was as unlike Duster's as a frown could be.

"No," she said more softly, "seriously. We worked something out and *I'm happy with it*. He took me in," she added, seeing from the solid state of his expression that he needed more. "He took me in when I was sick. He nursed me back to health. He's asked me for nothing. If it weren't for Rath, we couldn't have rescued Finch. If it weren't for Rath, you'd be crippled or dead.

"I don't know who he was," she added, lifting a hand. "I don't know what he did, or what he had to run away from. But whatever it was, it didn't include—" she took a deeper breath, "selling children. Or letting them sell themselves." She paused and then added, "Arann, I *know* this, okay?"

And those words, those last words, were enough.

But she felt odd, having to say them. Felt as if they had a texture and weight that not even her Oma would have granted them. And she felt, as well, some strange prickling in the corners of her eyes, her wide eyes.

Duster must have seen it all; she didn't miss much. But she snorted, and her snort was less angry than it had been. "You're all crazy," she said, to no one in particular.

Lefty surprised her by saying, "It's a good crazy."

"It's still crazy."

"You helped Finch," he shot back.

"Arann?"

"Leaving," Arann said, catching Lefty by his right arm and dragging him out the door that Carver held open. Jester followed quickly, and Fisher, a little less so—but Lander didn't move.

Duster swore. She swore impressively; it made Jewel feel like a Priest.

Or her Oma. "He can stay," Duster told Jewel. It was, yet again, a challenge. And Carver was standing in the doorway, waiting.

But as challenges went, it was a feeble one as far as Jewel was concerned. She looked at Lander, and nodded. "He's probably seen worse than us," she added quietly. She looked up at Carver, and saw him frown; clearly, whatever he was used to in a den—and she had no doubt he'd been part of one—it wasn't this easy shift of command.

But command didn't interest Jewel; it never had. Well, not since she'd turned five.

Duster nodded. Lander still held the hem of her tunic, and she didn't even bother to try to release it; she crouched there, knees bent, eyes as dark as any color Jewel had seen eyes get.

Rath left when it was quiet. He considered using the storage room's exit into the undercity, but the existence of these maps disquieted him. He had managed to keep that to himself, largely because Jewel was too afraid about the fate of her orphans to be perceptive. He doubted her ignorance would last, but doubted, as well, that it would be alleviated any time soon.

The sun was on its way down. He dressed with care, although he had less clothing to choose from than he had had a mere handful of days previous to this one. The cloak he had worn on his ill-advised raid was only good for rags now; there was too much blood and too much tearing to make repairs that wouldn't suggest old battles, and not of the winning variety. That and the singed edges would make him look too much the thug.

He had taken care to wash both face and hair; the face required some work. As he knew his hair would be under a hat for much of his walk, he was less scrupulous about its cleanliness. That, and he was weary. The mirror's reflection in magelight paled his skin, and made him seem ghostly, almost translucent. It wasn't a welcome reminder of mortality, but then again, little was.

Exhaustion had come upon him very shortly after Jewel had left his rooms; he had chosen to listen to the conversation that filtered out into the narrow hall, catching the cadence of both words and the silences that bracketed them. Jewel wasn't good with silence yet, but she would learn; she'd have to. She said too much, and said it too easily.

When he had finished dressing, and had taken inventory of his various disguises, paints, clothing, he placed the dull ceremonial daggers in the smaller of his satchels, and this he slung with care over his shoulder. He also carried money, but it was hidden in the folds of his sash.

He glanced at the fallen light, at the way it had faded, seeing the hours in its coloring of floor and desk. He was going to be late. But it would be a fashionable late, not a disastrous one.

Or not, he thought, eyeing the table at which his companion waited, disastrous had he not been on his way to see Andrei. He had half-hoped that Patris Hectore might accompany his most famous servant, but as with all faint hopes, this was doomed to be dashed. And, in the flickering candlelight of the damn Peacock, Andrei looked both annoyed and slightly menacing.

On the other hand, half of his disdain was reserved for the stemmed glass he held in his hand; he looked at the liquid as if it were what was left after dishes had been scraped clean in its depths. For a servant, Andrei was one of the most profoundly snobbish men that Rath had ever met.

He was also impeccably dressed; he wore a tailored jacket, and his hair was drawn back in a braid that fell beyond Rath's sight. He wore green velvet pants, and no obvious weapon, but then again, it *was* Andrei. Rath joined him, and Andrei nodded. He also placed a small and familiar stone between their plates on the surface of the table, where it was shrouded by the fall of wilting flowers. When he touched it, Rath felt his tension easing.

"Ararath," Andrei said, inclining his head, "I was wondering if you would deign to show up at all." His smile was genial, but as was so often the case, it failed to match his actual expression.

"I was detained," Rath replied, taking a chair. "But not, I hope, to our detriment. I see you've chosen to dress more colorfully than usual."

"An experiment," Andrei replied, with a shrug. "How was your morning?"

"It was eventful," Rath answered, as if he were speaking of some social gathering whose main event was boredom.

This was a signal to Andrei, and he treated it with the disinterested attention he did all matters that concerned him; his eyes were slightly brighter, and slightly narrower.

"I have some items to return to your care," Rath added, and he removed the satchel, handing it over the table to Andrei. "I fear they have sustained some material damage in transit, however; they are quite dull."

"Ararath. Did I not warn you?"

"You offered warning," Rath replied, pouring wine out of a heavy decanter.

"It's not a good vintage," Andrei told him.

"No doubt. But it will do. Your warning was, as usual, almost prescient."

"But not, as usual, heeded."

"I had undertaken the task; I could not, with grace—or without explanation—refuse it." He paused, and then, after confirming Andrei's opinion of the wine, added, "Nor would I have the explanation to offer, should I have desired to do so." He leaned slightly toward Andrei, which brought him closer to both stone and flower. "I desire explanations," he added softly.

Andrei's face was a mask. "There is explanation here," he said at last, as he lifted the satchel. He set it down beside him on the bench he occupied. "But it is not an explanation that bears examination."

"I met two men who could not be injured by the swords we carried."

"We?"

"I decided it would be wise to hire help."

Andrei's frown was prominent. "This is, of course, your usual definition of wisdom."

"Of course."

"And you trust these men?"

"They saw what I saw," Rath replied, with a shrug.

"And that?"

"A mage."

"You've seen mages before."

"Several times. I would have said I had better acquaintance with them than you, but it appears I would be mistaken."

"No doubt you have more numerous contacts."

"No doubt."

"We will have to return these," Andrei said quietly, motioning to the daggers that lay hidden. "And perhaps you will have some answer there."

"I have no desire to—"

"Rath, you have chosen to play the game."

"And you have not?"

"No, I have not. What I have done, I have done with discretion. What you have done—and I believe there was a fire in a large, old manse in the thirty-second this morn—was not."

"And this is of significance?"

"Where there are witnesses, yes."

Rath nodded.

"Patris Hectore is, of course, aware of the difficulty. And I will say that he is not ill-pleased by it, although some of this can be attributed to his fondness for a godson."

"How aware?"

"He is apprised of what the purpose of the manor was. From his discreet inquiries, you were seen leading children from the burning ruins, and age has made him sentimental; he believes he is proud of you."

"I see," Rath replied dryly. "And you, of course, did not see fit to explain that fires of that nature generally do not spread quite as quickly in our current weather."

Andrei's face lost some of its distance. "Your godfather has earned the right to some meager happiness," he told Rath softly, "and the belief that he holds is not essentially wrong. But now, he is concerned. Were he not, I would not be here."

"There was money involved, there."

"There was more than money involved. But yes, on the surface of things, more money than you can imagine." Andrei's smile was sharp, a hunter's smile. "It appears that some of the manse's visitors were rather surprised by the nature of the consequences of their visits."

"Blackmail?"

"Indeed."

Rath nodded; it made some sense. But only some. "My own research tells me that the manor was used for barely a month."

Andrei said nothing.

"It would take some planning and foresight; you would have to be aware of the foibles of the men you wished to entrap, and you would have to have the necessary contacts to approach them at all."

"Indeed."

"How, Andrei?"

"How is less of an issue. You have not asked where I heard of the fire."

"No. Asking questions is usually frowned on."

"It is in most cases. This one is interesting. I did not come down to the lower holdings; I did not do the research on my own. I merely . . . listened."

"When?"

"There was a luncheon at the Guild," he replied quietly. "And much is said in the presence of servants that would not otherwise be voiced."

This was generally true; it was not specifically true of Andrei. Rath did not point this out.

"Come, Ararath."

"Where?"

But Andrei rose and signaled the innkeeper. He did not answer. He expected to be followed. He did, however, pick up the stone from the table before he left.

It had been some time since Rath had ventured across the footbridge that led to the Isle. For one, foot traffic was less common than carriage traffic in the crossing; it was certainly less common than horseback. As either horse—if it were fine enough, and obviously meant for riding—or carriage, proclaimed a certain status or wealth, the guards upon the wider bridge were both more officious and less intrusive.

The toll across the footbridge was smaller, but more rigorously enforced. For this reason, Rath tended to hire a carriage when he made his visits to the Order of Knowledge, and his occasional forays into Senniel, the bardic College upon the Isle.

But Andrei led him to the footbridge, and he followed. There was, in Andrei, a certain officiousness that outmaneuvered all others, while at the same time implying no obvious threat. He was polite beyond any civilized bounds, and in his obvious courtesy, no one could point to any specific word or gesture that spoke of condescension.

But no one seemed to enjoy speaking with Andrei when he was in this mode, and if they were distant, they were also quick. Rath made himself a follower, rather than a leader here, drawing his shoulders in, and hugging the edge of the shadow Andrei cast; he spoke when Andrei had recourse to demand it, but otherwise kept his silence.

This wasn't natural; Rath had, however, become accustomed to donning personae as if they were clothing. He allowed Andrei to pay the toll on his behalf, and when Andrei strode off, he quickly followed.

Andrei was unimpressed, Rath unruffled.

"Have some dignity," Andrei said quietly.

"I have chosen to define dignity in a slightly different way."

"Not, clearly, a Weston one."

Rath shrugged. "Dignity isn't worth a man's life."

"Not especially when it's yours?"

"More or less. Dignity of the sort you favor is a luxury I can ill afford." He lifted a hand. "We've had this conversation before, Andrei; it's unlike you to retread old ground."

"Perhaps I'm bored."

"You've never looked anything but bored."

At that, the servant granted Rath a rare nod, his equivalent of a smile. The smile itself would probably have cracked his face.

The streets here were wide, and they were almost empty; there were no children in them, no old women with buckets, no buildings packed into small spaces. Instead, there were fences, magnificent structures that both excluded and yet invited the eye. Beyond these, there were grounds; they were not so large or fine as the grounds in the upper holdings, but upon the Isle, the rich made do with the lack of space; the Isle was the address of note to those in merchant families.

Upon the Isle, the bards could be found; upon the Isle, the Guild of Makers, and the Order of Knowledge. And above them, the palace of the Twin Kings towered.

But not so high in their reach as the great cathedrals at which the Kings paid their respects to the gods. There were three: The Mother's temple, the Temple of Cormaris, Lord of Wisdom, and the Temple of Reymaris, Lord of Justice. Other gods made their home here, but none in buildings so fine or old; these three were the heart of the Empire.

Seeing the direction of Rath's gaze, Andrei shook his head. "Not yet," he said quietly, "but later, if we've time. I am expected by the Patris before sundown."

"The Order of Knowledge?"

"The Order," Andrei conceded. "But not directly."

Rath said very little for a moment. "You think you've been followed?"

"I doubt it, but the possibility exists. Having seen what once followed you," he added, "it is not a risk I am comfortable taking."

Rath nodded. He had watched the streets less carefully after he had crossed the bridge, but he had watched them nonetheless. There was, in his life, no definition of the word safety that did not require—or even demand—caution.

But it was harder to be as cautious here, where no one approached them; where polite distance between strangers was defined in yards and not feet. Where guards, wearing the colors of the Houses they served, were more numerous than barefoot, underdressed urchins.

The rain was thin and fine. The air that left their lips hung before them like something that yearned to be fog. He could taste the salt of the surrounding sea on his lip and tongue; the breeze, where it existed at all, failed to send the clouds on.

But the buildings that rose in spite of weather, gray for the season, were capped or adorned by dank, heavy fabric that might otherwise reveal House crests, and these they passed quickly.

"We go to the High Market," Andrei said quietly. "There is an inn there of some quality, and it is there that we will pause and eat."

"Will we have companions?"

"One, perhaps, if it is a suitable time."

"And if it's not?"

"We will have had some exercise."

And no answers. Rath nodded. He had played these games for most of his adult life, but he had seldom played them here; here, games were played in parlors, foyers, great balconies; they were played in the special preserves used by the Kings for the occasional hunt; they were played in the halls which Senniel College's master bards filled. They were even played in bedrooms. But in all of these places, men with power, women with power, gathered.

That power, he understood.

This one? He had envied it, in his childhood. He did not envy it now.

"A Member of the Order of Knowledge?"

"And in good standing," Andrei replied. "Perhaps, if we are lucky, we will see two such. But their presence would be cause for gossip, were they to be recognized; I think it unlikely."

Rath thought the definition of lucky needed some fine-tuning. But he was weary of the cold and the damp, the stillness of air that spoke of, whispered of, the coming of true Winter.

Chapter Seventeen

THE INN WAS LIKE, and unlike, the Peacock. Proud Peacock, Rath reminded himself, as he entered through doors that were held by attendants attired in what was almost—but not quite—livery. They wore a uniform that was a deep, even blue, with hints of gold at the double-stitched seams; the jackets were perfectly fitted to the men beneath them, although they were of different sizes and ages.

The smiles they offered were both perfunctory and genuine, and the sympathies they offered, as they gazed out at an almost perpetual gray, were the same; they were men who were comfortable in the job they had chosen, or perhaps the job they had had chosen for them.

No owner came to greet Rath and Andrei, although at this time of day, it was likely that said owner was on the premises. No one paused to note Rath's lack of fine clothing; Andrei admittedly had the bearing and carriage of a man accustomed to power, and if his version of accustomed implied service, it implied such only to men who knew him.

Clearly, these two did not—but they expected that any man who crossed the threshold was a man capable of affording anything offered within, and it was not their job to keep the poor and less scrupulous on the other side of the door. Rich men—and women—could be notably odd in their habits; the accumulation of wealth might lead a man to a certain type of grandstanding or even obsequiousness, but the long custom of *having* it could lead them in any direction they chose. And one did not question the direction if one had breeding.

Thus it was in the Placid Sea, where men had occasionally been known to venture in without shoes, and been made to feel welcome. Rath was more at home here than long years of absence would have led him to expect; he did not blink when his coat was taken and handled with the same expert care that a more appropriate coat in the rainy season would receive. He felt some tension leave him as the coat did; his tunic was dry, and the warmth of the building warmed hands that had bunched into fists.

Andrei's coat was likewise taken, and Andrei offered the doorman a very civil nod in response; he also offered a coin, which the man accepted without comment or even, apparently, notice. Rath had no like coin to offer, and by the lack, made himself known as either guest or client.

They were led, after some small conversation, to chairs by one of the establishment's many fireplaces; they were offered cushions and towels, as well as a drink, and the fire was well tended; it crackled in silence as Rath observed it.

"You were always fascinated by fire," Andrei said quietly.

"Aren't all children?"

"Not in the same way, no."

Rath could have pointed out that Andrei's life lacked anything remotely resembling children, but it wouldn't have been precisely true; he had none of his own, of course, but he was almost a fixture for his godfather's numerous clan. Children, grandchildren, godchildren—all of these had passed before Andrei's steady eyes, and had often been passed into his patient care. In the great manor House Araven owned—upon the Isle—there was always noise, always light, always warmth; if there were questions, there was also an affability and a tolerance that were often absent in less well-established Houses.

"If this is a metaphor, Andrei, I'm well past the age where it might be of use."

"It is not, sadly, metaphor. And you were never of an age where my guidance might have been of use to you."

Rath shrugged; it was true. They sat in a companionable silence, but it was heavy with things unsaid. To Rath's great surprise, some of those did not remain that way. "My sister," he said quietly.

The word hung in the air between them; it appeared that not only had Rath surprised himself, but also Andrei. It was almost worth it.

The servant raised a brow, and then slowly bent his elbows above the armrests, shadowing them as he steepled his fingers beneath his chin. "She is well," he said at last. "The House Terafin is, for the moment, at peace."

He paused and fastidiously brushed wood ash from his pant leg. "She has, of course, asked after you."

"You've seen her?"

"Patris Hectore has been favored with an invitation to the House," he replied, as if this were commonplace.

"And you attended him."

"That is my privilege," Andrei answered quietly.

"Has she made many friends?"

"In House Terafin?"

Rath nodded.

"As many as one would expect of a woman of power and position."

"Which would be none."

"Ararath, that is beneath you."

"You might have noticed, Andrei, that very little is beneath me in my current life."

"But not nothing," was the grave reply.

Rath was silent. "I didn't think," he said at last, "that she would survive."

Andrei raised a brow. "You judge your sister harshly," he said at last, "And without your usual perception." He looked at his hands as he spoke, and in this, he was a consummate servant; he knew where to look, and when. "But as this is unusual, and you are in an unexpected mood, I will be more forthcoming than would ideally suit my position. She almost died in the struggle to take the House and make it her own; were it not for the intervention of a healer—from the House of Healing upon the Isle—she would have perished."

The words filled Rath with emptiness, or the appearance of it; something was opening beneath his feet, which, given they rested upon a cushioned stool in the heart of the Placid Sea, said much. "Healers seldom intervene," he said, groping for words and finding them somehow.

"Indeed. Almost never." He paused, and then added, "You might know the man; I believe you met him on one occasion."

"Alowan."

"Alowan Rowanson, yes. He is not young now. But I believe—"

"I know him," Rath continued. "He is old, even by my standards. He came when she called." Flat words, no surprise in them.

"He is resident within the Terafin House upon the Isle."

At that, Rath did sit up in surprise.

"He has not, however, seen fit to accept the offer of the Terafin name; he is still Rowanson, as he was born, and I do not believe that will change in the foreseeable future.

"The Chosen serve her," Andrei continued. "And she has built, within the House Council, an uneasy alliance of mutual interest. They look out-ward, now, rather than in, among themselves; if they sharpen their blades, they are now aimed at external enemies." He paused again. "The man who almost succeeded the man previously known as The Terafin—"

"Was called the Butcher, if gossip is to be believed."

"He was not called the Butcher in common parlance among his peers," Andrei said, with a hint of disapproval. But it was a hint that held no substance, no weight. "There is none, now, who will challenge her rule; it has been this way for many years, and I do not believe it will change while she lives."

Rath nodded bitterly. "And so she is now the most powerful woman upon the Isle, save for the god-born and the Twin Kings."

"And no one calls her the Butcher," Andrei replied calmly. "Nor will they. She is not the child she was. Nor are you."

Rath nodded. Thinking now, for one dangerous moment, about a statue with eyes of sapphire and a voice that contained the echoes of the voices of gods. Thinking of the darkness and the emptiness in which that statue had remained for centuries, waiting for Jewel's touch to invoke it.

And yet when it had spoken, its words had not been for Jewel, who lay insensate, but for Rath. He almost spoke of it, but Andrei's position shifted. It was subtle, but Rath understood instantly that their mo-ment of isolation was about to be broken, and he almost welcomed the interruption.

Andrei stood as two men joined them. Rath lifted a brow, and Andrei ignored it. Luck, it seemed, was with them. But there was enough of the streets in Rath to make him wonder which face Kalliaris now showed him: the frown or the smile. Perhaps both; she was a cagey god at best, and if she was the one whose name was most frequently spoken in the holdings, it was spoken with dread and hope in equal measure.

Andrei took the smooth carved stone from his pocket, but before he could place it upon the fireside table, one of the two men lifted a pale hand. He wore the robes of the Order of Knowledge beneath an oiled cloak that he had somehow managed to walk past the doormen.

Andrei nodded and pocketed the stone, and chairs were drawn closer to the fireside.

"Andrei," the man who had motioned said. His voice was smooth and colorless, the single word uninflected.

Andrei nodded again, but this time with more purpose, and Rath rose in greeting. "May I introduce you to Ararath Handernesse?"

The man lifted both of his hands and drew the hood of the cloak from the frame of his face; it was a slender face, and seemed at once aged and ageless. His hair, bound back in a braid that fell well beyond the hood itself, was all of white.

"Member APhaniel," Andrei said. "You honor us with your presence."

The words failed to register; the man turned steel-gray eyes upon Rath, and held him in a fixed stare for a moment. A long moment. "Handernesse?" he asked at last. "Are you, then—"

"I am a friend of Andrei's," Ararath replied. If words could be either window or gate, his were the latter, and at that the type of gate which stands beneath curtain walls, manned.

"As you will," the mage replied, withdrawing his attention, or at least the appearance of such. It was not, in Rath's opinion, a good start. The man turned to Andrei. "Understand," he said quietly, "that the nature of your inquiries is frowned upon within the Order of Knowledge."

Andrei inclined his head. His fingers still formed a perfect steeple; if he was uncomfortable in the presence of a man who wielded power as if it were thought, he gave no sign. "Surely," he said quietly, "the Order of Knowledge does not turn away from knowledge itself."

"No, indeed," the man replied, seating himself. His companion sat beside him, hood still high. "Although there is good reason that it is not named the Order of Wisdom.

"Recall if you will the old adage, 'knowledge is power.' Pretend, for a moment, that you believe it. There are some powers denied, by law and the Kings, to any who would otherwise make claim to *be* a power. What they gainsay, we, of course, do not seek."

Andrei once again inclined his head.

"But," the second mage said, speaking for the first time, "the fact that you make these inquiries is of interest to those who dwell within the Order." To Rath's surprise, the speaker was a woman. Although talent did not reside solely in one gender or another, it was seldom that Rath had

cause to speak with members of the Order, and he could count the number of times one of those members had been female on exactly none of his
fingers. As if she could hear his thought, she turned to look at him, and
as she did, she lifted her hood.

She was old, to Rath's eye, and bent with age; how much of this was
fact, and how much act, he did not venture to guess. It was, among other
things, impolite—and in the Placid Sea, he was reminded of the manners
of youth. And also of the necessity for such manners.

Her smile, however, was benign.

"May I present my colleague, Sigurne Mellifas."

As names went, it sounded vaguely familiar to Rath. Clearly, however,
it was more than vague to Andrei, whose eyes visibly rounded. And narrowed, just as quickly.

"Yes," the first mage said quietly. "The nature of your inquiries requires
a caution that I am unwilling to vouchsafe on my own behalf. My colleague has some interest in the antiquities, and no sense, whatever, that
knowledge has more value than life."

Andrei's nod was slight. "My apologies, Member APhaniel. I did not
intend to cause difficulty when I first requested your presence." He added,
before Rath could speak, "And I believe that House Araven has paid in
full for your time?"

"In advance, yes."

"Good. But we have not undertaken the hire of Member Mellifas; nor
was I aware that her time *could* be bought."

"You are not in our debt," the first mage said coldly. "But if the time
is granted freely, it is not less valuable. Do not waste it."

"As you say." Andrei removed the satchel that was tucked to one side.
"This, I believe, is yours."

"You believe incorrectly; it is not property of the Order of Knowledge. It
was, however, bartered for with some difficulty." He held out his hand.

Andrei set the bag on his palm.

To Rath's surprise, Member APhaniel chose to open the satchel. He did
not take the knives out; instead he gave them a single cursory glance. He
showed no surprise at what he saw. Instead, he passed the satchel to his
companion, and waited in silence.

She did not so much as look at them; she took the satchel and said, in
a voice several degrees cooler, "When were these used?"

"This morning," Andrei replied.

She turned to her companion. "Four," she said.

He nodded. "Four, and in so short a time. Andrei. Your explanation."

"I have little to offer; the four knives were used, in pairs, on two occasions."

"This morning?"

"This morning would be the second. Activities in the lower holdings have become somewhat suspect, and in the course of investigations, the use of the blades became necessary."

"Necessary?"

"No other weapons had any effect."

Member APhaniel nodded. "Magic?"

"If you mean, was magic used by the men whom these blades killed, the answer is yes."

"That is not what I meant."

"My apologies, Member APhaniel. I am not a member of the Order of Knowledge. Please be more explicit."

Explicit, in the case of the white-haired mage, involved the slow filling of a long-stemmed pipe. Andrei despised pipe smoke on general principles, but held his peace as he waited. While the pipe's bowl was carefully fitted with dry leaf, the mage said, "I wish to know if magery of any sort was used against these men."

"Once."

"To any effect?"

"To some. I have the writ," he added.

Meralonne APhaniel lifted a hand; the pipe hand. Had Rath not known better, he would have said that the mage was quite familiar with Andrei's fastidious disdain. "I am sure you have the required paperwork, Andrei. I would not, however, be surprised if the dates were somewhat stale."

Andrei shrugged.

"You play a dangerous game, as I have said."

"I do not seek to play games at all," Andrei replied quietly. "They are neither my desire nor my responsibility. But where my responsibility crosses their path, I will of necessity be forced to fulfill it."

"Understood."

"It is understood," Member Mellifas said quietly, "by Member APhaniel, but he is not known for his attention to fine detail."

"Which means, Member Mellifas, that the explanation is not enough for you?"

"Very perceptive."

Andrei shrugged again, and this time, he turned to Rath. "Ararath," he said quietly, "Sigurne Mellifas presides over the Order of Knowledge as its titular head. It is not a comfortable position, but a necessary one."

And in that many words, he offered Rath to the mages. Rath was both surprised and unsurprised; he was godson, not blood, to Hectore, and while his godfather was willing to sacrifice much for the sake of old ties and affection, the willingness extended only so far.

"I am afraid," Rath said quietly, "that I have even less familiarity with the Order than Andrei; what you wish to know, you must ask."

Sigurne Mellifas nodded, as if she expected no less.

"I live in the lower holdings," Rath added quietly.

She raised a brow, but held her peace. "And you have cause to suspect that things are amiss?"

"Where there is magic, there is usually both money and a great deal of influence and power," he replied quietly. "And demonstrably, there *has* been magic."

"Ah. And the nature of that magic?"

"Invisibility," he replied quietly.

She frowned.

"And fire."

The frown deepened. "It is unlikely that writs would be granted for the use of either."

"I consider it very likely," he replied. "Paper itself is frequently found, and writs granted in cases of emergencies to the members of the Magisterium who are responsible for the patrol of the holdings are not difficult to access."

"These were not magisterial guards."

"No."

"But you believe that the Magisterium has been compromised?"

Rath shrugged. "The Magisterium is a fine institution," he said, grudgingly, "but men are men everywhere."

"The Magisterium, in this, is beholden to the Order," she replied quietly, "and no such request has recently crossed my desk." Before he could speak, she added, "Recently, in this case, covering the period of time that is roughly equal to the last decade."

"There are the writs of exception."

"If a writ of exception *is* to be used in case of emergency, its use nonetheless requires a full report. A full and *timely* report." Her tone made clear that timely was about five seconds after its use.

"Believe, Ararath Handernesse, that such reports are read with care and a great eye to detail. Believe that those who tender those very necessary reports write them with care and precision.

"And believe, as well, that no such report has been offered me in the last several years."

He raised a brow, and she offered a grudging smile.

He nodded slowly. "Magic was nonetheless used. Money and power of the nature required to purchase the services of a less scrupulous mage is seldom found in the lower holdings; the lower holdings may claim few charms or virtues, but this absence would be among them."

"Granted. You were a witness to both of these uses of magic?"

"I was a combatant," he replied.

"Ah. And you used the daggers?"

"The second set, yes."

"Where?"

"In a large brothel of no legal standing."

"I see." She looked at him as if she did, and further, as if she might approve. "And what led you there?"

"A girl," he replied. "Before you make further inquiries, without her permission, I cannot in conscience speak more of her."

"A girl."

He nodded.

"Very well. She seemed normal to you?"

"As normal as any foundling who has been sold into slavery, yes." The words were harsher than he had intended, but he kept his tone neutral. That much, he could manage.

But the anger surprised him.

"Ararath," Andrei said dryly, "has never been known for a great love of sentiment, and he has seldom been called a hypocrite."

"Then this began as a matter of more practical concern?" The woman asked Andrei.

Rath wanted to kick him. As it was unlikely to be viewed in the correct social light, he refrained.

"Let us labor under the assumption that it was."

"And that the dealings of these men somehow naturally crossed his path?"

"Even so."

"And both uses of the daggers occurred in illegal brothels?"

"Ah. I have not made myself clear. The latter, I was not witness to. The former took place within the Common. Rath is something of an amateur historian," Andrei added quietly, passing the mess he had made of the conversation back to Rath.

"Ah. And your area of speciality?"

"I believe," Member APhaniel said, blowing smoke as he casually rejoined the conversation, "that it has something to do with Old Weston."

And Rath remembered Member Haberas, and was silent for a moment. But the pale-haired mage was waiting, and if he waited with perfect patience, there was something in his posture that implied veneer, not substance.

To his surprise, the mage added quietly, "The death of Member Haberas remains under investigation." It was both invitation and acknowledgment. Member Mellifas looked at Member APhaniel and frowned; the frown was slight, and seemed to contain no anger, no real criticism.

Hard, to remember that he was dealing with a woman who in theory ruled the Order of Knowledge. But remembering Haberas more clearly than he had in some time, Rath thought that this particular difficulty suited the Order, where a firmer, clearer hand might not.

"There were some irregularities," she said at last. "The Magisterium has not been entirely sympathetic to our requests."

Rath frowned. "To *your* request, Member Mellifas?"

"Even to mine," she replied, with a tired smile. Yes, hard to imagine that this tired, old woman could rule the mysterious and terrifying Order. "For this reason, we have not chosen to involve the Magisterium more closely than the rule of law demands."

He absorbed her words slowly.

"Yes," she said, before he could formulate a suitably tactful question. "This means we suspect that there are members of the Magisterium who have been placed in just such a position of authority to oversee our investigations, and not to our benefit."

"By who?"

"That is the question that we hope to answer. You will not, of course, be called upon in the course of these investigations. Any information you give us will therefore be considered collegial, but not legal." She paused, and then added, "Your friend, Andrei, has been most helpful."

"How?"

She lifted the satchel which contained the daggers.

"You'll forgive me if I consider the aid granted to travel in the opposite direction."

"Indeed. But the fact that these proved helpful—when so little else available did—tells us what we have begun to suspect. It is not welcome news, but we are long past the days of the Blood Barons, and we do not hold the bearer of unwelcome tidings responsible for carrying them.

"These are, of course, daggers. They will cut a man—"

"If he's standing still; they are far from the definition of sharp in any of the languages I know."

She smiled. "Very well. They are not new blades, and they were made in a time when the edge was less important than what was granted the blade as a whole. Andrei says you have studied some Old Weston." She waited for his nod, as if it made a difference. He almost believed it did.

She defined the term "grandmotherly" with her bearing, her obvious wisdom, her subdued affection. Rath found it disconcerting. He had had many reasons to deal with men—and women—of power in this City; he had hoped never to meet the person under whose sway the Order of Knowledge fell. He had taken care, during his rare visits to the Order, to use different names and a variety of odd disguises to further this goal.

"I know, dear," she told him, frowning as a circle of smoke crossed her vision. "I am seldom what anyone expects the first time."

"Nor," Member APhaniel said, having moved his pipe a fraction of an arm's length to one side, "is she what anyone expects a second or third time."

"Meralonne—"

He lifted a hand. "Time is at issue here. What Sigurne has said is true; the blades were not made to be common weapons. If you read Old Weston, you will see most of their purpose written on the flats of the blades themselves; if you have not mastered it, you will see some fragment of purpose; the metal, as I said, is not a hard one.

"But it was meant to endure enchantment, and to carry some hint of Lattan magic within it."

Rath frowned. "Lattan, as in the month?"

"As in the month, yes. There were other weapons made at one time that were meant as vessels for Scaral magic, but they serve little purpose now."

Lattan. Scaral. Opposite months in the Imperial calendar. Rath's frown deepened a moment. "The solstices," he said at last.

Meralonne clearly expected his words to have conveyed that information.

"The longest day," Rath added quietly.

"Indeed. In the ancient tongue, the height of Summer at the crossroads."

If Rath was not a mage—and to his great regret, he was not—he had more than a passing knowledge of the various branches of magic studied and practiced within the Order of Knowledge. Summer was not one of them. They were, after all, not agrarians.

"The blades contain that essence, when they are properly consecrated and prepared. It is not," Meralonne added, "a trivial task, and it is also not a task that can be undertaken by members of the Order."

"But the daggers—"

"They came from our hands, yes, but they were delivered to them, at some political cost and inconvenience, by the god-born upon the Isle."

The heads, Rath thought, of the triad of Churches whose spires were allowed, by law, to reach higher than the towers of *Avantari*, the palace of Kings. The only such spires.

"Had you stabbed a man with this—with either of these—it would have wounded him. That is not the effect such action had." He spoke with absolute certainty, and it was a warning to Rath: lying was not only unwise, it was pointless. Worse than pointless. Given that the head of the Order of Knowledge had chosen to involve herself, and given how little actual knowledge Rath possessed, it gave him only the opportunity to make enemies.

"No," he said quietly. "It—seemed to—burn them from the inside out."

The two mages exchanged a glance.

"You recognized these men?"

"No. In both cases, they were strangers to me."

"You've spoken of two incidents; the first?"

"I was followed in the Common, as Andrei has recounted," he said, speaking with care, "when I left the abode of a friend."

"Why?"

"Why was I followed?"

"That will do, for a start."

Rath shrugged. Lying was pointless, yes, but truth could be an art when used with care. "I had, in my possession, two old bowls that I hoped to sell. One of them was cracked," he added.

"And these?"

"I sold them; they are no longer in my possession."

"Who was their purchaser?"

This suited Rath. "A tall, bald man by the name of Patris AMatie."

Meralonne frowned. "The name is not known to me."

Andrei chose to speak. "He is a merchant, Member APhaniel, of some ten years good standing in the Merchants' Guild."

"And he has an interest in cracked bowls?" Member APhaniel took Andrei's information without once glancing at the man who had offered it.

"Of a particular vintage."

"You believe he had you followed."

Rath nodded.

"And you used the daggers—"

Andrei lifted a hand. "I used them," he said quietly. "Some discreet inquiries had been made by that time, and I chose to follow instinct."

"May it always serve you this well." Member APhaniel looked to Sigurne. "Four," he said again.

"Who were these men?" Rath finally asked.

"They were not, in our parlance, men, as I believe you already suspect," Sigurne replied. "But this is ill news, for those of us who labor within the Order. You were a child once," she continued, "and perhaps as a child you were told stories of the times before Veralaan returned to grace the Empire with her sons?"

Rath nodded.

"And you are aware of the wars that occurred between the Blood Barons?"

He nodded again. As perhaps the most significant of the holidays observed in Averalaan involved that history, not even Rath could fail to be familiar with it, although he understood well that history was remade by generations.

"During the dark years, the Blood Barons—those who were powerful enough—often summoned servants."

"From the Hells," Rath said with just the hint of a sardonic smile.

No answering smile was offered. "From the Hells," she replied gravely.

"If they had power, the possession of the creature's name, and the will and ability to use it to bind the summoned to service. Those creatures were called—"

"Demons."

Sigurne nodded gravely. "It is not, perhaps, what they would call themselves should you be in a position to ask."

"The ability to summon and enslave—"

"The arts are considered dark arts," she replied. Her voice was a shade cooler. "And the practice or study of such arts has long been forbidden any member of the Order of Knowledge."

Rath frowned. "Surely such creatures could be considered a superior form of servant or weapon," he began.

She met his words as if they were a physical threat—and she, the most powerful woman in the Order. The change in her posture was subtle, and the shift in the networks of lines that comprised her expression, equally hard to delineate—but they were there.

"It is a time-honored debate upon the floor of the Council of the Order," Meralonne told him. "And it is a debate which is, in its entirety, an intellectual exercise. Imagine," he added, "that you could force someone— anyone—to do your bidding with but the use of a single word."

"The bards—"

"The bards control a momentary action, not the whole of an existence." He waved a hand. "Those who are young and less experienced do not understand the particular mind-set such control involves."

"And even if they did," Sigurne added, "it would signify nothing. The Kings consider demonology a forbidden art."

And you, Rath thought, *would kill a man who broke that law without a second thought.* "Which means—"

"That we are in all probability dealing with a rogue mage, yes. There have, as you are no doubt aware, been a number of rogue mages in the history of Averalaan. Demonologists are rare, because there is usually only one mistake allowed them; if they make that mistake, they are no longer a consideration." Meralonne paused to draw smoke through pipestem before he continued. "The unknown mage in question has summoned at least four demons, and at least two concurrently. I did not fight them," he added, and Rath thought he heard regret's familiar edge between those last words, "and I therefore cannot judge their value, or their power.

"But if they were devoured by the ceremonial blades, they were not inconsequential. If they were immune to your weapons—" and here he actually did frown with distaste, "—your weapons were either of negligible quality, or the summoned creatures were of nonnegligible power.

"It is frustrating," he added. "But my assumption—our assumption—is that the demons summoned were of significant power only in the streets of the lower holdings."

"One used fire," Rath said quietly. "As a mage might."

Meralonne nodded. "But did he draw a sword?"

"Why would he need one? He had fire. And he could use it to far greater effect."

"They are arrogant by nature," Meralonne replied. "And you presented very little threat." But he seemed to relax. "Very well. You have found four demons—or they have found you—and you have dispatched them. Unlike mortals, their absence would be noted *instantly* by the summoner; if the summoner is skilled, it is likely that the cause of their disappearance might also be noted."

"They're aware of me," Rath said flatly.

"That is our supposition." Meralonne set his pipe aside and leaned forward in his chair. "For reasons we have already expressed, we wish to avoid a direct involvement of the Magisterium—beyond that which is legally necessary—at this time.

"Without their presence, however, we have little method of compelling you to part with either information or time; we must rely, instead, on your enlightened sense of self-preservation. Were it up to me, I would demand what information you possess; it is not, however, up to me, and Sigurne Mellifas has chosen to regard nicety of law as necessary."

"What he meant to say," Sigurne added, pointedly refusing to look at her companion, "is that we don't actually care what you're involved in, as long as it isn't the summoning of demons. We have taken the liberty of bringing with us two more of the blessed daggers, and we will leave them with you; we require in return—and will trust you in this—that you inform us of any need to actually use them.

"The bowls," she added. "If you describe them, we will look for them. We will undertake our own investigations into Patris AMatie."

"They were ringed with Old Weston," Rath told her. "Near complete."

Sigurne nodded, but it was clear that she did not like the way the information he had given her fit with the information she had withheld. "We must go," she told him. "But let me offer a word of warning."

He waited.

"I do not ask how you came across these bowls—or any other artifact of interest—because in the end, that is not my concern. But were I you, I would avoid a like discovery any time in the near future."

"Were it not for my discovery, you would not now be armed with what little knowledge you have."

"Aye, there's truth in that," she said softly. "But we are armed now; this is not your fight."

He nodded. He vastly preferred fights which were not.

"If you have need of us, Andrei knows how we may best be contacted." She rose. And then she smiled again, looking down on Rath. "Ararath Handernesse. Your sister—"

He lifted a hand. "I have no sister," he said quietly.

She nodded, as if this came as no surprise to her. "Amarais Handernesse ATerafin would not disavow you. Think what you will of her life and her choices, but understand this: She is worthy of House Terafin. The only question in my mind is whether or not the House can be made, in the end, worthy of *her*."

"And you say this because?"

"I have met her, of course." She turned to Meralonne APhaniel, and as one, they both drew their hoods up, shadowing their faces. "Think less harshly of her, if you can. What Handernesse surrendered to the Empire, even if it was surrendered unwilling, may well define much of its fate for decades to come."

"And what of Handernesse?" Rath asked, the bitterness in his voice beyond his ability to control.

"Handernesse had two children of note, or so it is said; the daughter, who gave up her name and her birthright in pursuit of her goals, and a son who apparently disappeared not long thereafter."

"You've met her," Rath replied. "Can you honestly say that I am her equal?"

"Not honestly, no," was the quiet reply. "But in life, there is fluidity and the possibility of change. The Terafin spoke highly of you, if briefly," she added, "and her words were not unkind."

He said nothing; instead, he turned his gaze to the warm and moving shapes of fire, contained by grate and burning logs. Nor did he look up until the shadows had passed, and he was once again alone with Andrei.

The servant said, "That went, I think, as well as one could expect." He rose. "I, too, have things to investigate, Ararath."

"Not on my account."

"Everything I do, I do at the behest of Patris Hectore." Andrei bowed neatly. "But I will say this: you do better than you know. I do not entirely understand the turn of events in the holdings," he added, "but it is clear to me that things are changing. You have always been cautious," he added, "and that caution has been both bane and blessing.

"But the child—"

"I will not speak of her, Andrei."

"As you wish." He bowed again.

Andrei left Rath at the door of the Placid Sea. His bow was curt, but it was not perfunctory, and when he rose, his eyes were dark and almost unblinking. Even rain, trailing slowly from his forehead, did not cause his regard to waver. He might have been made of stone, if stone lived. Rath had always admired that, in Andrei: he was a man who needed no one.

And lack of need defined strength.

"I have duties," Andrei said quietly, "and I am uneasy away from the Patris at this time. You will call upon me if you require my aid, but I feel it in the interests of Patris Hectore that your communications do not cross his desk."

Rath was momentarily silent.

"I have served Hectore for many years," Andrei replied, "and the manner and method I deem wise has always been accepted by the Patris himself. Patris AMatie *is* a merchant; I spoke truth, there. If the Order cannot find the information they require to secure his removal, it is best for future relations between House Araven and the Merchants' Guild that knowledge of these difficulties are kept from Patris Hectore."

"I doubt they would have missed any lie."

"Unlikely, and Member APhaniel is known for a somewhat mercurial temper." Andrei's smile was slight, and shadowed by more than the endless drab of passing cloud.

"The Terafin—"

"Leave it, Andrei," Rath replied wearily. "If I'm old enough to feel a twinge of nostalgia," he added, spitting the word from his mouth with distaste, "it is a problem I consider private."

Andrei nodded again. But before he left, he said, "you would not, even a year ago, have concerned yourself with the existence of a brothel."

Rath shrugged. "In a year, I probably won't be overly concerned with it either."

"As you say." Andrei turned then, and left.

Rath left as well, missing the fireside in the Placid Sea; missing the moment of warmth, the sense of belonging, that had crept up on him without warning.

Perhaps this sharp and bitter reminder of the past addled his brain; he was not a young man. He walked through the streets of *Averalaan Aramarelas*, gazing at the tall buildings that never crowded the wide thoroughfare. They were marvels of architecture; they used the scant—and expensive—land upon the Isle as if small space were divine, decreed, and much desired. Where the buildings of the poor holdings loomed at great height, their facades were often adorned by peeling paint or faded wood, barred and broken panes of once grand windows letting light creep in with rain and wind.

The height here was entirely majestic; it spoke of grandeur and drama; it spoke of wealth.

Such a house as this Handernesse had once owned. Such a house as this, he thought bitterly, with its large grounds, its high gates, its guards and its servants. If none of them were the equal of Andrei, they were nonetheless competent, and even trusted.

But Amarais? She had been their heart. From the moment she could speak, precocious child blossoming into something too quick and too subtle to long accept precocious as a relevant description, she had been the joy of their grandfather, Patris Handernesse. The Handernesse.

She had adored the old man.

So, in his fashion, had Rath.

He could not make his way to that home; it was no longer his.

"It could still be yours," Patris Hectore had told him. He had made that mistake exactly once, and two years had passed before Rath was ready to speak with him again. Rath's godfather learned from his errors; he was a canny man, and a cunning merchant.

But he had a weakness for his fledgling children, his wayward godchildren, and a belief that his guidance and wisdom could lead them to safe harbor; it was difficult for him to surrender beliefs so firmly anchored in sentiment.

Rath would have said that sentiment played no part in his life, and as the streets widened, as the carriages grew less frequent, he followed roads that he would have sworn were no longer familiar, lost in thought.

Averalaan Aramarelas had once been his home. He had not been proud of it; he had not been displeased by it. The Isle, with its stately, expensive buildings, its high manners, its proximity to the Kings and the god-born who ruled their followers across the Empire from the confines of the grand and glorious cathedrals to which many made pilgrimage—these were almost mundane in their matter-of-fact existence.

No; it was the land across the bridge that had always fascinated him; the lands where buildings could stoop and bow, and whole families could live in rooms that weren't fit for the meanest of the servants his family employed. There, hidden in pocked streets, roved almost legendary bands of child thieves, roving as they could among the well-to-do of their acquaintance like feral things.

There, in the low market, the great Common, languages of all color and fashion could be heard; indeed, it was hard, when in the Common, *not* to hear them, and be amazed that such guttural phrases, such loud and screeching vowels and abrasive consonants, could somehow be elevated to meaning.

The smell of the ocean was strong, either upon the Isle or in the holdings; the sea breeze swept across the lands as if land itself were of little concern. The ships floated upon the waves, waiting their turn to leave port, laden now with goods, now with men; they flew flags of the Houses to whom they owed a good part of their profits.

And Rath had not been the only child in Handernesse to find fascination in those mean streets, those areas in which the poor might, with impunity, approach those who lived on the distant Isle.

Amarais of Handernesse had been fascinated by them as well. She did not tell herself their stories; did not dream herself in the meanness of their odd exile from food, warmth, clothing, but like Rath, she did not turn away from the chance to cross the bridge in the Handernesse carriage, accompanied at all times by at least two guards.

What had she seen? he thought bitterly, gazing now upon the wealth that had been so commonplace. *When had it started?*

There, he thought. The buildings here were now widely and evenly spread, but although the ocean's presence could be tasted—it could always be felt—he could not see its lapping water against the farther shore; he could imagine it, and would once again dwell upon it when he found the bridge.

Imagination was treachery of a different sort, and his weakness was such that the question drove him back, to the past, to his sister, younger yet older than he; to the carriage, out of whose windows she perched, on elbows, to the consternation—and resignation—of their guards.

Yet she made no sounds of delight, that day, no cries of joy, nothing at all that implied happiness or discovery. She was still, perched there as if carved, and Rath, at her side, felt a twinge of worry.

The guards rapped the roof of the carriage; they wore mailed gloves, and didn't need to hit more than twice to get the driver's attention. The carriage slowed—although it never drove at great speed along the Old City roads.

Rath, peering out of his own window, could see that people were standing on the side of the street, as if waiting; it could have been the Kings' Challenge season, if it weren't the wrong time of year for it.

"What's happening?" he asked one of the guards. He had known the man's name, once, but the name—like the face—had receded into a place that only dream could recall. This waking reverie ceded nothing.

"The Mother's Children," the guard replied quietly. "They're coming down the street."

Being younger and less well behaved than Amarais, Rath thrust himself up under the thin perch of his sister's arms, craning out of the carriage for a glimpse of what had silenced her.

And he saw them: the Mother's Children, in their plain, harvest robes, green and brown, sun-faded and sturdy. They carried baskets on their arms, as they often did, but these baskets looked empty, they swayed so easily.

He could see the underside of his sister's face, the line of a jaw that had not yet become pronounced, let alone elegant. "Amarais?"

She said nothing. Just watched.

And behind the Mother's Children walked children. Some hobbled, working their way with crutches or canes upon the gentle slope of the Common street; the great leaves were in bloom, then, gold upon the heights of their thick and ancient branches. The youngest of the children gathered those leaves, slowing the procession; they were nudged back into line by acolytes, novitiates, and the older children nearest them.

They were not well dressed; they wore clothing that was striking in its lack of uniformity, its mismatched colors, its obvious age. But they were all thin as birds' legs, their cheeks hollow, their eyes dark; their hair was often long, but it had that wild look that reminded Rath of the coats of hungry dogs.

Amarais watched them walk, and her silence grew more oppressive, and at last Rath broke it. "They're poor," he said softly, as if only then realizing that poor was not a romantic story.

He reached into the thick pouch that lay twisted round his waist; it wasn't hidden, then; it didn't need to be. Guards were proof against the boldest of thieves the Common boasted. At least guards of the stature and build of Handernesse guards.

From this, he drew coins.

Amarais, taking this as her signal, opened the latch of the door; it creaked, but the familiar noise was lost to the protest of the guards. Amarais, young then—how old, Rath thought? How old?—had silenced them with a glance. He had thought her magnificent, then.

Now?

Now he remembered his own actions with an embarrassment that bordered on humiliation. He had taken the money, and he had run, his short burst of speed all but winding him, toward the elderly woman that seemed to head this procession. Her eyes, he recalled, were the color of pale honey, and there were creases around them, worn by smile or care or seawind. She had let him drop his coins in the basket, and she had nodded gravely when he had told her—ah, the pain of his self-importance, then—that this money was for *children*.

But Amarais, coming up behind him, had placed a hand over his shoulder; she did not stop him from giving away all of his money, but she did not offer hers.

Instead, she looked long at the matronly woman who led this odd parade, and she said, "Why are they on display?"

And the woman's eyes had narrowed, the lines there definitely verging on frown at this impertinence. But she searched his sister's face, and found no scorn in it. No ready emotion either. Even then, Amarais could be guarded.

"People forget what they cannot see," the woman replied.

"People forget what they can."

"They do. But these children—they are from the hundred holdings;

they are without family and without guardians. We tend them and we teach them, and once a year we walk, here."

"Why here?"

"The Common—"

"Why not on the Isle? That's where the money is."

The woman's eyes were gold, and they were an odd shade of gold. Not the cold of money, no, but they were no longer so warm or so sweet. "We could not afford the price of that passage," was the calm reply.

"What price?"

"There is a toll to be paid for all those who walk the bridge. And that toll would feed each child for a week. Perhaps more." She turned and said something that Rath couldn't hear.

"Should I have kept the money?" he asked, anxious now.

Amarais had smiled at him. But it was not a happy smile. "No," she told him quietly. "They need it."

"Then I did a good thing?"

"Yes," she said. "But it was an easy thing."

"But if everyone gave—"

"Yes," she said again. "But it's not enough, the money."

The Priestess looked down at Amarais. "You are not as young as you look," she said wearily. "But if the money is not all that they require, it is still needed. Let the boy feel generous," she added softly. "Generosity is never to be despised."

Amarais had nodded quietly.

That day, and the day that followed, she had spoken for a long time to their grandfather, the doors closed so that Rath might be spared the discussion. She had emerged from those closed doors and she had smiled at Rath, and she had asked him to join her in the garden, but she never spoke about what Grandfather had said, and Rath was too wary to ask, for Amarais did not look happy.

And Rath, now standing at the farthest edge of the fence that girded the greatest of all the mansions owned by House Terafin, looked up at the heights of that flat, wide building. At its stonework, its great, vast wings, its huge, sprawling gardens with their perfectly tended grass, their leaf-shorn trees.

Are you happy now? he thought bitterly.

And thought, too, that were he a different man, he might approach the guardhouse that was just barely visible from his position in the street;

that he might announce himself, enter into that coveted manse with its name, its law of allegiance defying and denying the loyalty owed blood and birth, and ask her.

But he was not that man.

And if he could now, at the remove of age, see the day on which his sister had begun to take her first steps away from Handernesse, the knowledge offered no comfort, and only a bitter glimmer of understanding.

Chapter Eighteen

FOUR HOURS LATER, Rath returned with boots. They were not perfect, but they were infinitely better than the bare feet or exposed thongs that the four newcomers were otherwise faced with. He offered them without comment, and when Jewel tried to ask him how he'd managed to pry them from the mendacious grip of the cobbler, he had stared her into an almost withered silence before retreating to the privacy of his rooms. He did not emerge from them in the following hours.

Around the ominous silence radiated by his presence, even hidden as it was behind the wooden panels of a flimsy door, the children moved in cautious silence. The rain on the window wells had grown loud, and often heavy. Jewel brought lit candles to the boys and, for herself, used the magestone that had been Rath's gift to her; Duster whistled when she saw it. Finch said little. They ate, divided blankets between them, and tried to sleep.

Finch succeeded.

Jewel tried to keep her breathing even in the darkness of the dimmed magelight, but she couldn't help listening to the breathing that wasn't hers. Finch's changed slowly, deepening and flattening into something that sounded like sleep. Duster's didn't.

Minutes were hard to mark, at night. Jewel didn't usually try; in fact, she usually tried to do the opposite. Sleep wasn't generally something that eluded her. But she hadn't slept well on the banks of the river, beneath the scant cover of Summer bridge. And she didn't sleep well, here, with a stranger in her room.

Which, given that she'd slept like a log—if logs had nightmares—when Arann, Lefty, Carver, and Finch had been pressing in on all sides, said something. She missed Carver and Arann, here, and that annoyed her enough that she sat up.

Duster was lying on her side, face propped up by a hand above bent elbow. Jewel could see her almost clearly; the magestone was like unveiled moonlight, here. Had she wanted it, she could have had sun.

But the dark of silvered light suited Duster better.

"They wanted to keep me," Duster said quietly. As if the light was just poor enough that speaking was safe. It was hard to see her expression, and she knew it; she must have, because Jewel's was likewise near-invisible.

"But not Finch?"

"Not Finch, no." Duster's brief snort of laughter was cold and ugly; it was an utter dismissal. "What could they have made of Finch that would have done them any good?"

There was only one question that the statement allowed, but Jewel was good at finding back entrances and exits that weren't as clear. "What did they intend for Finch?"

"She was going to disappear," Duster replied quietly. "Four other children did, in the month. Some of them were probably happy to go by the end of it. But those, they often kept. Like Lander," she added, her voice almost disappearing for the stretch of syllables. "It was the ones they didn't touch, didn't sell, that they took away."

And they had kept Duster.

"You were special," Jewel said. And the moment she said it, it was *true*.

Duster's head bobbed slightly as she shifted position, sitting in a curled hunch made of knees and bent back. "I was special," she said. The words were harsh, almost vicious. "They said that. Of me. That they could see me. See what I would become."

Jewel had always trusted her instincts. She trusted them now, speaking quickly. "They saw only *some* of what you could become," she said, a little too hotly.

Duster was utterly still. "What do you mean?" she asked, her first casual words of the evening. Casual and Duster were not a promising combination. Not even Jewel's optimism could paint it in different colors.

But she'd blurted it out, and having started, she struggled to continue; struggled to ignore the tension that was Duster, in a room that should have been safe haven.

"They saw the killer in you," Jewel said quietly.

Duster shrugged. She didn't even attempt words.

"They saw it. *I* see it," she added evenly. Not trying to ameliorate damage, but trying to be as clear as she could. Because this was important, and if she botched it, she'd already lost.

She had never questioned her visions before. She had viewed them not as possibilities, but as certainties. And for the first time, she saw that certainty was, like anything else, a blind. Duster was poised on an edge, and what Jewel thought she had seen clearly—no, damn it, what she *had* seen clearly—had not yet come to pass.

And it might not.

And this, too, she knew as truth. It was both unsettling and somehow liberating. She could be *wrong*. Even when she had seen something clearly, it could be *wrong*.

Had Duster been anyone else, Jewel might have told her. But Duster was Duster, Duster was the girl the mages had chained to a wall in a special room. The locks that Jewel had picked to gain entrance, the lock that she had picked to open the single shackle around her bruised ankles—they had been the least of the locks she would have to pick. And only by acknowledging what Duster was—by understanding *everything* that Duster was—did she have any chance at all of doing so.

And what if she did? What would she set free then?

Because she *knew* what the mages had seen in Duster. Killer. Death. How could she not? She'd seen it herself. She *knew* it was true.

So.

"You talked about that before. You asked me. If I'd killed."

Jewel nodded.

"And I answered."

Jewel nodded again.

"Did you like the answer?"

"Not much," Jewel replied. "Did you?"

Duster's eyes rounded slightly. Which meant they rounded a lot, if Jewel could see it this clearly in the level of light she allowed the magestone. She shrugged. "I didn't hate it," she said at last. "And I meant it." Defiance in those words, and a helluva lot of pride. She was proud of what she'd achieved. Because killing, for Duster, meant not being killed.

No, Jewel thought, seeing clearly in ways that she hadn't for some time.

It had *meant not being killed.* What it meant now, she couldn't say with certainty.

"They thought they could turn you into their killer," Jewel said softly.

"I would have killed," Duster said, with a shrug. "I wouldn't have killed for *them*."

"I don't think they would have cared why," Jewel answered, seeing now, as she had been born to see, but in an entirely new way. "They would have only cared that you did. That you killed. Their way."

"You think you know a lot," Duster said slowly. Jewel could feel the anger and the contempt in those words. She'd done nothing to earn contempt, but she understood its source: Jewel had found friends. She had been *protected*. She could never have survived alone.

And Duster had.

Even in that place, Duster had survived. She hadn't gone mad; she hadn't given into despair, sinking slowly into herself until she could barely see what passed beyond her. Either were options, and neither were ones she had taken. Instead, she had nursed the anger she now held against Jewel as a shield.

"Do you know what they were?" Duster whispered, moving closer, threat in the subtle grace of her slender limbs.

"No."

"I thought they were demons," the wild girl told her.

Demons were Southern stories. Demons were nightmares. Jewel had seen men.

But she had seen men with eyes of shadow, who walked and spoke in a voice that she would have said only death could use. If death walked these lands.

"They said they could see my soul," she added bitterly. "And they told me what they saw. How it changed, each time they gave me to someone. They promised that I would have a chance to kill my visitors."

"And them?"

"Them?"

"Your captors. Your demons. Could you have killed them as well?"

"I wanted to," Duster whispered. "But nothing could kill them."

And Duster had learned, in the streets of the holdings, that you could join or die. Jewel couldn't offer her that option. It wasn't in her. It wasn't what she wanted.

"We killed them," Jewel told her quietly.

"I know." So much in that word. So much anger, so much malice, so much hope. Twisted, all of it, around death and killing. Had anyone else spoken those words, Jewel would have shuddered. Here, in her place, she couldn't afford to.

And her Oma had taught her how to be practical.

"We didn't come to kill them," she added softly, not much caring that they had. "When we came to the—that place. We came for you."

Duster spit to the side. "You came back for the others."

"I didn't know for certain that there would be others; the only person Finch knew there was you. We came for *you*," Jewel said again, forcing the word to have the strength of conviction.

"Then you're an idiot. A pathetic idiot." Duster lay back against the blankets that rested on a flattened, old bedroll. She turned her back to Jewel, to the faint, pale light of magestone, and did not speak again.

But it was enough, for now. That she turned her back. That she could. That she considered Jewel—and Finch—so beneath contempt they couldn't possibly be a threat.

You had to start somewhere.

Lander spent only the first night with the girls, as the boys called them. After that, Duster led him to the room that housed Arann, Lefty, Carver, and Fisher, and she told him that it would be safe. She said other things, her lips at his ear, her face so close to his she might have been kissing him. He didn't appear to hear her, but he didn't try to stop her from leaving.

Maybe that was a good thing. It made their room more crowded, but the heat of bodies made up for the lack of other warmth.

Water was not in short supply. Rath had, reluctantly, purchased a rain barrel, and the trips to the well that afforded Jewel time with the people of the holding dropped sharply, which turned out to be a good thing. Rath made it clear that he was not precisely happy with the number of children she had chosen to take in, and he had also made it clear that he did not—yet—trust them enough to leave them unattended in his home.

His reservations were loudest—in that unspoken way he'd mastered long before she'd been born—when it came to Duster, and Jewel, often honest to a fault, couldn't bring herself to argue against his suspicion.

Over the next three days, Duster had started two arguments and one actual fight.

She'd drawn a knife on Arann.

And Arann had refused to blink or step back. Had Duster intended
to threaten Arann, and Arann alone, he would have given way instantly;
whatever pride he had, it wasn't the stupid kind. But she'd taken an instant dislike to Lefty, with his obvious fear, his obvious insecurity, and she
had pushed too far.

Arann, angered, had pushed back in one of the only ways he knew
how.

In all, it was not a scene that Jewel wanted to dwell on. Which meant,
of course, that she did. She couldn't force Duster to accept Lefty; she could
barely force Duster to eat or sleep. Nor could she comfort Lefty; Duster
had a cutting tongue, and between knife edge and word, Jewel was hard-
pressed to choose the more palpable threat.

Duster enjoyed it.

Jewel hated it. But she let it play out because she had to *see* how far
Duster was prepared to go. To know it, as fact, as something irrefutable.
Duster was no idiot—she didn't push far enough that Arann would be
forced to actually *fight*. But it was close, and in those cramped quarters,
the others as witness, Duster earned anger and a growing dislike that
bordered on hatred without quite crossing that boundary.

Because Finch could still reach her, and Lander—Lander, silent, almost
insensate, could also reach out to touch the hem of her clothing. And he
had, even when the knife glittered like the wrong kind of promise.

So Duster remained in the cramped quarters of Rath's home. Only
when they left as a group to go to the Common did they emerge into
what could laughingly be called sunlight; endless stretch of gray that was
colder with each passing hour. The ships in the far harbor could be seen,
flags and great sails furled as if they were leaves out of season, waiting
their chance to bud again. The ocean itself was choppy with wind, and
when the rain began to freeze, Jewel wondered—as she so often did—why
the sea itself didn't stop its endless motion.

Lander did not speak during the three days that passed beneath ground;
he ate when food was brought, and slept when the lights—such as they
were—were doused. But he slept poorly, and often loudly, and there were
grim circles under the eyes of the boys by the end of the second night.
Even Jester—Jester, red-haired, freckled, his skinny long face perpetually

turned up in an almost fey smile—found the nights difficult, and his humor developed an edge that amused only Duster.

Fisher was mute in sleep, but spoke a few words here and there when Jewel prodded him to see if he *had* a tongue. He didn't speak about the great house, and she didn't ask.

She couldn't speak to these newcomers as easily as she had spoken to either Lefty or Arann; couldn't plan with them, as she had, without thought, begun to plan with Carver or even Finch; they were strangers to her, and beyond her; she did not know how to draw them out.

On the morning, the third morning, after the great fire, she walked into the boys' room—the door was open, a signal that visitors were either welcome or desperately needed, Finch her shadow. What Duster was, Jewel still wasn't certain, but Duster followed as well, making room for herself just by walking. She wasn't much taller than Jewel, and she wouldn't surrender her age—which probably meant she didn't know it exactly. Duster considered almost everything a weakness, and it was still important *not* to be weak.

Lefty was sitting by Lander's side; Arann was sitting against the wall, watching them. Lefty wasn't speaking—he seldom did, when strangers were present—and had he been, Duster's shadow would have caused his jaw to shut so fast you could have heard its snap from Rath's room. But he was doing something with his hands.

It must have been important; he was using both of them. His right hand and his left, one short a couple of fingers, were moving above Lander's palms. And Lander appeared to actually be *watching* him. His own hands didn't move in response, but his eyes—the eyes that had been so vacant for all of the three days he'd lived here—flickered back and forth at the dance of Lefty's hands. Lefty was tapping his palm, left hand to right.

"Jay's here," Arann said quietly. In this room, with the single exception of his explosive shout at Duster, he always spoke quietly. He understood, without the need for words, what *was* needed of him. And he was willing to give it.

Had Jewel seen that in him, the first day, or the second? Had she failed to see it? He was the oldest of them, she thought. Certainly, if age could be judged by size. But he was more than that; she realized, at this moment, that he was also the *best* of them. What they could all hope to be, had they patience and grace.

And grace was a word that had seldom been used by her Oma.

"Lefty," Arann added. "Jay's here."

Duster crossed the floor, passing Jewel before Jewel could reach out and grab her arm. She knelt beside Lefty, and Lefty cringed, flinching as if her mere presence was a physical blow, a thing to be dreaded and feared.

Duster snarled at him, but wordlessly, her fangs hooded a moment by figurative lips. The contempt that she turned on Lefty at a moment's notice was never present when she looked at Lander.

But Lander's eyes were caught by Lefty's hands, or rather, by their sudden absence. If Lefty had been brave enough to risk approaching the strange boy—and Jewel admitted it didn't take much courage, given Lander's state—he was nowhere near brave enough to do it with Duster six inches away.

Finch crept up behind Duster, and stopped two feet away. This was safest, although Duster also seemed to have some sort of weak spot—no, that was the wrong word—tolerance for Finch. Finch didn't frighten Lefty, and she gently squeezed herself into the almost invisible space between Duster and the maimed boy.

"What were you doing?" she asked Lefty, without meeting his eyes. Which would have been impossible unless she laid herself out on the slats, faceup.

"Just—hand stuff," he answered lamely. Quietly. "He doesn't like voices," Lefty added. "But sometimes—sometimes he'll answer other things."

"Answer what?" Duster snapped.

Lefty snapped in a different way.

Jewel sighed.

But Carver, quietly sitting with his back to the corner of the room, stretched his legs and stood. "Lefty's been trying to teach him to talk with his hands."

"Lander can't talk?"

"He can talk. He won't." Carver's eyes were lined with dark circles, and he appeared to have lost weight. Or gained height. "But he responds to some things. We were talking," Carver added, "yesterday afternoon. Jester thought it would be useful—"

"I said neat," Jester interjected.

"Useful," Carver continued, "to be able to signal, between ourselves. He says other dens do it, when they're afraid of making noise or drawing the wrong type of attention."

"He did?" The fact that Carver had used the word den—and that Jewel had let him—escaped everyone's notice.

Jester nodded almost gleefully.

"You've been listening to too many stupid stories," Duster said, with easy contempt.

"They don't have to be stupid," he replied, completely irrepressible. "So we started to come up with one or two. We've got a really good one for danger," he added.

"What kind of danger?" Jewel asked, curious in spite of Duster's growing look of bored contempt.

At this, Jester slowed down. "What do you mean, what kind?"

The bored contempt flared into something a little more testy, but Duster held her tongue; she was still seated in front of Lander.

Jewel shook her head. "Later," she said. "Go on."

"Anyway, Lefty kind of made up something that goes like this—" He lifted his palm in the universal gesture for stop.

Jewel failed to notice Duster's expression, but it took work; any expression on Duster's face was always hard to ignore.

"And Lander kind of lifted his hand. Both hands. In the same gesture. One after the other."

"Why both hands?"

"Lefty doesn't like to use his bad hand, and Lander was making the gesture with both because it can be done with either. I think," Jester added. "I think that's why he did it. He didn't exactly say."

Well, no, he wouldn't. But in spite of herself, Jewel felt something a lot like hope. "Danger? Just that?"

"Well, sort of. I came up with a couple of other signals," Jester added, "but for some reason, he didn't repeat any of those."

Jewel could well imagine what they were; if Jester *had* a sense of humor, it wasn't actually funny most of the time.

"But Lander tried a couple more of Lefty's. It took an hour," Jester added, with a shrug. "And Lefty's been trying since then. Lander doesn't always respond. But he does sometimes."

"Lefty," Jewel said.

Safely bracketed by Finch, Lander and wall, Lefty took the risk of lifting his head.

"Can you teach me those?"

He nodded.

"I think," Carver said quietly, "that we should all learn them. If it's the only way Lander will talk, it's better than nothing."

But Duster had had enough. Enough of games. She rose, and her expression was smooth as merchant glass, barred and uninviting. "There's another way," she said grimly.

Jewel was on her guard instantly; Duster did that. Whatever it was that Duster was about to say, she wasn't going to like it much. But she nodded, not trusting herself to speak.

"You talk to that friend of yours?"

"Talk? About—"

"What you said you'd talk to him about. We need to find a few people."

"I don't think—"

Duster glared toward the door, and the hall beyond it. Jewel, taking the hint without the benefit of Lefty's hand language, stepped out of a room that had offered hope like the scant rays of cold sun in winter. She felt their passing, and missed it.

"Lander and I," Duster said, without preamble, "we had some of the same visitors."

The word *visitor* sank like a rock. Like a rock dropped through Jewel, and down into a darkness that she had never really explored. Didn't ever want to. She let it go before it dragged her with it.

"How will that help Lander?" she asked.

"How do you think?"

Jewel shrugged. "I don't waste time asking questions if I already have the answers. Or think I have them," she added, to be fair.

"He needs to know," Duster said coldly, "that they're dead."

"They're not dead."

"Not yet."

"How will that help him?" Because seeing a bunch of corpses wouldn't have done much for Jewel. She was smart enough not to say so.

Duster's glare was both hot and cold. Jewel thought the conversation had ended; when it was like this, it usually had. But apparently this was important enough to Duster that she was willing—barely—to make the attempt to get her point across. If she had to bury it to do so, that was just Duster.

"Because he'll know, if they're dead, that you're different. *We're* different." The we hung in the air for just a moment, it had been spoken with such heat. It was . . . an invitation. An opportunity. The first one that Duster had offered Jewel.

And it came cloaked in death, always death. Duster was still talking, and Jewel's hearing caught up slowly with the rest of the words. "He'll know that we won't use him the same way. Won't sell him. He'll know, if they're dead, that they'll never hurt him again."

"Doesn't mean that others won't."

"No. It doesn't." Duster seemed to deflate a little. "But you won't keep him here. Not like this. And don't think he doesn't know it. Don't think he's not waiting to be sent back to the place you dragged him from. Or sent somewhere else just like it."

"We can't send him anywhere else."

"The Mother's people will take him."

Jewel was absolutely silent.

"You think I don't know? You might be willing to keep the cripple because you get the giant with him—"

Jewel turned and walked away. Duster wasn't the only person who could end a conversation in anger, and it wouldn't be the first time—in a mere three days—that Jewel had proved this. Duster followed, but only so far as the door to Rath's room; if Duster was willing to show all her edges to anyone who could see them, she kept them sheathed near Rath.

"I'll talk to him. I'll talk to him even though you haven't yet given me the promise I *need* from you. I'll get your damn information," Jewel said, spitting the words out when she could unclench her jaw. "But damn you, *leave Lefty alone.*" And without knocking, she opened Rath's door. Kalliaris smiled upon her attempt at a dramatic exit; the door wasn't locked.

Rath was waiting for her, lit to one side by the magelight in its pedestal. He looked, in that lopsided glow, as if he had aged; as if his shoulders had suddenly taken the weight of years and bowed beneath them. The air in the room was cool and damp; although there was a small grate here, he hadn't bothered to feed it.

Jewel made her way toward it, and he lifted a hand, catching the bend of her elbow before she passed him.

"The door," he told her quietly.

She looked back; the light was moon bright, although day had not yet passed beyond the meager window. She nodded quietly, and he released her sleeve. The door clicked shut as she turned again.

His smile was slight. "I told you," he said quietly, "to let her go."

She nodded. She didn't mention Duster by name. "Maybe," she added grudgingly, "I should have listened."

His brow rose in mock surprise. "But you have no intention of ridding yourself of her."

She could honestly say she'd been thinking of nothing else for the last two minutes; Duster could rile her in a way that only her Oma had, while she lived. But—as her Oma had often said—thought and action were different. "I don't understand her," she said instead.

"No, you don't. I think it highly likely that you will never understand her, and if you have no cause to do so, thank Kalliaris."

"You do."

"Thank the goddess? Hardly."

Jewel frowned. Mockery was something she accepted in small quantities. Very small. But Rath's charity—inexplicable charity, as it seemed at this moment—was all that stood between Jewel and the cold Winter that was coming. And Jewel was the bridge between Rath and the snow for the rest of the children packed together in these rooms. She bit her tongue, held it. "You understand her," she said at last, when she could.

"I've spent more years observing people."

She couldn't argue with that, and didn't want to. She started toward the logs again, and he shook his head. "Leave them, Jewel." He gestured to the other chair in the room. "And sit. Your pacing makes me think of caged animals."

She dragged the chair across the floor, bringing it inches away from his knees. This was awkward, as it didn't leave any room for hers; she had to tuck them beneath her.

"Why does she treat Lefty like that? Arann almost hit her."

"She almost stabbed him."

Jewel, uneasy, said nothing; she looked at the magestone instead. "You heard that?"

"The dead would have heard it, had they bothered to listen."

She looked at her hands; brought them to her lap. They were fists. "If it weren't for Lefty, it wouldn't be so bad."

"Why? She questions your authority constantly."

"I don't *want* authority," Jewel told him quietly.

But his expression was odd as he met her gaze; she couldn't quite place it. "Don't you?"

"No."

"Why?"

"I don't want to tell other people what to do."

"You already tell them what to do."

"I don't—"

"You do, Jewel. Jay, then, if you prefer." He rose, pushing his chair back. The pacing he had denied Jewel, he kept for himself. "You tell them what to do, and they listen. Even she does."

"She *doesn't*. She won't leave Lefty alone. If Arann hadn't almost hit her, I *would* have."

"And she wouldn't have stabbed *you*. Next time," Rath said quietly, "hit her."

Jewel had no difficulty with the idea of hitting people who misbehaved; she'd certainly felt her Oma's hand often enough that she'd lost count. But she *wasn't* their Oma. "I can't."

He shrugged. "You don't understand Duster. Let me explain only this small part of her: she understands that life demands a victim. She understands that dens demand one. She understands that there is *always* a victim, and she's trying to ensure that it isn't her.

"Lefty is the obvious choice."

"Lefty wouldn't hurt *her*."

"Lefty wouldn't hurt a mouse. He sometimes tries to feed them," Rath added, with mild disdain. "It makes him ideal for her purpose."

"But she's not like that with Lander."

"No," Rath conceded. "She is not like that with Lander."

"Why?"

"Because Lander has *earned* her pity. Or her sympathy. With Duster, I think the two are the same. She knows what he's suffered; she suffered it herself. The fact that it broke something in him might be worthy of contempt in different circumstances—but she has Lefty here."

"That's not fair, Rath," Jewel said quietly, still clinging to the sides of the chair. "I don't think she'd treat Lander that way if there were no Lefty." She drew breath, and then said, "if she hadn't saved Finch, I wouldn't have taken her with us. I probably wouldn't have wanted to go there at all.

"I'm glad I did," she added, seeing for a moment the fire that had consumed the building. Feeling the heat as if it were her own. "She saved Finch," she added, turning the words over, revisiting them in the light of Rath's room.

"Yes." It was a grudging syllable.

"And I think she wants to help Lander." She looked at Rath carefully.

Rath, however, was not fooled. "What does she want, Jay? What did she ask you to ask me for?"

"Information."

"What information?"

Jewel hesitated. She could see Lander's blank face in the magestone; the light was like the color of day off his unblinking stare. She was afraid to touch Lander. Afraid to wound him. Aware that at the moment these two things were the same.

But Lefty had reached him, somehow. And Duster? Duster, who was always so damn cruel to Lefty it *almost* made Jewel want to kill her, could sit in front of Lander, speaking the silent language of shared experience. Ugly experience. All of it painful. Jewel had been spared that fate. By her Oma, her mother, and her father after them; by Rath.

"Duster wants to help Lander," she said at last.

Rath said nothing.

"Duster's not—she doesn't—" Jewel shook her head, and said in a strained voice, "She *saved* Finch, Rath."

"And you saved Finch. It doesn't make you the same person."

"No. It doesn't. But it gives us something *good* in common. I can't change who she is. I don't think—I don't even think I *want* to." The last, defiantly.

She didn't; he could see that. It should have disturbed him. But after his brief visit to the Terafin manse—its gates cold with rain and dark with lack of sun—he felt that nothing would.

He should have *seen* it. He should have understood it clearly. Jewel, Jay, *this* poor urchin, the weight of her odd morals still burdening her in the face of starvation, had looked, had spoken, so differently he had allowed himself the false grace of illusion. Now, it was gone.

He could see the ghost of Amarais in Jewel, and it haunted him; would haunt him, he thought, forever. He was not a young child now; not a young man; he would never be the younger, naive brother to Jewel Markess. And because he was not, he could see her clearly.

It was bitter, this clarity, this vision.

She did not tolerate Duster because she could pretend that Duster was someone—or something—she wasn't; she tolerated Duster because she felt, on some primal level, that Duster could be *of use*.

"What does she want?" he asked quietly although he thought he knew the answer to the question.

"Names," Jewel said flatly. "And places." She paused, and then added, "We'll do the rest." The edge in her voice was sharp, but it was hot. Untempered.

He did not pretend to misunderstand her.

"Do you think this will help Lander?" he asked softly.

"I don't know. I don't think it will hurt him," she added. Her voice had fallen, trailing into something that was barely louder than a whisper. She looked up at Rath, her chin steady, her dark eyes clear. "Those people—those men—deserve to die."

She surprised him, but then again, she always had. He had not thought she would put into words the whole of her intent. He almost told her how unwise it was. But Amarais was there again, in the straight, stiff spine, the width of determined eyes, the purse of lips.

Jewel hadn't the vision of his sister; she had never had the breadth of wealth and education that would give her that. The vision she did have was both more powerful and in the end, less ultimately useful in the situation she found herself in now.

"Do you deserve to kill them?" He asked her quietly, all motion ceasing as he knelt beside her chair, bringing their eyes almost into line.

She could have told him that she wouldn't be the one doing the killing. He waited for the words, expecting them, readying his reply. But he waited in vain; they didn't come. He felt a twinge of something that might be either pride or pain. If they could be separated.

"There has to be justice," Jewel said quietly.

"Justice is as simple as death?"

Jewel said nothing.

"The boys who injured Lefty—do they deserve death? Or did they learn to cause injury *because* they were injured, and became twisted the way Duster is twisted? Why are you willing to keep the one, and throw away the other?"

"Duster saved Finch," she said quietly. Clearly.

"And in her time, she may well have killed—or maimed—other children. Very much like Lefty was maimed."

She said nothing again.

"Answer me, Jewel, if you wish my aid in this."

"I'm not the Kings," she told him. "I'm not a magisterian. I'm not justice-born. I'm not a judge."

"If you're willing to kill, you are. And you feel yourself worthy to *be* that judge."

Some of her reserve left her as she leaned forward, her cheeks flushing. "Don't you? Don't you think they should die? Didn't you kill those other men—"

"It may have escaped your notice," he said sharply, "but they *were* trying to kill me at the time."

"It didn't. It doesn't. I don't know why you're doing this," she added. "But it doesn't matter. Lander's trapped inside himself. I can't get him out. Maybe Duster can." Her voice was low. "You killed those men. I *didn't care* that you killed them. I saw their bodies. I stepped over them. I saw the blood. And I didn't care.

"I cared about us. I cared about the us that were trapped in those damn rooms, or chained to the walls. I cared about Finch. I cared about the people that—" She stopped.

"Go on."

And closed her eyes. "I hated the bodies," she said quietly, her voice almost breaking. "I hated that they had to die. But if I had *seen* their deaths clearly, if I'd truly *known* it, it wouldn't have made a damn difference.

"You've killed men before," she added, opening her eyes. "And you can live with it."

"I wasn't ten."

"I'm almost eleven."

He didn't call her a liar.

"It's better," he told her, rising, "not to have to live with it."

"If you have the choice."

"You always have the choice."

"But some people *don't*, Rath. What choice did Finch have? What choice did Lander have? Even Duster—"

He lifted a hand, a bitter, angry gesture. "Enough." Thinking about Amarais, his sister; about the starving orphans who had evoked in her not pity but a cold and enduring anger; about House Terafin, whose siren call had beckoned her, fanning her ambition and depriving Handernesse of its one true hope.

About war in all its guises, the simplest of which was strangers with weapons who tried to kill each other because to do less was to die.

"I do not know," he told her grimly, "if I *can* find the information you ask for. It will be both costly and dangerous, and it is not something that can be done overnight, if it can be done *at all.*"

But her shoulders had slumped just a little, and the high color was slowly receding from her face. Her hands looked small and frail as she reached up and shoved unruly dark curls from her eyes. She looked so unlike his elegant, graceful sister it almost made him smile.

But the smile would not come; he had already made his decision. "If Duster has names, it would be helpful. I doubt she does," he added.

He was wrong.

Sigurne Mellifas looked up from a solitary desk upon which her reflection, around the neat stacks of vellum, could be glimpsed. In these chambers, high above the grand and almost opulent halls into which visitors were conducted, she worked and lived, and they reflected the complexity of that life: cases, glass doors carved with geometrical precision, the panes hinting at clarity, although they were themselves opaque.

The papers by which the Order governed, and was governed, were in tidy stacks, in descending order of import. The largest pile, querulous voices compressed into lines of varying widths and varying legibility, petitions and complaints from the various members of the Order itself, demanding, some in supercilious tone and some in bald outrage, her attention to perceived slights. The second pile, the results of various ongoing investigations in which the Magi of the Order played some part. The third, the writs by which magic—in the streets of the Empire—was governed. Ah, and a few admission notices, a few resignations, scattered among the whole.

The Order of Knowledge was, for many who journeyed through its doors, the end of a pilgrimage, rather than the beginning; those for whom this became increasingly clear would discover it in the months—or years—of their tenure as students. Many, some with the talent to master magic, some without, would reach this conclusion and depart.

They could not, by law, be required to unlearn what they had learned; nor could they be compelled not to practice it, inasmuch as such practice was legal. They could, however, be watched with care; this was the purview of some of the more fastidious of the members, of which Sigurne was simply one. She glanced at the list of names; the glance was cursory.

The Order was not a Guild, although it served in that capacity for the men and women who wished employment—and the concurrent income that arose from such—elsewhere. The mages themselves were oft fractious and argumentative, sometimes for the sheer joy of it. Sigurne, more practical, found little use in pointless debate, and her entrance into such discourse often signaled its abrupt end.

She watched the surface of the desk for some moments, frowning at the glimpse of her own reflection, wreathed in a light so pale it would have been hard to determine the color. But as it was Sigurne who had cast the spell, the color was obvious to her, and she set aside her papers and rose, feeling the chill of the air in the heights of the lofty stone tower. Had it not been so important that she occupy these rooms—rooms that came with the power and authority of the title she wielded—she would have gratefully set them aside and dwelled below with the students; the rooms in the main halls were never so cold.

But she would lose, without isolation, the privacy upon which she had come to depend. She caught the edge of her outer robe and drew it up from its mantle of chairback, donning it as she walked toward the door.

Not young, she was not yet so old that she was forced to bow or stoop; she did both, because she found the appearance of age useful. Still, the mild aches in her hands and knees were no act; the damp of the Winter sea air set her teeth on edge. She paused at the door, its dark, stained wood framed by peaked stone, curving upward in a recessed arch that seemed pretentious, given the space.

It was not, however, impractical.

Lifting her palm, she ran her hand across the smooth surfaces of those arches, her fingers trailing a pattern that not even eyes could see. These complicated wards were of her own devising; they were as comfortable as the hands that covered them, and almost as natural to Sigurne.

It had been perhaps two decades since she had taken the title of First Circle mage; it had been fifteen years since she had positioned herself as the head of the Order of Knowledge. The gray of her hair at that time had been the color of steel; it had whitened, and she had let it, as if the strain of governing the Magi naturally led to some premature aging.

But in truth it was less stressful than not governing would have been. She had come to *Averalaan Aramarelas* solely to do as she had done: to take the seat, to preside over the First Circle—and by default, the lesser circles in their turn—and to be vigilant.

The reward for her vigilance? She shook her head, lifted the hood of her outer robe about her face, and began her descent.

Rath was waiting for her when she entered the large room. It was narrow, this room, but the ceilings were high, the joists exposed, the windows—for it held windows of thick, colored glass along the eastern wall—poised to catch the sunrise hours hence. The view, he thought, would be magnificent at dawn; in the darkness it was less comfortable. Taking care not to touch the surface of the glass, he looked down to see the streets of the Isle; the magelights that lit the roads were bright and evenly spaced, and they marked the winding passage of flat stone so clearly the road might have been built of luminescent rock. Here and there, carriages could be seen, and the glint of bright breastplates indicated that men were on patrol.

Upon the Isle, they always were. Those crimes that could be committed in safety here were not committed on the streets or the causeways; they were sheltered behind the grand facades of the many, many mansions that stood almost shoulder to shoulder behind tall fences.

And perhaps in halls such as these, where the Magi gathered.

The doors opened slowly, their movement so perfectly smooth it seemed unnatural. Then again, much that happened in the Order usually did; Rath turned his back upon the windows, conveniently situated opposite the doors, and let his arms fall loosely to his sides, holding them in just such a way that it would be instantly clear that he was unarmed.

Sigurne nodded briefly and stepped into the room. The doors swung shut—just as smoothly, just as precisely—inches from the fall of her robes. Those robes were dark, a dusty black that no one could actually mistake for gray.

"You've carried a message?" she said, her eyes clear and cool. It was hard to judge their color; Rath thought they might be blue or gray.

He wore the tidy livery of an unidentified House; it was blue, with flashes of purple and gray—something that implied royalty, without the complicated illegality of actually mimicking it. Of all the clothing that Rath wore, this was possibly the most impeccably cared for; he brought it out in times of need. His early years in the presence of the rich and the powerful had exposed him to the hauteur of important servants—as opposed to those who must go unseen within the halls of a great House—and he had borrowed their posture, their distance, their hint of open disdain, quite liberally. His bearing was proud, and he had stretched himself to his full height; he did not mean his visit to pass unremarked within this tower.

But as Sigurne approached, she frowned.

"Member Mellifas," he said, bowing gravely.

She might have pretended confusion or surprise, and he thought she would attempt it; her face was momentarily devoid of expression, as if she could not quite decide which one to wear. But in the end, she chose weariness, and turned away.

"You . . . used the daggers again?"

"Ah, forgive me. No, I have had no cause to use them."

He saw her stiffen, and then saw the stiffness leave her in a rush; the loss made her look frail, as if in shedding worry she also shed strength.

The room, narrow as it was, was possessed of a great many window seats; these were not to her liking. It was not possessed of an obvious grate, but it was not chill; it held a long, narrow table, and at even intervals, chairs. They were simple chairs; heavy, but otherwise unadorned. They did, however, have armrests and cushioned seats.

"You will do me the grace," she told Rath, "of allowing me to sit while you explain your presence here."

He nodded, turning toward the windows again. This glass did not reflect light; he could see out, but any hope of watching the mage's movements without actually looking at her vanished.

"Ararath."

He accepted the inevitable. With some quiet grace, he pulled a chair out for her and held it while she sat. When she was comfortable—or as comfortable as one could be in this oddly sparse room—he took a like chair.

"I've come to ask you questions," he told her quietly, meeting her eyes. "I am aware that I have very little to offer in return; I am aware that I may leave these rooms without answers. I am also aware that I may never leave them, for it was clear to me when we met a week past that you have no desire to speak about the subject I have come to ask you about.

"But I have some hope, or I would have spared you the burden of visitors at this late hour."

She nodded, her gaze appraising. Not unfriendly, but not precisely friendly either. She seemed bent, to Rath, but Rath was also adept at disguise, at wearing or discarding as much of the burden of age as he could.

"I have in my keeping a child," he continued, when it became clear that only by continuing would silence be broken. "She was some days in the hands of the men who held her captive."

"Those men?"

"As you suspect, Member Mellifas. They were demons, the two I killed."

"The child is whole?"

"She was not uninjured," he replied with care, "but injury was not, I think, their goal." He had been wrong to sit; he desired the freedom to walk, to turn his back on this woman while he gathered thought. He had rehearsed his question with care, rephrasing it a hundred times, a thousand, while he made his way through the maze beneath the holdings. But as always, with such things, rehearsal had little bearing upon reality.

"Ararath."

"I did not come to ask how the demons were summoned; in truth, I would rather not know. But in such writings as are left from the time of the Blood Barons—and I assure you, I have read much—it is clear that if demons were used, they were used as intelligent weapons; they were given orders, and they were kept on tight leashes."

She nodded slowly.

"If the mage who summoned these creatures was within that building, I think we would have known it. Therefore, I have assumed he was not."

"It is a safe assumption," Sigurne said. She lifted a hand to her brow, massaging her forehead.

"It is not clear to me why a mage—any mage—would require the use of demons in the thirty-second holding as keepers of a brothel, however illegal; a man with money might have had the same service as they were providing from any of a thousand men, and again—from what scant writings remain—there appears to have been a risk to those mages who summoned demons in the past."

She chose silence, and Rath cursed it, although he often chose silence himself.

"Therefore one of two things is true: The mage you are looking for is one with a great deal of power who is not at risk when using demons for so trivial a task; or the demons were sent to pursue some other goal in the holdings, congruent with their running of a brothel." He paused. "I have been some days in my own investigation, and I can say two things with certainty."

"And those?"

"That the brothel offered services that were used by men of wealth and position upon the Isle, and that those services were costly. Had the brothel been left to run, it would have made a great deal of money for those who owned and operated it."

"It would not be the first time such an enterprise has been attempted. The lower holdings are not, perhaps, as tidy and lawful as the upper holdings—but they are not without the force of law; such enterprise would not have survived to make men rich; it might have survived long enough to ensure that some of those men were very dead. Very legally dead."

"Indeed."

She closed her eyes. "There is, of course, the third option."

"And that?"

"That both of the things you speak of are true: we are dealing with a mage—or mages—with exceptional levels of talent, *and* the demons pursue some purpose within the holdings, as far from the scrutiny of the Isle—and the god-born—as they can within the City."

Rath was not, by any measure, young, but when he looked at Sigurne's face, he felt the difference in their ages acutely. She spoke slowly, even smoothly, but there was a weariness in her words that went beyond fear. He leaned forward slightly in his chair, changing the line of his shoulder as he drew closer to this woman draped, almost incongruously, in the robes of the Order of Knowledge; in the magelights—recessed into the broad beams above—he could see the gleam of the quartered circle around her throat, but he could not make out the familiar symbols that graced it.

"Member Mellifas," he began, but she lifted a curved hand.

"Call me Sigurne. I appreciate the respect you attempt to show, but in this room it is unnecessary."

He nodded. "Sigurne, then. It was not directly of demons that I wished to speak, and of rogue mages, even less; they are not, in the end, my responsibility—and I am aware of my inability to deal with the danger they pose." He skirted the edge of the forbidden, and knew it. Knew also that in so doing, he was at risk. "I came instead to ask what they might gain from *us*."

Her eyes narrowed in a thoughtful way, rather than a cold one. "What an odd question," she said. "It is not one that I have often heard asked; the answer, it seems, would be obvious."

"Perhaps to the Magi, it is."

Her smile was slight and bitter. "Whoever summoned those creatures plays a dangerous game; I do not think it has occurred to them to wonder what the *demons* gain. What they themselves gain by the summoning is more clear and more direct: Power."

Rath shook his head slowly. "Power, Sigurne, I understand. And I understand malice as well." He hesitated. "Perhaps the demons had some task set them by their master that I cannot clearly see. But—the child I spoke of is a girl that we rescued a week past. I would not have considered taking her into my home; she is . . . dangerous. Unpleasant. If she has ever known anything but anger and pain, she hides it well."

"Ararath—"

"I am called Rath, or Old Rath."

"You are hardly old."

He smiled. "To you, no. But if I am to call you Sigurne, call me Rath."

"I am not fond of nicknames or diminutives."

"Nor am I fond of excessive familiarity." He shrugged. "We grow into our names, and perhaps mine is diminished, and I have become less than I was; I would not have said so years ago, and now, it is not of concern to me one way or the other, I have taken so many names."

"Rath," she said slowly. "This girl—"

"She is perhaps eleven or twelve; it is hard to gauge her age, and she has never offered it. If she did, I would revise my estimate either up or down around her claim, depending on the context; she would certainly be looking for some advantage, either way.

"She was taken from the streets—or so I believe—and kept prisoner by the two . . . demons. They sold her services, as they did the services of other children in their keeping. But to *this* girl, they gave the names of the men who had visited her." He watched the mage's face shade into darkness; beneath the weariness was a flicker of anger. He thought both genuine. It would be easy, with a woman such as this, to be caught unaware by such anger; easy to think her of little consequence, given her obvious frailty.

It would also be a mistake.

"And those names?"

"I will surrender them to you if you feel it will aid in your investigation. Without the cooperation of the children involved, it would be difficult to bring these men to justice by regular channels."

"Their cooperation is in doubt?"

"They are children of the poorer holdings," he replied. "And they do not trust where they are not forced to. For the crimes the men have committed, I feel it likely that the Magisterium would ask for the services of the judgment-born; money and position, as you know, mean little to the god-born when they are pursuing the duties laid on them by the blood and burden of their parentage. It would be impossible to lie to them."

"Why do you think they gave the girl the names of these men?"

"I don't know. Had I not begun my own investigation into this affair, I would say that the demons couldn't *know* the real names or identities of such men. But the names *are* real, and I have some cause to believe that the men who were born to the names the child was given were, in fact, her tormentors.

"But I cannot clearly see why. A mage must control the demons, yes? But a mage would gain *nothing* by this. I have thought long on the matter. I believe it possible that these men have provided, by their crimes, information that would prove fatal should it become public knowledge. Even private knowledge, in the wrong hands, would destroy their lives."

"You think the purpose of the brothel was to ensnare the foolish?"

"If so kind a word as foolish could be used, then yes, I believe it might be one such reason for the brothel's existence. It's the only one that makes sense to me."

Sigurne nodded slowly.

"But even so, providing the *child* with the names doesn't. The demons certainly killed some of the other children," he added softly. "If their master needed proof of any claims of grave misdemeanor on the part of the people being blackmailed, if he—or she—needed concrete threats in which to couch the terms of such blackmail, they might keep one child alive. But I don't believe that they intended to use *this* child in that fashion."

"Why?"

"I hoped you would be able to explain that to me." He paused, and then added, "The child herself believes that they intended to use her in a different way."

"She told you this?" Sigurne raised a platinum brow.

"Not precisely."

"Not at all."

He shrugged. "She told someone, and I happened to overhear it."

"You eavesdropped on a child?"

"A child I *do not trust*."

Sigurne rose. "Rath—"

"She has asked me for one boon, one favor, and I have yet to decide whether or not to grant it. She is driven by rage, but also by fear, and I wish to strengthen neither of these. But, Sigurne, I believe they did indeed have some purpose in mind for her; I believe it because she believes it. And fears it. But she did not fear torment, and I do not believe, in the end, she truly fears death."

"What, then?"

Sigurne, standing, gestured; a bright orange light ran across the room like a translucent curtain, a sudden gust of ethereal wind that had escaped her raised palms. She looked neither old nor frail in that moment. But when the light had passed, she looked down on Rath. "Speak the hint of lie to me, and I will know it," she told him softly.

"I did not come to bandy lies," he replied gravely. "Your answer, I think, will decide many fates, many lives, not the least of which are—" He stopped speaking.

"My answer, or what you make of it?"

"Either."

"Why do you assume that I *have* answers?"

"You are too wise to be fearful without cause," he replied. "And Member APhaniel clearly felt that yours was the greater knowledge. He is not, to my mind, a man who willingly cedes authority where such concession is not warranted."

At that, her lips twisted in a smile that was both bitter and infused with humor. "You've spent little time in these halls, if you can say that. He is merely less concerned with his precious authority than many a weaker man." She drew her robes tight, but did not resume her seat. "You ask much, Rath, and offer little."

"It is the way of men."

"Yes. But I am not a man. The child you speak of is not the child who truly concerns you," she added. "Do not stiffen into neutrality; it is clear that you do not care for the child you rescued from the demons; it is also clear to me that your preference would be to sever your fates, if you felt that were possible. You do not. And when we last spoke, you would not speak of a different child. It is clear—to an old woman, bereft of the comfort of grandchildren or children—that the child you protected and the child of whom you now so freely speak, are not the same; clear as well that the former has bonds with the latter that she will not break.

"I will answer your question," she told him, her eyes a bright, almost silvered, blue. "For reasons of my own, I will answer it. And then, Rath, you *will* speak plainly of your purpose here.

"Be aware that you will have what I grant, in the end, very few—including my colleagues. You will have my full attention. If I am unsatisfied with your explanation, it is unlikely that you will ever leave this tower."

Chapter Nineteen

SO MANY WORDS. And so few.

Sigurne looked at the world-weary man seated before her in his perfect livery, the telltale signs of manners learned in a rich and cozened youth still visible in the tilt of his jaw, the graceful and elegant nod of his head, the way he gave ground—and authority—to her not because she was the ruler of the Order of Knowledge, but rather, because she was the oldest woman present.

She considered the matter of House Handernesse.

Once a proud family, historically even a great one, it had survived the Blood Barons, and entered the reign of the Kings, sacrificing both sons—and daughters—to the Kings' war for the Empire. It had not been significant enough to be one of The Ten, and had it, Handernesse had, as so many Imperial families with them, sat on the balance of knife's edge, watching and evaluating the two untried Kings and their very determined war. When it became clear that *some* hope existed for their success, Handernesse had moved—as they say—with the times, and had come only in this last generation to a bitter halt.

A cousin, Sigurne thought, would rule Handernesse when Ararath's father finally made his final passage to the Halls of Mandaros, there to wait for his famous daughter and his lost son. In those halls, much might be said; she wondered if the words would be bitter. Having not passed through the halls—or not in a way she would remember—she wondered frequently what they might be like. There, one could lay the burden of life's responsibilities at last to rest, and know some measure of peace.

It was not peace that she thought of now, although, as always, she greatly desired it. So, too, must Ararath's father. And if he was not a small man in mind, he was not so wise or generous a man that he could ever fully understand the disavowal of family and blood ties that were necessary to join one of The Ten. If you had no family, what did you have? What loyalties bound you, or claimed you?

She could not remember the Handernesse cousin's name, and had certainly never seen his face; Handernesse was not a family who came often to the Order of Knowledge, and if they did, they did not petition for any use of magic that might distinguish them in her eyes.

But the son . . . She had not lied, although she was well past the age where lying seemed an invitation to a lurking, bitter discovery; she had met the woman who was now called The Terafin, and she had been much impressed by her. Amarais Handernesse ATerafin, she had been called then, her dark hair sleek as raven's wing, and drawn above her patrician face in a way that suggested severity without descending to it. She had reeked of elegance and power, as if they were more than mere birthright; she *owned* them. But she did not use them as weapons; they were hers as much as another man might naturally claim breathing.

They had spoken for some time, for the new Terafin ruler wished to purchase the services of a First Circle mage on retainer, should the need arise. For etiquette's sake, The Terafin had requested Sigurne's aid; Sigurne had, just as politely, refused. What work she did outside of the Order was not done at the convenience of The Ten; nor, if truth be told, at the convenience of the Kings. And Amarais was no fool, no uninformed petty lordling; she was aware of this fact. Her offer had been meant to convey the depth of her respect, no more, and it was taken as such by the woman to whom she had offered it.

Sigurne had taken much time and much thought before she had tendered a reply. "Understand, Terafin," she had said to the much younger woman, "that the Magi—even those of the First Circle, or perhaps, *especially* those of the First Circle—can be somewhat fractious, somewhat proud, and somewhat unpredictable; they are not beholden to the social niceties that are commonly considered good manners."

"People assured of their power seldom are," The Terafin had replied calmly.

"And your manners are so perfect, I am to assume that you are not assured of yours?" It was a more pointed question than Sigurne was given to asking when matters of rogue magery were not involved.

The Terafin had rewarded her with the blessing of her smile; it was fine and thinly edged, but genuine. "I am as assured of my position as any who have held it," she said. "But in the end, it is not the position that one is judged by. Some consider the title and the name worthy of fear, of respect, of sycophancy. But Terafin is one of The Ten because, in the years of the Blood Barons, when there was little hope of success, Terafin chose to support two who were barely come to manhood: the first Kings.

"And those of us who take the title and hold it must add to that legend; we must *live up* to those who risked all to create an Empire in which fear and power were not the only true measure of a ruler."

Years ago, Sigurne thought. *Years.* But she could remember the words so clearly, she needed no magical aid, no magical recall; they were cool and calm, and each was weighted. Heavy. It was a weight she valued.

And now she faced the brother, and looked closely for any sign of kinship that went deeper than high cheekbones or the set of eyes. She almost sighed.

"The Houses are not like the Order. When the man who previously held the title of The Terafin passed on to the Halls of Mandaros, divisions within House Terafin that had not been clear were instantly made manifest. But such things happen in any family; people are oft adverse to change, and squabbles arise out of past history over the remains left in the wake of a death." In so few words she dismissed the whole of a war that had savaged the House, from the Isle itself to the farthest reaches of its merchant runs. And in the same few words she made clear that she would not now—or ever—openly discuss the vulnerabilities that came with power.

Nor had she—in her first interview with the new ruler of House Terafin—discussed the man who now sat before her in his isolated, hard chair. Sigurne continued her study of his face, his graying hair, the length and line of his jaw; she saw in him some similarity of expression that spoke of Handernesse—but little else that spoke of the sister who had risen so high in the ranks of the powerful. He wore the uniform of a trusted messenger as if he had never worn anything else—and as she had seen him dressed very differently in the Placid Sea, she was well aware that this was not the case. Deception came easily to him.

This talent was not one he had learned in Handernesse, but it was often the way with the children of the powerful to learn their most useful talents on grounds other than the ones they called home.

She wondered, now, why he had come. She was not afraid of him, or rather, no more afraid than she was of any stranger who came asking questions about demons. They were few indeed, and usually they were both young and new enough to the Order that they could be cajoled into humiliating themselves in their utter ignorance by their more seasoned seniors; none of those pale, halting men and women were remotely akin to this aging and weathered man who wore his secrecy in so many layers.

And yet, to this man, who hid as much about his life as a man possibly could and still interact with people, she bent slightly. He was not one of hers; he would never be one of hers.

Perhaps because he couldn't be, she could speak. She wasn't entirely certain what she would say, and this was both distasteful and unusual; if Sigurne's age was not entirely feigned—and it was not—her reticence was deep and needful.

"I come," she said quietly, "from the far North of the Empire."

Ararath's expression shifted slightly. His eyes, dark, were going the peculiar blank she associated with slow memory. "The North?" he said at last. And then, in a different language, "How far to the North?"

In the same tongue, she replied, "Farther, I think, than you have ever had cause to travel. I do not believe that Handernesse had routes to the North, and even had they, the journey by land is unpleasant for all but a few months, and the journey by water is . . . unfriendly."

"Your land of birth is not commonly known."

"It is known," she said with a shrug, wanting very much to take her seat again. "By those who are curious enough to ask; I make no secret of it."

"How did you make your way to Averalaan—to *Averalaan Aramarelas?* It is seldom that the Order seeks the mage-born in the North."

"It is seldom they seek the mage-born at all," she replied with some asperity. "But when we are summoned to test those suspected of being mage-born—often at the behest of a local Priest—we travel in haste. And we can."

He nodded; this much, he knew.

"You have, perhaps, heard of the Ice Mage?"

Rath frowned for a long moment. When the moment passed, the frown had deepened; his eyes had narrowed. He nodded. "I believe he was called by other names."

"He was called many. In my youth, he was called Lord; we had no other." She felt the cold of the coming Winter less clearly than she now felt the Winters of the past. She would have turned away, but his gaze held her.

"Sigurne," he said quietly, "I am aware of the difference between our respective ranks. I am aware of your power and the threat it poses if you find me wanting. Nothing you could say or do to either emphasize or deny the truth of this knowledge will have any impact on it. Will you not sit?"

Her smile was wan. "My age is no act," she said quietly. "And my pride is misplaced. Yes, Ararath, I will sit if you will promise to remember those differences."

"In this tower, I am unlikely to have difficulty."

She took the seat with some gratitude—and some regret. In spite of herself, she found herself liking this wayward man. "What did you hear, in the South, of the Ice Mage?"

Rath shrugged. "Little. A small army was sent, and with them, the warrior-magi. He was not born to the North, although no history records the place of his birth. He is said to have arrived in one of the outlying villages, where he first killed the village elder, and then began to build a tower using the labor of the villagers he had not been forced to kill."

She nodded. "That much, at least, is true. What else?"

"That he was a rogue mage, of course; that when he was finally discovered—and confronted—he killed many of the Kings' men before the Magi destroyed him."

"Many good men—good mages," she added, "were also killed in that attempt; he had prepared many years for just such an encounter. Had it not been for the presence of Member APhaniel, I am not at all certain that he would have lost his battle."

"Member APhaniel?"

She watched Rath revise his estimate of Meralonne's age; it amused her for a few moments, and the amusement quieted her. "They took the tower down, stone by stone, and they destroyed what they found within it." She paused, and shook her head. "Almost all of what they found.

"I was one of the few things they did not choose to destroy."

"You?" His brown eyes rounded; his well-waxed brows—a conceit she despised—cracked slightly as they followed the curve of his eyes. "You were there?"

"In the tower. I was . . . much younger then. I was not without power.

And I was not without anger. But as I had played no small part in the summoning of the Kings' men, they could not find it within themselves to dispatch me. Some argument was made for my death," she added, speaking softly and without hesitation or resentment. "Had I been among the surviving Magi, I would have argued in just such a fashion."

"*Why?* You couldn't have been more than a girl—" He lifted a hand. "You learned," he said quietly.

"Yes. By his side. I learned what he studied. I aided him when I had no choice. Forbidden, all. All of the knowledge. All of the lessons." She could, in this tower, see the ghostly echoes of the other tower she had occupied. Feel the presence of the Lord in her room, her many rooms; she could hear the echoes of his voice. Had she been a different person, she would have let them go, dispersing them over decades, into the stream of murky past, where she would at last slip the tight bonds of memory.

But they steadied her now, in ways her master had never conceived of in the certainty of his power.

"But Meralonne APhaniel spoke for me."

"He holds you in regard," Ararath told her quietly.

"Perhaps. I do not think it was regard that moved him, then. He knew nothing of me, save that I was somehow thought to be responsible for the message that had drawn the Kings to the North. He could not know what I knew, and I did not lie; not then. Now, I lie far more frequently, and with greater ease. I had no desire to die," she added bleakly. "But no expectation at all that I would live beyond the battle. My only regret is that mine was not the hand that killed my master."

His eyes were narrow now, but not with suspicion.

"Do not think to offer pity," she began.

"I would not insult you, Sigurne. I am not unhappy that you did not die in the North. But you did not remain there."

"They chose to heed Member APhaniel's plea on my behalf—"

"I am attempting to imagine Member APhaniel pleading," Ararath said wryly, "but my imagination is not up to the task I set it."

"—and having made that decision, they did not execute me. Nor," she added quietly, "did they feel they could, in good conscience, leave me in the village that had been my home."

"Why?"

"I would not have survived it. I had lived in the tower for several years," she added, the emphasis she placed on the dwelling making, of the structural word, a thing with weight and substance that this distant mockery of history could not give it. "It was known to be my home, by the villagers."

"You were born there?"

"No. I was born some leagues beyond, in a village that was not dissimilar to the one the Ice Mage ruled. He did not dwell in the village of my birth, but he exacted tribute from it, and they paid."

"They sent you?"

"No. I was found and taken."

Rath, silent, watched her; she watched him. At last he said, "You were mage-born."

"I was."

"And the Ice Mage knew it, somehow."

"He did."

"May I ask how?"

Had it not been so cold, she would have abandoned the chair again. But even magical heat did not deny the chill of the wind that broke itself upon the heights of the Magi's towers. "You may ask," she told him. "And I will answer because it has bearing upon your question. But the answer to your question is not a matter of a handful of words, and in other circumstances, I would apologize in advance and beg your indulgence for the reminiscences of one old woman."

His eyes narrowed as the sentence drew to a close; he was shrewd, and missed little.

"It is not entirely an act, Rath. I am not young, and I am not particularly ferocious; I forget much these days, and such forgetfulness was not mine in youth. As a child, I would have considered myself a wasteful dotard."

"Children are often harsh critics," he replied, again with consummate care. So like, she thought, his sister in that unexpected kindness, that certain wisdom.

"You have encountered creatures that were once commonly known as demons. What impression did they leave upon you?"

He shrugged, the gesture both economical and automatic. "They seemed like men, to me," he said at last. "And were it not for your daggers and your insistence otherwise, I would have said they were mages. Rogue," he added carefully. "They looked neither more, nor less, terrifying than men do. In the stories commonly told to children demons are creatures out of nightmare; they have scales, or horns, or elongated jaws; they have wings, they spit fire, and they—" He paused.

"Yes?"

"It is said they can take a man's soul." He shrugged again, this time more slowly. "I confess I have given such tales little thought since my coming of age."

Sigurne nodded. "Most men—and women—do. They outgrow their bedside stories, conquer their fear of them, and move more freely in a world larger in all ways than they imagined when those tales had the power to frighten them.

"But there is always some seed of truth—no matter how twisted it has grown—in the oldest of tales." She closed her eyes; felt the hard curve of wood press into her shoulder blades. For a moment, she thought better of continuing, but the moment passed in the wind's howl. "The demons do not call themselves demons, of course."

Rath's brow rose slightly. "Then where does the word originate?"

It was not entirely the question she had been expecting, but Ararath had professed an interest in Old Weston, and she was not unaccustomed to this type of interruption; had she been one to take offense, she would have either died of frustration years ago, or would have strangled any number of the members of her Order. "We believe it has roots in Old Torra, but we are not entirely certain; it is not—quite—a Weston word. Nor for that matter," she added, "is angel."

"Are there?"

"Angels?" She shrugged. "If there are, they guard their names so well none has ever been summoned. Or perhaps the summoners chose not to write of their experience; history is a matter of both record and story, and of angelae, we have only story."

"And demons?"

"More," she whispered. "They are not men; there are some among their kind who can take on the shape and form of man, and some who can create and sustain the illusion of mortality. The latter are more common; they cannot bend flesh to their will, but they have the power to bend minds to suggestion.

"The former are more dangerous."

"Why?"

"We are not entirely certain. But the more human a demon appears, the more powerful it is." She paused. "Demons do not learn language in the way that we do; they appear to absorb it from their summoner. Nor do they appear to require sustenance; they neither eat nor sleep unless ordered to it by their master. They don't fear drowning because they don't need to breathe. They seldom fear fire or cold; the seasons are an echo of the elemental forces, and they can pass through the bitterest of Northern Winters untouched."

Rath lifted a hand. It was perfectly steady.

"Yes?"

"I fear to hear more," he said quietly. "I know your edicts, Sigurne. And I am aware—as perhaps few others are—that you have killed greater men than I for exercising their curiosity about this particular subject."

She nodded genially. Felt the smile that drew creases around the corners of her mouth. "You are not a member of the Order," she told him wryly. "There is not one among them who would seek to stop me from speaking at this juncture."

"I have learned, in the past few decades, to temper curiosity with caution; it is why I am now called old." His smile was fuller than hers, but his eyes were darker. "How much about demons must I understand to understand the answer to my question?"

"It is hard to say. Less, perhaps, than I have said. Or more. Judge for yourself, in the end, as you must." She gestured, placing one hand on the surface of the table. Rath was frowning.

It was often said that honest men could not be lied to, and she had often wondered why people *believed* this. It was men—like Rath—who skirted the edges of truth, mixing just the right amount of falsehood into the blend, who were adept at spotting prevarication; men, like Rath, who were capable of hoarding expressions, and offering them only where they might have the most effect, as if they were genuine.

"The Ice Mage studied the forbidden arts."

"He did not come to their study in the North."

"No. He was a full member of the Order of Knowledge; he claimed to be of the First Circle, and as that is an internal matter, I will neither confirm nor deny. But he lived some years upon the Isle, in this building, and while he learned to master the arts of the warrior-mage, his researches must have led him, in the end, to information that we have since eradicated.

"He was not discovered while he began to develop mastery of this particular craft within the halls of the Order; he was not discovered while he worked—as many of the more powerful mages do—under the auspices of the Houses. But he must have felt that discovery was inevitable; when he at last chose to abandon the Isle, he left in haste, and took with him only the most damning of the evidence that would have been used as justification for his execution.

"We have no records of how he traveled; we presume, given later investigation, that he chose to cloud-walk. It is a colloquial term," she added. "And for the purposes of this discussion, it means he traveled quickly by aid of magic. It is not an instant form of travel, but to travel instantly from Averalaan to *any* point, be it in the Empire or no, would be to invite investigation; the power required would leave a signature that could be read for miles by even the least talented of our students.

"He arrived in Brockhelm when I was perhaps eight years old. He had ruled in Dimkirk for two years before Brockhelm was subject to his whim, and we little suspected his existence until that day; in the far North, travel between villages is not common, at least not by those who dwell within the villages themselves. When he came, many died, and those that did not, chose to accept his rule. From us, he demanded little, but we were no longer free to travel. He expected pursuit, and he wished no warning of his whereabouts to escape before he felt himself ready.

"That pursuit was late in coming." She lifted a hand to her brow. "When I was twelve, I met the first demon. I did not know him as demon; I would have said he was a tall man with cold eyes, no more and no less. He wore clothing in the Northern fashion, and seemed little affected by the cold; were it not for the rule of the Ice Mage, we would have thought him a merchant far from home.

"But he came with the men who served the Ice Mage—and by this time, they numbered perhaps a hundred strong—and ordered the villagers to gather in the village center. There was some anxiety," she added, "but no thought of disobedience. We gathered. He came.

"And he left, after giving us each the barest of glances."

"He was looking for the talent-born?"

"Yes, but I did not know it at the time. He came once a year, after that."

"When did you leave the village?"

"I left Brockhelm at his command in my sixteenth year; I had turned fifteen two weeks before. I did not, at that time, understand why I was being taken from home; I understood only that I had no choice. The Winter makes us harsh," she added softly, "a harsh people for a bitter clime. My mother and father were silent; I was silent. My brother, younger, was only barely silent, but he understood that any word, any action, on his part would mean the loss—in one day—to my parents of both their children, and he said nothing. We accepted the inevitable."

Rath did not speak. He had no words to offer this woman. No words of comfort, no words of sympathy, no words of admiration. By her simple statement, her flat, uninflected voice denied him even the effort of finding them.

"Were there no Priests in your villages?" he asked at last, for the silence demanded something.

"No. We had perhaps three before the Ice Mage came, but none of them god-born. Had he found the god-born among the villagers, I believe he would have fled farther North; what the god-born see, the gods know, and what the gods know, the Kings, inevitably, will come to know. He was no fool. He desired power, but he was patient and cautious."

"Cautious in almost all things."

"But not the demons."

"Not the demons, no," she said softly. "Their first love is terror, primal terror; their second love is pain. For those creatures who look as if they stepped out of the rhythm of childhood story, the gratification of their desire is a simple—but bloody and messy—affair. But those who are more human in seeming are not without subtlety, and even in captivity, they are powerful."

"Is it not for their power they are summoned?"

"Ah, I forget myself. The past always makes an uncertain country of the present. Yes, it is for their strength or power that they are summoned, but even leashed, they can be compelling, and if they cannot satisfy their desire for fear or pain quickly, they will find another path to it; they think of it as a type of ripening. You are not talent-born," she added softly, "but with both words and weapons forged by men who were, likewise, born without such power, you are dangerous."

He nodded.

"Understand, then, that these creatures can see the darkness of even so slight an evil as thought almost before we can think it."

"They can hear your thoughts?"

"Nothing so concrete. They sense the darker thoughts the way sailors sense the storm. But sailors avoid the storm; the demons thrive on it. If they can find the seed, they will grow it; if the seed does not exist, they will plant it. And they will do so with subtlety, where subtlety is required.

"Where it is not, they will do so with glee and malice." She could not help herself; she rose. Her hand drifted away from the tabletop, and a web of light came with it, invisible, she knew, to Rath's eye.

"Understand that I was young," she said softly, "and away from home for the first time. Understand that I knew, from the moment the tower became my home, that I was never to return. I was not expected to be servant to the Ice Mage; he had those in abundance, although servant is too kind a word."

"They were demons?"

"He was not a fool. Where people would do, he used them. In the early years," she added softly. "In later years, he grew arrogant, certain of himself and his control, and in those years, he dismissed—often fatally—his household.

"To contain one demon is difficult. And the one that he had never released—the one who could sense talent, and find it—was a danger to him. He was, as demons are, arrogant; he was proud of bearing. But he was also almost human in seeming. He wore the clothing of the North as if he was born to it; he spoke the tongue. Where the lesser kin—for they are called, among other things, the kin—seemed almost bestial in their savagery, he appeared to consider such wildness beneath him.

"And he served for years. Served faithfully, as if unaware, in the end, of the leash. The Ice Mage was no fool," she added again, "but no man can be cautious and completely in control for his entire life."

"It does not seem—from my vantage—that he ever tried."

She laughed; it was a hollow sound, and spoke of age and pain. "He prided himself on his control."

Ararath offered no more.

"He summoned demons often. Testing himself against them, testing his hold over their names, became a matter of bitter pride, and it carried with it the edge of possible failure; I think he thrived on that possibility, while at the same time denying it."

"I remember the first day I saw him summon a demon. He spent hours tracing the necessary containments, and I was forbidden to move from the stool upon which he had placed me. He offered me to the demon," she added, "and I was afraid, then.

"But it was the fear he wanted. He understood that fear was their wine, and that some creatures were less immune to its effect than others."

"I was not the only witness," she said quietly. "The demon who had found me was present."

"Had he a name?"

Sigurne nodded. "They all have names," she said quietly. "But the names they give are not the names by which they are summoned; I do not think it possible to speak those names in any tongue save their own, and none without power can even attempt it."

"He told you this."

She was surprised. She knew that Ararath referred to the demon, and not to the Ice Mage.

"Yes. He told me."

"And much else."

Her eyes narrowed. "You are perceptive, Ararath. Yes. He told me much. It was a way of gaining my confidence; of gaining, perhaps, my trust—for we were both birds in a cage, and we both obeyed the same master, if for different reasons. I told you: I was young, and given to the thoughts of the young and the isolated. I lived in fear, those early years, and he—trapped, to my mind at the time—far more intimately and more invasively than even I—showed none. Where the Ice Mage was quick to anger—and to kill—the demon was not. And when the demon was sent to kill, when I was sent to witness, he killed cleanly.

"It must have taken a great effort of will on his part, those simple, clean deaths," she added bitterly. "But in all things, where he had choice—and where we were thrown together—he seemed to me somehow better than the Ice Mage. I did not fear him, then, although I had begun my lessons, and the Ice Mage was very clear on the nature of demons." She paused for a moment, remembering. To this place, unlike so many others, she seldom returned; it gave her nothing. Nothing, in the end, but pain.

"I was eventually sent to the villages when the Ice Mage was otherwise occupied. I think it pleased him; I felt I was on parade, and I *knew* I was hated. If I had dreamed—against all certainty—of returning to my family, these visits on his behalf, as his emissary, were death to even dreams.

"But he did not trust the villagers; he therefore sent the demon who found me as my guard. With us went a dozen men, armed and armored as is our custom, but these men were men I disdained. They served willingly, and even with pride; they were warriors, and they little cared which war they fought, as long as they *could* fight. But the demon and I—we were different. We had no choice."

Oh, the bitterness of the words, the *lie* of them. The worst lies one told were always the ones that one told oneself. Time and again she was reminded of this.

But the voice that reminded her was his voice, his velvet voice, the depths of it soothing and warm in a land where ice and stone ruled the heart.

"He told me of the Hells," she added quietly, "where the god we do not name rules. He spoke of the charnel winds, the great abyss, the demesnes ruled by the Dukes—his word—who served their god. He told me some of their history, much of it bitter, and some of their pride; the beauty of fire, red sky, and flight. And he spoke of the fallen."

"Fallen?"

"I think of them that way. The fallen. The lost. The souls of the damned."

Rath was silent for a moment. It was a long moment, as silences went, and he began—and discarded—several words. He did not pride himself on his great empathy, and his understanding of human nature had never led him to value people overmuch. But something in the voice of Sigurne Mellifas led in different directions than those he had previously willingly followed, and in the face of this particular type of unknown, he felt unequal.

Yet he was not so young that he could, with grace, abandon conversation, and after another long moment, aware of her too-bright gaze, he said, "My understanding of the nature of souls is almost entirely based in my understanding of religion."

A pale brow rose. "And that would be?"

"Very little," he replied, without shame. "But damned is not a word that I have heard used with any frequency."

"What have you heard?"

He shrugged. "Mandaros rules the Halls of the Dead."

"And he sits in judgment?"

"His children are called the judgment-born, so it stands to reason that he is, indeed, the judge. But it has never been entirely clear to me of what. It is said that there are souls that wait in his halls for centuries, and souls that abide no more than a handful of hours; it is said that none can, in the end, remain there, but that they also choose the time of their judgment; he does not force it upon them."

She nodded quietly. "All of this is true."

"Then perhaps I am not so ignorant as I feared."

Her smile was thin, but not cold; it was, however, slight. "I doubt that you are often considered ignorant."

He shrugged. "I was considered ignorant often enough in my youth, the sense of such opinion remains."

"And what, then, in your appalling ignorance, would you claim happens to the souls who wait for judgment?"

He paused. "They return," he said at last.

"Here?"

"I am not aware there are many other places to go. They are judged, and when found wanting, they return. They remember nothing," he added, "of their previous lives."

"Some few remember," she said, correcting him as if she were a schoolmistress, and not a mage. "But in general, your summation is not wrong."

"I have often wondered how any can be found unwanting."

"I, too." Her smile was tired now. "But the gods have said that there are those whom Mandaros considers cannot learn more, and they are let loose. To where, the gods either will not, or—in my opinion more likely—cannot, say. They are freed from the circle of the world, and if the gods no longer walk upon its face, they are of it, and tied to its fate."

"And the demons?" he asked quietly.

"Tied as well, in a different way. And if Mandaros can judge one soul incapable of learning, he can judge another incapable in a different fashion. They are not called damned," she added bitterly, "but rather, those who have *chosen*. As if, in living each life in ignorance of any others, they can make choices."

"We all make choices," Rath said quietly.

"We make the choices we are given in the context of our lives," she replied, "and our lives, until we return to the Halls, are the *only* lives we know."

He said nothing. In truth, the matter had concerned him little for the whole of his life until this moment.

"But those who *have chosen* walk the long road to the Hells, there to be kept by the demons and their Lord until the world ends." She looked down at her hands; they lay, now, palms down in her lap. "I do not hate the kin," she added quietly. "Oh, don't look like that. I hate what they *do*. At one time, I hated them with a ferocity that you cannot imagine I could now feel, and perhaps it is true—for I do not now feel it. I understand that they are what they were made to be; that they love pain and torment because it is to cause pain and torment, in the end, that they exist *now*. Such desire was probably considered a mercy to their kind when they made their own choice so long ago; what merciful gods would lay upon any creatures with empathy or pity such a terrible task?

"But having received the desire, they are what they are. And they cannot be easily turned aside. Indeed, if their Lord is aware, they cannot turn aside at all." She fell silent at once. "I say too much," she told him. It was not comforting.

"The *Kialli* lord told me much. Ah, I forget myself. *Kialli* is what they call themselves; in their tongue, it means memory. But more than memory. Not all of the kin are *Kialli*; there are some who are sunk into near bestiality, and they will not rise from it by any force known to us. There is, truly, a misery in memory—a pain and a viscerality—that make memory a great cruelty, but they cling to it, define themselves by it.

"The demon summoned by the Ice Mage, the demon who spent so much time in conversation with me, was *Kialli*. He remembered."

"What is there to remember?"

"They did not always serve the Lord of the Hells, although they always—as far as I can discern—served their Lord."

"Sigurne—"

"I speak in riddles?" She lifted a hand. "Things are not, now, what they were when the gods were young. And the gods *were* young, and proud. We are—in the eyes of the *Kialli*—a race that has sunk into dotage, as mortals must. We do not retain the memory of our golden age, our age of power—for it was said that in our youth, we had powers to rival the gods themselves.

"And I feel that this *must* be true, although it is hard now to separate the lies from the facts; if we had not known that power, we would surely have perished entirely during the wars that the gods made while they walked the face of our world."

Rath said nothing; the enormity of what Sigurne had just imparted was slow to settle, and if he professed to ignorance, it was a thin veneer; he disliked to speak from a position of profound lack of knowledge. "What has this to do with my question?"

"Everything," she replied quietly. "For the gods were persuaded, in time, to leave the world; to separate themselves in almost all ways from its doings. It was not a simple undertaking," she added softly. "And in some ways, it could never be complete; old magic and wild still walk the world, on paths we live in ignorance of.

"For although we *are* mortal, and fade quickly in the eyes of all others who were born to this place, there *is* some part of us that is not. It does not wither, and it does not die; it returns, instead, to the Halls of Mandaros. They can see it," she added softly, "the *Kialli*. I think all immortals can. And what they see in us, dark or bright, is some measure of the path we are tracing in our ignorance, either toward our final freedom or our final imprisonment."

The quality of Rath's silence changed sharply, as if it were a tangible thing. When it broke, the edges were apparent. "You are saying that all demons can see this?"

"I am, indeed, saying that."

"And this girl—the one of whom I spoke—the one they kept—"

"She must be dark indeed," Sigurne replied quietly. "And close, at last, to her final 'choice.' I deem it too great a risk otherwise."

"A risk?"

"What kind of people can be told of such things—of the darkness of their selves—without blanching? What hopelessness, anger, or despair, must such a person feel, when the truth is made known? We all fear to be less than we desire ourselves to be," she added softly, "and we perceive in ourselves wounds taken, and not as clearly the wounds we give. We lie, and in lying, we trap ourselves.

"But there are those who have come so close to that final edge, they might revel in it. Or they might accept it as a fate they cannot escape. And when they do, such people are profoundly dangerous. They will serve to cause what the kin desire: pain and destruction." She lifted a hand. "I have thought long on this, Ararath; it is both my responsibility and, I admit, my obsession.

"When the gods chose to leave this world, they bound themselves in such a way as to make return nigh impossible. But they did it for a reason, for they were not yet ready to give over their desire for dominion, their need to wage war against each other.

"We became the most subtle of the battlegrounds over which they might war. We, each of us, drifting one way or the other; toward the Hells, where the Lord of the Hells waits, or beyond them.

"What do the demons gain? What do they truly gain? Only this: our choice. The blackness. They are cunning and immortal; time is not their concern. It is my belief that they would know the souls they have seen, regardless of how many centuries—and lives—have passed.

"And to win their war, they need to be able to persuade us, to nudge us, with each life, toward their open arms."

She lifted the hands that had lain folded in her lap, and set them against the hard rests of her chair. "The danger in summoning is that, and almost solely that: that while they are here, they darken the world they can touch, laying the seeds for a misstep. Could the Lord of the Hells do so, I believe he would attempt to rule the world again, so that he might make it a place where only *one* choice, in the long and bitter end, is possible. It could take a hundred lifetimes," she added softly, "or a thousand; time is not their concern."

She rose, then. "None of the kin are modest. None of the kin would choose to be powerless. But I believe their names lie fallow in the pages of forbidden texts, in old works that have remained beyond the reach of the Magi of the Empire. I believe that some even ceded the names—the full power of the names—to those who might use them. Because *if* they used them enough, there would be the hope of freedom here. Old names," she added. "And bitter. I have spent my adult life destroying the knowledge of those names, and in some cases, destroying those who held that knowledge. You will never have it," she added, "for you were blessed—or cursed, as you sometimes feel—with a lack of talent that could lead you to them."

"As you were not," he said, without rancor or edge.

"As I was not," she replied, the words serene. "But Ararath, having answered your question, I must now demand answers in return.

"Why did you come, seeking this knowledge? To what use will you put it, if you even considered the use to which it might be put before you came?"

Rath was silent for a moment. Her expression, as he studied it, was now calm; she seemed to be the friendly, wise woman to whom one might come for counsel or solace. Everything about her bearing seemed to imply that she had seen so much the ability to judge others was beyond her, or possibly beneath her.

He wanted to believe it. And, being Rath, he didn't. "Understand," he told her, as he leaned back against hard wood, listening to the wind's howl as if it were harmony to his thoughts, "that I didn't know what you would tell me."

She nodded. "That is not the question I asked, Ararath. You are not a fool. You understood, in the Placid Sea, how important this issue is to me. Now you understand, as well, that it has informed the whole of my life, and that life has been long. Not," she added softly, "thankless, and not without joy. But long. Why did you come?"

He closed his eyes. "I have, in my care, a girl. She is not yet adult; she is not quite child. She is perched on a boundary she can't even see."

"She is not yours."

"She is not my child, no; I have none, nor am I likely to." He lifted a hand to forestall the words he felt must come.

She nodded, allowing him this much.

"And if I could choose a child, I have doubts that it would have been this one," he added, "given how we first met. But it matters little. I came because of her."

"And what is she, to you?"

"An orphan," he replied.

"You have no doubt seen countless orphans in your life."

"Yes."

"And this one?"

"I owe her my life. Once, possibly twice. I consider my life to be of considerable value," he added.

"No doubt." She graced him with a dry smile. "And it is because of this debt, in its entirety, that you chose to dare the tower height?"

He met her eyes. "You've cast a spell," he said, keeping accusation firmly out of the words, and making of them an acknowledgment by dint of that effort.

"It is unwise to lie, or to attempt to lie, but it is unwise to be here at all; yes, I have cast a simple spell. It will tell me only what you believe to be a lie, however; the lies that you believe are truths, it will hide."

"And my answer?"

"I would say," she said slowly, "that it is an answer that is not without truth; it is not the entire truth, although you may have believed it before you set foot in my tower. Not, given your reputation, a bad start."

"But not enough."

She was silent.

"She did not come from a bad family, in the less ambitious sense of the word 'bad.' She was, I think, attached to it, and in some fashion, she has begun to build a replacement for it. She has gathered—and gods help me, I have allowed it—some handful of children her own age; like she, herself, they are without family.

"And one of these children, the demons kept. She is . . . unpleasant in most ways. I would not have allowed her through my door in any other circumstance."

"And you allowed it because?"

He said nothing for a long moment, and then lifted his head, which had sunk into his hands, supported by the bend of elbows against arm-rests. "I don't know. I have asked myself little else these last few days, and there is *no* answer that I find satisfactory."

"The girl whose name you fail to mention; the girl the demons kept—"

"She rescued her, yes. She rescued them all."

"With help?"

"With help, yes; she's not yet eleven—" He stopped. "Even that, I would not have done a year ago; if you had asked me, if you asked it now, I would tell you I *would not* do it."

"You begin to understand the lack of efficacy of such spells as I have cast. If it helps, Ararath, I would have believed it had you said it. You have the air of a man who is uncomfortable with entanglement and responsibil-ity. And yet you are here, and against your better judgment.

"And the girl is there. Against your better judgment. This says some-thing about your judgment. Why this orphan, this other girl?"

He met her gaze, held it, and thought—for a brief moment—that his life was not worth the only answer he now suspected she would accept. Had his life depended on it, he would have sworn that he would accept death before speaking; that was the way of supposition. He faced death—and if it was a clean death, it was still death.

He was old, he thought, and bitter. He had pride—had always had pride—to shore him up and sustain him through all the long years after

424 ✦ Michelle West

the shattering of the only thing, short of his own life, that had mattered to him.

And he understood, as he watched Sigurne Mellifas, that that period of his life had come abruptly to an end. He had not made the choice, not consciously; he had simply reacted to something that he had chosen not to fully understand. That safety was gone, now: He understood, clearly, his own marked hesitations, his own foolishness, his own inexplicable decisions. Saw that she understood it as well.

"She is like my sister," he said, the words cold and curt. "Like my sister was before she betrayed and deserted us."

"And do you now hope to guide her so that she will be something other than your sister has become?"

He could not answer the question. He rose instead, propelling himself out of his chair as if its spindles were the bars of a cage that was slowly closing around him, too small, too confining. A different type of death.

"I will not answer any further questions about this," he said, in the same brittle voice.

She waited for a full moment, and then slowly inclined her head; her eyes seemed silver in the light, the way that polished blades seemed silver. "What, then, will you do about the other girl, the darkling child?"

"I had not decided, Member Mellifas. But I will tell you this much: she sent—" He almost used Jewel's name. Almost. "The other girl to me with the names of her tormentors, and asked only that she be allowed to kill them."

"Who asked it, Ararath?"

He lifted a hand. "And I," he said, not answering, "am left with the decision of whether or not to allow it. If I can be considered a vengeful man, my vengeance has taken the form of absence; it is seldom bent toward killing. But I have not suffered what this girl suffered, and perhaps, by killing, she will be free."

"If you believed this, you would not have come."

He nodded. "I don't believe it." This was neutral.

"And the other child?"

"I don't know what she believes." Rath began to pace the perimeter of the tower, forgetting one fear—the familiar, the old fear for survival—under the shadow of one less familiar, and far less welcome. "She understands that the girl is—what she is. The girl has made no lie of it, and even if she tried, it would fail utterly.

"But she is willing to *ask* it. She is willing to come to *me* and speak of murder on behalf of this foundling, this feral girl."

"And you do not trust your own child—forgive me, but as you will not use names, I will choose attribution of my own devising—to withstand the temptation of such an action? You believe that your child will turn to murder, in the end, as a solution?"

Rath was silent, grimly silent. He tilted his head up toward the ceiling, so that he might have no sight of her eyes, her watchfulness; so that he might see no unwelcome change of expression.

"I believe," he said quietly, "that my sister, in her war for her House, had many men and women killed. That she knew they must die, and that she—like you, yourself—was worthy to be judge of who, of how." The words escaped him, all the words, twisted, bitter, and utterly true. He had hated her for years for abandoning their line, but he had never stopped believing in her. He faced that fact, and had it been something as simple as a mirror, he would have shattered it with a fist.

Nothing was ever to be that simple again. "I believe that my child—as you call her—understands, at a remove, the *need* for this. The need to have someone who *can* kill, when killing is required.

"I do not believe she will ever desire death or suffering. But she will accept its necessity in time. And I came to you because I wanted to know that the girl for whom she *will* accept this truth, this knowledge, is not somehow cursed or controlled by demons.

"And perhaps you have given me the answer to that question, and in the end, it is no answer."

"Then let me give you a different answer. The demons do what they can to twist a life; it is the only measure of permanence they are allowed. What they destroy—if they can—they color for lifetimes. But theirs is not the only hand that can be so lifted. We are not divine, Ararath, and we are none of us without flaws; we cannot see at the outset where the path we walk will bring us, no matter how neatly we plan, how cleverly we lay out stones."

"And you think that my—that the child is somehow poised to push back the darkness? When she can accept it?"

The look she gave him was oddly gentle. "She accepts what *is*," she told him. "But she is young, and I think she is not without ambition, even if it does not wear a shape you recognize. She understands that all things that live can change, and believes—in the arrogance of youth—that that change might be affected in this darkling child you so fear.

"But it is not of your child that I spoke, Ararath. I will not keep you here longer. I am satisfied, for the moment, with what you have said. And troubled by it, as well; I fear that we are not looking for a single mage, but many. If fate is kind, you will have no cause to use the daggers placed in your care." She rose. "But you must make peace with your past, Ararath."

He watched her go, aware that in his past, there was no peace to be found. Aware, now, how much of his past haunted him, like a baleful shade, an inimical ghost.

Jewel.

Amarais.

Chapter Twenty

IT SNOWED IN THE CITY. Across the whole of the hundred holdings, rich and poor alike were greeted with the cold ice of winds laden
with frozen water. Streets were made new, white, pristine; buildings were
adorned, from roof to street, with inches of brilliance. At a remove, the
City had been made, overnight, one thing: cold, pure.

To Jewel Markess, waking to an oddly transformed patch of light, cold
made itself felt; she rose, her feet bare against floors that had never felt so
bitter. Finch was curled into a sideways ball, adorned by blankets that had
never been meant to fend off this deep a chill. To Jewel's surprise, Duster
also slept. She slept with her hand curled round the hilt of a dagger, but
her breath was deep and even. Almost, she looked content.

Jewel's breath hung a moment in the air. She looked at the small,
forlorn box in which all her money lay, no doubt now painful to the
touch; she would have to buy blankets—if blankets could be had for a
decent price. Merchants were famed for their ability to profit from the
unexpected—and in Averalaan, snow was *always* unexpected. Maybe once
in six, even eight years, it fell, bracketed on either side by the rain that
made ships stay in harbor.

She made her way to that box, moving completely silently. She'd been
in this place long enough to know which boards creaked, and which only
groaned, and she chose her steps with agonizing care.

And yes, damn it, the money was like ice. She picked through it; there
was a lot there. If it wasn't spent.

Rath had chosen this place for a variety of reasons, but the one that most interested Jewel at the moment was the wood stove. Her family had owned such a stove—or rather, the apartment in which Jewel had spent the longest part of her life had—and although it had been used sparingly, at such a time as this, it *would* have been used. Her Oma had despised the cold; it reminded her that her home was no longer in the South of her distant birth.

Given what she had often said about her home, Jewel wondered why the reminder would be so bitter. She had never been allowed to ask.

Nor had she been encouraged to ask about the price of wood, and the cost, to the family, of spending money on wood when so much else was needed. Bitter choices, her Oma had said, made stronger people. In Jewel's opinion, it also made for broken people. Her mother and father had hoped to spare her the truth; her Oma had cursed them all for fools. *Because the girl has to learn,* she said, could still be heard saying, *and if those that love her don't teach her, who will? She'll have to make decisions far worse than this in her time, and she'd better start now.*

But then, the weight of all decision had been borne by her parents. Now? Rath, if he was not still angry. Jewel, if he was. Perhaps both.

She opened the door; it was stuck.

On Lefty's foot.

She heard his bark of pain, and the door—which, admittedly, she'd put most of her weight behind—flew wide, bumping into Arann. Who grunted.

Carver, on the other hand, had either the grace or wit to be standing in the narrow arch between hall and kitchen; he was uninjured enough to find it all funny.

"What," she asked, as she carefully shut the door at her back, "are you doing?"

"Waiting for you," Carver replied. "We thought it likely you'd head out to the Common today, and we wanted to join you. You'll need help," he added, glancing at Arann.

She started to argue—out of habit—but her thoughts caught up with her tongue and she shrugged instead. "I don't know what we'll find," she told them all. "If the snow's been heavy, we won't find much; the wagons won't pass the gates."

Carver lifted a brow in Arann's direction. "I told you," he said nonchalantly.

"You knew it would snow," Arann said, when Jewel turned her glare on them both.

"I knew it would snow *sometime*. I didn't expect it this morning. If I had, I would have bought everything already." She paused. "It *did* snow, didn't it?"

Lefty nodded. "It's still snowing," he told her. "You can come and see it, if you want. We've been out a bit. Streets are real empty; if it weren't cold, it would be pretty."

"But it is cold," she said quietly. "And pretty, in this case, is death."

"He knows that," Arann said, with the extra heat he reserved for defending Lefty. He'd been more prone to show it, this last week. Jewel looked at her closed bedroom door, and made a decision. It would be good to be out of the house, with these three. Living with Duster was like living in a special cage. She felt it most when Duster was anywhere near Lefty.

She nodded. "I know he knows. I was just talking Oma talk. Is that *all* you're going to wear?" she added.

Arann smiled, the tension easing off his face. "I told you, we already went out for a bit. Our stuff's by the door on the chair. Or under it," he added, looking at their feet.

"Is Rath awake?"

"Who can tell? We can't even tell if he's in."

She nodded. "That would be no. Or as good as no." Just a brief hesitation.

"You want to leave Duster here if Rath's not?" *And thank you, Carver,* she thought grimly, *for putting that thought into words.*

"She's going to be here one way or the other," she said quietly. "Might as well begin as we mean to continue." She put a hand on Arann's arm. "I know it's hard," she told him. "But bear it. It'll get better, if she stays."

"If?"

"I'm not sure she will," Jewel replied. And this, the moment she said it, was true. "But if she leaves with the money, I don't think Rath will hold it against us for too long. If she leaves with *his* stuff, we won't be alive for long enough to regret it. Come on; it's not going to get any warmer."

"Well, if there's sun—" Lefty began.

She cuffed the side of his head gently.

It wasn't windy. The cold was no surprise, but the lack of wind in the early morning made the City seemed a hushed, new thing, adorned in a blanket of white. Chipped paint, warped wood, broken boards—all of these things were blessed by snowfall, forgiven the signs of age and decay; they were, and could be, forgotten for a moment.

Jewel's breath came out in a dense cloud that hovered above her head; it was joined by Arann's, Lefty's, Carver's. They stood a moment in the open door, staring; it was Lefty who moved them, leading them in a sudden whoop of high delight into the streets, his boots leaving the prints that the falling snow would soon hide.

For snow *was* falling, but driven as it was by no wind, it fell like a drift of soft, cold fluff. Jewel reached out with her hand, and then, casting off the shadows, with her tongue, her face turned toward the sky. Snow melted across her cheeks, clinging last to lashes; she heard Arann's muffled shout, and turned to look at his face. More snow adorned it, and Lefty was off in the street, bending unmindful of his knees to scoop it, pack it.

"I'm only laughing until it hits me," she shouted, shoving her hands into her pockets.

"You're not laughing," Carver pointed out.

"Well, no. Standing too close to Arann."

Arann snorted; mist, like dragon's breath, fled his mouth and nostrils. He bent himself, and picked up a handful of snow.

"You're not going to throw that at a cripple?" Lefty shouted.

"No," Arann replied, his smile slightly lopsided. "I'm aiming at *you.*" And he did.

To Jewel's surprise, Lefty's was the better aim. And Lefty danced back and forth across the snow, moving the group who followed his leaps and little rushes away from Rath's place. Their place. She was almost silent in her astonishment, for here, Lefty was transformed. By snow, still falling.

They must know, she thought. *How deadly it is. How many people it will kill.*

But if they knew it, it didn't matter; they found a gift in its presence that fear didn't dislodge or dampen. It was snow, she thought. Winter. And even falling, it was peaceful.

Carver bent. He came up with snow, with a smile not unlike Arann's, and he sent a ball of white in an arc through the air. It was a slow, lazy arc, and Lefty avoided it with ease. *Both hands in play,* she thought, and realized that she so seldom saw him use *both* of his hands. *When was the last time? With Lander.*

But the weight of Lander's isolation had left him; the concentration with which he sat by Lander's side, hour by hour, speaking in silence with the deft, swift movement of hands, no longer weighed him down. He seemed younger.

Stronger, somehow, for the youth.

It helped that the streets weren't so crowded; there was no one to run into, no one to run away from, except each other. She wanted to join them, but damn it, the snow was *cold*.

Still she watched, and laughed, and walked.

When it came, it caught her by surprise; it was like a physical blow. She buckled at the knees, and Arann, walking by her side, stopped, catching her shoulders before she could fall. She shook him off, covering her eyes against the glare of sun on snow. Breath was shallow, uneven; her cheeks were wet.

Just like that.

"Jay?" Arann asked. Not more than that, just her name.

Lefty caught Arann's sleeve and shook his head. This much she saw without seeing, shadows and habit blending into something just shy of certain knowledge. "Let her think," Lefty said quietly.

"Let her see," Carver added.

They knew. They waited quietly, while she struggled to breathe. Wiping her eyes with the back of her hand, she straightened slowly.

"Jay?" Carver, this time.

She said, "We need to take a slight detour on the way to the market."

"How slight?"

"I don't know."

"Now?"

"Now or never," she replied.

"You lead," Carver told her, his hand falling to the hilt of his barely visible dagger. "We'll follow."

"I don't think we need to worry about fighting," she replied, glaring his hand off the hilt.

"What do we need to worry about?"

"Snow," she said bitterly. "Cold. The normal things."

The silence was broken by Lefty. "But, Jay," he said quietly, "You're crying."

She would have slapped him if she could; her Oma had not been a woman who could abide the sight of tears, and for this reason, Jewel had learned not to cry where anyone else would see her. But she held her hand, held her temper, and looked at his face.

"Not my tears," she said at last.

"Whose are they?"

"Don't know. His."

"Should we go back for Finch? If—"

"No. If we get Finch, we might get—"

"Duster."

"Duster," Jewel said heavily. "And Duster—wrong person. For now. We'll do this without. I'll have to be more Finch-like."

Carver coughed. Lefty surprised Jewel by kicking him.

But she felt it now; the cold, the terror of it, the anonymity of white changing streets and the shape of the City seen at dawn.

"Who are we looking for?"

"You'll know," she said curtly. "You'll know, one way or the other." She should have given a better answer, but she didn't have one. She expected only that she would know, and that had always been enough for her. In a very short time, it had become enough for these three.

Fear didn't lessen the cold. Fear that remained unnamed made it worse. She had no specific vision to guide her; this was visceral, a thing of gut and emotion, unadorned by external reality. Had she had so little to go on, she would never have been able to save Finch's life. But Finch had been days away; this was *now*. The imperative needed no images, and no thought.

She followed streets made unfamiliar, and all play, all joy, was buried, like the city itself. Behind her, beside her, white clouds of mist flitting past from their open mouths, ran Arann and Carver and Lefty. Snow was both blessing and bane; at no time of day was it usually safe to charge headlong through these streets, this holding.

But safety was not a concern, couldn't be—there wasn't room for it. Someone was running through these streets the same way she was—but dressed so poorly for them, his feet had passed over the bridge between pain and numbness. He didn't notice. Jewel did.

She had to. She *had* to. She was Jewel. The stranger—the boy?—was not. His fear was overwhelming, and hers couldn't be. Couldn't be allowed to become so. Different fear, she told herself. She wasn't running through the streets in growing terror. She wasn't searching for—

The dead.

Arann skidded to a stop, snow spraying airward in his sudden halt. Carver stumbled. "Jay?" Urgent question.

"He's lost," she whispered. Hard, to whisper or to speak, her throat felt so thick.

"We're not much better," Carver told her, looking around him at the tall buildings that were wedged together in narrow peaks, like a man-made gully.

But Arann said only, "What is he looking for, Jay?"

And she answered before she could think of finding different words. "His mother."

Lefty and Arann exchanged a glance. They left it to Carver to ask. "She's dead?"

Jewel nodded.

"He knows?"

She shook her head. "Not yet," she whispered. "Not for sure." She felt so cold it seemed strange to see mist rise from her lips. "But he'll know. We have to find him," she added.

"We got that."

She hadn't run like this when she had lost her Oma, or her mother. She hadn't run like this when she had faced her father's death, her last link to family and the bloodline that her Oma had placed all trust and faith in. She had felt the fear, but it was a fear that was imbued with certainty. No hope was in it; no room for hope. She had *known*. Her father was dead.

She had waited. She hadn't run like this. She'd had a lifetime to get used to knowing.

When her Oma had passed away, her life had become so silent. Not even her mother's tears could be heard, although they could be seen, touched, and even tasted. Her father had been absent, away at work—because work wouldn't wait and it didn't come often enough.

"She's gone to join your grandfather," Jewel's mother had said, rubbing her eyes with the mound of her palms, spreading her tears, with dirt, across her cheeks. Those cheeks, lined, had been pale.

Jewel had been six. Or seven. It was hard to tell; hard to mark the passage of time by something as singular and final as death. That would come later.

"How can you tell?" she had asked.

Her mother said nothing, holding her grandmother's hands. Those hands had shrunk and dwindled with the passage of time. It was the High

City fashion to be slender, but in the streets of the hundred holdings, and especially in the poorest of those holdings, it was a mark of poverty and hunger.

Her mother struggled for an answer. Jewel recognized the expression; her mother's words were heated, but unlike Oma's and her father's, they were few, and chained to the service of the practical. Not for Jewel's mother the flights of fancy, the lively delight of the old, grim stories that her grandmother had so relished; not for her mother the steady, fanciful optimism of her husband.

After a while, she said, "I just know it, that's all."

And Jewel, tainted by the gift and the curse of the foresight her grandmother had called thunder and lightning, saw nothing, knew nothing, except this: her Oma was gone. She would not smoke a pipe or sit in the corner chair again, would never offer her lap, her stories, her bitter advice. That she would never again raise her hand in anger was no comfort.

The apartment was quiet when they had at last taken her body away. Jewel had never asked where it had gone.

She *knew* that it was consigned to flame; that there was marker and no grave. And she knew why. They were poor.

One day, she vowed, but quietly, that would all change. She would be rich. She would have money. She would buy a big house—on the Isle—and everyone she loved could live there with her, even if they were poor.

This boy, this stranger, this *impulse* who had as yet no face, no name, nothing but a growing frenzy too strong to be simple worry, was poor. Poorer, Jewel was suddenly certain, than even her family had been. She could almost see him, for a minute; could almost see his home, small and narrow, defined as it was by only one other person.

He wasn't Jewel. He couldn't be certain his mother was dead. There was hope, but it was a hope of dread, of terror. There were some certainties that were almost more than she could bear, but she understood at this moment that uncertainty was worse.

And in the Winter, with death hovering in the air, it was a bitter gift, and came wrapped in memory. She accepted the memory; it was strong and it kept the cold at bay.

The first time:

"Mommy?"

Jewel's mother had stopped beneath the huge bower of the ancient trees that lined the Common. Her basket half-full, she had frowned, turning to the side to let people pass her by. The trees provided some cover, but in truth, not much; it was a market day, and while there was sun, there would be crowds.

Her mother's frown had deepened. "Jewel, what is it now?"

Jewel pointed. "The dog," she said. "The dog will get hit by the wagon."

Her mother looked, and failed to see, the white dog across the crowded thoroughfare. Market flags flew above the crowd, and the crowd moved, one long, loud mix of color, voice, height. "There's no dog," she said at last, grabbing her daughter's hand and holding it too tightly. "And if we don't get to the farmer's stall soon, all of the good vegetables will be gone, and we'll be left with the spoiled." No need to add what would happen in that case.

But Jewel looked over her shoulder, seeing the white flash of fur, the triangular head, the big, dumb, friendly face of the old dog. "He's there," she said, pulling against her mother's hand.

"Jewel, I can't see a dog, and even if it's there, there *is no wagon*. Now come." She had dragged her daughter from the shade of towering trees and into the crowd, holding her carefully, balancing the weight of one hand against the weight of the other, basket laden with some of the food they depended on.

On the walk back to their apartment, Jewel saw the dog again. Across his body, in furrows, the long mark of wagon wheels.

Her mother saw him this time as well. She looked at her daughter's face, her own pinched with worry. "Don't," she whispered, as Jewel tried to free her hand. "It's too late."

"But—"

And her mother shook her head again. "I told your Oma," she whispered, shaking her daughter's hand. "Do *not* speak of this," she told Jewel in a louder voice. "Never speak of this. They'll call you bad names, here. They'll blame it on you. They'll say you caused it."

But Jewel knew she hadn't.

She just hadn't been able to *stop* it.

Not the first time that she'd failed. Not the last time that she'd tried. But that one stayed with her, like a scar. Her Oma had had scars. On her wrists, on her arms, one on the side of her neck. They fascinated Jewel; they were always white, even when her Oma's skin was at its most sun-dark.

Her Oma, smoke spraying from the corner of her mouth, had snorted. "These? Feh. These aren't scars," she told her granddaughter. "They're marks, that's all."

"But how did you *get* them?"

"How does anyone?" But the old woman had lifted her wrists to the light, and her expression shifted, the way it sometimes did when she was about to tell a story. "These," she told Jewel, "are for the Lady."

"The Lady?"

"Aye. In the South, we call the Lady. In the North, you call the Mother. They're almost the same." She shrugged. Inhaled acrid smoke and closed her eyes. "Sometimes if we bleed—if we *choose* to bleed—it's enough. We offer the Lady our thanks that way. For life," she added. "For our lives."

"But the scars—"

"You'll learn, girl. These *aren't* scars. They're nothing. The scars you carry with you? The ones that never leave? They're all in here." She'd tapped her chest. "Regret," she said softly, "for the things you didn't do. Or the things you couldn't do. They haunt you enough, and you see things like this," and she put her hand to her neck, "and they mean nothing."

"What things do you regret?"

But smoke answered; smoke and silence. The old woman had finally smiled, but it was a bitter smile. She pulled Jewel into her lap. Held her there.

And Jewel, curious, knew better than to speak. But it frightened her anyway; until that moment, she had always believed that her Oma could do *anything*.

Oh, the boy made it hard to *breathe*. She had never, ever felt vision as strongly as this; it was as if they were joined by experience—by lack of experience—and nothing would separate them. She was weeping, and she was not; she was breathing too heavily, too shallowly, for the running. Her legs were numb with cold, her feet worse; the shadows the sun cast, short, were all that she could see.

When her mother had passed away, Jewel had been older, but not by much. The air in the room had been cold and damp; the windows, open to Winter, let in the sounds of the street below. The room was close to the market.

Her father, unemployed now that the port was closed, had been with her mother, with them both. He was grave and silent.

"Will she go to see Oma?" Jewel had asked him.

He had nodded quietly. "Oma," he said, "and her brothers."

Jewel had never met the mythical uncles of whom her mother had so infrequently spoken.

"How do you know?" she had whispered. She couldn't talk in more than a whisper; the Winter fog was in her throat and chest, and her breath was weak, a rasp. Her mother's had been like this, but worse.

He placed a hand on her head, pushing aside dark curls; he left it there, as if she were an anchor. "Mandaros," he said quietly, "is the god who sits in judgment, and he loves his people."

"Who are his people?"

"The dead, Jewel. He lives in halls so large that the entire City could be built between the first columns, and he sits on a throne that can be seen for miles."

"Like *Averalaan Aramarelas?*"

"Like the High City, yes."

"Is it beautiful?"

"It is beautiful," he told her quietly. "But sometimes it is very far away."

"As far away as the High City?"

"For us? As far," he said. He smiled. It was not a happy smile. His hair was wild, fringed in white, his cheeks hollow. Cold Winter, and lean. His sweater was threadbare. Oma had done all the knitting, all the mending, and all the scolding for the family, and when she had died? Her mother had tried.

"For some of us," he continued softly, "the throne is so far it takes years and years to reach. We walk," he added, ruffling her hair, "and sometimes we run. But it is distant, that throne."

"And the god?"

"He waits."

"Is he angry?"

Her father shook his head. "He is seldom angry, Jewel. He is often sad."

"Will he be sad for Momma?"

"He will be sad for you," he told her. "And for me. But not for Momma. She was very tired."

"Did he take her away?"

"No."

"Will he keep her there?"

"He will let her stay by his side for as long as she wants," he replied.

"Will she wait for you?"

His brows drew close together. He paused a moment, and then said, "She will wait for you."

"Why?"

"How could she not? She will miss you, and even if she can never come back to you here, there's a place where you'll meet her again. You have to be good," he added.

"I was good. But she died anyway."

He said nothing to that. Nothing at all.

Jewel had never seen a ghost, and she didn't believe in them. Her father hadn't either. Her Oma had—but her Oma's voice was still, this day. Still, cold, distant; death had silenced her. Jewel wanted to believe in ghosts. Even angry ones. She had seen all of her family angry at one time or another, and if she hadn't enjoyed it—and she hadn't—it would still be better than this: silence.

She had lived with her father for years. He had struggled to teach her what he thought she should know: How to read. How to write. How to count, how to meld one number into another, as if they were liquid. He spoke sometimes in Torra, her mother's tongue, and sometimes in Weston.

It was hard, to be alone.

She learned to cook, and to mend, where it was possible. She learned to keep the room clean, for when her father returned from his day's work. She learned many things, in this place. The names of the gods. The names of the days, so like the gods; the names of the months, so different, that passed, one after another, in slow concert. This was time.

But as the years passed, she learned that there were things her father could not teach her; things he feared to speak about. Her strange vision was one of those things. Only Oma had listened, had cared to listen. Only Oma had given her advice when it could be offered, and even Jewel's mother had been uncomfortable when she did—but no one argued with Oma. Not and won.

The sight came and went, like seasons, but less predictable. She learned not to speak of it; not to her father, not to anyone. She learned to keep things hidden, to keep them secret.

Five days before her father died, she *knew*.

She sat in bed crying, disconsolate, and her father had come to her side; they shared the room, after all. It was only a few steps. He was not sick, not as Oma had been, not as her mother had been.

Her father had taken her in his arms, drawn her up across his lap, found a place for her beneath his chin, although she was ten, and too large to fit easily. She had babbled into his chest, and he had cradled her, rocked her, whispered into her hair. About nightmares. About fear.

She had tried to tell him. That she *knew*. What she knew. He had both listened and failed to listen.

He is a man, her Oma's memory whispered. *He's not one of us; he can't be. He is not a bad man, but he is not a woman.* And because he wasn't, she knew that he would hear nothing.

Jewel knew how to count. And she counted the bitter passage of days. She cooked for her father, and cleaned, and wept; she begged him not to go to work. But the words were poor words, and useless. *It's just one day,* she said. *If I miss one day,* he told her quietly, *they'll find someone else to take my place. Hush. If it's death, it's a faster death than starving.* Work was life, in the twenty-fifth holding.

It's death, she tried to tell him, and when she met his gaze on that last day, when she ran to him, hugged him, squeezed the words out of his lips, she thought he *must* know.

But he kissed the top of her head, disentangled himself, and left her anyway.

She had waited in the cavernous, empty room, the table clean, the floor clean, her few possessions gathered on the far corner of her bed in disarray. She had slate, and some chalk; she had clothing, three days' worth, before it had to be beaten with stone and soap. Food? Not much. And no money.

The knock came at the door. She rose to answer it.

A tall man stood in the frame, hat in hands, his face grave. "Jewel Markess?" he said. Her whole name. She looked up, and up again, until she saw the end of his beard.

She nodded. She didn't ask him to come in, because she knew he wouldn't. She'd seen it, seen this.

"I'm sorry, lass," he said, bending, his broad shoulders folding slightly, his beard drawing closer. "There was an accident at the port. A timber beam fell."

He must have thought her cold, uncaring. She had nodded, but she hadn't said a word. She'd listened, but the words had already been said, already been heard.

She didn't ask about the money. He gave it to her anyway; three days' pay. Her father's. This man, bearded, tall, was a good man; he could have kept the money.

But he looked beyond her into the empty room, and his face twisted. He mumbled something. Gave her an address. Told her to come to him if she were ever in need. They weren't empty words. Not yet.

But they would be, come Winter. He was married, and he had several children. She waited for him to leave, and after the door closed, she looked back.

Thinking about the sounds that she had once heard, here. The things she had seen. The people she had touched, and the people who had loved her. Everything was gone; soon enough, the room would be gone, too, home to another family, a larger one. Home to people who could pay the rent.

And Jewel?

She ran to the windows, threw them wide, looked down into the streets below. They were busy; carts and wagons rolled past, men and women shouted at each other, children played in the lee of the building opposite hers.

If she had a home, it was there.

She didn't weep; she didn't cry; she didn't pray. She just watched people pass by, as if this were any other day, as if her father had not died across the distant city, within sight of *Averalaan Aramarelas*. After some time had passed, the shadows growing, the sunlight fading, she returned to her bed and began to pack the things she owned into a sack.

Then she found the other items that she thought she might need: old needles, half-balls of carded wool in the least expensive of colors, the single-edged knife that her father had used for carving when the Winter was cold. She bound these in cloth, depositing them with care into her sack. Last, she took a box, her father's box, from its hidden place beneath the false bottom of a dresser drawer. Old and tarnished, it had become the center of their lives in many ways; it was where he put the coin he earned.

She opened the lid with care, and put three days' worth of pay into the hollow, dark interior.

He'd taught her well enough; she knew just how far that would get her.

What was the point of knowing? Of seeing things before they happened? She hated the vision, the helplessness that came with it, the utter failure that marked her whenever it came. Why had she been cursed this way?

And yet, she had an answer, now, in the streets of this holding, her father—her whole family—nothing more than memories, some bitter and some sweet. No one listened to a child. No one heard what a child said clearly. No one but other children.

And Rath, maybe.

Her Oma was gone, and her mother, and her father, all of whom would have stopped her from her headlong flight into Winter streets. They would have held her back, held onto her, kept her safe from the cold and the danger.

She missed them bitterly. She missed the safety of their arms, the warmth of their stories, even the heat of their anger, the bitter sting of their worry.

And yet . . .

She didn't. Because the safety they offered had been a type of cage, and she understood that now. The cage came with love, was born of it, but in the end—in the end, had she still been under its lock and key, Finch would be dead, and Rath would be dead and Arann and Lefty, and Lander, Fisher, Jester. Duster would be something else, and might still become that.

And this boy?

She *knew* his fear. Felt it as if it were her own because it *was* her own. He spoke to her, wordlessly, and she, unable to speak in kind, spoke in a different fashion, running faster and faster as his fear peaked, as it shifted, as it grew so damn big he could no longer contain it.

It would devour him. It had already begun.

She cried out, she couldn't help herself; what he couldn't contain, she didn't even try. She stumbled in the snow, her hands plunging through it to the hard, frozen dirt beneath. She tasted it, felt it melt against her hot cheeks, her warm skin.

Arann was there in an instant, and he hauled her to her feet as if she weighed no more than Lefty. Carver waited in silence, and Lefty stared at her as if—as if this were normal.

Quiet, succinct, he said, "He found her body."

Jewel swallowed and nodded. It was true. He had.

They didn't ask her why.

Why this boy? Why this one? She had no time to think it, although she knew—who better?—that there would be many deaths in the city over the next few days. She couldn't save them all. It had never truly occurred to her to try.

And how did the gift—the cursed gift—choose?

Like this, instinct and more driving her, herding her, taking her through twisting lanes of the oldest part of the City. Tears had frozen, had stopped; everything had stopped. The world had ended.

She made no noise because he made no noise. It was trapped inside him, as if, by silence, he could stave off knowledge. She stopped a moment, hand against a wall that was leaning at an awkward angle. Cold wall, snow running between her fingers like a winter web.

Lefty caught her elbow. Arann caught her shoulders.

She started to speak, but Lefty spoke instead—in silence, in the language of hands and fingers dancing across palms. As if she were Lander.

And as if she were Lander, watching his hands, his missing fingers some part of their movement, she understood what he was saying, and she swallowed. She could breathe now.

She had found him.

But as she turned the last corner, as she came shoulder to almost-shoulder with Carver, it was almost too much.

He was a boy. Smaller, she thought, than Finch. Possibly younger, it was hard to tell. His eyes were ringed with dark circles, his hair darker with snow, wet and flat against his unadorned head. No hat, of course. No heavy sweater. She couldn't see his feet, couldn't tell if there was anything between his soles and the snow.

But she could see that he was struggling with a burden several times larger than he; that he was trying to *pull* that burden across the snow, toward the mouth of the alley in which they all stood in silence, bearing witness.

He looked up as he approached them, struggling, pulling. She met his eyes, thought of them ever after as a brown so dark it was almost black. He did not let go of his burden.

His mother.

And Jewel found herself kneeling in the snow. She didn't know what had killed his mother; whether it was the cold or something else was impossible to tell at this distance. Nor was it important; it was fact, it was the past.

The present was here.

She held out a hand to him, both hands, palms out to show that they were empty. She might have approached a starving or injured dog in the same way, but it was the only way she knew *to* approach; she was afraid he would startle, or run, and if he did—he would be lost.

Lost to snow, an orphan among orphans.

She said, distinctly, forcing her breath to even out, "My name is Jay. These are my friends. We've come to help you."

He stared at her as if she were speaking a foreign language. And she was; she was speaking in Torra. Her Oma's tongue. The language of comfort and disapproval. She shifted into Weston, spoke again, slowly.

He said, "My mother's not well. She has to go home."

No one spoke.

He knew now. He had to know. But knowing something wasn't the same as accepting it; never had been. This boy—she shook her head. Lifted it, made certain he could see her eyes as clearly as she could see his.

She could have asked him what his name was; she didn't. Instead, she said, "If you'll let us, we'll help you. We'll help you take her home." And she turned a pleading gaze on Arann, the only one of her den that might be able to make truth of the statement.

Arann didn't even blink. He nodded, but he approached the boy very slowly, and his hands, as Jewel's, were exposed and empty.

The boy was beyond shivering, and his skin was so white it was almost blue. His hands were bunched in fists, frozen in shape.

Arann knelt, slid his hands and arms into the snow that surrounded the body, and lifted; he tried not to grunt or stagger. He did them all proud. But Carver understood and moved to help him anyway, handing Lefty something as he did.

Lefty held Carver's dagger in his good hand; his maimed hand he had slid into a pocket rather than under his armpit. The boy watched them all, but his gaze was like a trapped butterfly, a frantic moth; it came at last to rest upon the thing that burned.

His mother's face, her open, sightless eyes, her slightly parted lips.

She was stiff with cold, possibly frozen. Jewel knew that you *could* freeze to death, but she had never seen it.

They walked, and the boy walked with them, his hand on his mother's face, or on her arm, the entire way. It took a very long time, and by the end of it, not even Arann could pretend the burden was insignificant. It wasn't so much that she was dead; it was that she was heavy. But heavier by far, he would have still tried; she saw it in his face, and loved him for it, the sharp kind of love that was mixed with pride and pain. He didn't notice; he barely looked at anything but the stranger, the young boy, and his expression had the same unguarded worry that he often showed Lefty's back.

They had missed most of the early market by the time they reached the building the child called home. He led them in. Stopped to speak, and then stopped again; she could almost hear him say: *I have to ask my mother*.

It would have torn out her heart if he had, but she was spared at least that much. She didn't know him yet. She couldn't touch him. But for a moment, she wanted to pull him into her arms and shield him from the simple truth of death. To make it a lie.

And so she came to understand completely how the complicated cage she had lived in almost all of her life was built, just as she had come to understand that it existed at all. She watched him open the door, torn between the two lessons that had been long in coming, and would never leave her.

"She's tired," he said faintly, and led them to the bed that occupied the far wall, stepping across bare, dry boards in an almost empty room. He pulled the single blanket back; the bed itself dipped in the middle as if it would fold beneath weight.

Arann was red with exertion, but silent and steady as he carried his burden the final few steps, and with Carver's help, laid her down. Jewel brushed the snow off as best she could. Saw that the woman's feet were bare.

Wondered what the last words she had spoken to her son had been. Wondered, as well, what the last words her son would speak to her would be.

And found that she didn't need to know, didn't want to. She nodded abruptly to the door, and when Arann and Carver just stood there awkwardly, lifted her hands in an abrupt and clumsy mimicry of Lefty's fluid language: Go out there.

She said, "We'll wait for you." Uncertain that he heard her at all.

They waited for fifteen minutes, standing in a heavy silence that was broken only when Lefty sat and the floor creaked beneath him. Arann sat heavily by his side, and brought his large hands to his face, covering as much of it as he could. Carver stood, watchful, waiting. Jewel began to pace.

"You want to take him home," Lefty said, looking up.

Jewel nodded. No point in lying to Lefty. "He belongs with us," she told them all quietly. Carver nodded, and Arann removed his hands, lifted his head, and looked up at her. His eyes were red, but he wasn't weeping; it might have been exertion that colored his face.

"Why?" Arann asked her.

"He just does."

But the giant shook his head. "Why us?" He gestured at Lefty and Lefty nodded. "Why any of us?"

"I don't know," she whispered. "I just *know*. He belongs with us. And we belong together. We don't have to like it," she added.

"We don't hate it," Carver told her. "But—"

"But?"

"There are so many people *like* us, Jay, we all want to know—why *us?*"

She had never really wondered. She shrugged. "I can't explain it," she told them quietly. "Not to you, not to myself. But I don't worry about explaining things I *know* to me.

"You're there, in the future, you're part of my life, and part of each other's. And we need him." The words were true in a way that dawn was; inevitable, unstoppable.

She was cold and tired, and relief robbed her of the driving force that had carried her this far. "He has nowhere else to go," she added.

They didn't point out that this was true of many, many people, not all of them children. They understood that in some fashion, they'd been chosen.

But so had she; she bore the gift, but she didn't control it, couldn't direct it, couldn't force it to tell her things she needed to know. She could accept it or deny it; she could be helpless or she could act.

And that was true of everything. She squared her shoulders and said, "he's coming now."

The door was still.

But Lefty and Arann stood quickly, backing away from it to give the boy room; the hall was narrow and not at all well lit.

He came, opening the door with one hand, while in the other he held the gathered edges of a patched, thin blanket, a kind of pack. He was white as snow, just as blinding to her eyes, and so small, so frail, she thought he might be Finch's brother. His eyes were red, and his lips were swollen, and he looked gaunt. She had never believed in ghosts, but she could see one in him now.

"I'm Jay," she said quietly. "This is Carver, and this is Arann. The boy behind him is Lefty. None of us—" She stopped. Held out a hand.

He looked at it.

Arann very gently removed his belongings from his hands, and the boy let them go without suspicion or dread; anyone who had carried his mother home could carry anything he owned, anywhere, and he would not question what they meant to do with it.

He slid his cold fingers into hers, and she caught his hand, holding it a little too tightly. "We're going home," she told him. "We have to go to the Common, but we're going home after that." She knew he wouldn't ask.

But he nodded, sagged a moment and closed his eyes.

Chapter Twenty-one

RATH CAME HOME TO a more crowded house. It was, of course, in his nature to notice even the minute changes that occurred within his domicile—or indeed within anyone else's—but even had it not been, he would have been aware instantly that more than just numbers had shifted.

There was a good deal of silence, something he prized and often grew weary of repeating demands for, but it was a layered silence, a thing both born of childhood and yet outside of it. The beginnings of something different.

And there was a new boy.

He was perhaps Finch's size, perhaps smaller; it was hard to tell. He did not have Lefty's obvious skittishness, nor Lander's mute silence; he did not have Jewel's wariness, or Finch's flutter, and if he smiled, it was a quiet smile, unlike the manic and aptly named Jester's. There was absolutely nothing of Carver or Duster in him. Only in Arann, a boy twice his weight, and at odds with his coloring, did there seem to be any kinship; the new boy was quiet.

He was, Rath thought, in shock. But it was a shock that did not displace the ability to observe, or the necessity for it. Rath knew at once that this was another of Jay's orphans, and in this cold and bitter weather, he grudged the addition only slightly.

Jewel looked up when he entered and made a direct line for him, her hand reaching out for his sleeve. He let her grab him and lead him to his room, as if this were natural; he could tell that she was nervous, and had every reason to be. But Rath was weary, and in this act—the saving of this boy—he saw the opposite of the act that now tormented him; this boy was Duster's opposite.

He opened his door and entered, which was difficult because Jewel did not choose to relinquish his arm. Only when the door was shut did she slump, her shoulders folding inward gracelessly.

"You have a new boy," he said quietly, his voice measured and deliberately distant.

She nodded. "You noticed."

"Where did you find this one?"

She shrugged. "Lower holdings," she said at last. And then, when his gaze did not waver, she muttered, "I don't know which one. I just ran."

"You just ran?"

"I—I just ran. To him."

"Another one of your premonitions?"

"My what?"

"Your visions." He paused. "You knew where he was."

"It was different, with Teller."

"Teller?"

"What we'll call him. He doesn't talk much."

"I'm surprised you think he'd have the chance."

She frowned; she was on the edge of an age where teasing of any sort made her prickly. It was why Rath enjoyed it. But he waited. He found himself wanting this story, so different in texture from Duster's, for he had already made his decision, and he didn't like it. He wouldn't change it; he understood that it was, in all ways, a test. But of who, in the end, only time would tell. Time and death, as it so often did in war.

And this was a war, personal, small, but necessary in all the usual ways.

"Why this boy?" he asked quietly, when she looked away.

"I don't know," she replied. He'd expected as much; it was almost always her response at times like this.

"He's not like Duster."

"Nothing like Duster." She hesitated, and then said, "It was different, with Teller, Rath. I didn't so much *see* as *feel* him. We were on our way to the Common. To buy extra blankets, clothing. Stuff."

He nodded.

"Arann, Lefty, Carver. Me. We were most of the way there—and I . . ."

She shook her head. She would have to become more adept with words in the future; they deserted her when she required them, and in the end— but it was not the end, that nebulous future, and it might never come to pass. He held his breath, exhaled. "I am not angry, Jewel."

"Jay."

"Jay, then. I'm not angry that he's here. I surprise even myself with my tolerance."

She didn't smile. She looked . . . surprised. If it were in him, Rath might have taken umbrage. He smiled instead, deliberately adopting a casual expression. "But I'm curious. You said this boy was different."

"The feeling was different," she said. Her brows furrowed as she frowned. Time would etch those lines in place, but when the expression passed, they were gone, as if written upon the surface of moving water. "His mother didn't come home last night. He waited for her. Waited most of the morning. And then he went out searching."

"His mother—"

"We didn't ask," she said, and her voice was so curt, there was command in it. Or warning. She could surprise him in so many ways, he wondered if that wasn't part of her charm. Not all of it, but part. "But, Rath—I felt as if he were part of my future. An important part. I felt as if I *needed* him, somehow."

From Jewel, this was an admission, and perhaps a costly one.

"Needing people," Rath said carefully, "is not a crime."

"You don't."

"And my lack would be considered criminal by many, and has been, Jewel. Do not look to me for an example to follow; it would not suit you. Ever. Be Jewel Markess; allow me to be Old Rath. We are what we are."

"People can change."

"They can. But for me, need *is* a weakness. And for you, Jewel, I believe it is a strength. Do not deprive yourself of the strengths you have."

"You didn't say that about Duster."

"You don't need Duster."

"She's a part of the den."

Den. He stopped himself from smiling, and found that it wasn't hard.

"But yes, he's different. Calmer. Rath—his mother died. He found her body in the snow."

"The others saw this?"

She nodded. "They were with me," she added softly. "They didn't even ask questions; I ran, and they followed. As if I were—" But she didn't continue, and he didn't force the issue.

"She was the only family he had," she added.

"And yet he came home with you."

"Where else was he going to go?" She paused, and then added, "Arann and Carver carried his mother's body home. He put her in her bed and pulled the covers up and waited. He knew she was dead," she added bitterly. "And he didn't scream or weep or wail or—anything. But she was his world," she added.

"And you know this—how?"

"I felt it all, Rath. I—it was—" but she shook her head again. "He was willing to trust me. I don't know why. He was willing to come here."

"You said yourself he has nowhere else to go."

She nodded almost absently. "He can stay?"

"For as long as you do, Jewel, he can stay. But please—no more."

"I promise."

He raised a brow. "It would be wise, Jewel Markess, not to make a vow you cannot keep."

"I—"

"You cannot be certain that you can keep this one. Do not make it. I don't demand it."

"But you do."

"I value my privacy, but you've already destroyed that. No," he added, seeing the shifting lines of her expression, "I destroyed it. And I accept the consequences of my choice. We have between us enough money to see us through the Winter, and beyond that, we will see."

"You haven't gone hunting in the maze again."

He said nothing for long enough that she realized the subject was a closed one. "Go back to your Teller, Jay. And your den. See that they're fed; see that they're warm, or as warm as they can be. He will feel the loss of his mother, and feel it deeply, as the days pass. But in this, you are building a family of sorts, and perhaps that will counter what he feels."

"Rath—"

There was a knock at the door. It was not a timid knock; it was a demand. Because of this, Rath knew who was on the other side. And from the way Jewel stiffened, so did she.

"Answer it," he said curtly.

Duster glared into Rath's inner sanctum. It was not a place that she saw often; in fact, Rath was certain she had not seen it at all. What she expected, he could not say, but he was certain that she noticed everything; all the little details. The papers, the ink, the desk with its closed drawers, the clothing that denoted both rank and its utter lack, strewn across chairs and bedding.

"Duster," Jewel began, "now is not the time—"

"But it is," Rath said quietly. "Duster, please, come in. Do not touch anything, or I will have you removed."

"By who?"

"I don't need aid." His tone made clear that the possibility of fatality was not low.

She was not a child to show fear. She did not surprise him by showing vulnerability either. But her gaze wandered for just a moment to Jewel's before she crossed the threshold, and this surprised him.

She trusts you, he thought. *Even this one trusts you, inasmuch as she can.*

"You may sit, if you desire it. You may also stand." Rath himself took a chair, but Jewel didn't; she sat on the edge of his bed. This caused Duster to tense, but whatever she thought she would see in Jewel's face was utterly absent. Rath would have found her suspicion amusing had it not been so insulting.

Duster stood.

"I have made the inquiries that I agreed to make on Jewel's behalf," he said with care. "And I have reason to believe that the names you were given were, in fact, real names. The men to whom they belong are men of both power and social standing; your presence alone would cause them grave personal difficulty. Do you understand what this means?"

Duster shrugged.

"That is not an answer," he replied coldly.

"They'll want me dead," she said sullenly.

"Good. You understand then that what you propose to do—or what Jewel proposes to do on your behalf—"

"I don't need her help. I just need the places."

"You need me," Jewel said quietly, and with a ferocity that volume should have made impossible. "Or I tell him to shut the Hells up. He won't give you what you want."

"I don't need your *help*—"

"You will need a good deal more than that," Rath broke in quietly. "They are not men who are accustomed to going unescorted anywhere;

even when they visited you, it is likely they had their guards stationed close by."

She said nothing.

"Understand that were you to take your complaint to the Magisterium, it would be treated with the utmost gravity."

She frowned.

"They would treat it—and you—seriously. What these men did is in no way legal."

"They have enough money to buy their way out of trouble."

"Not all the money in the world would do that here," he replied. "If some of the magisterial guards are not above bribes—and human nature dictates that some are not—the god-born are entirely incapable of that mendacity. The men would be summoned, and they would be questioned by those to whom they cannot lie."

Duster said nothing.

"I offer you this alternative. If you want these men stopped—"

"I want to kill them," she replied quietly. "I don't give a damn what they do to other people."

Jewel flinched, but said nothing. And Rath was content with this; let her see Duster clearly, if she had not already done so. But seeing her stiffen, he doubted that Jewel was capable of the self-deception required to see in Duster any charity.

"Very well. I thought that would be your answer, and I am willing, against my better judgment, to aid you as much as I can."

She looked at Jewel again, and then back. "Tell me where," she said.

"Not so quickly," he replied. "I will tell you that I know where three of these men can be found."

"You know where they live."

"Oh, indeed. But that is not where you will find them if you wish to kill them. I will start with whichever of the three you choose. But I will give you the location and relevant information for one man at a time. Not more, and not less. If this does not suit you, you are free to leave to pursue your vengeance in your own way.

"But if you require aid, you will compromise."

Duster glared at him, and Jewel rose, taking Duster's arm just as naturally as she had taken Rath's. Duster started to shrug her off, aware of Rath's observation. But she hesitated. Interesting.

"He's right," Jewel said quietly. "I didn't go through all the trouble of rescuing you to lose you to anger. We need to plan."

"That is exactly what we need to do," Rath told them both. He turned to the headboard of his bed and extracted from a long, narrow ledge a rolled length of paper that, when unfurled, would cover his desk. This he cleared with care, handing the magestone holder to Jewel while he placed weights on the corners.

Duster stared at it for a moment. "What is this?" she asked, almost in spite of herself.

"A map," Jewel told her quietly. "These lines are streets. And these are street names. This is the Merchant Authority," she added, choosing the right building with care. "It's like what you'd see if you were a bird."

Duster tried very hard to look unimpressed, and succeeded well enough that Rath thought there was half a chance it was genuine. But her words undercut her. "And that?" she said, with contempt. "Priest scrawls?"

"I told you," Jay said, her words developing some heat, "that you didn't have to learn to read if you didn't want."

"And let that one-handed gimp lord it over me?"

Jewel's lips compressed into a thin line. This, Rath thought, was interesting. "Rath," she said, her eyes never leaving Duster, "Duster and I need to talk for a minute."

He understood that she was asking for privacy in *his* personal quarters. She must, indeed, be very angry. For all her caution, she had a Southern temper, and burying it hadn't killed it. Although this, too, was interesting, it was less amusing. He did not hesitate, however.

He rose and headed toward the door, hearing the hiss of breath escape Jewel's clenched teeth. He opened the door quickly, and closed it in the same fashion, but not in time not to hear the distinct sound of a slap.

He hesitated now, torn between the desire to protect the orphan he'd dragged away from the banks of the river and its slender roof of bridge, and the desire to let her begin as she must continue. But he knew that he'd kill Duster if she hurt Jewel, and this was too much knowledge.

Children or no, they could play deadly games, and their sense of consequence was not yet profound. In some, it would never be.

Jewel knew that Duster wore a dagger; she also wore a white hand's imprint on her cheek. Jewel's Oma had been quick to anger, and Jewel herself had often felt the sting of that open palm. It hadn't hurt much, not physically, but it was humiliating.

And Duster did not take humiliation lightly.

But Jewel was past caring. She'd found Teller today. Lefty had helped. She'd found Lefty first, and his vulnerability, his utter dependence on Arann, had not yet left him. He'd opened up, in her house; he'd learned to talk and to leave his hand out of the sheath of his armpit. Until Duster had come.

Until, Jewel thought, *she* had brought Duster in.

It was enough. Duster was staring at her in mute and growing anger; her hand had fallen to the hilt of her dagger, clenching it until her knuckles were white.

"There are rules here," Jewel told her quietly. Had to speak quietly; the words that were straining to leave her lips would start a war she couldn't quell. It almost didn't matter. "I want you here," she added, still speaking in measured tones, and choosing her words with painful care. "And I made you a promise I intend to keep. Rath has helped; we couldn't do it without him.

"But you aren't the only person I promised to help. No one else has asked so much," she added, "and I accepted what you asked of me. But Lefty belongs here *as well*, and if you make his life miserable, it doesn't matter how much I think we need you. You're free to go. I won't keep you. I'll give you whatever information Rath is willing to part with. But you go on your own. And you don't come back."

"You think I won't go?" Duster snarled back. "Because it's *cold* and there's *snow* on the ground? You think I'm so desperate I'll suck up to—"

Jewel had lifted her hand; it was bunched in a fist. "I don't care," she said, abandoning quiet. "I don't care if you go. I care about the den, and if you're part of it, you have to care, too."

"No one cared about *me*," Duster shouted, and the knife left its sheath.

Quiet settled into Jewel, or perhaps it spread out from the core; she couldn't say. "I cared," she told Duster. "Enough to go back, to put us all in danger."

"You didn't know me."

"I knew that you saved Finch," was her quiet reply. "How is Finch so much different?"

Duster said nothing for a moment; the dagger didn't waver. But Jewel saw it, understood its presence, and let it be.

"If you saved her to spite your captors, you still saved her. It's not why that counts, Duster. It's what you did. Find that, here."

"They're not here."

"Aren't they? Why are we here, then? Why are we looking at this map, and waiting for Rath? Why are we—"

Duster drove the knife into the tabletop. Rath was going to be so pissed off. But the table was better than the alternative, and Jewel acknowledged this truth in the only way she could.

"You said they thought they could make something out of you, and you didn't like it. I don't know who they were," she added, "but it's pretty damn clear they like pain. Yours, ours, anyone's. You need to spite them? Spite them, then. *Don't* be that person. Don't cause pain." She paused.

"I know you think there always has to be a victim; I know you don't intend it to be you. But Lefty's important to me—to us, Duster—and in this house, there are no victims."

"You don't slap Lefty," Duster said.

"No."

The wild girl smiled almost crookedly. "So even Saint Jay has limits."

"A lot of them," Jewel replied. "But Lefty's been hurt enough, and he doesn't need more of it. Leave him alone. You need to snap? Snap at me. I had an Oma with a tongue sharper than your knife; I can take it."

"But I need you. For now."

"Now," Jewel said, "is all we ever have. I'm going to get Rath," she added.

"He'll be worried about you." The words were a sneer with syllables.

Jewel shrugged. "I worry about him sometimes. It's fair."

She started toward the door, and Duster said, "The new boy."

Jewel stopped.

"Why did you bring him home? He wasn't there. At the house. He didn't—"

"He found his mother's dead body in the snow today," Jewel replied, snow in her voice. "And he would have frozen there with her, trying to get her to move."

Duster said nothing. She didn't snort; she didn't make a gibe.

"Arann carried his mother to their home, and we waited for him. I brought him here because I need him here," she added. "Same as you."

"He's nothing like me."

"No. *I'm* nothing like you. Arann's nothing like you. So what? If we were all the same, I'd only need one of us."

"He's never killed."

"He's never had to."

Silence. Duster tried to remove her knife from its place in the table. And Jewel, aware that she had barely managed to skirt a crisis, said nothing. Nothing more. But whatever she had said was enough for now. Duster needed to hate something. Jewel had found enough of it to hold her, for now.

And now, as she had told Duster, was all they could be certain of.

Rath didn't even acknowledge the exchange when he returned. He looked bored and slightly frustrated. He failed to notice—and this took no little effort—the deep gouge in the table that happened to also coincide with a slash in the delicate map's surface. He wasn't certain what had been said—what could be said—but knew, as he entered the room, that it had been enough.

And it was not his job or his responsibility to add more.

"You are both aware that I spend much of my life cultivating different appearances."

Jewel nodded. Duster nodded as well, but there was an edge in the way she looked, once again, over the contents of his room. "You are both untutored in the art of assuming a different station in life, and this is unfortunate. I am not by nature a patient man, and I am not a teacher. There is a man who taught me much, and I wish you to meet with him. He will explain the art of appearing to be something you are not.

"You will learn everything he is willing to teach," he added quietly. "I am willing to help you in your errand, but I am not willing to send you into a combat unarmed and ignorant."

Duster bristled visibly; Jewel, however, did not.

"He is a somewhat quirky man, and he was never patient. Do *not* play cards with him if he asks. He always cheats; he is never caught."

At this, Duster perked up.

"It is not card tricks that I wish you to learn," Rath added, seeing her expression. "You must be able to pass unseen while being seen by everyone. Wherever it is you will go, you must be both noticed and so much a part of the scenery, no one will actually pay attention.

"The Lords live in manors upon the Isle, and they leave seldom, usually on business affairs. I do not intend," he added darkly, "to cause difficulty in the Merchant Authority; nor do I feel it wise to attempt to accost said lords in alleys in which they would not otherwise travel.

"They are, however, victims of their own proclivities."

"*They're* victims?" Jewel said, almost outraged. The fact that she didn't know what the last word meant escaped her attention.

"Very well, they are fools. Does that suit better?"

She nodded. Duster said nothing.

"You have responsibilities here that are entirely your own, Jewel. When you have seen to your newest arrival, and you have taken the time to purchase the clothing and blankets we require—I have taken the liberty of seeing to wood—I will take you to meet the man who will be your guide."

"What will we tell the others?" Duster asked him.

"You are not so fond of the truth that you are incapable of lying," he replied sweetly. "Come up with a lie that suits you. I should warn you, however, that Jay is famed for her inability to lie; if it comes at all, it must come from you."

Duster said, "You don't like me much, do you?"

"At the moment? No. But things change, and people have been known to change as well. You are not without that ability; you simply lack the desire."

This suited Duster. Had Rath given any other answer, it would have been the wrong one. He knew it, and saw from Jewel's expression—relief—that she knew it as well.

Hate and contempt were things that Duster understood. Jewel and Rath were things she didn't—and she needed some stability.

"I will take a few days to arrange the meeting with my associate," he added, as he nodded vaguely in the direction of the closed door. "In which time, tend to your own."

Things were not exactly lively when they escaped Rath's room, but Duster had lost the look of anger that usually informed her face. Jewel had hit her hard, and the mark lingered like a white accusation against her ruddy skin, but Duster had forgotten it, as if it were nothing.

Jewel was ashamed of herself. And of her temper. It had taken all of her meager self-control to wait until Rath had left the damn room—but not waiting would have been worse, and she knew it.

Finch approached her quietly, as she often did. "He's in our room," she said.

"Our room?"

"There's more room there; the other room is too crowded."

"You don't mind?"

Finch raised a pale brow. "Not more than you do."

Duster said, "I don't give a shit. He's just a kid."

Jewel shrugged. "I don't mind," she told Finch, and only Finch. "Has he eaten anything?"

"Not hardly. But . . ." Her voice trailed off, and fell until it was almost inaudible. "Lefty told us what happened. I didn't want to push him."

Jewel nodded. "What do you think of him?"

"He seems nice," Finch replied with care. "But quiet."

"I think he'll always be quiet. It's when he's not that we'll have to listen."

"He loved his mother," Finch added. And Jewel remembered what had happened to Finch and said nothing. But she touched Finch's shoulder, wanting the contact, or wanting to offer it. Nor did Finch pull away. "He's talking to Lander," she added.

"Talking to him?"

"Well, gesturing at him. Lefty taught him a bit, and he picked it up really quickly. I think Lander likes him."

Jewel nodded quietly. "Lander will talk to us," she told Finch, and knew it for truth. "In his own time, he'll talk."

"Maybe Jester will stop," Duster added, but without much malice. Fires banked, here. It gave Jewel hope. "We have to go to the Common," she added, "before the day is out."

To Teller, the noise was almost overpowering. The rooms were crowded, and the kitchen large compared to his home, but every corner seemed to be filled with something or someone. He wanted to feel lucky; felt, instead, a simple lack of anything but cold. His fingers ached with it, and his chest was tight. He could no longer feel his toes.

He watched them all. Especially Jay, because everyone seemed to look to her for guidance. She was dark-haired, and her hair curled around her face so awkwardly she was constantly shoving it to one side or the other; she was slender and neither tall nor short. Her eyes were dark, and her skin Southern.

And she understood his loss.

He understood hers. He had no way to speak of either, no words for the certainty. But some part of him had been waiting for her in the snow; for her or for the gods. She had come first. His mother had believed in fate, and in the malice of Kalliaris, the goddess of luck. Teller had believed in his mother, and had accepted the way her world worked. This world, however, was new to him.

New, and yet, still his own. Because Jay was here; she had found him, he had followed. He had watched the silent giant carry his mother home. He wouldn't have asked it; couldn't have demanded it—he had no words, not then.

But she had seen it and understood it, and what she asked, they offered. He labored under no illusions; he knew that she could never ask him to do what Arann had done. If he had a place here, it wasn't Arann's place. But he had one; he had to find it, and hold it.

He liked Lefty, although he thought it odd that Lefty spent most of his time with his arm wedged under his armpit. He only stopped that when he spoke with Lander, the mute, pale boy that Jewel had also taken in. Lefty told Teller how Lander had come to be here, and Finch stood by, correcting him gently when she felt he needed it. Fisher could talk, but didn't; it wasn't so much that he was quiet—you knew when he was in the room—as that he didn't feel a need to talk at all. He nodded often, grunted once or twice, ate three times as much as Arann, and kept mostly to himself.

But he was willing to learn what Lefty was willing to teach or share: the movement of hands, the silent language that Lander responded to. Not one of these children had family. Not Jay either, according to Finch.

Carver told him the story of Finch's rescue, and Finch let him talk. When he had finished, Teller said, looking up at Carver from the patch of floor he'd made his seat, "I don't understand one thing."

"What?"

"Why you were there."

Carver shrugged. "I don't understand it either," he said at last.

"But you helped her—in the tavern—you started the fight."

Carver nodded.

"Why?"

"She needed help."

"A lot of people need help," Teller replied quietly.

"She needed help *I* could offer."

Teller nodded at that. It made sense. "What do you do here?"

"Do?"

"What kind of work?"

"Work?"

Finch looked at her feet. They weren't bare. "We do whatever Jay tells us," she said at last. "She's teaching us to read. And to write. Well, most of us. Not Lander, yet. But she says he'll learn."

"She's teaching you to *read*?"

Finch nodded.

Teller felt a peculiar hunger then, the hunger that had entirely escaped him when Finch had offered him food or blankets. "Read what?" he asked carefully.

"She says anything, in the end," Finch told him. "But we're learning letters first. And our names."

"Why?"

Finch shrugged. "Her father taught her, before he died. And Old Rath told her she had to keep learning if she wanted to stay here."

"He's teaching her?"

Finch nodded.

"Why?"

"I don't know. You ask a lot of why."

Teller smiled. "It's the only way I'll understand anything."

"Jay would ask, too. Why," Finch added. "I asked her why. Why she saved me. Why she saved the rest of us."

"What did she say?"

"She didn't. I think if she could, she'd save the whole city, or die try-ing." Finch's eyes were bright, and wide, as she spoke. "And I want to help her," she added, looking down at her slender arms, her orphan hands. "Whatever she wants to do—it can't be bad. And I'd rather help Jewel than do almost anything else. If it means reading, I'll learn to read. If it means fighting, I'll learn to fight."

Teller frowned, and Carver shook his head. "She's been trying to teach Finch and Lefty to fight a bit. Not like soldiers," he added, "but just enough to be able to get away if they have to."

From what? He didn't ask. Enough, to have the questions answered. Enough, because it made him think of something other than his mother. She had died alone, in the cold; he hadn't even *been there*. He couldn't remember if he'd told her he loved her before she'd gone. He couldn't know for sure that she knew it, while she lay in the street dying.

"Teller?"

He smiled and shook his head. "Cold," he said. "Just cold." Winter death in the tone of the words. And Finch didn't ask more. He liked Finch. He liked Carver. And Lefty, so nervous, and yet in his own way so generous; Arann, who stood over Lefty like a shadow or a guardian; Jester who tried so hard to make people laugh, when there was so little to laugh about. Even Fisher, who in his own way tried to make Lander more comfortable.

But Duster scared him.

"So we learn to read?"

"And we go to the market with her, sometimes. We get the water, we help some of the older people. She doesn't ask much, Teller."

And you want her to ask more. Again, he didn't say it. "She will," he told her gently. "From both of us, even us, she will."

"You're not afraid of her?"

He shook his head. "I feel like I've known her forever," he said, meaning it. "I don't know anything about her, but . . ." He shrugged. "I know she wants me here, and that's enough."

Finch nodded. "It's good, this place."

"Crowded," Carver added. But he smiled when he said it, his hair hanging over one eye as he leaned back against the wall. "She's got a bit of a temper."

"And she speaks Torra," Finch added. "Do you?"

"A bit."

"I think—" Finch shook her head. "You'll like it here."

"And what about Duster?"

"Duster saved my life," Finch replied. But her expression was troubled. Teller didn't ask more; Carver's expression had frozen in place. Teller was new here; he would learn. Was determined to learn.

Jay went out with Carver and Arann and Lefty, and when she came back, snow melting in the curls of her hair, she had blankets, clothing, food. The blankets, she handed to Teller. "We don't have beds," she added. "These will have to do for now."

She paused for a minute, and then said quietly, "Kitchen." It was to Teller she spoke, and only to Teller, and the rest understood it; when he rose, they stayed where they were. He followed her. On the scant counter space, she was carving bread that had almost frozen; it was like chipping soft rock. She nodded toward a chair, and he took it, waiting by the table.

"I don't know what they've said about me," she began, back turned toward him as she worked, "and most of it probably isn't true."

He had to smile at that.

"But you should know something if you're going to stay here. You haven't asked me how I found you."

"No."

"Why?"

"When Kalliaris smiles, it's not a good idea to ask why. She might frown instead."

Jewel chuckled. "Good answer. You would have liked my Oma."

He said nothing.

"But you should know that—" she put the knife down with a curse, and he saw she'd cut her finger; saw blood ebb into bread that seemed too frozen to absorb it.

He rose quickly and handed her a towel, and she took it without a word; the cut itself seemed beneath her notice.

"I want to apologize," she said at last, looking down at bloody bread without dismay. "But to do that, I have to explain. Sometimes I know things, Teller."

He waited.

"I just *know* them. I can't predict what I'll know, or when, or even how—but when I know something, it's true."

He nodded.

"I knew you would be there. We were on the way to the Common in the snow. We were playing in it," she added, and her eyes seemed to look beyond the wall, as if it were a window. "And then I—I knew I had to go. To you, to where you were. I knew what you were looking for. I knew you weren't dressed for the cold. You don't have Winter clothing, do you?" She paused when he became motionless. "Not clothing that fits," she added.

He shook his head.

She nodded. "But I didn't know that your mother would die. Only that she was dead. I'm sorry," she whispered.

He understood what she was apologizing for. "You didn't kill her," he said as gently as possible. Older than his years, as his mother had often said.

"No. But I couldn't save her, and if I could—" she held out her palms almost helplessly, one wound in towel. "You would still *have* a mother. You wouldn't have to be here."

"You're apologizing because my mother died?"

"No. Because I couldn't see that in time. Only you."

"Jay—"

"That's all," she added. "I wanted to tell you I'm sorry."

It never occurred to him—then or later—to doubt her. To doubt what she said about her ability to see, or to doubt her regret. He stood, pushing the chair to one side. But he didn't touch her; he had noticed that no one did.

"My mother would have liked you," he told her. "She would have been happy I met you. She would have told you to think about the things you did well, not the things you couldn't do anything about."

"She would?"

He nodded. "It's what she used to tell me." And stopped. The silence stretched out between them. "I was afraid," he said, seeing now through the same wall that Jewel gazed beyond. "That I would never see her again. I was afraid that the world had ended."

She said, "I knew when my father would die."

"I'm sorry."

"It was horrible. The worst thing in my life. Even worse than being *right*." She had begun to knead the towel that bound her cut hand as if it were part of her flesh and she sought to remake it.

He still didn't touch her. But he came to stand closer, to stand within touching distance. "I don't think I want your gift," he said at last. "But if it didn't exist, I think—I think I would be dead. In the snow."

"But you'd be with your mother. At least that's what my mother believed. And my father."

"I'm not ready to be with her yet." Hard to say the words, but in saying them, he found comfort, and not guilt.

"Good," she told him firmly, "because I'm not ready to lose you." She added, turning away, "I feel as if I know you, or have always known you. Or will always know you. I can't see the future—not all of it, and not when I want to. But I know that you're part of it, that you *have* to be part of it. That's why I ran," she added. "That's why you're here."

Only at night did he cry. At night, in a room full of strangers pressed together on the floor. His mother had always gone out when the sun began to set, dressed in what had seemed at first finery, and in the end just pieces of cloth stitched together in such a way that meant she was leaving; as it grew darker, as the sounds of the streets quieted and changed, he was on his own, when all words, good or ill, didn't matter. The walls had listened, and the gods, but neither interfered.

Here, they slept, or pretended to sleep, these strangers and Jay, and no one asked him questions, no one offered him any comfort except the pretence of ignorance. That, and their presense, their silent acceptance. Even their understanding: they were all orphans, in this place. All they had was each other. This was the only privacy the den would ever offer, and he accepted it, as he accepted all else.

In this fashion, Teller began the journey toward home.

Duster, to no one's surprise, was good with knives. She could even throw them and actually hit the large wooden target that Rath had set up in the boys' room. It hadn't been their room to begin with; he had used it for training. And he had been at his most unkind during those sessions, his voice rising and falling like a dog's bark or growl.

He asked Jewel, Carver, Arann, and Duster to join him there; the others, he said, wouldn't fit, and he would see to them later. But Jewel knew he was lying; she didn't call him on it. Rath always had reasons for what he did.

Rath gave them long sticks; longer than short knives, but shorter than swords. They were heavy, too—heavier, Jewel thought, than wood had any right to be. He carried a stick of the same size, and he had height and reach as an advantage.

"Not fair," Jewel told him curtly, when her wrist had taken its third sharp slap, and she could feel the bruises beginning to form.

"There is no fair in a fight like this," he snapped. "You go out into the streets and tell the roving dens they're not being fair, and if you're lucky, they'll only laugh."

Duster had sneered at Jewel's comment, but not at Rath, and Jewel noted that this was the first time she treated Rath with anything approaching respect. Because it was clear—even to Jewel—that Rath was *good*. Better, she knew, than she herself would ever be. But maybe not better than Duster.

Arann got clouted on wrist, shoulder, and the side of the head; he was big, but almost ambling, and he did not strike hard when he chose to try. Rath cursed him roundly, and with heat. Jewel had to bite back words—all of them Torra—and she threw herself into Rath's damn lesson with ferocity and focus. She managed just once to strike his elbow, and to strike it hard enough that it threw him off.

"Good," he said, withdrawing.

She relaxed, and he tossed the wooden stick, catching it with his left hand and lunging toward her before she'd had any chance to feel pride at her meager achievement.

She found that he was at least as good with his left hand as he had been with the right, and she took the bruises there, too. Accepted them as the price for carelessness.

Carver was not as foolish, and nothing Rath said or did angered him. Rath hated Carver's hair, considered it a gift to any opponents of "worth" as he called them, but could not convince Carver to cut it or push it up under a bandanna. He had much less luck with Carver than he'd had with either Arann or Jewel; Carver could *move,* and his movements were like a dance. He didn't stand to fight; he didn't stand at all. He leaped from foot to foot, seeking not so much flight as unpredictability.

Rath caught him in the chest in the end, but it took about five minutes, and when it was done, and Carver was gasping for breath on one knee, Rath nodded. "Not bad," he said, in a grudging way. "You fight like a street boy, but you fight well enough to survive."

He turned last to Duster. "You," he said quietly.

Duster looked dubiously at the weight of wood in her hand. "This?" she said, with barely concealed contempt.

"I could kill you with it," Rath replied evenly. There was no threat in the words, just certainty, and Jewel expected Duster to bridle, to give in to anger. But Duster shrugged instead. She looked different in this small room, with its boards along the wall and its creaky floors; it was girded by rolled blankets, the odd pillow, a pile of clothing, all pushed aside to make space.

"If you prefer, use your knife."

Duster looked up at him; had to look up at him, he had straightened to his full height. Gone was the element of the scholar, the seeker of knowledge; gone as well the gentleman that he sometimes chose to be. What was left was something that made Jewel uncomfortable, because it reminded her of . . . Duster.

But Duster had her pride. She threw the stick over her shoulder, and

Arann dodged it; it clattered, skidding across the floor into a gray blanket. She pulled a dagger, tossing it from her right hand to her left, crouching slightly, knees bent, shoulders curved inward. She looked comfortable here. She looked, suddenly, as if she truly belonged to this room, and to the man who now ruled it.

Rath did not draw a knife; he merely shifted the position of his stick and waited. Duster waited as well, observing him. The sneer that was almost her only expression had melted into something serious, something that bordered on respect. Because she believed he *could* kill her. They all believed it. Jewel knew he wouldn't. Mostly.

But he had never liked Duster.

They drew a single breath—watchers, and combatants alike—as if they were one thing, audience and performers. And then Duster began to move toward him. She didn't dance the way Carver did; she didn't shift her position, make the position itself unreliable. She didn't smile, she didn't crack a joke; these things she couldn't have done anyway.

But she showed none of Arann's hesitation, was marred by none of Jewel's. When she at last struck, she struck up, from a low stance, and she moved damn fast. Rath parried, a glancing blow that sent Duster's arm just off to the side; he continued his single motion toward the base of her throat, and she threw herself back before his stick's point could make contact.

Rath nodded. "Good." And then it was his turn, and he showed her no mercy at all. Which was good; Duster wasn't much for mercy. He hit her; she swung round, and caught his sleeve, slicing it open. But he'd given her that; he caught the underside of her jaw and sent her reeling. She staggered back, blade still in her hand. He gave her nothing; she found the space in which to ground herself before he was on her again.

But she managed to back up enough, managed to make contact again, this time with his forearm; there was blood, and Jewel stopped breathing. Rath didn't notice. Duster didn't.

When he switched from right to left hand, she was prepared, and in the switch, she backed up suddenly and *threw* the knife. Rath parried it, but only barely, and it flew to the side, landing on the ground behind him.

Duster stared at him, and he stared back, but he made no further move. "What do you have left?" he asked her quietly.

"Another knife."

He nodded as she pulled it. But he lifted a hand. "Enough. I wanted to take your measure, and I believe I have it. I will train you," he added. "It may mean you have less time to spend in reading and writing."

Duster spit. So much for reading or writing. But she looked—almost happy. Almost.

"Duster, Jewel, I would like to speak with you in my room. Carver and Arann, you may return the room to its previous state." He paused and then added, "Clean up."

They didn't wait to be told twice.

"Lord Waverly," Rath said, bending over the map, "lives here."

Jewel whistled. "That's on the *Isle*," she said.

"Yes. For that reason, his domicile is unsuitable for any encounter we may plan. It is guarded, and you will not be able to cross the bridge to the Isle without being noted. But he does not spend all of his time in his home, as Duster is well aware. Of the men whose names you gave me, Duster, I believe Patris Waverly is the most driven by his own desires, and the least cautious.

"We may lure him out of his dwelling with the right incentive," he added quietly.

Duster said, "And that?"

"Jewel."

Jewel startled.

And Duster said, in a cold, even voice, "What do you mean?"

"Finch would be better as bait; she is, I think more to his liking. But—"

"No." Jewel's voice was cold and clear. To Jewel's surprise, Duster's was just as cold, and the word she spoke was the same.

Rath smiled. It was not a friendly smile, but it was genuine. To Duster he said, "So, you have some limits. If Finch was the only way—"

"No."

"Good. I do not consider it wise, although I believe if you asked it of her, she would do whatever it was you required."

"Don't ask." Duster again. Jewel had fallen silent, watching Rath and listening to the words. He was testing, now. She wondered if they had just passed or just failed; it was a test of resolve.

"I will, of course, respect your wishes in this," he said, his tone very formal. "But I must ask why. I believe she is the most suitable, and the most likely chance you have of success here."

Duster's eyes were black; they glittered like . . . like the eyes of the men who had held her captive. She opened her mouth to speak, frowned, bit the words back. "She's suffered enough."

Jewel was staring at Duster. At words that she would have bet would never leave Duster's mouth, even if she was also certain they weren't the first words that tried. "Her parents *sold* her," Duster added. "And she knows it. She'll always know it.

"I won't sell her that way."

"And yours?"

"Mine died," Duster said with a shrug. "I don't remember them. I grew up in the Mother's temple until I was old enough to run away so they couldn't find me. We can do it without Finch. I can look helpless, if I have to."

At that, Rath raised a brow. "And Jewel?"

Duster shrugged. "Up to her."

And Jewel understood then that Duster considered her an equal. It was a compliment, of sorts.

"Jewel?"

"I'll do what I have to. I owe her that much."

"Good. I have taken the liberty of procuring clothing, but clothing alone will not be enough. If the two of you feel you are ready—and determined—I will begin negotiations with Patris Waverly." He pointed at a different spot on the map. "Do you recognize this?"

They both shook their heads. "It's in the older holdings, but near the Merchant Quarter. It is there that you will meet Patris Waverly when you are ready." He rose. "Duster, you fight well enough; I believe you are capable of killing should the need arise."

He turned and looked at Jewel. "But you, Jewel Markess, have not yet been tested."

"I'll do what I have to."

He said nothing for a long moment, and it was not a silence she liked. "Then come," he said at last. "There is a man you should meet; he will teach you about the art of disguise. It is not as simple as clothing; you could dress as the Princess Royale and you would be spotted in an instant as a fake."

He opened the door, and Jewel was aware that this opening was different. But she followed where he led, Duster in tow. Wanting to see the future. Wanting not to see it. Torn between these things, as she would so often be.

Chapter Twenty-two

WASHING HAIR IN the Winter was about the last thing on Jewel's mind. It was a waste of wood, a waste of heat, a waste of time—with her hair. But she didn't say much because she didn't have the chance to slide any of her words between Duster's curses. Rath looked slightly unamused, but mostly bored, which meant he expected no better of Duster. Duster failed to notice; Jewel didn't.

The clothing he had taken the liberty, in his own words, of securing was neither too fine nor too poor—but it was a dress. Well, two dresses. Duster was livid.

Rath was cold. "How much do you want this, Duster?" he asked, and Winter air seemed warm around his words.

She fell into her habitual sullen silence in Rath's presence. But she dressed, and even allowed him to help with the ties that bound the back of the dress in a crisscross pattern. "The skirts are wide enough," she said at last. "You could run in these."

He nodded. "They are meant to be as practical as base fashion will allow; indeed, they are not considered high fashion. But among the less poor, they would suit for visitors and possibly the Challenge season; they will do." He eyed Duster critically. "Try to smile," he said, "as if you weren't contemplating removing the limbs of a helpless cat."

He turned to Jewel. Frowned at her hair.

"I could cut it," she offered.

"No."

"But it's not—"

"No. We don't have time. Now if you will both be so kind, I, too, must make myself presentable." He nodded meaningfully toward the door but did not tell them to get out; they left awkwardly, aware of sleeves and skirts, of bodices that were too tight and too unnatural.

"You say one word," Duster said loudly as she exited the room, "and I'll break your arm."

She said it to no one in particular, or to everyone. Jester, Jewel was certain, had bitten off his tongue; he liked his arms.

Finch said, "You look beautiful!" before she could stop herself, and Duster turned a glare on her. But it wasn't much of a glare; there was almost a hesitance in it. She touched the skirts; they were soft and shiny. "I look like a—a fop."

"You look like a *girl*," Finch replied. "I never knew your hair was so long."

And it was long; long, fine, dark. It framed her face, made it seem less threatening and more regal. Well, as much as someone with Duster's mouth could ever look regal. She cursed a bit, but only a bit. She wanted to look at herself, to see what Finch saw, but the only mirror in the apartment was in Rath's room, and Jewel knew she'd die before asking to use it.

"You look nice, too," Lefty told Jewel. Jewel almost laughed. "I don't look like Duster," she said. He shook his head. Mumbled a few words she couldn't catch, but could understand anyway. She touched his right shoulder gently. "We're going out with Rath," she told him. "Make sure Teller's okay."

He nodded. "Can I teach him the letters?"

"If you want. You're better than Arann with letters."

"I have to be better at *something*."

"You talk a lot more, too," Arann said.

Jewel laughed. "Everyone talks more than you do," she told him. Everyone except Lander. She didn't say it.

"When are you coming back?" Finch asked.

"Don't know. It's Rath; it could be any time. Don't let anyone in," she added. But she always said this.

Rath joined them in the hall, and everyone fell silent; he looked like a lord. His face was the same face, his expression the same expression, but the clothing he wore—dark purples and blues—somehow made everything seem more severe. More distant.

Jewel wasn't sure she liked the difference.

"Are you ready?" he said, and then added, "Stop playing with the skirts."

"No pockets."

"No. Young ladies are not expected to carry things in their pockets; it ruins the fall of the fabric."

So, as young ladies—as uncomfortable young ladies—they followed Rath where he led. The apartment, the crowded and messy noises of home, made way for the noises of cold wind and half-empty streets. Snow had been carved into tunnels by footsteps, paths had been made; what had been new in the morning had become just another part of the City, an inconvenience, even a deadly one, but not more.

Duster had none of Lefty's wonder or glee, and no desire for it; weather, like anything else, was beneath her. She lifted her skirts when Rath told her to lift them, but it was impossible not to trail snow at the hems; impossible not to be touched by it.

"Where are we going?" Jewel asked.

"The Common."

She nodded. "By the—"

"We will walk the normal way, yes." Warning, in the cool words. Jewel subsided. She thought the tunnels beneath the streets would be both warmer and drier, but knew also that for Rath, they were a hoarded treasure. Not something she could share with Duster; not yet. Maybe never.

Duster didn't ask. Curiosity was a weakness, in Duster's eyes—because curiosity implied ignorance, and she wasn't about to look stupid for Rath.

There were a few wagons in the snow, but they moved slowly; everything seemed to except Rath. The snow didn't touch him, and it didn't hold him back.

He led them through the stalls, where voices were carried by clouds of breath, human mist that wreathed faces red with cold. There were fewer of them than usual, but Winter or no, the Common was still busy. People had to eat, even if the food itself was Winter food, and scarce. Prices would be higher, in most places. She wondered how her farmer was doing. Wondered if he still had the voice to berate his sons for their imaginary wrongs, or to praise his daughter.

She wanted to bring Teller to meet him. But she was afraid to take Duster. Maybe later. And maybe, always, never.

The beggars were out in force, and the Winter made them look genuinely afraid; it lent an edge to their pleas for money or food that the Summer robbed them of almost entirely. She had taken some small amount of coin in a pouch she had tied to her waist, but Rath's single forbidding glance made her walk around them.

It was hard. And harder not to resent this other Rath, this nobleman.

Duster, however, was unmoved by their plight. In this, she could have been Rath's daughter, for if she lacked his grace of movement, she didn't lack his callous indifference. Jewel had neither, and wanted neither.

But she had given Duster her word, and she meant to keep it. Her eyes begged forgiveness, but she did not apologize or make excuses for her lack of generosity; she followed Rath.

The stalls passed by as she struggled with her anger, and the streets suddenly cleared of snow; she could see its white between the stones that made the road where the actual shops hovered, crushed together like birds in a nest. He led them to a dressmaker's store. It had a wide window, one that bowed in the front in a half circle, displaying dresses that only a princess might dream of wearing. Light caught them; magelight, she thought with disdain; light made them seem unnaturally lovely.

And someone would buy these dresses instead of offering food to the starving and the freezing. Whoever that someone was, she hated them.

There was a bell attached to the door; it rang as the door opened, jostling its gleaming brass dome. A woman looked up as they entered; the store itself was almost empty. A man sat behind a counter, surrounded by beading and needles, by spools of thread, each a different color. He wore glasses and a ready frown, and did not bother to look up from his work.

He was a bald, slender man, and seemed bowed with age, but that was artifice; he bent over whatever it was he crafted as if it were the only thing of consequence in the world. And perhaps to him, it was.

Jewel had always liked to watch people work when they were consumed with their particular vision. Clothing itself had rarely interested her, but she found, in his focus, some hint of passion or fire, and if she stood close enough, she might catch some of its heat.

But Rath cleared his throat as the woman curtsied before him, and as if that were the signal, the man at the counter looked up with a frown. His eyes narrowed in a squint, and he reached for his glasses.

"Hannerle," he said curtly. "My glasses?"

"They're on your head," was her soft reply. She shook her own; clearly, this happened often.

He reached up and pulled them down from one perch to settle them on another: the bird beak drift of his nose. His eyes were a pale blue, and they were clear. "Is that young Ararath?" he said, with affected surprise.

"It is, as you well know," Rath answered.

"It's been a while since you've come visiting. And in the Winter, too." The man hopped down from the stool upon which he'd perched. "Don't touch anything," he said to the woman on the other side of the counter.

She rolled her eyes. "Yes, Haval."

"What is that you're wearing?" Haval asked, looking Rath up and down—and failing entirely to notice his companions. "It's not this season, Ararath."

"No, Haval; I've never been one to follow fashion."

"No, nor common sense, from what I hear. But come, come, enough pleasantries. I've work to do; you can keep me company in the back while I tend to it. It's damn cold in here and I want my tea."

Tea, as far as Jewel could tell, was mostly alcohol. She and Duster exchanged a single look, but Duster was carefully not casing the place. It made Jewel realize just how aware she was of Duster's constant probing. Duster was uncomfortable, but then again, so was Jewel; they stood side by side for a moment in genuine companionship.

"Well," Haval said, indicating not one chair but three—his first acknowledgment of either girl—"you might as well sit and have a drink, Rath. Business hasn't been bad," he added, "so we can afford it."

"Given the quality of what you drink, business had better be booming," Rath replied, with a smile. He nodded to Jewel and Duster and they sat, Duster fidgeting slightly with her skirts.

The older man noticed, his eyes narrowing slightly over the rim of his cup. "I won't ask you your business," he told Duster, "or yours," he added to Jewel. "But I'll tell you both that you've taken up with a rather odd patron."

"Enough, Haval."

"Better they know."

"You think they don't?"

"I've known you for half of my life, and I'd lay odds that *I* don't."

Rath laughed. It was a clear sound, free for a moment of either edge or worry. "I wouldn't take any odds you were willing to bet on," he said at last. "These two are friends, my charges if you will."

"And you brought them to me because they have no fashion sense?"

"That, too."

Jewel could not stop herself from grimacing. She didn't even bother to try; there was something about this man that set her at ease.

"Girl," Haval said, "don't sneer. Fashion is a statement that people listen to whether or not they know they're paying attention. They have that luxury, most of the time; if Rath brought you here, you don't."

He was now serious, although he still perched over his cup as if it were three sizes larger than it actually was. "I don't like it," he said at last, to Rath. "Did I mention business has been good?"

"At least once."

"I'm out, Rath. I've set up a decent shop here, and I don't have to blackmail more than a third of my customers to keep them coming back."

Rath laughed. Jewel, however, wasn't entirely certain Haval was joking. "You can relax," he said, when his mirth had diminished. "It is merely your knowledge we wish to tax, not your actual ability."

"I never betray a confidence."

"Not if it won't get you somewhere, no," Rath replied. "And we're not here for that type of information. I can't afford it," he added. "Tell me a bit about the two girls here."

Haval shrugged almost genially. "That one—what did you say her name was?"

"I didn't."

"Ah. Well, the one with the nest of hair."

Jewel grimaced.

"Torra, I'd guess, by descent. Probably speaks it. Lives in the hundred, probably between the twenty-fifth and the thirty-fifth. She can read some, which suggests she might be able to write. She pays attention. She never wears dresses. Enough?"

"Scratching the surface of enough, but it will do. The other?"

Haval's frown deepened. "Steals for a meager living when she can. She's trying too hard not to notice what she could take if she thought I wasn't paying attention. She's a beauty," he added, "but so are some of the running hounds that will rip your throat out for sheer pleasure. Her hands are scarred," he added, which caused Jewel to turn to Duster in some surprise, "and I wouldn't be surprised if she has other scars as well; knows how to survive a fight, if not unscathed. She doesn't know how to read," he added. "She also doesn't wear dresses."

"And her station?"

"Worse than the other's. Poorer, leaner. I'd say thirty-second if I had to pin it down, but I'd guess she's made a habit of moving around a bit."

"Tell them how you know this."

Haval set his cup down for the first time. "I owe Ararath a great deal," he told both girls, "or we wouldn't be having this conversation at all. Very well. Neither of you are comfortable in your clothing; you fidget, you play with your skirts, you chafe at your sleeves. You, curly, you've been reading the signage all over the store, not that there's much of it. You're curious about why you're here, and who I am, and it shows.

"But you, raven, you wouldn't be here at all if you didn't think it would gain you something. You want whatever it is Rath has promised you badly enough to try to be something you're not—you just haven't figured out what that something is yet. I'd say you're hunting," he added. "But again, you aren't reading anything here; you're paying attention to where the money is, to where the small textiles—the lace, the beads, the crystals—are, you've taken note of entrances and exits, and how many of us there are.

"You probably think we're unarmed."

Duster relaxed, crossing her legs and pulling them up off the ground so she could rest her elbows on her knees. "You're good," she said, not grudging the words. There was genuine respect in them.

"Either of you could clean up well; either of you could pass as the daughters of struggling merchants in the Middle City. But not as you are now." He turned to Rath. "Is that enough?"

"It's a fair assessment, but I expected no less."

"What do you want of me, Ararath?"

"I want you to teach them what you once taught me."

Haval's gray brows rose into his receding hairline, changing the shape of his narrow face until he looked almost clownlike. "Impossible."

"We don't have a lot of time," Rath added, without pausing to ac-knowledge the single refusal. "We have a meeting in less than ten days with a Patris of some import in the city. And no, Haval, I will not bore you with the details; if you need them, you'll figure them out on your own."

"What is the purpose of the meeting?" Haval asked. Everything about his voice had changed, and his posture had altered significantly as well; there was steel in his spine, and he'd found it.

Rath said a very loud nothing.

"You will, of course, give me the name."

"You don't want it."

"Probably not. But want and need are two different creatures, as you and I well know by now. Who, Rath? The answer you give me, and the answer I give you, are now linked."

Rath was silent for a long, long time. Jewel was wise enough to know that she didn't know him well, but had she been asked, she would have said he would have walked before answering. His answer, when it came, surrendered little. "I wish to involve you very little in this affair," he told Haval. "Were it not for necessity, I would not trouble you at all."

"That bad?"

"It is bad, Haval. Bad, as you might say, for business."

"Then it's not your business you're here on. And which of these two hold your strings?"

Jewel was almost shocked.

"School your face, girl," Haval told her. But he spoke gently. "It gives away much that Rath wishes to hold secret. Very well; he is here because of you. I hope you're worth it. I will now assume, from Rath's reticence and your open shock that the Patris in question is not aware of your existence at this time."

She said nothing, and tried, very hard, to school her expression. Haval winced.

"Rath, is this wise? They are not—"

"It is not wise."

"Very well. You know your own business." Haval rose. "But I will have the name."

"The name will tell you too much."

"The name," he said quietly, "will tell me whether we have business here at all."

And Rath surrendered. "Patris Waverly."

Haval's face did not change at all; he seemed the same pleasant and oddly stern man who had led them to the room. But Jewel *knew* he recognized the name, and more, the unspoken history that surrounded it.

"Not that Patris, Rath."

"We have little choice, Haval. Either you will aid us, or we will go without your aid. There is no one else I care to ask."

"Two weeks, you said? There's no one else you *could* ask."

"That's more or less what I said."

"He doesn't play games," Haval continued, staring now at Jewel and Duster, before once again giving Rath his full attention. His expression had become utterly impassive. "Ararath, I have long held some affection for you, but affection is like any other coin once spent; it is gone. If you intend to use these girls as bait—"

Duster rose, shoving her chair back so quickly it toppled. Jewel rose almost as swiftly, catching her den-kin by the arm in a grip that could have broken bone. There was a moment in which silence was strained almost to breaking, but it eased. Jewel was relieved to see that Duster did not draw her dagger.

"I see," Haval said, and Jewel thought he just might. "Forgive me, Ararath. I felt I had to speak plainly, and if insult was about to be offered, your friends have spared our friendship that.

"If you do not play this carefully, you'll be dead," Haval continued, looking at the two girls and testing their resolve. But he said it absently, in a tone of voice better suited to discussing the variants in shades of blue fabric. "What role, then, will the two of you play?"

And Duster said, "I'm going to kill him."

Haval did not laugh. He met Duster's gaze and held it for a long moment. "You've met him, I see," he said at last, his tone completely without inflection. Without pity.

She nodded her defiance, her trembling anger.

"Very well. I will help you as I can, because I am fond of Rath. I do not consider this wise," he added. "And I will need two full days of preparatory time before I can be of use to you.

"But I would suggest, if you have any other recourse, that you consider it carefully."

Rath's smile was thin, but it was there. "Believe that we have considered it carefully, and believe that," he added, as he bent down and righted Duster's fallen chair, "all other options were gently refused."

Haval nodded. "They'd almost have to be, with the current state of the magisterial guards in the lower holdings."

Rath frowned. "What news, Haval?"

"It is not appropriate to discuss it here," Haval replied. Jewel silently added *in front of the children,* and clenched her teeth to stop herself from speaking.

"Perhaps not, but it bears discussion and study. You are not the only friend I've visited in the past few days."

"Then I will trade information for information," Haval replied serenely. "I will do what I can to help your young friends to adopt suitable roles, and you will share what you deem wise when the information is in your possession."

"Wisdom plays little part in this," Rath replied.

"It seldom does. But if you were wise, we would never have met. And I? I would be elsewhere, I think. In the Kings' service."

None of the words made sense to Jewel.

"Come back in two days," Haval said to them, rising. "I have work to do in the meantime; House Havani has commissioned three very fine dresses, and Lady Havani has specifically requested that I see to their details myself. We all have to eat," he added.

Rath laughed. It was not a kind laugh. "And Lady Havani is well?"

"She is, of course, as hale as a horse. On a rampage."

Duster and Jewel walked back to the apartment in lockstep. Rath walked ahead in silence. The cold made itself felt in every step, every breath; the streets were as empty as they were when the moon was at nadir in the rains. Rath was angry, of course. Jewel knew it, and knew as well that there was nothing she could offer to ease his anger.

"You shouldn't have said anything," she told Duster quietly.

Duster was sullen, her shoulders bunched together, her skin red with either cold or embarrassment. "I had to," she said, through clenched teeth.

"Why?"

"He—" She shook her head. "I'm not *bait*. I'm not—" She stopped walking, and Jewel stopped two steps ahead of her, and went back. Rath, however, kept walking, dwindling into the distant, crushed white of Winter. "I don't understand you," Duster said softly. Or as softly as she ever spoke. "And I don't understand your Rath either."

"He cares about you. He wouldn't help me if I asked; he wouldn't lift a finger to help me."

"He's not like that—"

"He's *exactly* like that," Duster snapped, but without scorn. "He doesn't like people much, and he sure as Hells doesn't trust them. But you?" She shook her head. "He likes you well enough. I thought maybe the two of you . . ." She shook her head. "But that's not it. I don't understand it."

"Does it matter?"

"No. As long as I get what I want, I don't give a shit."

"My Oma used to say—"

"Spare me."

Jewel shrugged. Started to walk. It was Duster, this time, who caught up to her. "I said it because I didn't want him to think that Rath was like—like the others. The ones who kept me chained in that damn room."

"Why do you care?"

Duster shrugged. "Damned if I know," she said at last. And it was true. She didn't.

"Rath can take care of himself."

"And you."

"And me." Jewel shrugged. Felt something like happiness, but thinner, and more fragile, as she met Duster's dark eyes. In Torra, she said, "The hardest thing to figure out is what will make you happy."

"Your Oma said that?"

"All the time."

"Why?"

"I don't know. It was just something she said. You would have liked her."

"I doubt it."

"She would have liked you."

"I *really* doubt that."

Jewel exhaled, her breath a mist wall between them. "I do," she said quietly.

"Because I saved Finch."

She nodded.

"You like Finch."

"Yes. She's important to me."

"Why?"

"Because she's Finch. She's not very harsh, and she's not—she's not like me. Or you. Sometimes we need people who aren't. My mother was never hard enough, according to my Oma, and she's some part of me. But

Duster, Finch didn't save herself. If you hadn't decided to help her some-how, she would have died."

Duster said nothing.

"If I hadn't decided to help her, she would have died." She paused, searching for the right words when so many wrong ones waited like traps. "She didn't need you to kill for her. She didn't need me to do that either. But she needed *both* of us."

"And we were there." The words were bitter. "What about what I need?"

"I don't know what you need," Jewel replied. "Sometimes I don't know what *I* need."

"Your Oma again?"

"No, that's just me. I'm making it up as I go. We only have now," she added, "and yes, that part's my Oma."

"I'm not afraid of dying," Duster said, as they walked. "I'm not really afraid of pain either."

Jewel nodded. "I'm afraid of both."

"But you came to the mansion."

She nodded. "There are things that I'm more afraid of."

"Like what?"

Jewel shrugged. An invitation to expose herself to Duster wasn't going to happen every day. Thank the gods. But she felt that she owed Duster the truth. Or as much of it as she could actually see. "I'm afraid of fail-ing," she said quietly. "I'm afraid that I've made promises I can't keep. I'm afraid," she added, stopping again and turning to face Duster, "of losing any of you."

Duster's laugh was harsh and grating. Jewel accepted it, let it pass her by. Duster didn't have any other way of laughing. Maybe she never would.

"Finch doesn't need what you need. I don't think any of the others do. Except Lander," she added softly, her vision suddenly sharpening as she spoke. "I think Lander needs what you need."

"Lander doesn't even talk."

"No. And I don't think he will until we—" She stopped. Wherever this was going, she didn't like it. But she was Jewel, her Oma's little fire. "Until we kill Patris Waverly." Her eyes widened a little. "You said that, then. I didn't—I wasn't—" She shook her head.

"I want them all dead," Duster told her, not even noticing.

"I know. But we start where we start." She closed her eyes. Opened them. "Thank you."

"For what?" Duster seemed genuinely surprised.

"For trying to spare Rath. Even if you know he can take care of himself."

Duster shrugged, retreating from the moment. Or so it appeared. But when she spoke, she said, "I've never had much I was afraid to lose. I wonder what it's like." The bitterness and envy that inflected the words weren't all they contained; it surprised Jewel.

But today, so had Duster, if only a little.

"It's like any other fear," Jewel replied. "But some weaknesses are good and some are bad. I think this is a good one."

"I don't want it."

Jewel said, quietly, "I know. But you saved Finch. That counts for something. It has to."

Duster didn't laugh. She said, "I'm trying. Not to be whatever it was they thought I'd become. But you keep harping on Finch. You want to know *why* I saved her?" She spoke the words with enough force, they were like a blow.

And behind that, Jewel *knew* she was afraid, for just a minute, of what effect those words would have. Was fighting fear the only way she knew how: By ignoring it. Worse.

"Doesn't matter."

"It should. I saved her because they needed her dead."

Jewel frowned. "They *needed* her dead?"

"They needed her dead. That's what they said. They wanted her 'cause she wasn't all damaged and dark, like me." Bitter, bitter words. "I *wanted* her to die. She's never had a hard life—" So unlike the words she'd spoken to Haval, and yet, they were *also* just as true; Jewel could hear it. Duster was never going to be simple. "But I wanted them to suffer more. That's it. That's the only reason."

Before she could think, Jewel said, "That's not the only reason."

Duster flinched. Started to speak. Stopped. In the cold, breath like a whirling cloud all around them, she stared at Jewel Markess. Jewel stared back.

"It's the only reason," she said again. But the words were thinner. "It's—the only reason that matters."

"What's the other one?"

Whispered words. But Duster surprised Jewel. She answered. "She was the only *good* thing I did there. The only thing I—the only *right* thing. They never guessed I could do it. They never guessed someone as fallen as me could do anything good. But—if I only ever do one good thing—she's alive. She's not me. She can do the rest. And she can do whatever good—" she said the word without her usual sneer, "*only* because of me."

Jewel understood, then. Why Duster had looked so angry when she had laid eyes on Finch.

"That has to count for something, right? In Mandaros' Halls, that has to count for something."

"It counts," Jewel said softly. "And with more than just Mandaros. He won't care until you're dead."

She fell silent, and the mists parted slowly around their faces.

Duster said, "I killed my uncle."

And Jewel, to her own surprise, said, "He probably deserved it." And meant it.

"That's it?"

"What's it?"

"That's all you're going to say?"

"I know that the Patris deserves death," Jewel replied quietly. "All of them. I don't see why your uncle was different; if you killed him, you had your reasons."

Duster just stared at her, hand on her dagger, her eyes wide, dark eyes. Animal eyes.

"We have to get back."

"I don't know if I can stay. With you. With them."

"You can. But not if you don't want to."

They started to walk again, two girls in dresses that were too fine, in a Winter world where anything was possible, and ice of all kinds was both deadly and thin.

Teller made a place for himself in the kitchen, at Finch's side. Jewel should have been surprised, but she wasn't; he had probably done the same thing at home, and finding something familiar in the midst of all that was strange just made sense. Lefty was with them, both hands by his sides; he spoke with his hands and with his voice, alternating between them, depending on whether or not they were looking. Jewel stood in the hall that was only inches away from the kitchen's frame, looking in at their world.

It was a warm one, with fire in the woodstove and bodies radiating heat. Duster, to no one's surprise, avoided kitchen duties with a sullen passion. Carver avoided them adroitly, and Arann did the heavy lifting—the wood, for instance. But Finch directed when Jewel wasn't there, and Jewel was content to let her be.

When Jewel's family had been alive, the kitchen had been their gathering room, the place at which all discussions of import were held. Her Oma would sit in the corner, smoking, which irritated her mother; her mother would cook and clean while her Oma would hold forth with gossip—she called it information—and the stories that Jewel so loved. Her father would help here and there, but he said two women in one kitchen was one woman too many, and his mother had affectionately called him a coward.

Jewel shared some of that cowardice, and some of that affection, watching her den-kin work. And they were her den; she accepted that now. They didn't have to steal—not yet—to live and eat. Later would be later; for now there were pockets of safety, of things that were familiar.

When Finch looked up from her work, she paused, glancing at what they were wearing. But she didn't ask where they'd gone; she said only that they must be hungry. The last was a question. Jewel's stomach answered. Like a little mother, her Finch. Like her own mother might have been when she had been ten.

"Where are the boys?"

"Carver and Arann are trying to beat the crap out of each other," Lefty said cheerfully. "They call it *training*." The cheer wavered when Duster stepped into the kitchen, and the hand that had been flying in mute conversation now returned to his armpit; his spine bowed and his head sank inward, as if he expected to be hit.

With Lefty, words and blows were kindred spirits.

It was this meekness, this obvious fear, that so goaded Duster. Jewel knew it, and knew also that Lefty was incapable of being anything else.

Duster did sneer. That, too, was a part of Duster, and it wouldn't change any time soon. But she curbed her tongue and said instead, "Sounds like fun. Maybe I'll join them." She paused. "Can I lay bets?"

"You've got money to bet with?"

Duster shrugged. "Some."

"No."

She laughed, then, and it was almost genuine. Surprising in its burst of warmth. Jewel felt fear, not of the laughter, but of losing it; she wanted to hold it, cling to it, nail it down. But she let it go, because if Duster was to be here, to be *hers,* she would have to accept Duster.

Duster walked down the hall, and Lefty slowly unfolded. "She's in a good mood," he said hesitantly. Even hopefully. It hurt Jewel, to hear the fear and the uncertainty. But she nodded.

Only Teller was silent, his face drawn. "I'm not a good cook," he began.

Finch hit his arm with her little fist. "He's not a bad one."

"The rest of us suck," Jewel told him cheerfully. "Not good is better than very bad."

"Mostly, we don't," Lefty added. "Cook, I mean."

Teller nodded. "Wood is expensive." They all looked toward the stove.

"Rath can afford it, for now."

"And now is all we have," Finch said, in mimicry of Jewel's voice.

"You've been spending too much time with Jester," Jewel told her, laughing.

"He's silly," Finch replied, her expression grave. "And I don't know how he *can* be after—" She shook her head. "But I like him."

"Good. We're all going to be living together for a long time; we might as well like each other if we can manage it."

Finch nodded. "We'll eat in the room?" she asked, looking dubiously at the kitchen table. They could crowd around it in theory, but not unless they were sitting in each other's laps.

"Sounds good. I'll go and get what's left of Carver and Arann."

"Rath said they should practice," Finch told her.

"Sounds like Rath. We should eat. We have lessons in the afternoon."

Teller perked up a bit. "Lessons?"

"Reading, sort of. It's mostly just learning the letters," she added. "But I bought another slate or two; we can share for now."

"Torra?"

She shook her head. That was the language of the street, for too many people. "Weston."

He nodded again. His eyes were bright, too bright, and she *knew* he was thinking of his mother. Would think of her often, in this place. But so did Jewel. Nothing wrong with that.

* * *

"Carver's good," Duster said, when they had finished eating. She spoke quietly, and only to Jewel, although everyone in the room could hear what she said. People tip-toed around Duster. Wasn't the smartest thing to do, but it would change. She hoped.

"Good how?"

"He knows how to handle himself. I'd have trouble taking him down."

"And Arann?"

"He's big and he's slow," Duster replied. "And he's afraid of hurting anyone." She said it dismissively.

"He'll defend what he feels needs defending," Jewel told her.

"He'll do that, yes. But only that."

"Not asking him for more."

"No. You wouldn't." The words were sharp. They were meant as a criticism. But they had enough truth in them that they couldn't sting. "Not much of a den," Duster added. "You've got two of us, two and a half if you really count Arann. I think Fisher's got the right build to fight, but he just sits back and watches. Jester couldn't fight a mouse. Lefty—" she bit back the words, although the contempt in the name was damning anyway.

"And the others, Finch and Teller. They won't be worth much in a fight."

"Neither will I."

Duster looked at her dubiously. "If you say so."

"We're not that kind of a den," Jewel said quietly.

"I know. I just don't know what kind of den you *are*. And I know what's out there," she added, nodding up in the direction of the street beyond the walls. "We're not going to carve out much of a territory the way we are now."

"We're not carving that kind of territory."

"You said you wanted to protect your own," Duster said, facing her squarely. "How are you going to do that if you can't stake a claim and hold it?"

"I'll figure it out. We've got other things to worry about first."

At that, Duster was satisfied, or mollified. She nodded. The dresses were gone; they once again wore the loose pants and tunics that best suited them. They were heavy wool, and Jewel found they chafed at her neck, but they were at least warm.

Jewel rose and took out a stack of heavy slates, and these she passed around. Duster glared at them. "You have to learn, too," Jewel told her quietly. It wasn't a command. It was not, however, a request.

"And what in the Hells am I going to do with this?"

"Gods know," Jewel said crisply. "But you'll find something. Hopefully, something legal."

There was a lot of silence around Jewel and Duster as Duster stared at the slate. People waited.

"We're not going to stay in this holding forever," Jewel told Duster, aware that she was speaking to them all. "We're not going to be poor forever. If we have to steal to eat, fine, we'll steal—but there are other ways to make a living, and we're not going to have even a chance at those if we can't master a few crooked lines.

"We need to do this. We're *going* to do this."

Duster took the slate and said, "Only until I'm finished what I need to do."

"All we have is—"

"Now. Yeah, I heard you. Damn your now." But she didn't rise, she didn't stalk out. It was a start, and a better start than Jewel had hoped for.

Two days passed in this fashion. Teller was still silent, but he spoke to Finch and Lefty, and he struggled to memorize letters with a hunger that Jewel dimly remembered as her own. There was a world that words opened, if you could read them. Not a world of money, not a world of opportunity—a different world. A different place.

He asked her questions. About the letters, about the forms, about where they came from. In the end, she borrowed some of Rath's books— his prized books—and she opened them for Teller. He stared at the pages with a mixture of dismay and open hunger.

"This is a book about the history of the Blood Barons," she told him quietly. "It's grim. But it ends with the story of Veralaan and the Twin Kings—the first Kings—so it's not all bad."

"You can read this?"

"With Rath's help. The language is kind of strange. People talked differently then, I guess."

"I recognize these ones," he said, pointing out letter shapes. His smile was bright and open; a studied contrast to Duster's. She nodded, because he actually did. He was fascinated by the pages, by the texture of the paper, by the binding of the book itself, by its obvious age.

But when he closed it, he turned to her and said, "I talked with Finch and Jester."

She frowned.

"They're worried about you."

"Are they?"

He nodded. "What are you going to do?"

It caught her by surprise, and Jewel wasn't good at surprises. "Do?"

"You went out with Rath in those dresses, you came back, Rath shut himself in his room."

"Oh, that. He always does that."

"He left again." Which was obvious, or they wouldn't be in his room, in front of his books.

He stared at her, and she felt the weight of his observation pinning her down. In the quiet corner of this room, book in her lap, she struggled with lies, and gave up on them.

"Duster was—"

"Finch told me." He spared her the words themselves, and she was grateful for it.

"Duster only wanted one thing, when we rescued her," Jewel said quietly.

"Finch told me."

"We're working on that."

Teller was silent. It was a long silence, and a drawn one. "You don't want anyone else to help you."

"*No.*"

The force of the word would have stopped anyone else; it didn't seem to surprise the meek and compliant boy in front of her. "Why? Anyone here would help you in any way they could if you asked."

"I don't want their help. I don't want yours," she added, the words harsh. That would have silenced Finch or Lefty. Teller was unmoved. "I owe you my life," he whispered.

"Yes," she replied. "And I want you to have *your* life, and your life isn't Duster's."

"Neither is yours."

It wasn't what she expected. "It's mine, or part of mine," she told him quietly.

"Why?"

"Because it has to be. Teller—when I came home—the kitchen, the cooking—it reminded me of my home. When my family was alive. I miss them," she added, "And I *want* that for us. That home, that type of home. I want that more than I want anything else. And asking for this from any of you—it would change that."

"Will it change you?"

She closed her eyes. "I don't know," she said quietly. "But if you get involved, if all of you get involved, there's no way back. For me," she added. "Or for Duster."

He nodded. Just a nod. But it contained everything.

"I think I like it here," he told her, as he closed the book and handed it back to her keeping. "I want to stay."

"I want you to stay."

"I know. Don't change too much."

"I'll try." Her expression shifted. "You haven't been talking to Rath, have you?"

Teller shook his head. "Don't need to," he answered. "And besides, he never talks to anyone but you."

"You know that after two days?"

Teller shrugged. "I want to be able to read this," he told her, touching the book's cover. "With you. With them."

"You will."

He said nothing, and she felt the room as an empty place, a cold place. Premonition.

And Rath walked in.

Finch was shy; if Jewel had been asked, she would have said that Teller was shy as well, for they seemed alike in many ways. But Teller offered Rath diffidence without fear. And Rath accepted Teller's presence in his inner sanctum as if he expected to find him there.

"Haval will see us this evening," he told her, without preamble.

She nodded, but she saw that his gaze was not actually on her, although it skirted her face: he was watching the new boy's reaction. Whatever minimal reaction Teller had—Jewel would have said it was none—was exactly the right reaction.

"I offer you what sympathy I have for the loss of your family," he added, to Jewel's great surprise. "Loss of kin, in any way, is a blow. We're all defined by how we handle loss, and I think you may prove my better in this." And he bowed his head with genuine respect. Jewel remembered to shut her jaw. It kind of snapped.

"I have some work to do here, and I would prefer to do it without interruption. Teller," he added, and the boy nodded, "you may, if you handle them with care, borrow my books, save for only a select few. Jay will let you know which ones those are, if it is not obvious."

Teller nodded again.

"But I must ask you both to leave me."

Jewel was halfway out the door when Teller turned.

"Thank you," he said. Just that. But Rath smiled.

Chapter Twenty-three

H AVAL WAS WAITING for them when they arrived; it was dark, although the Common—and more important, his store—had not yet closed for the day. Magelights glowed brightly above the snow, lending it beauty and grace, neither of which deprived it of deadliness. Like Duster, Jewel thought, surprising herself.

He was at work at his counter, and glittering beads were spread out between needles and spools of thread that were colored and almost gleaming. Fabric covered the counter as well, possibly the length of a skirt. He was working with it when they entered.

His aide—Jewel couldn't quite think of her as an apprentice—approached them with her fixed and weary smile, and Haval motioned her back to her place with a nod of the head. "We'll want tea," he said.

This was clearly not the woman's regular job, and she frowned. Jewel jumped up. "I can make that," she told the tight-lipped woman. This did not endear her.

"I don't like this," the woman told Rath. "I'm happy enough that Haval sees his old friends, but I don't want him involved in your business. We have a respectable shop now, Rath. We have a real business."

"I assure you, Hannerle, that we have no intention of—"

"I don't want your damn assurances."

Jewel was surprised, but said nothing; this was Rath's problem.

"Very well. If they bore you, I will leave them for now. We are not here to involve Haval in anything that would require his absence from your establishment, and it is clear that the commission over which he labors is a significant one; he does not stop for much. No doubt he will be working as we speak," he added.

Hannerle snorted. "No doubt," she said. "It's the type of work I question. We're not young, Rath, and we've got something to lose. I *don't* want to lose it."

"Hannerle," Haval said curtly, "enough. Rath understands that I'm an aged, respectable citizen. He has not come here to tempt me back to a life of crime in the streets. He doesn't have that much money."

"He has enough influence."

"Hannerle."

Hannerle had the hair that Haval lacked, pulled back in an overly severe knot and fastened by a bronze pin. She also had lines worn into her brow and around her mouth and eyes, and it seemed that they were perpetually on the edge of a frown. Or, in this case, in the middle of one. "I'll show you the kitchen, girl," she said curtly.

Jewel nodded and followed her. "I won't be a minute," Haval said, to her retreating back.

"She will," Hannerle snapped back.

But Jewel understood Hannerle, so much like her Oma in her distrust of strangers, and she felt oddly comforted by the woman's presence here. "He's your husband?" she asked, when the door to the shop had been closed firmly behind them.

"Aye," Hannerle said wearily. "And he's as dishonest as the day is short in this season, but for all that, he's got a good heart, when he can be bothered to find it.

"He was in another line of work when we met," she added, her expression grim, but softening as she spoke. "And I adored him for it. I was young and foolish then. But not so foolish that I'd tie my fortunes to his if he didn't make a few changes. He has talent," she added, her anger relenting to a grudging pride, "and an eye for detail that can't be matched. We've built a clientele in the Common that would belong in the High Market on the Isle if we could afford the taxes and the rents there.

"He built it," she added. "I don't know why you're here, girl, and I don't know why Rath brought you. But Haval won't say no to Rath."

"Why?"

"He owes him too much, he says. He won't tell me why; believe that I've asked. But if he wasn't entirely honest, he was almost entirely honorable, in his own way. He means it. Nothing I say is going to change his mind. So I'm going to ask you not to destroy our lives for the sake of a simple favor."

Jewel nodded quietly, taking the responsibility that the older woman handed her as if it were food, and she were in need of it.

"This," Hannerle said, "is the kitchen."

It looked very much like the counter at which Haval was working. "I'll help you," the older woman added grudgingly. "Don't touch those bottles; they're expensive dyes and you'll be dark blue for months if they spill."

Jewel nodded again. She was accustomed to taking care when walking among the things other people treasured. Rath had taught her that much. Hannerle donned an apron, and offered one to Jewel as well; it was far too large, but she took it and put it on anyway.

They worked in silence, until Jewel said, "I won't let him do anything to hurt himself, or you." She spoke gravely.

The woman's facial lines were still etched there, but they were transformed by a weary smile. "Rath has a good heart," she said quietly, "but he never lets go of anything. He could have been a Patris on the Isle, did you know that? He could still go back, if he wanted."

"He doesn't talk about his past, and if he doesn't, I can't."

"Smart girl."

"Sometimes."

"I can give you something for your hair," Hannerle said, when Jewel had shoved it out of her eyes for the fiftieth time.

"Won't help," Jewel replied. "It's been tried. My hair is just like this."

"Rath doesn't usually involve himself in the lives of strangers. But you're too young to have any sort of links with his past. You're not the child of a friend?"

Jewel shook her head. "I'm just an orphan he found in the Common," she said quietly. "I was new to the streets. It was warmer then."

"And he took you in?"

Jewel shrugged.

"Then maybe he's changing, too, and high time. He's never married," she added. "And I doubt he will, now."

Jewel nodded. "He won't," she said softly, and as she said it, the knowledge took sharp and sudden root, and she was paralyzed with a sense of foreboding. She forced herself to pull out plates, cups, to tend to Hannerle in spite of the sense of unease. No, of dread.

It would pass; it had nothing to anchor it. No vision, no image, nothing at all.

"Why are you here?" Hannerle asked, as she set water to boil and dried her hands on her apron.

"I'm not sure. Rath says Haval knows things he can teach us. That's all."

"What things?" Sharper question.

"Observant things. He says Haval can tell you almost everything about a person just by watching them for a few minutes."

"Aye, that's true."

"And he thinks we need to learn some of it. Whatever we can," she added. "But that's all."

"What does he want you to learn?"

"I don't know." She was entirely honest; she didn't. But she had a guess or two. "But it's important enough that we *will* learn whatever it is he's willing to teach us. We don't have much time," she added, "and we won't bother you much, I promise."

"It's not you that worries me," Hannerle said, setting the cups on a tarnished, silver tray. "But you've a solid head on your shoulders by the sound of you."

Jewel wondered. But not aloud. Hannerle didn't ask her anything else, which was a kindness. But she made Jewel carry the tray, which was not.

"You both carry the streets in you," Haval said without preamble, cup in his hands, silk—or so he said—making a blue spill on his lap. "Rath does as well, but he can either embrace it or cast it off. We will begin, today, by studying your speech patterns. Tell me a bit about yourselves," he added, looking at the two girls. Rath, sitting across from Haval, was silent; he offered no warning and no guidance.

Jewel, knowing that Duster would not speak first—and might not speak at all—began. She spoke of her family life before she'd lost her family, and spoke a little, and more hesitantly, about the days in which she had wandered the streets, without a familiar roof above her head.

"Where did you end up?"

"By the river, under one of the bridges," Jewel replied. "It was hotter, then, and I needed to be clean."

"Practical. Don't use the word Oma," he added.

"Why not?"

"It marks you as lowborn here."

"I *am* lowborn."

"Yes, but you wish to either use that information to your advantage or conceal it for the same reason. You speak well," he added, "given your background."

"Rath's been teaching me."

Haval laughed. "You also sit as if you spend most of your time on the ground."

Jewel shrugged. She often did.

"You will need to practice better posture. You will need to imply, by the way you sit, many, many things," Haval said. "Now, I want you to watch me."

She did. She didn't expect magic, but Rath had often said magic was subtle—at its finest, almost impossible to detect, and yet, likewise impossible to miss. Haval was, cup in hand, suddenly imperiously cold; everything about him seemed to radiate a distinct distaste for the room. He made it, by presence alone, seem messy and shoddy, and its occupants—his guests—completely beneath him.

Duster rose instantly, and Jewel, reaching out for her den-kin's arm without looking away from Haval said, "He's not suddenly showing us what he's *really* like, or what he really thinks. Sit down."

"Very good, young lady. Very good." His enunciation had also sharpened, and the syllables fell like geometrical stones, each in its perfect place.

But he had changed nothing; he had not touched his hair, his face, or his clothing. In spite of herself, Jewel was almost shocked. "Hide that," he told her quietly, his voice changing again, its tone and cadence familiar and even comforting. Gone from it was every hint of superiority and disdain; instead, it held a weary annoyance.

She watched him again, and again, he was a different man—he had done nothing at all to change his look; he was still bald, and still old, and still surrounded by the tools and materials of his chosen trade. But he now seemed like a rather peppery uncle to whom she had gone for advice.

He shook that balding head as he bent over his cup, and set it aside a moment to examine the stitches he'd made. She wasn't fooled; she knew his attention was riveted to her. But he no longer seemed too large or too fine for the room; he seemed entirely *of* it.

"Men are not made by their clothing," he continued, picking up a needle. "Although they make a statement by the wearing of it. The poorest of men and the richest of men are separated by far less obvious things. Ararath gave you the dresses you wear, and you wear them as if they belonged to a different life; you aren't *in* them; they're simply on you, and they fit poorly."

She nodded now.

"It is not a difficult thing," he added, and she watched him transform again, his shoulders bending inward, toward the sudden weight of the work he had chosen, as if it were his entire care. His arms seemed thinner and more fragile as he lifted fine silk in the pale Winter light that was fading. She wondered, then, if he might not need an assistant, someone to help him or guide him; he held the cloth a little too close to his face, and his eyes were narrowed in a squint.

But this, too, she realized, was not Haval; it was yet another disguise, another appearance. When he looked up and set the work aside on his lap once again, his expression was softer, more vulnerable. "So you see," he told her gently. "And you *do* see."

She nodded. "I'm not sure—I don't think I can do this."

"You may not do *this,* as you call it, with ease—but it is *this* that you must learn. Had I the proper clothing, you might fail to recognize me at all should I desire to go unnoticed; you might be unable to ignore me, should I desire to be noted.

"In either case, it is my choice. And it is a choice you will learn, if I am still capable of teaching it."

"But I—"

"You will be aided by the perceptions of those who observe you," he added. "In a way that I am not aided in this room. There are men who will consider you helpless simply because you are young; your carriage and bearing will change almost nothing. You *are* young," he added quietly. And he glanced up at Rath for the first time.

Rath was impassive.

"Patris Waverly is a predator, but he is a jackal, not a wolf. He does not seek strength, but weakness; he does not desire companionship, but rather humiliation. What he sees in you, if you are indeed to suffer his company, will be a young girl. If you are haughty, you will simply be more easily destroyed." He paused and frowned. "But you must do something about your hair."

"Short of shearing it off, you mean?"

"You could go with bald; it would be a bold statement," Haval replied, treating flippancy with unusual gravity. "But I do not think you would be able to carry it off; you don't have the bearing, and I don't have the time to teach it to you. Your friend," he added, nodding toward Duster for the first time, "could, but it would be a pity to shave *her* head." He shook his own. "She has other difficulties. I assume that you will not speak much about your own past," he added, shifting the weight of his focus to Duster.

Duster shrugged sullenly. She was on edge here. Rath had once again forced them to dress in ways which neither girl found comfortable. "Not much to say."

"No. And it is not by your words—although your cadences are of the street—that you are being judged at the moment. You *do* know how to sit straight?"

"I can," she snapped. "But what's the point?"

"In this room? There is no point. However I would like to see your version of sitting up straight."

Jewel caught Duster by the arm. "Remember why we're here," she said quietly. "And do as he asks."

Duster froze for a moment.

Jewel said, "How badly do you want this, Duster? How badly do you need it?" Her voice was quiet, almost a whisper.

Duster swallowed.

And Haval came, unexpectedly, to the rescue. "You do not prize honesty," he told Duster quietly, "and I am teaching merely a more refined form of lying. It has less to do with words than is your wont, but it is essentially the same. It is a way of hiding," he added, "what must be hidden until the last moment. Come. Sit."

Duster swallowed air, and then she sat, pulling her shoulders slightly back. Haval's frown was almost gentle. "No," he said, quietly, "that will not do. It is, however, a start, and we must all begin somewhere." He turned to Rath, and said, "You must have things that will occupy you."

Rath frowned.

"Leave the girls with me, and come back for them in two hours; by that time, I am certain we will have had enough of each other for the day."

Rath did, indeed, have other things to do, but he did them reluctantly. He left Haval's shop and headed for the Proud Peacock. For this reason, he dressed well; the innkeeper there was not so fine or perceptive a judge of character as Haval, and clothing was the signal by which he tuned his behavior.

He greeted Rath obsequiously, found him a good table, and offered him a few solicitous words. Rath returned them curtly—which was not as much effort as it should have been—and after a few moments spent hovering, while Rath explained that he was waiting upon a companion, he left.

That companion was Andrei.

Andrei was dressed as he always dressed—like the finest of servants money could buy. His bearing and carriage were a testament to the import of House Araven, and if he was not himself a noble or a man of worth, he nonetheless served one in a position of responsibility, and was led—his jacket taken to the safety of the coatroom—to the table at which Rath waited with barely veiled boredom.

Andrei sat, and after a moment, he once again placed a stone in the table's center. Rath noted it with distaste, but the glance was fleeting. He nodded a wordless greeting, and Andrei returned it; they faced each other over fine brass candlesticks and silver plates.

"You are determined," Andrei said, a hint of question in the flat statement, no more.

Rath nodded.

"And you will, therefore, ignore any advice I offer."

"Indeed."

"Then I will come to the business at hand. Patris Waverly is, as you suspected, on the periphery of the merchant circles in which Patris AMatie moves. They have been seen on occasion together, but not frequently." He paused, and then added, "He has, however, been called upon to visit Patris AMatie three times since we began to observe the AMatie household."

Rath nodded.

"The servants of which I previously spoke are no longer present; they have been replaced. And the replacements are remarkably similar; they are all foreigners, they are all new to the city, and it is impossible to trace their past to any known city or distant country."

Rath paled. "In what numbers, Andrei?" he asked, in a low tone, unmindful of the secrecy bestowed on them by magecrafted stone.

Andrei nodded briefly, a sign of approval. "There are five.

"His household has, however, established accounts with some of the finer bakers in the High Market, and in the past two weeks he has been entertaining more frequently than was previously his wont. His personal life, however, is still nonexistent."

Rath nodded.

"Patris Waverly has been, of late, distracted. Much of his previous business dealings have been moved to AMatie's mining concerns, and Patris AMatie has also proved to have some influence in the importing of pearls and other similar trinkets."

"And Waverly?"

"He has not left the High City since the incident. When he leaves his abode, he travels with no fewer than four guards. The guards have been in service to Waverly for at least a decade; two of them are sons of the men who served Patris Waverly's father. If there is a weakness in his escort, it will not be found with his guards."

Rath nodded again; he had expected no less.

"Patris Hectore, my lord, is not well pleased by your inquiries, Rath."

"I am aware of this."

"He is afraid that you will fall in with bad company," Andrei added, and both men exchanged a brief smile.

"He hasn't changed much, has he?"

"He has, in my opinion, softened considerably with time," Andrei replied. "But he is essentially the man he was when I agreed to a lifetime's service."

"How much have you told him?"

"I have discussed little of your affairs with him," Andrei replied. "I deem it wisest that he know as little as possible. But if he has softened, he is by no means a fool. Waverly has a reputation that even Hectore has become aware of over the years."

"He knows, then, that we hunt Waverly?"

"He knows that you are interested in the men that AMatie has gathered about him, and he is also less than impressed by the quality of those men." It was a neutral answer, a careful one. "Ararath—"

"Rath."

"Rath. Old Rath. Seek a different route."

"If it were available, old friend, I would. I hope that it will end here, with Waverly, but I cannot leave it until I see it to its end."

"Ah. And the end?"

"I cannot say."

"Or will not."

"No, Andrei, although you might choose to believe otherwise. I do not know what the outcome will be. I only know that a certain invitation must reach Waverly, and it must *not* reach AMatie."

"That may be difficult."

Rath tensed, although he had expected as much. "AMatie keeps watch?"

"It is subtle, Ararath, and were it not for the connections I maintain with the Order of Knowledge, I would myself be unaware of just how intent his scrutiny is. But, yes, he does watch those that he has gathered. And it is not a surprise to me that, of the three names you requested information about, all belong to his circle."

"I wish only to separate the one for now."

"And the others?"

Rath said nothing for a long moment. "Mandaros will judge," he said, when he at last spoke. "In his own time, he will judge. Of you, of my godfather, I will ask no more than Waverly."

"Very well. Among Waverly's acquaintances and servants, there are those who might be of use to you. They are in his pay, but they are—as is so often the case with men of his particular character—beneath his notice."

"To whom do they report?"

"That is beneath you, Ararath."

Rath shrugged. "It is an old habit, Andrei, and I meant no harm or insult by it."

"Then I will endeavor to take none."

Rath nodded.

"Do you expect a similar difficulty to the one you encountered in the Common?"

"I am not yet certain. I hope not."

Andrei nodded. Wine was brought to the table, and Andrei sniffed it with barely concealed disdain; the goblet did not touch his lips.

"If you wish word to be sent, if you wish an offer of a particular type of . . . service to be made, it must be done with care, and it will take time."

Rath nodded. "Have you begun?"

"Not yet, Rath; I hoped that you would think better of your decision."

"It is not entirely my decision," was Rath's measured response, "but for my part, I am committed."

"Then I will do as you ask. Waverly himself will not be without suspicion, but he has his weaknesses. I will make certain that there is no trail for the magisterial guards to follow, should they seek one; he will no doubt be making inquiries of his own, and it would be prudent if they, also, lead nowhere."

"If things go as planned, that would be not only wise, but utterly necessary."

Andrei nodded. "I will take my leave of you," he said, "but I will meet with you again in three days."

"At the same time?"

"And in," Andrei said, with obvious distaste, "the same establishment."

Duster was in a foul mood. The cold contained most of it, leaching heat from her mouth in dense, almost rumbling clouds. She didn't like the pompous old man, who did he think he was anyway, what the hell did he think he knew about anything, living it up like that, the litany went on for blocks.

Jewel, having grown up under the eye of her watchful Oma, had truly believed that a person existed who could see everything she was thinking, had thought, or worse—had done—and found the man oddly comforting. Her Oma had never stooped, as she called it, to lying. Lying was a Weston word, as far as she was concerned, and it belonged with the pale Northerners in their hearts of ice.

When pressed to speak about something she felt honor bound not to talk about, her Oma went as silent and cold as stone, folding her arms— after she'd lit her pipe—and sitting in her chair with a glare that could have frightened a dragon, if it had managed to peer in the window. *Lying's just another way of hiding, girl. Best not to do things you want to hide, unless the lives of your kin depend on it. That's the worst thing you'll ever have to face—the choice of upholding only one of two vows. That can break strong men,* she added. But her grim silence implied that this should *only* happen to men.

Jewel's mother was softer spoken and far less harsh, and she loved her husband dearly, so it was clear that not all men were beneath notice.

It hit her as she walked beside Duster: She missed her Oma. Her mother. Her father. She had to swallow, to stop, to force herself to breathe.

And to her surprise, the sounds that were mostly verbal grunts paused, and Duster was by her side with something that might have passed for concern on her dark features. She didn't like to acknowledge weakness, especially not her own; it was natural that she assume that everyone felt the same way. So she was awkward in her concern, almost tongue-tied.

Jewel shook her head. "He reminds me of my Oma," she said quietly. "I think she would have liked him. She wouldn't have trusted him, but she never trusted anyone who wasn't kin. I miss her," she added, her voice dropping. "I don't know what she'd say, if she saw me like this."

"Do you care?"

"Sometimes. When I was little, I thought she knew everything. Sometimes I still do."

"I never knew mine," Duster told her. Jewel had already guessed this much. "I liked my grandfather, but he died early. And I don't like the old man."

"I know. He doesn't dislike you," Jewel added. "But he wants you to see things as clearly as he does."

"As he thinks he does."

Jewel shrugged. Stopped walking. "You wanted this. You still do. We don't have what we need to do this on our own."

"We could get it."

"We couldn't, Duster. I mean to survive this. I know you don't care if you do—but I do. I care if *you* do."

"Why?"

Jewel shrugged. "Why do you always ask that?"

"Because I want to know. You're the one who speaks well for her station in life," she added, in bitter mimicry of Haval. "You find the words."

But Jewel didn't have them. Not then. All the words she had were mourning words, lost words, and she could not bring herself to expose them to someone who had never felt the same way.

Nor, in the end, did she expose them to Teller. He came to sit by her side when she retreated into the relative privacy of the kitchen. He didn't speak, and he didn't touch her; he just took a seat beside her, and ran his fingers across the wood grain. He was only Finch's size, smaller even than Jewel, and his arms were as fine as bird legs, although they were pale and smooth. His eyes were pale brown in the odd kitchen light, and his face was drawn, the circles under his eyes pronounced.

"You aren't sleeping well," she said, to fill the silence, but not to obliterate it; she spoke quietly.

He said, "Neither are you."

She shrugged. "I never sleep well. I dream too much."

Teller nodded. After a brief hesitation, he added, "Lefty told me. Arann tried to stop him, if that helps."

Jewel almost laughed. "Lefty didn't speak to me for days," she told him, "but he spoke to you and Finch after a few hours. Am I so scary?"

Teller shrugged. "Yes," he said, "and no. You're sort of fierce, but you're not terrifying."

"Then why do you think they're more comfortable around you?"

"Because they don't really care what I think about them; they care what I think about you."

She looked up and met his gaze. "I was thinking about my family today," she told him quietly. "About my Oma. I miss her."

"My mother used to say that if you remember someone, they're not really gone."

"Feels gone to me."

"Me, too. I figure I'll understand it better later." Silence again. She took his hand in hers, and was surprised at the feel of it; it was cold to the touch. He did not withdraw it.

"Carver's worried about you," Teller said at last.

"He said that?"

"No."

"But you know it."

Teller nodded. "Arann and Lefty aren't so worried, and Lander's in his own world. Finch worries about everything, but only a little, and Jester worries about gloom. Everyone worries about Duster," he added, with just the hint of a smile. "But not the same way."

"No. They're afraid of her, not for her."

He nodded.

"And you?"

"You want her here."

Jewel nodded as well. "But it's hard. Don't ask me," she added. "Don't ask me to explain. I'll explain after. If ever."

"I think Rath is worried as well."

The boy almost reminded her of Haval. "Probably."

"I didn't ask what happened to Duster," Teller told her. "I didn't have to. What is she going to do?"

"Kill a man," Jewel replied. There wasn't much point in not saying it; he already knew.

"And you're going to help her."

"I'm—yes. I'm going to help her." And the words, when they left her lips, left like weights.

"Rath would kill him for you," Teller said quietly.

Jewel was surprised. "He won't."

"He won't because you don't want it and wouldn't accept it—but if you would, he'd do it tomorrow. Tonight."

"I can't ask that of him."

"But you're asking it of yourself."

"Myself is different. I'm me. I can decide what I do. And live with it."

"Rath has killed men before."

She nodded absently. "Probably a lot of them. But I'm pretty sure they were trying to kill him first. He's not—he's not a bad man." Lame, lame words. Duster would have sneered. Teller didn't waver.

"I want to help."

"You are. By being here. By talking to Lefty and Lander. By helping Finch." She met his gaze and held it, her own unguarded. "Don't be anything else. Not right now."

He nodded again. "Finch left dinner for the two of you," he said, and rose. "I'll get it."

"I'm not hungry."

"Doesn't matter."

"Teller—"

He shook his head. "Finch is worried. We all are. Just eat."

And because he was right, she ate, and if the food tasted like sand in her mouth, it was good sand in its way. It reminded her of all of her promises.

Haval was waiting for them when they arrived, but although he was perched on his stool behind the vast, chaotic stretch of colorful counter, he rose. He wore a coat, a waistcoat, and carried both hat and cane. The hat was almost comical, its brim was so wide, and the cane looked thicker than his arm.

"I've decided," he told them, as they huddled in the room for warmth, "that some fresh air would do us all a world of good."

Jewel stepped on Duster's foot before Duster could describe "fresh air" in more colloquial terms. "Ararath," he added, speaking to their silent shadow, "if you wish to accompany us, you may; if you have business elsewhere, I suggest that this would be a reasonable time to conduct it."

Duster, frowning, attempted to pick meaning from his complicated words, and Jewel whispered, "He's telling Rath to get lost."

"All that means get lost?"

"Pretty much. It's politer."

Duster said something about manners under her breath, and Haval wisely chose not to hear it. He made his way to the door, and lifting their snow-fringed skirts, they sighed and followed him, drawing their sweaters tightly around their arms and chests.

As he left his store, he straightened slowly, gaining inches in height. He did not seem nearly so old in the streets as he had in the magelit quarters behind which he ruled his small world; nor did he seem frail. The cold seemed to bolster him, to remind him that there was an outside world of which he was still part. Or, more likely in Jewel's opinion, he didn't want to look harmless out here.

"I do not know how much Rath has discussed with you," he told them genially as he walked, pausing to look at the sparrows that were feather puffs in the snow, picking at invisible grains. "He has discussed nothing with me, but I am not a man to rely on words, as you will both no doubt have observed."

Duster gave up and nodded.

Jewel, however, listened carefully.

"Duster, please, lift your shoulders and your chin; you are not heading toward a fight."

This produced almost the opposite effect, but Haval must have expected no less. He frowned a moment, and air left his mouth in a cloud, like a bubble of silent conversation cut free in the winter air.

"Patris Waverly is not widely known for some of his less respectable inclinations; were he, he would be ostracized. He is feared, with cause, and he is not loved by many. It is rumored that even the Astari—" He shook his head. "Too complicated. The Kings would not weep to attend his funeral."

Jewel nodded, aware that Haval was observing them both, although his gaze seemed to be caught by everything that Winter ice had transformed.

"It is seldom that he has the opportunity to indulge himself, but not, unfortunately, never." His gaze did not pause or linger on Duster, but it didn't have to. "He is cautious, but between caution and desire there are always many slips and many errors in judgment made.

"It is upon such an error in judgment that your plan depends, if I am any judge."

Jewel nodded again.

"And it is not, in the end, the lovely young lady who must be offered as his entertainment, for I fear he would recognize her." And he looked at Jewel. There was no insult offered in the carefully chosen words.

Jewel had carefully refused to think this through until this moment. Thinking, however, changed nothing. As if Haval was a window through which she could gaze, she watched him. "Your hair," he told her gently.

This time, she did not argue.

"We can iron it out. The air is dry, and it will hold some semblance of length for a small time, if you will consent to it."

Jewel nodded.

"I believe Rath means to introduce you to the Patris, in a location of his choosing. It will be as safe a location as he can make it," he added, "and Ararath has always been a canny man. But if the location is not entirely safe, there is a risk, and I judge it to be a large one. For you."

"It's mine to take."

"Indeed, young woman, it is. Were I you, I would not, but I am no longer young, and in my youth, I might have been just as foolish, just as determined. Our youth—should we survive it—teaches us much. But you must face the fact that there is every possibility that Ararath will be unable to come to your aid in a timely fashion, and that what is offered the Patris, he may well take."

Jewel closed her eyes.

And Duster snarled. The sound drew Jewel back into the now of cold streets, Common streets, tall, bare trees girding it as if it had grown up within an ancient forest.

"I won't let her be hurt," Duster said, heat instead of cold transforming both her words and her expression.

"You want two different things," he told Duster, without pause and without apparent concern. "And you are willing to let her take this risk in order to achieve one of them."

"I'll be there."

"How?"

"I'll—" The words faded. Duster was not a planner; she reacted, and she reacted quickly, but she had to react to *something*.

"You begin to see," Haval said quietly.

"Leave her alone, Haval," Jewel said, equally quietly. "I've already made my decision. There's no point in talking about it."

Haval was silent for a full minute. "It is not for your sake," he said at last, and more heavily, "that I make the attempt. It is not even, in the end, for Ararath, although any harm you take will scar him. It is for Duster that I speak."

Duster startled. She hadn't given the old man her name.

"Because if you die, Jewel Markess, do you think it will have no impact on your friend?"

Jewel expected Duster to snarl; expected her to deny any friendship, any ties. But Duster said nothing; she stared mutely at the old man. "For me?" she said at last, the two words harsh and grating.

Haval nodded, but it was a slight gesture, framed by bitterness. "You will have to live with the outcome, whatever that outcome may be. Be certain that you can."

"She can," Jewel said again. "Let it be, Haval."

"And are you so eager to see your friend kill?" There was no heat or anger in the question; he might have been talking about the weather.

"Eager?" Jewel asked him, turning the syllables over on her tongue. "No."

"Then?"

"She's Duster. She is what she is. And she'll become what she'll become. But she *has* to do this, and because she does, I have to do my part."

"And you are so certain?"

"Always," Jewel replied, with complete confidence. Because at this moment, in this street, she was. If there was fear—and there would be, she could feel it coiling in the pit of her stomach, and waiting, biding time—she would face it then.

"Then you must learn. You are not highborn, and Ararath is no fool; Lord Waverly would not touch a highborn girl for all the money in the world. But you cannot be lowborn."

"What do I have to be?"

"The naïve child of grasping, merchant parents," he replied. "Parents who are ambitious enough to desire any means of elevating themselves above their circumstances."

"You've talked to Rath."

"No, Jewel. He will say nothing at all to me of this; he gave me the name, and that was a surprise to me."

"You wouldn't have helped him without it."

The old man favored her with a sharp smile. "You've got good instincts, girl," he told her. "And you are, of course, correct. Remember this about Ararath: He gives what must be given, no more and no less."

"And me?" Duster asked quietly. Quietly enough that Jewel turned to look at her. "What do I have to be?"

"You will be, no doubt, a waitress or a barmaid, possibly even a servant." He frowned for a moment. "A personal servant would not be unknown; the highborn have their attendants, and merchants who are desperate to be associated *with* the highborn will often ape them."

Duster shrugged. "I could do that."

"You could, yes. But you will have to do it *well*. Lord Waverly must both see you and see through you; you must be in all things what a capable servant is: invisible. Part of the furniture. Nothing you do must draw attention to who you actually are. Everything you present must be a surface, a mask, and it must fit you so perfectly it seems utterly natural." He paused before the rounded curve of a wide, wide tree, and reached out to touch the ice that smoothed out the surface of ancient bark. "If I had two months," he said, almost to himself. "If only I had two months."

"Why don't you?"

"I am not entirely certain. I assumed it was because your friend, your Duster, will seek redress without patience or concern for her own safety. But . . . it is never wise to make assumptions based on so little knowledge. Rath is not hasty," he added, "except when the need forces haste upon him.

"And he has chosen the time. Could he, I believe he would choose differently. But enough idle chatter, and enough of this damnable cold. Let us return to my shop, and let us begin there as we must continue."

And so it began: Jewel, seated, her back straight, the folds of her dress arranged and rearranged by a very focused Haval, and Duster, fidgeting and agitated, carrying everything: trays, silks, cups, and—yes—a duster. She was not, Jewel thought, good at any of it; she resented the lessons.

But she did as Haval ordered. It gave Jewel an odd sense of hope to balance a growing anxiety.

Ararath Handernesse sat, once again, with Andrei. They did not dine in the formal rooms of the Proud Peacock; instead, they chose drinks by the fireside in the round room that was the Peacock's pride. The mantel that surrounded the fire was a gleaming piece of redwood, oiled and stained so that it caught and transformed flickering light. Above it were silvered plates that were polished and obviously unused. Above those plates rested a painting of the seascape, waves battering the seawall beneath the proud rise of Senniel College.

Rath recognized the scrawl of a signature in the corner of that painting, and was impressed in spite of his dislike for the pretensions of the Peacock's owner; this was not a masterwork, but it was the lesser work of a known artist. Emory Blackwood. A man who, in his august years, was often invited to paint the portraits of the patriciate, and whose brush strokes and fine sense of light had captured the likenesses of even the Kings.

Andrei nodded in recognition, if not quite approval. "It is small wonder the man can afford so little potable wine," he said grudgingly. "It is a lesser work, but it is unmistakably a Blackwood."

Rath nodded as Andrei touched the round stone that was a constant third party in their conversations. He did not allow Rath to touch it, which was wise; Rath wished to see how it was marked, and by whom. He would not ask, and Andrei would never volunteer the information.

There were other questions to be asked, however. "I received your note," Rath said quietly. "And you must know that it is not to my liking."

Andrei nodded slowly. "You've been speaking to Haval."

"And if I have?"

"You've been in the company of two young women."

"Andrei, do not play these games."

"They are not games, Ararath. You are canny enough to pass through the streets unnoticed should you desire it; they are not."

"You think I'm being hunted."

"You don't?"

Rath shrugged. "I would play another game of distraction," he said softly, "but I fear that it would end in a fashion less to my liking."

"I assume that your timing is due in large part to the presence of the young women."

"In part," Rath replied uneasily. "But only in part. There are games being played in AMatie's circle, and if I am not privy to them—and I am not, yet, in such a position—I fear they are coming to a close."

Andrei frowned. "Your information?"

"That is unlike you, Andrei."

"There are things at stake that you are beginning to understand," Andrei replied evenly. "Why do you feel the time is pressing?"

"We were hasty in our burning of the brothel," was Rath's reply. "And in the timing of other ventures. I do not pretend to understand the nature or goal of our enemies, but were I in their positions, I would not now sit idle. I would find me," he added, "or those around me."

"Not so easily done."

"Nor so difficult as it would have been a few months ago. I will have to move," he added softly, "before the month is out. But the fact that I cannot be found should be cause for concern."

"It almost certainly is."

"And such concerns are often enough to force a hand that might otherwise remain hidden."

"You could wait," Andrei replied.

"So you've said. Would you?"

Andrei said nothing, which was answer enough. "I've come with the information you requested. I do not think my inquiries have yet come to light."

"But they will."

Andrei shrugged. "It is hard to see how, but having seen what you faced in the market, I would not say anything was impossible. All of the men of whom you made your queries, save one, have had business dealings with the Patris."

"And the one?"

"He is a friend—a cousin, I believe, once removed—of Lord Paletos. Who *is* involved in some fashion with the AMatie concerns."

"Paletos is not one of the names I was given."

"No."

They watched the fire for a long moment, drinking idly as they did; they were somber, but men who drank in this room often were. Rath missed The Den, with its boisterous shouting, its offhand lewdness, its poor food, rich ale, and stacked games of chance. Inasmuch as he had a place, it was there.

But it had not always been there. The past was a burden that had bothered him so little in the last few years he thought it had been laid to rest; it woke now, to his very real regret. You could leave many things behind, but one of them was not yourself.

And who was Ararath Handernesse? He had not paused to ask himself that question for decades. And yet, had he never been worthy of the name, avenues of information that opened naturally at a single word would be not only closed but invisible.

"It's the magery," he said at last. "I understand blackmail as well as I understand any game that men play. But magic is no necessary part of those games."

Andrei nodded. "You've spoken with Sigurne and Meralonne."

"And Haberas, poor fool," Rath said bitterly. "And although I cannot see how, or perhaps cannot see why, they are connected, this game and the games the Magi play. I feel that time is short, Andrei, and it does not run in our favor while we labor in ignorance."

"What, then, would you do to alleviate that ignorance?"

Rath smiled and shook his head. "Faithful servant of my godfather," he said, "there are questions which you know better than to ask."

"It is not from the answer that I expect to glean information," Andrei countered, the sudden stillness of a face that was never very expressive lending him a patina of a power that Rath had always felt, but had so seldom seen. "But rather, by the way you decline to answer." He reached for the stone and placed his hand upon it, but did not remove it from the table. "You have never followed advice, Ararath, and I respect your choice, for in this we are somewhat alike. But I ask you now—as a favor for anything that I have done, rather than as advice: Do not do this."

Rath felt surprise, but did not deign to show it. "Ask anything else," he replied at length, noting that Andrei's stone still masked their conversation.

Andrei looked down. When he lifted his face, it seemed aged. "I am not the man you think me," he said softly. "Nor am I so young that loss does not grieve me. You will, of course, do what you feel you must.

"But you have given me leave to ask a question, and I will ask one. Why, Ararath?"

He began to say *I don't know,* but caught the words and held them; they were not the truth, and he had offered, in an oblique fashion, truth if it were requested. "This must go no further," he said quietly.

"Do not feel the need to insult me, Ararath."

"It is not need, but habit," Rath replied. "And accept my apologies for it. You saw the girl in the alley the night you came to my aid."

Andrei nodded.

"She lives with me, and has since I found her. Were it not for her interference, I would already be dead."

"For her, then?"

"Yes. And no, Andrei. Nothing is ever that simple. For her, I would wield sword and kill if the act were required—but it would be a blind act, an instinctive act. It would require no planning. She is special. She is aware of the ways in which she is special—but she is also unaware of the ways in which she might be more."

"And you are not."

"No, to my regret, I am not. I see much in her, and perhaps I, too, am old—addled by the past that has always decided my future. Her future is tied into these demons, as the Magi called them." He watched his godfather's servant for any flicker of surprise the word "demon" might cause; there was none.

Andrei said, "And you know this—how?"

"I have answered the one question you asked," he replied, thinking of the statue that had flared to life in the undercity, and thinking as well of Amarais, the sister who had deserted him for reasons he had not—then—been willing to understand. "Trust that I know it. She is part of this, and if she is to survive, I must know more than I now know."

"My information—"

"Not even the Astari have the information that I believe I will be able to obtain." The silence that the single word caused was textured and heavy. Ararath, like Andrei, knew when to keep his peace; it was in the abandonment that all risks were taken, and some less wise than others.

"I see," Andrei replied. "I will aid you as I can."

"I know. And I know to ask is to burden you. But I can achieve two goals in our meeting with Patris Waverly."

"His death?"

"That, yes, but it is *not* his death that is of interest to me now; it is the manner of his death, and only that. A test," he added quietly. "What

I do from that point on will be determined by whether or not the test is passed or failed."

"Assume that it is passed."

"I will join the AMatie circle. Jewel's presence, as a gift to Patris Waverly, will be a sign of my intentions."

"His death will surely cause some difficulty when they question your sincerity."

"Perhaps. Perhaps not. I chose Waverly for a reason," he added.

"And if the test is failed?"

"I will live as I have lived," Rath replied. "It will be a welcome—and peaceful—change."

But Andrei knew which of the two outcomes Rath now desired. He lifted the stone, palming it. His hand seemed to tremble, as if the act were final. "You should have stayed with Handernesse," he said quietly. "You doubted yourself much in your youth, but I see in you now a Patris that might have lead the House to glory."

"Had I, I would never have met the girl," Rath replied, and he said it without rancor. "She shows me much that I refused to understand in my youth; had I stayed, I would have been a bitter—and weaker—man. I will never return to Handernesse; it is no longer my home. But I regret its passing now, in a way that I did not; all thought, then, was for what I had lost."

"Many a man would have thought, instead, of all that he had gained, for your sister would have inherited the title and the responsibility had she not left."

Rath nodded. "I understand her better now than I could then, and in a fashion, this is all the apology I will ever be capable of making."

"And she will never know of it."

"No," he said quietly. "If pride is a sin, I am still a creature of sin." He, too, rose. "It will be difficult to arrange a meeting with Patris AMatie, and in truth, it concerns me; I am not entirely certain I will pass unrecognized, for all my skill."

"That is your only concern?"

He nodded. "I will linger in the outer circle if possible. Thanks to his generosity in the purchase of a few broken pieces of stone, I have funds with which to entertain the men I despise. They will last some time."

"Then I will find the information you requested."

Rath had never doubted it.

Chapter Twenty-four

IF DUSTER HAD ever considered herself an accomplished liar, Haval's lessons wore away her sense of confidence. Jewel could see it clearly in their long, slow walks through the Winter streets. Even Duster's anger, ever ready, had dimmed beneath the weight of her weariness. She was like and unlike Jewel; Jewel wondered, as they walked in silence toward home, what Duster would have been like had she had an Oma, and a home, where warmth was not simply a matter of wood and the clothing one could steal.

Or an uncle she had been forced to kill.

She was even too tired to continue her constant sniping at Lefty, and a strange peace descended upon the crowded rooms in which the den huddled. Jewel wished she could be home more often to see it or enjoy it.

But when she was home—as she was now—she was absorbed with the duties she had undertaken: she taught them how to read. The writing was hard. From Lefty, she expected no less, and was surprised at how he struggled to master what should have come easily to anyone else; of her students, only Finch and Teller worked as hard.

No, if temper frayed in the den, it was Jewel's. She snapped at Carver and Jester when their attention wandered. She cursed liberally at the absence of anything she wanted—water, wood, even the food that was her responsibility.

And in the end, on the way to Haval's house, it was Duster who dared to bring it up. She said, "You've been a real bitch the last couple of days, you know that?"

Jewel stopped in the street and stared at Duster as if she'd lost her mind. "*I've* been a real bitch?"

"That's what I said."

"You've been sulking in the corner and doing almost *nothing,* and I've been a bitch?"

"Pretty much. If you slap me again, I'll break your arm."

But Jewel hadn't even begun to raise her hand. She glared at Duster, and Duster shrugged. "No one else will say it," she told Jewel. "But it needs saying. Everyone else is worried about you," she added. "Me, I just wonder what in the Hells your problem is."

They had stopped walking, and Jewel, realizing how highly Haval prized his punctuality, began to stride down the streets, leaving heavy prints in snow that only barely paused its fall.

But Duster hadn't finished. "You've got everything," she said coldly. "Rath adores you, even if you're too dense to take advantage of it. The others do anything—or would do anything—you asked them. You've got a place, you've got food, you can afford to buy clothing that fits all of us. You've never had to do anything you hated in your life, just to get by. You've got anything any of us could ever want. So what is your problem?"

Jewel had no answer. She was busy seething. But Duster's barbed words found their mark. And the words she offered next put Jewel off her stride enough that they were to be late to meet Haval. She said, "If it's the killing, I don't want your damn help."

Jewel swiveled, snow dusting her feet. Her hands were bunched in fists.

"Without my help," she said, the words almost a hiss as they escaped a clenched jaw, "there's no killing. Isn't this what you wanted?"

Duster shrugged. "Maybe," she said at last, and looked away. "Maybe this is what I wanted. But not like this. Look, I don't think I've ever liked you; you've always been too *good* for me. But this . . ." she shrugged. It was a common gesture. "I don't like it." She said the words as if they were strange, and given how much she disdained, this was a surprise. "The others—I thought they were weak and stupid. And some of them *are,* and I don't give a shit what you think.

"But not all of them. And they don't need you to be me." Her laugh was bitter, but restrained. "No one needs me to be me," she added. "Except *me.* But they all need you to be you."

"And that's your business now?"

"You made it mine," Duster told her. "I didn't ask for it, and I don't even want it. But no one else will tell you what you need to hear." She laughed again, and again, the laughter was familiar in its bitterness. "You said you needed me," she told Jewel, the words both a taunt and an accusation. "I didn't know you'd be right."

Jewel wanted to hit her.

But the desire escaped, and the anger went with it, slowly draining into the winter streets, the cold of the air, the damnable snow of this horrible season. She tried to see herself as the others might see her, or even as Duster obviously did, and the glimpse the effort gave her was more than she wanted.

"It's not enough that I have to do this," she said, her bitterness an echo of Duster's. "I have to be cheerful too."

"Or not. You're not exactly cheerful, normally." Duster shrugged. "I'm not having fun either," she said. "This servant shit—it's hard."

"If we don't do it—"

"I *know*. The old guy may be a smug bastard, but he's not stupid." She hesitated, and then added, "He thinks if I screw up, you'll die. We both will."

"You're not afraid of death," Jewel said, trying to keep the edge from her voice. Trying to think of Duster as someone who could care enough about anyone else to say something like this.

Duster shrugged. "Not afraid," she said, evasively. "But not exactly rushing toward it with open arms." She paused. "He doesn't like me."

"Haval?"

"Yeah. Haval. Rath doesn't either."

And you care? But the words would have been said to wound, and Jewel bit them back with effort.

"They think this is my fault."

"It's *not* your fault." The edge slid back in, and Jewel didn't bother to struggle with it. She caught Duster's arm. Duster stared at her hand.

"No one tells me what to do," Jewel added, removing her hand. "Not you, not them."

"If it weren't for me, you wouldn't even try."

"Maybe not. Does it matter? If it weren't for you—"

"Finch would be dead. I've heard it before."

"Still true. It's my decision."

"And you'll live with it. Yeah, heard that too. But you—"

Jewel lifted a hand. "I'll try harder," she said, meaning it. Angry, but meaning it. "To keep it to myself. But nothing that happened there was your fault. And nothing that happens now is your fault either."

"Unless I screw up."

Jewel nodded.

"And we're late."

She cringed.

Haval was, indeed, annoyed when they arrived; he kept them waiting by the door for twenty minutes while he puttered about his counter, absorbed in either his work or his annoyance.

Aware that they'd earned it, Jewel was content—barely—to stand and be ignored. To breathe warmer air, in a quiet place. The fact that an angry man sat at its center wasn't much of a concern. She'd grown used to his type of anger.

Eventually, however, satisfied with their apparent compliance, Haval rose, his pale brow a gathered line across a sour face. "If you ladies are ready?"

They nodded, and Duster did not even look sullen.

"Then today we will learn about fear."

"I think we understand fear," Jewel told him.

"Good. I note, however, that Duster has not chosen to speak."

And didn't.

He moved around the counter, calling his wife to take his place. She came, looking slightly harried, and also slightly disgusted; he really wasn't the neatest of craftsmen. "We will be in the back for the afternoon," Haval told her, "if an emergency arises, you may interrupt us."

"Fear," he said quietly, "is something we all face. We face it in different ways. Sometimes we deny its existence. Sometimes we thrive on it. In either case, the fear itself isn't necessarily the defining factor." He paused. "Understand that men like Waverly live on the fear of others; it keeps their own at bay. Understand as well that he is never without fear. Men with much to lose will never be without it."

"And you?"

"Fear is a constant companion," he replied, his expression so serene it was hard to believe the words. "Believe that no life is lived without fear.

When you are too tangled up in your own, and especially when you are young—" he allowed them to express their quiet outrage at being called "young" in that particular tone that implied ignorant, "—it is easy to believe that no one who does not obviously show fear feels any."

"And what are you afraid of?" Duster asked, and not perhaps in the servile tone of voice she had been practicing so damn hard.

"Funny you should ask that today," Haval replied. "Today I am afraid that I will fail you both. That anything I can teach you will be superficial at best; that you will learn to behave in the appropriate ways only in my presence, and that it is my presence alone that anchors your efforts."

Duster glared at him.

Almost wearily, he added, "You will be able to perform *here*, where in the end it doesn't count."

Jewel nodded. "It's easier here," she told him quietly. "For me." She glanced at Duster; Duster was silent. In all, better than she usually hoped for. "I can watch your face. I can hear your tone of voice. I know when I'm doing something right, and when I'm doing something wrong." She paused. "But I think I'll have that anywhere else as well."

"Do you?"

She nodded. "Other people will react. Not the way you do, not exactly—but they'll be expecting something of me, and if I do the wrong thing, I *think* I'll be able to tell. And fix it."

"Most of your life will be made of a series of perceived crises," he told her, after a pause in which Duster poured tea. "If you are lucky, they will seldom be so intense, and the outcome so uncertain. Do you understand that you could die?"

Jewel started to answer, and stopped. Because until he had said the bald words, she hadn't. The nebulous fear of discovery had been enough to drive her; the fear that discovery would end in death? It hadn't really occurred to her. And now that it had, it wouldn't leave her. She *knew* it was possible.

"I have endeavored not to speak openly of it," he continued, when she did not. "Because the nature of fear for some is paralyzing; because fear might make you clumsy and incapable, rather than more honed, and more wary.

"But I have spent the better part of a full week in your company, both of you, and I am better able to understand your fears and how they motivate you. You, Jewel Markess, I understand well. Your fear surprises me;

it is seldom found in those in your circumstances. And Duster's fear, as well, is uncommon because her life has been lived at the extreme edges of our society, for better or worse.

"In most your age, the fear of not being liked, the fear of disapproval, is enough motivation; it encourages people to wear outlandish styles and behave in even more outlandish ways; it causes them to group in packs, there to peck out a social order. This is not what drives you, either of you."

Jewel was quiet, waiting for Haval to finish his thought; his thoughts were often long and meandering.

"It does not, however, matter. People will assume your fear—when exposed—means what they expect it to mean. But it is in the exposure, in the *use* of the fear, rather than the fear itself, that you will find some protection. And today, we will begin to teach you how to show that, how to let it seep through the cracks of your facade as naturally as if it were breath." He turned and lifted his cup, and Duster was there by his side in an instant, filling it, her face a study in complacent neutrality.

"What does a servant fear?" he asked her, when she had set the hot tea aside, and was in no danger of spilling any of it in his lap.

Duster shrugged. "Don't know."

"Then think."

Of the words he often used, these were perhaps Duster's least favorite. She wasn't stupid, but Haval's manner of speech made her feel as if she were, and it also made her angry. He could see this clearly, and added, "We will discuss the nature of anger at a later date. At the moment, it is fear that you must understand. Think of it as a language, Duster, and one that you must master if you are to survive."

"I'm not afraid of death," she said coldly.

"No. But it is not of your fear that I speak. You are a servant; that is your role and your sole function. Your daily wages are earned by cleaning up after others, and by serving them when service is required. What, in that role, do you fear?"

She closed her eyes. Her lashes, dark and long, changed the look of her pale face. "I don't want to lose my job?" she asked at last.

"Very good. Most don't. You are more aware than Jewel that some people have power. You are now required to serve a man of power. How is that fear expressed?"

Duster swallowed. "I don't know."

"No. You don't. It is why you are here. But time is not our friend in this place. Try again."

"If he's powerful, he's more important. If he's more important, any mistake I make can mean—"

"Yes. Instant dismissal. Possibly public, if your employer wishes to mollify an angry lord. You yourself do not fear this; it has never been your desire to serve. What you *do* fear—the loss of opportunity, the possibility of discovery—must express itself *only* in a way that a negligent man of power might interpret as fear of his rank, of the differences between his rank and yours.

"Men of station generally do not notice servants. There is a risk that Lord Waverly may, in fact, notice you, and not for the reason of servitude. How will you handle this?"

"By ignoring it," Duster replied, with some effort.

"Yes. By ignoring it. But if Lord Waverly senses the fear, it would be better; he will—as I said—make his own translation. He expects to be feared; he expects to be waited on. He expects that the people who wait on him understand that their very livelihood is dependent upon his goodwill. If you are afraid for any reason in his presence—*any* reason, Duster, do you understand?—you must work to channel it, to express it in ways that will be expected, and can therefore be overlooked."

"Jewel," he added, "your fear is a different fear. It is upon you that Lord Waverly will—should this foolish and ill-advised plan be set in action— focus the brunt of his attention. What, then, will you fear?"

Jewel swallowed. But she did not answer immediately. She thought about it. "I'm the daughter of a merchant?" she asked at last, although she knew the answer by heart.

"Yes. A younger daughter, and not terribly lovely, but neither are you repulsive. You have been raised in a somewhat sheltered environment, but your mother has recently passed on, and your father is in a position to benefit from Waverly's merchant interests, if Waverly is well-disposed toward him."

Jewel nodded. Thinking not of herself, but of Finch. Of being sold by family, for that meanest and most necessary of things: money.

"Again, it is in Waverly's nature to assume that all men seek advantage and position. If they seek it from him, and they are servile, they are *almost* servants. There is safety in that, for such a man. He does not seek a circle of friends; at best, he surrounds himself with like-minded rivals.

An ambitious man of low birth will not be a surprise to Lord Waverly. But there are many ambitious men, and many of low birth, who would not seek to obliquely offer their daughter as the price of entry into his circle.

"What is offered, cannot of course be *legally* offered. Therefore, it will not be discussed openly. Ever. Waverly is aware of this, and aware of the risk involved in taking what is offered. He will assess you, when you meet, but he will feel relatively safe in the certain knowledge that he has the advantage of your father's ambition.

"And you will fear him," he added. "Even if you do not fear him now. How your fear is expressed will define everything.

"How you dress, and how comfortable you are in that dress, will not matter; he will expect you to be both ignorant and nervous. I believe it will amuse him. Defiance," he added, "will likewise amuse him, because he knows why you are there; he may well expect that you will not; that you will be naïve. I think that this approach is best; if you are confused and you lose your way, he will again interpret it in a fashion that fits his view of the situation."

Haval rose, and set the cup aside. "At no time must your fear be for anything other than yourself. At no time must you pay heed to the presence of either servants or guards."

"Guards?" she said sharply.

"He'll have guards there," Duster whispered. "He won't send them away."

Haval closed his eyes for a moment. "No," he said at length. "For humiliation is important to men like Lord Waverly, and anything done in private will offer him less of what he craves."

"If we're to kill him," Jewel began, "we're going to have problems with guards."

"Oh, indeed. And I assure you that some thought has been given to the matter of the guards. It is not clear how many—"

"Two," Duster said quietly. Too quietly.

Haval did not pause. "Two guards, then. You will be attended by guards, and by Duster. But to Duster you will not look, do you understand? She will not be in the room, in any case, for the worst of it. You may look at the guards as chaperones, initially, and I consider this wise; you may treat their presence as safety.

"Do not make the mistake of believing it."

Jewel swallowed, throat dry. "Where will Rath be?" she asked him, her voice almost too quiet to be her own.

Haval closed his eyes for a moment, but his expression was thoughtful, not fearful. When he opened them, he said, "I don't know. It is not for your Rath, as you call him, that I am concerned. He has survived worse than this.

"And in my opinion, it is better that you not know. Fear has an edge when it is genuine. Were I younger, Jewel, I would accompany you. You are—neither of you—the children I would have chosen for a ruse of this nature."

"We're not children," Duster said.

"To me, you are," he replied. "Experience alone does not change this fact." He rose. "I will leave you both to think about what I have said today; I am weary, and I have not finished the work that will actually pay me."

Fear was a constant companion from that moment on, but really, when in their lives had it been absent? They were aware of it, and Duster, aware that she had somehow been exposed. This vulnerability was worse for her than for Jewel; Jewel took a blunt pride in her ability to accept the truth. If she hadn't developed that skill early on, she would never have survived a woman as sharp-tongued and clear-witted as her Oma.

But if Duster was ever to learn, it wasn't now. Her silence was heavy, twitchy, a nervous and caged thing. What would spring from it—and Jewel felt certain something would—would not be pleasant.

"I'm using you," Duster told her as they walked.

Jewel shrugged.

"Don't you care?"

"Not much."

Steam streamed from Duster's slender nostrils as she snorted. "People use each other," she said. "What are you using me for?"

Jewel shrugged again. "Don't know," she said quietly. "I don't think about it much."

"What do you want?"

"Impossible things."

"Like what? Money? Power?"

"Safety," was the curt reply.

"You don't get safety without money or power," Duster snapped back.

She was spoiling for a fight. Would have to be; she'd been so damn attentive for Haval, it had to come out sometime.

"Money and power just get you attention," Jewel snapped back. Better her than Lefty. "There are a lot of dead people who had money and power."

"You get more safety with than without."

"You never have safety," Jewel answered. "It's just something to want. Like happiness," she added, squaring her shoulders. "Or peace."

"*Peace?*" Duster stopped walking, her hands by her sides, bunched into incongruous fists around folds of loose skirting. "What kind of drivel is that?"

Jewel shrugged for a third time. "You don't want the answer, don't ask. You don't like the answer? Tough."

"Do you even understand what could happen to you? Do you have any idea what Waverly can do?"

"I can guess," Jewel said bleakly. "I'd rather not talk about it, but I can guess."

"I *know*."

"If you didn't, we wouldn't be meeting him."

Duster nearly shrieked, and Jewel felt slightly guilty; she was almost enjoying this. Almost. "I could die in the snow," she told Duster, before Duster could let loose again. "I could freeze to death, the way Teller's mother did. I could *be* Teller, finding her there. I could starve to death, the way Lefty almost did. I could have drowned on the riverbanks if the rains had come early and Rath had never found me.

"Dead is dead," she added quietly, willing herself to believe it. "And everybody dies sometime."

"That's your Oma again, isn't it?"

"What if it is?"

"Everybody dies sometime. I want to be old when I do it."

"So do I. So did Teller's mother. What we want doesn't matter. Doesn't always matter," she added. Thought about it a bit, and said, "No, that's not true. It does matter. It's just not everything. You want to kill Waverly. We're trying to. We wouldn't be trying if it wasn't what you wanted.

"But after that—have you thought about after?"

Duster shrugged. Which meant no. And almost meant she wasn't about to start.

"Think about after," Jewel told her, hoping to divert her anger.

"I'll get there when I get there."

We'll get there, Jewel thought grimly. She said nothing else. Let Duster fume. Let the cold of the walk bleed off some of the heat of her anger. Jewel shortened her stride, drawing her shoulders down her back and lifting her chin as Haval had taught her.

"What the hells are you doing now?"

"Practicing," Jewel told her. "Rath hasn't given us a day. He hasn't given us a place. But when he does, we *have* to be ready."

Rath was seldom home, and when he was, he was not in a mood for company or discussion. Jewel was, but she wanted Rath's. In his absence, however, she arranged the early outings to market, she stocked the cupboards, and she fetched the boots that had finally been finished from the rather truculent cobbler. In bits and pieces, the children in her care became less gaunt and less cold; Fisher even ventured a few words here and there, although he would never be much for talk.

Only Lander's silence was persistent, a reminder of the things that lay both in the past and the future.

At the end of the ninth day, Haval told them he thought they had come as far as they could under his tutelage.

"So we come to the last and the least of things," he told them, and he headed toward an armoire against the west wall, one that had never been touched or opened in their presence. "Appearance. It is easy to alter appearance," he added, "but harder to live *in* it. What I have taught you will carry you through much; you can suggest training and birth by carriage and speech, and if you must spend any time under scrutiny, that subtle suggestion is more powerful than all of the dyes and superficial artifice in the world.

"But the world is superficial, and now that we have come as far as we can in the time we have, I will teach you how to alter your appearance."

"Your appearance," he said, turning to Jewel, "is unfortunately distinctive. Especially your hair."

She said nothing. Distinctive was not the word that was usually used to describe it, but mess was nothing she wanted to offer as an alternative when Haval had that particular expression on his face.

* * *

Everyone gaped in their own special way when Jewel finally opened the door, took a breath, and walked in. Duster was almost skulking *behind* her. There was a loud moment of silence that was broken by Finch.

Unfortunately, Finch didn't exactly *say* anything.

Rath, watching in silence from the door to his room, which had remained slightly ajar for the better part of the two hours they were late, was surprised to find that he *was* jarred, as unsettled for a moment as the rest of the children here, although he'd been witness to far more spectacular transformations.

If there was one thing that defined these two—besides their ability to curse in Torra—it was the fact that they were who they were. Duster, capable of lying when it suited her, also loudly proclaimed the fact, whittling away at any possible gain subterfuge might lend her. And Jewel? Practical in the extreme, she barely paid attention to what she was wearing as long as it was either warm enough or cool enough to suit the weather. Her hair, which had always been a tangle of curls, was like a visual punctuation to the statement of who she was.

And neither of them looked precisely like themselves.

He recognized them, of course; would have recognized them anywhere and under any circumstances. But Duster's sleek hair had been both cut and dyed; it was a pale, almost platinum blonde. Her faced had been powdered, and were it not for the color of her eyes, she would have been able to pass for a cold Northern servant. Were it not for her eyes and the way she was uncomfortably crowding behind Jewel, her shoulders hunched inward as if expecting a blow.

Jewel herself? Her hair had been ironed. Rath was aware of the custom; had seen it several times in his youth. But Jewel's hair was actually quite long when it was straightened. Haval had not chosen to change its color; it was the same auburn that it had always been. But it reached for her back, and in the dress she now wore, it was striking. Her eyes, Haval had also left alone; he had powdered her skin, paling her natural complexion, but he had done little else.

Yet what he had done was enough; she looked only slightly less wary than Duster as she confronted her group.

But she was still Jewel; something caused her to look past her den down the hall; to see Rath as he stood in his open door. To say, "Sorry we're late. Haval insisted."

"Given what he's done, I'm surprised you arrived before dawn," Rath replied. "You look . . . different. Both of you." He took a breath, like a pause, and held it. "The timing is not, perhaps, poor. I have some business that will keep me away this eve, and some part of tomorrow, but I believe that tomorrow night, or the day after, we will be ready."

Jewel nodded. Her nod was entirely her own; it was all business. Duster, behind her, said nothing. And Teller, watching as Rath watched, offered no words, but he turned and met Rath's gaze with something akin to disapproval. It was not a bold glare, such as Duster would have offered; it was not—quite—an invitation to argument. In fact, it invited no response at all, and Rath was almost at a loss for words. Which, considering how often he spoke with Jewel's den, was just as well. He retreated, leaving them, and returned to his room, where the letters he had written lay unfinished. They were in various stages, and no single one of them had been left untouched or unmarked; he had sifted each word for tone and weight, choosing first one and then another. Tonight, however, at least one must be finished and sent, and before it was posted, he had one more visit to make.

The Den—the bar—was dark and noisy when he arrived; this was not his preferred time of day, but he was not there to enjoy the rather unfortunate atmosphere. He was there to speak with the men of *The White Lady*. Northerners all, they sometimes referred to themselves as sea wolves, an incongruous term that nevertheless suited them.

Here, with snow in the air and on the ground, they were beached and stranded; the port itself was nothing short of hazard, for it was not the job of the port authority to maintain passages in and out of the shipyards when the ships themselves were in harbor for the season.

And among those, of course, Harald.

The smoke was thick, but the scent of ale and the sweat of men too smart—or too stupid—too remove their winter vests, was almost as tangible. In a youth that troubled him enough he seldom dwelled on it, he would have shuddered just passing the doors. And now, a world away, he felt at home here, where death was evident, and manners not layered so thick that they could hide it easily.

Harald was quiet; this was not unusual; he joined Rath by the simple expedient of glowering his way through the crowd. Reputation—in context—was always valuable; it obviated the need for Harald to actually injure the fools who might otherwise stand too long in his way to prove a point. He sat and Rath waved one of the brothers over; the man came and plunked two mugs across a table that had already seen at least one good spill.

Rath nodded; Harald nodded. That was all the time left for social intercourse when the bar was busy.

"Well?" Rath said, as they bent over their drinks. The question was casual, but it held weight. Harald did not answer immediately, which was usually a bad sign; when he gathered his thoughts, rather than his weapons, things were often slow.

But Harald only looked like a thug; had he been, in fact, no better than an ill-tempered warrior, he would not now be alive. "The report handed to the Magisterium by the magisterial investigators spoke simply of a cooking fire," he said at last.

"A cooking fire."

"Aye."

"And the dead?"

"Trapped in an old building. Probably drunk; it was morning, after all."

"The Magi were not summoned?"

"No."

Rath was silent. "The investigators?"

"Their names were attached to the report," Harald said quietly. And he removed a sheaf of papers from within his cloak. "This was costly," he added.

Rath nodded and handed him a small bag. The tinkle was lost to the crowd, but it didn't matter overmuch; no one would think of taking the money by force when Harald would gamble at the tables sooner or later. No one smart, at any rate.

"They thought a kitchen fire started in the grand hall?"

"They imply that little enough was left standing; the fire spread."

"Incompetence?"

"The magisterians are not my domain, Rath. If they're anyone's here, they're yours. You tell me." He paused. "You made a report?"

"I sent rumor with a runner," Rath replied. It was an evasion. Harald clearly expected no less. "But there were other witnesses in the streets; mage fire was clearly used there."

"They didn't speak with your witnesses then," Harald replied. "If any of them are still alive. You gave names?"

"I failed to retrieve names," Rath said. "It did not, at the time, seem necessary."

"Then perhaps no one was willing to come forth."

"I told you—"

"Beyond your rumormonger," he added.

But they were both disturbed. The use of battle magic in the streets was not a daily event; it was perhaps an event witnessed every decade or two, and that with both dread and fear. Mages *were* feared; they could, by dint of both birth and training, do the impossible. It was only the iron grip of the Kings, and the watchful eye of the Magi themselves, that kept that fear at bay.

And it had slipped here, and slipped badly.

"You expected this?" Harald asked, draining half his mug. He was still stone sober.

"Not this," Rath replied, drinking less heavily. "But something, yes. I would not have said it would be possible to . . . prevaricate to this extent."

"Money buys silence."

"So does death."

And trouble. They were quiet for a long moment. "I owe you for this."

Harald laughed. "You couldn't pay what you owe," he replied. "But I'll keep it on the books."

"One of your men is part of the magisterial guards now?"

Harald shrugged. "Does it matter? You have the report. You can read it at your leisure. But I would say it's a bad sign for this holding."

"I'd say it's a bad sign," Rath nodded. "But not for the holding alone; for the City as well. Concealment of this type would be less obvious in the holdings, where the powerful seldom travel."

"Something's going on down here."

Rath frowned. "Something must be," he said at last. "But I can't make sense of it yet; I don't have the whole picture."

"If anyone can see it, it's you. Not that I'd suggest it," Harald added. "You're Old Rath for a reason. This one—it reeks of trouble."

Rath nodded. "The magisterial guards have been less present in the streets of late."

"And the streets have become more dangerous."

"A place where men can die."

"Or disappear," Harald said agreeably. "There are two other reports there. One's about Jim," he added.

"Same station?"

"Same station. Different names on the documents."

"Good." Rath rose almost hesitantly. He did not want to leave The Den, or his chair.

"You think uptown is involved in this."

"I think," Rath said, "that the Isle itself may be involved in it."

Harald shrugged. "Not my problem," he said curtly.

"No, thank the gods, it's not."

"Not your problem either, Rath."

But Rath didn't answer.

"Don't get mixed up in mage business."

"A good piece of advice if ever I heard it," Rath smiled. "And worth every copper paid for it, as well."

Harald reached out; caught Rath's arm. There was no humor in him, although he was capable of it when the mood struck. Lightning would strike first, tonight. "I mean it, Rath."

"I know. And were I in a position to take your advice, I would sojourn in the country."

"That bad?"

"Bad enough," Rath replied, "that this is the last favor I'll ask of you for quite some time. Take your own advice," he added. "You've already lost men to this."

"Aye."

"The money there should cover some of their responsibilities, if anyone was fool enough to marry them or bear their children."

"Aye, and in at least one case, it'll be more welcome than having him back. Sea's good for something." Grim humor. "This isn't a fight."

"Not your kind, no. But it is a fight in the sense that there will be deaths by the end of it. If the whole City isn't affected," he added, "we can offer thanks to the gods."

"Which ones?"

"Doesn't matter. Choose one, and be sincere while you're there."

Harald did laugh at that. "You know my god's Cartanis."

"Cartanis," Rath said quietly, "would not frown on this. I will take what you've brought. If there's trouble that follows, I'll send what word I can."

"And I'll know it's from you?"

"I'll make sure it's obvious." Rath nodded and rose.

"Pay before you leave," Harald said, reaching for what remained of Rath's ale.

"Already done, old friend. And a round's worth as well if your crew shows up."

"If? Not much else to do in this town at the moment. Damn snow," Harald said, with a vigor that was surprising, given his homeland.

Rath took the reports home. It was quiet when he arrived, if by quiet, one meant a scattering of barely muffled voices behind closed doors. He made his way to his room, and saw that the slates were not in their usual unwieldy stack; Jewel was teaching, then.

He liked to watch her teach, on the rare occasions it was possible. He found some comfort in it, and if she was a somewhat waspish teacher—and she wasn't particularly gentle—she was also a determined one. Arann had the most difficulty absorbing the shapes of letters, and his memory was poor; he tried several times to give up. Lefty spoke only when Arann was in a state of frustrated despair. Had Jewel wanted to excuse Arann, Lefty would have pinned him there. And, struggling with his off-hand, his good hand sometimes visible, he could silently shame Arann into continuing.

She allowed only Lander, however, to be excused. If Teller and Finch were her most able students, the others surprised, for Carver was quick with chalk and Jester, ebullient in his humor, only a whit slower. Duster swore loudly, especially when the answer to a question was beyond her. Jewel allowed her to hide her ignorance, but did not allow her to keep hold of it. She whittled away at them all.

Her father's gift, no doubt; Rath did not know what part his own teaching played in Jewel's. His role, when he had the time for it, was to teach the rougher things, and he had already begun—to Jewel's mute amazement and concern—to teach Duster and Carver the rudiments of what might best be described as illegal entry.

Jewel was trying to prepare them for a different life. Rath, in his practical way, was trying to prepare them for the life they might have to lead instead; he was old enough to have witnessed failure, endured it, and survived. Noble cause did not, in the end, guarantee success.

Determination often did. He marveled at Jewel's. It did not stem from

530 ✦ Michelle West

ignorance or naivete, although she *was* undeniably naive. She wanted more for these orphans than the streets were prepared to grant them, and she was willing to wrest it from the streets, through dint of will and struggle if need be. He did not desire to take that from her. Hope had its place.

And it was a better place, he thought wearily, than these reports occupied. He read them carefully, and with growing contempt and weariness. The Magi had not been called; they were not even mentioned. And the fire itself was indeed, as Harald had indicated, blamed on the kitchen which had probably been among the last of the places to burn; it was tiled there, and wood was scarce.

He took note of the names of the two investigators—for only two had signed this report. One was a man of little rank, and probably scant years; the other was a Primus of the magisterial guards. The second name, Evanton Billings, was therefore of more interest.

Money could buy men. It always had.

But seldom among the magisterians, who answered to the judgment-born. It was not merely their jobs that were at risk.

The second report, scant, was more annoying. It was not a missing person report, as Harald had suggested—for Jim was undeniably missing; it was instead a domestic complaint. From the report, Jim had taken what money he and his wife had, and had left the city. His wife was described as hysterical, and angry, but no credence was given to the idea that he was "missing."

The other report was similar. It detailed the description of a young girl who had run away from home. It gave her name, the names of her parents, her address.

These, Rath filed away; he thought he might pay a visit at some point. And soon. He wondered if that girl had been in the mansion at some point, before the mansion had simply ceased to exist in gouts of magical flame.

And he wondered, not for the first time, what would have become of Finch had it not been for the interference of Jewel and—yes—Duster.

He set the reports to one side and returned to the letter he had seen through so many drafts. Duster. If he had been stupid enough to walk blindly into Jewel's life—and he could almost acknowledge that he had, and in that direction—he could understand it.

But Duster?

Jay, he thought. *Jewel.* And then, of course, his sister's name. All of them. Terafin. Handernesse. Amarais.

Had he always known that their lives were, in the end, too large for his? Or were they both simply too arrogant or ignorant—or both—to acknowledge the burden of the responsibilities they accepted, and even fought to bear? Had he, he thought, pen hovering over paper again, while he stared dully at magelight, failed his sister? Had it gone in that direction, rather than in the one that he had built an angry life upon?

He could ask the question now. It was more painful, and less painful, than the questions he had asked for all of his adult life. And as in so many questions, he did not have an answer ready; no one, after all, was waiting upon it but he himself.

But he thought, as he penned this letter, that he knew what the answer was, because he felt a grim determination. What use mistakes if not to learn from them? What use learning if, in the end, one clung to the old? If he had indeed failed the sister he had once adored, he could not now fail the child he had grown to care for.

Because her life would be larger than his.

But only, in the end, with his help, and only in the end if she survived.

Chapter Twenty-five

JEWEL WAS NOT a patient teacher. Her Oma had not been patient. Her father and mother had, but Jewel had often been left in
her Oma's care, and it was her Oma's blood that ran true—or so the old
woman had taken some pride in saying.

But Duster's words still stung her, and she bit back her anger and her
frustration, channeling it into words that were less harsh and less quick. It
was harder work than running the maze had been, the night she had gone
to save Rath. Harder than finding Finch. Because there was no end in
sight to the need for it; it was a constant worry, and a constant burden.

For the first time since she had invited Lefty and Arann into her home
and life, she wanted privacy, the space in which to scream and swear and
punch the wall in fury. She wanted to let her hair down—where had that
phrase come from, anyway?—and just be herself. But herself in this case
wasn't what was needed.

Hard, to change it.

But necessary. Tiring, vexing, and necessary.

She did the work. Because she could see, from the moment she started,
that Duster—damn her—was *right*. It was Jewel's moods that set the tone
for her den; it was her anger—or her lack of anger—that either destroyed
peace or let it settle. What she wanted for her den-kin wasn't simple, and
when they didn't obviously want it for themselves, she wanted to slap
them. Her Oma would have.

But she couldn't be her Oma here. No one could. She had to be, not
better, but different. Her father, or her mother. Or maybe Finch, although

that was beyond her reach. She was learning while she was teaching, and if the others had trouble with their lessons, it was fair; Jewel was struggling with hers.

Duster, to her credit, didn't fight Jewel. She bit back her sullen words, her angry threats, her declarations of independence. She stopped herself from chewing on Lefty when she was bitter and resentful, and it was at least as much work for her as Jewel's hold on her temper was for Jewel.

They were *all* trying. She wanted to be proud of them. Was, in fact, proud.

But she was frightened as well. Because Rath had grown silent and withdrawn, and she knew, she *knew*, that tonight he would lead them away from this basement apartment, this crowded home, and into the unknown. Haval had done his best to explain what they *might* face. But the waiting was killing her; her imagination was far worse than reality.

She hoped.

But she didn't know what would happen if they failed. What would happen, not to her—although she was worried about that as well—but to them: To Lefty, Arann, Carver, Finch, Teller; to Jester, Fisher, and Lander. Even to Duster, although she imagined that Duster would land on her feet and run.

So she sought Rath out on the morning of *the* night, and she inserted herself quietly between his door and its frame, waiting to catch his attention. She didn't wait long, but he was slow to turn, slow to face her. She didn't like what he was thinking, even if she didn't know for certain what it was; his face looked worn and haggard, as if sleep had eluded him for days.

"Jay," he said, motioning toward a chair.

She took it, drawing her knees up to her chin. "I wanted to talk to you," she told him, armored in that way, her arms wrapped round her legs.

"About what?"

"My den."

"Ah."

"I want to know—" She hesitated. "I still have money," she told him. "From the other stuff. Not as much, but it's still a lot. It'll hold us through the Winter, and maybe through the next one as well, no problem.

"It's mine," she added. "You said it was mine."

"It is yours."

"If we fail—no, if something goes wrong—I want you to set them up someplace. With the money. Because I won't need it then."

534 ✦ Michelle West

"They're not my den," he replied.

"No, they're not. They're mine. But I have to do this, and—"

"And?"

"I'm not certain, Rath. I don't have the visions. I know you'll take us somewhere tonight. I can see the rooms; I can almost see the place. But I can't see the people. I can't see where the danger is, or where it will come from. It's like I'm blind."

He watched her, neither nodding nor shaking his head, and after a moment, she continued. "They're special."

"Are they?"

She nodded forcefully. "You know it," she added, half accusing.

"I know you think they are."

"Can you do this for me? They don't have to live here," she added awkwardly. "You don't have to keep them here. But the money—their own place—"

"Jay—"

"I need to know you'll take care of them at least that much."

"Or you won't go?" Soft words. Almost dangerous. They were an offer, one last chance to back out. And the damnable thing was that she *wanted* to take it.

That he wanted her to take it.

He watched her carefully, neutrally, the desk at his back. This was a test, and some part of him wanted her to fail. He knew it, and was not diminished by the knowledge; he was curious instead, in a calculating way.

A minute passed; he could see the indecision across her features, and it was so clear, he could almost touch it. Could, if he wanted, tease it out and make it stronger. That tempted him.

But he waited instead, like a judge, or a teacher.

And after a moment, she said, "No, I'll go anyway. I'm not demanding it," she said quietly. Almost desperately. "I'm—"

He lifted a hand. "I will do as you ask," he told her. "I will make sure they have a place, and the money, and even the slates that you use. But, Jewel, they won't be what you want them to be if you're not here to lead them. You do understand that?"

"I'm just one person," she told him flatly. Believing it. Maybe she had to. Because this was possible, he offered no argument.

"I will do as you ask," he told her again. And then he said, "You know."

"Tonight."

He nodded. "I should have guessed."

"I just can't see what's going to happen."

"Nor can I. If you were trained somehow—" But he shook his head. "It doesn't matter. Your instincts are good; *trust* them. When you are there, when you are in the lion's den, trust what you feel or think. Don't let fear guide you, but let fear make you cautious."

"Did you learn that from Haval?"

Rath raised a brow. He laughed, but the laugh was brief and almost bitter. "No," he replied quietly. "I learned it from my own mistakes. I survived them," he added, "where others did not. Mistakes are made constantly; it's what you do with them after that counts."

"Will this help Duster?"

"That, I cannot answer; you know her better than I, and I admit that she has surprised me in the last ten days." He paused, playing with his pen. "I think that it will either help her or free you."

"Free me?"

"You will let her go."

Jewel nodded. She couldn't see how, but she heard truth in the words, and it was her truth, not Rath's. Here, just Rath and she, she was comfortable in a way that she hadn't been in weeks. Since she had brought Duster home.

"You'll know," he added, with no hesitation and no doubt. "When the moment comes, you'll know, and you'll make your decision only then."

"Will she survive it?"

"I don't know."

Will I? He could see the fear in her face; she was not capable of hiding fear. Not from Rath, who understood its nuances so well. But because she knew better than to ask, he was kind; he did not answer.

"Spend the day with your den. Do what you feel necessary to prepare them—if you think it wise. But by sunset, be ready to travel."

She rose. "I'll tell Duster."

He nodded; he had no intention of speaking to Duster except in this fashion: through Jewel. Through the leader of this misfit den.

"She doesn't believe in you," he said, as Jewel unfolded and rose.

"I know. But, most of the time, neither do I." And she smiled as she said it. Some hint of the child she would not be for much longer was in that movement of lip, the crinkling of eye.

Rath could not speak a word. But he let her go.

That evening, they ate early, at Rath's command. It was phrased as a polite request, but he so seldom entered the rooms in which Jewel was teaching that everyone instantly deferred to him. Even Jewel. Especially Jewel.

The kitchen was quiet. Finch was quiet, and not in her usual way. Teller was utterly silent; it was a very funereal meal. But Rath joined them, and ate with them, sitting cross-legged on the floor of Jay's room—the room in which they usually ate if everyone was there.

Then Jewel kicked them all out, so that she and Duster could change into fine dresses. Jewel's was almost beautiful; it was not the dress that she wore to Haval's, but softer and shinier than that. It had sleeves that would trail in the snow, skirts that were full enough to rustle; it was a deep blue, a dark color that was neither the azure of the clear sky at day, nor the dark of the night.

Duster, however, wore the dress that she wore to Haval's, and beside Jewel's, it looked practical, serviceable, fine enough for work. They stared at each other; Jewel with her hair still long and straight—or as straight as it would ever be—and Duster with hers a pale platinum, knotted as Haval had shown her, behind a fine web of netting.

They took time to color each other's faces, to change the tone of their skin, to shade their cheeks to imply cheekbones, or perhaps heighten them; they did this with shaking hands, for each other; there were no other mirrors.

And when they were done, they drew a single breath and opened the doors. The den gaped at their transformation, but before they could freeze or speak, Rath stepped forward.

"It's time," he told them all, almost gently. "Come. All of you."

Lander did not look up, but Lefty touched his shoulder gently with his maimed hand, deliberately exposing the lost fingers, as if to ensure that the touch held no threat. Lander met Lefty's eyes and rose obediently, following Lefty.

"You will not speak of this," he told them all, "to anyone. I would be happiest if you did not speak about it among yourselves either, but I am realistic enough to hold little hope for that. Finch and Carver, you've seen some of what I will show the others."

Finch nodded hesitantly. Carver, bangs obscuring one eye entirely, nodded more forcefully.

"We will not chance the streets tonight," Rath told Jewel. She stared at him in surprise. Of all the things she had been careful not to share with her den-kin, the existence of the maze beneath their home was foremost. It was Rath's, to give or withhold. And tonight, he chose to give it, like a benediction.

Or a doom.

He held out a magestone to Carver. "Hold this," he said quietly. "Jewel, you have yours?"

She nodded; she always had it. Hidden, light eclipsed by fabric and lack of command, it warmed her pockets.

"Good. We will have need of it, I think." He led them, not to the door that led out into the hall, and from there to the streets, but in, toward the closed storeroom door that was never used.

There, the magelight brightening at Rath's command, even though it rested in Carver's palm, no sunlight shone, and there were no window wells, with their pathetic offering of scant light.

Duster looked at Jewel. Jewel shook her head. Silence reigned, and not even Jester was fool enough to break it; you could hear breathing. Only breathing.

But Rath said, "this is not a grave, and we are not attendants at a funeral. This is a hidden world, and in many ways, it has been mine. If you are not careful, you will fall and injure yourselves; no more and no less."

"Where are we going?" Carver asked quietly.

"You? Not far. Jewel, Duster and I will travel farther this eve. But we may have need of the maze in the next few days, and you will know when we use it."

"But not why?"

Rath didn't answer, which was answer enough. Instead, he bent and retrieved the packs that held rope. He handed one to Jewel and after retrieving the twine from the other, shouldered it himself. To Duster, he handed nothing—nothing but this knowledge.

Jewel understood that it was almost a vote of confidence in the evening, in what might follow. She felt momentarily overwhelmed by the knowledge, and she bit back words because they would come out garbled. Or worse, they would come out choked.

He led them down, through the trap, and into the subbasement, ordering the taller among them to watch their heads. Carver still held the magestone aloft.

"Jay," Rath said, "go first. When you are down, and safe, light your own stone so the others can see."

She nodded, and he wrapped the rope around her, knotting it loosely. It was a guide, no more.

"You have an escape tunnel here?" Duster whispered.

Jewel smiled. "Not exactly. Watch." And Rath lowered her down, and down again, the rope pinching her underarms. He never tied it around her waist.

When she hit bottom, and felt the uneven dirt and stone with the flat of her palms, she drew out her own magestone, and held it in much the same way that Carver was holding Rath's: so that they could all see. There was a magic in the moment that had nothing to do with stones.

They all followed, even Lander, who unfolded in the unnatural quiet as if he were waking from a dream. Or perhaps entering one, when the waking world was too damn hard to bear. He blinked, although the light was not harsh, and even reached out to touch the rough-hewn tunnel walls. And he said, "They're cold."

Jewel almost tripped over nothing; she would have, had she been moving. He spoke to Lefty, and Lefty didn't even startle. The others all did, and Finch's mouth was a rounded O of shock, quickly suppressed.

"No sunlight," Lefty replied with a shrug, as if Lander had always spoken and these two words—his first—were not a surprise. Lander nodded, because it made sense.

The tunnels were cold, but they were not the Winter cold of the streets above; no snow graced or hid their surfaces; no ice crunched beneath their boots. Here, they might weather a bad Winter, if the lack of light didn't drive them all mad. It certainly seemed to have the opposite effect on Lander, who seemed more alert than he had been since, well, ever.

Jewel thought that Rath would order the others out, but he didn't; he led them instead farther in, to where the walls *were* walls, through the doorframe that seemed to bear too much weight, and beyond it. Here again, Lander stopped to touch everything. As if Lefty's silent language had become some part of his movement, his gestures conveyed wonder, even awe. Rath must have noticed, although she never caught him looking at Lander, for he led them a little farther in, and he walked slowly, for Rath.

But when he reached the first branch, the first hint of road, he stopped and looked at them. "If someone comes for you fight as you must, and flee *here* if you can," he told them quietly.

Jewel understood then that this was not a gift; it was practical. "Duster, Jewel and I must continue, but we will not leave by the door; nor will we return by it.

"However, on another day, I will take you farther; I will show you some of what lies beneath Averalaan. History," he added, and he looked at Teller.

Teller nodded quietly.

"You can find your way back?"

"I can," Carver answered firmly. He hesitated, and then said, "But we'd like to go with you."

"Not tonight."

"If we can help—"

"If we need your help," Rath replied, and then stopped. "Not tonight," he said again, but more gently.

"Jay—"

"No, Carver. Arann, cut it out. Take Lander and Lefty and Finch home." She paused, and then said, "We're going to be with Rath. We'll be as safe as we can possibly be. Go *home*."

They still hesitated, and instead of resenting it, she found it oddly comforting. But Rath was waiting, and he was watching her with that peculiar testing expression he so often wore these days. "What are you afraid of?" she asked instead.

Carver and Arann exchanged a glance; they said nothing. It was Teller who lifted his chin. "We know why you're going," he said at last. "And we're willing to help."

"That's not an answer."

"We'd like you to come home," he replied, after a brief pause, "And it's clear that you all think there's a chance you won't make it back. If we can help—"

Jewel lifted a hand.

But Teller kept talking in his quiet, soft voice, "And we don't, and something happens, we'd rather not live with it."

This, she could understand; wasn't it how she felt herself most days? *You have to be able to live with yourself.* Her Oma's voice. Her Oma's sharp words.

"You all feel this way?"

Jester nodded. Even Fisher, whose silence was less a matter of trauma and more a matter of personality, nodded.

"You can't speak for Lander," she began.

"I want to go," Lander said.

She hesitated for a moment, weighing all options. And then she nodded. Saw Rath's brows rise. "You told me to trust my instincts," she said, and if she sounded defensive, it was mostly because she was.

"You'll risk them?" he asked, the words stark, like all accusations stated baldly.

Carver said, "It's not her choice. It's ours. I'm older than she is," he added, drawing his lanky shoulders back and gaining a couple of inches in the process.

"She is the den leader," Rath told him quietly. "And I will not question her decision further. I merely want to make clear—"

"You want her to worry," Carver said, cutting him off, "but she'll do that anyway. She's been leaving instructions for days, just 'in case.'" He paused. "I don't know where you grew up, Rath." It was the first time he had ever addressed Rath by name, and he did not flinch or step back as he said it. "I know where I did. This *is* my home now. I want to keep it. I don't want to go back to what I had before. None of us do."

"You've discussed this?"

"We don't have to," Carver replied. "We all know. She found us," he added. "We probably wouldn't have found her. Sure, we'd be able to skip the reading lessons," he added with a grimace of distaste, "but the food and the fire are kind of important."

"I . . . see."

"You don't."

"Carver—"

"No." Carver's arms had folded across his chest, and he no longer leaned against the nearest wall. His eyes—well, the one you could actually see—were slightly narrowed, and his lips thinned; he was angry. And he was afraid. Then again, being afraid made him angry, so no surprise there.

"We could send Finch back with the others," Arann offered. Lefty kicked him. "Or not."

Duster stared at them all, and then she looked at Jewel. There was, for just a moment, a hunger about her expression that Jewel couldn't look at for long. "We might die," she told them bluntly, using words that Jewel had so carefully, deliberately avoided. "And if you're there, if you're anywhere near, you might die.

"Don't you follow her because she *saved* you? You want to throw that back in her face? Throw it away?"

"Without her," Carver said willing to face Duster down where even Arann was not, "I'd still be alive. Don't bother trying that with me."

"Then why do *you* care?" Duster shot back. Her hand had fallen to her hip.

"Because she does," Carver said steadily. "She wants us, we'll come. No, never mind, we *want* to be there, and if she'll let us, we will be."

Rath said, "It is up to you, Jewel, but decide quickly."

Jewel nodded. Her throat felt tight, which was stupid. "Come," she told them all, even Lander. "I don't think we'll need help—but right now, I don't know."

And she had not been allowed to follow her father to work the day he'd died. *You're not their parent,* she told herself, but the words didn't take, couldn't hold her.

As if, in the end, he had expected no less, Rath nodded. She didn't understand him; she was certain she never would. But as she glanced sideways at him, it came to her that he was testing, yes, but this one—this one was not for her, and not, in the end, directly about her. It was for them, for the den that she had told him, time and again, was special.

She wondered if they had passed or failed; nothing in his expression gave the answer away. "I don't want anyone to follow who doesn't want to be here, Carver."

"Everyone wants to be here."

"Can they speak for themselves?"

"Why? You speak for us most times. I'm speaking for them. Do they look like they're being forced?"

She looked at them all, and they all met her gaze and held it, even Lander. So she nodded. "It's fair."

Rath paused and then said, "I suppose these will be useful." And he pulled, from his pocket, three magestones. "They are mine, and are to be treated as if they are mine. But distribute them; we are too long a line to have only two such lights."

Success or failure, he had anticipated them.

* * *

Rath watched as Carver gave a stone to Teller, Finch and Lander. Finch and Teller, Rath could easily see as wise choices; he could also understand why he did not choose to grant that responsibility to Arann, their only giant. But Lander? That took perception or kindness, or some mixture of both.

But Carver alone had not come to Jewel through vision; he had aided her, and he had followed her, his past veiled and less threatening than the past of the other children. He was not a calm child, and he did not have Teller's obvious penchant for quiet but intent observation. Yet he must have observed what Rath himself only guessed at. Lander stared at the stone for a long moment, and then nodded quietly. He kept his hand out, extending the gift of that light to those around him.

Rath did not carefully observe the words they exchanged in their hurried odd movements; they spoke only with their hands. A secret language, he thought, and it pained him, for his sister and he—as children—had devised so many, and it was a reminder to Rath of both his own childhood, and the fact that these *were* still children, although they bridled at the word with the obvious arrogance—and ignorance—of youth.

Having given Rath back his own magestone and distributed the other three, Carver kept for himself only his daggers, and not even both of them; he handed one to Arann who nodded grimly—for Arann—and accepted it. Just as the others had accepted the gift and responsibility of light.

Jewel was not surprised, or did not appear to be surprised; she merely nodded her thanks to Carver as he approached her. But where the den had spoken with their hands, as if words would somehow break or damage the spell of the undercity, Jewel chose—as she often would—words.

"Keep an eye out," she told him. "Both now and then. If we don't come back, get them home, if you can. Get them out somewhere crowded and safe if you can't."

He nodded. Interesting. That she had chosen Carver, and not Arann; that he accepted.

They traveled more slowly than they might have had they been just three; Jewel couldn't be certain if Rath was annoyed or not. He set the pace, however, and he held her back when she tried to forge ahead. He didn't show them the stone garden, or anything else that Jewel would have shown them had she had time; those wonders, like quiet promises, lay in the dark, waiting.

But in the dark, other things waited, and although the air was cool, it wasn't cold enough that she could think about warmth instead. She thought about death as she walked; she thought about it a lot.

Everything she had said to Rath was true; she had seen him kill. She had stepped over bodies that hadn't stopped bleeding, they were so new. And she hadn't cared. But she hadn't killed them either. She could accept responsibility for their deaths, could say that her hands weren't clean—but in the end, it wasn't the same thing. The desire to kill was a visceral thing, like a flash of rage; it came and went, so much daydream and idle intent.

This—this was colder, its conception darker and more deliberate. She was walking to an inn somewhere in the upper holdings. By the end of the night—if everything went according to plan—someone would be dead. That he deserved death wasn't in question. He did. She would have smiled had Rath told her he had died, messily and horribly. But being told was different, and the sense that she could control the fear of it vanished with each step she took.

What are you afraid of?

Her voice, and her memory of voice: Oma. And when her Oma asked a question, she got an answer, one damn way or another. Jewel had no answer ready. She should have.

Was she afraid of failing? Yes. Of being caught? Yes. But what did failure mean now? That he survived, or that he died? She wasn't certain; couldn't define success well enough to know what failure meant. Could only be certain that failure felt a lot like this: walking toward the unknown, with a sinking heart and a growing certainty that she was not up to the task she had undertaken. The promise she had made.

Promises are not an accident of fate.

No, Oma.

They are an act of will. They are a responsibility. You are measured by the worth of your word, and if you give it, girl, you will keep it; break it and you break a blood debt.

Yes, Oma.

She looked at Duster, or at Duster's profile; Duster was watching the ground with care, and placing her feet—in tight, uncomfortable boots—with deliberate weight along a road that was often cracked and broken. She did not share in the den's wonder, or in their silent language; she had barely troubled to learn it, and then, only to speak with Lander. More often, she had chosen to just sit by him, to whisper to him; what she said, Jewel had never fully caught, but she could guess.

But she *had* taken that time. And it meant something.

"You afraid?" Duster asked, with an edge of contempt in her voice. She didn't bother to look up to see the reaction her words had caused; she said them so carelessly, she must have been certain what they would be.

But Jewel said, quietly, "Yes." And this did make Duster look at her. "But it's just fear," she added. "Haval said fear was good if you could control it; bad if you let it control you."

"And is this a *bad* fear, or a *good* fear?"

"Don't make me slap you."

At that, Duster's face did change, allowing for expression: she laughed. It was—for Duster—genuine laughter, shorn of edge, but not of surprise. And it ended quickly enough.

"It's just fear," Jewel repeated remotely. As if it were weather. But she knew, as they all knew: weather could kill. She didn't ask Duster the same question; she knew what the answer would be, and didn't feel like hearing it.

"Why did you bring them?"

"I couldn't stop them."

"You could have."

"I could have told them to go home," Jewel conceded, stepping over a large, cracked stone, something that looked like a fallen slab. "and yes, they might have done it. But it wouldn't have been fair."

"Fair?" The laugh was different, short, brutish. "You just wanted them here."

Jewel shrugged. "Maybe. Maybe I wanted to know that they *wanted* to be here." She stopped walking, faced Duster, and said, "We're all we have. Each other. I let my father leave the day he died. I knew he would die, but I couldn't stop him. He wouldn't take me with him—and if he had, I might have saved him."

"And that has what to do with them?"

Jewel shrugged again. She was growing angry, and there wasn't much incentive to keep it to herself. "Everything, but I don't expect you to understand that yet." Wrong words, and harsh ones; they bounced off Duster. Angry words almost always did. "I don't want them to have what I have: the guilt. The sense that if they had come—"

"They'll just get in the way. Well, most of them."

"You don't know what they'll do. You don't know what will happen."

"Neither do you."

Which was true. There were whole days when Jewel hated the truth.

"They'll be one more thing for you to worry about."

"A better thing," Jewel snapped back. And then she calmed, because there were also days when the truth was like a little bit of necessary light. "You don't love anything that doesn't make you worry," she added softly.

"I don't love anything."

"Maybe not. But I wasn't talking about you."

She expected Duster to answer, but heard instead the stiff rustle of fabric, her shrug in the shadows and darkness.

Then, silence, and walking.

In the darkness, all nuance of expression was lost, all subtle gestures, the minute downturn of lip, the slight gathering of brow; everything silent was mute here, except where light was brought to bear. And given the nature of the road they walked, with its sudden cracks, its wide chasms, it was never brought to bear.

Jewel felt uneasy as she walked. Uneasy as they approached the wide gap in the road she recognized. Finch and Carver recognized it as well.

But Rath said, "Not this way," as they approached it, looking for an anchor; he led them instead to the left of where they were standing, along the edge of the wide gap, until the gap narrowed. "We are not going to the Common," he told her quietly.

"Where are we going?"

"To an inn, of sorts."

"And we can reach it from here?"

"We can reach most of the City from here," he replied. He paused, aware that she was surprised by what he had said, although he had hinted at it strongly many times. "I should have showed you the ways."

Jewel shrugged. "I probably wouldn't remember them."

"No. You wouldn't. I think Teller might."

She looked at him; he was a silhouette. A shade. "You like him, don't you?"

"I don't know him," Rath replied.

"You're hedging."

"Perhaps. If one hedges, best to use truth where possible." He undid the top button of his jacket. It was not nearly as fine as the clothing he had provided for Jewel, and not, in the end, as fine as the servant's garb that Duster wore. If she had wondered how far he intended to lead them, she had her answer the moment she saw what he wore. But she had hoped. Still did, if she were truthful.

"Be careful of those stairs," he said, looking back. "They are not as solid as many of the others, and they will likely not bear Arann's weight well."

She turned herself to see light bobbing around the facade of a building that did look—from this distance—to be solid. It was like and unlike the massive old buildings that girded the Common; it was not overly decorated with statues or carvings or brass plates that shone in the morning light. But she couldn't see the height of the building as it crept into invisibility above.

"What was it?" she asked Rath.

"I don't know," he replied. "I don't know what most of these buildings were. There is little enough left in them to indicate what use they were put to."

He walked past it, as if it were of no interest, and because he did, they followed.

"How did this get here?" Teller asked.

Rath's smile flickered briefly in the glow of magelight. He did not hold it; she could not be certain how long it lasted, or even if it were there at all. She could see him smile or frown when she closed her eyes.

"I don't know," he replied. "I imagine that there was a cataclysm of some sort that plunged this city into darkness."

"But we—"

"It is very old," he added softly. "Old enough, I think, to be forgotten. No one lives here anymore," he added.

"Were there bodies?" Jester's voice.

"There are some," Rath replied carefully. "Not bodies, but bones. Old armor. The armor itself is worth a great deal, where it is found; it is seldom found." His tone made clear that they were not to start looking now. "And when it is, it must be handled with care."

"If it's lasted this long—"

"Idiot," Duster snapped. "He meant *sold* with care."

Jester stopped talking. Duster always had that effect; her contempt bred silence, and there was usually a lot of it.

Rath led them down a broad, broad road, and Jewel knew that she had never walked it before. From this vantage, it was a night city, with guttered magelights instead of the ones that girded the streets of Averalaan when the sun began its slow fall. But there were no stars and no moons above. There was cloud, if one wanted to pretend, and air that tasted of dry dust.

"Here," he said quietly, "we turn right. The road will narrow significantly, and it will bank sharply when it goes up."

"Where does it go?"

"Out." Final syllable. But Rath relented and added, "You'll see. Practice patience."

And out it went, out and up, into—of all things—a yard, a stable yard, with wagons in various states of repair. Some were missing wheels, and some missing axles; some seemed almost worthy of travel, if not capable of bearing a load. They were bunched together like refuse.

"What is this?" Jewel asked Rath; she was the only person who spoke as they at last returned to the land of ice and snow, with its cold, damp air, its clear night sky, the stars bright, even beside the pale face of the full moon; the pale moon could not be seen.

"These are the old yards that were once used by the Merchant Authority," Rath replied. "They are still used during the Festival Season," he added, "and during the Kings' Challenge. At all other times they are as you see them now. Do not," he added, "attempt to use this exit—if you can find it—when the Kings' Challenge is in progress; there are royal guards posted everywhere at that time, and they are not idle or lazy."

Now, however, they were absent. A small group of children could easily make their way between the press of wagons, leaving footprints in the snow.

"This is close enough now," Rath said quietly, "that some caution would be wise. But they will not be looking for us here."

No one asked who "they" might be.

"We will proceed to the Common from here," he told the den. "The Common is poorly patrolled at this time of year; it is, however, patrolled. We will leave the Common and head toward the upper holdings, but our destination is not far from there."

He glanced at Jewel.

She stopped, then, and before Rath could rearrange her dress, she hugged them each in turn, holding them a little too tightly. She had nothing else to say to them, nothing that she could put into words. They didn't ask, and they held her, briefly, just as tightly—all save Lander, who retreated again into silence when they breached the invisible barrier between what lay hidden by the streets, and what lay upon them.

To Lander, then, she made a few gestures, visible in the bright moon, and after a moment, he offered a tentative response, his hands rising, his palms turning, his fingers twisting—all with a grace that surprised her.

This might be good-bye, and this was all she allowed herself. Then she turned, as Rath waited, and followed where he led, taking Duster with her, and leaving the rest behind in the cold of the growing night.

Chapter Twenty-six

THE COMMON AT NIGHT was not Jewel's favorite place. One chance meeting with would-be assassins had changed it, as events often changed the meaning of a place. It was linked, now, with a terrified run through the undercity, two strangers by her side—one that she had set out to rescue, and one that had come to her by the grace of Kalliaris' smile, and had stayed. She looked back once at Carver and Finch, and smiled; her smile was lost to shadow, but it lingered a moment.

They had not quailed or argued; they had not doubted for a moment that wherever she was going was someplace she *had* to be.

And they didn't doubt her now.

She doubted, but kept it to herself; there was no point in sharing. Rath would hear her, or Duster would, and either of these would be bad.

But as she emerged from the scattered wagons, some sitting like the cavernous bodies of beached ships on the drifts of Winter's bitter white snow, she shook herself, straightened her shoulders and lifted her chin. No, she thought, changing posture again, that was wrong. She lowered her chin slightly, and she let her nervousness show—and knew that that was better. She could almost hear Haval's voice guiding her movements.

But she had always heard absent voices. They were often clearer than the voices of those who walked with her; they became some part of her thought, some part of her way of looking at the world. Crowded head, hers. Her Oma's voice was mercifully silent. She didn't try to call it back. She had been a grim woman, in her way, and her sense of justice was acute and profound; she would no more allow a man like this lord to live than she would a cockroach found crawling near the food.

Jewel clung to that belief, and no argumentative voice came back to pry it from her.

She could breathe, here, and the air was sharp and cold; it was also so clear it felt as if she'd stepped into a different country. The night was piercing, almost beautiful, as it hovered above the city; the magelights were glowing softly. No missing stones here, and no long gaps between the poles; this was a place where people who had no fear of starvation lived.

They weren't lords, she thought, looking at the houses on their small parcels of land. Whether or not the lawns were bright and well tended she couldn't say; the snow covered all in one forgiving blanket. But the snow on those lawns was clean; no wheels cut into it, and very few footprints muddied or sullied it.

But they owned no horses, no great carriages, the people who claimed these houses as their own. They had fences, but they were short, and not the grand fences that had all but fallen over in some parts of the old holdings, where legend said great men—and women—had once chosen to live.

Not even their ghosts remained. And here? No hint of ghosts at all. The houses rested upon the earth and above the snow, unaware of the history that lay beneath them in silence and darkness.

But it was not to these houses that Rath led them; he walked the road, pausing here and there beneath the magelights. Patrols were not infrequent, but Rath merely waved as they passed, and was rewarded with a curt nod—or sometimes a friendly one—as he did. Duster kept her head down when they passed, but this, too, was appropriate. Jewel thought Haval would be pleased with her, but didn't say as much. No telling what Duster would say in response, and they didn't really need a fight here.

But Jewel found the patrols unnerving.

"They are here for our protection," Rath told her grimly. "And only that. You have nothing to fear from them unless you bolt."

Jewel nodded. She understood every word, but some part of her didn't believe it, and she had to squelch all the noise it made. With effort.

"Do you know where we are?" he asked at length.

Jewel shook her head. Duster was mute, which was pretty much a No. That was just her way.

"This," he said quietly, "is where the foreign merchants have housing when they are forced to Winter here. The houses are often owned, not by the merchants, but rather by the companies they work for, or through; they are sometimes owned by the owners of the Kings' charter." He waved briefly to one side. "This is the Northern quarter. The Southern quarter is just beyond this."

"Is that where we're going?"

Rath shook his head, but not with impatience. "Some merchants do not work with larger companies; they own little land here. But they find homes or rooms in some of the inns built for that purpose."

"We're going there?"

He nodded. "To one of them, yes. It is quite large, and during the height of the trade season, it is full. At this time of year, it is almost empty." He paused. "And therefore houses men who are perhaps less reputable. But innkeepers require some sustenance, and as long as the occupants break no laws, they are vastly less strict in the stormy season." He led them down blocks of Winter street, until they were pulling their heavy cloaks around their shoulders and hunching their bodies against the inevitable cold.

"Here," he said quietly, and stopped. He handed Jewel a letter. "Do not open it. It is for Lord Waverly," he told her, although her hands were now shaking enough that opening it would have been a challenge. Dresses of the kind she now wore were not designed for warmth, or rather, they were designed for people who didn't have to contend with the damn cold. And she told herself it was only the cold.

"I must go. I may not see you, but I will be there."

"Rath—"

He waited. She knew that she could, even now, turn back, and part of her wanted to. But only part.

"You will arrive," he told her softly, "and you will wait for Lord Waverly."

She nodded. Nodding was easier than speech.

She entered the inn, Duster at her heels, Rath nowhere in sight. Haval's lessons were firmly entrenched in her bearing, but they hadn't prepared her for what she would see: The floors were made of marble that gleamed in the evening lights. Magelights, adorned by glass sculptures, in pale hues that made light their heart. She was still a moment, tilting her head up, and up again, toward the tall and rounded ceilings. They were pale, and the shadows diffuse that lay against their surface.

Her whole den could have made a spacious home of the room that lay empty beyond the desk—and the desk itself might occupy three kitchens' worth of space. But the wood here, gleaming as if it were a dark reflection of stone, was unmarked, unscored, utterly untouched.

She had never expected so much money could feel so . . . empty.

The warmth melted snow; she stood dripping in the glare, and tried not to feel self-conscious. A man appeared behind the desk. It was not so late that he looked tired or grouchy with lack of sleep—but given his expression, and the perfect drape of his stiff, pale clothing, she doubted that he ever slept. He nodded politely in her direction, and this, too, came as a little shock. But the clothing she wore spoke of affluence, not poverty; she was not out of place here. Or she didn't *look* out of place.

Drawing her chin up, she walked slowly toward the man behind his fortress of a desk. "I'm here," she said quietly, "to meet a friend."

"Your name?"

Her name. She hesitated for a moment. "Amber," she said at last. "Amber Hartold."

He paused, and then opened a drawer to his right; he pulled out a long piece of paper, and studied it. It neither annoyed him nor amused him; his expression was like the stone she walked across. Since her parents had died, she had learned that being unnoticed was *good*; therefore it didn't bother her much.

The wait did; she had never been patient. Even when awaiting punishment, the wait was a torment, the punishment almost a relief. She didn't glance at Duster; she studied her boots instead.

"Yes," he said at last, and this time he did look at her, and a brief expression, flickering by too quickly to be pinned down, touched his face. "You are expected." He clapped his hands, and a man appeared from the other side of a small door she hadn't noticed. His perfect clothing was almost exactly like that of the man behind the desk, but he was younger, and a bit less stern. He even smiled—when the older man's back was turned.

"The Arboretum dining hall," the older man said.

This stilled the smile. "But that's—"

"Now. Ask no questions," the older man added severely. "And do not trouble our guests."

At least one of the guests didn't like his tone, but Jewel was now, as Haval would say, in character. She pretended not to notice. And it was hard.

* * *

Rath had said the inn would be almost deserted.

He was right. And wrong. Inn was a poor word for a building this fine and grand; it could almost be a *cathedral,* with its high ceilings, its perfect floors, its visible stone and hanging tapestries; a cathedral, she thought bitterly, for the gods of money, whoever they were. Wealth was supposed to be hers, and this display of wealth should therefore be beneath her notice.

But it was almost impossible to just walk past unmoved; it was certainly impossible to move quickly in any case; her feet were now sore with their unfamiliar confinement, and the height of her heels made the back of her calves ache. It took effort not to wobble.

Duster caught her when she almost tripped; her grip was like steel, and Jewel was certain her fingers left bruises. She met Duster's eyes, and saw that they glittered in the opulence of the light; glittered, and yet, were as dark as Jewel had ever seen them. There was, about her expression, something that made avarice seem chaste and tame, a hunger that made starvation seem paltry.

What did you expect to see? Fear?

No answer, there. Duster had never been a mirror.

And yet . . . she shook herself, smiled weakly, banished that smile, and continued to walk.

The air smelled oddly sweet and musty; incense was burning in the halls, fine, slender sticks that were dense and fragrant. Fires burned in hollows made for wood, and chimneys drew the smoke up, and up again; she was not cold in this place. And at this time of year, cold was always an issue.

Better cold, she realized, better hunger, than this.

She had come to kill a man.

No, some part of her said, *Duster's come to kill a man. It's not murder. It's execution.*

But another part of her answered, bleakly, *She would never have come this far without me. If she's the knife, I'm the hand that's holding it.*

Then turn back. Turn back while you can; run. Give it up. What do you have to lose?

And behind her, steps soft and firm, walked a shadow, some vague accusation whose name was Duster.

But the next question, she had no answer for: *Why are you afraid to lose her?* And she asked it, because there was no way to still that voice.

* * *

Rath watched from the shadows; they were some part of him now, as was the Winter. He waited until Jewel and Duster, two incongruous steps behind, cleared the decorative guards at the grand front doors of the inn before he began to move. He felt uneasy, in the clean open light of the Winter moon. She was gone; he could not watch her or hear her.

He was an accomplished liar; he could not tell himself that he thought she'd be safe. He had made his plans, but plans seldom survived first contact with the enemy—and first contact would be hers in its entirety. Not for the first time, he wondered why he had agreed to this, and not for the first time, he accepted the answer: This was her test.

And had he tested Amarais? Younger and smarter than Rath, smaller and more steely, had he tested her? He had thought, in his youth, that she had failed them all, betrayed them all. Perhaps, he thought bitterly, she had tested Rath—and Rath had failed.

He was determined not to fail now.

He checked the one pouch he carried, leather thick and Winter-cold to his touch. At some cost, he had procured large quantities of a medicinal herb—the only one with a subtle flavor that would be easily masked by wine. He made his way to the servants entrance, and there, handed the guard on duty a small sum of money. It bought, for a few seconds, a very necessary blindness.

The Arboretum was the biggest shock. Jewel was vaguely aware of what the word meant—Rath was not a kind teacher, and certainly not a lenient one—but vague knowledge and reality were in no way the same. There was *green* here. It was the type of green that even the streets didn't see during the height of Summer; the leaves seemed to glow with magelight, as if they absorbed it. And the leaves themselves were as wide in places as her thighs, as narrow in others as her smallest finger; they were long and short, emerald and magenta, and among them, nestled at times in the heart of those leaves, and at others, upon leaves that seemed to bear them like a crown, were flowers that were so brilliant her clothing's expensive dyes seemed dull and flat by comparison.

This was life, she thought, and forgetting herself, bent to touch a leaf with a shaking hand, to stroke the thin membrane of red and violet. She could remember sensation clearly when other things escaped her: words to describe it, visual memories to fasten it. She could, if she wanted, think of bark, and know exactly what it felt like to bite it or suck on it, although she had no memory of ever doing so. And there was ivory bark here, thin trees with slender, rising branches, that almost invited her to make that memory. But she had enough dignity to pull back and rise.

Duster waited by her back in perfect, subservient silence. It was . . . unsettling. Jewel had never thought to miss her cutting words, her cruel curses—but she missed them now. There was nothing of Duster in the servant; the servant had become her. Then again, Duster had always said she was a damn good liar. Lying, to Jewel, was like a foreign language; she struggled with its consonants and the shape of its vowels.

And tonight, she had to sound like a native.

She was, of course, afraid, and she remembered clearly what Haval had said about fear. Coming here, in the cold that was so familiar it was almost like kin, it had been easy to believe that she could channel fear; in this bright room, this beautiful, impossible place, belief faltered.

But the boy who was leading her—and he was a boy, although older than she by a few years if she was any judge—now offered her a pained smile, a hesitant one. "Lady," he said formally, "your host is waiting." And in his tone she heard the words he wanted to say, and didn't: that this host did not like to be kept waiting.

"Of course," she said, in a pale, thin voice. "It's—I'm sorry to keep you." But hadn't Rath said she would wait for him? He was early. Lord Waverly was early. Jewel was well aware of how their plan could go wrong—but all of the disasters she'd imagined, and she'd done little else, did not include this.

He shook his head. "In the Summer, hardly anyone notices the Arboretum. But in the Winter, it's different. It's almost like a harbor."

"Do you come here often?"

"Me?" He laughed. Caught himself and folded laughter into awkward silence. "No. The Master Gardener would kill me if I so much as dribbled water across his precious flowers."

She laughed, and her laughter sounded almost natural. "I can almost understand why," she told him. "I'm not very good with plants."

"He doesn't call them plants. He has names for all of them," the boy added.

"Flowers have names."

"He calls that one Fossie."

"Oh."

"But if he saw you touch them, he couldn't say a word. You were care-ful," he added, "and you—appreciate them."

"We don't have flowers like this."

"No, not unless you sleep in a flower bed." He began to walk, and then slowed. Turned to look at Jewel. And to look away. It was painful and awkward, and she wanted to tell him, "It's okay." But her own words wouldn't come, maybe because she just didn't trust them to be the *right* words.

That was the problem with lying, she thought; *you had to have the knack of using the right damn words at the right damn time.* She had the knack of using the wrong words at the right time on a good day.

"If you—" he smiled, but it was the ghost of a smile—something that might once have known life, but now knew only cold and fear. "There are bells—" He stopped again. "Do you—have you met your host before?"

"He's a business associate of my father's," she replied smoothly. "I haven't met him yet, but I'm told I'll like him."

He said nothing at that. But the smile was gone, and he was pale and cold, like the Winter outside. Even the passing garden—and it still ex-isted all around them—leeched color from his face.

"The dining room here is part of the Arboretum," he said formally and stiffly. "The walls are made of special glass. Your host has—the Arbore-tum is his for the evening. There will be attendants to serve dinner," he added, "but they will leave when the lord commands them."

She nodded.

Nothing else to say, really.

Rath made his way to the spacious and—given his experience—the sur-prisingly clean kitchen. As it was Winter the staff numbered four; during the busy merchanting season, when the port was not occupied by empty ships, there were at least triple that number. He knew this because it was not the first time he had used this fine inn for business transactions. Admittedly, the tour of the kitchens that he had insisted on making had been entirely secondary to his goals, but the role he had taken for that particular job had required no less.

He glanced around the large room and frowned. There were two aproned cooks—a woman of Rath's age, and a young man; the man who ruled the kitchen could be seen nearer the large stoves that occupied the far wall. But the man he had come to see, briefly, was nowhere in sight.

The woman, however, rose as Rath paused. She eyed him dubiously. But if she was brisk, she chose to be polite; it was, after all, a sparse season, and everyone needed to eat.

"Here," she said. "You've taken a wrong turn. These are the kitchens, and they're no place for guests."

"My apologies," he said. "I serve as a courier for Landsdon's, and I was instructed to carry a small parcel for Marrett. His daughter's been unwell," he added.

She frowned. "Aye," she said after a long pause. "She has, at that. But maybe whatever it is that made her unwell has also caught Marrett—he's not come into work today." She lowered her voice and added, "and the Cook's fit to be tied; we've an important guest for the off-season."

"I beg your pardon," Rath said, running a hand through his hair. "But you said he hasn't been in this evening? Perhaps I have the wrong shift."

"Oh, no, you've got the right shift. But he's not come in, and he's sent no word." She shook her head. "Maybe you should take that parcel you're carrying off to his home; he might find it more useful there."

Just like that, the world shifted. Rath was a practiced liar, a practiced con man. He nodded briskly to the woman and apologized, just as briskly, for the interruption, before retreating from the kitchen.

But if the Arboretum was a surprise, the man who waited, at a long, perfect table, was no less of a surprise. Jewel had, she realized, built an image of him in her mind, and that image and the man clashed horribly, the one shattering like the glass walls wouldn't.

She had expected someone who looked like Rath's friends—tall, forbidding, and very dangerous. She had expected someone handsome and cold, with dark hair, dark eyes, and an obvious penchant for cruelty. She hadn't really thought of his age, of how old he must be, or how young—but this man could have been her father. Or someone's father. He was not tall, at least he did not look tall, and he was not so lean and scarred as Rath's almost unnamed friends. His hair was shot through with gray, and he had a beard that was almost unkempt. His hands were thick, like carpenter's hands, although the rings were out of place, and many. She looked at him as if, by making this list, she would understand what she saw.

Understand, perhaps, the difference between what she saw and what she had expected to see. She had expected guards; Duster had been *so cer-*

tain there would be guards; there were none. But Haval had been certain as well—and that meant Haval could be wrong.

It should have comforted her: this stranger, this unexpected man, shorn of guards, no obvious cruelty in his expression.

Her Oma had always told her that life was a series of lessons, and most of them were harsh. It was a pride to the old woman to have survived so much hardship, and she was never so happy—in a grim sort of way, pipe cooling in the corner of her mouth—as when Jewel swallowed either fear or disappointment with a grim child's acceptance. Not cowed, never that, but not broken.

She had cautioned Jewel to be suspicious of all things, especially appearances: the appearance of wealth, the appearance of poverty, the ways in which children would pretend to be crippled to swindle money out of the foolish. She cautioned Jewel not to be led astray—*never* to be led astray—by the whim of a foolish heart, a stupid kindness. But she also waited for the inevitable, because Jewel was her father's child, and it *did* happen.

So you've learned something, she would say, and then slowly pad the bowl of her pipe. *And you're still alive. You're not bleeding. Nothing's broken. You've no scars and you've lost nothing important but stupidity.* Not a kind woman, her Oma, never that.

Now, Jewel looked at this man, sitting casually in a chair at a table that was neither too long nor too intimidating. Certain, watching him, that he had children, and that he was even kind to them.

Had she been another person, she might have looked back at Duster, looked askance, demanded acknowledgment that *this* was the man who had so hurt her. But she was Jewel Markess, and before she could do any of those things, she understood what she was supposed to learn here.

She swallowed, and then offered the man a formal half-curtsy. "My father," she said, in a quiet girl's voice, "asked me to deliver this letter." And she walked toward him, slowly, as if aware of his importance. His title.

She was. She hated it with a ferocity that did not banish fear, but deepened it. It was harsh and unexpected, and her hands were shaking as she extended them, Rath's carefully sealed letter the bridge between them.

He nodded genially and took the letter with care. But he didn't open it immediately. Instead, he said, "How old are you, girl?"

"Fourteen," she replied carefully. In the dress and the cloak, it might even be true, but it was a young fourteen.

He raised a brow, not believing her, and there was genuine amusement in the smile he offered. "Fourteen," he said. "Almost an adult."

She nodded hesitantly, stiffly, letting her fear inform her movements. Working with it, as Haval had taught her. When he returned her smile, he looked almost gentle.

Almost.

"Please," he told her, lifting a hand, palm up, and gesturing around the table as if he owned it, "take a seat. It is cold outside, and you've traveled some distance; join me while I eat. Your father is waiting?"

"I am to call a carriage," she replied, "when I'm ready to leave." Lifting her chin, now, and striving to look the elevated age of fourteen.

This seemed to amuse him, and she remembered dimly that amusement was often one way of stemming rage, of averting danger. It had been so when she had been a child in her Oma's home. But what amused this man?

She did not look at Duster when Duster came and retrieved, in perfect silence, her winter clothing; the fine cloak, the gloves, the scarf that Rath had taken pains to arrange so carefully.

"That will be all," Lord Waverly told Duster, in a tone of voice that was both cool and dismissive. "Your mistress will call for you when she requires your service. Wait in the servants' quarters until you are summoned."

Jewel had not believed that Duster could come here and be unrecognized. Haval had promised her that she would pass unnoticed, and she had accepted his word as truth—but she hadn't truly believed it until this moment. Duster was beneath the lord's notice, here.

And Jewel was increasingly aware that she was not.

She didn't want Duster to leave. But she nodded in silent agreement with the officious command. To do anything else might be to lose this unexpected miracle of anonymity. It might be the only miracle of a long evening.

She listened for the sound of retreating steps, aware that she was the only one who did. It had not occurred to this man—would probably never occur to him—that his careless, casual command might be disobeyed.

Duster had hated Jewel. This was the truth.

The fine woolen cloak she had draped so carefully over her servant's sleeves trailed the edge of the leaves that had failed to catch her attention as she walked away from Lord Waverly.

Hated her, yes. Hated what she could offer from the comfort of her easy, easy life. Hated the fact that somehow, for *Jewel*, Rath had been there, offering her both food and shelter in return for—nothing. For nothing at all.

She had hated the fact that the others had deferred to Jewel, had listened to her, and had treated her as if she were somehow important. Resented the fact that Jewel, who had suffered so damn little, had so damn much.

In the dark of night, when Jewel slept, she had wondered what Jewel might be like, left alone with Waverly. No; wonder was the wrong word; her imagination was vivid, lurid, angry. In the silence of the small room, kept warm by distant woodstove and breath, she had imagined just what Waverly would do to an idiot like Jewel, had laughed at how easily Jewel would break, at exactly how she would come to truly *understand* what life was like.

And it was here, now: a gift. A daydream, a night thought, come true. Offered to her by a fool, handed to her without any scheming or planning on her own part. The robe draped so carefully over her arm slipped beneath her feet, and she tripped over its hem. Stopped herself from cursing, because cursing here would draw attention that she didn't want.

She hesitated, just outside of the glassed-in room, taking refuge behind plants that were almost overpowering, they were so sickly sweet. She could hear Waverly's voice. Could not fail to hear it, although memory gave it words and cadences that were absent in fact. When he had been introduced to Duster, he had not bothered to hide what he was behind this civil mask; in the holdings, he had paid a great deal of money to dispense with pretense. He had come with her jailers, and he had treated her like a dog, like less than a dog.

And his laughter had been almost gentle. She could hear it now. What was he saying to Jewel? What was Jewel thinking? Did she even understand the danger she was in?

No, she expected rescue; her whole life had been one damn rescue after another. She didn't have to lie for it, or beg for it, or pay for it in any of the ways with which Duster was painfully familiar. She could *afford* to be high and mighty; when had anyone ever let her fall?

Duster reached up and tore a leaf in three pieces, absently destroying the peaceful arrangement. Wanting many, many things; seeing in the light just another way of casting shadows. Enjoying the possibilities of suffering that wasn't her own.

Duster had hated Jewel.

And if it weren't for Jewel, she wouldn't be here. If it weren't for the fact that she had saved Finch—to spite the damn demons, nothing more—she wouldn't be here. If Jewel didn't trust her, she wouldn't *be here.*

Her grip tightened around the slender knife her servant's clothing hid. Hating was easy. It came as naturally as breathing. Contempt came that way too; and anger, and irritation. Even fear, although she would never admit it where anyone could hear it.

If you had had Jewel's life, what would you be?

There. She'd asked it. In this place, leaf bits strewn in her shaking lap.

It wasn't the same question as, *If you had what she had, what would you do with it?* She knew, because she'd considered stealing most of it from the moment she'd first entered the old man's apartment. It was a different question.

Duster wondered what she would be, with friends and guardians and people she could *trust*. People who wouldn't sell her out, wouldn't sell her, wouldn't casually beat her to show others how strong they were.

Would she be Jewel? Could she? Could she have cared for some sniveling wreck like Lefty, some flighty girl like Finch? Could she have shopped and cooked and cleaned and argued and tried to make some sort of family out of a bunch of losers without killing one or two of them to make a necessary point?

No.

Honest answer. Even if she had had Jewel's life, she wouldn't be Jewel. None of them would. And who was to say that the inverse was true? Who could really say that if Jewel had had Duster's life, she'd end up being Duster?

The demons had said Duster was special.

Not death, not for Duster. Not freedom, either. But something else. In the shadows. In the darkness they could see in her.

If darkness was what she had, why not use it?

Because they win, she thought. And no one beat her.

But she sat there, in the Arboretum, listening, and dreaming, and knowing that part of her *wanted* Jewel to suffer at the hands of Waverly. Because she would enjoy it.

"Yes," a soft voice said, above her, "you would."

She looked up, then.

Ten feet away, in clothing that spoke of riches and finery, stood a man she had never seen before. But his eyes—the darkness of them, the lack of white—were familiar.

"You are a resourceful girl," the man said, examining his gloved hands with care. "And I admit that you eluded the lesser of my kin." He wore dark colors, black with a hint of purple, a hint of coal gray, and cold gold around his neck. He had very little hair, but the lack didn't speak of age.

He was also taller than Arann.

"You are far more resourceful than we had assumed, but it does not displease me, Duster. You have had some time to contemplate your past; contemplate your future now. I assume," he added, his voice growing so soft it might have been a purr, "that you intend to have a future."

She was not chained now, not bound; she was no one's captive. But standing ten feet from this stranger, she could not say she was free.

"I am Patris AMatie," he told her, inclining his head. "And I have lost a number of servants in the last month. It is not to my liking, and it leaves my household bare. You were to take your place among my servants," he added, "later, rather than sooner; you were not deemed ready."

"And now?" she asked, hedging, knife still in her palm, her dry, shaking palm.

"Now?" His smile was slight, like the edge of a sharp knife is slight. "You are mortal," he replied with a shrug, "and few indeed are the mortals judged worthy of service to the Shining Court."

"And me?"

"You are close enough now to make that decision. To prove your worth," he added, "or to fail to prove it." Again, he smiled. "But there is, in you, the darkness that beckons. You are almost with us," he added. "This life, or the next, little one, and you will be among us, and mortality will be a simple illusion.

"But you can be victim," he said, voice colder, "or victor; the choice is yours. There will always be suffering; cause it, or be consumed by it."

Duster straightened. "I want Waverly," she told the man evenly. "Give me Waverly, and I'll serve you."

But the Patris shook his head. "Serve me," he said, "and you obey me. That is the law of power. When you have power greater than mine, you may force me to surrender that which I hold. Only then." And he reached out to touch her face.

Ten feet? Five. Four. He had moved; she hadn't even noticed. But his fingers felt like claws against her skin; claws beneath it, when he flexed them. Her cheek stung; she knew that she was bleeding.

It wasn't even a cut worthy of notice; she didn't blink.

"You came here with another child," he said. "And you have been contemplating her fate as you sit here. You have been enjoying what you imagine."

She said nothing. She didn't even ask him how he knew; she *knew. We can taste it, we can sense it, we can see everything about you that makes you almost . . . kin.* "Waverly is there, but it is not of his death that you dream; it is of the pain he will cause. Is that not so?"

She nodded grimly.

"Then watch," he said softly. "Take what you can. Waverly is mine; he serves my purpose here. Pass only this test, and his purpose will be yours as well."

"I want—"

"And I will give him to you, when I am ready. We will see how creative you can be then."

Rath had approached the Arboretum with caution.

He could. He had spent every favor owed him by those who inhabited the dim and forbidding reaches of the Magi's tower; he had badgered Andrei, cajoling and threatening by turns, until he had obtained some of what he desired. He was not invisible—that, no amount of bribery would allow him—but he walked completely silently, and even his breathing could not be heard by anyone who was not paying attention. But the familiar cadences of a voice that he almost recognized had drawn him into the Arboretum; he had intended to skirt its edges, to go to Jewel, or as close to Jewel as he might come.

And this, with Patris AMatie in attendance *was* as close as he could safely come. He had written his letters, had set his stage, had prepared for all eventualities he could think of. But this, he had not seen.

He wondered, briefly, what had become of Marrett. Wondered how he had failed in his attempts at secrecy, how he had drawn AMatie here. He stared at Duster, at the answer that presented itself.

If he had been a different man, he would have assumed that Duster had betrayed them all; he had trusted her so little that he had not explained all of his plan to either of the two girls. But . . . her carriage was wrong.

He was a betting man, and he thought—reluctantly—that she was as surprised as Rath himself.

He had intended, of course, to be present. To be where Duster and Patris AMatie now sat. And all of his plans, the knife's edge of his deception, the *risk* of it—were made manifest. He was numb with it; beyond something as simple as fear.

He had never trusted Duster. His first advice had been to have her removed. His last advice had been no different. And Jewel had remained unchanged. But beyond them, behind the glass walls whose adornments were living and growing plants, she might not remain so for much longer. And yet, in the end, he had given way to Jewel's quiet determination; to call it demand was unjust. He had allowed her the freedom to choose, and with choice came consequence.

He watched the Patris, and the girl who stood quietly before him in her perfect servant's clothing, green flecks catching light as they nestled in the falling wrinkles of her skirts.

Her hair was pale, her skin pale, she looked in all ways like a different child. But the Patris had recognized her instantly. She had not recognized him; Rath would have noticed that. But she either knew of him, or recognized something about him. She was not yet terrified.

She was not angry.

Nor was Rath; if anger came, it would come later; now, he felt cold, and even weary. Jewel was to be tested here; he had told himself that, and believed it still. But he knew that part of Jewel's test *was* Duster. And so Duster, herself, was to be tested.

But not like this.

She had been with Jewel scant weeks. Before that, she had amassed a lifetime of specialized knowledge, and he could see it in her expression: Power ruled. Only power.

And the Patris was powerful.

Jewel, Rath thought, almost numb.

"We shouldn't be out here," Finch said quietly, her breath hanging in the air before her slender face. Arann's, a full head above her, came out in a silent cloud.

"She said we could come," Teller told Finch quietly.

"She told us to wait."

Carver, following the trail left in snow that had not yet been obliterated by other footsteps, other pedestrians, shrugged. At this time of night, pedestrians were few, although the magelights still shone that guided them from one place to another.

Lander had followed; he was silent now. The words that had come to him in the undercity had deserted him the moment he left, and only Lefty had the composure to speak to him in the silent gestures of their moving language.

Fingers danced in the cold, shaking slightly; Lefty used both his hands, and the absence of two fingers seemed right, here. They spoke of loss, but also of healing. He would never have them back; what he might have, instead, was a lack of shame at the mutilation that he had never asked for.

"Old Rath's not going to like it," Carver said quietly. But as Carver was leading them, they only nodded. He wasn't going to like it, and they had chosen—mostly—not to care.

"You know where we're going?"

Carver shook his head.

But Teller spoke up. "I know," he said quietly.

They all stopped to look at him, but with a lot of gaping. Teller shrugged. "He was writing a letter," he said, finally. "A lot of them. They were on his desk. I saw them. I saw the addresses."

No one asked how much rifling it took to see those addresses; better not to know. There was only one important question to be asked, and Carver asked it. "And how do you know which *one* of those addresses is the right one?"

"There was only one in this part of town," he said, "or close to it." He looked at the streets, the empty, wide roads with buildings that were not actually packed into each other's armpits. It might as well have been a foreign country, and they all knew it.

"But you don't know the city—"

"He's been teaching me. To read his maps."

"Why?"

"Because I asked," Teller replied, with a hint of question dragging his tone up at the last syllable. "I don't know. I—I like his maps." It was lame. He knew it was lame. He didn't care.

Then again, neither did anyone else. Jewel had taught them that strangest of things: hope. They now took it as they found it, and they clung to it as they began to move.

Not even Finch asked the question they all kept to themselves, although it was hard. *What are we going to do once we get there?*

"Your father understands business," Lord Waverly was saying. He had said a variant of this about six times over the course of a very uncomfortable ten minutes, and each time he said it, moving a word around and changing its tone, as if the rearrangement somehow added weight or meaning, he drew slightly closer to where Jewel now sat.

She had taken care to mind her posture, and her spine was stiff and straight. Her hands were folded in her lap, as Haval had taught her, and she pressed them into her legs to stop them from shaking.

"I don't know very much about his business," she said, for perhaps the fourth time.

"No, no, of course you wouldn't," he replied, which would normally have annoyed her. It was clear that he expected her to be stupid. At any other time, she would have done what she could to correct his assumption; now, she wanted to hide behind it.

Because she knew—of course she knew—why she was here. Knew that he knew it, that he expected her to be ignorant. That she very much *wanted* to be ignorant.

He poured her a glass of a pale, yellow liquid, and placed it on the table before her, very close to the glass he then filled for his own use. "I appreciate a canny man," he told Jewel quietly, lifting his glass. "And should your father choose to ally himself with my business interests, I assure you your family will be well taken care of."

He waited for a moment, and Jewel understood that she was meant to lift her own glass, with its fine, slender stem. Which meant she would have to raise her hands. "I—I don't drink very much," she said, apologetically.

Still, he waited, and his smile seemed to freeze in place, becoming not so much a frown as an ill-fitted mask. A warning, there. She understood it as such, and also understood that he would, if pressed, put that warning into far less pleasant words—and she was not yet willing to see him stripped of his facade of pleasantry.

She took the glass.

His smile became fluid again as she lifted it to her lips and took a small sip. The wine—if it was wine—was almost bitter to the tongue; it was neither sweet nor sour, but acrid, biting. Haval's lessons stopped her from spitting it back out.

"So," he said, "you are fourteen?"

She nodded, drinking only enough to taste. The motion, she could mime, and she wondered—briefly—if the liquid would kill plants, and if she could discreetly experiment. He really didn't look away at all.

"Fourteen," she said quietly. "Do you have children?"

"Three."

She waited, but the subject did not engage him. The awkward pauses in adult conversation had seldom been filled by her, and she struggled. "The plants here are very lovely."

"They are, especially in this cold season; it is for that reason that I often spend time here."

"You like flowers?"

"I like," he said quietly, "all things that are delicate and lovely; they seldom remain so, and it is best to appreciate beauty while it lasts."

Before you destroy it, she thought. *Before you consume it.* The anger was brief and intense, and her lips were closed to prevent the words from escaping. No escape, here.

"You don't find the wine to your taste?" he asked her, after a moment.

"I don't drink often," she replied. "It is only this past season that I have been invited to spend time at the table with my father's visitors. He doesn't approve of my drinking."

"Ah," Lord Waverly replied, his voice lowering, softening. "Then we shall keep this between us; a secret if you will. The forbidden is often enticing."

No, Jewel thought. *It's just forbidden.* And she meant it, and again, she swallowed the words, remembering Haval. Remembering why she was here. There would be food, soon. Duster was supposed to help with that, to help just enough.

But Duster was nowhere in sight, and Lord Waverly was much, much closer than he had been. Walls of glass, she thought, and leaves, and flowers. Surely, here—

His hand touched her leg; his palm was warm.

And Jewel was very, very cold.

"She is afraid," the Patris said quietly, standing beneath the fronds of large, smooth-barked trees, as if he were the entirety of the shadow they cast.

Duster knew who he referred to. She didn't ask how he knew. Instead, she shrugged, and was rewarded with the edge of a smile that was almost approving.

"You will wait here," he told her. "And I will wait with you. Judge for yourself how strong—or weak—your little friend is. She was there, was she not? She was present when you chose to leave us."

"I never chose to join you," Duster told him, defiant now, the hand around hilt a comfort, even if it was almost useless.

"You were not ready, then," he replied. As if he had always intended to grant her some measure of choice or respect. She tried to remember the chains at her ankles, the bare room, the bed itself meant for anything but sleep. She wanted to kill him, but then again, she wanted to kill almost everything that lived or moved and had ever crossed her path.

"It is not in death you will find your salvation," Patris AMatie told her, as if he could hear the thought. "Death is too simple. It is in pain that you derive power, or will. Pain, fear. Especially fear." He drew closer. "Do you fear me?"

And she met his gaze. Held it a moment. There was only darkness there, in the lights of the Arboretum, and it was a darkness that was familiar. Desirable. It was so like her own, she felt an echo of herself in its depths.

"No," she told him. "I don't. I don't fear death."

"I told you—"

"It's still death," she replied.

His frown was not slight, and it was not pleasant. It changed the shape of his face, and he straightened to a height that Duster would never reach. He was close to her now, as she sat, and he touched the side of her face. A sharp touch, and shallow; she felt it burn. Knew she was bleeding.

Knew that this was nothing at all but a caress and a warning. "What you desire," he told her softly, "you cannot hide."

"I'm not trying."

"You want her to suffer."

It was true.

"Suffer as you did. And be broken as you were not."

All true. It didn't even make her squirm.

"I myself would like to witness it," he added, his hand, slightly crimson along the edges, drawing away. The blood would never show unless you knew it was there; knew what to look for.

"Why?"

"Her friends have caused me some difficulty," he replied. "And in ignorance. But ignorance is not an excuse. Do you know where the others went?"

Duster shrugged. "Do I care?"

He smiled again. "We want them back," he told her.

"I could find them for you."

"I suspected as much. Find them," he told her, but his glance strayed over her, past her, and to the walls of glass, their lead bars spread to contain transparent color, a hard tapestry, a mosaic of a type.

She nodded.

"Then let us wait."

She had little choice in the matter.

It was choice that had always confounded her. She made the wrong ones, over and over again, and she paid. She had scars—ones she could see, ones that were hidden and therefore worse—as proof of that. She had wanted power for herself because only with power was there any chance of safety.

And safety meant? Freedom. The freedom to cause suffering rather than to experience it.

She thought of them, then: Finch, Fisher, Jester. They were ridiculous, stupid, *happy* in Jewel's illusion of safety. They *wanted* to call it home.

Her hands were moving in her lap, her fingers dancing slowly, even around the hilt of her knife. Familiar movements, this odd dance, although it took her a moment to realize what they were: Lefty's language.

Lefty's attempt to speak to Lander.

No, she thought. Worse than that: they were her words. Her silent words, her own way of conveying her meaning and her intent to the silent boy whose tongue might as well have been cut from his mouth by what he had suffered.

She said, "I saved the girl to spite them."

And he laughed. "I know. I know you well, Duster."

Her name, from his mouth, had a power and a resonance that Jewel's thin voice would never, ever give it.

"And the girl might even believe that you cared about her life."

Duster shrugged. "Only if she's stupid."

"The beauty of humanity," Patris AMatie replied, "is just how stupid it can be in the face of fact." He paused, and then added, "Do not be stupid here."

She nodded. Waiting for the first scream, the first crack in the silence. Waiting now in the shadow of a man who could give her—she knew it—everything she had ever desired.

They approached the building with dwindling confidence; it was large and fine, and it boasted a gleaming fence that even snow did not dare to cling to for long. There were guards in livery at those gates, men with swords and armor. Not one of the children who called themselves Jay's den had any fondness for armed men.

"What do we do now?" Finch asked softly.

Teller drew his shoulders back. Instead of making him look taller, it made him look younger; he was all bone, and his skin was Winter-white, pale with lack of sun. And pale, as well, with fear.

But it was a fear they *all* felt; these men were not their deaths, but they were obstacles that might never be passed at all.

"Do we go in?" Carver asked. "I don't think that was the plan."

"What plan?" Teller replied. And then he added, "It wasn't Old Rath's plan, no. But we were never a part of that; we have to make our own."

"Great. Standing in the middle of the street and freezing to death isn't much of a plan—" Arann grabbed Carver's arm. Tightly. And Carver's thoughts caught up with his mouth as he remembered a frenzied run through streets newly white and unwalked. Remembered his first sight of Teller, and the body over which he lay like a blanket that was too small and too slight to provide warmth.

But if Teller was offended, it didn't show. Finch watched him, watched his face, realized that she was holding her breath. A white wreath escaped her lips, rising upward like a ghost. Teller was not Jay, and not Arann; he wasn't Carver. But although he was as quiet as Finch herself, although he found the same comfort in the kitchen that Finch did, although he seemed to have more in common with Lefty than with anyone else, he was *not* Lefty.

"I have a letter," he told them all.

They stared at him. "You wrote a letter?"

"I didn't say I wrote it," he replied. "But I have one." And he pulled, from the inside of a jacket that Jewel had paid for, an envelope with a red wax seal.

"That's Old Rath's—"

Teller nodded.

"You asked him to—"

"No. He would never have agreed. I have no idea what's in it."

"You took a letter—"

"From his desk, yes."

"When?"

"Does it matter? He's been teaching us all how to take things when we need them. I was practicing."

"And we need this."

Teller nodded. "It's official. To look at, it's official."

"It's got a name on it."

Teller nodded. "That might be a problem. But not yet." And shoulders still stiff and straight, he made a direct line for the guards at the gate.

After a moment, the others joined him, Lefty bringing Lander into Arann's orbit and holding him there. Lefty had not spoken a word since they had reached the building; his language—not a movement of hand or lip—was in his eyes, in the way he watched Arann's face and back.

"You should wait," Teller told them calmly.

"Hell with that," Carver replied. "We all go, or we all wait."

"We can't wait," Teller said. "But it's going to look suspicious if there are seven messengers."

"We'll take that chance."

"Rath is going to be angry," Finch told no one in particular.

"Rath is always angry," Arann replied. His way of making it clear that he, too, had no intention of being left behind.

"What would Jay say?"

"Go home," Carver answered. "She'd tell us to go home or go back to the compound and wait. But she's not here, and we are."

"But she's—"

"She's in there," Fisher said, speaking for the first time. "She's with one of the—" he couldn't bring himself to finish. But after a moment, he said, "She came for us."

And that was that.

Teller approached the guards carrying his very official looking document. The guards looked up as he approached, and their hands fell to their weapons, but they looked—if anything—both cold and bored. They counted without counting; numbers of this type came naturally to them. Finch could see it; she could feel the gaze sweep over her without really stopping.

"We've been sent by my uncle," Teller told them, the letter in his hand unwavering. "We're to deliver a message. It's a surprise," he added. "It's my cousin's birthday, and she and her father are guests here. She likes it here," he added, speaking with sincerity that never once faltered into either fear or obsequiousness.

"We'll see about that. You'll speak to the innkeeper before you go anywhere."

Teller nodded, and the guards parted. But he kept the letter as he walked between them, and the others followed in silence. Aware that they were clothed now, and if the clothing was not fine, if it was not grand, it was still new and clean.

Aware of both this and the fact that Jay needed them.

Chapter Twenty-seven

JEWEL HAD ALWAYS been aware that money could buy almost anything. She had seen it, and envied it, at a distance, her Oma's disapproval quelling any words she might have spoken. Her Oma had been a staunch believer in knowing one's place. That, and living up to it.

This place was not Jewel's. She knew it, and knew better why her Oma had been so harsh in her judgment, so quick to be cutting.

When Jewel had lost her home, and it had been both slow and instant, she had learned that having no money was kin to death, but slower and less dignified. She understood, dimly, that there were things she could sell. Herself, her services. And that, in the end, they were hers *to* sell, if she were desperate enough.

She had never despised the women who did; she had been close enough to death and starvation, even with a family, that she, like her Oma, had refused to judge their desperation. Nor did she judge it now, a stranger's hand creeping across her thigh, light glancing off glass that would allow anyone who passed by to see everything.

Instead, she pitied it. Because she was certain it was men like this to whom they sold what they could. At ten, she had never shown much interest in boys; some of the girls who lived in her building had started to, but Jewel was still more interested in shoving them into the bushes and taunting them than in anything else.

She was certain, now, holding her breath, trying not to be overwhelmed by nausea and—yes—fear, that she would *never* be interested in men. Not like this. That she would never want them touching her, or holding her, or owning any part of her time, or her attention.

And yet, she thought, stiffening, unable to relax in any way, she *was* here by choice. Duster, Finch—all of the others—had had none. And this man? He hadn't cared. He had cared about money, and about what he wanted; the fact that they didn't want it meant nothing.

Or maybe, she thought, as she noticed the shifting lines of his expression, it meant something. She wanted to be ill. She almost was.

But her Oma's voice was there, steadying her with its harsh anger. She had chosen, and not in ignorance, and she could abide by the choice. *You put your hand in the fire, it burns. You live with the pain. You pray there are no scars.* She meant to. She honestly meant to.

But when his hands touched her face, cupping her cheeks, her body reacted before she could confine it; she shoved his hands away and almost fell back off her chair in her haste to put distance between them. Any distance at all.

And she had been right about one thing; although his expression mimed a frown, there was something in his eyes, something etched in the weathered lines of his face, that was like . . . glee. Glee made dark and personal, where there should have been light and life.

He said, "You don't understand why you're here, do you?"

She rose quickly, trying to put table between them; he was slower, but more assured. She said nothing.

"Come here."

And held her ground.

"Your father's future depends upon what you do. It depends upon my goodwill. *Come here.*"

There was no Rath in this room. No Duster. No one to interrupt them; hadn't there been a plan? Food? Something drugged? It was hard to recall, now. Now was Lord Waverly, a man with the power and money to make a cage of even the most beautiful of rooms.

And she had walked in through the door, in this dress, with that letter, determined to be what she had to be. Determined to somehow give Duster a choice. She had not thought—had not honestly thought—that she would have none beyond the first act: walking in. Sitting down.

She *could not* bring herself to obey him.

And she saw that this was both the right thing and the wrong thing to do. He was not ill-pleased with her refusal, but his words were ugly, ugly words. In her rising panic, the only ones she understood clearly were *teach you something you will never forget.*

And she knew that he was right; that he could do this; that she could do nothing but remember.

Patris AMatie stiffened slightly, lifting his chin, exposing the underside of a jaw that seemed so smooth it might have been made of glass. Or steel. His eyes were wide and so dark they did not reflect light, or the life that grew fettered in pots and dirt.

Duster sat by his feet, felt his hand brush her shoulder gently, possessively. But her eyes were on the plants, on the place where their stems and trunks emerged from, yes, dirt. They were beautiful, they were expensive, they were cared for in ways that she had *never* been cared for—and yet they relied for their beauty and life on . . . dirt.

And she was dirty.

Jay had said something. Sometime. Someplace that was not this fine, fine building, with its glass, its impossible ceilings, its paintings and tapestries. Someplace that did not offer privacy to men who—

She heard it, then. What she had longed to hear.

Short, muffled, but sharp as dagger's edge: a scream. A high scream. It did not linger. It did not echo.

And yet it did, and Duster understood something about desire, and hated herself for the understanding.

She did this for me.

I didn't ask her to do anything.

You did. You asked. You demanded. And she did it.

And without thought, thought was too harsh and too ugly, she rose, shedding the Patris' hand in a smooth movement learned in the streets of the poorest quarters of this horrible city. Bringing the dagger she clung to to bear, cutting his skin.

Cutting skin that did not shed blood.

She was away before he could grab her; away before he even seemed to notice what she had done; he seemed mesmerized by what they had both heard. But if he seemed caught in a trance, he was not slow, not clumsy; he was not weak enough to be caught off guard.

He simply didn't care about her dagger.

She'd seen enough fighting in her life—enough death—to recognize this immediately. And she *knew* what to do to preserve her life. Knew it intimately, she had done it so often.

But she couldn't bring herself to do it here—that required thought, acting, planning. It required *caring* one way or the other whether or not she survived.

He reached out as casually as Duster might have were she to crush a bug. And Duster traveled halfway across the room, tumbling through the stalks of slender plants, crushing fragrant blossoms. Finding dirt in her face, and beneath her hands.

"Do not," he said, although he didn't even look at her, "disappoint me."

Even now, she had a chance. A chance to preserve her life. A chance to take back the dream of power and twisted, bitter justice.

But it wasn't a dream—it was a nightmare. *This* is what she had so loathed when she had been chained in the crumbling manse, visited by guest after guest until all touch and all sensation blurred into pain and humiliation.

Herself. She had loathed herself. Because she had known, even then, what they hoped for; she would grow stronger and angrier and darker until only the killing lust remained. Then, only then, would she be free to move and act.

And she had told Jay what it was that frightened her. Why? She couldn't remember.

Only that she had told Jay.

And that Jay had told her she would be judged by her actions. Oh, she had hated the answer, had known it would come, had despised the pathetic attempt at comfort.

But—and this was another lesson, another terror—she had *wanted* it as well. The bitter double edge of desire.

And she stood on it now, bleeding in so many ways that her time in the manse now seemed a distant blessing. Because in that room, chains around her, she *had had no choice.* And gods forgive her—if there were gods that could—she had had a choice here.

"Jay!" One strangled word. A name.

The Patris approached her as she scrambled through the foliage, breaking it, destroying it, bringing it at last to just dirt, to her own level.

"So," he said softly. But the softness filled the room, rebounded off the ceiling, off all the broken things that lay beneath her and within her. She was still free of him, her dagger twisting in the air before her as she tried to make a wall of its edge. It had worked before, a time or two. It had failed just as often.

It would fail here, she saw that.

She cried out louder, louder now. A name. Not hers.

And if it did fail? If it couldn't protect her?

It would be *over*.

She was wild with panic, and fear, and neither of them were familiar to her; they were all wrong.

She cried out the name a third time, her whole body shaking with the single syllable, the weight of it, the need to have it answered.

But if Jewel's single scream, curtailed, went unnoticed by any save Duster, the clear cry of Jay's name did not.

Patris AMatie noted it, and understood it for the denial it was. He approached Duster as she rolled to her feet in her dirty, awkward clothing, her pale hair—false as everything about her had been false, *was* false—mired in petals and soft soil.

"They failed me," he told her softly, moving like a cat moves, a great cat, a hunting beast. "They failed me by allowing you to escape. You were so very close to the choice; so close to making it, and becoming one of ours.

"I do not have the time, in this life, to fashion more out of what I see in you. But you will return, and I will see you when you do; we will begin again in earnest, because, little one, when you *do* return, we will once again rule over these pale lands, and the world will be ours."

"The world that is yours," a new voice said, "is not this world."

Duster recognized the voice, but it was cold and hard, and in its way, it was as terrifying as the Patris. It was not as terrifying as the silence that followed—that still followed—Jewel's single cry.

Rath stood in the room, framed by an arch that was covered with vines that drooped flowers. He was tall, and well-dressed; he was also armed. But armed, he appeared to be at ease, as if this were simply an unpleasant conversation, a trifling negotiation.

"Duster," he said, without once glancing away from the Patris, who had stopped and pivoted to face him, "I do not know what part you have played in the plans that have gone awry, but you are not needed here, and you are not wanted here. Go where you must go, and do what you must do. The Patris and I have matters that cannot be discussed openly."

"There will be little discussion," the Patris replied, and he seemed to grow taller and wider as he spoke, as if he were shedding the patina of vulnerability—such as it was—that he had worn throughout the evening.

"Rath—I—"

"I don't know," he said, his voice lower. And she knew that he suspected, and that she would pay.

And the price seemed almost like a promise of peace, although it was death. She who could deal death could recognize at least that much.

She struggled to her feet, shoving broken things from her lap, her arms, pushing her hair out of her face. With it came makeup, the color that Haval had chosen; beneath the surface of powder, swept away in a gesture, she exposed her true face.

And then she turned and ran, and once again, she lifted her voice, crying out a single name, as if by uttering it she could cling to it.

You wanted this.

Gods. And what gods could forgive, what gods could understand, what gods could care for someone who *could*? They would never forgive her, the others, Jay, this Rath who would be her death.

And tomorrow, if she somehow survived her awkward flight, she would find excuses and reasons and she would make them walls so tall she would never see over them again. Because she *had* seen over them in this room, and what she had seen had hurt her far more than even Lord Waverly and the demons who had given her to his care.

Across the building, Carver lifted his head so quickly, his hair flew, revealing the eye that was almost always hidden. He froze, his hand dropping to the dagger he concealed in the width of Winter clothing. He ran into Arann's back, and felt the stiffness there as if it were a slowly burning heat.

Teller, letter clutched in hands that had balled into fists, was white and silent; Finch was shaking. They had heard Jay's name, and in the white of bright light and beautiful floors, walls, ceilings, they saw the bars of familiar cages.

Cages that Jay had opened, so that they could live.

Lander was shaking. Lefty was utterly silent, his hands still. Finch could not see what Jester and Fisher were doing; she didn't care. She recognized the voice that uttered the name so strangely it sounded strangled and horrified.

"Duster," she said, her voice a whisper. They were frozen for just a minute; the whole damn place was *so* big.

But before they could move, or run, or shout, someone cut them off.

Not now, Finch prayed. *Kalliaris, not now. Goddess, smile, smile please. We'll bear your frown later; we'll pay. But smile now.*

Gods didn't answer prayers.

But Kalliaris was a god of whim and if she chose to listen, if she chose to find amusement in this overdressed, undermonied den of misfits and orphans, Finch could only offer gratitude.

For the person that approached them was perhaps a handful of years older than they were, and he was pale, his face pinched with indecision and worry. Fear, maybe, but it was not of them, and there was no contempt when he reached Carver's side.

Carver said, "We've come for a friend." All pretense, all lie, even the official and officious letter that Teller now held as if it were garbage, forgotten.

And the man—the boy?—said, "I'm sorry." It was the whisper of a word, two words. "I think you may be too late."

Rath was not dressed for the political; he was not dressed to impress. He was—barely—well enough turned out that his presence in the inn would be tolerated, and at that, only in the off season when business was poor.

The Patris was, of course, finely attired. His clothing was dark, and perfect, and it stretched a little too much at the shoulders and chest as he faced Rath, shedding now even the pretense of humanity. Of mortality.

"You should not have come here," the Patris said, and he smiled, and his teeth glinted, long and strange in the bright light of the inn. Too bright, Rath thought, to contain what he saw. "But I offer my thanks for your consideration, *Wade.* I have lost a number of my servitors to your intervention, and had almost considered hunting you myself." His expression darkened as he spoke the words, and the nuance in them was not lost on Rath.

Rath knew, both instinctively and intellectually, that he had no advantages here; in this fight, height or speed were lost him, and he did not doubt that the Patris was capable of fighting. That he carried no sword and no obvious weapon were of little concern; he expected Rath to provide him with amusement.

Not pain, and certainly not death; not his own.

Rath shrugged. "I am always willing to be of service," he replied, his tone neutral. "And perhaps had we had this conversation at a different time, or in a different place, we would not now be adversaries."

The Patris' frown was thin. But he was not stupid; he understood exactly what Rath intended.

"The child," the Patris said, "suffers."

To anger him. To goad him. All the old tricks, the old warnings that had informed so much of Ararath Handernesse's early training, were brought to bear now; had to be. He could not fight on uneven ground when he was either afraid or enraged—and he was very much both.

He could see Duster darting away, and he spared her no more thought than this: *If Jewel's hurt, I'll kill you myself.*

Duster followed the marbled floor, broken by metal into something that made it look almost cobbled. She trampled on the flowers that Jay had been so damn careful to step around; she did not bend to see them, to smell them, to touch them. They were just plants, and she didn't give a damn about them one way or the other.

She would have said—would still say—that she didn't give a damn about *anything* that wasn't Duster. But she ran, and her knife was out and glinting. She knew where Jay was; she'd left her there. Left her, forgot about food, and kitchen and plans. Left her to dream about—to think about—

She wanted to throw up.

The nausea hit her like a physical blow to the stomach. Her breath was noisy and uneven, as if she were gasping at air, as if even air was too clean and too pure for her to take in, to swallow.

And she broke through the archway, careening into plants and the steel that they so artfully twined around, clutching at them to steady herself, cutting her own hand in her haste. Physical pain here was *good.* It brought her back to the now. To the room.

To Jay and Lord Waverly, the chairs that had fallen to one side or the other, the table that shadowed them both as they struggled, each in their own way.

She didn't have time to *think* anymore; she leaped across the room, cursing skirts and everything else that had led her to this point: her whole life. The life she didn't much care if she lost now.

She could even remember the chains that had bound her, physically, in the presence of this man; could barely remember the fear and the humiliation that had been all he had left her. The only impulse she had—at this moment—was to separate them: the man who she had wanted so badly to kill, and the girl that she had wanted so badly to see broken.

And she would be, Duster thought, and again, nausea caused the walls of her throat to collapse. Jay would be broken, as everything in Duster's life had been broken in the end—by her own failure, her own desire, her own actions. The demons—she could not think of them as anything else—were right, had always been right, about what they had seen in her. Darkness, death, cruelty beyond measure.

Her legacy. Hers.

She leaped past the trellis that she had all but torn from its moorings, trying to ignore the *sounds* here that were so famliar they were almost suffocating. Hearing in the whimpering and the anger and the fear the only thing she recognized as her own.

It was such a short distance to Lord Waverly's back; his exposed back. Such a short distance to the disarray of his clothing, half on, half off, the expanse of white, heavy flesh, the bulk of him.

He had not removed his shirt; his collar was stiff and she almost straddled him—straddled *them*—as she grabbed it, bringing her knife at last to bear against the underside of his throat.

He froze as he felt it; she let the edge cut into his skin. She could end his life here, cut his jugular, let him bleed. But that was *not* what she wanted. It was too easy, too quick, and too painless. She wanted him to know who he was facing, and why—even if some part of her, wild and howling behind the silence of compressed lips—was no longer certain why.

He moved so very carefully as she yanked him to his feet; his face reddened as his collar cut off the breath that was heaving in both directions from his mouth. He was ugly, in all ways, but ugliest in a way that Duster recognized for her own.

Jay had no part in this.

But without Jay—

No. No. No. She tried not to see Jay, pressed against the floor, her dress torn, her skirts in disarray. She tried not to look at her face, at the intimacy of this forced contact, this humiliation, this helplessness.

"Get up," she snarled, her voice guttural and low, barely human.

And he obeyed—he *obeyed*—as her knife hugged the side of his throat.

As he lifted his bulk, Jay rose as well, gathering her dress to her as if it were armor. Her face was pale, her eyes wide—she had passed beyond fear to a place that nothing might reach again.

Now you understand, Duster thought, with a painful self-loathing. *Now you understand my life.*

"Remember me?" Duster whispered softly. "You and I met in the thirty-second holding." She let him turn—slightly—the knife bearing into flesh again, the blood beading slowly, the cut was so shallow and clean—to see her face.

His look of confusion enraged her.

"You have delved into places where you should not have delved," the Patris said quietly. Everything about him was contained and quiet; he was in control here, and knew it.

Rath's weight was on his back leg; he was ready to move, to dodge, to feint. But the Patris did not approach him; not yet. Instead, he smiled. "You have come too late," he continued. "And whatever you keep from your expression, you *cannot* keep from me. You know what I am," he added.

Rath nodded. He could not think of Jewel here. He could not think of Duster. In the end, the moment was defined by something that was not human, not mortal, not afraid of whatever it was that Rath could bring to bear in his own defense.

The Patris drew himself up to a height that Rath had not imagined, his robes flowing around him as if they were liquid, not cloth; as if they were shadow, and bent to his will as naturally as all darkness should. But out of the back of his robes, unfurling like a dark cloud, Rath recognized the dim shape of wings, leathery wings that had never known feathers or grace.

His arms lengthened, his hands extended, and from each of his fingers, claws grew that were longer than the daggers Rath now held in either hand. Even his face lengthened, changing in shape until it was almost unrecognizable.

"You do not understand what you face," the Patris said, and his voice was thunder's distant rumble. But the lightning had come and gone, and voice alone was not enough to kill Rath. "And you are privileged to witness it."

Rath shrugged. It was habit, and it was not a habit that he had any desire to break. "We must agree to disagree on what amounts to privilege," he said, in his lazy drawl. "I have seen things more fell than you in my life."

These last words were not pleasing to the Patris—if he could be called that with any truth anymore—and the wings that had seemed so insubstantial in the clouds solidified. "I will eat your heart."

"You will have to find it first," Rath replied bitterly.

"Believe that it is a trivial matter," the demon replied.

And then there was no more time for words. What had been still and almost—almost—majestic, became a frenzied blur of motion.

Rath knew when to accept a blow; he knew when to take the lesser wound in order to strike the greater one. But this creature moved so quickly, the lessons that had become instinct failed him; he dodged, and felt claws rake his back; knew blood blossomed there, in red and black, like a dark flower.

The Patris, in this room with its grand ceilings, its boast of height, had the advantage: he was not confined by as simple a thing as gravity, and his reach was the greater reach. Had he been human, the fight would have been over before it started; he left himself open, he moved with contempt and an easy arrogance, a certainty of victory that would have been misplaced given his knowledge of his enemy's strengths and weaknesses. Rath knew this well; he'd taken advantage of it many a time.

Honor, his weaponsmaster used to say, *is for the idle, and the bards. You want to survive. If survival means playing to their stupidity, play that hand.*

But his enemy was not human, and in spite of appearances, had never been close.

Rath had not expected the Patris to be present.

But nothing in Rath's long life had ever gone according to plan, and part of planning was the attempt to second-guess himself. To have contingencies, something in reserve in case of emergency.

Today was no different than any other day.

And it was horribly different. He struggled with all knowledge, and paid: Claws cut his shoulder, laying it open to bone. He was not as fast as he had once been.

But neither was he as callow, as easily disappointed or frightened. He bore the wound as if it were a simple fact of life; bleeding was. But if the

Patris, or whatever it was he was now called, seemed arrogant beyond ken, he was *fast*, and the opening that might have existed, eluded Rath.

And it couldn't. Because in order for Rath to execute the plan that had been weeks in the making, the Patris had to die, here, before he could speak to another creature, human or otherwise.

"Too late?" Carver grabbed the young man's arm, and the young man winced. But he did not withdraw. "What the Hells does that mean?"

"She came to visit—a patron. An important man. Here."

Carver's eyes narrowed. Only his eyes. The rest of his face was utterly still. There had been anger and even desperation in the way that he'd grabbed the finely accoutred arm, but it bled away as the words sunk in.

"He rented the entire Arboretum," the young man continued, oblivious to Carver's grip, Carver's unusual stillness. "And ordered it cleared."

Carver had no idea what the Arboretum was, and he didn't give a damn. It could have been a dungeon.

"Take us there."

"I can't."

Finch tensed. Teller tensed. They were standing side by side, and they could almost read the meaning of their own stillness, it was so strong. But when Carver's free hand dropped to his side, the tension melted from Teller, replaced by the urgency of movement. He caught Carver's arm and when Carver turned slightly to look at him, shook his head.

No knives here. No daggers. No threats. Short sentences, all of them spoken in the sign language Lefty and Lander had made their own; the language that had spilled out of their communication, and into the rest of the den, gaining strength at first by the pleasure of secret communication.

No pleasure here.

They'll make us leave. They'll call their guards.

Jewel. Leader.

Teller spoke, his hands stilling. "You can't lead us there. We won't ask. But tell us where it is. We've never visited this building before, and we may not get there in time—"

The boy struggled a moment, not with Carver, but with himself. His indecision was a quiet rictus that transformed his features, causing them to pale further, which shouldn't have been possible. Shame did that. "I'll show you," he said at last. "I'll show the way. But I can't go there myself. I'll get sacked."

The words made so little sense the rest of the den ignored them. But Arann's shadow was very, very close to the young man, and he was taller and wider.

"Show us, then," Carver managed to say. "Take us as far as you can; forget you ever saw us after we've left."

The young man nodded.

This, Finch thought, was cowardice. But it was a cowardice tainted by courage or decency, and she felt no anger or contempt for him. She looked to Lefty and Lander, both silent; caught Jester's eye before he could open his mouth. Fisher's silence was the only silence she could not read.

But she saw only determination in all of their faces, and wondered if she was seeing something she wanted to see, or something that was real. It didn't matter. When the young man moved, they followed, as if together they had become a cloak that was too long, and dragged in his wake.

"Don't you recognize me, *Lord* Waverly?" Duster said, her voice low and guttural, her knife finding a little more flesh to pierce. "Don't you know who I am? We've met before."

His eyes narrowed, his confusion and his lack of recognition unchanged. That and the stench of his fear. Duster loved it. Loved it, at last: his fear. He had made her suffer. He had even laughed, at the end, when he had finished, and she would never be free of his memory.

Jewel, however, he had already forgotten, and she struggled to her feet. Duster was aware of her. But the awareness was tinged with the triumph she felt now that this man was in her power.

"I wore chains," she told him. "I was unarmed. Did you really think I'd stay that way?"

And this time his eyes rounded.

She could almost taste his fear. But . . . it was not her moment, not *just* her moment. She said, without looking away from his face, "You've got a dagger, don't you?" Speaking to Jewel.

And Jewel said, her voice raw and distinct, "Yes."

"Then get it," Duster told her softly. Offering to share.

The Patris' eyes widened further, almost bulging in his flushed face, the folds of his skin. "Who sent you?" he managed.

"No one," Duster replied, and she cut him again, shallowly this time. "We came on our own." She looked up. Jewel had not moved. But she now carried a dagger in her hand, and in the light, it glinted.

And it looked wrong, to Duster. Wrong and right, at the same time. She didn't understand it, and she didn't much care. This moment, this dream, had kept her sane, and she wanted to live it, fully and finally. To replace one memory with another, or perhaps to answer it, and have peace.

And Jewel Markess stood in a room that had almost become a tableau. Beneath the stillness there was frenzy, fear, desperation, and a deep and abiding sense of hatred and loss. All of these things were hers.

But not hers alone.

Her throat was raw, and her lips were swollen where they'd cut her teeth; it hurt to stand, and the only thing that felt *good* was the hilt of a dagger; it was cool in her hand, and solid, and familiar.

Lord Waverly was whimpering. And bleeding. She watched him as if from a distance, and when his eyes met hers, she smiled. Sharper edge in that smile than the knife held.

It hurt to walk. She walked anyway, breaking the stillness, adding a stilted motion to the noise, the breathing, the little sounds that spoke of fear and . . . and something else.

Desire. Death. Here, in the end, weren't they one and the same?

Rath had no time to think; just time to react, and even that was in scant supply. There was, however, freedom in the momentary pain of new wounds, the promise of obvious scars; fear took thought. Guilt took thought.

He had no time for either, now; just time to dodge, to roll, to maneuver awkwardly in a space that should have allowed him some grace. Awkward was almost death; he skirted the edge of it, looking for an opening. He would have one, and only one; to waste it was to lose not just this fight, but the game.

The Patris could not now escape him, or it was over.

But the wings were like swan wings in force, if not in appearance, and they drove him back, and claws raked his arms. They should have finished him; he was being toyed with.

But even that, he could use.

This combat was like a conversation, a visceral way of exchanging insults and threats. There was blood, and it was his, but in the end, the only thing that mattered—as in all such bouts—was the final word.

Rath was devoid of words.

But in the distance, Lord Waverly was not, and his words, high and pained, did what Rath had not yet been able to do—they drew the demon's attention from the fight, as if even Waverly's pain and fear were a physical chain that he could not quite escape.

Only a moment, a second, an eye blink, but Rath had survived to be called Old Rath for a reason; he knew that this was the opening he wanted. And the sound of a dead man's pain did not trouble him or stir him at all.

Ararath Handernesse dropped his knives; they were forgotten before they clattered across the floor into the invisibility provided by crushed foliage. They had never been the weapons he meant to wield in this fight, even if he could not have predicted the fight itself.

He drew the weapons Sigurne Mellifas had given him, and he launched himself directly at the creature who was physical shadow, winged and crowned by darkness. They were too awkward a shape, to unwieldy, to be thrown; he could not afford to miss. He met the creature's outstretched hand with his ribs, felt claws glance off bone, and kept going.

And the blades struck flesh, and flame gouted from the wounds they caused, and the creature was shorn in that instant of arrogance and certainty. Rath let go of the hilts, throwing himself backward, too injured to roll. But no death followed him, no death dogged his awkward retreat.

Instead, flame, fire, the heart of it almost blue, the edges a golden yellow that Rath would never forget. They curled out, up, reaching like hands across the whole of the Patris' form, stretching to encompass even the wings, gaining speed and breadth as they moved and consumed what lay beneath them.

The creature spoke; Rath did not understand the single, harsh word. Nor could he take meaning from tone; he could take a vicious satisfaction from the pain it held, but that was all.

Ash fell like rain in the room, and it was hot where it brushed his skin, but in the end, it did not burn him, and in the end, it did not linger.

Bleeding, he touched his side and winced; he'd had broken ribs before, and knew by touch that he had added to that tally. But he could not afford to fall here, or to stop; he was a room away from Jewel, and it was one room too many.

*   *   *

The boy in the perfect uniform faltered only once, but when he did, he seemed frozen in place. Finch thought Carver could stab him and he wouldn't feel it; as she approached him, she saw that he was now completely white, his lips tinged almost the gray of death.

And it was not hard to see why; Finch froze in spite of herself as she saw the wreckage that waited for them around the corner: the broken glass, the piles of greenery that lay trampled and flat against the bright floors. Trellises, delicately built for the weight of vines and flowers, no more, had also fallen, tilting and listing in turn; an army might have moved through this room and caused less destruction.

But there was no army here; there was only one man, and he was staggering and bleeding.

Finch lifted a hand to her mouth to stop sound from emerging, but he must have heard it anyway, the choked little cry of recognition that might have been a name.

He turned to look at them, and as he did, pain passed from his face, to be replaced by weariness and an utter lack of surprise. She would have gone to his side had he been any other man. Had he been one of them. Had he belonged, as they all did, to Jay.

But everything about his bearing warned her to stay back, and the others—they all must have felt it.

"So," Rath said quietly. "You're all here. I should have known."

And it was Teller who spoke first; Teller who broke the silence that followed his words. He was standing just off to the side, and he straightened out before saying a word, but he lifted his chin, his pale face, and said, "We've come for Jay."

Rath winced again, and this time, Finch did move. They all moved, except for Lander and the boy who belonged in this hollow wonder of building, with all its glittering darkness, its lords, its money.

"Where is she?"

"There," Rath said quietly. "Come, now. But do not—" He stopped himself. "Come," he said, and the word itself was a warning.

Chapter Twenty-eight

JEWEL HAD NOT even thought to hate him; the fear and the pain had been so strong that she had lost, for a moment, all ability *to* think. She struggled now with things she couldn't find words for—would never find words for; struggled to see what was there, beyond the envelope of her body, which had itself become foreign and painful.

Duster watched her. Duster, her hands red and slick, her eyes wide, wild, her face both flushed and pale. Her oddly colored hair, the slippage of all disguise, was ghostly; they belonged in a different place. Jewel looked at her and saw—Duster. Saw her truly, as Duster, no more and no less.

This was what Duster had come for. Not death, not that, but the fear and the pain, the humiliation.

Jewel's throat was raw and dry, and she swallowed air as if it would once again be denied her by the weight of, the pain of, his lips, his teeth, hoarding it in her lungs until she was dizzy. But she did not let the knife slip as she walked. As she continued to look. Upended chairs, the tablecloth, the fallen, shattered glasses; dark stain of wine that would always taste sour.

She saw broken flower pots, the story of struggle, saw also that when the chairs were righted and the tablecloths washed or replaced, this room would look as pristine as it had when she had first entered it, in a different life.

Saw, beneath Duster's knife, Lord Waverly. He was not the man he had been, only moments before; the cruelty was gone from his face, and the cowardice was so naked it was numbing.

And Duster waited, now, cutting skin almost casually, and never fatally; threatening death because the threat itself evoked fear and a terrible whimpering, a pleading, a useless attempt at negotiation with a force that was larger and darker than he himself had been.

"What are you waiting for?" Duster said, and although there were no sibilants in the sentence, it was a hiss of words over clenched teeth, as if this much control, this much of an offer was a struggle to make.

This offer to share. This offer of vengeance.

Jewel had no answer. She could walk. She had thought the pain would cripple her, but apparently that had been fear's voice, and as always, the truth was different. She was not without fear now.

She looked at the man, and he met her eyes, his own wide, and she could not recognize him, although everything in her screamed at the sight. Raw scream, fear and rage. What had she told Rath?

He deserved to die.

She had believed it then. She believed it now. The difference in the quality of that belief did not change the fact of it. *You chose to come here,* her Oma's voice said, at its most remote, its coldest. *And you've survived. Learn, girl.* Her Oma had always despised tears. Jewel rarely shed them. Not when there were witnesses. Sometimes the only witness she needed was herself.

But she had said he deserved to die.

And she had meant it.

"Jay!" A single, sharp word. It took her a moment to recognize it as her name. The name she had chosen because Jewel was such a precious conceit. She looked to her right, and there they were: Lefty and Lander in the shadow of Arann, Teller and Finch behind Carver. Carver himself, dagger glinting, eyes bright and dark as he surveyed the ruin of her clothing, the fallen tangle of her straightened hair, the bruises on her jaw, her swollen eye.

She saw Jester, utterly pale, his freckles unchanged; she saw Fisher, grim now, his silence weighty with things that would—must—remain unsaid. She saw shock in their faces, and saw the beginning of its crumble into something else.

And behind them, darker by far, Rath.

She saw Rath.

Saw that he was bleeding, that he favored his side, that he was smudged with dirt like fine ash. He did not look away when she met his eyes, did not flinch when she flinched. But she saw in him an anger that was already implacable and untouchable. She was not afraid of him. Nor was she afraid for him. But for the first time, she felt her throat swell, and the tears she now held back with effort, a dint of will that she had, over the years, mastered.

And she remembered why she had come.

Remembered that she had always seen Duster clearly.

Understood that although Rath was struggling with something akin to guilt, he was also measuring her, as he had always measured her. But against what, and for what purpose? She had never asked him.

She could not ask him now.

She turned to look at Lord Waverly, at Duster, felt the stillness breaking. Her hand shook but she did not drop the dagger; it was now her only anchor, and she needed it. Guide and guardian, she needed it.

She swallowed.

"I want you all to leave," she told them. Her den. They had come for her, and if they had come late, they were here. She didn't ask them how, and there was no need to ask why, and if she had thought to love them before, she knew now that she did, and that she would never stop. They were here for her.

And she was here, in her own fashion, for them.

But there were some things she hoped to spare them, and this—this was one. Had she truly thought this far?

She shuddered, she struggled for composure, she held it. There were *so many* things that were worse than this. She was not alone. She had not been forsaken. She had not been sold, or abandoned. Nothing had been taken from her.

No.

No. She would *not go there.*

She told herself the story of her life, forming and re-forming it, finding in its threads something strong enough to bind her, to hold her together. She needed to do this, because they were here, and they were watching, and she *was* the den leader. She accepted this now, because if she wasn't—

If she couldn't be—

But where had they been when she needed them? Treacherous, horrible question, and it was so visceral, she could not uproot it; it echoed, the words and syllables merging into something so sharp it was more than accusation.

And as she heard Lord Waverly whimpering, as she heard him begging for their help, as she heard his voice die into pain again, and yes, sobs, she understood that the answer to that question *had* to be: here. They were here.

Because *this* was what she needed of them.

She had planned to come here.

She had planned to kill Lord Waverly. Or to let Duster kill him. But she had also planned to deny Duster what Duster was taking now: the pleasure of the sadist. It had been her only real thought, her only clear thought, and it *was not* clear enough now, but it remained there *because* they were here, her den, the people she had chosen.

And yet . . . she wanted to walk out on him. To leave him to Duster. To find, in the hollows of her imagination, a death for him that would linger, a death that he would greet, in the end, with relief. A death that she could set against the other memories that would not leave, her own bleeding, her bruises, her own loss.

She saw Duster clearly. Saw Duster, for a moment, in herself. Understood that what she had planned so clearly, and so easily was no small thing to ask.

But it had to be possible, to ask it.

And she *had* to be able to ask it.

Carver said, "We're not leaving without you."

She could have ordered him to leave. She could have done that. But she had asked. And she had been rejected. And perhaps, in the end, that was for the best. She said, "I'm fine." And sounded fine. To herself; perhaps to them.

Rath said nothing.

But when she turned to Duster, when she looked again at Lord Waverly, she asked a single question. "Duster, is that what I sounded like?"

And Duster's face contorted, as if the question itself had been asked in a language that she had heard so long ago she had to struggle with the memories to even understand it.

Jewel *hated* the question. But it was the right question, and something surrounding her snapped as it left her, breaking cleanly in the middle, and allowing her to emerge. Not unscathed, never that, but the shadows no longer engulfed her; she could reach out to either side and touch them; she could draw them back in and hold them in what she had idealistically called her heart, or she could deny them: but she could never again be unaware of them.

She said, again, with a slowly building revulsion, "Is that what I sounded like? Did you hear me?"

And Duster shook her head in confusion, although her knife hand did not waver, and her determination did not break.

"He *deserves* this," she hissed. "After what he did—to me—to you—he deserves this. You must know that."

Jewel beckoned Carver forward, and he came instantly, wordlessly. She held out her knife, and he understood what she asked of him; he took it. He was the sheath.

"He deserves this," Jewel replied calmly, coolly now. "But you don't."

Confusion, uncertainty. This, too, was Duster. It was the only way in which she showed vulnerability, and it was close to the edge.

"I kept my word," Jewel said, as proudly as her Oma would have said it, and with just as much determination. "But this is not what *I* want."

"And if it's what *I* want?"

"Then you'll take it," Jewel replied. "Just as he did. You'll take what you want. But you'll be him, Duster. You'll *be him,* and I will not have you in my den if you make that choice.

"Kill him," Jewel added. "But kill him quickly."

"But *why*—"

And something broke again, and it was a good break, and Jewel looked at Duster, met her eyes, held them. "I'm not strong enough," she said, soft voice now, almost a whisper although no one in the room could have missed it. "I'm not strong enough for this. I could kill him," she added. "I want to kill Lord Waverly. I do want that. I'm not ashamed of it.

"But I *can't* kill this man. I could have killed him, when he was—" She shook her head. "But not like this." And it was true. All of it.

Because Duster had not answered her question, Jewel did. "I did sound like that." It was costly. To say it. To admit it. But more costly, in the end, to hide it. She would not always be strong. She was not her Oma. But *if* she could somehow manage to be strong at the right time, at the right minute, if that was all the grace that was allowed her—that would be enough. Had to be.

He tried to speak to her. He saw the weakness. He understood that, were he now in a room without Duster, he would be allowed to crawl out. And it would be wrong. He would recover, and he would have power again, and he would use it in the way that he had used it, time and again.

"Kill him," Jewel said quietly. "But understand the difference between an execution and . . . what he does. What he did. Be an executioner," she added. "Be my executioner. But only that."

"That's—that's Rath talking!" Duster almost spit. But the knife did not cut again; she was held there, staring.

And Rath said, "No," in a quiet voice. "I would leave him to you."

Finch had turned away, and Teller was staring at his feet. Carver, by Jewel's side, had not moved an inch, but she could not see his face in the shadow of his hair. Arann, silent, was expressionless. Lefty could not be seen. But Lander? Lander, silent and voiceless, came out of the shadows. Lander moved across the room as if the invisible boundaries which split it into so many disparate pieces did not exist at all. As if Duster was beside him, beside them.

And he knelt, and Waverly *must* have recognized him.

But it was not to Waverly that he looked. Not to Waverly that he lifted his hands slowly. He did not touch Duster. No one did. But in the air between them, the movement of his fingers made his gestures spinnerets, and a web of simple words formed that even Jewel could read.

Do what she says.

Duster could not answer in kind without losing her knife and her grip, without surrendering the power she had gained. She used words instead. "I promised you," her voice was low now, "I promised."

And because Lefty's slow labor was not yet up to the task of the discussion, because the den, in spite of their delight in their own secret tongue, did not yet have a signal for something as weighty and defining as *promise* or vow, he spoke.

"You promised you would kill him," he told her. "Kill him. And come home."

"But I—"

"Cleanly," he told her. "Because Jay is right. You don't have to do this."

"I *want* to do this."

"Yes. But you don't have to. You are not Lord Waverly."

So many things had broken this evening. So many silences. So many beliefs. "I *am*."

There it was: the despair. The thread of it. Jewel wanted to catch it and hold it, because this was the only hope that she held for Duster, and she accepted it. She had not known whether or not Duster would come home with her at the evening's end; she hadn't *seen* it. She could not clearly see it now, and if she had called the sight a curse, she wanted to be cursed, truly, forever.

She hadn't known, until this moment, whether or not she wanted Duster. And she knew now, and this, too, she accepted.

So she said, in Torra, in a language she knew Duster would understand, "You aren't judged by what you want. If we were, you and I would be no different. It's only what you do, in the end, that counts.

"It was easy for me. That's what you want to say. It was *easy*. Let me say it for you. It was. It's *not* easy now. And maybe . . . Kalliaris' frown, maybe I had to *learn* what it is that you—what *hard* means.

"And it *doesn't matter* whether it's easy or not." Breath was cleaner, clearer. "That's your trap. You think it's only about what you want. You think you only want one thing. You can only *have* one, but that's not the same." She turned to look over her shoulder. "We don't have much time. Decide."

Rath closed his eyes. It was brief, this momentary denial; it could have been a long, slow blink. But for just a moment—for less than a moment—he could not look at Jewel. He could meet her eyes; he could force himself to do that much, could mime neutrality and distance. He could pretend to be unmoved, for the moment, by what held him fast: the sight of her, the words that she had just spoken.

For as long as he lived, he would remember them clearly, not because she had spoken them—but because of when, because the context itself made them almost incandescent to a man of his age, to a man who had made the choices he had made in angry ignorance. He wanted to apologize to her, but apology itself was a thin and pale thing, and it felt hollow enough that he could not bring himself to say the words.

Or perhaps, he thought bitterly, he had *never* been capable of speaking the words. Apology and pride were at opposite ends of a long life, and having chosen the one, he could not now lower himself to the other. Or, in this one moment, elevate himself, rise above himself. Become, he could see this clearly, like *her*. Like Jewel.

Like Amarais.

Duster was silent, as silent as Rath. Rath understood all the nuances of that silence, and he thought—although he could not be certain—that Jewel *did not*. That Jewel did not understand how much of what had passed here had passed *because* of Duster, her choice, and her bitter, ugly envy, her hatred, her scarred and twisted thoughts.

If you understood her, if you truly understood her, he thought, *would you offer her this much? Would you take her in?*

And looking at Duster's face, which now concealed *nothing*, he knew that word for word, it was her thought, and her fear. But it was also her hope, who deserved none. He wanted to kill her.

And knew, even as the desire was mastered, that it was misplaced; that it was not Duster, in the end, who had failed, but Rath himself. He had laid out a clever and sophisticated trap; it was a simple one. But he had not seen clearly enough, and if in the end, the trap had closed, it had closed in ways that only the foolish or the sadistic would be glad of. Rath was neither.

He would have killed Lord Waverly himself. He would have given him the death he deserved. He saw, for just a moment, that Duster was like a mirror; something he could look into. Liking what he saw was not even in question. He had always understood her.

And yet.

"Jewel is correct," he heard himself say quietly. Every word measured, because it had to be, for Jewel's sake. Perhaps for his own. "You have little time. I think the boy—" He shrugged. "If you are here when the magisterial guards arrive, it will go ill with you."

The death of Patris AMatie would never be traced, if it was even discovered at all; what did fine ash mean, to the magisterians? Fire, perhaps, or something equally inexplicable. They might summon their mages, or even those who could bespeak the Lord of Judgment, but in the end, he thought they would do no such thing. Lord Waverly was not a man wellloved or well-respected.

But he was a lord.

What will you do, Duster?

Duster was afraid.

She could not—at this moment—remember a time in her life when she had not been afraid. Afraid of pain, yes. Of loss. Of starvation, which in the end made everything else look so much more appealing. You could force yourself to do almost anything to stop the hunger.

But there wasn't very much you could do to stop the pain. Pain was something that other people caused. And pain was something that other people—like Duster—could learn from. Like a lesson, like the most valuable of lessons, the right pain taught you everything about life you needed to know.

Everything about power.

Power was supposed to be the guarantee. When you had power, the fear belonged to someone else. Fear existed like that; it was always there. Somebody had to bear it. She knew this. She had *won*. Waverly was here, and he was hers.

But the triumph she had felt—and she *had* felt it, and she tried to cling to it as it burned to ash—was crumbling. She knew she'd won; it wasn't her blood on her hands. Or her face. It wasn't her who was whimpering, pleading, it wasn't her who—

She had suffered. He deserved to suffer.

And Jay understood that, now.

But she stood there, still stood there, holier than thou, offering with one hand and demanding with the other. She *understood* what Duster had suffered, and she had *let it go*.

Duster should have hated her for it. She *wanted* to hate her. She almost ignored her; she could do that, here. She understood Jay, or thought she did, and she knew that if she made the choice, Jay would just walk away, same as she had just walked in.

And the bad part was: Duster didn't want her to leave. She had, she had told herself she was quit of Jewel once she'd gotten what she wanted. And here it was, but she wasn't certain that it *was* what she wanted. No, she was certain she wanted it.

But there was something else here that she couldn't—didn't dare—put into words, not even in the privacy of thought, where no one but the gods, curse them all, could hear her if they bothered to listen at all.

Jewel had seen, and understood, and Jewel was waiting. She was waiting for Duster. She was offering her something that Duster had never had and had always said she never wanted: a home. A place.

"What—what do you want from me?" she managed to say.

"I want you to kill him quickly and come home," Jewel replied.

"No," Duster said. "Not that. I don't mean that. If I—if I come home, what then? I'm not going to work in your kitchen. I'm not going to cut your vegetables. I'm not going to run your errands. I'm *not good at that*." She looked at Jewel, the words heated and angry.

"You don't have to be," Jewel replied steadily.

"Then *what*? What am I good *for*?"

"I don't know," Jewel told her softly, still quiet in the face of her flash of anger, her teeter across despair's edge. "But I don't know what I'm good for either. I know that I'm not good for this. I know that I don't want you to die here, or to die in a jail, or in the shadow of the gallows. I know that you can do things that I can't."

"Like this?" Duster asked bitterly.

"Like this," was the serene reply. "But what I need from you now, what I need to know now—the rest can wait—is that you can walk away from this when you need to. No," she added, holding up her hand, stemming the words, "that's not fair. I need to know that you can walk away from this when *I* need you to.

"We won't always live where we live," she added, and her eyes changed, shifting almost imperceptibly into something darker and rounder, something like black but warmer. "We won't always be safe."

"You call this safe?"

Jewel winced. She should have looked away. But she didn't. "Yes," she whispered. Hard to say the word. Duster knew the tone. But she said it. "This is safe compared to where we will be, later.

"And when we're there, you'll know. Finch is never going to raise a sword in my name or in my defense, and if she did, she'd only cut off one of her legs. Teller will never be able to do it either. You can," she added. "You're like a walking sword. But you've got no sheath, Duster, and you need one."

The urge to say something lewd came and went. "You want me to be your muscle?"

"Something like that."

And that, Duster understood. As much as she could understand anything about Jewel, she could understand that.

The rest could wait, would have to wait.

Because whatever it was Jewel could see in Duster, whatever it was she *wanted*, was not what the demons had seen. It was different.

It was something that Duster wanted, for a moment, to believe of herself. And there was only one way she could do that, and that one way, that narrow path, was standing there like Judgment, waiting on an invisible throne.

She swallowed.

She said, without thought, without the desire to hide, "He *hurt* me. They always do."

And Jewel flinched, and nodded. And said, "I know." And her voice broke on both syllables, and her eyes narrowed, and Duster could almost taste the desire that was so much like her own—Ah.

So much in those two words. Too much. But they were *true*, and if they were true, and Jewel could stand there and *be* Jewel . . . then the rest just might be true as well.

What rest? What else? She could mock herself in the silence of thought. Deride herself. Call herself weak where she'd kill anyone else who even started the syllable.

But she could find just enough to believe, and she wanted that belief so badly it terrified her.

Jewel said, "It's always harder when you have something to lose."

"What do I have to lose?"

"Us."

"I don't give a shit about any of you."

"Then choose, Duster, and we're gone."

And Duster did choose. Eyes closed, hand trembling, the future opening before her like a pit from which there might be no escape. She slit his throat cleanly and quickly, and if her hands were drenched in the sudden gout of his blood, she barely noticed. Because when she opened her eyes, when she could see the world again, it was wavering.

And Jewel was pale as a ghost, and her eyes—she was crying. Not sobbing, not that—but there were tears now across her cheeks which had not been there five minutes before.

"For him?" Duster said, feeling anger's bite. Something like jealousy.

"For you," Jewel told her softly. "Because it's hard, what you did, and I didn't know if you *would*. I knew that you could, but it's not the same thing." She held out her hand, her bruised arm, and Duster stared at it.

Stared at it until Jewel took another step forward, hand still outstretched.

So many choices, to be here. To be in this place. Duster had not lied to Jewel. She didn't care about "us." Whatever that was. But she had nothing against lying anyway.

Was it a lie, then, to reach out for Jewel's single hand with both of her own? Was it a lie to pull back just before they touched, because her hands were so red and slick with a dead man's blood she was—for just a moment—afraid that all that would remain when she pulled her hands back would *be* that blood, that death?

But Jewel didn't allow her to find out. The blood, she ignored as she could; the single hand became two as she caught Duster and pulled her to her feet. It was awkward, with Lord Waverly between them; Duster stepped on him by accident, as if he were a cumbersome and broken bridge.

"Rath," Jewel said, without looking away, "we need to leave quickly. We need to go home."

Carver took command then, but quietly, his words so short and pointed he could sign them. Lander had been standing outside of the door, as if death and only death waited there, but when they came out, following in Carver's wake, Rath had not moved an inch. "Take the tunnels," he told her quietly. "Go back the way we came. Don't stop, Jewel. Tonight is not the night for a tour." And then he stopped, and covered his hands with his eyes as if he were greatly weary and ached with it. "No," he said, his voice soft. "You have the magestones. Use them, and take the time you need.

"You've seen enough tonight. See as much as you want, as much as you think you can manage. And then *go straight home,* and stay there. Don't answer the door. There shouldn't be anyone at it."

By which, Jewel understood that he meant to join them through the streets of the undercity, but later. She didn't ask what he was going to do. She didn't want to know. She was herself in pain, and walking was hard, at first. Breathing was painful.

But the other sharp sensation was both painful and joyful, and it was the latter that she clung to, as hard as she could. Duster's hand. Duster's choice. This was the better way: to find joy, to find the single beam of light in the darkness; to see it, know it, absorb it. To know that it was *just as real* as the bad things; that the bad did not destroy all good.

And it was hard.

She thought about the undercity, and she walked out of the room, still clinging to Duster's hand, as if afraid that at any moment Duster would change her mind, withdraw, and be gone. But even if she left *now,* she had made a choice that she would never have made before, and that was its own hope, and Jewel lived on hope.

What had she said to Duster? That it was always harder when you had something to lose? Maybe. But was it really easier when you had nothing at all?

She looked at Finch, at Teller, and they met her eyes, searched them, did not, this time, look away. They were afraid for her, afraid of what she might be feeling, and she was their den leader. What she felt now, she felt; what she showed them of that, she *chose*.

And she would have to choose wisely.

She almost bumped into Lander, who was standing there, waiting. He looked at her, but it was a glance, no more; almost all of his attention was on Duster.

Duster started to speak, and then she said, "Let go of my hands."

Jewel shook her head, and Duster added, "Just for now, then. Let go of them for now."

And understanding came to Jewel, and she did as Duster had asked. Not commanded, not demanded, but asked. Her hands—both of their hands—were red and wet, but Jewel didn't care. She watched as Duster lifted hers, the evidence of her deed there, darker where the lifeline ran.

Those hands moved slowly, the fingers shaking as she did the small dance in the air with deliberate care.

Lander understood the two words. He closed his eyes.

Duster did not immediately return to Jewel; instead, she stepped forward, and Jewel watched as a girl that demons would foster—in their cruel, terrible fashion—now touched both shoulders of a boy who had been mute for so long. That she left the imprints of blood on either shoulder should have felt accidental, but it wasn't; Jewel could see that Duster now made a deliberate choice.

I don't give a shit about "us."

And Jewel's Oma said, *Words are cheap. They don't say what we mean. The don't mean what we say. Judge, learn to judge, by other means.*

Judgment had always been a top priority for her Oma.

Jewel tried not to judge now. Not Duster, who had done, in the end, what Jewel herself was afraid she could *not* have done; not the boy who had waited—she saw this clearly now—for Duster to keep her word. To kill the man who had hurt them both in their captivity.

The blood might never wash out, Jewel thought. But that was fair. The memories wouldn't either; they were just harder to see unless one knew how to read their signs and shadows in the ways the people who held them behaved.

Lander bowed his head, bowed it low enough that it could touch Duster's forehead; they stood this way for a long moment. Long enough, but Duster was not Jewel, and was not Finch; she was justice, judgment, death—but she could offer comfort for only so long before it became just another cage.

And Lander said, "Thank you," so softly it might have been signed. It was enough. Duster's eyes widened slightly. It was her version of surprise, and even gratitude. But she didn't tell Lander that she hadn't done this for him. She didn't deride him. She had always somehow managed to be, if not gentle, then not cruel, while dealing with Lander.

Because damaged people were the people she best understood, and she wasn't terribly perceptive. It took very little to see Lander's wounds; it took more to see what might exist beneath them, when all the scabs had cleared. Let Duster do the former; let Jewel do the latter. They each had a role to play, and as long as they *could*, they would have a home, and a family. Blood bound them, and if it was not birth blood, it was enough.

"Go out the kitchen doors," Rath told her. "Left, here. They'll swing in. No one will stop you," he added, his voice slightly lower. "I have business here to which I must attend, but I will meet you at home before dawn."

"And if you're not there?" Jewel asked, with just a trace of hesitation. It was not a question she had really dared to ask before. But many things had been torn from her this evening.

"I *will be* there," he replied.

She could not doubt that tone.

"We'll be waiting," she told him, and then, in a slightly louder voice, "Kitchen, then; we'll leave that way. Do you remember how you got here?"

Teller said quietly, "I do."

"Good, because I have *no idea* how to get back."

His smile was slight, almost shy, but there was a shadow across it that he would never, ever put into words; she saw that clearly as well. "I know."

She would love him for it for a long, long time, if the gods smiled, and if they were kind.

Rath watched them go. In silence, he watched, stood guard over the dead. The dead that would cause them all so much trouble, if the situation were not handled carefully, correctly. This, Ararath Handernesse, heir to a House among the patriciate that he would never claim, could do.

But there were other things that he could not do. Watching as they walked, this odd group of strange children who now circled and hid both their leader and her adopted killer, he felt a strange sense of something that was almost pride, and a bitter certainty that he had failed them all; that they were strong enough to *bear* his failure because Jewel was strong enough to bear it.

He had opened up his home to Jewel's intrusive presence, and he had lied to himself about his reasons for doing so. Or perhaps not; was ignorance truly lying? He had encouraged her in the end to do what he said he would not accept: invade it, by stealth and by determination, take it over, make it her own.

She had chosen her den, although she would never have called them that at the time; she had chosen as wisely as she could, given her circumstances—and never in ways that he could have conceived.

He had always known that she would be tested. He had intended—from the moment he had agreed to help her—that *this* would be her test. And it had been. And she had not only passed it, but risen above his expectations in ways that were bitter and horrible to him now.

Pride in her, yes, and wonder.

But for himself he felt only loathing, and a blacker loathing than he had ever felt. He had fallen lower than he now stood many times in his life, starting with his abdication of all responsibility in the face of what he had thought of as his sister's betrayal. But *he* had fallen; he had paid the price for the fall, and he had struggled to stand, to walk, and to survive, aware of it.

This time, it was not his price to pay. He had never intended this to happen; he had never intended for things to go so far, so quickly. And he *should have seen it.* He should have known that Duster would fail in her duties. He should have known that somehow—somehow—the demons in the brothel and the Patris AMatie were so intimately tied, that AMatie would be a concern.

He had failed to see. He had failed to plan accordingly. And there she was, in the wake of his failure.

She could walk, surrounded by them. She could smile, or cry, or speak, could ignore it in their presence. But Rath was not Jewel; he did not live on hope. He lived, rather, by bitter experience, and he knew that the scars she bore would never truly fade.

And yet, in the end, she had all but denied what was completely obvious to every single child in the room, because to do less was to damage *them.* He had seen what was on her face; he had seen the dagger in her

hand; he had seen the uncertainty, the revulsion, the horror and—yes—
the desire for vengeance and death. And she had handed Carver the dagger
instead, and by managing to do just that, she had become—did she know
it?—the sheath for Duster that she had spoken of so carefully.

The ghost of his past was his sister, at that moment, his sister and her
pale face, her abiding anger, her slow determination.

I did not understand you, Amarais, he thought, bitterly. *And if I understand you now in some small measure it is because of Jewel Markess. An orphan
in the poorest part of this city.*

She had been hurt, and he knew why. Knew that in the end, Waverly
was simply a tool. Knew, as well, that the hands that had wielded him had
not yet been fully revealed; there was work to do.

He would dedicate his life to doing it, because only by doing so would
he be free of the image of Jewel standing in her torn and bloody dress, her
bruised face silent and still. And perhaps not even then.

Epilogue

MAGELIGHTS IN DARKNESS. No moon, no sky, no lamps to hold them aloft. Held, instead, in cupped hands, carried with care and worry, they lit a small path, revealing cracked stone, fallen pillars, rocks with sheared edges that might have cracked centuries ago. Or days.

No snow here, and no rain; no weather to trouble the undercity. The only movement that could be seen was theirs; the den's. Jewel watched them, her hands empty. She had given her stone to Finch. She could not hold it herself.

But hold it or no, she followed where the light led, finding comfort in its presence. There was secrecy in this place, and in secrecy, a promise of safety. But more, there was history, and beauty, that lay untouched and undisturbed. The walk through the streets above had been cold and numbing, and she had welcomed that.

Duster walked by her side in utter silence, and trailing her like shadow came Lander, his shoulders black in the shadowed light, and not the red of blood. No one spoke. No one touched her. No one offered her words of comfort. This, too, was a blessing. She was shaking, and could pretend that this was because she was cold; they let her be.

Carver offered her his coat, and she shook her head; she had one, and she wore it. It hid much. Had she eaten, she might have thrown up.

But instead, she followed and led, surrounded by her den, the kin she had chosen, and the kin who had chosen her. She did not find the path into the undercity; Lander did. And Lander led only as far as the entrance, before giving way in silence to Arann. They entered it as they left it, aware of the things that had changed.

So much silence. The silence of the dead. The silence of a city that might be filled with ghosts, all mercifully still. The silence of fear, of regret, of anger. Too much silence.

The voice that broke the silence was hers. In the future, she thought, it would always be hers. But here, in the now, she had to struggle to break it, and when she did, she found surprise and some flicker of memory that was both attenuated and strong enough to cling to.

"I want to show you something."

They stopped walking, as a group, and turned to face her, and she realized she was at the center of a circle. It was a good circle, if a bit lopsided.

Teller said, "Here?" and light bobbed in his hand.

She nodded. Even managed a smile. There were so many things to cling to, all of them memory. But too many of those memories could be shared only with words, which were all that were left.

This one, this was different.

"Come," she told him, told them all. And they nodded.

She didn't remember the way, not consciously. Maybe her feet did. Or maybe she could *see* it in a way that did not give her nightmares. But she found a path over the cracks in the stone; paused once or twice so that they could navigate the more treacherous byways. She was not afraid here. Fear would come later, if it came at all. Accidents did not frighten her, they had now become so impersonal. There were worse things.

She looked once or twice to see if Duster was with her; Duster failed to meet her eyes, failed to meet anyone's eyes. But she followed, and that was enough for now.

You got what you wanted, she could hear her Oma say, in her bitter voice. *Didn't I tell you to be careful of what you want?*

Always, Oma.

And would you do it again?

No answer. She wasn't sure what the right answer was. No. That wasn't true. *It doesn't matter,* she told the past. *It happened; I can't change it.*

And if you could?

I can't.

Her Oma's ghost seemed to shrug at that, to offer something like a smile, twisted and laced with both anger and a grudging approval. That had been her Oma, in life, and in death, her voice was still strong.

You be practical, be a practical girl.

Jewel nodded. But it wasn't the practical that led her, in the end, to the tall face of a building she had seen only once. She heard Teller's sharp intake of breath, and said, "More light, Teller."

He looked at her, and she spoke a word, and the magelight flared in his hands with its cold fire. The face of the building grew sharper and clearer as the light blazed up from his hands—from all their hands—at once.

"Someone lived here?" he finally asked.

"Maybe. No one lives here now. Come."

And she led them into the terraced stone of the Maker's Garden, as she now thought of it, and she led them among the flowers that age and seasons did not wither.

"This is a secret place," she told them, and it was easy to speak in a whisper because no other voices intruded. "This is Rath's place, and he—" She shook her head. "And he'll share it with us, for now."

She bent to touch a petal, her hands drawing webs as she pulled them back. "It never ages," she said quietly. "And it never changes."

"It's—" Finch, now. Finch, kneeling with as much care as she would have had the flowers been real. "It's like magic."

Jewel nodded. It was. But she couldn't feel it, here. She could feel it in memory. Perhaps you couldn't go back. Or perhaps you could only have it once, and that once—she wanted it for these people.

But they failed you.

She closed her eyes, let the words echo, hating them. Hating them, believing them, denying them.

And Duster said, in a voice that was quiet in this quiet place, and so unlike her own that Jewel almost couldn't recognize it, "I don't deserve this." Laying herself bare.

Or blossoming, in a way the stone couldn't.

Beauty, Jewel thought, *in the things that never changed.* Whoever had made these flowers, those twining stone leaves, those trellises—they had captured a moment in time, and held it; you could almost feel the reverence in the creation itself. But they could not capture the beauty of the things that *did* change; only by being there could you see it, and only with memory could you hold it.

She turned, lifted the hands that touched petals and the webs that had been spun around them, and faced Duster who was crouched by her side like a wounded creature. "Maybe," she said, with a shrug. "Maybe you don't. But who's to say that any of us do? We get what we get, most times. We just have to deal with it." She paused, and said, "Judge what you have to judge. Change what you need to change.

"If you don't deserve it now, earn it."

Duster was shaking. Just . . . shaking.

Her hair would grow out, the pale blonde edges eclipsed by natural darkness. Her skin would grow ruddy again, and no doubt her face would lose this wounded wonder. But Jewel would remember it.

For both of them, if she had to.

Teller whispered something to Finch; Finch said something to Arann, words crept into the stillness, like a breath of warmth and life.

Jewel reached out for Duster's hand, and she held it tightly for just a moment before letting go.

Duster raised that hand to her face, and the other hand joined it, and she sat there, huddling into her knees, her face now hidden.

It was the only way she would cry. It was something else they had in common, now, this need to gather and hide their weakness.

Rath sat in the Magi's tower, waiting. Hard, to sit, and wait. Hard to sit at all, to be confined; he had rarely been driven by the anger that drove him now. Anger was for the young, and he had spent it carelessly in his youth. Had spent enough of it that he had grown to realize how much energy and effort it took to sustain anger, to nourish it.

He had thought it left behind, like all else about his youth, and it was a bitter surprise to find that he could not shake himself free of its grip.

But then again, why should he? It was wed to guilt, here; to his absolute certainty of failure. That Jewel had somehow emerged, that she had proved to Rath that his testing had not been in vain—it galled him. It sickened him. She was a *child*, and he had given her a test that she should never have been given. Not even as an adult.

But he had thought of his sister, then. In the planning, and even in the execution—he had thought of Amarais, who had never been vulnerable. And Jewel had paid for that.

What Rath would pay had not yet been decided. That he would was not in question. Here, now, he understood that he had already chosen his fate, and if he could not clearly see where it lay, the ignorance made little difference.

He sat at the end of the long table that he had seen only once before, but he wore no messenger's garb, no disguise; he no longer needed one. Or perhaps he had passed beyond disguise to come to this point: he could not discern who he *was* anymore, and he did not wish to hide.

Upon the table, the daggers lay, dull and flat, their runes no longer glowing. Both daggers. He had used them, and as he had promised the Magi—and only a fool broke a promise given to a woman like Sigurne—he had come to make his report, and to return them.

But that was not all he had come for, and sitting here, his hair in a warrior's braid, a hint of his year in the North, he faced those daggers, and he waited, and he longed to cut all waiting short, to take up sword or knife, to hit the streets fighting. To kill.

Long, long time, since he had felt such a pointless, visceral desire. But even so, the distance of years could not lessen it. Wisdom had failed him. Everything had failed him.

He had failed Jewel.

But she? She had not failed *herself*.

And because she had not, he could not now kill Duster, although the desire was strong. He remembered that anger was like this; like fire, it burned everything in its wake; it did not discriminate. Perhaps this was not true of other angers; perhaps Jewel, trusting, implacable urchin, was not possessed of this, and her anger was something that could be appeased, could be put out. Not so the anger of Handernesse, slow to wake, and impossible to quench with anything less than blood.

He heard the door open; it creaked. He took the sound as a courtesy, and not a lack of attention to the oiling of door hinges, and in this, he knew he was not wrong; that door could open so silently a man could die in this chair before he was aware that someone had entered the room.

But it was thus that Sigurne Mellifas announced her presence, and he rose at the sound, and turned to face her. She stood framed by peaked arch, and she seemed slight and frail as she saw who waited, even though she must have known who it was long before she made the onerous walk in the cold from the height of her tower to this room where strangers might meet in safety.

In safety for the Magi.

But she offered him no threat, and indeed, the courtesy of a nod, and he closed the distance between them and offered her his arm, his elbow bent at the correct height, his bearing, so often discarded, the bearing of the son of a noble family of old blood.

She glanced at his face, but made no comment; she did, however, accept the use of his arm, and she let it bear some of her weight. If she was not ancient, as she often chose to appear, she was not young.

But then again, neither were the trees that girded the Common from great height. She chose frailty as her mantle, but it was one she could put aside at will or necessity. And she saw no need, in this room, to do either. Not yet.

But she saw, as well, the daggers that lay in isolation across the perfect sheen of a long table, and her steps faltered. Her hand, in the crook of his arm, shook. He could feel it, although he could see none of it in the seamless neutrality of her expression.

Were all women of power so guarded?

Jewel, in her youth; Amarais in her prime, and this woman in her aged wisdom—they could have been kin, for a moment. He saw traces of each in Sigurne's face, and knew that he would search, in future, for such traces in Jewel's. But his sister, he did not intend to see again while he lived.

And for the first time, he regretted it; the bitter pride. But regret was not enough to break what had given his life meaning to this point. Now? He had to find a different meaning, for the anger he felt had shifted and changed. His sister's betrayal had become a shadow, a ghost; it no longer lived in him, and through him.

His *own* betrayal was greater, and more personal, and there was only one way to expunge it. He had done this. And he could live—barely—with the loathing he now felt for himself. Because to die was to leave it unanswered; to leave Jewel unavenged. This, he would not do.

For he was certain, and meant to be more certain, that this had not ended with the death of the Patris; that it had not ended with the demise of Lord Waverly. Even that—even that had been denied him; Jewel had taken it from his hands, had offered it—demanded it—of Duster.

He could have interfered—but she had suffered everything for just that demand. And having paid the greater price, he could not sunder the possible failure or success from her without paying a heavier price than the one he paid now.

Sigurne said, in a flat voice, "So."

"Yes," he told her, equally uninflected. He walked her to the table, and there, removed his arm so that he might pull out a chair. She accepted it wordlessly, as if it were her natural right. And it was, in this place, although he knew she had not been born to it.

"Who?"

"Patris AMatie."

"Where, Ararath?"

He did not deny her the use of the name he despised. Because he owned it now. Son of ancient Handernesse.

"In the Ivory Retreat," he told her quietly.

Her brows rose slightly. "There were witnesses?"

"None." He paused, and added, "No body." Not of the demon; Lord Waverly was a different concern. But Lord Waverly was not entirely Sigurne's concern, and he did not intend to share everything.

She nodded. "Both daggers," she said. "What was he?"

He frowned. Understood the question only after a moment's pause. "He had wings," he said at last, joining her in the chair closest to her side. "Large and dark. He had talons that were the length of these daggers, but in other aspects, he was not dissimilar from either you or I."

"He was a lord, then," she said, and age seemed to weigh more heavily along the slump of shoulders. "And not merely kin; he was of the *Kialli.*"

"He is dust now."

"They are not so easily destroyed," she replied, "although we will not see his return in our lifetimes. And for that, we must be grateful."

He was not grateful, but did not tell her so; it would have been beneath his station. And he had thought nothing beneath it, in his time. But the thought that the Patris would return, and that he could be killed again and again, had an appeal to Rath at the moment that mere words could not contain.

All of his times, all of his life—it led here. He had never thought that it would lead to this place.

She said, "You are not here merely to return these to my keeping."

"You grace me with your perception, Member Mellifas."

She looked at him carefully, as if attempting to glean some humor in the words, some lightness of expression, some hint of triviality; there was none. "Why, then, are you here, Ararath? You are not . . . calm, now. Nor are you frightened, and given your evening's work, you should be."

"You do not—and gods willing will not—understand my evening's work," he replied bitterly. "And I am not man enough to admit or confess it. But I know that it is not yet done. The Patris was not here alone."

She was silent. Almost, she rose, but he caught her frail hands in his, and she subsided. "You suspect that there are those within your Order who have been compromised in some fashion; you suspect that because of the investigation that is ongoing in the death of Member Haberas, a man I admired, and held in some esteem." He paused and said, "Yes, I mocked him, but never without affection; he was what he was, and he was of aid to me."

She nodded. "All that you have said is true, Ararath. But all that we might speak of is forbidden. Do you understand?"

He nodded.

"What help you offer—I cannot accept it in any legal fashion. I cannot acknowledge it plainly; I cannot claim it. You cannot work with the magisterial guards; you cannot work with the Order itself. There is only one other that I would trust completely, and you have met him. There are few indeed within the Order who could work either under him or by his side; we are known for being somewhat fractious."

"I don't care," he said. "I have not cared for decades about the official and the unofficial. I have not claimed a role for myself—"

"You have claimed many, Ararath." Her eyes were now intent and pale; he could not see his reflection in them. *Magic,* he thought; she used some sort of magic. But let her. Let her understand the intensity of his intent. The truth of it.

"If I cannot come to you," he told her quietly, "I will not. But what I do, I must do."

"And if I ask why?"

"You will not ask me why."

She nodded after a moment. "Your girls—"

He shook his head. "Nor about them. I have played my first hand, and played it poorly."

"But you did not lose them."

"No," he told her, and he told her more than he had intended and more than he desired. "But not through any skill of my own. I have learned much about myself that I would have been happier not to know, Sigurne.

"And I accept it as truth and judgment. There are demons in this city, and they play a game that neither you nor I fully understand. But I want them. I will have them, with or without your help."

"You are mortal," she said slowly. "Do you understand that they have seen millennia pass? That they have witnessed the death of gods?"

"I neither understand nor care. Give me the weapons that you have given me, and I will return them with my reports. Or deny me them, and I will find other weapons."

"You play a dangerous game," she told him, and her tone, rather than hardening, softened. "And it will consume you, Ararath. You can only play with fire so often before you get burned."

"It will likely kill me," he replied. "War does that. But I have learned one thing in my life, and I offer it to you now: all things are games, and the games that I have chosen have consumed me in one way or the other. I am called Old Rath by many, and I intend to survive. But intent and success are not the same, to my great regret.

"What will you do? I will not let go of this. I cannot."

"I will, as you guessed, give you everything within my power to give. Not more, Ararath, and not less. But if you walk this edge, you risk more than just death."

"I know. But in the end, it is mine to risk."

She nodded. And then she reached out to touch his face, as gently as a mother might. His, long dead, had often brushed his hair, not as an act of grooming—there were of course servants for that—but as an act of wonder and affection.

And he thought of that, now, when he was so long past her. He thought of peace—and death—and wondered if for him they would be one and the same.

"Then come," she said. "We have much to discuss, you and I. I should turn you out of this tower, and send you back to the tenuous safety of the life you have chosen.

"But the life you have chosen would not allow it, and in the end, I am a practical woman, and I will use what you will not set aside."

"Don't speak with such bitterness on my account, Sigurne. It is all that I desire."

"So speaks youth, to the elderly, and with just such focus. But desire is illusion, and illusion is a tool."

"Then if I am to be your tool, let me be a sword, and let me fall as I must, and swiftly."

*   *   *

When he returned to the apartment, it was quiet. Dark. The evening had started and ended, and although dawn had not yet paled the sky, it was coming. He could feel it in the ache of shoulders, the tension of muscles that had not once relaxed during his conversation with Sigurne.

But he was still Rath, and although the apartment was silent, he knew instantly that not all of its occupants slept. The door to Jewel's room was closed; the door to the room that the boys now occupied—a much more crowded room—was likewise closed, and all was still.

But he turned toward the square, unlovely arch that led to the kitchen, and in it, he saw just the barest hint of magelight, glowing, cupped as it was in fingers through which light bled.

Jewel sat on a chair, huddled over that light, her eyes wide and dull. She was rocking on the chair in absolute silence; her lips were so tightly pressed together they were white.

He felt it all then: his failure, his horror, his self-loathing. They did not lessen his pride in her, and this—this waking nightmare—did not stain or tarnish it, but made it stronger until it was almost unbearable.

"Jewel." He spoke her name from the arch, just her name. He was grateful that he had come up with a false identity; had she used her name, he might never be able to speak it again in the darkness, like this.

She startled and looked up, and her eyes lost some of their unfocused, blank horror. She even smiled, although her lips gained no color. "Rath," she said wanly. "You're late."

"I'm always late." He smiled down at her. Seeing, now, the things that he had lost. Aware that he would discover more in the days and weeks to come. Because before tonight, he might have gone to her. He might have lifted her, carried her in his arms, offered her that comfort.

And it would be no comfort now, and he could not do it; could not stand to see what must follow; the flinch and the silence.

"I couldn't sleep," she told him.

And because she did not dissemble, he could not. "Vision?"

"Nightmare. Just—nightmare."

"Does the light help?"

She nodded, holding it before her like a talisman, like a captive ray of hope. That was Jewel. But in the darkness, the fear was balanced with that hope, and she sat immobile.

He could not touch her, no. But he had met many people who

could not easily be touched. "Come," he told her quietly. "You need to sleep."

"I can't."

"You can. Not there," he added, nodding to her room. "But I have work to do, Jewel. I will not sleep for some hours yet."

No fear of him shadowed her face, and for that, he could be grateful; had it been there, he might have gone insane. Trusting him, still, after his failure—it was almost too great a gift, too large a burden. But she levered herself out of the chair, and as he walked casually down the hall—and it was hard—he could hear the light fall of her steps as she followed him.

She had slept in this bed before, when she had been ill. When he had first found her. Before he had understood how much she meant to him, and would mean; how much she would change his life. He had, in his arrogance, assumed that his life could not be changed.

But he turned back the covers as she entered the room, and she hesitated. "You need to sleep," she said. And he heard the other words that she did not say.

"I need to work," he told her, "and you need to sleep. Sleep, Jewel. I will work here. I will watch over you."

He stepped aside, and she sat on the side of his bed, watching him, her eyes shadowed and heavy. But she was exhausted, and after a moment, she fell over, her knees curled almost into her chest, her hands still clutching the magestone. His own, he set upon the pedestal on his desk.

"I will watch over you," he said again. "No one will enter this room without my leave. Here, you are safe."

She nodded.

He waited until she stopped moving, and then with care not to touch her, he pulled the covers up and over her, letting them fall as gently as he could. He started a fire in the grate, for the room was cold, indeed; he had been in it so little, there was only ash for warmth.

And for heat, and fury.

He would endure the dreams she had, the sounds she made, the way she struggled with what sleep held. Endure it all, because he expected it.

But his own loss was harder to accept.

He stood guard, this first night, as he would stand guard on later nights, but only when her breath was even and there was a lull and a silence, did he bow his head to his arms. They all had something to hide.